PAINTING KATHERINE

To: Jennie,

Godspeed,

Diane Meholick

PAINTING KATHERINE

Diane M. Meholick

iUniverse, Inc.
New York Lincoln Shanghai

Painting Katherine

iUniverse, Inc.

For information address:
iUniverse, Inc.
2021 Pine Lake Road, Suite 100
Lincoln, NE 68512
www.iuniverse.com

ISBN: 0-595-27340-8

Printed in the United States of America

To my sister, Connie Merchant, and my niece, Rachael Meholick, with love.

CHAPTER 1

"I once was a painter," Vincent Vermay said as he stared at the empty canvas sitting expectantly on the easel. He ran his hand through his brown wavy hair and sighed. "Once upon a year ago," he clarified. The canvas stared back at him. Waiting. Always waiting. He reached out and touched the empty surface. It felt both smooth and rough beneath his fingertips. He had filled many such canvases with beauty over the course of his forty years. But since his fortieth birthday, he'd painted nothing. Nothing he'd dare show the public anyway. Nor had he shown them to his dealer. Kate had seen them though. He'd shown her the few pitiful paintings produced during his fortieth year and all she'd done was shake her head. Words had not been needed. Words would have stung far worse than the shake of her head.

Vincent turned away from the easel and went to the window. He looked down on the quiet Georgetown street below. The street, like the façades of the 19th century townhouses that lined it, was brick. Vincent liked his brick street. He remembered the day fifteen years ago when he and Kate—newly married and tired of apartment life—had met the realtor to look at the townhouse where they now lived. He'd fallen in love with the brick street. It was an archaic anomaly in the bustling, modern world. It harkened back to a simpler time. To a romantic time when neighbors gathered on front porches after dinner to visit and horses' hooves clopped as carriages drove by. Vincent smiled. Yes, the brick street remained. He and several of his neighbors, especially the elderly ones, fought an ongoing battle with the city fathers who wanted to pave over the brick. He and his fellow homeowners would never let that happen.

Vincent grasped the window's brass handles and slid it up. A cold breeze blew in and he shivered, goose bumps rising on his bare forearms. He wore his usual painting clothes—blue jeans and an oversized, one hundred percent cotton, beige-colored shirt. Kate called it his Williamsburg shirt because it reminded her of the craftsmen at Colonial Williamsburg. At present, he had the sleeves rolled up and held in place with black garters. He wore penny loafers on his feet. He took several deep breaths of the cold winter air. It burned inside his chest but that was okay. It made him feel alive. Something he rarely felt these days. He would be forty-one on Saturday. He prayed this birthday would end his artistic block. After all, or so it seemed, last year's birthday began it.

He heard the furnace kick on in the basement. He started to close the window but stopped, catching sight of Kate's red Mercedes turning onto their street. What, he wondered, was she doing home in the middle of the day? He finished closing the window and turned back to his empty canvas. What would she say when she saw it? Would she accuse him of wasting another day while she was out working, actually supporting them now, since he no longer was? She hadn't voiced these feelings yet, but Vincent knew they were there. He saw them in the resentment that lived in her eyes these days. She didn't have to see the blank canvas though. She didn't have to know he still wasn't painting. He snatched a white sheet off the couch where he sometimes slept if he'd stayed up too late working. He threw it over the easel and covered the canvas. He'd never lied to her about his painting before. This would be a first for him. He hesitated, one hand reaching for the sheet to remove it. He heard her come in the front door. "Vincent!" she called. "Vincent, are you upstairs?"

"Yes, I'll be right down."

He left the studio. He left the sheet covering the canvas.

He met her on the second floor landing. Sunlight poured in the large stairwell window, lighting her up like an angel. She wore a dark green skirt and blazer with a pale green blouse. An ivory scarf covered with ivy encircled her neck, an emerald pin holding it in place on her left shoulder, the pin the exact color as her eyes. She had her long, curly, chestnut brown hair pulled back with a hairclip that matched her scarf pin. Round, steel-framed glasses rested on her long, delicate nose. She wore very little makeup; her fair skin and natural long eyelashes didn't need much embellishment. He looked at her perfectly angled face, her cheekbones high yet subtle, her chin square, and couldn't help but feel exactly what he had felt the day he'd met her in his college economics class. He was bowled over by her beauty. As he did that day so long ago, he grinned a big, old, country-boy grin.

Her green eyes questioned him.

He kept on grinning.

"What?" she asked, setting her leather briefcase on the window seat.

"You're extraordinarily beautiful, Kate."

Her right eyebrow shot up. "Okay. And now this is when you tell me you haven't painted a blessed thing all morning."

The words cut him. His grin disappeared. "Thanks for your faith."

"Well, have you?"

"Yes," he lied, surprised at how easy the lie came out.

She started up the steps toward his studio. He followed her. "You can't see it."

She stopped and turned back to him. "Excuse me?"

"You can't see it."

"And why is that?"

"Because…" He took her hand. "Because this might actually be something good. I want to wait until it's done before I show anyone."

"I'm not anyone."

"I know that."

She pulled her hand free and continued up the stairs. He let her go. He sat down on the stairs and waited for her explosion. She would lift the sheet, see the blank canvas, realize he'd lied to her and she would blow. His hands formed into fists. He waited. He heard the studio door squeak open. He really should oil the hinges. Her high heels stomped on the hardwood floor. Then silence. She was lifting the sheet now. He knew it. The eruption was about to begin.

Except the eruption was not the shouting he expected. Instead, laughter floated down the stairwell. He sat still, not believing his ears. Footsteps on the floor again and then she was on the stairs next to him. "Vincent," she said, still laughing. "You're serious. You've got the damn thing covered."

He couldn't believe that she hadn't uncovered the empty canvas. He sat there on the step, unable to speak. How could it be, he wondered, that his lie would go undetected?

Kate sat down next to him and patted his knee. "You artists sure are some-thing," she said, shaking her head. Mirth filled her eyes. "So you think I'm your artistic jinx. Is that it? If you don't show me what you paint, it'll be spectacu-lar."

"No," he said, taking her hand. "It's just…well…I thought that if I painted the whole painting to completion without anyone seeing it or commenting on it, it might…you know…"

"Time was when you couldn't wait to show me your works in progress."

"I know but…" He didn't know what to say. Not really. He was lying to her for the first time since meeting her. He was lying and not getting caught. He hung his head.

She slipped her arm around his shoulders and pressed close against him. Her body touching his made him feel more ashamed than he already did. "I guess I can live with this new painting method. The suspense might kill me though." She kissed his cheek. "You need a shave."

Still not looking at her, he asked, "You're really okay with this?"

"Yes. Although it does hurt a little."

He looked at her. "What hurts?"

"The fact that I might no longer be your muse."

He saw traces of sadness creep into her eyes. He touched her cheek. "Don't think that. That's not it at all."

"Then what is?"

"I can't explain it. I just think that no one, not even you, should see this painting until it's done."

"A feeling you have?"

He nodded.

She smiled. "Then we'll go with your feeling. But you know how impatient I am." She stood up.

"Where are you going?"

She started down the stairs. "To pick you out a suit."

"A suit?" He followed her. "For what?"

She stopped outside their bedroom. "Okay, now I know you've definitely been painting and all those creative juices of yours have been flowing."

"Why?"

She lightly patted his cheek. "Because you've forgotten. You're not dressed. Didn't answer any of my phone calls. By the way, what did you do with the answering machine? The phone keeps ringing off the wall."

"Shut it off. The phone is turned down. What have I forgotten?"

She shook her head and went into the bedroom. "The reading of the will, Vincent." She stuck her head out the door. "Remember, my grandmother died three weeks ago. Not that anyone in my family was ever going to tell me."

He slapped his hand against his forehead. "Damn! The appointment with the attorney in D.C. That's today."

"Give the artist a prize. Now, come on. I may have missed her funeral, but I don't intend to be late for the will."

❈   ❈   ❈

Vincent sat beside Kate in the huge conference room. She was nervous. He knew that because she kept playing with her earrings. She was angry too. He knew that from the fire in her eyes. The flames grew with each relative she looked at. There were four of them: two men and two women. Vincent had never met them before. They were, Kate had informed him earlier, from the "filthy rich and we know it" side of the family. Vincent didn't quite know how these four people were related to the deceased—knowing, according to Kate, wouldn't matter a hill of beans—but there was no doubt they were Kate's relatives. The women, especially, shared her same green eyes, and her chestnut brown hair. The four did not speak to Kate. In fact, they stared at her with open hostility.

The conference room door opened and a young, slick-looking lawyer in a designer, pinstriped, navy blue suit entered. He carried a leather briefcase. "Good afternoon," he said as he sat down at the head of the table. All eyes turned towards him, murmured hellos spilled forth.

The lawyer set his briefcase on the mahogany table and opened it, the latches snapping, the sound echoing off the mahogany walls. Pointing at a sideboard loaded with bagels, muffins, donuts and a full coffee pot, he said, "I trust you've helped yourselves to the refreshments."

No one had and no one explained why he or she hadn't.

Vincent stifled a chuckle as he winked at the lawyer.

The man looked at him with blank eyes.

Vincent wondered just how much hairspray the fellow used to keep his golden hair in place.

The lawyer removed a file from his briefcase and opened it. Clearing his throat, he said, "As some of you already know, I'm Derek Clausterman and for the past ten years, ever since my uncle died, I've managed Katherine Malloy's affairs."

"We know, Derek," the elder of the two men said. "Just get on with it."

Derek glared at the man then turned to Kate. "You must be Katherine Vermay."

"Yes. This is my husband, Vincent."

"Oh, I know who he is, Mrs. Vermay." He smiled at Vincent. "I own two of his works."

"Which ones?" Vincent asked, curious.

"*Laughing at Winter* and *Gloom in Spring*."

Vincent inclined his head. "I'm honored."

Kate pinched his leg beneath the table.

"For God's sake, read the damn thing and let's be done with it," the elder man said.

"Yes, Derek," the younger man said. "I have a meeting at four."

"Which was exactly why the dear man couldn't attend his own grandmother's funeral," one of the women said. "A meeting, you know."

"Caroline," the man practically hissed.

Lovely people, Vincent thought. Maybe it was a good thing that Kate had no contact with this side of her family.

"Okay," Derek Clausterman said. "We'll get on with it." He turned back to Kate. "The reason I've included you in this reading of Mrs. Malloy's last will and testament is because she's mentioned you in it. From what she told me during her last days, you've been a great source of joy to her over the years."

Kate tugged on her right earring. "I spent summers with her when I was a girl. I stopped going there for the summer after I went to college."

"After you sucked your college tuition out of her you quit going to see her." The words had come out of the woman who looked most like Kate. She had to be close to Kate's age as well. "Isn't that right, cousin?"

Anger flared in Kate's eyes. "You know nothing about it. You never did understand her."

"She was a crazy old woman. What else was there to understand?"

"She wasn't crazy."

"Oh, really? Then why did you stop going to see her? Especially after she gave you the money."

"That is none of your business." Vincent touched his wife's arm. She ignored him. "What I had with her was special. You never understood her."

"She was my grandmother too. Don't tell me I didn't understand her."

"You understand her? I think not Lydia. You never understood her. If you had, you never would have forced her to leave her home and move into your cold, ugly mansion."

"Why did you care, Kate? You stopped going to see her."

Kate shot out of her chair. "I had the right to know she died. I had the right to attend her funeral."

Vincent stood up as well. "Kate," he said, taking her arm. "This isn't the time."

Lydia rose to her full height, leaned over the table and said, "You gave up those rights when you left her that day."

Kate trembled but she said no more. Vincent gently eased her back into her chair. He held on to her hand. Tears welled in her eyes.

"Now that the pleasantries are out of the way," Derek Clausterman said, "May I continue?"

Lydia sat down. "Please do, Derek."

"As you know, Katherine Malloy was worth in excess of fifteen million dollars."

"Wow," Vincent said in spite of himself.

Lydia glared at him.

"Anyway," Clausterman continued. "You are all here because you are the only ones of her surviving relatives who are bequeathed anything."

The elder man sat forward in his chair. "And rightfully so. I am her only surviving child after all."

Lydia rolled her eyes.

Clausterman turned to Katherine's son. "To you, Jethro, she has left one million dollars."

"What!" Jethro explained. "That's all?"

Clausterman turned to the younger man. "To you, Edward, she has left one million dollars."

"You're joking." He grabbed Jethro's arm. "Dad, he's got to be kidding."

Lydia stood up again, a sick smile on her face. "I don't think Mr. Clausterman is kidding at all. Tell me, Derek, I take it one million is exactly what she left Caroline and myself."

"That's correct."

Vincent turned to Kate. She sat stock still beside him, her skin white, her body trembling.

Lydia leaned over the table, rested her hands on its top and, eyes boring into Kate, said, "She left the rest to you, Kate. You bitch."

Kate bowed her head. Vincent could feel her fighting for control with every fiber of her being. He laid his hand on her forearm.

"Sit down, Lydia," Edward said.

Lydia ignored him, shifting her gaze to Clausterman. "Am I right?"

The lawyer nodded as he said, "Yes, Lydia, you are. Mrs. Malloy left the remainder of her estate to Mrs. Vermay."

Kate gasped and clutched Vincent's hand.

"In addition, Mrs. Vermay, she left you another item which she felt only you and your husband would appreciate."

Kate looked up. "The house?"

"Yes, Mrs. Vermay. Katherine left you the house in North Tonawanda. The house and all it contains." He held out a manila envelope. "The keys and deed are inside. It's all yours."

Kate took the envelope. She stared at it in wonder.

"Where is North Tonawanda?" Vincent asked.

"In upstate New York," Derek replied. "The house there has been in the Malloy family since it was built by Katherine's husband."

"It's the house Lydia forced her to leave," Kate said. She turned to Vincent. "She hated it down here. She never wanted to leave that house. She wanted to die there. She belonged there. She always said that."

Vincent rubbed Kate's arm.

"Sentimental crap," Lydia said. "It's a dilapidated old house in a Godforsaken city. Besides, I got her fulltime help and gave her a wing to herself. What more could she want? I looked after her in her old age and look how she repays me."

"She wanted to be in her home."

"The home you stopped going to see her at."

Kate opened her mouth to speak but checked herself. Instead, she turned to the attorney. "Is this all?"

"For now, Mrs. Vermay. We will need to meet so I can discuss Katherine's holdings...well, your holdings now."

"I can go?"

He nodded. "I'll call you Monday to set up a meeting."

Kate rose from her chair. "Thank you, Mr. Clausterman." She walked towards the door.

"What's the matter, Kate?" Lydia said. "Nothing more to say."

"Shut up, Lydia," Vincent said. He took Kate by the hand and led her from the room. Out in the hall, he slipped his arm around her and asked, "Are you okay?"

She handed him the manila envelope then removed her glasses and wiped at her eyes with her hand. "Thanks for telling her to shut up."

"Why didn't you tell her that you have seen Katherine since you turned eighteen?"

"Katherine didn't want her to know."

"Why?"

She sniffed. "I don't know. She never told me why. Drive me home, okay?"

"Sure." He pressed the elevator button and massaged her upper back while they waited. "When are you going to show me your new house?"

"Soon."

Vincent woke with a start. He knew before he checked her side of the bed that Kate wasn't beside him. He glanced at the clock on the nightstand. It was three o'clock. His heart beat wildly in his chest. What if she'd snuck upstairs to see his supposed painting? He jumped out of bed, slipped on his pajama bottoms and went looking for her. He ran up the stairs to the studio. She wasn't there. He sank against the door, relieved.

He tried downstairs next and found her on the front porch, wearing his flannel robe, light snow falling upon her. She was crying, oblivious to the cold and snow. He sat down beside her and took her in his arms. She buried her face in his bare chest and cried harder. He stroked her hair and held her. *Idiot!* She had been out here crying and all he'd thought of was himself. No, more specifically, what he had thought of was his lie.

He looked over her head at the snow gently falling in the pale light of the old-fashioned street lamps. It hit the brick street and melted. Snow did not often stick here in Georgetown. Licking his lips, he said, "Hey, babe?"

She pushed back from him and looked up. Sniffing, she said, "I didn't want to wake you." Her voice wavered and cracked.

He smiled down at her. "You not being next to me woke me." He wiped the tears from her cheeks. "It's freezing out here."

She nodded, gripping his hand.

"Let's go inside. You're soaking wet."

She nodded again.

He led her inside, switching on the foyer light as he said, "Give me that robe."

She removed it, revealing mauve flannel pajamas decorated with small peach roses and green petals. He'd given them to her last Christmas and it pleased him that they'd turned out to be her favorite.

He hung the wet robe in the closet. "Come on." He led her into the living room. He didn't turn on any lights; the light filtering in from the foyer was enough. He sat down on the leather couch and pulled her down beside him. Arm around her shoulders, he said, "Now, what are all these tears about?"

She laid her head on his shoulder. "You're skin is cold."

"That's because I was sitting out on the front porch with you without a shirt on in the middle of winter."

"Sorry."

He kissed her forehead.

She took his right hand and entwined her fingers in his. "You have marvelous hands, Vincent. Hands with talent that create beauty."

Not anymore. "I don't think you were sitting on the front steps crying because of my hands." He pushed a stray lock of hair back from her face. "Any chance it had to do with Lydia Malloy?"

"Not really her."

"Then what."

"Katherine's death. And her life too."

"What do you mean?"

"It's a very long story, Vincent."

"So tell me. I'm not going anywhere."

"But I am. I have to be at the Capitol building early. Senator McMartin wants the whole staff there by seven."

"And what the good Senator wants, he gets."

"Don't do that." She moved away from him, releasing his hand.

"What?"

"Use that tone."

"What's the difference, Kate? You know I don't like the man."

"That man happens to be my boss."

"A choice I've never understood."

"The job pays quite well, you know. More than the one with Congressman Freeholder."

"Freeholder was a better man."

"Maybe so. But the job with McMartin affords me a higher profile. And, I'm making more money. A fact, by the way, which has been our saving grace this past year."

There it was, the resentment he knew she felt towards him because he was no longer pulling his financial weight. "Thanks for pointing that out, Kate," he said, rising.

She reached for him. "Wait, Vincent, I didn't—"

"Yes, you did. It's how you feel. You think I haven't picked up on it? How naive do you think I am?"

"I don't think you're naive."

"I know what all your Washington cronies are saying about me behind my back at all the functions you drag me to. I'm a leach. I'm a failure. I lost my artistic touch."

She jumped to her feet. "Stop it, Vincent!"

"Tell me, Kate. Do you agree with them?"

"No."

"But you resent me."

"No," she said. "I love you. I believe in you."

He looked away. She was lying. What she said aloud was not what her eyes said. Even in the dim light from the foyer, he could see the truth. She loved him. He didn't doubt that. But she no longer had faith in him. Lies, their relationship was nothing but lies now. What had happened to them?

"Vincent," she said. "I love you."

"But you think I've lost my talent."

"No."

"Don't lie to me."

"I'm not lying."

"Yes, you are."

She grabbed his hands. "Please, Vincent, drop this."

"You won't admit it."

"Vincent," she pleaded.

He pulled his hands free. "Don't admit it. I know. You can't fool me." He started to walk away, but stopped when she said his name, her voice quiet, trembling. He turned back to her. "What?"

"I need you. I just lost Katherine."

He ran a hand through his hair. "I'm not going anywhere. Besides, where would I go?"

"Will you do something for me tomorrow?"

"What?"

"Book us on a flight to Buffalo this Saturday. North Tonawanda is not too far from the airport. I want to show you Katherine's house. I can explain things better there."

He stared at her, considering. Maybe a trip together would help. He did want to see Katherine's house. "Okay."

"I know I've never really explained my relationship with Katherine."

"She was your grandmother. That's explanation enough."

"She liked you, Vincent."

"I only met her once at one of your clandestine meetings. And that was years ago."

"She said that you were perfect for me. She said if I married you, I would never be lonely and never unloved. She said you were one of the few special men in the world."

"Then I guess she was wrong."

"No, she wasn't. Painting isn't everything you are, Vincent. You're gentle and kind with a heart as big as the universe. You love with every fiber of your being. I could never be unhappy with you."

"If that's so, why has the way you looked at me changed, Kate? Explain that one."

She stood silent, staring at him.

"Thought so. No explanation."

"Vincent…" She trailed off.

He held up his hands. "Forget it. I'll book the flight."

He left her standing in the living room. He went up to their bedroom, climbed into bed and rolled onto his right side, his back facing her side of the bed. She followed him to bed moments later. She lay down close to him. He felt her breath on his neck. "Vincent," she said. "What you see is disappointment. Not in you, but in life."

His heart picked up speed. "Life?"

"Yes."

He rolled over on his left side and faced her. "What do you mean, Kate?"

"I mean that life is ugly. And that over time, it creeps into your heart and destroys your hopes and your dreams, and in your case, the outpouring of beauty in art."

He took her hand. "You don't resent me."

She smiled. "No."

"But what you said about the money and taking the McMartin job?"

She laid a finger on his lips. "Is fact. We needed money." She smiled. "But now, thanks to Katherine, that's no longer an issue."

Now that she had said it aloud, it suddenly hit Vincent. "Shit," he said.

"What?"

"We're filthy rich."

Kate laughed. "Yes, I guess we are."

Vincent sat up. "If Katherine was worth 15 million dollars and she gave the others a total of 4 million. That means you got…"

"Eleven million, Vincent."

"Oh, my, God, Kate." He let out a long whistle. "Technically, I don't have to ever paint again."

"Oh, but, Vincent, you must. You must paint."

He lay back against the headboard. "And you, Mrs. Vermay, don't ever have to write another political speech."

She shook her head. "Don't get carried away with this, Vincent. You know we both love our work."

"Okay, I'll give you that. But now, we can do it just for the fun of it."

"You are impossible." She kissed his shoulder. "Now go to sleep. And don't forget to book the flight before you start painting tomorrow."

"Promise."

She rolled onto her back and closed her eyes. He rolled onto his back and stared at the ceiling. He didn't dare tell her that he would have plenty of time to book the flight tomorrow because, just like today, he wouldn't paint a thing.

CHAPTER 2

"It needs work," Kate said, crossing her arms over her chest.

"It's pure Victorian," Vincent said, his arms open wide. "It's magnificent."

They stood on the sidewalk in front of the old house.

"The paint is peeling," Kate added. "Or should I say what paint is left on the shingles is peeling."

"It's huge," Vincent said. He walked up to the wrought iron gate and squatted. He brushed snow and ice from the gate's emblem. "J.M.," he read aloud.

"Jethro Malloy."

Vincent glanced back at Kate. She stood hugging herself, shivering in the frigid air. He straightened, went to his wife and put his arm around her. She laid her head on his shoulder and said, "This is not how I remember this house. It was beautiful once."

"It still is." He pushed his gray tweed, newsboy cap further up on his forehead and leaned his head back. The house was a symmetric beauty of Victorian architecture. Bay windows dominated the front façade. Vincent counted four gables, two red brick chimneys and a classic widow's walk, surrounded in wrought iron. The third and second floors had fish scale shingles and the first floor shingles were long and narrow. "Incredible. Three stories of magnificence and those bay windows; I bet they have big old window seats on the inside. Look at the cornices, brackets and eaves. The trim has to be hand-carved. Those posts on the porch have to be hand-carved as well."

"The porch wraps all the way around the first floor of the house. I loved that when I was little."

"The shingles were white and the trim was rose. Right?"

"You're close. The trim was mauve. But when I first came to stay here, the house was painted many colors. And then one day, when I was still a little girl, Katherine had all those beautiful colors scraped away. The house was painted white and the trim mauve. When I asked her why, she just shook her head and turned away from me." Kate shivered against him.

He rubbed her arm with his gloved hand. "Let's go inside."

He unlatched the gate, took her hand and led her through the snow to the front porch. They stopped at the bottom of the steps and Vincent admired the mahogany, double doors; an arched stained glass window above them. The right door had a stained glass window at about waist level. The window portrayed the likeness of a man wearing a derby bowler. Vincent pointed at the likeness. "Anybody we know?"

"That was Jethro."

"Liked himself, did he?"

"I guess he did."

Vincent shook his head. "That is somehow both weird and fascinating."

"You get used to it after awhile. At least I did when I stayed here."

Vincent brushed snow off the porch steps with his gloved hands. "After you, my lady."

She climbed up the steps, pulling the skeleton key from her jacket pocket. He stopped on the top step and looked back out at the street. "What's the name of this street again?"

She unlocked the doors and opened the right one. "Goundry. Come on."

He grabbed her arm. "Not so fast, my lady."

"What?"

He picked her up.

"Vincent, what are you doing?"

"Why, I'm carrying you across the threshold."

He carried her inside, set her down, and closed the heavy door. "All Victorian houses should have a beautiful woman carried across their threshold."

She laughed. "You are such an incurable romantic."

He looked about him in wonder. They stood in a foyer facing a wide mahogany staircase. A hall ran the length of the house. If they turned left, they entered the parlor. To the right was a room big enough to be classified a ballroom. The kitchen and dining room took up the back of the first floor. Vincent went into the parlor. All the furniture was covered with white sheets and sat where it had obviously sat for years. "My, God, Kate," he said. "Look at the crown molding and wainscoting and the cornices above the windows. Look at the mahogany fireplace. It's a masterpiece." He knelt down and touched the hardwood floor. "Original." He pointed at the oval, flowered area rug. "Beautiful."

"Look at the cobwebs," Kate commented, staring up at the molding.

Vincent stood up and sprinted to the kitchen. He stared down at the floor. "Ceramic tile."

"Cold and slippery tile you mean, Vincent."

He looked about him, his eyes widening. "Is that what I think it is, Kate?"

"What?"

He went to the black wooden box beside the back door and opened it. "It is!" he exclaimed, gleefully. He grinned at Kate. "It's an honest to God icebox."

"Yes, it is. Katherine would never part with it. Look at those." She pointed at the stove and refrigerator. The stove was black with gold detailing. The refrigerator was red. "Very old appliances, I presume."

Vincent chuckled. "Boy oh boy, take away your modern conveniences and you just go all to pieces."

She stuck her tongue out.

"Be careful I don't bite it off."

"You wouldn't dare."

"Let's go upstairs." He took her hand. They went up a narrow back staircase to the second floor. There were four bedrooms and two bathrooms. All the bedrooms had armoires instead of closets. The bathrooms had pedestal sinks and claw-footed tubs. "Wonderful," Vincent said. A room at the end of the hall, at the west end of the house was a library. Dust-covered books lined the shelves. A mahogany desk sat in the room's center. "Every room, Kate," Vincent said, sitting down in the desk chair, dust flying up around him. "Every room has gorgeous hardwood floors."

She sat on the corner of the desk, sneezed twice and said, "Every room needs a good scrubbing." She ran her finger along the desktop. "I hate dust." She sniffed. "Stale air. Mold too."

"Look at those books." He got up and went to the nearest shelf. He pulled out a volume and wiped the dust from the binding. "Charles Dickens."

"Which one?"

"*Great Expectations.*"

"I loved that book."

"You read it?"

"Yes."

"No, Kate, I mean you read this book I'm holding?"

"I guess so. I read it while staying here one summer."

Carefully, he opened the book. "Look at this."

She came to him. "What?"

"See the date. This is most likely a first edition."

"No kidding."

Vincent shook his head in wonder. "Do you realize what we have here? God, did Katherine give us a gift."

"Maybe so, but it's a gift that requires a lot of work. And money. We'd have to hire somebody to restore this place to its former grandeur."

Vincent closed the book and put it back on the shelf. "Hire somebody. Why would we do that? I could do a lot of the work myself. It would be a hell of a lot of fun, actually."

"What do you mean?"

Not answering her, he walked out of the room. "What's on the third floor?"

She hurried after him. "What do you mean you'll do it?"

He gestured at the stairs. "You haven't told me what's on the third floor."

She looked up the stairs and went suddenly pale. "I'm not going up there, Vincent." She backed away from the steps.

"Why not? What's up there?"

"Just forget that floor exists. Please, Vincent?"

"Oh, I get it. You had a fright or something up there. Well, Kate, you're all grown up now." He charged up the stairs. Grabbing the doorknob, he said, "Open sesame."

"Vincent, don't!" Kate yelled from below.

He looked down at her and met eyes laced with fear. He released the doorknob and rushed down the steps. Hugging her, he said, "Okay, okay, we won't go up there now. Hey, you're trembling."

"I don't like it up there, Vincent."

"Apparently not." He kissed her cheek. "Tell you what, let's go have a nice dinner somewhere and discuss just what to do with this old place."

"We could sell it."

"Why would we want to do that?"

Before she could answer there was a knock on the front door. "Look at that, company already."

Vincent hurried down the stairs to the foyer and opened the double doors. A woman about Kate's age stood on the snowy porch. She wore gray wool slacks and a black overcoat. A gray fedora sat atop auburn hair that cascaded about her shoulders. "Well, hello," Vincent said.

"Hi. This is embarrassing."

"What is?"

"You have my dog."

"I do?"

"Yes. If you'll just let me in, I'll show you where."

Kate peered around him. "Liz? Is…my God, it is you!"

The woman squinted at Kate, recognition flooding her green eyes. "Kate," she said, her tone not quite hostile but not welcoming either.

Kate gestured with her arm. "Yes. Come in."

Liz entered and Kate hugged her close. Liz was stiff, her arms straight, not returning the hug. "Look at you," Kate said, stepping back. "You look great."

"So do you."

Vincent coughed.

Kate took his hand. "I'm sorry, sweetheart. Liz, this is my husband, Vincent. Vincent, this is a very old friend. Her name is Elizabeth Reilly. Unless, you're married now."

Elizabeth shook Vincent's free hand. Her grip was strong. "Not married. And it's Dr. Elizabeth Reilly."

"So you did it," Kate said, smiling. "I always knew you'd end up a doctor."

"I did. What about you, Kate?" Although her tone was cold, her voice held curiosity.

"I work for a U.S. Senator. I'm his words."

Liz did not look surprised. "You always were good at making speeches."

Vincent could not tell if Liz was making a joke or being insulting. Trying to lighten up the atmosphere, he said, "I can vouch for that."

Kate nudged him in the ribs. Seemingly oblivious to the fact that her "old friend"—a friend Vincent had never heard of, by the way—did not appear all that thrilled to see her, Kate plunged on, asking, "How's your mom and dad doing?"

Liz faltered, her legs threatening to give way beneath her. Her skin turned deathly pale.

Kate slipped an arm around her. "What is it? Are you all right?"

Liz latched on to Kate's arm. "My mother died shortly after I finished my last residency."

"Oh, Liz." Kate's face filled with sorrow.

"I always planned…hoped that Dad and I would work together. That…" She trailed off, fighting back tears. In spite of her efforts, one slipped from her eye. Impatiently, she brushed it away.

"I remember. You wanted to join his practice even when you were five."

Liz sniffed, her voice cracking as she went on. "I took over Dad's practice. He's...well...he's not the man you remember. He can't work."

"What happened?"

"Mom's illness was very long and painful and it tore him up inside. He needs a lot of help now."

Kate gave her a reassuring squeeze.

"You remember Miss Whiting?"

"Your dad's receptionist? Of course I do. How could I forget her? I remember that we thought she had a crush on him."

Liz smiled through her sadness. "And we were right. She lives with us now. She takes care of him while I'm working. We still live in the house next door."

A blast of cold air blew in and Vincent closed the doors. "Good thing we're not running the furnace while we're standing here with the door open in the middle of winter."

Neither woman heard him. They stared into one another's eyes and Kate said, "You're angry with me, Liz?"

Liz pushed Kate away. "You just left. I didn't hear from you for twenty-one years. What did you think I'd be?"

"There were reasons."

Liz shook her head. "You threw away what we had. I thought I meant something to you. That we were best friends."

"We were. But...I had to get away from here. Something happened and—"

"And that meant you had to get away from me too?"

"No. It wasn't like that."

"Then suppose you tell me why, Kate? Why you took off without saying goodbye, without ever calling me. Do you have any idea how much that hurt?"

"You might not believe it but I do. I haven't spent a day where I didn't think about you."

Liz turned away from Kate and called up the stairs, "Duke! Come on, boy." A yellow Labrador retriever came bounding down the stairs. He stopped at Liz's feet, his tail wagging. She scolded him. "What have I told you about coming over here? This is not your house." The dog lay down and buried his nose in his paws.

"Don't turn away from me, Liz," Kate pleaded. "Don't leave like this."

Liz turned back. She didn't speak, but stared at Kate with fury in her eyes.

"Please, Elizabeth?" Kate begged. "Talk to me."

Silence hung heavy in the air. Vincent knelt down beside Duke and scratched the dog's head. "Hey, boy, nice to meet you. Why don't you show me how you got in here? We'll let these two ladies talk."

Still staring at Kate, Liz said, "There's a doggie door in the kitchen, Vincent. Our yards share a fence and Duke's dug his way under it. I gave up filling in the hole."

Vincent straightened. "He's welcome anytime. So are you."

A brief smile crossed her pale face and then she asked, "Why are you here?"

"Katherine died," Kate said. "She left me the house. And eleven million dollars."

Liz gasped. "You're kidding?"

"No, I'm not."

Liz grinned. "What did Lydia say?"

"I believe she called me a bitch."

Liz looked from Kate to Vincent and back at Kate again. "So you really own this place?"

Kate nodded.

Liz knelt down and wrapped her arms around her dog. Duke licked her face, his tail thumping on the floor.

"Vincent wants to restore the house to its former grandeur," Kate added.

"What do you want?"

Kate knelt beside Liz. "To spend time with you again. Explain things."

Liz laid her cheek on the top of Duke's head. The dog's tail thumped faster. Vincent saw the struggle going on inside of her. Dare she get close to Kate? What's to say Kate wouldn't take off again? Could she afford to take the chance on someone who had let her down in the past? In the doctor's beautiful face, Vincent saw these questions and more. Elizabeth Reilly, M.D. had experienced a great deal of pain and loss in her young life and Vincent had a hunch she'd lost more than just her mother and Kate. There was sadness deep within her. Sadness she concealed well, but sadness that was there nonetheless.

Finally, Liz nodded. "Okay. We can talk."

Kate glanced up at Vincent with joy in her eyes. She gestured at Liz and mouthed, "Dinner."

Vincent nodded. "Hey, Liz, Kate and I were just going to get some dinner. Come with us?"

"Yes, Liz," Kate said. "Come with us. We're celebrating Vincent's birthday today."

Liz shook her head. "No. Not tonight. I should catch up on some medical journals."

Vincent waited for Kate to press further, but she didn't. Sighing, she got to her feet, looking helpless.

Vincent held out his hand to Liz. "Please, Liz, come with us. Don't you think twenty-one years was long enough?" He smiled reassuringly. "Start getting to know each other tonight."

She accepted his hand and stood up.

"Now, that's more like it," Vincent said. "Let's get going. I'm starving." He led Liz outside, Kate and Duke following.

"Is it always this cold here in winter?" Kate asked as she locked the door.

"It is," Liz said. "Summer girl."

Liz's teasing brought a grin to Kate's face.

"Let me put Duke in the house. I'll be right back."

"Okay, Vincent and I will wait in the car."

Liz walked down the porch steps and Duke bounded after her.

Liz had just reached the gate when Kate called, "Liz, wait. I'll come with you. I'd love to see your father again."

"I'll wait here," Vincent said.

He watched the two women walk down the snowy sidewalk towards the Reilly house and disappear up the driveway. Turning his attention back to the Victorian, he ran his hand along one of the carved porch posts. "Thank you, Katherine Malloy," he said. "Thank you for this perfect house."

They went to Zebb's Bar and Grill on Niagara Falls Blvd. Leaving the snowy parking lot behind, they entered a world of movie star photos, bright colors and rock music blaring around them. They opted for a booth rather than a table and ordered burgers and fries. As if she believed it her job to fill the air with conversation, Kate rambled on about Senator McMartin and political life in D.C. Liz listened, nodded now and then and even flashed a couple of smiles. But it seemed to Vincent that her mind was elsewhere.

During the drive back to Goundry Street even Kate ran out of conversation. The ride was uncomfortably silent. Vincent thought about turning on the radio but didn't. When they pulled into the Reilly driveway, Kate turned in her seat and said, "I'm glad you came Liz."

Liz nodded. She opened the car door.

Kate grabbed her arm. "I want to see you again."

Liz sat in the backseat with one leg out of the car and one in. She gazed at Kate. Again, Vincent saw the struggle within her. After several minutes of cold winter air pouring into the car, Liz said, "The phone number at the house is the same as it always was. Call me when you come back into town."

"How about if I call you whether I'm in town or not? Just to talk."

"Whatever you want, Kate," Liz said then slipped from the car, closing the door and running up the driveway.

☙   ☙   ☙

They lay in the dark in their hotel room; Kate snuggled against him. He could tell by her breathing that she wasn't asleep. He ran his fingers through her soft hair.

"That was one awkward dinner," she said in the darkness.

"It was."

She eased herself away from him and sat up.

He propped himself up on his elbows. "It's going to take time, Kate. You know that."

She sighed. "Will she ever understand, Vincent?"

"I don't know. I still don't know why you left North Tonawanda. Or why you never called your supposed best friend all these years."

"She was my best friend, Vincent."

"Then why did you spend twenty-one years without her in your life? I never knew she existed until today."

"There is so much you don't understand."

"Try me."

She let out a long breath then said, "I never wanted to…I…" She pounded her forehead with her palm, the smacking sound loud in the quiet hotel room.

Vincent sat up and grabbed her wrist. "Hey, are you trying to hurt yourself?"

She wrapped her arms around herself and rocked back and forth like a baby.

"Kate?" He took her by the shoulders. "What is it? What is torturing you?"

She shook her head and tears rolled down her cheeks. "I can't," she said. "God, I just want to forget it."

"What happened, Kate? What drove you from North Tonawanda that night?"

She reached for him, her wet cheeks pressing against his bare chest. She choked back sobs.

"Okay," he whispered into her ear. "We don't have to talk about it. Not tonight."

He lay back down with her, holding her close, stroking her hair. Gradually, she quieted down and her tears ceased flowing. Still, he held her. A car horn beeped outside. Voices floated in from the hall. Someone in the next room switched on the television. It came on loud but was turned down immediately.

Kate's fingers toyed with the hair on his chest. "Vincent?"

"What, babe?"

"Did you mean what you said? That you want to fix up the house?"

"Yes."

"Katherine would like the house restored, I think. Even if it was just painted white and mauve again…"

He heard the "but" that she didn't say and so he said it. "But?"

"This is an election year for McMartin. I can't leave D.C. right now."

"You could come for long weekends."

"We've never been apart for more than a few days since we married, Vincent."

He brushed a lock of hair from her forehead. "I know. It's not a pleasant prospect for me either. I hate getting into a bed without you."

"Then let's hire it done."

"Or, thanks to Katherine, neither one of us has to work. You could quit your job, Kate."

"How many times do I have to tell you it's an election year?" Her words came out in a sudden flurry, causing him to jerk. "I can't just walk out on McMartin. Besides, I have to work. I want to work. I won't just walk out on my career."

"Easy, Kate." He placed a hand on her shoulder. "I promised you the day I proposed that I'd never stand in the way of your career. So, you need to do your work and I need to fix this house. It's a feeling I have. The minute I saw it, I just knew it was a cause for me to champion, just like politics is your cause. This past year, Kate, while your star has brightened, mine has faded."

"And fixing a house will brighten it again?"

He shook his head. "It's not just the house. It's…I don't know…kismet or karma. I just know that if I'm to succeed painting again, this house is where it will be."

"How do you know that?"

"Honestly, I don't know. I just know it. I'm the one who should restore Katherine's house, not some contractor."

Kate slipped away from him. She got out of bed and went to the window, pushed the curtain aside and peered out. "It's snowing," she said. And then, immediately, she asked, "When do you plan on moving up here?"

"Right away. I can start working inside. Work my way out. I was thinking of checking out the third floor to see if it would be a good studio."

"The third floor isn't right for your studio, Vincent. It doesn't have the correct lighting. The room that would work best for your studio is the room I used to sleep in when I stayed there. It gets the most natural light all day."

"The one with the large, really wide windows?"

"That's the one."

"Okay. I could ditch the frilly curtains and the canopied bed."

"You would most assuredly want to do that. Unless you plan to sleep instead of paint."

"Oh, woman, you've pierced my very heart. One does not sleep when one can paint."

She turned back from the window. "Is that so?"

"It's true, my lady."

She gazed at him with sad eyes. "God, I'll miss you."

He went to her and took her in his arms. "This separation won't be all that long, Kate. You'll come visit. We'll be okay, you'll see."

She managed a smile.

He cupped her chin in his hand. "I'll make sure I put in lots of good words with Liz for you too."

"Thanks, you're swell, Vincent."

"Of course I am."

She playfully punched his chest. Sighing, she rested her head on his shoulder. "I love you, Vincent," she said.

"I love you, Kate," he assured her.

They crawled back into bed together and she snuggled close, arms encircling his right arm. Her body was familiar and warm against him. Her hair smelled of lavender. She was the only woman he would ever love. He knew that without a doubt. But there was much about her he didn't know. Even after fifteen years of marriage, there were secrets locked within her. He wondered what he would find when he moved into the Victorian. What had happened on the house's third floor that still tortured Kate?

When at last sleep claimed him, he dreamt he stood on the stairs before the door that led into the third floor. He tried in vain to open the door, but it wouldn't budge.

❧   ❧   ❧

Vincent closed the back of the Rodeo and turned to Kate. She stood on the townhouse steps, arms crossed over her chest. Her eyes were bloodshot. She wore his red, blue and gold plaid flannel shirt. It hung over her blue jeans, reaching to her knees. "Liz and Miss Whiting should have the house livable for you. Do you have everything you need?" she asked, her voice hoarse from crying.

He held up a gloved hand and dropped his fingers as he listed the items. "Clothes, wallet, shaving kit, and contents of now empty art studio." He patted the Rodeo. "All packed and ready to go." He walked up the steps and stood in front of her. He rubbed her upper arms. "Minus one shirt of course. And one wife."

She looked away, her eyes filling with tears.

He pulled her close. "I'll call you when I get there. And in two weeks, you're coming up for the weekend."

She nodded.

He gently pushed her away. Touching her cheek, he said, "I love you, Kate. Don't doubt that. I'll be counting every minute of these next two weeks."

"Me too," she managed, sniffing.

He kissed her trembling lips. She clung desperately to him for a few minutes then set him free. He went down the steps, around the Rodeo and opened the driver's side door. Saluting her, he said, "Give Senator McMartin's rivals hell."

"I'll do my best, Vincent. Drive safe."

"You bet."

He climbed into the Rodeo, started the engine and then with a final wave to Kate, he dropped the vehicle into drive and pulled away from the curb. As he turned the corner and left the brick street behind, Vincent thought of the still blank canvas in the back of the Rodeo and was not at all surprised to find that while he would miss his wife desperately, he was also relieved to be leaving her.

CHAPTER 3

Darkness had fallen by the time Vincent pulled the Rodeo up to the curb in front of the house on Goundry Street. He shut off the engine and got out of the vehicle. Cold air hit him full force and he shivered, wrapping his arms around himself. A light shown in the left bay window of the old house and he smiled. Liz had taken care of turning on the utilities as she'd promised Kate she would.

Since he wasn't sure if there were phones in the house, Vincent unzipped his leather coat, reached inside and pulled his cell phone out of his breast pocket. He re-zipped the coat, flipped open the phone and dialed the townhouse in Georgetown. Kate answered on the second ring. "Hey," he said as he walked around the Rodeo and up onto the sidewalk.

"Vincent." Her voice was soft and warm. "You made it."

"Yep." He walked past the house to the driveway and found it was filled with snow. The white stuff reached to his knees. He pushed his way through it and headed for the carriage house. "Drive got nasty right after I crossed the New York border. I had to drive through a virtual blizzard."

"You should have stopped for the night."

"Nah. I just drove cautious."

"Are you inside?"

"Nope. I'm literally plowing through snow to reach the carriage house. Do you know if there is a shovel in there?"

"No. I was a summer visitor only, remember?"

"Oh, yeah. I need to get the Rodeo in off the street."

"You are huffing and puffing, old man."

He laughed. "What did you do today?"

"Worked on a speech for a dinner Monday."

"How exciting."

"This place is lonely without you, Vincent."

He reached the carriage house. "Are you still in my flannel shirt?"

"It's mine now and yes, I am."

"Are you in bed?"

"On the living room couch."

He pictured her sitting there, her slender frame dwarfed by his shirt, and much to his surprise, the image brought a rush of loneliness. "I love you, Kate," he said.

"I hate you being so far away," she said. There were tears in her voice.

"You'll see me in two weeks."

"That's forever."

He closed his eyes. In a way, she was right. Being separated from her would be torture. He thought of the empty canvas in the back of the Rodeo. It would also be his saving grace. It would be easier lying to her from three states away. "Maybe you should get a cat."

"No. I should have my husband here."

"You'll have me there again. Once this old house is in ship shape."

"Well, I don't mind telling you that I'm jealous of that house."

"Don't be. She's not nearly as beautiful as you."

"She better not be."

"Hey, I better get to work on this driveway."

"Okay. I love you. I miss you."

"Ditto for me."

"Goodnight, Vincent."

"Night, babe."

He shut off the phone and shoved it into the back pocket of his blue jeans. He tried to open the carriage house doors but they were locked. He pulled the key ring from his coat pocket and prayed the second key on the ring would open the doors. It slid into the lock perfectly. Smiling triumphantly, he turned it and the lock slid over. Due to the snow, he could barely open the doors wide enough to squeeze through. Once inside, he searched the wall on either side of the door to see if there was a light switch. He found one to his right and switched it on. The building flooded with light and he squinted against the brightness. What he saw before him sent adrenalin shooting through his veins. Sitting side-by-side, both covered with dust, but in decent condition, were a 1924, two-door Model T Ford and a hansom cab, brass lamps on either side and driver platform on the back. The Ford sat up on blocks and had no tires.

"My God!" Vincent exclaimed, going to the cab. He opened its door and ran his hand along the leather interior, gritty dirt coating his fingers. He wiped them on his coat then climbed in and sat back, dust flying around him. He banged the ceiling, sneezed then ordered, "Home, James." Chuckling at his foolishness, he climbed down from the cab. He went to the car and wiped the dust from its hood. Its blue finish was faded. He opened the hood and stared at the engine. "I wonder if you still run." He closed the hood then stepped back, gazing from one vehicle to the other in awe. "Incredible."

Taking a deep breath, he looked at his watch. 9 p.m. It was getting late and he had to get the Rodeo into the driveway. Looking around, he saw horse bridles, garden tools, and shovels hanging on the walls. He grabbed a sturdy, wooden shovel and headed back outside. Snow fell, but it was a gentle snow, the flakes large. He trudged down to the end of the driveway and began shoveling. He'd only been at the job a few minutes when he heard a familiar bark. Turning around, Vincent saw Duke charging towards him.

"Hey, Duke," Vincent called. "Come on boy." He stuck the shovel into a snowdrift and knelt down. The dog jumped into Vincent's arms and licked him furiously. Vincent hugged the animal and planted a kiss on the top of his head. "How you doing, boy? How's Duke tonight?"

"Very happy to see you."

Still petting the dog, Vincent looked up. Liz Reilly stood on the sidewalk. She wore sweatpants and a ski jacket. A ponytail stuck out the back of a Buffalo Bills cap.

Rising, Vincent said, "Hey, Liz."

She motioned Duke to her with a hand signal. He obeyed and sat down beside her. "Just get here?"

He nodded. "A little while ago. Thanks for leaving the light on."

"I turned it on before Duke and I went running."

"Kate says, 'Hi.'" He pulled the shovel from the snowdrift. "I'm just going to get the truck in off the street."

"I'll help." She ran up the driveway and disappeared inside the carriage house. Duke followed her. Mistress and dog emerged minutes later, Liz carrying a snow shovel.

"You don't have to, Liz."

"I know," she said then started shoveling.

They worked in silence. Duke watching them. When they had shoveled enough so that the Rodeo would be far enough up the driveway to avoid blocking the sidewalk, Vincent stopped and said, "That's good enough for now."

Liz paused. "You sure? We could finish."

He held up his hand. "Neither one of us needs to have a heart attack. Besides, it's still snowing."

"I'll put the shovels away."

"No. Put them on the front porch."

"Sure thing."

Vincent ran to the Rodeo and moved it into the driveway. He retrieved his suitcase and his box of paints from the back of the vehicle and went inside the house. Liz sat on the stairs removing her running shoes. Duke had disappeared.

Closing the front doors, Vincent set his suitcase and box of paints down and looked around. Liz had removed the sheets from the parlor furniture. The floors were vacuumed and the stands, coffee table, and shelves were dusted. He turned to thank her, but she held up her hand. "Not me. Miss Whiting did it. I just handled the utilities."

"Then I must thank Miss Whiting."

"You'll get your chance. You're invited over for dinner tomorrow night."

"I accept."

"Good. Miss Whiting is a great cook."

Vincent removed his coat and hung it on the coat rack in the corner. "So the good Dr. Elizabeth Reilly doesn't cook."

Liz stood up. "Not if she can avoid it."

Vincent untied his hiking boots and kicked them off. "Where's Duke?"

"Most likely lying on one of the beds upstairs. I think he likes this house better than his own."

"Well, he has great taste." Vincent ran his hand along the mahogany stair rail. "This place is magnificent."

Liz nodded. "All these old houses are."

"When was the one you live in built?"

"It was begun in 1902 and completed in 1903."

"Who built it?"

"My father's aunt."

"Aunt?"

"Yes. Aunt. She was the first Reilly doctor in North Tonawanda. She never married. Remind you of anyone."

"You're young yet. Don't count yourself out."

Liz smiled. "Oh, but I do, my friend."

Vincent removed his newsboy cap and tossed it at the coat rack. It landed on top.

Liz clapped. "Score."

Vincent bowed. "I'd offer you some hot chocolate, but I doubt I have any."

"Oh, but you do. Miss Whiting again."

"Don't you grocery shop either?"

"Not if I can help it."

Vincent led the way to the kitchen and switched on the overhead light. Liz went to the pantry, retrieved a box of instant hot chocolate, held it up and said, "One for you too?"

"Most assuredly." He sat down at the rectangular shaped, white kitchen table and watched her fill a teakettle with water. He was happy to see that her mood was greatly improved over the day he'd met her. She set the kettle on the stove and turned on the burner.

"The stove is electric," she said, opening cupboards in search of mugs.

"What makes you count yourself out?" he asked.

She found some coffee cups and removed two from the cupboard. They were white with blue flowers and looked too delicate to actually use. She rinsed them out and dried them with a dishtowel he figured Miss Whiting had hung on the refrigerator handle.

"Well, Liz?"

She set the cups on the table. "It's a long story."

"I'm a good listener."

She brought the box of hot chocolate to the table and opened it. She tossed him a packet then stood gazing at him with uncertain eyes. He could sense that she wanted to talk. She needed to talk. And just maybe, she needed to talk to him, someone she hardly knew, someone who would listen objectively, someone who was married to the woman who had once been her best friend and had known her deepest dreams and fears.

"I am a good listener," he said again.

His words broke the camel's back. "I was in love once," she said, her voice soft but baring raw emotions. "We were engaged."

"No wedding?"

"He died." The words were abrupt and laced with pain.

She pulled another packet of hot chocolate from the box and as she opened it, he saw her hands trembling.

"I'm sorry, Liz."

She poured the brown powder half into her coffee cup and half onto the table.

He reached out and took her left wrist.

She stared down at the mess she made for a few seconds then said, "Maybe you should pour your own powder."

He gently squeezed her wrist before releasing it. He ripped open his packet and poured its contents into his cup.

"I didn't hook up phone service for you," she said, still staring down at her mess. "There aren't any phones in the house so I figured you could do it when you buy a phone."

"Sounds good."

"When will Kate be coming to visit?"

"In a couple of weeks. She'll do a long weekend thing."

Liz nodded, but didn't comment. She rested her hands on the back of her chair and glanced around the kitchen.

Vincent wondered if he should press her about her fiancé. He wasn't a psychiatrist, but he could see that she needed to talk about what had happened to him. She was a time bomb of pent up emotions. Not quite sure how to bring up the topic again, he bought himself some time. "Why don't you take off your jacket?"

She unzipped the jacket and removed it, revealing a white turtleneck with a blue sweatshirt overtop. She hung the jacket on the back of the chair.

"You run every night?"

"Pretty much."

The teakettle whistled. She turned off the stove, carried the kettle to the table and filled each cup. Her hands were steadier. She set the kettle back on the stove and said, "Now, where do you suppose the silverware is?"

"If there's any here, I bet it's in that drawer right there." He pointed to the cupboard beside the refrigerator.

She opened it and said, "You're right." She came back to the table with two spoons. Handing him one, she sat down and stirred her hot chocolate. Watching her, Vincent wondered how best to prod her and thus he was surprised when she volunteered, "He got me into running. We'd go together, usually at night."

"Your fiancé."

"Yes. His name was Alan. Alan Rourke."

"You would have kept your same initials."

"He was a paleontologist. We were living in Salt Lake City where he worked at a museum. He'd also go on digs."

"And you were?"

"My last residency. I worked in the emergency room."

"And?" He spoke softly, gently probing her onward.

"It was the year before my mother died." She stopped stirring her hot chocolate. Her eyes looked at Vincent, but they didn't see him. "I was working the night they brought him in. He'd been riding his motorcycle back from a dig. He'd said he'd be home by midnight. The paramedics brought him in on a stretcher. I ran to meet them like I had done so many times before when a stretcher came in. This time it was Alan. His body was broken and twisted and the blood…God, Vincent, the blood." Tears rolled down her cheeks. "His blood."

Vincent reached out and laid his hand on her arm.

"Dr. Myers pushed me aside. He knew who Alan was. They went to work—Myers, the nurses, another doctor. I don't remember any of them, but Myers. While I stood there, frozen, they tried. But he was gone." She bowed her head. She continued the story, her voice cracking and filled with tears. "When they pronounced him dead, I went to him and took his hand. He looked peaceful then. I kissed him goodbye and pulled the blanket over his face. They wheeled him away and I went outside, sat down in the grass and cried. And you know what, Vincent? You know what person I wanted at that moment? I remember because later, I thought how strange it was because I hadn't seen her since I was eighteen and I was still so damn mad at her. I wanted Kate. I wanted her to put her arms around me and hold me. I would have called her if I'd known where she was." Liz wiped at the tears on her face. "My mother was too sick to travel and my dad couldn't leave her. I went to the funeral alone. I wasn't Alan's wife yet so I had no say in the arrangements. His parents took over. They'd only met me twice, when they'd come to Utah to visit so I guess they didn't think I should have a say. They took his body home to Detroit to bury him. I flew there. I attended the funeral. I was his fiancée, Vincent, but at the funeral, I was a stranger. And I was so alone. And again, I wanted Kate." Liz shook her head. "I needed her." She slammed the tabletop with her fist. "But she wasn't there."

Vincent waited a few minutes, giving Liz time to regain control before asking, "What did you do afterwards?"

"Flew back to Salt Lake. I had two months left on my residency. I worked them. Then I came back home."

"Went to work with your father?"

She shook her head. "He'd already stopped working to care for Mom."

"So you took over the practice."

She nodded.

He rubbed her forearm. "You've had some rough years."

She looked down at his hand. "You have a gentle and warm touch, Vincent." She smiled at him. "Kate is very lucky." She laid her hand over his and stopped its movement. "I miss Alan. I miss him every day. I lie in bed at night and I wonder what my life would be like if I'd married him and stayed in Utah."

"You'd still be a doctor."

She nodded. "Yes. But I would also be a wife. And maybe a mother as well." She removed her hand from his and folded her arms over her chest. Gazing at him through tears that still filled her eyes, she asked, "Why did Kate leave here, Vincent?"

"I honestly don't know, Liz. She hasn't told me yet."

"When I first saw her the other day, I couldn't believe my eyes."

"She was happy to see you."

"I know. But twenty-one years...Twenty-one years of silence and missing her and wondering if she's all right and...Wondering what I did to make her take off like that."

"I don't think it was you, Liz."

"We'd gone to the movies. We were going to go shopping the next day. But she was gone." Liz wiped her eyes with her sleeve. Sighing, she said, "I asked Katherine where she had gone but she didn't know. For days afterwards, I waited for Kate to call me." Liz sniffed. "She never did." She leaned forward, resting her arms on the table. "You didn't know about me, did you?"

"No. I only met Katherine once. I knew Lydia had brought her to Maryland from somewhere, but Kate never told me about North Tonawanda."

"Did she tell you about her parents?"

"Not much. I never pushed her to talk about her past. She said that except for the time spent with her grandmother, her childhood sucked. I believed her. Over the years, I've thought she should talk about it, but have never been able to open her up."

"So you accepted not knowing?"

"I love her. I accept her the way she is."

Liz circled her hands around her coffee cup. "You are a rare man, Vincent Vermay."

He shook his head and then took a few sips of his hot chocolate. "I'm just a guy who loves his wife."

They fell silent, each drinking their hot chocolate. It was not an uncomfortable silence, but a peaceful one that was broken by a shrill beeper. "That's me," Liz said, lifting her sweatshirt. The beeper was hooked onto the band of her sweatpants. "It's the hospital." She stood up. "I better go home and call them."

Vincent pulled the cell phone from his back pocket. "Use this."

Taking it, she flipped it open, pressed power and dialed. Her conversation was short. Switching off the phone, she said, "Got to go. They brought one of my patients to emergency. Abdominal pain." She handed him the phone and grabbed her jacket.

He followed her down the hall to the foyer. She slipped on her jacket, zipped it, and then put on her shoes. "I'll see you for dinner tomorrow."

"Sure."

"Six. Don't be late. Miss Whiting is very punctual."

"Promise."

"Duke!" she called up the stairs. "Duke. Come, boy." When he didn't come, she said, "He's probably sleeping up there."

"Leave him. It's okay."

"You sure?"

"Very." He opened the front door. The wind had picked up outside and the snow fell harder. "Be careful driving in this, Liz."

"I will."

She slipped out the door, turned back and said, "How do you do it, Vincent?"

"Do what?"

"I barely know you and yet you get me to talk about things I don't want to."

He shrugged.

Turning away, she took off running. He closed the door and leaned back against it. He stood like this for a long time. He was here at last. Here in Katherine Malloy's house, in a strange town miles away from his wife. And strangely enough, he felt at home.

❧   ❧   ❧

The first thing Vincent did the following morning was set up his studio. Duke watched as Vincent took down the canopy bed and moved it into the adjoining bedroom. He leaned the mattresses, the headboard and the footboard against the wall. He moved the chest of drawers out into the hall. He left the armoire where it was. Down came the frilly curtains and up went his easel, complete with the empty canvas. He moved the dresser beside the easel so he could use it for storing his palate and sketchpads. The armoire was empty so he set his box of paints on the shelf at waist level. Standing with hands on his hips, Vincent grinned. Kate had been right. The light that poured in the windows was perfect. The room's walls were painted a cheerful light blue and the carved woodwork and crown molding were white. The floor was yellow pine. He could definitely paint here. He removed the sheet from the canvas. He could and he would paint here, starting tomorrow. Then when Kate came, he would have something to show her.

Happy, Vincent went downstairs. Some searching in the kitchen yielded a coffeemaker and coffee. Once he got that going, he searched further and found cereal and milk. He ate two bowls of Cheerios—Duke had one as well and ate it with relish—and drank two cups of coffee. Donning his leather jacket, cap, and hiking boots, he led Duke outside. While the dog played in the snow, Vincent shoveled the remainder of the driveway, moved the Rodeo up closer to the carriage house then cleaned up the snow that had fallen around the vehicle during the night. Lastly, he shoveled the walkway from the front gate to the front porch.

He was just finishing up when he saw Liz's Saturn pull into her driveway. She got out of the car and Vincent saw she was still wearing the same clothes as last night. Seeing her, Duke barked and ran to her. Carrying the shovel over his shoulder, Vincent walked down to her driveway. "Have you been at the hospital all night?"

She petted Duke as she said, "Yes."

"You look like you've been through a war."

"I was."

"Your patient?"

Liz smiled in spite of her tiredness. "She's going to make it." She looked down at Duke. "Come on, boy. Mama needs some sleep."

Vincent glanced at his watch. "Hey, it's noon. Would you rather skip dinner tonight and sleep?"

"No. Be here at six. Don't be late."

"Miss Whiting is very punctual."

"Don't you ever forget that, Vincent Vermay."

She started up the driveway, Duke at her heels.

"Hey, Liz?" Vincent said.

She turned. "What?"

"No doctor I've ever had would spend a whole night with me at the hospital."

"Guess you just never found the right doctor."

"Guess not."

He watched her go inside before returning to the old Victorian. He showered, donned blue jeans and a blue turtleneck then tried calling Kate. He got the answering machine. He left a brief message telling her that he would call her again later. Map in hand he left the house and headed out to buy a couple of telephones.

❧   ❧   ❧

Vincent was just getting into the shower when his cell phone rang. He eagerly snatched it up off the back of the toilet. Standing in his robe, the shower already running, he said, "Kate?"

"Sarah," his sister's voice replied.

"Hey."

"So when were you going to tell me that you moved out on Kate?" she asked.

"I didn't move out on Kate."

"And when were you going to tell me that you and Kate inherited eleven million dollars?"

"I take it you've talked to my wife."

"Sure have. Congratulations."

"For what?"

"The money. The house. She tells me you're enamored with it. I think she's jealous."

Vincent leaned against the pedestal sink. He saw Sarah in his mind. Long, chestnut brown hair and hazel eyes, body small and thin, yet athletic, and lovely face with a tantalizing mole next to her nose. She was five years his junior, fiercely independent and owner of Sarah's Colorado Excursions in Silverton, Colorado. She'd quit college and left Philadelphia at nineteen years of age, much to his parents' protests, and struck out on her own. She'd landed in Colorado and after working for a ski resort in Aspen had headed west to Durango. She'd driven a jeep for a while, taking tourists up into the San Juan Mountains on a wild ride. Ten years ago, just to kill time on one of her days off, she'd taken the Durango to Silverton Narrow Gauge Railroad up to Silverton with some friends and had fallen in love with the former mining town. Less than a year later, Sarah's Colorado Excursions was born. A few years back, Vincent and Kate had taken one of Sarah's hiking trips along with five other people. The physical exertion of the trip had nearly killed him. It hadn't put a dent in his sister's strength or energy. New respect for her had grown within him by the end of the six-day trip.

"Do Mom and Dad know any of this yet?" Sarah pressed, breaking into his thoughts.

"Not yet. They're in Paris right now. Business for Dad, pleasure for Mom."

"No kidding?"

"You'd know that if you called them more."

"They know my number."

"Not that you're ever there."

"So they could leave a message at the office for me, couldn't they?"

Vincent ran his hand through his hair. "When are you going to stop playing this game with them?"

"Don't badger me. Besides, I'll see them on Thanksgiving."

"Come on, Sarah. That's nine months away."

"Tell me about the house," she said.

"Not unless you promise to see Mom and Dad before Thanksgiving."

"Okay, okay, damn, you are exasperating. I'll hook up with them for Easter. Is that good enough?"

Vincent cringed. "That would be great except they'll be on a cruise with some friends."

She laughed.

"So pick another time. And one sooner than Thanksgiving, Sarah."

Still laughing, she said, "Okay, I promise. You need to stop worrying about my relationship with our parents. We get along."

"Barely."

"That's not totally my fault, Vincent. Flights to Colorado go both ways." Accusation hung heavy in her voice.

Vincent sighed. "Look, I know they've never come out to Silverton, Sarah, but they're the only parents you have."

"I shouldn't always have to come to them."

Vincent scratched his chin. "Sarah, couldn't you just cut them some slack? You know they never wanted you to—"

"They've visited you and Kate in Georgetown, Vincent."

He heard the hurt in her voice. He couldn't deny her statement. He stood in the bathroom holding the cell phone to his ear and wondering how the hell he could talk his parents into visiting Sarah in Silverton.

On the other end of the phone, she cleared her voice and said, "Shit, Vincent. Let's not dredge all this up again. Tell me about the house."

"I'd love to but not now. I'm actually getting ready to go have dinner with a neighbor. Will you take a rain check?"

"Sure."

"Good. I'll call you later."

"Better make it in a week. I've got some errands to run, and then I'm hitting the sack early. I'm going on a ski trip with some friends early in the morning."

"Where to?"

"Telluride. I'll call you when I get back."

"Be safe."

"Always. Take care, Vincent."

"I will. And Sarah?"

"Yeah."

"I'm proud of you. I think what you've done with your life is pretty wonderful." He heard the breath catch in her throat. "I love you, little sister."

"I love you too, bro," she said then hung up the phone.

He switched off his cell phone, took of his robe and got into the shower. As the hot water streamed down over him, he realized that he really should stop being the mediator between Sarah and their parents. He should leave them to their own devices; let them sink or swim. Yes, he should stop. But he knew he never would.

Dressed in black slacks, a white button down and a maroon and black striped tie, Vincent knocked on the Reilly door at six sharp. As he stood on the porch waiting, he turned and looked back at the street. Large snowflakes drifted down in the light of the street lamps. A car drove by; it's wheels crunching the fresh snow.

The Reilly's front door opened and Vincent turned around, finding a tall, rail thin, white-haired man staring at him. Holding out his hand, Vincent said, "Hello. You must be Dr. Reilly."

"Not anymore," the man said. "Come in."

Vincent stepped inside and found himself in a foyer, a crystal chandelier hanging above his head. The walls were covered with a colonial era mural, depicting, Vincent guessed, a view of Monticello, Thomas Jefferson's famous Virginia home. The floor was classic black and white tile. To his left was a high-backed bench. A winding staircase led up to the second floor. A light burned in the second floor hall.

Dr. Emmett Reilly held out his hand. "Coat and hat," he said, expectantly.

Vincent removed his leather jacket and tweed cap and handed them to Liz's father. He hung the garments in a closet under the stairs. He pointed at an arched door to Vincent's right. "This way."

Vincent followed Dr. Reilly into a massive dining room. Its walls were pale green, dark green ivy stenciled below ivory-colored crown molding. An oak table, oval in shape, devoured the room's floor space. Twelve Windsor chairs surrounded it. A maple sideboard held bottles of brandy, whiskey, and scotch. Crystal glasses sat beside the alcohol, beckoning. The far wall held the largest hutch Vincent had ever seen. It contained a collection of blue and white colonial china. Plain white china sat on the table, which was resplendent with a burgundy tablecloth and napkins held in sterling silver napkin rings that matched the flatware. A basket of fresh wildflowers adorned the table's center.

Dr. Reilly went to the sideboard. "Drink?"

"Yes. Some scotch would be nice."

Vincent stood just inside the door while Dr. Reilly retrieved ice from the ice bucket then poured the brandy into one of the crystal glasses. He held out the drink, forcing Vincent to go to him to accept it. "Thank you, Dr. Reilly." The old man squinted at him.

"Call me Emmett. Liz is the doctor now."

Vincent bowed. "Thank you, Emmett."

"Miss Whiting is making lamb. Do you like lamb, young man?"

"Yes."

"Liz will be down soon."

"Great."

Dr. Reilly looked away and Vincent suddenly realized that Liz's father was very uncomfortable playing host. Vincent wondered when the last time was he had done so. "Are you going to join me, Emmett?" Vincent asked, holding up his drink.

The old man shook his head. "Can't." He looked at Vincent with sad eyes. "My wife decorated the house," he said, searching for something to talk to Vincent about.

"She did a lovely job."

"Liz says you like old houses."

"I do."

"Marlene fell in love with this place when I brought her home. Changed the décor from what it was. I told her to do whatever she wanted. Just have fun."

"And did she?"

"Yes. She was so full of ideas and she did a lot of the work herself. She called it her labor of love. I enjoyed watching her and listening to her ramble on and on about the next room she wanted to do. It was…"

"What?" Vincent gently prodded.

"One of the best times of my life. The best was when Liz was born." He wiped at his eyes. "That was the best."

"What did she weigh?"

A trace of a smile crossed his face. "Five pounds, 9 ounces. She was a peanut." He held up his hands to show Vincent her size. "Small one, she was. All delicate with curly auburn hair."

Vincent sipped his drink. "Did you have any others?"

"Kids?"

"Yes."

"No." He looked past Vincent into nothing. "Marlene lost the next two. We quit trying."

"Well, at least you've got a beauty in Liz."

"She is a miracle," the old man softly said. His eyes filled with sudden joy.

Vincent turned from Emmett Reilly and saw Liz standing in the doorway. She wore a black dress and her hair hung free, waving about her shoulders. "Good evening, Dr. Reilly," Vincent said, bowing.

She entered, went to her father and slipped her arm in his. "I see you've met my father."

"Yes. He's treated me quite hospitably." Vincent held up his drink.

Liz looked up at her father. "Thank you, Dad." Emmett looked down at his daughter with wonderment in his eyes. Standing on tiptoe, Liz kissed his cheek. "Any estimated time of arrival for dinner?"

"Your mother didn't tell me," he said.

Liz took her father's hand. "Dad, Miss Whiting is cooking dinner."

His eyes filled with confusion. "Why isn't your mother cooking?"

"Dad, you know why. Mom passed away. You remember."

He shook his head.

Liz nodded as she said, "When I was living in Salt Lake City."

Emmett trembled as the memory flooded back to him. "Yes, of course," he said, reaching for a chair. Liz helped him sit down in one of the table's end chairs. He buried his face in his hands.

"Vincent, could you get him a drink of water? There are some bottles of spring water in the bottom of the hutch."

Vincent quickly retrieved a bottle and poured it into a glass with ice. He handed it to Liz. "Dad," she said, holding the drink in front of him. "Drink this."

He shook his head, his face still hidden in his hands. "I'm sorry, Lizzie," he said, starting to cry. "I tried. I didn't want to embarrass you. I'm sorry." His shoulders shook as a sob escaped him.

Liz knelt beside him. "Oh, Dad, you could never embarrass me. I love you." She set the glass of water on the table then massaged her father's back. "Dad, look at me." He did as she asked, tears still rolling down his cheeks. "It's okay. Vincent understands. Don't you, Vincent?"

"Yes," Vincent said, smiling at the old man. He knelt on the other side of Emmett. "Hey, things happen. No need to let them spoil a whole night and, from what I can smell, a fine dinner."

Emmett swallowed hard. "I'm sorry," he said again.

Liz hugged her father. "You have nothing to be sorry for, Dad."

He pushed her away and, reaching out, touched her cheek.

Liz placed her hand over his and pressed it tighter against her cheek. Vincent saw tears in her eyes. "Dad, why don't you go wash your face?"

He nodded. Liz stood up then helped Emmett stand. She turned him toward the door and with a gentle push, sent him on his way.

Still kneeling, Vincent smiled up at her. "You're terrific with him."

Liz forced back her tears. Unable to speak, she shook her head. She went to the window and looked out at the darkness.

Vincent rose and went to her. He rested his hands on her shoulders and gave them a squeeze. "It's snowing," he said. "In Georgetown, we don't get snow like this." She didn't reply. "Liz?"

She laid her head against the frosted windowpane. "Kate didn't enlighten you, did she?"

"No. I didn't ask her."

"It shocked her." Liz's voice wavered. "His condition shocked her." A tear slipped from her left eye. "I've lived with him like this since my mother's death and still, it shocks me."

Vincent kept his hands on her shoulders. "Maybe so, but you handled him beautifully."

A sob escaped her. "He was my hero."

Vincent squeezed her shoulders again. "He still is. In your heart and in your memory."

"I love him."

"I know."

She sniffed. "I try to keep his life as comfortable and simple as possible." She looked up at Vincent. "I know he's not happy. I don't think he knows how to be happy anymore."

Vincent smiled. "Yes, he does. He's happy in his memories. Didn't you hear him talk about your birth?"

She shook her head.

"He called you a miracle. And he smiled. More than that, the minute he saw you in the doorway, his eyes lit up."

She wiped at her eyes. "Really?"

"Really."

"Lizzie!" Emmett called from the hallway. "Lizzie, Duke is back." Liz's father appeared in the doorway with a snow-covered Duke at his side. Seeing Liz, the dog hurried to her.

Petting him, Liz said, "You are all wet." He licked her hand.

Vincent reached down and petted him as well.

"Duke loves all that attention," Emmett said, entering the room. "Miss Whiting says dinner is ready. She says to be seated."

"Then we better get to it," Liz said.

Emmett sat in the head chair with Vincent on his left and his daughter on his right. Duke crawled beneath the table, hoping, Vincent supposed, for dropped food. He rubbed the dog with his foot.

Miss Whiting came in, carrying a dish with green beans and a dish with mashed potatoes. She was a lovely woman with short gray hair. She had a figure some twenty-year-olds would die for. She wore a green dress beneath a white apron. She smiled at Vincent as she set the dishes down. "Elsie Whiting," she said. "You are Vincent."

"Yes, Ma'am."

She left the room and returned moments later carrying a plate loaded with sliced lamb. She set the platter down and turned to leave, but Emmett stopped her. "Elsie, you will join us."

"One's housekeeper doesn't join the dinner party, Emmett Reilly," she scolded.

"Apparently in this house they do," Liz said, gesturing toward the chair beside Vincent.

"But Elizabeth—"

"No, buts," Vincent said. "I insist as well."

Shaking her head, Miss Whiting went to the hutch, retrieved another place setting and sat down beside Vincent. "Most improper," she mumbled.

Laughing, Vincent said, "Don't worry. I'm an artist. I do everything improperly. So let's eat?"

❧   ❧   ❧

Liz insisted on walking him home. Duke ran ahead, playing in the snow. The night was cold and dark, the street lights nearly obscured by the falling snow.

"If it keeps this up, I'll have to shovel the driveway again," Vincent said, seeing his breath as he spoke.

"We have a plowing service. I could give you their number if you're interested."

"Nah. I don't have to get anywhere first thing in the morning. Besides, I need the exercise."

"Just be careful. You don't want to end up hurting your back. Shovel the proper way."

Vincent laughed. "Always the doctor."

"I guess I am."

"Kate told me on the phone that you came here to fix up the house and to paint. She said you have recently experienced an artist's block."

"She did, did she?"

"Yes. But she also said that you've begun a promising painting."

"She told you that?"

"Yes."

They reached the Victorian's front gate and Vincent opened it. Duke ran up the path to the porch. He stopped in front of the double doors, his tail wagging.

"Duke, you come," Liz said. "You're going home with me."

The dog turned and looked at her, but didn't budge.

"Apparently, he doesn't like your decision, Liz."

She smiled. "He doesn't like many of my decisions." She started up the path. "You, Duke, are being bad."

Duke's wagging tail flopped, but still he didn't budge.

"Looks like he wants to come inside. How about his mother?"

Liz laughed. "His mother…I guess that's the right term for it. And, yes, I would love to come inside."

Vincent unlocked the right door and held it open. Duke shot inside and up the stairs. Liz entered as she said, "I think my dog believes he has two houses."

Vincent followed her inside. "Let him believe it. No harm."

Liz removed her ski jacket and fedora and hung them on the coat rack. She kicked off her boots. "You're very kind, Vincent. Not everyone will put up with the neighbor's dog."

Vincent waved his hand. "No big deal. I like him." He shed his outerwear and set his boots beside Liz's next to the coat rack. "Come on, let's get comfortable." He led her into the parlor and turned on both floor lamps. They lit the room with a soft yellow glow. Vincent gestured toward the couch. "Sit."

She sat, curling her legs up beneath her. "I always liked this room. Will you change it, Vincent?"

Vincent sat down in a red velvet, wingback chair and looked about him. Beige and navy blue striped wallpaper covered the walls. White wainscoting and crown molding matched the built-in oval topped bookcases on either side of the bay window. Books and vases sat on the shelves. The window seat beckoned one to take one of the books, sit down and wile away the afternoon. Another wingback chair, across from Vincent's own, bore the same pattern as the wallpaper. White and red velvet pillows, sporting the same floral pattern as the couch on which Liz sat, surrounded her. A red, blue, and white flowered oval rug covered most of the hardwood floor. There were also two mahogany Queen Anne stands, a coffee table and a sideboard behind the couch. A brass floor lamp with a crystal shade sat beside the couch and its twin sat beside Vincent's chair. A painting of roses in a gold vase on a table hung on the wall beside the door that led into the kitchen. Beneath it, Vincent had sat a twenty-seven inch television he'd bought along with the phones. The television and the entertainment unit it sat on looked out of place in the room. Turning from the intrusion, his eyes fell on the magnificent fireplace, constructed of hand-carved mahogany with red brick insides that stretched out into the hardwood floor. Family pictures sat on the mantle.

Turning back to Liz, Vincent said, "No. I like it just the way it is."

Liz smiled. "Good."

"You spent a lot of time here when Kate came to stay?"

Liz nodded. "Kate and I were inseparable. We had sleepovers. Mostly here though. I liked escaping from my parents."

"All kids do."

She sighed. "God, we had fun. My parents got me a doctor's bag for Christmas when I was five. I swear, every year I made Kate let me listen to her heart, take her temperature. Sometimes, we'd pretend she had a disease that I had to diagnose."

"And did you?"

"Of course. And I was never wrong and she always got better."

"Which turned out to be good for me."

"Most definitely."

Liz got up from the couch and went to the fireplace. She studied the pictures a moment, before picking one up. She held it out for Vincent to see. "Kate and I at age ten, I believe."

"You were both very pretty."

She set the photo back on the mantle and picked up another one. "Katherine. She was beautiful."

Vincent held out his hand and Liz gave it to him. A woman with dark hair curled into a bun stood beside an older man. She wore a white flowing dress. The man wore a dark suit and held a cigar in one hand. Vincent stared at the woman's soft, delicately boned face. He saw traces of Kate in her face. "How old was she here?"

"I'm not sure. But that's her husband. He was in his fifties when she married him."

"So this is the man whose initials are on my front gate and whose face is on my front door."

"Afraid so."

Vincent gazed at Jethro Malloy's face. It held no kindness. "He was dead long before you were born, I presume."

"Yes."

"But you knew Katherine?"

Liz returned to the couch and sat down. "Katherine kept mostly to herself. She looked after us, but…"

"What?"

"If Kate and I weren't over here, she spent her time on the third floor."

"Were you ever up there?"

"No. The third floor was off limits to children. The only person that went up there was Abe, the caretaker."

"But Kate was her granddaughter. Surely, she let Kate up there."

"I don't know. You'll have to ask Kate."

Vincent got up and returned the photo to the mantle. He scanned the other pictures. "Hey," he said, pointing at a photo in a gilded frame. "This your mom and dad?"

Liz joined him at the mantle. She peered at the picture. "Why, yes, it is. Now, that's odd."

"Really?"

"Yes. I didn't think Katherine really socialized much with them. Guess I was wrong. Look at my father with dark hair. He went white in his forties." She touched the picture, running her finger along her mother's auburn hair. "Mom," she said. "God wasn't she lovely. We have the same hair color."

"You do. But you have your father's face."

Liz didn't acknowledge his comment. "She was so beautiful. I miss her, Vincent."

He folded his hands across his chest and leaned against the fireplace. "That's understandable."

"She made childhood fun. She encouraged me in everything I wanted to do."

"And your father?"

She turned her eyes to Vincent. "What about him?"

"Did he encourage you?"

"He would always say, 'Whatever your mother thinks is best.' He trusted my mother's child raising skills implicitly. But then he was a very busy doctor so I guess, in a way, he had to trust her."

"She did well."

"If she were here, Marlene Reilly would thank you." She was silent a moment then said, "You should have known my father before, Vincent. He had such confidence. He enjoyed life. Every day was special to him. I was in awe of him. He was a doctor and I wanted to be one too. And then my mother got sick." Liz closed her eyes. "She wasted away right in front of him and he could do nothing. This man, this doctor, who had cured so many." She looked at Vincent, the pain of her memories in her eyes. "He tried everything. He called in doctor after doctor, calling in favors, even begging. He had to watch her suffer every day for two years. It was easier on me. I was out west. I talked to her on the phone and could pretend it wasn't happening."

"But you came home during that time?"

"I did. Each time I came, she was weaker and thinner."

Vincent laid a hand on Liz's shoulder.

"But you see, Vincent, I didn't live it day in and day out like he did. I didn't have to face the fact that after a lifetime of helping people, I could do nothing for the person I loved most in the world. He had to face it." She ran a hand through her auburn hair. "You saw him. That's how I found him, the night she died. I came home from the office and he was sitting beside her bed, holding her hand. I knew the minute I stepped into the room that she was gone. I went to him and hugged him. I asked him why he hadn't called me. He looked up at me with...his eyes...they..."

"Were filled with overpowering sadness," Vincent said for her.

She nodded, blinking back tears. "I've taken care of him ever since. Miss Whiting left the office to come care for him too. I hired a new receptionist."

"Miss Whiting who has always loved him."

"He never knew. He was totally oblivious to that fact. Now, he wouldn't comprehend it even if she told him."

"Liz, when was the last time you had a dinner party?"

She shook her head. "Not since before Mom died."

"I suspected that. He was quite upset with himself."

"I know. But he'll forget it tomorrow."

"Have you tried..."

"A psychiatrist? Oh, yes. We've tried several different therapy approaches. To no avail."

Vincent drew a long breath. "Like I said before, he has his memories. He has you and Miss Whiting to care for him."

"I will never desert him, Vincent. But if you could have only seen his brilliance." She went back to the couch and sat down, her face buried in her hands. Vincent sat down beside her. He thought she was going to cry but she didn't. He sat next to her, remaining quiet, hoping that just his presence would comfort her. He had no comforting words to offer her. What could he say? Her life had been one loss after another the last several years.

Breathing deeply, she lifted her head and, managing a small smile, said, "You did it again."

"Did what?"

"Tell me, Dr. Vermay, what do you charge per session?"

"I'm no psychiatrist, Liz."

Her smiled widened. "No." She took his hand. "But already you are a dear friend. I can see why Kate fell in love with you." She got to her feet. "I better get going. I have early rounds at the hospital tomorrow."

He walked her to the front foyer, helped her round up Duke and watched as they walked down the front path. Once they were outside the gate, he gave a final wave and closed the door. Heading upstairs, his thoughts went to the third floor. Liz had said that Katherine had spent most of her time up there. So if Katherine had been comfortable up there, why was Kate terrified of it? Reaching the second floor, he walked down the hall to the stairs that led up to Katherine's sanctuary. He took the steps two at a time. He tried the door but it didn't budge. "Locked," he said aloud.

He ran back down the stairs to the coat rack and dug in his jacket pocket. He found his key ring and hurried back up both flights of stairs. Clausterman had given Kate just two keys—the skeleton key and the key to the carriage house. He hoped the skeleton key worked in this door as it did in the front and back doors of the house. It slid into the lock and it turned without a problem. He pushed the door open and searched the wall for a light switch. He didn't find one.

He stood in the doorway a few moments, letting his eyes adjust to the darkness. Gradually, he saw shadows. A little light filtered up from the second floor hallway and between it and his widening pupils, he saw an object glittering in the room's center. It seemed suspended above the floor. Walking to it, he reached out and took hold of it. It was a piece of crystal on a string. He pulled it and light filled the room. He looked up, squinting. A crystal chandelier hung from the ceiling, suspended on a board that ran between the ceiling's arches. His eyes followed the slanted ceiling down to a double bed, its headboard and footboard white wrought iron, its comforter ivory with pink and red cabbage size roses. He scanned the room, noting a wooden rocker with a seat pad that matched the comforter and a pine armoire and dresser. A white porcelain bowl and pitcher sat on top of the chest. A chamber pot sat on the floor beside the bed. In front of the room's long and narrow window stood a wooden music stand. The window glass was frosted over. The white ceiling slanted down to maple wainscoting and the wall beneath was covered with wallpaper with a white background and red roses. Plain white drapes hung on the window. The room was simple, yet plainly pure Victorian.

Turning back to the bed, Vincent caught sight of a closed violin case. He opened the case. A plaque on the inside cover read, "Katherine Mann." He lifted the violin from the case and gasped. It was a Stradivarius. "Wow,

Katherine," he said to the empty room. He plucked a string. The instrument was grossly out of tune. Returning it to its case, he wondered how long it had sat here no longer making music. He closed the case then looked around the room again. So this room had been Katherine's escape. She had come here to play her violin. Just like he escaped to his studio to paint. He shut off the light and went back down to the second floor. He knew he should go to bed if he wanted to get any work done tomorrow. But he wasn't tired and Jethro Malloy's library beckoned.

He went in, sat down at Jethro's desk and switched on the desk lamp. He opened the center drawer and found a pen and stationery. He pulled a piece from the drawer. The letterhead boldly proclaimed, "Malloy Lumber Company." So Jethro had been a businessman. He wondered if there was anything of Malloy's business left in North Tonawanda. Certainly, there was no longer the forest necessary to sustain a lumber business. He would check into it while he was here.

He picked up the pen. Grinning, imagining her face when she opened the envelope and saw the old stationery, Vincent put pen to paper and wrote, "Dear Kate…"

CHAPTER 4

The incessant ringing of the cell phone woke Vincent the next morning. He sat up and discovered he'd been sleeping with his head on his letter to Kate. He fumbled with the cell phone, trying to remove it from the holder on his belt. At last he succeeded, flipped it open and huskily said, "Hello."

"Hi, handsome. Got that painting done yet?"

"Hi, Kate," he said, smiling.

"Well, do you?"

He sat back in the chair. "I've only been here a day, love."

"I miss you dreadfully."

"That's nice to hear." Vincent glanced at his watch. It was 9 a.m. "Aren't you working today?"

"I'm in my office right now. I'm supposed to be writing a speech on the NRA."

"National Rifle Association?"

"The one and only."

"McMartin's stand?"

"You don't want to know, Vincent."

"You're probably right."

"Have you set up your studio?"

"Yes, first thing yesterday. I had dinner with Liz and her father last night."

"How was it?"

"Why didn't you tell me about his mental condition, Kate?"

"Because I didn't want to predispose you."

"It was actually a lovely evening. He lapsed a few times, but I tried to smooth things over. His condition breaks Liz's heart though."

"Her's and Miss Whiting's."

"Elsie is definitely devoted to him."

"She always has been. I always wondered if Mrs. Reilly suspected."

"Who knows?"

"Mrs. Reilly knows and she took the knowledge with her to her grave. Not to change the subject, but I am. Guess who came to see me?"

"Your old boss?"

"Nope. The visitor was of the relative persuasion."

"Yours or mine?"

"Mine."

"Lydia Malloy?"

"Close, Vincent. Her son Jeff knocked on the townhouse door yesterday. Her illegitimate son, I should add."

"Scandalous."

"Actually, the whole affair surrounding his birth was scandalous."

"Have I ever met him?"

"No. He wasn't at the reading of the will. He's an arrogant, nineteen-year-old. He's going to George Washington University. He's quite full of himself."

"Impressed with his own unimportance?"

"Precisely."

Vincent brushed at his whiskers with the back of his hand. "What did he want?"

"You've been inside the carriage house, right?"

"Yeah."

"He wants the Ford."

Vincent gasped and sat forward. "What?"

"He wants the 1924 Ford."

"I hope you didn't agree."

She didn't answer.

"Kate?"

"You want it, Vincent?"

"Yes. I want it and the hansom cab. Please tell me you didn't give either of them away."

"No, darling, I didn't give either of them away. I told young Jeff to stuff it. Although not quite that kindly I must say."

Vincent let out a sigh of relief. "Thank God."

She chuckled at the other end of the phone. "You are so damned old fashioned, Vincent."

"So?"

"So I do so love you for it. God, it seems so damned long until I get to see you."

"You, Kate Vermay, are impatient."

"You bet I am. What are you going to do today?"

"Paint. And call the phone company and get the phone hooked up. You?"

"Write a speech about the NRA. And attend one of those political functions tonight. You know, the political functions that you love so much."

Vincent smiled. "I hate them."

"No kidding."

He could feel her smiling on the other end of the phone. He didn't want to shock her smile away, but he had to tell her. So, in a soft voice, he said, "I went up to the third floor last night, Kate."

She didn't respond.

"I couldn't figure out what frightens you up there. It's just a bedroom."

"Katherine's bedroom," she said, her voice tinged with sadness.

Confused by her tone, Vincent said, "It's a beautiful room, Kate."

"Don't judge a book by its cover, Vincent."

"What does that mean?"

She breathed heavily into the phone. When she spoke, her voice carried fear. "Is the violin still there?"

"Yes, it is. It needs tuning, but it's a magnificent instrument."

"No, Vincent. It's a magical instrument."

"Why do you say that?"

She didn't answer right away.

"Kate?" he prodded.

Finally, she said, "It's too bad you never got to hear Katherine play it."

"She brought out the magic?"

"Very much so. Look, Vincent, I better get back to work. And you better go paint."

"Wait, babe. How did you know the violin was on the third floor?"

Because that's where Katherine always kept it."

"Why didn't she take it with her to Maryland?"

"To quote her, Vincent, 'Because I couldn't. The violin must stay in North Tonawanda.'"

"Why did she think that?"

"I don't know. She refused to answer any more questions about the instrument."

"Wow." Vincent scratched his chin."

"Now, I really have to hang up."

"Okay, babe. See you in…let's see…twelve days."

"I'll be counting the hours."

"Me too. Goodbye, Kate."

"I love you, Vincent."

The phone clicked in his ear before he could say the words back to her.

Beethoven's fifth symphony filled the Victorian as Vincent painted in his studio. He'd been working for six hours. He was so absorbed in his work that he hadn't heard Duke come up the stairs and lie down on the studio floor. The dog lay with his face on his paws, watching Vincent's every move. The symphony ended and the CD player shut off. The silence smashed into Vincent's ears and he stepped back, palette in one hand, and paintbrush in the other. He studied his work.

The once blank canvas held what could very well turn out to be a brilliant painting. So far he'd painted a winding road lined with stark, black trees without leaves. Snow covered the bare branches, a bright moon shining down. "Okay," Vincent said. "There is potential here."

Duke barked and Vincent jumped. Looking towards the door, he saw the dog and asked, "You trying to give me a heart attack?"

The dog got to his feet; tail wagging furiously.

Vincent pointed at the winding road. "Do you know what I'm going to have coming down that road, Duke? Do you?"

Duke cocked his head.

"That magnificent hansom cab stored out there in the carriage house." Vincent nodded. "And that, my new found canine friend is the genius of it. Who expects a hansom cab to be out here in the middle of nowhere? Hansom cabs belong in cities. Get it?"

The dog sat down.

"Well, you don't have to get it. Patrons of the arts have to get it. My fans have to get it." He set the palette on the dresser. "I'm famished. What about you, boy, hungry?"

Duke barked.

"Right answer." Vincent set his brush beside the palette and closed the tubes of paint he'd been using. "Beef hash sound good, Duke? I've got two cans, courtesy of Elsie Whiting." Vincent wiped his paint-stained hands on a rag and looked at his painting again. "I like it, Duke. And the beauty of it is Kate will never know it wasn't started in Georgetown. Think about it. The background is…well…represents anywhere. See what I mean?" He tossed the rag on the table. "Come on, Duke. Let's eat."

Downstairs in the kitchen, Vincent washed his hands then prepared the beef hash. He ate one can and Duke ate the other. Not bothering to change out of his painting clothes, Vincent donned his hiking boots, leather jacket, gloves, and newsboy cap then led Duke outside. He stood on the front porch and breathed deeply of the cold winter air. A royal blue sky with white puffy clouds greeted him. Rubbing the dog's ears, Vincent said, "This is beautiful." He pointed at the snow glittering in the sunlight. "Look at it, lying on the fence and trees. Incredible." He glanced down at Duke. "Let's play."

Vincent ran down the porch steps, Duke following him with the enthusiasm that only a dog has. Vincent made snowballs and threw them, Duke chasing after them.

"I don't know who is having more fun—you or Duke."

Vincent turned. Liz stood by the gate, her fedora low on her forehead.

"Hey," Vincent said, tossing the snowball at her.

She ducked. "Don't you dare!"

Duke ran to the gate and looked up at her.

"Come inside the gate. I promise I won't throw anymore."

"You better keep that promise." She came inside, petting Duke and accepting his jumping up and licking her without scolding him.

Vincent glanced at his watch.

"Just after three. Home early today?"

Liz pushed Duke down. "Amazingly, my last office patient was at two. I shot over to the hospital to visit those who are incarcerated, then came on home."

Vincent laughed. "Think highly of being in the hospital, do you?"

She laughed as well. "No, I don't. I'm a terrible patient. I was hospitalized a while back and I think, by the time I was discharged, the nurses hated me."

"They say doctors are the worst patients."

"And they, whoever they are, would be right."

"What hospital do you work out of?"

"DeGraff. You must have passed it on your way in Saturday."

"Ahh, yes, it's at the corner of…" He snapped his fingers.

"Tremont and the Twin Cities Memorial Highway. In fact, you can walk right down there to Whiting, turn right and walk down to the hospital."

"I'm in good shape here then. I got a doctor living next door and a hospital just around the corner."

Liz crossed her arms. "You must learn about North Tonawanda, Vincent. It has a rich history."

"I guess you'll have to teach me." He gestured at the driveway. "Speaking of history, do you know what's in that carriage house?"

"Yes."

"Fantastic."

"Want to see what's in my garage?"

Vincent grinned. "Sure." As they walked to her garage, Vincent asked, "Do you know if any of Malloy's lumber mill is left?"

"You mean any of the buildings?"

"Yeah."

Liz scratched her cheek with a gloved hand. "Yes, one. It's over on River Road, along the Niagara River. It's a marina now."

"How do you get there?"

"Just go down Goundry until you hit River Road. Cross the road, turn right and you'll run into it. It's a huge, blue building."

"I can't miss it."

"No, you can't."

They reached the Reilly driveway and started up it. Duke ran ahead of them. "Do you know how long the lumber mill operated, Liz?"

"Not really. Katherine had sold it by the time I was born. My father might know."

"I'll ask him, if it's okay with you."

"Of course. You can visit him anytime you want. That is if you can take…you know…what happened last night."

Vincent took Liz's arm, stopping her forward progress. She looked up at him with questioning eyes. "Your father's condition doesn't scare me off, Liz. I would be honored to visit him."

She smiled. "You mean that, don't you?"

"Yes, I do."

"None of his former colleagues or friends feels that way. They never call or come to see him. My father was once highly regarded in this city. And now…" She trailed off, her eyes misty.

"They are all idiots. Besides, he has the best two people in the world with him."

"He was on the town council and the Board of Education. His practice thrived. A lot of his patients defected when I took over."

"Some people don't like change, Liz."

"Guess not. But I can't complain. I've built a new practice."

They entered the garage through the side door. Vincent saw the familiar Saturn. A covered automobile was parked beside it. Liz pulled the cover back. Vincent stared at the grill and hood of a 1965 red Mustang. "Oh, my God," he said.

Liz grinned. "Like it?"

"It's really yours?"

"Yes. It belonged to my mother. She left it to me in her will." She removed the cover completely. "Hop in."

Vincent got in behind the wheel and Liz climbed into the passenger seat. He turned to her and asked, "Do you drive it?"

"In the summer. We use salt on the roads here in New York during the winter. Destroys cars like you wouldn't believe."

Vincent ran his hands along the steering wheel. "You keep it insured year round, don't you?"

"Yes. Classic car insurance."

"You have to take me for a ride this summer."

"It's a date."

Vincent smiled at her. "You rode in this when you were a kid?"

Liz nodded. "So did your wife."

"No kidding."

"I don't kid."

Vincent sat quiet a moment, enjoying sitting behind the wheel of a 1965 Mustang.

Liz broke the silence. "You have to promise me something."

"What?"

"That you'll take me for a ride in the old Ford."

"I don't know if it runs, Liz."

"You'll get it running, Vincent."

"You think so."

"I know so." She opened the car door and got out. Leaning back inside, she added, "Because you, Vincent Vermay, are a man who accomplishes anything he puts his mind to."

Vincent painted until noon the next day then showered, put on jeans and a tartan plaid flannel shirt, donned his outerwear and stepped out onto the Victorian's front porch. Once again, a rich blue sky and puffy white clouds greeted him. It was warmer than yesterday. He thought about taking the Rodeo then changed his mind. He could use a walk. He stopped in front of the Reilly house. It was not quite as big as Katherine's house. Still, it was a large old Colonial, shingles painted beige; trim painted dark brown. Its windows were long and narrow, except for a double, multi-paned window on the first floor, to the left of the door. A porch with thick, round columns ran across the front and west side of the house. Smiling, Vincent continued on his way. As he walked, he admired the huge, stately old homes that lined Goundry. There were other Victorians like Katherine's as well as Colonials like the Reilly house. Many, he could tell just by looking at the added outside staircases and non-symmetrical additions, had been converted into apartment houses. He shook his head, saddened by each house he saw like this.

He crossed over Payne Avenue then Oliver Street, passing by an apartment building. Its sign proclaimed it to be the Carousal Apartments. He waited at Main Street for the signal to change, and then crossed both Main and Webster. On the corner of Webster and Goundry was a restaurant called Nestor's, housed in a tall, red brick building. Vincent could smell hot dogs. The sidewalk took him down an incline and where the ground leveled off, he saw an auto parts store to his right and what was obviously River Road straight ahead. Again, he had to wait for a signal to change, but once he crossed the road, he reached the former Malloy building within moments. The sign on its front proclaimed "Steven's Marina." The smell of fish was strong and the river lapped against the riverbank with short slapping sounds.

Vincent walked around the side of the building and found a door. Letters carved into the wooden trim above the door read "Malloy Lumber Yard." He walked around to the other side of the building and discovered a smaller building. It sat on a gray stone foundation and was painted white. Squatting, he brushed snow away from the cornerstone. The date read 1868. Straightening, he peered in the building's side window. It was an office filled with modern office equipment.

"Can I help you?"

Vincent jumped. Twirling around, he faced a burly man in a blue parka and a white, sea captain's hat. "I hope you can. You own this place?"

"I do."

"This little building; was it part of the old lumber mill?"

"Malloy's place?"

"Yes. I'm doing some research on Jethro Malloy."

The man rubbed his chin. Vincent noted he wore no gloves. His hands were huge; his skin dry and cracked. "It was. Malloy's father started the mill back in 1868. My father bought these buildings from Katherine Malloy when I was a boy."

Vincent judged the man to be in his sixties. "Your dad turned it into a marina?"

"Hell, no, I did that. My dad ran it as a museum. You know, pay to see the biggest lumber mill North Tonawanda ever had. Which is saying something, I guess, since the town had lots of mills back then. That's why it's nicknamed the Lumber City."

"What did you do with all the old equipment?"

"Sold it to collectors. Made a bundle." The man pulled keys from his coat pocket. As he unlocked the office door, he said, "People were up in arms when I closed the museum. Claimed they'd boycott the marina. Claimed I was stealing the town's history."

"I think I agree with them."

The man looked at Vincent with laughter in his eyes. "Think whatever you want, but go over and see how many boats I'm storing for all those people who hated me ten years ago. Hypocrites." He opened the office door. "I got paperwork to do." Without saying goodbye, he went inside and closed the door behind him.

Vincent left the marina. He thought about exploring downtown, but changed his mind, thinking of Emmett Reilly. He picked up his pace. As he turned on to Goundry Street, he hoped that the old man was up for a visit.

❦   ❦   ❦

Elsie Whiting opened the Reilly front door. Seeing Vincent, she smiled, she stepped back and said, "Come in."

Vincent entered, removing his cap. "I hope this isn't a bad time. I was hoping to visit Emmett."

Elsie's smile widened. "I've just finished making lunch. Have you eaten?"

"No, I haven't."

"Please join us. The company will do Emmett good."

"I would be honored."

While Elsie hung his coat in the closet and stowed his cap on the closet shelf, Vincent removed his boots. "Emmett's in the dining room, Vincent. He likes to eat all his meals there. Go on in while I get lunch."

Vincent entered the big room and found Liz's father sitting in the head chair. "Emmett," Vincent said, pulling out the side chair on Emmett's left. "Miss Whiting has invited me to lunch. I hope you don't mind."

The retired doctor looked at him but did not speak.

"Is it all right if I sit down, Dr. Reilly?"

"Elizabeth isn't home."

"I know. Do you remember me?"

The old man studied him a few minutes before saying, "You are the painter."

"I am. Vincent Vermay." He held out his hand.

Emmett shook Vincent's outstretched hand and said, "Sit down, boy."

Miss Whiting came in just as Vincent sat down. She carried a tray of cold cuts, a relish tray and a loaf of bread. A crystal pitcher filled with water, a jar of mayonnaise, a bowl of potato chips, and three place settings already occupied the table. "I'll be right back with the soup," she said, setting the trays and loaf of bread down. She left the room, returning a short time later with a large crock. She set it on the table, opened the lid and filled a ladle. "Vincent," she said, holding out her hand. "It's chicken noodle. Emmett's favorite."

Vincent handed her his bowl. "Mine too, Elsie."

Once she had filled three bowls, Miss Whiting sat down. Bowing her head, she said a short prayer then indicated they dig in. Vincent was pleased to see that Emmett ate with relish, first his bowl of soup and then a giant ham sandwich. He also downed three glasses of water. Whatever had disrupted the normal function of his mind hadn't stolen his appetite.

"So, Liz tells me that you have a wife and a home in Georgetown," Miss Whiting said.

"Yes. I believe you know my wife."

Miss Whiting smiled. "Lovely little girl. When she came over not too long ago with Liz was the first time I'd seen her since the girls were eighteen. She told me she works for a senator."

"Senator McMartin. She writes his speeches, his newsletter…she writes pretty much all of his communications."

Miss Whiting took a bite of her turkey sandwich. "She likes it?"

Vincent nodded. "She's a marvelous writer."

"Doesn't surprise me. Although, with the imagination the child had, I thought she would go into fiction writing."

"She's thought about it."

"Well, tell her I said she should do more than think about it."

"I will." Vincent took a long drink of water then asked, "When did you go to work for Emmett, Elsie?"

"Which time? Now or when he was working?"

"When he was working."

"Let's see…" Furrows appeared in her forehead as she thought. "Liz wasn't born yet and she's…"

"Thirty-nine?"

"Yes." Elsie counted on her fingers. "I started four years before she was born."

"And you've been with him ever since?"

"I have." She averted her eyes. "He's a good man."

And you love him. "It's hard these days to find an employee that loyal."

"She's my friend," Emmett said, breaking into the conversation for the first time. He set his second sandwich down and repeated, "She's my friend."

"I'm sure she is."

He looked at Vincent as if suddenly realizing Vincent was there. He turned to Elsie. "Where is Elizabeth?"

She touched his forearm. "She called, Emmett, and said she couldn't make it today. She's very busy at the office."

He looked at Vincent again. "You were here before."

"Yes. For dinner."

"You are the painter named Vincent."

Vincent nodded.

Emmett stood up. "I want to show you something."

"Emmett, we're not done eating yet."

"We can come back, Elsie," he said. Vincent rose and followed Emmett out into the hall. "It's upstairs, Vincent." Dr. Reilly led him up the winding staircase to the second floor. They went down the hall to the last room on the left and entered. A queen-size, four-poster, walnut bed dominated the room. Emmett pointed to the painting hanging above the headboard. "Marlene bought it. Liz was still in medical school."

Slowly, a smile formed on Vincent's face. He went to the foot of the bed and stared at the painting, not believing what he was seeing. It was a painting of

Thomas Jefferson sitting in a pavilion at Monticello. The former president, then retired, was reading a book on the different varieties of legumes.

"It's one of yours, isn't it, Vincent?" Miss Whiting asked from the doorway.

Unaware that she had followed them, Emmett turned and looked at her, obviously confused.

Vincent said, "Yes, Elsie. It was the first painting I ever sold. My God, Emmett, are you telling me that your late wife bought it?"

"Thomas Jefferson was her hero. She saw this at an exhibit and fell in love with it."

Still shaking his head in wonder, Vincent said, "Small world."

"Marlene always wanted to know what inspired the painting."

"That's easy. Kate and I went to Monticello shortly after we met. The creativeness and unique structure of the place impressed me. It inspired me."

"It was Marlene's favorite painting."

Vincent looked Emmett in the eyes as he said, "I am honored."

"I will never take it down from there." The old man turned and headed for the door. Miss Whiting moved aside so he could pass by her.

Looking back at the painting, Vincent said, "It nearly broke Kate's heart when I sold it."

"I don't doubt it."

"Amazing. Marlene Reilly bought my first sale. And now...now here I am living right next door to her husband and daughter."

Miss Whiting nodded. "Life is funny that way, Vincent. Come, let's finish lunch."

🍁   🍁   🍁

"Why do I have a feeling that you didn't come here for a casual visit?" Miss Whiting said as she washed the dishes.

Vincent stood beside her, dishtowel in hand. The Reilly kitchen was a cozy room with a marble tile floor, yellow pine, glass-front cabinets and white appliances. A square pine table with four chairs occupied a small breakfast nook. The walls were pale yellow, and small-checked, yellow and white curtains decorated the windows. Standing at the kitchen sink, one looked out on the backyard where Duke currently lay inside a doghouse.

"Why is Duke outside?" Vincent asked, accepting the plate Elsie held up. He dried it as he awaited her answer.

"He's moping. And, he's mad."

"Why?"

"Emmett brushed him today. He hates that."

"So he exiles himself?"

"At least until Liz gets home."

"Of course," Vincent said, continuing to dry the dishes. "And yes, you're correct. I actually came to ask Emmett some questions about the Malloy Lumber Yard."

Miss Whiting rinsed the glasses. "He's not in shape today to answer, Vincent. He had a rough morning."

"Regarding Mrs. Reilly?"

She nodded. "He woke up around eight. Liz had already left. I was down here mixing pancake batter. He'd dreamed about the day she died. It took me an hour to get him calmed down. It breaks my heart to see him continually go through it again. Anyway, he usually spends most of the day after an episode like that confused and rattled. He wouldn't answer you too coherently."

"I see. What about you?"

"Me? My grandfather worked at the Malloy yard. Once the forests played out around here, Jethro Malloy found other ways to make money. He got into real estate, both residential and commercial. He started a construction business. And, he made furniture. My father was a cabinetmaker in the old mill.

"How old was he when he married Katherine?"

"Fifty-five. The story was he'd gone to New York on business. Saw this young violinist there and fell head over heels in love with her. She was twenty. He brought her back with him a week after he left to go on the trip."

"A week?"

"Yes. Guess he wooed her quick."

"Guess so. What year?"

"September of 1925 I believe." Miss Whiting rinsed the final dish then emptied out the dishpan. The drain sucked the water down in a loud rush. Still holding the dishpan in her hands, Miss Whiting continued, "It was the talk of the town, my grandfather said. Katherine was beautiful and from exotic New York City." She dried the dishpan with a paper towel and stowed it beneath the sink. "Funny thing was, you'd think he'd want to show her off around town. But he never did."

Vincent hung the dishtowel on the stove handle. "What do you mean?"

"People hardly ever saw her. She never went anywhere with him."

"Really?"

Miss Whiting crossed her arms beneath her breasts. "Emma—Emmett's aunt who built this house—well, she was the town doctor then. She kept a journal too. Emmett's shown me excerpts. Emma noted on several occasions that she heard Katherine playing the violin, but that she never saw her. Until, let's see, 1955 when Katherine knocked on the door one night and asked Emma to come over because Jethro was dying. Fact was, Jethro was long dead before Emma got there."

"He lived to be eighty-five."

"He did."

"What did he die from?"

"Coronary."

"They had children. I met some of the descendents at the reading of the will."

"They did. None of them grew up here though. Jethro shipped them all off to boarding school. There were three boys and two girls."

Vincent shook his head. "Amazing. What kind of guy was he?"

"Not a very nice one."

"Then who delivered the babies if not Emma Reilly?"

Miss Whiting shrugged. "I don't know."

"When did Katherine sell the mill?"

"From what I understand, immediately after Jethro's death. He'd left her millions, Vincent."

"Did Katherine become involved in public life at that point?"

"No. She kept to herself. None of her kids came to see her much. Her youngest son, however, dumped Kate off every summer like clockwork. But Katherine never took Kate anywhere. Marlene did that. If you ask me, if it wasn't for the fact that Kate and Liz became friends, your wife wouldn't have had any fun. A kid needs to get out."

Vincent shook his head. "Damn! What would make an accomplished violinist who played concerts in New York turn into a recluse?"

"That, Vincent," Miss Whiting said, "Has long been a North Tonawanda mystery."

CHAPTER 5

Vincent paced impatiently in the airport terminal. Kate's plane was on the runway. What was taking them so damn long to get to the gate and disembark? He couldn't wait to see her. He couldn't wait to show her the painting. He had completed it last night just before midnight.

People milled around him, also waiting for friends and loved ones. Some paced like him, others stood staring at the gate, and others sat in the chairs. Vincent glanced at his watch—10:45 p.m. He turned his attention to the gate again. At last, passengers started coming down the ramp. Vincent craned his neck and saw her. He pushed through the crowd and met her just as she reached the end of the ramp.

"For heaven's sake, Vincent," she said as he crushed her in a bear hug.

"You're here at last," he said, kissing her full on the lips.

She giggled and pushed him away. "We're making a scene."

"Who cares?" he said, kissing her again.

She untangled herself from him, slipped her arm through his and started him walking. "Let's get my suitcase and get to the house. I am dying, Vincent. Totally, completely dying."

"From what?"

"From sleeping alone for two weeks," she whispered in his ear.

He laughed and pulled her closer.

"Are you proud of me?" she asked.

"Why?"

She stopped walking. "Look at me."

He did and grinned. "You're beautiful."

"What else?"

He looked her up and down. She wore blue jeans, boots, and a blue parka. Her purse strap rested on her shoulder. Her glasses were the same as when he'd left her. His grin widened. "No briefcase."

"Give that man a prize. Now, come on."

She started him walking again with a gentle push.

"I am proud of you," he said. "I have you all to myself for four wonderful days."

"That's right, Vincent. So let's get moving. The clock is ticking."

❧   ❧   ❧

Vincent pulled the Rodeo into the driveway and stopped abruptly. Duke stood in front of the truck, tail wagging.

"I take it he's become your best friend," Kate said, opening the truck door.

"Something like that." Vincent jumped out and went around to the back of the truck to retrieve Kate's suitcase. Duke followed him. He gave the dog some quick pets before pulling the suitcase from the truck. Duke headed down the driveway, turned left and headed for home.

Kate watched him go, her arms crossed beneath her breasts. "He looks forlorn."

"Most likely is. Liz must not be home yet."

"Ah. He's waiting for her."

"Yep. Does every day, babe."

Kate stamped her feet. "Lord, it's cold here. Let's go inside and start a fire."

"We can't. The chimney needs some repairs that I can't do until spring."

Kate laughed. "Not that kind of fire, silly."

"Oh," Vincent said, chuckling.

"You've definitely been painting again," Kate said, heading for the porch.

Vincent followed her, carrying her suitcase.

Once they were inside and their outerwear removed, Kate stepped up on the first step, looked at him with raised eyebrows and said, "Ready, Mr. Artist?"

"Can I show you something first?"

"And that would be?"

"The painting. It's done."

She smiled at him then shook her head. "No, darling, not tonight."

"But, I…"

She held up her hand. "No, not another word. I want to see your painting in the morning light. Tonight, I want to see your naked body." She turned and ran up the stairs.

He ran after her, calling, "I sleep in the fern room." He reached the top of the stairs just as she turned into the bedroom. He hurried down to the room and entered, dropping her suitcase on the floor. She was ripping her turtleneck off. He watched her undress. "You are shameless," he said, his body responding to her beauty.

Naked, she fell on the bed. Her long hair curled around her shoulders and breasts. Kate's breasts were wonderful, just the right size and blemish free. She lay back on the pillow. "Ravish me, Vincent," she said, her eyes flashing fire.

She didn't have to ask him twice. He jumped on the bed, and together, they tore off his clothes. He kissed her shoulders, her breasts, and her belly. He forgot his finished painting. He forgot where he was. He thought only of Kate. He made love to her that night for hours. And their lovemaking was more passionate than it had ever been.

✿   ✿   ✿

He woke before her. Sunlight streamed into the bedroom. Kate lay beside him, her right hand on his chest. He looked down at her with complete love. He kissed her forehead and she stirred, her eyes fluttering a few times then opening. Seeing him, she smiled. "Hi," he said, brushing her hair back from her forehead.

"Good morning, Vincent." She snuggled closer to him and said, "God, you don't know how good it is to wake up next to you."

"You really did miss me, huh?"

"Intensely." She stared at him with serious eyes. "I've been incredibly lonely." Her voice caught in her throat as she said the words.

"Hey, don't cry. This arrangement isn't forever."

"It seems like forever."

"I love you too, Kate," he said, tenderly.

"I know." She rolled onto her back and sat up, leaning back against the brass headboard. "I can't believe you picked this room."

"Why?"

"I feel like I'm sleeping in a jungle."

He shook his head. "I happen to like this room because it's unique."

She rolled her eyes.

Not only did Vincent find the room unique, but he also found it to be—along with Jethro's library—the more masculine than any of the other bedrooms. He liked the wallpaper in this room with its white background and green ferns, the comforter and bed sheets baring the same pattern as the walls. The room was octagon in shape and had two built in arched bookcases on either side of the window, repeating this decorative detail from the parlor. The floor was light maple as was the woodwork. A white, beige and green striped rug covered most of the floor. A maple stand beside the bed held a crystal lamp. A cedar chest sat at the foot of the bed. To the right of the bed stood a tall maple armoire. Unlike most of the other room's in the Victorian, this room had no crown molding. Instead, a border matching the rug traveled round the room just below the ceiling. Dark green cushions lined the window seat between the bookcases. In keeping with the room's fern theme, a giant fern sat near the door, basking in the morning sun. Vincent's favorite feature in the bedroom, however, was the double French doors that held beveled rectangular panes of glass. The door latch and scroll knobs were brass like the bed.

"You know, Kate, he said as he sat up and leaned back against the headboard. "It must be the artist in me who finds this room so appealing."

"It must be." She looked over at the fern. "That couldn't possibly have been alive when you got here."

"I bought it."

She laughed. "How original."

"I thought so." He took her hand. "You were incredible last night."

Her cheeks turned slightly red. "So were you."

They fell silent, gazing into one another's eyes, each seeing the love the other felt. Looking away, Kate drew a long breath and said, "You may be surprised to hear this, Vincent, but this was Jethro's room."

"Which he didn't share with his wife?"

She turned back to him. "Who told you that?"

"Elsie Whiting."

"What else did she tell you?"

Vincent told her everything Elsie had said. When he finished, he saw tears in his wife's eyes.

"She had a miserable life, Vincent. She could have continued being a famous violinist. Instead, she…" She trailed off.

"She married Jethro Malloy."

"It was 1925. Things were different for women then."

"Even so, Kate, the twenties were a wild time. Women were breaking out."

Kate shook her head. "That wasn't Katherine's way. Ah, Vincent, you would have had to know her to understand."

"I'll buy that. Let me tell you, Kate, I know I wish I'd heard her play. Elsie said that she was wonderful."

"Pure genius, Vincent."

"She played for you?"

"Yes."

"Did you ever record her?"

"No. She wouldn't allow that." Kate ran her hand through her hair. "But enough about the past. It's making me melancholy." She threw back the covers and got out of the bed. She opened the armoire, rummaged around until she found his blue, gold and white flannel shirt and slipped it on.

Still sitting in the bed, Vincent asked, "Are you going to steal all my shirts?"

She grinned at him. "Maybe."

He admired her shapely legs as she sat down on the window seat and curled them up beneath her. She stared out the window for several minutes then she looked back at him. "It's a virtual winter wonderland out there."

He got up, found his jeans on the floor and slipped them on. He joined her on the window seat. Fresh snow had fallen during the night and it lay on the shrubberies, the tree branches, the fences and the cars parked in the driveway across the street. The plow had been by, large mounds of snow lying on the sides of the road. He could hear a distant snow blower.

Kate pointed at the house across the street. "Lydia lived there with her parents for a while."

"Your cousin Lydia, the witch?"

"Yes. I think her father bought it just so he could sit over there and wait for Katherine to die."

Vincent looked at the house. It was three stories tall with a round tower on its right side. Its shingles were painted dark green, its trim painted light green and its large, third floor, single gable sported a design of pink, green, and tan. It sat on a narrow lot. The driveway, holding three cars, led up past the house to a garage. There was a for sale sign in the front yard. "Not a bad looking place. Like this one, though, it needs some work."

Kate pointed at the window in the top of the tower. "Uncle Nelson used to sit over there in that window with a telescope."

"You're kidding?"

"Nope."

"What happened to nosy Nelson?"

"He died before Katherine did."

Vincent chuckled. "Serves him right. Any guy who would sit over there, spy on his mother and wait for her to die, deserves to die first."

Kate laid her head on Vincent's shoulder. "Uncle Nelson never came over here and visited Katherine. Lydia came though. God, she was a spoiled, pain in the ass. Liz and I used to hide from her." Kate sighed. "Katherine had the patience of a saint to put up with her the way she did."

"She was her grandchild, of course she would put up with her, Kate."

"Probably because she didn't get to raise her own children. They were all sent away to boarding school when they turned five. Prior to that, Jethro made sure that she had limited contact with them."

"Live in nanny?"

"Exactly. My father was Jethro and Katherine's youngest boy. The only time he saw Katherine was when he dropped me off for the annual summer visit."

"How old were you when you came here for the first summer?"

"Four. The year my parents divorced. The divorce was ugly. They hated one another and used me as their volleyball. They shuffled me back and forth. They fought over me. God, it was horrible." She shuddered. "Even though I was only four, I remember it all vividly. That first summer, I was terrified when my father left me here. I'd never met Katherine before. I'd heard about her. She was the strange recluse in the family."

"What was it like, that first meeting?"

Kate smiled. "She was sweet and patient. She didn't force herself on me. She let me get used to her and the house. Of course, the second day I was here, I was sitting on the front porch crying when Liz saw me. She marched right over and asked me why I was crying."

"What did you tell her?"

"That my father had left me here and I was scared."

"What did Liz say to that?"

"She took me by the hand and dragged me to her house. She said that her mother could make any fright go away."

"And did she?"

"Yes, as a matter of fact, she did. Marlene Reilly told me that Katherine was a lonely lady in a big house who sure would love it if I stayed the summer and kept her company. She said that Katherine was just shy around people but that she had a big heart that would love me forever." Tears welled up in Kate's eyes. "Marlene Reilly was right. Katherine Malloy had a lot of love in her heart for me."

Vincent massaged his wife's back. "And you loved her in return."

"I did. I guess she knew that even though…"

"Even though what, Kate?"

Kate wrapped her arms around herself. "Even though I let Lydia have her way."

Vincent slipped his arm around Kate and drew her close. "Don't beat yourself up over that. You didn't desert her. You still visited her."

Kate swallowed hard, her voice cracking when she spoke. "I don't deserve what she's just given me."

"She thought you did." He kissed Kate's forehead.

"Eleven million dollars, Vincent. God, what does one do with that much money?"

"Damned if I know, babe. Keep in close touch with Derek Clausterman."

"My father gambled his money away. I've told you that, I'm sure."

"Yes."

"He died buried in debt in a Las Vegas hotel room. He refused to ask Katherine for help. So he put a pistol in his mouth and blew his head off because he was too proud to ask his mother for money. Pathetic, isn't it? Funny, though, how his death didn't bother me. I've often wondered why that is. The man was my father and yet…" She shook her head. "All I knew of him was anger and gambling. I remember when he died, shortly after you and I met, that you kept thinking I should be crying and sad."

"I did. But once you explained your history with him, I understood. He was the man who fought your mother for time with you and then once he had you, basically pawned you off on servants or Katherine."

Kate stood up and held out her hand. "Enough family history. Show me your painting."

He took her hand, but he didn't stand up. Instead, he asked, "Are you going to tell your mother about the inheritance, Kate?"

"Way ahead of you, husband of mine. I drove down to Richmond and told her last week. She was happy for me. I tried to give her some money, but she refused. She said that she and my stepfather are doing just fine."

"And are they?"

"They are. They love one another. He's a good man. Their life is simple, but joyous. She just asked that I visit her more."

"Then you should."

Kate grinned. "And I will. Now, show me your painting."

He led her down the hall to his studio. He opened the door and, swinging his arm with a flourish, he said, "Ta da."

Kate entered and gazed silently at his painting. She took a few steps toward it then stepped back again. Vincent stood just inside the door, heart banging in his chest. After what felt like an eternity, she turned and said, "It's good. The cab in the woods instead of the city…" She took another step back. "Isn't that the hansom cab from the carriage house?"

Vincent swallowed the rock in his throat, wondering if this were the moment she would discover his lie. Praying his voice would come out steady, he said, "Yes, it is. When I saw the cab in the carriage house, I knew it would complete the picture." He moved closer to the painting, his hands gesturing around the cab. "It belonged on this road. See what I mean?"

She nodded. "I do."

"I think that's why the house called to me, babe. What I needed to complete the painting was here."

She raised her right eyebrow.

"You don't believe that, Kate?"

"It doesn't matter what I believe, Vincent." She took his hand. "It worked for you. That's what matters."

"And the painting…"

"I like it."

"Like it?"

"Yes."

He studied her a moment then looked back at the painting. "But you don't love it."

She took his chin in her hand and turned his face back to her. "I don't think it's brilliant. But I do think it's the best thing you've painted in a long time. It shows that you still have talent and are on your way."

"On my way to what?"

"Another breakthrough painting."

"But this one isn't that painting."

"No, Vincent, it isn't." He tried to turn away from her but she kept a tight hold on his chin. "Now, don't pout, my darling artist. You've made great progress here. You know I've always been honest with you about your work."

"Kate, I—"

"Quiet. Would you rather I lie to you?"

"No."

"Then be still and accept the progress you've made. This painting will sell. You ask David. He'll agree."

"You're sure about that? I could take this to David?"

"Most definitely. Your dealer will like it. But I'm also sure that there is more greatness within you." She held up his hands. "These wonderful hands will paint that greatness. So don't despair. Keep painting. It will come." She pointed at the painting on the easel. "It's very close to the surface."

"If anyone knows, you do," he said, softly.

"That's right. So don't get all down on me here. We've got four days together before I must go back to Washington. Let's enjoy them."

He nodded. "We will."

"Good. Now, let's eat some breakfast and go have an adventure."

"An adventure where?"

"Niagara Falls, my dear. We must see the ice bridge." She headed for the stairs. "Feed me."

"I'll be right down."

She started down the stairs but stopped halfway down. "Vincent!"

"Yes."

"No pouting."

"I'm not."

"Yes, you are."

He heard her walk the rest of the way down the stairs as he stood staring at his painting of the hansom cab on the wooded road. She was right and he knew she was right. In fact, if he were honest, he had known before showing her the painting. "Can't blame a guy for hoping," he said to the painting. He looked down at his hands. Was Kate right about them? Was the greatness ready to come forth?

"Vincent Vermay!" his wife called from the first floor. "Get down here right this minute."

Sighing heavily, Vincent exited the studio, closing the door behind him. Heading for the stairs, he called back, "Coming!"

✤   ✤   ✤

"Isn't it magnificent?" Kate asked, leaning over the icy rail to get a better look at the thundering falls.

Vincent stared down at the frozen water that formed a bridge across the Niagara River. "It sure is, babe." His eyes followed the ice up the riverbank, noting the frozen trees and how they glistened in the late morning sun.

Kate pointed at the falls. "See how the water is just frozen there in spots?"

"Yep."

She smiled at him. "This is worth shivering to see."

He slipped his arm around her. Although bundled up in her parka, her body shook. "Maybe so, but I don't want you getting pneumonia. Come on, it's almost time to meet Liz at the Hard Rock."

She took hold of his gloved hand and they started walking back towards the visitor's center. Kate reached up with her free hand and broke an icicle off a tree branch. She held it up. "Looks like a little sword."

He broke a larger icicle off and said, "My sword is bigger than yours."

She laid her head on his shoulder. "You win." Still, she banged her icicle against his. Both broke in half. Dropping her remaining half on the ground, she said, "It's magical here. The very air shimmers."

Vincent looked around. Everywhere was snow and ice. "It's definitely worth painting."

"Done before."

"True."

She raised her head from his shoulder as she said, "You would need a new twist."

"I'm sure I could find one."

"And you shall." They walked a while in silence, passing others on the path. They were nearing the top of an incline when she said, "This is nice, Vincent."

"What?"

"Just walking together. Seeing something special together. We don't do things like this back home. We used to." She sighed. "What happened to us?"

"Work and worry."

She stopped walking. "That was a fast answer."

He gazed down at her lovely face. "It's the right answer. We get caught up in our everyday existence that we forget about the little, enjoyable things. Think about it, Kate. When was the last time we took a vacation and just spent time together? No demands on either of us. Just time to be together and do whatever we want to do."

She let out a low whistle. "Years."

"Exactly. So maybe this little separation of ours isn't so bad after all." He grinned. "You did come without work in tow."

A small smile crossed her face. "I did at that. Which means that you can't paint until I go back to Georgetown."

He stuck out his hand. "Deal."

They shook on it.

"Hey, Vincent, Kate!" Liz stood at the top of the path.

"What?" Kate replied, shielding her eyes with her hand.

"Hurry up. I have an idea."

Waving, Vincent said, "Just a second." As they continued up the path, Vincent leaned close to Kate's ear and asked, "How's it going with you two? Has she warmed up to you more?"

Softly, Kate replied, "I've talked to her everyday on the phone. I've made it a point to do so and I think, yes, she's warming up."

"Good. She needs a friend."

Kate shot him a questioning look, but they were nearly to Liz so he muttered, "Later."

"You're not too hungry, are you?" Liz asked when they reached her.

Vincent looked at Kate who shook her head. "Not really, why, Liz?"

Liz grabbed Kate's free hand. "Good. Come on. The rink is open."

"The what?" Kate asked, following her friend. Vincent tagged after them.

"The ice rink by the Convention Center," Liz said.

"Ice skating?" Vincent asked.

"Yes, why?"

"Oh, just that I never have."

"Ice skated?"

"Bingo."

Liz chuckled. "Great. You'll love it even more."

"No doubt," Vincent mumbled.

Liz led them past the visitor's center and down a path to a street in front of a glass building. They waited for the signal to change then crossed the street and entered the building, which was filled with exotic plants. Glancing about him, Vincent saw a wrought iron stairway that curled up to a second floor. It was warm in here, a stark contrast to the winter cold outside. "It's called The Wintergarden," Liz explained. Moments later they exited the tropical paradise and walked through a long courtyard lined with trees. They reached another street, waited for traffic to clear then crossed it and walked up a staircase to the top of a bridge. Stopping, Liz pointed over the bridge's stonewall. "Ice rink, my friends."

Vincent looked down at the oval rink that was filled with skaters of all ages and ability. He pointed at a guy who clung to his companion. "That's a perfect picture of me."

Kate laughed. "Oh, come on, it will be fun."

"If you insist."

"I do."

Fifteen minutes later, Vincent found himself standing on a pair of skates, Kate holding him upright. His legs shook beneath him. Liz grabbed his left arm and said, "Now, just go with us, Vincent."

"What should I do?"

"Relax."

"Easy for you to say."

Kate and Liz skated slowly around the rink. Vincent stared down at his feet and watched the blades cut into the ice.

"How's it feel?" Kate asked.

He looked at her. "Spooky. I can't balance."

"You will. Just relax and let us skate you around a few times."

"If you were a summer girl, when did you learn how to do this?"

"Boarding school during the winter."

"Lucky for me."

After they had completed their third time around, Liz said, "Okay, Vincent, see how I'm moving my legs?"

"Yes."

"Try it. We'll keep hold of you."

He started to stroke with them and he thought he had the hang of it. "This is cool," he said. "Let go."

"Are you sure?"

"Yes, Kate, let go."

They did and he skated on his own.

"Bravo!" Kate called behind him. "Bravo!"

He turned to wave at her and promptly fell on his rear. His wife laughed, shaking her head. Liz skated over to him and stopped, ice shavings showering his lap. "Can you get up?"

He looked up at her sheepishly. "I have no idea."

"Try."

Kate skated over and held out her hand. "Come on, Vincent."

She pulled him up and after a few seconds of fumble feet, he stood on his own again. "Keep practicing, darling, you'll catch on." Winking, she took off.

"Hey, wait!" Liz called, charging after her.

Vincent gingerly made his way over to the railing and latched on to it. He watched Liz and Kate chase each other. Kate squealed with delight as she pulled farther ahead of Liz. As he watched her, Vincent thought how long it had been since he'd seen her this carefree. As she sped by him, Kate said, "Chicken, Vincent."

"And don't you forget it!" he called after her.

Liz zoomed by and Vincent laughed. He didn't doubt the good doctor would catch his wife. She was determined. He watched them a few minutes more then wrestled up the courage to try skating again. His skating was sloppy, but at least he stayed upright. He was actually gaining some confidence in himself when Kate and Liz came up alongside him, each taking one of his arms.

"Having fun yet?" Liz asked, her face red from the cold.

"Tons."

The women skated him over to a bench and the three of them sat down. Kate gasped for air and leaned against him. Between gasps, she said, "That was a riot."

"Told you it would be fun," Liz said.

Vincent looked from his wife to Liz and back again. Both women were exhilarated, the exhilaration adding to their beauty. Vincent slipped an arm around each of them and said, "I am one lucky guy. I'm sitting here with two beautiful women on a beautiful—"

"That's your first mistake," Liz said, cutting him off. She jumped to her feet and grabbed his hand. "You're sitting." She tugged him off the bench.

Kate got up and took his other hand. "Skate with us, Vincent."

"But…hey…wait…" They were speeding with him. "Stop…you guys are going too fast!"

"Oh, quit your whining," Kate said, laughing.

They spent the next forty-five minutes skating. By the time they called it quits, Vincent had become quite proficient. As they walked to the Hard Rock Cafe, Kate said, "You did excellent, sweetheart. I'm proud of you."

"Here, here!" Liz agreed.

"How could I go wrong with you two as my teachers?"

They reached the restaurant and Vincent held the door open for them. Inside, Billy Joel blasted from the overhead speakers. Pictures of rock stars as well as Rock'n'Roll memorabilia covered the walls. The hostess showed them to the only remaining booth in a corner near the kitchen. Vincent said very little during the meal. He downed his burger and fries and enjoyed listening to

Kate and Liz reminisce. Liz had dropped her guard completely, talking and laughing with Kate as if the twenty-one years without seeing her had never occurred. His wife's face glowed in a way he'd forgotten it could. Grinning, Vincent tipped his bottle of beer skyward and silently said, "Thanks, Katherine."

❧   ❧   ❧

Freshly showered and bundled up in a white terrycloth robe, Kate sat on the window seat gazing at the frosted windowpane. Her wet hair waved about her shoulders. Vincent switched on the pole lamp and leaned against the doorframe. She turned to him with questioning eyes. "One would think you don't like the fern room, sitting here in the dark like this."

She smiled. "The streetlights make neat designs in the frost." She pointed at the window.

Vincent switched off the lamp and went to her, joining her on the window seat. He studied the designs. "Cool."

"Fascinating," she said.

He lightly rubbed her back. "Today was fun, wasn't it?"

"It was. But tell me, what did you mean back there on the path, about Liz needing me."

"In any of your conversations, did she tell you about Alan?"

"Who?"

Vincent sighed. "I didn't think so." Briefly, he told Kate about the fiancé Liz had lost. "Between Alan's death and her mom's death and her father's condition…well, she's sad Kate. Sad and lonely and I see it in her eyes."

Kate touched his cheek. "You always have been able to see into a person's very soul, haven't you, Vincent?"

He took her hand. Her skin was soft and warm.

"I will be her friend, Vincent. If she'll let me."

"She will. She needs you. Subconsciously she knows that."

Kate moved closer to him and he took her into his arms. They sat quiet for a time and then she surprised him by saying, "I like it here, Vincent."

"Better than D.C.?"

"That's not a fair question."

He held up his hands. "I take it back. But I hope you've put any thoughts of selling this house out of your head."

"Who said anything about selling this place, Vincent? Certainly not me."

"Then who was that nutcase?"

"Damned if I know."

He ran his hand through her damp hair. "There's a nice bed over there, Kate."

She grinned. "There is, isn't there?"

He grinned back.

Kate rose from the window seat, took his hand, and led him to the bed.

❧   ❧   ❧

The phone woke him with a start the following morning. He reached for the infernal contraption, his hand searching the nightstand. Finally finding the receiver, he pulled it from the cradle and barked, "Hello." His voice was husky and his mouth felt like the Sahara.

Kate moaned beside him, rolling from her side to her back. "Who is it?" she mumbled at the same time as the person on the other end of the line started talking in his ear.

While he didn't hear the exact words the man said, Vincent recognized the voice. "Hang on," he said, holding the phone out to Kate. "It's your boss."

She frowned. "You're kidding."

"Nope."

She took the phone from him and said, "Darren?"

Vincent rolled onto his side and stared at the alarm clock. Its red numbers proclaimed 5 a.m. "Christ," he muttered, throwing back the covers. He swung his legs over the side of the bed and sat up. Resting his elbows on his knees, he buried his face in his hands.

He heard Kate talking, but didn't have a clue what she was saying. All he could think was that her asinine boss had called them at 5 a.m. He raised his head. But for faint moonlight filtering in the frosted window, the room was dark. *What day was it anyway?* But the thought that crossed his mind next didn't answer this question. Instead, it informed him he had to pee. Yes, that's what he felt that was so damned uncomfortable. He had to pee. Vincent got to his feet and stumbled to the bathroom.

Standing in front of the toilet, naked and urinating, he tuned into his wife's voice.

"Can't this wait, Darren?" she asked.

Then, "I know. Yes, but…"

A short, tense pause followed by, "Darren, you promised me these days."

Finished, Vincent flushed the toilet and washed his hands. He returned to the bedroom, knelt beside his wife and touched her bare shoulder. She looked at him. "You're not going," he said. "Not until Tuesday."

"Yes, Darren. It's Vincent. Obviously, he doesn't want me to leave early."

"Kate," Vincent insisted.

She shrugged helplessly. "Okay, I'll be on the one o'clock plane. Yes."

Vincent reached for the phone, but Kate pushed his hand away. "No," she mouthed. Into the phone, she said, "I'll see you then." Stretching across the bed, she hung up the phone.

"What are you doing?" Vincent asked.

She leaned back against the headboard and drew a long breath.

"Kate?"

She gazed at him with sad eyes. "I'm getting on a plane this afternoon and going back to D.C."

"What the hell for?"

"What do you mean what for? My boss needs me."

"What's his problem now?"

She pushed her hair back over her shoulder. "Does it matter? You wouldn't—" She stopped in mid-sentence, but it was too late.

He finished the sentence for her. "I wouldn't understand. Politically stupid Vincent just doesn't get the picture. Isn't that right, Kate?"

"That's not what I meant!"

"What did you mean?"

She pulled the blankets up over her breasts and folded her arms. "It's just not something that would interest you. You have other things going on. Like painting. Repairing this house."

"And my wife. My wife here with me until Tuesday night, as planned."

"Vincent, I don't want to go anymore than you want me to."

"Then don't go."

She stared at him with wide eyes.

"You heard me. Don't go."

"I have to go. I have a job and a boss who is counting on me."

"So let him hire someone else to count on."

Kate shook her head. "I'm not giving up my job."

Vincent stood up. "Why not? You don't need it anymore. In case you've forgotten, you've just inherited eleven million dollars."

Kate stared at him, dumbfounded.

"I take it you had forgotten."

She threw the covers back, got up and walked past him. She scooped up her robe from the floor and slipped it on. She headed for the French doors.

"What are you doing?" he asked, following her.

She turned back to him. "I'm going to take a shower, eat breakfast, pack and be on the one o'clock plane back to D.C."

"And I don't want you to go."

"I have to go, Vincent. I signed a contract to do a job and I'm not going to break that contract. I'm not going to shirk my responsibilities and turn my name into mud in the Capitol just because I inherited some money."

"Eleven million dollars."

"I don't care if it were seventy million dollars!" Her voice rose as she spoke. "I am not just going to give up my work!"

"Why not, Kate?"

"Because it's my work! Don't you get that? Does the fact that we're suddenly rich mean you're going to give up painting?"

"No, of course not."

"Then don't think that I should give up what I love."

She started moving again and he followed her to the bathroom door. She barred him from entering.

He took a step back.

"Now, may I take my shower in peace?" she asked.

"It's different, Kate. My painting is a part of me. Working for McMartin—"

"Is how I do what is a part of me. I'm a speech writer, Vincent."

"No, you're a writer."

"Semantics. Right now, I write for Senator Darren McMartin. I have a contract. I'm not going to break it. Now, please let me take my shower."

He held up his hands in defeat. "Do whatever the hell you want." Angry, he went back to their bedroom, dressed in jeans and a tan turtleneck and ran downstairs. He put on his boots, cap, and jacket and went outside. Grabbing a shovel from the porch, he began shoveling the driveway. He worked furiously; sweat building up beneath his clothing. He took harsh breaths, his heart pounding. Still, he shoveled. He felt his chest would burst, but he didn't care. He had to shovel. Had to. Otherwise, he just might get on a plane, go to Washington and kill Darren McMartin—the man who was spoiling his weekend, the man who seemed to always have Kate at his beck and call, the man who always came first.

"Vincent!" Someone grabbed the shovel handle below his grip. "Vincent! Stop it. You're going to have a heart attack."

He stopped and stared at his wife, his chest heaving, burning with pain.

She pulled the shovel from his hands and tossed it into a snow bank. "Vincent," she said again.

His legs gave out and he collapsed, falling to his knees. She went down with him, hugging him. He buried his face in her parka and fought for air. She held him close, her lips kissing his forehead. "I love you," she said. She was crying.

His breathing eased and he looked at her. Tears were rolling down her cheeks. He wiped them away with his gloved hand. "Don't," he said.

"Come with me, Vincent. Fly back with me today, and when I'm done with Darren, we can spend a few days at the townhouse. Does it matter where we spend those days as long as we're together?"

He didn't answer her. He pushed back from her and stood up. Taking her hand, he pulled her to her feet. He led her inside the carriage house and opened the hansom cab's door. She climbed in and he followed her. Sliding his arm around her, he said, "It matters, Kate. Now, to me, it matters."

She laid her head on his shoulder and squeezed his hand. "I have to go, Vincent. Please understand."

"Imagine what it was like to live when this was the mode of transportation. No cell phones, no television, and no zero to sixty in two-point three seconds. Imagine, Kate."

"You have a better imagination than me, Vincent. You always have."

"Maybe so." He sighed.

"I'll be back in a few weeks. Then you can show me another painting."

"Sure."

"Don't be angry with me."

"I'm not." And he wasn't, not really. But he didn't understand her. Not like he once had, when they were first married. Then she had been passionate about him, and life, and writing. She'd started a novel. It was in her desk drawer in her office in the townhouse. Over the years she'd pull it out and write every now and then. Vincent loved watching her work on the book. She looked so alive and full of fire when she worked on the novel. He couldn't remember the last time he'd seen her pull the manuscript out of the desk drawer. It had to be before she went to work for McMartin. Now, Vincent no longer wondered how she would end the book. He wondered if she would end the book.

CHAPTER 6

They left for the airport at noon. He said very little during the ride. He carried her suitcase into the terminal, sat waiting with her until they called her flight and dutifully kissed her goodbye before she entered the ramp. Before disappearing up the ramp, she turned, smiled and waved. He waved back but he did not smile. He had nothing to smile about. In fact, if the truth were told, he was downright pissed. Maybe he was just being selfish, but damn it, he'd wanted her with him until Tuesday afternoon. *Damn you, McMartin.*

He drove back to the Victorian surrounded by Kate's lavender scent. He saw her hopeful face just before she disappeared up the ramp leading to the airplane. *Don't stay mad,* her eyes had begged. *Please, Vincent, understand.* Well, doggone it he didn't understand. She'd promised him four days. She'd broken her promise. Why? She didn't have to jump whenever McMartin barked anymore. Why couldn't she act accordingly?

He spent the rest of the afternoon in his studio but didn't really produce anything promising. He quit at five, showered, put on black slacks and a blue and white striped shirt and left the Victorian. He didn't know where he was going so he just walked. He ended up on Tremont Street, heading towards DeGraff Memorial Hospital. He was nearly at the hospital when he saw the sign. It stood in the front yard of a brown, two-story Victorian. Maroon letters on its white background read, **Elizabeth Reilly, M.D.**

So this was where her office was located. Smiling for the first time since McMartin's phone call, he walked up the porch steps. He stood on the top step, one hand on a square, decorative column. The hospital sat kitty corner from Liz's office. She didn't have far to go to see her incarcerated patients. He chuckled, laughing at the term "incarcerated." But then, she'd coined it first.

He turned from the street and studied the front door. It was definitely the original door, the wood cracked but sporting a recent coat of paint. The windows were stained glass, portraying red, yellow and purple tulips. He grasped the shiny brass door handle, only wanting to feel its solidness. To his surprise, the door opened. He found himself in a marble tiled foyer, a huge staircase facing him. Turning to his left, he saw Liz's name painted in white letters on a beautiful walnut door. He tried it and it opened. He stepped into a waiting room with a wood floor covered by a maroon, tan, green and ivory, flowered oval rug. Tan leather chairs lined the walls. Two walnut coffee tables held magazines. A tall, meandering philodendron stood beside the bay window that looked out on the street. A pale green cushion covered the window seat. The reception area faced the door. At present, the sliding glass window was closed, the receptionist and nurses obviously not working on a Sunday.

He was about to call out to see if anyone was there, when he heard a woman crying. Thinking it might be Liz he hurried past the reception area and ran down a hallway past examining rooms. He followed the crying to the last room on the right. Liz was there, but she wasn't the one crying, although she looked like she wanted to. A young, blonde-haired woman sat in a chair in front of Liz's desk. Liz squatted next to the chair, her arm around her patient. Seeing Vincent in the doorway, she gestured him away with her head. He obeyed, returning to the waiting room. He sat in one of the chairs and waited. What was the woman crying about, he wondered? And what was Liz doing working on a Sunday?

Fidgeting, he unzipped his jacket, removed it and tossed it on an empty chair. He picked up a copy of *Muscle & Fitness*, turned its pages but absorbed nothing. He glanced at his watch. It was 6:30.

Another fifteen minutes crept by before Liz came down the hall with her patient. Now that he could see her face, Vincent realized that the blonde was a girl of no more than nineteen. She wore gray sweatpants and a red sweatshirt. She walked with a pronounced limp, favoring her right leg. Bald spots shined on her head and she was much too thin, her face carrying the gauntness of one who has lost weight too quickly.

They reached the waiting room and Liz removed a blue and white ski jacket from a hook on the waiting room wall. She held it out and said, "I'll drive you home, Jill."

The girl shook her head as she accepted her jacket and put it on. Vincent noted that her hands trembled.

Liz removed a white and blue checked scarf from the hook and put it around the girl's neck. She tied it into a loose not. "I insist. I'm going to drive you home. You shouldn't be walking on that leg."

"I want to walk."

Liz gazed at Jill with love in her eyes. "You're mother is going to kill me for telling you by yourself."

Jill looked away.

Liz brushed a stray lock of hair back from Jill's shoulder. "I'm going to be by your side. You know that."

Jill nodded then burst into tears. Liz pulled her close, holding her tight, Jill's tears wetting her white lab coat. "You can get through this, Jill," she said. "You can beat this."

But while her voice came out strong and confident, Vincent saw doubt in her eyes. He saw fear in them too. Who was this girl, he wondered? She had to be more than a patient.

Jill fought to control her tears. She wiped her face with her coat sleeve. "I'm sorry, Aunt Liz," she said, stepping back. "Maybe…maybe you should drive me home."

Liz opened her mouth to speak, but before she could get any words out, the waiting room door opened and another teenager entered. She was younger than Jill but was obviously her sister. Her blonde hair was pulled back in a ponytail that stuck out the back of a Buffalo Bison's cap. She wore a navy blue pea coat and blue jeans. She went immediately to Jill and took her hand. "I came to drive you home."

Jill stared at her in wonder. "Tracy, how did…"

"I know you were here? Some snooping. You can yell at me later." She turned to Liz. "She can go home, right?"

"Yes."

She tugged her sister's arm. "Come on. We'll have time to talk before Mom and Dad get back from Rochester. Let's go."

Still bewildered, Jill went with her sister.

"You have your parents call me tomorrow, Jill," Liz said, closing the door behind them. She pressed her forehead against the wood and took a deep breath.

"Is it bad?" Vincent asked.

Startled, she turned to him. "I forgot about you."

"Is it bad?" he asked again.

"Follow me." She led him down the hall to her office. It was a cozy room with floor to ceiling bookcases stocked full of medical books. There was a warm green carpet on the floor. Just to the right of a doublewide window sat an oak desk with two leather chairs in front of it. "I'm breaking every medical ethics rule here, but I have to talk to somebody right now or I'll go crazy." She went to the far wall and flipped a switch. An x-ray viewing panel lit up. She pulled a pen from her lab coat pocket and pointed at an x-ray. "See that?"

"What is it?"

"A knee."

"Couldn't prove it by me."

"This is the kneecap." She circled the area with her pen. "It's not in the right position." She circled another area. "And this is why."

"What?"

"It's a mass that shouldn't be there. And as you can see, it's worked its way up a good portion of her thigh."

"Jesus," Vincent said, peering at the x-ray. "It's in her bone."

"Jill has been dealing with knee pain since September. She goes to college in Boston where she is a member of the indoor cycling team. At first the trainer told her the pain was from overuse. Then he gave her cortisone shots. And through all of that, she continued cycling and suffering. Her mom and I are old school friends. I went to a Christmas party at their house in December and noticed that Jill was favoring her right leg when she walked. I asked her about it and she shrugged it off. Said that she hurt it cycling."

"You thought it was more."

"Not then. But I was over their house again when she was home for a weekend in mid-January. Her limp had gotten more pronounced and when I watched her climb the stairs, I saw just how much pain she was in."

"So you confronted her."

Liz nodded. "I slipped away from the adults and went up to Jill's room. She was lying in bed, crying, with an ice pack on her knee. My initial examination was enough to tell me that something was up and that it wasn't just a sport's injury."

Liz pulled the x-rays down, went to her desk and slipped them into a gray folder. She set the folder on the desktop and sat down. She pointed at the chairs in front of her oak desk.

Vincent sat down.

Liz sighed and when she spoke, her voice was laced with pain. "It's bone cancer, Vincent."

"Sweet, Jesus."

"Biologically, she's not my niece but…" She placed her hand over her heart and looked at Vincent with troubled eyes.

"I noticed they both call you, Aunt Liz."

"I was in the delivery room when Jill was born." She slammed a fist on the desktop. "Damn it!"

"What did you tell her tonight, Liz?"

Liz shook her head, unable to speak. She buried her face in her hand.

Vincent went to her and knelt beside her chair. "Hey, Liz," he said, rubbing her shoulder.

"She's only nineteen," Liz cried. "Oh, God, Vincent, she's my goddaughter. She's just a kid."

Vincent took her in his arms and held her while she cried. He couldn't think of anything comforting to say. There was no denying the fact that Jill's situation stunk.

Liz pushed back from him. "I'm sorry," she said, wiping her face with her sleeve.

"It's understandable, Liz." He pulled a handkerchief from his pocket and offered it to her.

She took it and wiped her eyes. She drew in a long breath then said, "Get up off your knees, Vincent." He returned to his chair. She stared at him with grateful eyes. "Thank you."

He smiled and gave her a quick wink.

She kneaded his handkerchief in her left hand. Her eyes suddenly widening, she asked, "Where's Kate?"

Vincent scratched his whiskered chin. "Back in D.C. by now."

Liz frowned. "I thought she was staying until Tuesday."

"So did I. But king McMartin called."

"And she went back?"

"Pretty incredible, right?"

"No, it's just that…well…I mean she really wanted this time with you."

"So she said."

"You don't think she wanted to be with you?"

Vincent drew a deep breath. "Honestly, Liz, I don't know what to think. She says one thing but does another."

"I detect a note of frustration, Mr. Vermay."

"You detect correctly, Dr. Reilly."

A faint smile crossed Liz's face. "Your maleness is showing, Vincent."

"Excuse me?"

"Damn, my woman should be home barefoot and pregnant."

Vincent pointed at her. "That's not fair. And that's not it."

Liz sat forward and rested her elbows on the desk. "Then what is 'it'?"

"She doesn't need to jump when that man barks anymore, Liz. She just inherited eleven million dollars, remember?"

"I remember."

"Well, my wife doesn't."

"Sure she does."

"Then why did she go running back to McMartin?"

"Ooh, jealousy rears its ugly head."

"I'm not jealous."

"Of course you are."

Vincent glared at Liz.

"Oh, stop that. And don't pout."

"Now you sound like Kate. She always accuses me of pouting."

"And she would be right. You should see your face."

"Women."

Liz laughed. "Oh, Vincent, Kate most likely went back because she has a job to do. Does she have a contract with him?"

"She does. But she doesn't need to work for him anymore."

"You're still pouting."

"Shut up."

"Nope. Give her time, Vincent. Let her adjust to the fact that she's a multi-millionaire. She'll figure out what she really wants to do."

"How long do you suppose that will take?"

"As long as it takes."

"Hope I can last that long."

"You will," she assured him.

"I guess." He flicked a piece of lint off his thigh. "You eat dinner yet?"

"No. I'm not really that hungry."

"You should eat." He stood up. "Come on, I'll buy you dinner."

She hesitated.

"Hey, if you're going to be there for Jill you have to take care of yourself."

"Okay." She picked up her pager from the desktop and hooked it on her belt. Next, she let her hair down, shaking her head. She exchanged her lab coat for her fedora and leather coat. "Where do you want to go?"

"Your pleasure, Madam?"

"I think…yes," she said smiling.

"What?"

"I think it's time you went to Nestor's."

"The place on the corner of Webster and Goundry?"

Liz grinned. "You've been exploring. That's good. Now, let's go."

He waved his arm. "Okay. After you, my lady."

As she walked past him, she said, "Just one thing."

"What?"

"Prepare yourself for a true gastrointestinal delight."

"Lay it on me, baby," he said, following her out of the office.

Inside, Nestor's was reminiscent of a 1950's diner, it's décor sporting bright orange and beige. Upon entering, they bypassed a long counter with stools, one of which was occupied by a gray-haired man. He was eating a hot dog and reading a newspaper. Liz led Vincent around some tables and to the right to one of the booths lining a wall across from a soda fountain counter. Pictures of North Tonawanda in the twenties and thirties graced the wall to the left of the soda counter. Vincent made a note to check them out on another visit. Tonight, Liz needed his full attention. They sat down across from one another on simulated wood benches. The table was bright orange. Liz pulled a menu from a metal holder and tossed it at him. "The décor is simple but they've got great food."

Vincent slid the menu aside. "And what is the good doctor eating tonight?"

"Texas red hot with fries, my friend."

"Very healthy, doctor."

"Glad you approve. Even doctors go off the straight and narrow sometimes."

"So I see."

The waitress, a thin woman with dark hair, gave them each a glass of water and said, "Hi, Dr. Reilly. The usual?"

"You got it, Deb. What about you, Vincent?"

He looked from Liz to the waitress. "Give me her usual."

The waitress smiled. "Brave man." She wrote the order on her pad and left them alone.

"What have I gotten myself into?"

Liz laughed. "You'll see."

Vincent rolled his eyes. "Thanks for warning me."

Liz sipped her water. "Vincent?"

"Yep?"

"What I said in the office about Kate, I meant it. Give her some space. Give her time."

"That's not so easy."

"Have you forgotten that coming here to North Tonawanda was your idea? That's why you two are separated."

"I know, Liz. That's not the point."

"What is?"

"Our planned time together should be just that, our time together. She shouldn't just run back to D.C. because McMartin has a crisis."

Liz grinned. "Oh, Lord, Vincent, you could never be married to me. God forbid my pager goes off during dinner."

"That's different."

"How so?"

"You being with a patient could mean the difference between life and death. Kate's job, on the other hand is not life and death. Hell, all she does for him is write speeches."

Liz sat back and crossed her arms over her chest. "When we were teenagers, Kate wrote all the time. She had notebooks full of stories. Does she still write fiction?"

Vincent shook his head. "No. Has a novel half finished but hasn't touched it in years."

"That's too bad. I loved reading her stories."

Vincent scratched his cheek. "You know, Liz, now that she doesn't need to work, she could write full time."

"True."

"She could finish her novel and publish it herself if she wanted to."

"Again true."

"I'll suggest it to her."

"You could." Liz leaned closer. "But remember something, she'll need time to process the idea. Don't expect her to jump right into it."

"Why wouldn't she want to stop working and finish her novel? Hell, she could work here, in the Victorian. We could both work—"

Liz held up her hand. "Whoa, pardner."

"What?"

"Hold those horses a moment. Doing what you're suggesting would be a major life change for Kate. And a big one at that. Let her think about it."

"But—"

"Oh, hush. Promise me you'll let her think about it."

"Okay. I promise."

"Good. Now, get prepared. Here comes dinner."

❧   ❧   ❧

"You're throat and esophagus on fire yet?" Liz asked as they exited Nestor's.

"No. When it comes to hot foods, I can match you."

Liz donned her fedora, laughing. "It's snowing."

"That surprises you? It is winter after all."

She held up her gloved hand. "It's a snow globe kind of snow. Nice, gentle, big flakes."

He understood what she meant. "Nice to walk in," he added.

They walked side-by-side down Webster Street past shops and restaurants, and Vincent silently read their names; Pepperday's Clothiers, Walker Bros. & Monroe Jewelers, Teddy Bear Carpets, and American Skin Art. Liz pointed at a tanning salon and said, "That used to be a department store named Murphy's. They had a lunch counter where Kate and I hung out a lot." She pointed across the street. "The building a few doors down with the marquee is the Riviera Theatre. You should check it out. It's been restored."

Vincent gazed at the building, it's façade decorated by a triangular marquee advertising an upcoming organ concert. He couldn't tell for sure what color the building was, but he admired the arched windows, heavy wooden doors and the two lady statues atop the façade. "How old is it?"

"Opened in 1926. It has the original Mighty Wurlitzer Organ inside. It's a beautiful instrument."

"Thus the upcoming organ concert.

"Yes. The organ was manufactured at the Wurlitzer plant on Niagara Falls Boulevard. Have you driven by it yet?"

"I don't believe so."

"Now that building is busted up into offices. But back in 1926, the organ business was booming."

"For silent movies."

"Exactly. The organ in the Riviera rises up and down on a platform."

"Cool."

"It is cool. When I was a kid, they used the theatre for movies. Back when it was built, they showed silent movies and also ran vaudeville shows."

"And now? Anything beside organ concerts?"

"Lots of things. It's a vibrant theatre again. There are movies, concerts, and Christmas shows and sometimes plays. Next time Kate is in town, you should take her to the theatre."

"Maybe I will."

They crossed Tremont Street and Liz looked back over her shoulder. "You can't really see it at night, but there's a mural on the side of the Riv. It's beautiful. Depicts Charlie Chaplin and a drawing of the organ. You should check it out during the day."

"I will."

They passed a store called Udderly Country. "Love that store," Liz said. Further up the street, she pointed at The Canalside Bakery. "You should try their cookies, Vincent. To die for." Right beside the bakery was The Hodgepodge. "I like this store too. Lots of unique things in it."

They reached a bridge. "Goes over the Erie Canal into Tonawanda," Liz said. She pointed left. "Lets go down here. It's the old brick walkway in front of the Packet Inn. Which is no longer the Packet Inn. Since they put in new landscaping here along the canal, they've closed this road to cars. Damn, I think I've turned into a tour guide."

Vincent looked down at the brick as they walked. It felt hard and familiar beneath his feet. It brought his Georgetown Townhouse to mind. He wondered what Kate was doing.

"There are offices and restaurants in the old inn now," Liz said, pointing at the long brick building to their left. "So many changes." Her tone was wistful.

Vincent stopped and looked about him. Ice flowed down the canal. Snow piles lined the road beside them. Except for the traffic back on Webster, they seemed to be alone.

"What?"

Vincent squatted and ran his hand along the brick. "Can you feel it, Liz?"

"What?"

"The past. I can almost hear the clip clop of horses' hooves on this brick." He stood up, grinning. "Or the honk of early horns on Model T's."

"You definitely are a history nut."

"Yeah, I sure am." He walked to the edge of the road and climbed up on a snow bank.

"Hey, be careful, Vincent. You're awful close to the canal."

"I'm all right." He gazed at the old Packet Inn, liking its red brick, square columns and balconies. His eyes moved along its façade back towards Webster Street and he saw his next painting, a blending of time periods.

"What are you doing?" Liz asked.

"Seeing a future painting." He jumped down from the snow bank.

"And that would be?"

"I'll show it to you when it's done."

"You haven't even shown me the one you just finished. So how can I believe you?"

"Come on, I'll show it to you right now."

Duke was sitting in the Victorian's driveway when they arrived. Seeing Liz, he barked excitedly and ran to her, tail wagging.

Liz hugged and petted him. "Hi, boy." He licked her face. "Oh, I love you too, Duke," she said.

Vincent opened the front gate. "After you."

Duke followed them into the house and while they removed their outer-wear, he charged up the stairs.

"I hope he doesn't sleep on your bed when he's all wet like that," Liz said.

"He does. It's okay though. I've come to think of him as my little buddy. Come on up to the studio." She followed him up the stairs and down the hall to the studio. Vincent snapped on the light and said, "There she be."

Kate looked at the painting of the hansom cab on the wooded road and said, "It's wonderful, Vincent. Are you going to sell it?"

"Most likely."

"It appears that you are out of your slump."

"Not according to my wife."

Liz frowned. "What did Kate say about it?"

"That it's good, but it's not a breakthrough painting. It's not brilliant. But I'm progressing towards brilliance."

Liz's frown deepened. "Wow, she's tough on you."

"I suppose so." He moved closer to the painting. "But while I hate to admit it, she's right. I see where it fails." He pointed at the dirt road. "Like right here, there should—"

"Stop," she demanded, holding up a hand. "I don't want to know. You'll spoil it for me."

"Okay. How about some hot chocolate?"

"Deal."

Ten minutes later they sat in the parlor, each holding a cup of steaming liquid. Liz sat on the couch. Vincent sat in the striped wingback chair. "Once I fix the fireplace, it'll be perfect in here," he said.

"I know a guy who could check the chimney out for you. He does ours once a year."

"Great."

Liz gazed at him. "It hurt didn't it, what Kate said about the painting?"

"Yes." He sipped his hot chocolate.

"But…"

"But she told me the truth. In spite of the fact that it hurt, it's good that she was honest. I need honesty." Still holding his cup, he rested it on his thigh. "This weekend didn't turn out at all like I wanted it too."

"Because you'd rather be sipping hot chocolate with your wife instead of her friend."

"You're my friend too."

"Even so, you'd rather be with your wife."

"Guilty."

"So call her when I leave. Call her and tell her you love her."

"Maybe I will."

A wide smile crossed Liz's face. "Good, God, Vincent, you are so head over heels in love with her. It's written all over your face."

Vincent felt his cheeks go red. He opened his mouth to speak but before anything came out, Liz's pager went off. She looked down at it. "Who is it?" he asked.

"Jill's parents. At least it's their phone number."

He pointed at the phone. "Call them." He stood up. "I'll be in the kitchen."

He sat at the kitchen table, drinking his hot chocolate. Liz came out ten minutes later, her eyes filled with tears. "I'm going over there."

Vincent got to his feet. "Do you want me to drive you?"

She shook her head. "I'll walk. They're just over on Louisa Parkway."

"Okay."

"Jessica, that's Jill's mother…"

"You're school friend."

"Yeah." Liz rubbed her eyes with her sleeve. "She wants to…Oh, damn, Vincent."

"She wants to have the conversation you planned for tomorrow, tonight."

"Exactly." She breathed deeply. "I'll see myself out. Call your wife, okay?"

"Definitely." He slipped an arm around her. "And I'll see you to the door."

They walked in silence down the hall to the foyer and she donned her outer-wear. He held the door open for her and smiled encouragingly.

"Thanks for being here," she said.

"Call me later if you need to."

"Thanks. I just might."

"No matter what time."

She managed a smile. Stretching, she kissed his cheek and then walked out into the cold, snowy night.

❧   ❧   ❧

Vincent called Kate on the living room phone. He tried the townhouse in Georgetown and got the answering machine. Frowning, he glanced at his watch. It was nearly 9:30. He tried the cell phone next, but the call was forwarded to her voice mail. Again, he left a message. His last option was her office in the Capitol Building. He dialed the number. Once again he was pleasantly informed, by Kate's voice, that she was unable to take the call. Cursing, he slammed down the phone. What the hell did McMartin have her doing, anyway, he wondered? Folding his arms across his chest, he sat back on the couch and counted to ten. *Calm down, Vincent, and don't blow a gasket. Remember what Liz said. Be patient and understanding.*

He heard dog nails on the foyer floor and seconds later Duke entered the room. The dog sat down, his tail thumbing the floor, his eyes hopeful. Vincent smiled. "She left, boy," he said. "Duty called."

Duke barked and stood up. He walked to the front door and sat down. Vincent got up off the couch and followed the dog to the door. Opening it, he said, "Go on, boy."

Duke continued sitting there, staring at Vincent.

"What?"

Duke barked again.

"Oh, I get it," Vincent said, petting the dog's head. "You want your nightly run."

Duke jumped up excitedly.

"Okay. But I don't run. I walk."

Vincent put on his boots, coat and cap and followed the dog outside. Snow still fell and it was colder than it had been earlier. Even so, Vincent let the dog lead him down Goundry Street, past Nestor's, and across River Road to the banks of the Niagara River. While Duke sniffed around, Vincent stood in the snow and stared down into the dark, icy water. Shivering, he backed away. He called Duke and started back to the Victorian. The dog walked ahead of him, stopping every now and then to eat snow.

When they reached the Reilly house, Duke turned up the driveway and disappeared in the dark. Vincent continued on home. After removing his coat and boots, he checked the answering machine. The message light glowed. He pressed play.

"Hi, Vincent," Kate said. "I'm sorry I missed you. I'll probably be sleeping by the time you get this. God, I'm tired. I'll call you tomorrow. Love you. Bye."

He lifted the phone from the cradle. He'd call her back. So what if he woke her? He needed to talk to her. He had the number half dialed before he stopped himself. Maybe he'd better let her sleep. Lord knew how long McMartin would make her work tomorrow. He set the receiver back in the cradle. He snapped off the living room and kitchen lights, made sure the doors were locked, tossed his cap onto the coat rack and went upstairs to bed.

🍁   🍁   🍁

Violin music woke him. It called to him; its sound sweet; its song unidentifiable, but still alluring. He got up and followed the sound down the hall. It came from the third floor. He stood at the bottom of the stairs, staring at the closed door. Was this real, he wondered? Or was he dreaming? Who was playing it?

A harsh ringing cut off the violin and Vincent jerked. *The phone!* He ran back to the bedroom, snatched up the receiver and fell onto the bed.

"Hey," Kate said in his ear.

"Hi."

"Did I wake you?"

"No, why?"

"It's not yet seven. But I have an early day."

"It's okay." He ignored the urge to bad mouth her boss.

"Anyway, I hope…" She trailed off.

"What?"

"That you're not still mad at me."

"I told you before you left that I wasn't mad at you."

"But at the airport…well…you seemed so distant."

Vincent ran a hand through his hair.

"You really were, Vincent," she added.

"Sorry. Sour grapes, I guess."

"Did you paint after I left?"

"Not much. But I'll paint today."

"Good."

Vincent heard a clicking in his ear.

"Damn," Kate said. "That's the other line."

"Ignore it."

"I can't. It's Darren."

"It's Darren," he mouthed.

"Hold on, okay?"

"Sure."

He sat listening to dead air and growing more annoyed. He sat there on hold for five minutes. He watched the numbers change on the radio alarm and he thought if he were there with her right now he would grab the phone out of her hand and hang up on the bastard.

"Vincent?" she finally said in his ear.

"One and the same."

"I can't hang. I really have to go."

"I see. Well, Kate, when do you think I'll be able to talk to my wife without interruption?"

"You're mad," she said.

"Gee, I wonder why. Look, call me when you can spare the time." He hung up before she could reply. He punched his pillow. "Shit."

The phone rang and he stared at it. One ring. Two rings. Three rings. "Oh, damn," he muttered, picking up the receiver. "Kate?"

"Yes."

"It's okay. Call me later."

"You've never hung up on me before."

He heard tears in her voice. "Look, I'm sorry. Call me when you can and we'll…well…we can plan your next visit."

"I'd like that." Her voice held a smile.

"Have a good day. I'll keep an ear open for the phone."

"Even if you're painting?"

"Promise."

"Okay. I'll talk to you later."

"Bye, babe."

"Bye."

The phone went dead in his ear. He hung it up and headed for the bathroom. While he showered, he decided on his next plan of action. He would, as Liz suggested, be patient. That is until Kate returned for a visit. Then they were going to talk. He would make her see that multi-millionaires don't have to be slaves to Senators anymore.

❦   ❦   ❦

Vincent painted the next two days away. The painting of the old Packet Inn was shaping up just fine. Kate called as promised Monday night and Tuesday night. He listened to her talk about work and politics, thought how uninteresting it all was and forced himself not to voice his thoughts. Instead, he replied in all the right spots. He told her he missed her and he did. She could come visit him the first week of April. She was taking a week's vacation. Vincent smiled, thinking how that visit would change things. After exchanging "Goodbyes" on Tuesday night, he watched TV. He shut off the television at midnight and went upstairs to bed. He fell instantly asleep and dreamed of Katherine Malloy. She stood before the window in her third floor bedroom playing the Stradivarius. She played Mozart. The piece was soothing and beautiful and Vincent smiled in his sleep.

He awoke just before eight and found Duke in bed with him. He hugged the dog, accepting his licks. "When did you get here, boy?" The dog laid his head on Vincent's chest. "Where's Liz?" Duke stared at him with big, sad eyes.

Vincent lay petting the dog for a bit. He had just decided to get up and get them both some breakfast when the phone rang. It was Liz, her voice, though steady, held exhaustion and tears. "Hey, what's going on?" Vincent asked, sitting up and leaning back against the brass headboard.

"What are you doing, Vincent?"

"Actually? I'm lying in bed with Duke."

"I'm at Roswell Park Cancer Institute," she said, not commenting on her dog. "With Jill. Can you come down?"

"Sure."

"I need you." Her voice broke.

"What happened?"

"Just come down, okay? Can you find the place? I can give you directions."

"No need," he assured her. "I'll find it."

And he did, using a map. An hour after getting Liz's phone call, he stood in the doorway of Jill's room. The girl lay in her hospital bed surrounded by machines, tubes in her nose and arm. She looked small, dwarfed by the blankets. Her eyes were closed, her skin pale, what was left of her blonde hair fanned out on the pillow. Liz sat in a chair beside her bed. She wore her white lab coat, her hair held back by a clip, a stethoscope around her neck. Her face was buried in one hand and her other hand held Jill's. Her shaking shoulders told Vincent that Liz was crying.

He went to her, knelt beside the chair and gently touched her shoulder. She looked up, saw him, and reached for him. He took her into his arms and held her. He let her cry, massaging her upper back, his eyes falling on Jill.

Liz fought for control, got it and lifted her head from his chest. "Thank you for coming," she said, wiping her checks with her hand. "I'm sorry."

"It's okay."

"I'm supposed to be the strong one, you know. I'm the doctor."

"You're also human."

She nodded, turning back to Jill. She laid her hand on the girl's forehead. "She's too warm."

Vincent straightened but remained beside Liz's chair. "Why is she here?"

Liz turned down the blankets. Jill's right leg was gone. It had been amputated about six inches below her pelvis.

"Christ," he said. His stomach flipped over and he was glad he hadn't taken time to eat breakfast.

"Yesterday," Liz said. "Dr. Fornier, her surgeon, couldn't...couldn't save her leg." She pulled the blankets up to Jill's chin. "The chemo hadn't..." She trailed off, unable to go on.

Vincent laid his hand on Liz's shoulder.

Liz stroked Jill's hair. Almost whispering, she said, "And there's more chemotherapy to come. Which may work or may not. Either way it's devastating to the body." She held up a strand of limp blonde hair that had fallen out in her hand. "As you can see."

He nodded.

"Why didn't she come to me sooner, Vincent? Why?"

"Because she's young and an athlete. And the cortisone shots kept her cycling."

Liz shook her head. "If I ever get my hands on that trainer."

Approaching footsteps pulled Vincent's attention to the door. Jill's parents and sister filed in. Tracy, dressed in jeans and a white sweater, her blonde hair pulled back with a gold clip, went to her sister's side. She bent over her and kissed her forehead.

Jill's father was a tall, muscular man with brown hair, gray sprouting at his temples. Bits of gray flecked his mustache as well. He wore jeans and a blue button down shirt. His wife, her blonde hair hanging in waves about her shoulders, held his hand. Wire-rimmed, round shaped glasses rested on her thin nose and she wore tan Khakis and a pink turtleneck sweater. Her cheeks were tear-stained. Her eyes were bloodshot and looking questioningly at Vincent.

Liz stood up. "This is my friend, Vincent."

Jill's father held out his hand. "Mike."

Vincent shook it. The man's grip was strong. "Hi. Vincent Vermay." He nodded at Jill's mother. "You must be Jessica?"

She nodded. "Do you know my Jill?"

"Not well. Liz asked me to stop by."

Dismissing him, Jessica turned to Liz. "Did she wake up while we were gone?"

"No. Did you eat?"

"We did," Mike said.

"Shouldn't she be awake by now?" Tracy asked.

Liz walked around the bed to where Tracy stood. She put an arm around the girl and said, "Soon. You have to remember that the surgery was hard on her. She needs sleep."

Tracy managed a small smile. "Okay."

Jessica sat down in the chair Liz had just vacated. "We'll be here when she wakes up."

Liz gestured towards the door with her head. She mouthed, "Wait for me."

Shooting Jill a final look, Vincent stepped out into the hall and leaned against the wall. The hospital corridor was alive with action. Nurses and doctors bustled about. An orderly went by with a three-decker cart piled with clean blankets and sheets. The walls were painted cheery blue, pictures of flowers hanging on them. The attempt at the cheerfulness in the décor almost made Vincent laugh. After all, it was a cancer hospital when all was said and done.

Liz came out of Jill's room. Vincent smiled at her. "How do you do it?"

"Do what?"

"Turn it on and off. They had no idea you were just crying."

Liz signed, "I don't know. Years of doing it, I guess."

"What's Jill's prognosis?"

Tears filled Liz's eyes. "It's not good."

"She's a fighter though, right?"

"She is."

"She's got you and her family by her side."

"Yes."

"Then I'm betting on her. What about you?"

Liz blinked and tears rolled down her cheeks. Swallowing hard, she said, "I have to bet on her. Because I don't know if I can survive another death in my life right now."

CHAPTER 7

Vincent made up his mind during the drive home from Roswell. Liz needed a friend and Kate was that friend. She may have deserted Liz before, but she would be there for her now. He kicked off his boots in the front foyer, went into the parlor and dialed Kate's office number. Her secretary answered on the second ring.

"It's Vincent," he said and was put through.

"Hi," Kate said, pleasure in her voice.

"You need to come here," he said. "Liz needs you."

"What?"

He filled Kate in on Jill, Liz's relationship with the teen, and her involvement in the cancer treatment. "She's on the verge of a breakdown here, Kate. She needs a friend. I can't give her what you can. I don't have the history with her."

"The girl is Liz's goddaughter?"

"Yes."

"Wow. I've missed so much."

"So make it up to her now, babe. She's been through a lot these past few years. She lost her fiancé, her mother, not to mention her father's current condition. I'm afraid she could—"

"End up like her father," Kate finished for him.

"Exactly. Can you come?"

"Lord, Vincent, my schedule is jam packed."

Vincent closed his eyes and silently counted to ten.

"There's a lot going on here," she continued.

"Damn it, Kate!" he shouted. "Aren't you listening to me? Your friend needs you. And you said yourself that you never should have walked away from her. You said you should have been there for her when Alan and her mother died. Now you have a chance here. Don't blow it!" The force and anger in his voice surprised him.

But it got through to her. "You're right," she said. "You're absolutely right. What am I thinking? Okay, hold on."

He sat back on the couch, unzipped his jacket and shrugged it off. He removed his cap and twirled it around on his finger. Ten minutes crept by before she came back on the line. "I'll be there Friday morning. Pick me up at 10:45 a.m. at the airport."

"How long can you stay?"

"Until Monday afternoon."

Vincent smiled. "Thanks, babe."

"No, thank you. Don't tell Liz I'm coming. Let me surprise her."

"Okay."

"I love you."

"Back at you."

Still smiling, Vincent hung up the phone and went upstairs to paint.

He knocked off around 8 p.m. He took a shower, realizing as he stood beneath the hot stream of water, that he was starving. He slipped on a pair of black jeans and a white button down, sat down on his bed and debated. Should he or shouldn't he? Deciding he should, he picked up the phone and dialed the Reilly house. Miss Whiting answered and informed him that Liz was in bed.

"How's she doing?" he asked.

"She's exhausted."

"No doubt. I just wanted to get her some dinner."

"She ate. Not much, but enough. I made sure of it."

Vincent didn't doubt that Elsie Whiting had matters well in hand. "What about Emmett? How would he like to go out?"

"Good Lord, Vincent," Elsie said. "You're a brave man."

"Come on. Don't you or Liz take him out to dinner every now and then?"

"No."

Vincent scratched his chin. "Well, there's always a first time."

"I suppose so. But tonight wouldn't be it, young man. Trust me on that."

"Okay. But I just might ask again."

"You have a good night," she said.

"You too." He hung up the phone, pondering his next move. He went downstairs and rummaged around the kitchen. Settling for a bowl of canned chili and a few slices of Italian bread, he ate it in front of the television, laughing at a rerun of *Barney Miller*. His stomach full, his eyes heavy, he stretched out on the couch. He drifted off to sleep just before eleven.

The melodious sound of Katherine Malloy's violin lulled Vincent from his sleep. He opened his eyes. The room was light. Sun shone in the big bay window. He glanced at his watch—7:30 a.m. Katherine Malloy played her violin early, he thought, rising from the couch. His shirt half-unbuttoned, his hair disheveled, he walked toward the sound. Listening, smiling at the the beautiful music, he walked up the stairs and down the hall to the staircase that led to the third floor. He stood there, listening. "Incredible," he said. He climbed the steps and found the bedroom door cracked open. In the back of his mind, he thought it odd that the door was open. He could have sworn he'd closed and locked it behind him the night he'd gone up to the third floor.

He stepped into Katherine Malloy's bedroom and she was there. She stood in front of the wooden music stand by the window playing her violin. Her lustrous brown hair fell in gentle curls about her shoulders. She wore a lacy white dress, its skirt nearly touching the floorboards. Its cuffs and collar were ruffled. She played with her eyes closed, not needing to read the music that lay open on the music stand. He couldn't name the piece she played, but Vincent knew it was Mozart.

He stood just inside the bedroom door, speechless. *What the hell was happening*? Was he still sleeping? Surely this had to be a dream. While he watched, Katherine finished the piece she was playing and lowered her violin. She looked down at the music on the stand and shook her head. "I'm sorry, Wolfgang," she said, her voice soft and as lovely as her violin. "I don't do you justice anymore." She turned from the music stand and went to the bed. She closed the violin in its case and sat down on the bed, its springs creaking. Burying her face in her hands, she began crying, her shoulders shaking.

Vincent wanted to go to her. He wanted to put his arms around her and comfort her. But he was unable to move. He begged his legs to function, but they refused. The phone rang downstairs and he involuntarily turned toward the sound. Silently cursing the distraction, he looked back into the third floor room. Katherine Malloy was gone. Shaking himself, wondering if he'd been walking in his sleep, he hurried downstairs to the bedroom and snatched up the phone. It was Liz.

"Hey," he said. "How ya doing?"

"I'm here. Getting ready for work."

"Will you be going to see Jill today?"

"This afternoon."

"Want some company?"

"No. But thanks. Besides, you have painting to do."

"Sure?"

"Absolutely. Anyway, the reason I called is to thank you."

"For what?"

"Thinking of my father. Elsie told me about your call last night."

"Oh."

"Are you sure you would want to take him out, Vincent? I used to try but…well, it usually turned out to be a disaster."

"I don't doubt that, Liz. How long has it been since you tried?"

"Over a year."

"Maybe it's time to try again. In any event, I'd like to give it a shot."

She was silent a moment then said, "Go for it, Vincent."

"Good, I will."

"I have to get going," she said. "I'll be seeing you.

"You too. Bye."

He took a quick shower, slipped into black cotton slacks and a tan denim shirt, and then went downstairs to the kitchen. He had a bowl of oatmeal and a cup of coffee for breakfast. He knew he should paint, but he didn't feel like it. It was time to start thoroughly cleaning and redecorating the house. He set his dirty dishes in the sink. As he walked up the back staircase, he wondered which room to start first. He wasn't going to change the fern room, unless Kate wanted it changed. He'd ask her about it. He wandered down the hall to Jethro Malloy's library. He stood in the doorway, leaned against the doorframe and said, "Now, here's a room that needs lightening up." Everything about it was dark—the carpet on the floor, the draperies, the woodworking, the desk. He went to the window and looked out on the snowy side yard and further on to the Reilly house. He pushed the curtains as far to the side as they would go and turned back to face the room. Yes, he thought, smiling. This would be a perfect place for Kate to finish her novel. The wooden floor, the woodwork, the book-shelves and the desk could stay. But the walls, those he would lighten up. His smile widened. Brighter curtains and a new rug and the room would inspire.

He would do it for Kate as a surprise. Hell, he'd even buy her a state of the art computer with an Internet hook up.

The doorbell rang and he went downstairs to the front door. He opened it and found himself staring at Tracy Woodward. She stood shivering in her ski jacket, her hair hanging free about her shoulders.

"Come in," he said, opening the door wider. Frigid air hit him and he shivered.

"Thanks," she said, entering. She stamped her feet, snow falling from her boots. "I need to talk to you."

Vincent closed the door. "Okay." He held out his hand. "Your coat."

She shook her head, hugging herself. "I'll keep it on. I'm freezing." But she took off her boots.

"I see. Follow me."

He led her into the parlor, pulled the afghan off the back of the couch and handed it to her.

She sat down on the couch and covered herself. Her entire body shook and her cheeks, nose, and ears burned bright red. "Aunt Liz told me where you lived. Don't be mad at her."

"Why would I be mad at her?"

"You being famous and all."

"Trust me. I'm not a celebrity."

"But you are. You are to Jill. Even as upset as she was Sunday night, she recognized you. She's wanted to buy one of your paintings but…" She trailed off, looking away. "Well, being just a student, she can't afford it."

"I see. Tell you what, let me get you a hot chocolate."

Still shaking, she said, "I'd like that."

He made two giant mugs of hot chocolate, gave one to Tracy, and sat down beside her on the couch. She sipped the hot liquid, her eyes filled with gratitude. "How far did you walk out there?"

"I took a bus from the hospital. It ran as far as Main Street in Tonawanda. I walked the rest of the way."

"That's a good hike in this temperature."

"Yeah. The wind chill is nasty today."

"And you didn't know I'd be home."

"I would have just gone home then. It's not far."

"Far enough on a day like today."

She didn't argue.

"How is your sister doing?"

"She's depressed. Last night, when Mom and Dad were out of the room, she made me pull the covers down so she could see. She cried. I've never heard her cry like that before."

Vincent didn't have a clue what to say. He sat there, staring down into his mug of chocolate.

"Anyway," Tracy said. "I came here because I want..."

"What?" He gazed at her with encouraging eyes.

"I want to buy her one of your paintings. I have a part time job and I could make payments on it. I think it will cheer her up. She might die soon and at least she would have achieved one of her dreams."

"Wow," Vincent said, shaking his head.

"Please, Mr. Vermay, don't say no. I'll pay it off. Please."

Vincent held up his hand. "I'm not saying no, Tracy."

Tracy's eyes questioned him.

"I think it's pretty terrific that you're here asking me this. And the answer is, Jill will have one of my paintings."

"Really?"

"Really. Besides cycling and my artwork, what does she like?"

Tracy took a long drink of her hot chocolate before answering. "Let's see. She's a history major. She's nuts about the 1800's. She's dragged me to the Genesee Country Museum several times. It's an 1800's village made up of old New York State houses that were saved and moved there. That's why she likes your paintings. They're so historical."

Vincent set his mug of chocolate on the coffee table. "Okay, wait here. I think I've got just the painting for her."

As he ran upstairs to his studio, Vincent found it hard to believe, as he always did, that anyone, let alone a nineteen-year-old girl, would dream about owning one of his paintings. Entering the studio, he lifted the painting of the hansom cab on the wooded road from its resting place against the wall. He hurried back down to the living room. He held up the painting, "It's called, *Road of Possibilities*." He pointed at the lower left hand corner. "My signature is down here."

Tracy stared at it with wide eyes. "It's great, Mr. Vermay. She'll love it."

"Good. I'll wrap it up for her."

"How much is it?" Tracy asked. "I can pay you twenty dollars a week."

"No, you won't pay me anything. You'll take it and give it to her."

"But—"

"No, buts. I'll wrap it up."

"Thank you," she said, her lower lip trembling.

"You're welcome. Finish your hot chocolate while I get this ready."

Back in the studio, he sorted through some extra frames he had accumulated over the years. While packing up his studio in Georgetown, he had thought about leaving the frames behind. Now he was glad he hadn't. He chose an ornate gold one and framed the painting. Next, he wrapped it in paper and taped the paper shut. Walking back downstairs with the painting, he decided that he would drive Tracy back to Roswell. Not only would she have a warmer ride, but the painting would be safer as well. Anything could happen to it on a bus.

He reached the living room and found Tracy fast asleep on the couch, her empty mug sitting next to his on the coffee table. Wet tears on her cheeks told him she had cried herself to sleep. He set the painting against the wall in the foyer and went upstairs to the bedroom phone. He dialed Roswell and asked for Jill's room. Jessica Woodward answered. She sounded exhausted and worried.

"Hi, it's Dr. Reilly's friend Vincent."

"What can I do for you?" she asked.

"How's Jill?"

"Sleeping a lot. And she's running a temperature. Dr. Fornier and Liz are watching her closely. Thank you for your concern."

"Sure. Look, the other reason I called is that your daughter Tracy is here."

"I sent her to school."

"She didn't go. She came here."

"I'm sorry she imposed on you."

"No imposition. She came to pick up a present for Jill. Anyway, she was pretty exhausted so I let her fall asleep on the couch. I just didn't want you to worry about her."

"Thank you. But she should have done what I said."

"Well, sometimes kids will be kids."

"I guess. I'll call my husband and have him pick her up on his way home from work."

"No need. I'll drop her home when she wakes up."

"Are you sure, Mr. Vermay?"

"Positive. Don't worry about her."

"Thank you."

"You're welcome."

He hung up the phone. Shopping for paint for Jethro's library would have to wait. He couldn't leave Tracy alone. Who knew what condition she would be in when she woke up. He changed into his jeans, loafers and Williamsburg shirt and went to his studio. He stood in front of his painting of the old Packet Inn and smiled. He needed to play a little with the sky, maybe a little more shading on the brick street. He scratched his chin. The painting cried out for something more…something unusual on the brick street. But what did it need? Not the hansom cab. He couldn't use that again unless he did a series of hansom cab paintings. No, the hansom cab painting should stand-alone. It should be unique now that it had a very important owner.

He stood pondering his painting in the morning light. He stared at the brick street and he thought about what he could place there. His mind flashed pictures of people, cars, horses, plants, and shoes and then, Katherine Malloy's violin. He smiled broadly. Of course, the violin, abandoned on the street. He sprinted down the hall and up the stairs to the third floor. The violin lay on Katherine's bed, shut in its case. He snatched it up and ran back downstairs to his studio. He set the case on the dresser, opened it and looked down at the violin resting in red velvet. Carefully, he removed the instrument, pushed the case aside then laid the violin on the table. He laid the bow over it and studied it from all angles. He readied his palette, snatched up his brush and began painting. He didn't stop until a voice said, "Mr. Vermay?"

He turned, his brush in hand. Tracy Woodward, still wearing her ski jacket, stood in the studio doorway. He smiled at her, wondering if he looked like a wild man. "You're up," he said, hoping he didn't have paint on his face like he usually did.

She nodded, hugging herself. "Yeah." She pointed at his painting. "I like it."

"Thanks." He set the brush and palette on the dresser. "What time is it?"

"Four."

He picked up a rag and wiped his hands. "I called your mother and told her you were here."

"She's going to yell at me."

"Probably. But you'll survive it. Let me drive you home."

"I'd rather go to the hospital."

Vincent eyed her. She was pale and still exhausted. In fact, she looked as if she hadn't slept at all.

"No, you'll go home. Tomorrow you can go to the hospital and give Jill her painting. I'll pick you up at your house at 8 a.m. Deal?"

"Deal," she said without further argument.

❦   ❦   ❦

The Woodwards lived a few streets over from Vincent in a Tudor cottage. Bushes surrounded the front porch, ivy climbing around the arched doorway. Ivy also climbed up the house on the driveway side. A white arbor between the house and the garage invited one to step into a snow-covered, English garden. Tracy was standing on the front porch waiting for him, painting in hand.

Vincent pulled into the driveway and rolled down the window. "Wanna ride?" He jumped out of the Rodeo and took the painting from her. "Hop in." She did while he stowed the painting in the back. Once back inside the truck, he said, "Did you get some sleep?"

"Yes."

"Good." He put the truck in reverse and backed out of the driveway. As he shifted the vehicle back into drive, he shot her a quick glance. She looked rested. Pleased, he pushed down the accelerator and headed to Roswell.

Their conversation was sparse. Her mother had indeed lectured her about blowing off school, but Tracy thought the lecture had been half-hearted at best. Especially after she learned about the painting. Permission had been speedily given for Tracy to skip school long enough to deliver her gift.

"My dad is going to drive me to school afterwards. He spent the night with Jill."

"I see."

"We're taking turns. But between you and me, Mr. Vermay, I don't think Mom rests when she's away from her."

Vincent nodded but kept his eyes on the road. "You're probably right. I doubt your dad sleeps much either."

"Yeah." She fell silent.

Vincent didn't press her further and they spent the remainder of the ride in companionable silence. They left the Rodeo in a parking garage and walked to the hospital. The building towered above them, ice cycles gleaming around its eaves and windows. He escorted Tracy as far as Jill's door then stopped. He held out the painting. "Here, you go on in and give it to her."

She took it, but said, "You come too."

He shook his head. "This is your gift and your thunder."

"But—"

"Nope." He held up his hand. "This is yours." He pointed at the closed door. "Go on."

"Will you wait out here?"

"No. I have to pick up a lady at the airport."

"What if Jill wants to see you?"

"Tell her I'll stop by and see her soon."

"Promise."

"Scout's honor."

She stood on tiptoe and kissed his cheek. "Thank you, Mr. Vermay."

"No problem."

She disappeared into the room. He heard her say, "Hey, Dad, Jill," before the door closed behind her.

He didn't go straight to the airport. He had time to kill so he stopped at the hardware store and purchased the paint for Jethro's library. After some consideration, he decided on a pale yellow. He arrived at the airport at 10:30, parked the Rodeo in short-term parking and went inside. His eyebrows shot up when he read the arrival postings and discovered Kate's plane would be arriving fifteen minutes early. He hurried to her gate, dodging people as he went. He removed his cap and fluffed his hair with his hands. She was the fifth person off the plane. She wore a blue parka and navy blue, pinstripe slacks. Her glasses were crooked on her nose. She had her purse slung over one shoulder and her laptop case over the other. One hand held an overnight bag and the other a box wrapped in gold paper with a blue bow.

"So much for hugging you," he said, kissing her lips. "Damn, it's good to see you."

"You too." She held out the box. "Peace offering."

He took the box. "There was no need."

"Open it."

People milled around them. He untied the bow and opened the box. Inside was a brand new red, blue and gold plaid, flannel shirt. He grinned at her.

"To replace the one I stole."

He kissed her cheek and closed the box. "Thank you. Let's get your suitcase."

"Didn't bring one. Everything's in here." She held up the overnight bag. "I'm starved. Feed me." She slid her free arm through his and started him walking. "How's Liz?"

"Holding up. What did McMartin say about your leaving?"

"Just that it was poor timing."

"That's all?"

She stepped around a toddler. "Pretty much. Except he said I have to be back Monday."

"And are you?"

"What?"

"Going back Monday."

"Yes, I really have to, Vincent."

He refrained from voicing his thoughts on King McMartin. Instead, he said, "I think you need to go to Nestor's for lunch."

"It's still open?" she asked.

"Yeah. You know about it?"

"Best Texas Red Hots in North Tonawanda. Take me, Vincent."

"You're wish is my command, my lady."

She chuckled. "After that, though, let's go see Liz."

"That's the plan. She should be at her office."

Kate leaned closer and whispered in his ear, "And after that..."

Grinning, he replied, "Yes, and after that..."

❧   ❧   ❧

Vincent parked the Rodeo in front of the Paperback Swap'N'Shop and jumped out. Kate got out of the truck, closed the door and stood gazing down the street toward the canal. Vincent walked around to her side of the vehicle and said, "What?"

She shielded her eyes with her hand. "Webster Street."

"What about it?"

She smiled. "Lots of memories." She took his hand. "Lead on."

They walked down to the signal, crossed Groundry, made an immediate left and crossed Webster. The day was warming up, trickles of melting snow traveling out from the snow banks onto the road. Vincent held the door open and Kate entered. A middle-aged woman sat at a cash register directly to their left. She bid them hello and Vincent nodded his greeting. There were no empty stools at the counter so Kate bypassed them and headed into the dining room. She stopped suddenly and Vincent almost ran her over.

"Look," she said. She pointed at the booth in the far corner.

Liz sat alone. She wore forest green slacks, a white blouse and a pale green, beige and white rose-flowered vest. Her auburn hair was pulled back with a green suede clip. Her fedora sat on the table next to a plate of untouched food. She didn't see them because her face was buried in her hands.

"Oh, Vincent, she's devastated," Kate whispered.

"Yeah, she is, babe."

"Come on."

They went to her. Kate knelt beside her childhood friend and laid a hand on her shoulder. "Liz," she said.

Liz jerked then looked up. Her skin was pale, dark bags under her eyes. Seeing Kate, she said, "How…when did you…" She looked from Kate to Vincent.

"Just now, Liz."

Liz looked back at Kate again. "Why?"

Kate massaged Liz's back. "Because you need me."

Liz stared at her with incredulous eyes. "You came for me?"

"Yes. Don't you think it's about time I show up for one of your life crises?"

Tears spilled from Liz's eyes. A sob escaped her and Kate took her into her arms. Vincent backed away, aware that the restaurant's current crop of customers was shooting Liz and Kate glances. Liz was well known in North Tonawanda. He had no doubt that she would be the topic of conversation at several dinner tables tonight.

One of the stools at the counter had opened up and Vincent slid into it. The waitress, a young woman with blonde hair approached him, pad and pen in hand. "Just a glass of 7-UP," he said. He removed his cap and set it on the counter. He could hear Liz's sobs and Kate's murmurings of comfort. He sighed.

"Sucks, don't it?"

The voice came from the elderly man next to him. The man wore a brown, white and black plaid, flannel shirt and blue jeans. His hair, white as the snow outside, was clipped close about his head. Black, plastic framed glasses sat on his long nose. His beard and mustache held streaks of gray in the white. "What sucks?" Vincent asked him. The waitress set his glass of pop on the counter and moved on.

"Her life."

"Whose life?"

The man chuckled. He held out his hand. "Doug Lassiter."

Vincent shook the hand. "Vincent Vermay."

"I know who you are. You're living in the Malloy house." He gestured over his shoulder toward Kate and Liz. "That's Katherine's granddaughter. She used to spend summers here."

Vincent gazed at him but said nothing.

"She and Elizabeth were fast friends back then. Then Kate disappeared. Left one summer and never came back. Until now that is."

"Did you know Katherine Malloy?"

"Nope. Knew Emmett Reilly. Was my doctor for years. Until he went…well, you know."

"You go to Liz now?"

"Nope. Moved on."

"I see."

"I doubt you do. I don't hanker to women doctors. Nothing personal."

"Ahh." Vincent took a swig of his drink.

"Anyway, back to what I said originally. That girl hasn't had an easy life. No, sir, she sure hasn't. First, her best friend disappears. Then her fiancé dies and soon after that, her mother. Then Emmett…" He shook his head. "He was one damn fine doctor too."

"Ever visit him?"

The man shook his head. "Naw, I wasn't on his level. Just a patient."

"I'd bet that doesn't mean he wouldn't like to see you."

Lassiter removed his glasses, folded them and slid them into his breast pocket. "You think he'd know me?"

"Only one way to find out."

"Suppose so." The waitress came over and set Lassiter's check on the counter. Ignoring it, he asked, "You married to Kate?"

"I am."

"How long you plan on staying in the Malloy house?"

"I don't know for sure. Why?"

"I live over on Tremont. Before Katherine moved down to Maryland, I used to walk by her place in the evenings and I'd hear her play that violin. Damn fine violin player she was. You should've heard her play."

Vincent almost said, I have, but stopped himself. *More like dreamed I've heard her.*

Lassiter pulled his wallet out of his back pocket and said, "After she moved, every now and then, when I'd take my walk, damn if I didn't think I could still hear her playing." He pulled a five-dollar bill from the wallet and tossed it on the counter. "Sounded so lifelike, you would've sworn she was still there playing."

Vincent stared at Lassiter.

"I know." The old man waved a hand. "Sounds crazy." He stood up, rubbing his back. "Damn arthritis. Hey, you really think I should go visit Emmett?"

"Wouldn't hurt to try?"

"Maybe not." He tipped a thumb towards Kate and Liz. "You two going to help her? I heard about the Woodward girl. She's Liz's goddaughter, you know."

"I know. Yes, we're going to help Liz."

"Good." He turned to go.

"Mr. Lassiter?"

He turned back. "What?"

"What you said about still hearing Katherine play the violin after she moved away. Did that happen often?"

"Nope. But when it did, it sure stayed with me." He glanced at his watch. "Gotta pick the wife up at the library. Bye, now."

"Goodbye."

Vincent watched him remove his parka from the coat rack by the door. He shrugged it on and headed outside. Vincent kept staring at the door long after the man had disappeared from view. All he could think of was that he wasn't the only person in the world who had heard Katherine's violin even though Katherine wasn't there to play it.

❧   ❧   ❧

"Vincent?"

Startled, Vincent whirled around on the stool. Kate sat next to Liz in the booth and she was motioning him over. He picked up his cap and glass of 7-UP and went over, sitting across from them. Liz was wiping her face and eyes with a napkin. "Hey," he said.

She managed a smile. "Hey."

"You okay?"

She nodded.

He pushed the cold plate of food towards her. "When was the last time you ate anything?"

She barely gave the hot dog and fries a passing glance. Instead, she said, "That was wonderful of you."

"What was?"

"Giving Jill the painting. It's hanging next to her hospital bed."

"I hope it cheered her up."

"Deep down, I think it did."

"But?"

"She's experiencing all the normal things. She's grieving for her leg. She's depressed and terrified."

"How's her godmother?"

Liz's lower lip trembled. "Losing control."

Kate slipped an arm around her and Liz laid her head on Kate's shoulder. Sighing, she closed her eyes.

Vincent couldn't say anything comforting. What was there to say? Hell, Lassiter had said it. Liz had experienced so much loss lately that it was no wonder her strength was dissolving on her. "I was talking with an old patient of your father's."

Liz opened her eyes. "Doug Lassiter."

"Yeah. Seemed like a nice guy. Said he might stop in to visit your dad."

"I don't know how that would go."

"Wouldn't hurt if he tried, though, would it?"

"I don't know, Vincent." She raised her head. "I can't seem to think of anything but Jill right now. I got a colleague to see my patients for me today."

"That's good."

Liz looked at Kate. "I'm so glad you came."

Kate smiled.

Liz absently cracked her knuckles. "This is so hard. God, I hate feeling like this. I can't get a hold of myself."

Kate laid her free hand on top of Liz's hands. "You trying to break a finger there?"

Liz looked down at Kate's hand on top of hers. "I need to sleep," she said. "Why can't I sleep?"

"Because you're worried," Kate said. "Why don't Vincent and I take you home and you can lie down for awhile?"

"Okay."

"Good, let's go."

While Kate helped Liz get into her jacket and hat, Vincent walked over to the cash register by the door. "How much for Dr. Reilly's lunch?"

The cashier shook her head, her blue eyes filled with compassion. "On the house."

"Thank you."

"Anytime," the woman said. "Folks take care of one another around here."

Vincent gave her a smile. He held the door open for Kate and Liz. As they headed for the Rodeo, Liz walked as if in a daze. She climbed into the backseat and let Kate buckle her seatbelt. As Kate got into the truck, she shot Vincent a worried glance.

They reached the Victorian and Vincent parked the Rodeo at the end of the driveway. He got out of the truck and walked around the back of the vehicle to the passenger side. Kate was already unbuckling Liz's seatbelt. Liz let Kate take her by the hand and lead her home. Duke sat on the front porch. Seeing them, he jumped up and charged. Vincent greeted the dog, but Liz walked by him as if he weren't there. She was on autopilot, functioning just enough to walk.

The three of them climbed the porch steps, Liz between them, supported by Kate. Duke raced around the front yard, barking. Vincent fished through Liz's pockets for her keys and came up empty handed. Kate rapped on the door. While they waited, Liz turned to Vincent and said, "My keys."

"Where are they?"

She stared at him, at a loss.

The front door opened and Vincent fully expected to see Elsie Whiting. Instead, Emmett Reilly stood there.

Liz looked at him. "Daddy," she said.

A troubled look entered Emmett's eyes. "What's wrong, Lizzie?"

"Jill has cancer Daddy. They amputated her leg Wednesday."

"Little Jill Woodward? Jessie's girl?"

"Yes." Liz was trembling; tears close to spilling yet again. "I can't help her. Daddy she could die." The tears came and with them, Liz collapsed.

Kate held her upright. "Mr. Reilly," she began.

But Emmett Reilly needed no prodding. He scooped his daughter into his arms and carried her towards the stairs.

Vincent saw Elsie Whiting running down the hall. "Emmett," she called. "What's going on?" Emmett ignored her. He carried Liz upstairs, away from them all. Elsie turned to Vincent and Kate. "What happened?"

"She's exhausted," Kate said. "And worried about Jill Woodward. She needs some sleep."

Elsie came to the door, fear in her eyes. "Oh, Lord, it's happening again." She pushed stray locks of hair back from her face. "It's just like when Marlene got sick. Emmett couldn't fix it. And now Liz can't fix this."

Vincent touched Elsie's forearm. "Liz will be all right. We're all here to help her."

Elsie looked towards the stairs then back at them again. "I hope you're right, Vincent. You have no idea how much I hope you're right."

CHAPTER 8

❀

"It's good, Vincent," Kate said. She stood studying the painting of the Packet Inn and the abandoned violin, arms folded across her chest, head slightly cocked. Her hair, freshly wet from a shower, hung in waves about her shoulders. She wore moccasins and a white terrycloth robe.

He came up behind her and put his hands on her shoulders. She leaned back into him and he felt her wet hair through his shirt. "I wondered what was taking you so long in the bathroom."

"In fact, it's wonderful. The violin, laying there with the bow broken, is just…it says so much."

"I thought twilight was fitting too. That works, right?"

"Oh, yes. It makes the violin look so…lost and forlorn. Even abandoned and forgotten. It looks like it misses her." She turned and faced him, slipping her arms around his waist. "I think I told you that she never played it unless she was in her room."

"On the third floor."

He felt Kate shudder. "Yes."

"What is it about that room that bothers you so?"

She pulled him close and laid her head on his chest. He rested his chin in her wet hair. "It's old news, Vincent. Don't worry about it. Is the lasagna ready?"

"The timer should be going off any minute."

"Good. Because that shower brought my appetite back."

The dining room was at the back of the house beside the kitchen. Vincent had set the table with two brass candlesticks, each holding a white candle. He'd lit the candles and they gave off a soft glow of yellow light. Delicate, crystal glasses filled with white wine sat in front of each plate. The table, a perfect oval, filled the center of the old room. It was matched with a maple hutch and sideboard. Maple paneling climbed halfway up the walls, separated from the maroon, green and ivory flowered wallpaper by an elaborately carved white chair rail. The same design repeated itself in the molding beneath the ceiling. Maroon lacy curtains, pulled back with white sashes, decorated the room's two windows.

Kate stopped in the doorway. She pointed at the crystal chandelier that hung over the table. "Doesn't that work?"

"Ye of little faith," he said, chuckling. He flicked the switch on the wall and the chandelier blazed.

Kate laughed. "Okay. But I like the candlelight better."

He switched the light off. "Sit, my lady," he said, motioning to the table. "I'll be right back."

The timer went off just as he entered the kitchen. He removed the pan of lasagna, from the oven and returned to the dining room. He set the entrée in the middle of the table, next to a huge bowl of tossed salad. Sitting down across from her, he raised his wine glass and said, "To us." They clinked glasses and drank.

"I love you," she said, watching him cut the lasagna.

He smiled at her. "I love you." He set her piece of lasagna on her plate. "Take some salad. Sorry there's no Italian bread."

"It's fine." She put some salad on her plate.

He watched her eat and he wondered if he should start the discussion he'd been planning since her last visit. Dare he bring up her quitting her job and returning to novel writing? He could feel their harmony, tight and comfortable at this moment. Dare he break the spell?

She looked up at him. Forkful of lasagna halfway to her mouth, she said, "What?"

In his mind, he said, "I want you to quit working for McMartin and come live here with me. We'll redecorate Jethro's library and you can write there." But he didn't say it aloud. He saw something in her eyes, way in the back of them. *Resistance*? Or maybe what he saw was defiance or just plain old-fashioned independence? He wondered if she realized it was there, holding its ground, controlling her. He grinned at her and said, "You have never looked more beautiful, Katherine Malloy Vermay."

She wrinkled her nose. "Right, with wet hair and dressed in a robe. What have you been drinking?"

He chuckled. "That's just it, Kate. When women think they're the least attractive to a man, they're actually the most attractive."

She rolled her eyes and ate a bite of lasagna. She chewed it, swallowed and said, "That's weird."

"What?"

"Whenever I'm called Katherine, I don't think of myself as a Katherine. Not really. I'm a Kate. You know?"

He nodded. "Like I'm a Vincent, not a Vinni."

She laughed. "Vinni? Oh, Lord, Vincent, you are definitely not a Vinni."

He loved the way laughter enlivened her face, softening it, turning her eyes into shining green orbs. Her smile brought joy to his heart.

As suddenly as her laughter had erupted, it ceased. The light faded from her eyes and the smile dissolved. She looked at him with profound sadness in her eyes and said, "Seeing Liz like that. God, Vincent, I'm worried."

He reached across the table and took her hand.

"I feel guilty as hell right now. She's over there an emotional wreck and I'm here having a really great time with my husband."

He shook his head "Don't feel guilty about that, babe. You're here for her now. Focus on that fact."

"Vincent, do you suppose she's snapped like her father? Can conditions like that be inherited?"

He held up his hand, silencing her. "Don't think like that. Think positive and tomorrow, go over and see her, talk with her, and give her all the support she needs. She can get through this."

Kate sighed. "And if Jill dies?"

Vincent could only gaze silently at Kate.

"It sucks to not have the answers, doesn't it, Vincent?"

All he could do was nod his head.

When they had finished eating, they cleaned off the table and did the dishes. She washed and he dried. It felt wonderful, having her there beside him in the Victorian's kitchen, her lavender scent warming his soul. They didn't speak while they worked. There was no need. They were as one, feeling one another's contentment in their being together.

He dried the last dish and stowed it in the cupboard. Folding the dishtowel, he set it on the counter and watched as Kate wiped the faucet with the sponge. "What?" she asked, shooting him a glance.

"You're looking very domestic."

"Gee, thanks."

"You're welcome. It's after eight. Want to go to a movie or something? We could catch a nine o'clock show."

She hugged herself and shook her head. "I don't want to be with other people tonight, Vincent. I just want to be with you. Can we stay here and watch TV?"

"Sure."

She led the way to the parlor. She sat down on the couch and patted the cushion beside her. He sat down and she curled up next to him, resting her head on his shoulder. He reached behind them and got the afghan. He covered her. "Good?"

"Wonderful."

He picked up the remote from the coffee table and hit the power button. Actress Melina Kanakaredes filled the screen. "*Providence*," he said.

"Leave it on."

They watched Melina, playing Dr. Syd Hansen, work her way through two problems, one involving a patient, the other a family member. This time it was brother Robbie.

Kate yawned and snuggled closer. Vincent absently stroked her hair. "This is a good show," he said and when she didn't answer, he looked down at her and saw that she'd fallen asleep. Smiling, he kissed her forehead. *Providence* ended and *Dateline* began. He turned off the television, hoping the sudden quiet didn't wake her. He sat with her on the couch, enjoying her closeness and rhythmic breathing.

He carried her upstairs and put her to bed shortly after 10 p.m. He took off his clothes, tossed them on the floor and crawled in beside her. He was nearly asleep when the phone rang. He snatched it up, praying it hadn't awakened Kate. "Hello," he said.

"Vincent?"

He sat bolt upright. "Emmett?"

"Yes, son."

Kate stirred beside him.

"Is Liz okay?" Vincent asked.

"Who is it?" Kate asked, stretching.

"Liz is sleeping," Emmett said in Vincent's ear.

Vincent put his hand over the mouthpiece and said, "It's Emmett." He uncovered the mouthpiece and said, "How long has she been asleep?"

"I gave her a sedative."

Kate sat up and reached for the phone. "Let me talk to him."

Vincent blocked her hand. "You did what?"

"I gave her a sedative."

"Are you allowed?"

"I may not practice anymore, but I'm still a doctor. And Elsie helped me."

Vincent breathed a sigh of relief. "Hold on." He turned to Kate. "He and Elsie gave Liz a sedative. She's sleeping."

"Ask him what she said. How she is mentally."

Right, Vincent thought, lifting the receiver to his ear again. Ask a guy who's just about crazy himself if his daughter has joined him in Never Land. To Emmett he said, "Did Liz eat anything or talk before you gave her the sedative?"

"We talked. Don't know as I helped her much though. She's really upset about the Woodward girl. I know how she feels, Vincent. When Marlene..." He didn't finish his sentence.

"Well, anything Kate and I can do to help, you call us."

"Could Kate come over here? Liz needs someone strong to be there when she wakes up. I'm not that person. And Elsie..." He trailed off.

"Elsie is not Kate," Vincent finished for him.

"Right."

Vincent gazed at his wife. She was beautiful in the moonlight, her curly hair falling haphazardly about her shoulders. He didn't want her to leave his bed. "She'll be over in a few mnutes, Emmett."

"Thank you. I'll put the front light on for her."

Vincent bid Emmett goodnight then hung up the phone.

"Where am I going?" Kate asked.

"Next door. Emmett thinks you should be there when Liz wakes up."

"Then I better get going." She kissed him then got out of bed. She switched on the light and dug into her overnight bag. He watched her as she put on a pair of blue jeans and a pale blue turtleneck. She brushed her hair and piled it up on her head, holding it there with a clip. She looked stunning even though traces of sleep still lay in her eyes.

"I'll miss you," he said.

She smiled. "I'll lock the door on my way out. Don't be too lonely."

"Maybe if I'm lucky Duke will come over."

She bent over him. "You poor boy," she said, kissing his lips.

He touched her forearm. "Call me if you need me over there."

"Don't worry, I will."

He listened to her walk down the stairs. He pictured her slipping on her parka and boots. He heard the front door open then close. Sighing, he rolled onto his side and pulled her pillow to his chest. It took him a long time to fall asleep.

Warm lips on his forehead woke him. He opened his eyes. Kate leaned over him. "Hey," he mumbled.

"Good morning." She straightened. "We're downstairs."

"Who is we?"

"Liz and I. Come on down. We're in the living room."

"How is she?"

"You'll see." She left the room.

Vincent threw the covers back and got up. Quickly, he hurried to the bathroom. He splashed some water on his face, ran a comb through his hair and brushed his teeth. Back in the bedroom, he put on a pair of green khakis and a white button down. He gave himself a final look in the mirror, deemed himself presentable and headed downstairs.

Liz sat on the couch beneath the afghan, Duke on the floor at her feet. Kate was setting a tray with three cups of coffee on the coffee table. She motioned for Vincent to enter. "Come on in."

Duke's tail wagged as he approached.

"Hi, Vincent," Liz said. She spoke softly, her voice hoarse from crying.

"Good morning." He patted Duke's head. "Hi, boy."

"Thanks for driving me home yesterday."

Vincent knelt beside the dog and petted his back. Kate sat down on the couch beside Liz.

"You're welcome."

"I lost it," Liz said. "I'm sorry."

"I already told you not to worry about it," Kate said.

Liz closed her eyes. "I was with Jill yesterday morning. I changed her bandage and..." She shuddered, her eyes opening and looking at Vincent. "I just couldn't take it any longer." Kate laid a comforting hand on Liz's thigh. "It just all came down on me. I just couldn't be strong anymore. And all I could think is am I going to lose Jill too?"

The pain in her voice tore at Vincent's heart. It tore at Duke's too. The dog jumped up and licked Liz's face. She hugged him. "Thank you, Duke."

Duke made soft whining sounds, his tongue working furiously.

Liz let him go a few minutes then gently pushed him down. "You sit," she said.

The dog obeyed but he didn't take his eyes off of her.

"Do you realize that yesterday was the first time my father has comforted me since before my mother died? For a brief time it was like he was back." A wistful smile crossed her face. Kate patted Liz's thigh. Liz looked at her. "First Alan. Then my mother and—"

"Don't, Liz," Kate said. "Don't dwell. As hard as it is, you have to move on."

"I never got to practice medicine with my father. Instead, I practice alone. Everything, always I'm alone."

"You're not alone anymore." Kate took hold of Liz's hand and squeezed it. "If I'm not here physically, I'm only a phone call away. Vincent is here too."

Liz looked from Kate to Vincent then back at Kate again. With fear in her eyes, she said, "I feel like I'm on the edge of a cliff, Kate."

Kate pulled Liz into her arms and held her close. She gazed over Liz's shoulder at Vincent with worried eyes.

❧   ❧   ❧

Beethoven filled his studio while Vincent put the finishing touches on his painting of the Packet Inn and the abandoned violin. He had the music jacked up loud and he didn't hear the phone ring. He was in his painting zone, a place he reveled in. Duke watched him work and while he was aware of the dog, he didn't pay him any attention. Kate had talked Liz into a day away from hospitals and doctoring. They had gone to a movie together. Then they would stop for dinner. Vincent was supposed to meet them at Roswell at 7:30 to visit Jill.

After the last brush stroke, Vincent set his palette and brush down and stepped back from the painting. A wide smile crossed his face. It was good. No, it was better than good. While not quite brilliant, it was even closer to brilliant than the painting of the hansom cab on the wooded road had been. He rubbed his hands together. He was almost back.

The CD ended, but the studio did not fall silent. The doorbell was ringing. Duke jumped up, barked and ran for the stairs. Vincent followed him. "Easy,

Duke." He pushed the dog away from the front doors and opened them. Doug Lassiter stood on his front porch. "Mr. Lassiter," Vincent said, motioning him inside.

Lassiter entered and Vincent closed the doors behind him. "Been trying to call you," he said, stamping snow from his boots. He held out a scrapbook. "Thought you'd might like to look at this."

Vincent took the book and opened it.

As he petted Duke, Lassiter said, "My uncle kept that. He lived in New York City and worked on Broadway. Never amounted to much. Just had steady work as a character actor. No big stardom or anything."

Mystified, Vincent flipped through the book's pages. Katherine Malloy, although in the newspaper clippings pasted into this book she was Katherine Mann, had been a child prodigy. She'd played her first concert in New York City at the age of 13. By the time Jethro Malloy had married her and whisked her away to North Tonawanda, she was a renown concert violinist. Vincent scanned the articles. Words jumped out at him—*brilliant, genius, gifted, beautiful*. Critics loved her. Orchestras begged her to play with them. She traveled all over the world performing. She had preformed in Paris, Vienna and London by the time she was 19.

Lassiter said, "The last picture on the last page. That there is my Uncle Norman."

Vincent stared at the young man standing beside Katherine Mann. He had wavy dark hair and a thick mustache. He wore a pinstripe suit with a vest and tuxedo collar shirt. He was handsome and by the look in his eyes, hopelessly in love with the lady beside him.

"He knew Katherine?"

"Yep. Introduced her to Jethro, in fact. Always said it was the worst mistake of his life. Norman wanted to marry her."

Vincent closed the scrapbook. "Did he ever see her again after she moved here?"

"He did. Whenever he came to town to visit my father, he'd march over here and demand to see her. I don't think the visits went well though."

"Mind if I borrow this book for a few days."

"Nope. Figured you might want to." Lassiter opened the door that had Jethro's stained glass image. "Now I gotta go. I have an appointment next door."

"Really?"

"We'll see how it goes."

"Let me know."

"Sure will."

Duke followed Lassiter outside. Vincent bid them both goodbye and closed the door. He wanted to read every article in the scrapbook, but he knew his reading would have to wait. Daylight was fading outside. He had to get ready and meet Kate and Liz at the hospital.

Vincent heard Jill screaming the minute he stepped out of the elevator. "It hurts!" she cried. "God, it hurts!" He ran down the hall to her room. Liz, Kate and Tracy were with her. Liz held her right hand. She was bent over Jill, talking to her. Tracy held her sister's other hand, tears rolling down her face. Kate stood next to Liz. Hearing Vincent enter, she turned to him, helplessness in her eyes.

Jill thrashed in the bed. Liz held her down. "Jill," she said, her voice strong and penetrating. "Jill, look at me. Jill."

Jill obeyed. "Make it stop," she begged her godmother. "It hurts so much."

The out-of-control, dazed Elizabeth Reilly of yesterday was gone. Dr. Elizabeth Reilly was back. She eased Jill back down into the bed, holding her there with a firm hand on each shoulder. "Jill, listen to me. Your leg is gone. What you're feeling is called ghost pain. It's normal, honey. But it's not real."

Jill stared up at Liz, tears spilling from her eyes. "It hurts," she cried again. "Make it stop."

Liz bent closer. "Easy, Jill. Calm down. It'll stop, but you have to relax."

Harsh, gut-wrenching sobs escaped as Jill said, "I...can't do...this. Let me die. God...please...let me die."

Tracy Woodward could stand no more. She ran from the room. Vincent followed her past the nurse's station to the stairwell and down the stairs. Tracy didn't stop until she reached the cold outside. She slid on a piece of ice and fell, landing on her rear. She sat there, hugging herself, rocking and crying. Vincent knelt down and put his arms around her. She buried her face in his leather jacket. People walked by them, casting them questioning looks as they left or entered the hospital. Vincent held the sobbing teenager. At last Tracy's tears stopped falling. She looked up at him. "I'm cold," she said, her voice cracking.

Vincent carried her back inside. She clung to him as if he was the answer to all her problems. He set her down on a couch in the lobby and then sat down beside her. He held her hand.

"I'm sorry," she said, shivering.

He unzipped his jacket, took it off and put it around her shoulders. "You're allowed to cry."

She shook her head. "I have to be strong for Jill."

"Maybe so. But you need release, Tracy."

She reached for his hand again and he gave it to her. "She's been having these attacks all day. She's feeling pain that really isn't there. Before Dr. Reilly got here, she begged me to kill her."

"Where are your folks?"

"I talked them into going home and spending some time together. I told them I could handle things here. Pretty dumb, I guess."

"No. They need time away. But you do too."

"Tomorrow was going to be my day off."

"Then you should take it."

She wiped at her tear-stained cheeks. "I will."

"Good."

She looked towards the elevator doors. "I should go back up."

"You sure you're ready?"

She gazed at him with sad, tortured eyes. "I'm not sure."

"Then why don't we sit here until you are?"

"Okay."

They sat together, Tracy clinging to Vincent's hand. She didn't talk. She just stared at the tiled floor. Vincent wondered how things were going upstairs with Jill. Tracy's eyes slipped shut, her head sagging. Vincent put his arm around her shoulders and she automatically snuggled close to him, her head resting on his shoulder. He glanced at his watch. It was nearly 9 p.m.

Another half hour went buy before the elevator doors opened and Kate and Liz emerged. As the two approached, Vincent studied Liz's face. She was not happy, but she was not in Never Land either. She squatted in front of Tracy and gently touched the girl's cheek. "Tracy," she said.

Tracy jerked, her eyes flying open. "What? Jill?"

Liz took Tracy's hand. "Jill is sleeping."

"I have to go to her."

Tracy tried to get up, but Liz stopped her. "I'm going to spend the night with Jill, Trace. I want you to go home. Vincent and Kate will drive you."

Tracy's breaths came in short blasts. "But…Jill needs me"

"No, honey. You need to go home and get some sleep. I'll stay with Jill. She won't be alone."

Fresh tears fell from Tracy's eyes. "She wanted me to kill her, Aunt Liz."

"I know."

"I don't want her to die."

"None of us do, kiddo." Liz wiped Tracy's tears with her thumb. "Just remember that Jill is going to have bad days and good days. And today was a doozey of a bad day. But I'm here now. I'm going to take care of her."

Tracy nodded. She looked at Liz with trusting eyes.

"You go on home."

"Okay. What should I tell my parents? They're going to ask me how she was today."

"Have them call me." Holding on to both of Tracy's hands, Liz pulled her up from her seat. "You go on into the bathroom and wash off your face." She turned Tracy towards the bathroom door and gave her a push.

Once the girl had disappeared behind the door, Liz turned to Kate and said, "Will you be in town tomorrow?"

"Yes. Are you sure you're up to this tonight?"

"I have to be."

Liz was teetering on the edge. Vincent could see it in her eyes. Right now the strong side was winning, but for how long? Kate must have sensed it as well. She hugged Liz and said, "You call me if you need me. I don't care what time it is. Understand?"

Liz nodded.

Tracy came out of the Ladies Room, her face freshly washed. Liz hugged her, kissed her cheek and said, "You go home and get some sleep. Don't worry."

"Thank you, Aunt Liz," Tracy said, clinging to her.

Liz eased her away. "You're welcome." She pushed a lock of golden hair away from Tracy's face. "Don't you forget, I love you too."

"I love you."

They left Liz standing in the lobby, alone. She gave them a final wave. And while her smile looked genuine and encouraging, her eyes held sadness and pain.

Vincent rolled over, reached for his wife and found only air. Her absence penetrated his sleeping brain and he awoke with a start. The radio alarm glowed 3:10 a.m. He got up, snatched his robe from the end of the bed and put it on. As soon as he stepped into the hall, he saw the line of light beneath the door to Jethro's library. He hurried down the hall and pushed open the door. Kate, wearing one of his flannel shirts, sat behind Jethro's desk. Her laptop was open and on, but she wasn't working. Her arms hugged her knees, her feet resting on the chair. She stared at the frosted windowpane.

"Kate?"

She turned her head. "Hi. I couldn't sleep."

"What are you writing?"

She shrugged. "Nothing really. It's supposed to be a speech."

Vincent walked to the desk and perched on the corner. "You like this room?"

"I always have. I used to come in here and read when I was a kid. I wrote in here too."

"So you thought you'd write in here again."

"I guess. But I'm afraid I don't feel much like writing. At least not about what I'm supposed to be writing."

"Then write something else."

She chuckled, shaking her head. "Oh, you mean my great American novel."

"That's exactly what I mean."

She shook her head. "That's in the past, Vincent. I'm over that desire."

"You could do it, you know. You could quit working for McMartin and finish your novel. We have the financial means now, remember?" His heart pounded in his chest as he voiced his desire. He prayed she didn't blow up at his suggestion.

To his surprise, she didn't. She looked thoughtful a moment before shaking her head again. "I think not, my dear. I wouldn't have a clue where to begin."

"You wouldn't even consider it?" He watched her face closely, his gaze peering into her eyes.

For a second, he saw a flash. He was sure of it. And even though she again assured him she wouldn't consider it, he didn't believe her. There'd been a flash. He could build on that. And the minute she left for D.C., he would begin transforming Jethro Malloy's library into Kate Vermay's writing office.

Vincent stood before the studio window holding Katherine Malloy's violin. He watched as the morning sun danced off the strings. He ran a finger across the smooth, solid wood. He wondered what it felt like to make this instrument sing like Katherine had.

"What is it telling you?"

Vincent turned from the window. Kate stood in the doorway. Her hair was a tangled mess and traces of sleep lay in her eyes. She wore her white robe.

He smiled and replied, "It cries for another painting."

She folded her arms beneath her breasts. "Then you should give it what it wants."

"I have some ideas." He carefully laid the violin in its case and picked up a sketchpad from the dresser. "Let me show you."

She came to him and he showed her three different sketches. She pointed at the third one. In this one the violin sat on a wooden chair on a stage, the bow leaning against it. An audience looked on, waiting for someone to play the violin. "This one intrigues me."

"Me too." He kissed the top of her head. "This one it will be. Thanks, Kate."

"Hug me."

He took her into his arms, resting his chin in her hair. "You know I value your opinion. I value it most of all."

She looked up at him. "For awhile there, you had me wondering."

"Don't ever wonder." He thought about the lie that still surrounded the hansom cab painting. He thought about telling her the truth, but knew he was too much of a chicken to do so. Instead, he kissed her lips.

They stood together in his studio; Vincent savoring their closeness and wishing the moment wouldn't end. But it did end, harshly, when the phone rang. "I'll get it," Kate said, disengaging herself.

Running his hand through his hair, Vincent trailed after her. She answered the phone in the bedroom. It was Liz and Vincent knew before Kate said the words, that she would not be his today. She hung up the phone and said, "I know my way down to Roswell so why don't you stay here and start your painting?"

"Are you sure?"

She reached out and buttoned his Williamsburg shirt. "Yes. Don't get any paint on that gorgeous chest of yours."

He took her hand. "Is Liz all right?"

"I think so. She sounded level headed. I'll meet her for breakfast down there and see what develops."

"I'll miss you."

She stood on tiptoe and kissed his lips. "And well you should, Vincent Vermay." She grinned. "Now, let me take a shower."

She went off to the bathroom and Vincent collapsed on the bed. He spread his arms wide. She was right, encouraging him to paint this day away. What she didn't know, however, was what he really wanted to paint. He thought of the paint he'd hidden away in the basement, the paint that would transform Jethro Malloy's library into her new office. But he couldn't start the transformation with her here. Forcing his desires down, he got up and walked down to his studio.

※   ※   ※

He was still painting when he heard Kate and Liz come in. They tramped up the stairs and down the hall to his studio.

"Hey, handsome," Kate said, entering. She studied what he'd painted so far. Her right eyebrow shooting up, she nodded admiringly. "You have most definitely been a busy boy."

"I should say," Liz said. "It's excellent, Vincent."

"Thanks. How's Jill?"

"Better. At least she isn't begging me to kill her."

Kate slipped her arm through Liz's. "Our friend here had a rough time last night. Which is exactly why I dragged her away. Jill's parents are with her."

"I see."

"And," Kate continued. "We are due next door in a half hour for dinner. Elsie likes punctuality as you know, so you better get cleaned up."

"I'm on it," Vincent said, beginning to clean up his paints.

"Vincent," Liz said. "Thanks for letting me have your wife today."

"No problem."

Liz gazed at Kate. "I don't know what I'm going to do when you go back to Washington tomorrow. I really don't."

Kate smiled and gave Liz a slight squeeze. "You'll be fine. I'm only a phone call away. And besides, I'll be back the first week of April."

But she wasn't.

CHAPTER 9

Vincent found his wife in Jethro Malloy's library on Monday morning. Freshly showered, wearing only her robe, she sat looking through the scrapbook that Douglas Lassiter had dropped off. Her damp hair hung freely about her shoulders. The light coming in the window lit her in a soft, angelic glow. He stood in the doorway, watching her a few minutes. He didn't want to put her on the plane back to D.C. He didn't feel good about this parting, even though it would not be cold and distant like the last one. He couldn't explain the feeling. It didn't make sense. She would be back the first week of April.

She glanced up, saw him and said, "This is fascinating."

"Yes, it is."

She smiled as she looked down at the pictures in the book. "My grandmother was a knockout."

Vincent walked over and stood behind Kate's chair. He looked down at the photo of Katherine and Norman Lassiter. "Handsome couple."

"Yes, they were. Katherine told me once that she should have married Norman. They were close in age, I think."

"Did she love him, Kate?"

"That I don't know. She didn't use the word."

"Did you meet him, babe?"

"No. He died young."

"From what?"

"I don't know." Kate flipped a few pages back towards the beginning of the book. "Did you read some of these reviews, Vincent? They praise her highly."

"I know. She was considered a natural, a phenomenon."

"This reviewer calls her divinely gifted." Kate closed the book and hugged it to her chest. "I never realized how talented she was, Vincent. And what she gave up when she married Jethro." Vincent massaged Kate's shoulders. "I could see," she continued, "If she'd given it up for a loving husband and a family life. But that's not what he gave her."

"What did he give her, Kate?"

"Hell on earth."

"Don't you wonder why?"

"Oh, Vincent, I've always wondered why. Only thing I can figure is he thought of her as a possession, one he didn't want to share with anyone, not even her own children." She set the scrapbook on the desk, slipped from beneath his hands and stood up. "I better get dressed."

She was halfway to the door when he said her name. She turned, her eyes questioning.

"You're gifted too," he said. "You're a gifted writer. You should pull that novel out of the drawer and reread it. I bet you'd be pleasantly surprised."

She laughed, shaking her head. "More like I'd be mortified. Besides, I don't have time for that nonsense."

"It's not nonsense, Kate."

"Yes, it is, Vincent. You are the creative one in this family."

He went to her and laid his hands on her shoulders. Her damp hair was cool against his skin. "Remember when we were first married and living in that cramped apartment in D.C.? You would sit at the kitchen table in front of that ancient typewriter I bought you and pound away on those keys. You were so alive. I would watch you and know that you were writing pure genius. Why did you stop, Kate?"

She reached up and tenderly stroked his whiskered face. "Because it wasn't pure genius. Ask the agents and publishers out there. They'll tell you." Her eyes watered over and she looked away.

He pulled her close and held her. "It could be, Kate. I'd bet money on it that it could be."

"No, Vincent," she said, her words muffled by his flannel shirt. "That dream is over."

As he held her, Vincent became more determined than ever to see her dream reborn and brought to fruition. He would keep on encouraging her. He would see to it that she came to her senses and finished her novel.

❧   ❧   ❧

"You look like a lost, forlorn little boy," Liz said, when Vincent entered Jill's hospital room.

Vincent removed his newsboy cap. "I just saw Kate off at the airport."

Jill stared at him with sullen eyes. "Your wife?" she asked, her voice hoarse, barely more than a whisper.

"Yes." He stepped closer to her bed and pointed at the painting of the hansom cab. "Do you like it?"

"Very much. Tracy told me you didn't charge her for it. Thank you, Mr. Vermay."

"You're welcome."

Jill pointed at the painting. "I feel like I could just get into the cab and ride forever through the woods. And I wouldn't be wearing modern clothes. I'd have on a white, lacy long dress with a round collar. I'd have a straw hat on my head and ankle-high, laced up shoes on my feet. Two feet because I would still have both legs." She looked to Liz who rose from her chair. She took Jill's hand and leaned close, kissing her forehead. A tear slipped from the girl's right eye and Liz wiped it away with her fingers. "I'm sorry," Jill said.

"Don't worry about it," Vincent said. He picked up a book that lay next to Jill on the bed. "Renoir. You have good taste."

"Aunt Liz was reading it to me."

"I see. Tracy said you like art. Have you painted?"

"Some. They're not that good but my parents insisted on hanging them at the house."

"I'd like to see them, Jill."

"They really aren't that good."

"I happen to agree with your parents," Liz said. She squeezed Jill's hand. "I have to get back to the office. Your mom and dad will be here in a couple of hours. Hang in there."

"Okay."

"Want the television on?"

"No. I'm going to sleep."

"All right. Let's flatten you out a little." Liz pressed a button on the side of the bed rail and the head of the bed descended.

Jill grimaced. "That's enough, Aunt Liz."

Liz straightened the blankets. "If you need something for the pain, you buzz the nurse."

"I will." Jill managed a smile. "Thanks for coming, Mr. Vermay."

"Take care."

Once outside Jill's room, Liz leaned back against the wall and slid down to the floor. Vincent sat down beside her. She looked over at him. "Your painting has been a God send, Vincent. She stares at it constantly. I think she's using her fantasy about it to keep herself going."

"Then I'd say that's a good thing, Liz."

She nodded. She sat silent a few minutes then said, "So Kate really left?"

"Sure did."

"She left all her phone numbers?"

Vincent unzipped his jacket and pulled Kate's business card from his shirt pocket. "Right here." He handed it to Liz. "She instructed me to tell you to call her whenever you need her no matter what the time."

Liz slipped the card into her lab coat pocket. "She may regret saying that."

"I doubt it." He pointed at Jill's door. "You really think Jill's paintings are good?"

"Yes. Why?"

"I'd like to see them. Seriously. If there's talent there, it might give her a new focus."

Liz looked thoughtful. "Turn the athlete into an artist."

"Why not? If there's talent there."

A slow smile crossed Liz's face. "You would do that? You would take the time to teach Jill?"

"I would." Two doctors stopped in front of them and looked down. One, a tall, red-haired man, said, "Liz? Are you all right?"

"I'm fine, Bryan."

"There is a lounge with couches and chairs just down the hall."

"I know. We're fine."

The doctor shrugged, gave his colleague a light push and the two continued on their way.

"You know, Liz, we probably do look kind of silly here sitting on the floor in the hall."

"Who cares," she said, waving his concern away. "I would pay you, Vincent. You wouldn't have to—"

"No," he said, raising his hand. "No payment. I would teach her because I want to help her. Just think, Liz, if we can fill her heart with a new passion and give her a reason to live, then she'll have a better chance of beating the cancer."

For the first time in days, Vincent saw hope in Liz's eyes. Even so, she said, "She's got a long, hard road ahead of her, Vincent. Once she gets her strength back from the surgery we have to start the chemotherapy. She may need several rounds of it. It'll be devastating to her when the remainder of her hair falls out. There'll be vomiting, lack of appetite."

"And there will be good days too, I presume?"

"Yes."

"Then we'll paint on those good days."

The hope grew in Liz's green eyes. "Does Kate know what a wonderful man she married?"

Vincent shrugged. "Who knows?" He got to his feet. "Make sure you tell her the next time you talk to her." He held out his hand. "Now get up, Dr. Reilly. You have patients at the office to see and I have paintings to check out."

❦   ❦   ❦

Vincent reached the Woodward home at 2 p.m. He parked the Rodeo in the driveway and sprinted to the back door. He opened the storm door, grinned at the pineapple knocker then banged it against the door. While he waited, he looked out over the English garden. It held stone pathways, shrubs, and snowy flowerbeds that begged for Spring.

The door opened and Vincent turned. Tracy stood there, bundled into a pale blue and white striped, flannel robe. Her hair hung in greasy locks about her face. She was flushed, her eyes heavy with sleep.

"I woke you," he said. "I'm sorry."

"I wasn't really sleeping. Come in." She stepped back and he entered, closing both doors behind him. "I got the flu," she said, her voice nasally from congestion. "Big time got it. Enter at your own risk."

"Bummer," he said, following her.

She led him through a kitchen that had yellow pine cupboards and mosaic multi-colored tile on the floor. They emerged into a family room decorated in beige and forest green. One wall housed an entertainment center and shelving unit. The movie *Titanic* starring Kate Winslet and Leonardo DiCaprio played on the television. The ocean liner had just hit the iceberg. Tracy collapsed on a green, white and beige checked couch and pulled a white blanket up to her chin. She was shivering. The coffee table in front of the couch held a pitcher of water, a bottle of prescription medication, and a bowl of untouched soup. A round garbage pale sat between the couch and coffee table.

"Where's your mother, Tracy?" Vincent asked, removing his jacket and cap. He tossed them onto a wingback chair.

"The store. For ginger ale." Her teeth chattered. "I can't keep anything down."

Vincent knelt beside the sick girl and laid his hand on her forehead. Her skin was hot. "Have you taken anything for the fever?"

"I will with the ginger ale." She pointed at the prescription bottle. "I have to take that too."

"How long has your mother been gone?"

"Not long. What are you doing here?"

"I just came from seeing Jill."

"How is she? I can't go see her."

"She's hanging in there. She didn't look as pale today."

"Good."

Vincent heard the back door open. He stood up. "Mrs. Woodward?" he called.

Tracy's mother appeared in the doorway, a bottle of ginger ale in her hand. She was surprised to see him. "Mr. Vermay? What brings you by?"

"He saw Jill today," Tracy said.

Mrs. Woodward set the bottle of ginger ale on the coffee table. She removed her parka and laid it on top of Vincent's jacket. "How nice of you, Mr. Vermay." She knelt beside the couch and touched her daughter's forehead. "You are hot, baby girl."

"I'll live."

"How's the tummy?"

"Crampy."

Mrs. Woodward stroked Tracy's hair. "You didn't eat your soup."

"I can't, Mom."

"You can't take what Liz prescribed on an empty stomach, honey. Sit up and try a few bites."

"I don't want to throw up anymore."

"Come on."

Vincent watched, amazed, as Jessica Woodward skillfully coaxed her daughter into eating half a bowl of soup and drinking an entire glass of ginger ale with her medication. She eased Tracy back down on the couch, made sure she laid on her left side with her legs curled up then covered her with the blanket. Tracy's head no sooner hit the pillow then her eyelids slipped shut and she was sleeping. Mrs. Woodward went to the TV and turned the sound down. She motioned Vincent from the room.

They stepped out into a foyer decorated with a white and green tiled floor and four white busts on mahogany pedestals. The busts were of George Washington, Thomas Jefferson, Patrick Henry and Abraham Lincoln. The foyer's wallpaper had gray, stone arches on a pale green background. Mrs. Woodward slid the family room door closed. She gestured towards the busts. "My husband is a history professor. Jill inherited his love of history. Tracy inherited his sculpting talent. She made those. He helped her though."

Vincent peered at the Thomas Jefferson bust. "Wow. Excellent work. Will she be pursuing an art degree in college?"

"Tracy? I'm not sure what she wants to do"

"Tracy said Jill is studying history."

"Yes. How was she when you saw her today?"

"Pretty good. Better than last time I saw her anyway."

"This whole thing has been horrible for her."

"Maybe so, but from what I just saw in the family room, she'll get great care when she comes home."

Mrs. Woodward's cheeks turned red. She brushed a stray lock of blonde hair away from her face. "I'm not a doctor."

"No. You're a mother. And a good one at that. That will help Jill a lot."

"I pray so."

"It will," he assured her again.

"Jill will be waiting for me today, but I can't go. Tracy needs me here. I told Mike to go down when he's done teaching."

"She'll understand."

"I hope she does." Tears welled up in Mrs. Woodward's eyes. "It's awful, seeing both of your babies sick. Even if it's just the flu Tracy has." She sniffed. "Anyway, did you stop by just to see Tracy?"

"No. I understand you have some paintings hanging that Jill painted."

Mrs. Woodward's eyes lit up. "Why, yes, I do. They're along the stairs here."

Vincent walked up and then down the stairs, studying the four paintings carefully. They were all landscapes.

"They are all of the area around my sister's cottage at the Finger Lakes. Why are you interested? I mean you're an accomplished artist."

"She has wonderful technique. It needs developed, but...See this?" He pointed at a painting of a stone winery. "See how real the stone looks. You can almost feel its texture. The shadowing is very good too." He turned to Mrs. Woodward. "When did she stop painting?"

"When she discovered indoor cycling. She'd just entered eleventh grade, I think."

Vincent scratched his chin. "Well, Mrs. Woodward," he said, grinning. "I believe it's time she starts painting again."

Vincent was painting Jethro Malloy's library when Sarah called him. "Where the hell have you been?" he scolded her. "I've been calling and calling you. You said you'd only be gone a week."

"Careful, Vincent," she replied. "You're sounding more like a parent than a big brother."

"Well?" he persisted.

"Everywhere and anywhere," she said, ducking his question. "What are you doing?"

Vincent looked around the library. Sheets hung over the bookcases. He'd moved the desk to the center of the room, covered it with plastic so he could use it to set the paint tray and cans on and he'd masked off all the woodwork. He had one more wall to paint. He set the paint-filled roller in the tray, wiped his hand on his jeans and said, "I'm painting."

"I'm sure you are. I've been out of touch, what else is going on there?"

"I should say you were out of touch. How was Telluride?"

She chuckled. "It was the start of a very interesting time."

"I see. And his name would be?"

"Don't pry, Vincent."

Annoyance erupted within him. "Sarah, you've got to stop doing this. You're not getting any younger, you know. It's about time you settled down with someone." Once the words were out of his mouth, he wanted to kick himself.

"Well, I didn't realize I'd called Mother. Let me see, what number did I actually dial?"

"Damn it!" he cursed. *Lord, she was a handful.*

As if reading his thoughts, Sarah said, "A handful I am. But you love me anyway."

And he did. She was his baby sister. He would always love her. Sighing, he ran a hand through his hair and asked, "Are you back in Silverton?"

"I am. Actually been on a couple of excursions since Telluride. Sorry I haven't called, Vincent, but you know me. I get involved and lose track of time."

Yes, he knew how she was, because when in the throes of a painting, he could be exactly the same way. So, he let her off the hook and said, "Don't worry about it. You're all right, that's all I care about."

He knew she was smiling when she said, "You're the best, bro."

He drew in a long breath of air, the paint smell pungent and strong. Cradling the phone between his shoulder and ear, he went to the window and opened it wide, cold air pouring in. He realized he was wet with sweat and the air felt refreshing on his skin. Duke was chasing a ball in the Reilly yard, fetching it and bringing it dutifully back to Emmett.

"So, what's been going on with you, Vincent?"

He turned around, leaned his rear on the window ledge and he told her everything that had happened since he last spoke with her. He told her about Liz and Jill. He told her about his plans to put a new fire into Jill's life so that she would fight for and win the battle to keep that life. He told her about his dream of Kate leaving McMartin and returning to writing her novel. And the whole time he talked, he once again found himself amazed that their conversations were always about him and not her. But then, she had always been his sounding board, especially about matters concerning Kate.

When he had run out of words, Sarah said, "I like your vision, Vincent. But you can't push it on Kate. Go easy. Wheedle it in on her. Make her come to her own conclusion."

"Wheedle?"

"Yes, you know."

"Inch by inch?"

"More like milli-inch by milli-inch."

"There you go, Sarah, making up words again."

"I'm serious, Vincent. You don't want to alienate her in the process."

Duke barked outside, the sound bringing a smile to Vincent's face. Maybe he and Kate should get a dog, he thought, and then shook his head. Now was not the time.

"I'm sorry about what your friend, Jill, is going through," Sarah said in his ear. "I hope you can pull it off with her, Vincent."

"Yeah, me too. Now, tell me about your past month."

"I already did. I went skiing, came back here and led a couple of excursions."

"Hiking in the middle of winter?"

"No, silly, snowmobiles."

"So, give me details."

"How boring would that be for you?"

Vincent scratched his whiskered chin and knew his quest was hopeless. Unlike him, she never talked much about what she did or how she felt about it. In fact, unlike him, his sister was the silent type. He found himself grinning as he realized that in his need to talk things out, he was more like a woman while she, a woman, felt no compulsion to pour out her heart. Which was exactly why when it came to the rift between her and their parents, he'd only heard their side of the story. Sarah had simply said, "It is what it is, Vincent. It happened. It's done." And of course, "The airplane between Philadelphia and Silverton flies both ways."

Bracing himself, he asked, "Have you called Mom and Dad?"

"Wouldn't you be surprised if I said, 'Yes'?"

"Can you say it?"

"Nope."

"Sarah, come on. Call them."

"I sent them a postcard from Telluride."

He growled into the phone.

"I'll call them, Vincent. I will. Promise."

"Soon?"

"Okay, soon." A bell jingled in the background and Sarah said, "Be right with you?"

"Who's there?"

"Someone looking for a snowmobile adventure I hope. I'll be talking to you, Vincent."

"Be careful, Sis."

"Always. Bye."

Vincent turned off the portable phone and returned to painting the library. As he worked, he found his spirit renewed, seemingly washed clean of the pain he'd witnessed over the past few weeks. And all it had taken was a call from Sarah.

❋   ❋   ❋

"It's wonderful," Liz said. She stepped into the library. "Absolutely wonderful."

"Thanks. I hope Kate thinks so."

"How could she not, Vincent? She'd be crazy not to love it."

During the course of the past three weeks, Vincent had transformed Jethro's dark, brooding library into a bright and beautiful room. The walls were painted a warm pale yellow. The woodworking, shelving and desk had all received a thorough scrubbing and shining. All the books had been re-organized on the shelves. He'd replaced the old area rug with a new one of yellow, beige, ivory and mauve stripes. Yellow curtains with mauve and white cabbage roses hung on the window. A new computer sat on the desk.

"She claims she no longer wants to write fiction."

"I see." Liz looked up at him. "And you're trying to show her otherwise."

"Exactly."

"Well, I hope you succeed. Being a novelist was all Kate talked about when we were kids. I always thought she'd be a good one."

Vincent grinned. "Then help me by mentioning it when you talk to her."

"Sure. Is she still coming Friday?"

"As far as I know, Liz." He turned for the door. "Let me show you something else while you're here."

She followed him. "I can't tell you how many times I've wished she were here these past few weeks, Vincent."

"Have you told her that?"

"Many times."

Vincent entered his studio and pointed at his just completed painting of Katherine's violin sitting untouched on a chair. "You like it, Liz?"

"Yes, I do." She peered at the painting. "The audience waiting is...it's pure...genius."

Vincent felt his cheeks flush. "Thank you."

Liz folded her arms beneath her breasts. "You have certainly been a busy boy, my friend."

"Keeps me out of trouble. So, tell me, what brings you by this afternoon?"

"News I thought you'd be interested in. Jill came home today."

"Really?"

Liz nodded. "Yes. She had her first dose of chemo on Monday. She was pretty sick afterwards. Vomiting. She had the shakes. But this morning she felt a little better and begged me to convince Fornier to let her come home."

Vincent squeezed Liz's shoulder. "And you couldn't tell her no."

"God, no, I couldn't, Vincent." Liz shook her head. "Psychologically, she needed out of the hospital. Fortunately, Fornier agreed. I know that Jessica will take good care of her."

"Maybe I shouldn't ask this, but what's her prognosis now? Are her chances better?"

Liz sighed. "It's a crapshoot, Vincent. I don't know." She walked to the studio window and gazed out at the cloudy sky. She sighed again then turned back to him. "She could beat it. There's a chance. But I can't say that she'll lick it for sure."

Vincent scratched his chin. "Think she's ready for some art lessons yet?"

"Give her a few more days. The chemo took a lot out of her."

"Okay."

"She might refuse, Vincent. Be prepared for that."

"Oh, I'll work on her, don't you worry."

A faint smile crossed Liz's face. "Enough about Jill. How would you like to come over for dinner? Doug Lassiter and his wife are going to be there."

"You're dad is okay with that?"

"Very okay. Mr. Lassiter has spent a great deal of time with Dad lately. He even convinced Dad to go with him over to his house for dinner one night last week."

"You're kidding?"

"No."

"Damn! I've called over and asked Emmett to go to lunch several times. I always get a flat out no."

"You're not a former patient who is the same age, that's why. Anyway, will you come?"

"I'll be there with bells on, Elizabeth."

❦   ❦   ❦

Elsie Whiting answered the door and she looked downright beautiful. She'd curled her hair and the curls softened her features. Diamond earrings dangled from her ears. She wore a black evening dress with an intricate lace design on the bodice. Its collar was high and round. Smiling, she motioned Vincent inside.

He removed his black raincoat and handed it to her. As she hung the coat in the closet under the staircase, she said, "I hope you don't mind wearing that tux, Vincent. Emmett insisted this be a black tie affair."

"No problem," he said.

"Come on in then."

He followed her into the dining room. Emmett, in his tuxedo, sat at the head of the table. Doug Lassiter, in a gray tux, stood at the sideboard, He was pouring a glass of wine. Hearing them enter, he turned. A petite woman with gray hair stood beside him. She wore an elegant blue gown, diamond studs in her ears.

"Mr. Vermay," Lassiter said, bowing. "Please, meet my wife Mary."

Vincent bowed. "Mrs. Lassiter. Please call me Vincent."

"And you call me Mary."

Soft music, harkening to the Thirties, played in the background. The table was set with the Reilly's best china. Lassiter held out the glass of wine and Vincent accepted it.

"Young man," Emmett said. "Where is Katie?"

"Katie?"

"You're wife." Emmett stared at Vincent as one would a moron.

"Oh, yes, Kate. She's still in Washington, D.C. I expect her this Friday for a lengthy visit."

"Tell her I would like to see her."

"I will, Emmett."

Emmett looked towards the door. "Where is my Elizabeth?"

"She's upstairs, I believe," Elsie said.

"Well, call her down. She's holding up dinner."

"Speaking of dinner let me check on it. Then I'll get Elizabeth."

Elsie left the room and Emmett pointed at the door leading to the foyer. "Vincent, go get my daughter."

"Certainly." Vincent hurried out to the foyer. Liz stood on the stairs, resplendent in a sleeveless red gown. Her hair hung in waves about her shoulders.

Seeing Vincent, she said, "Don't you cut a striking figure?"

"Speak for yourself, beautiful lady." He held out his hand.

She walked down the remaining steps and took his hand. She smiled up at him, but the sadness in her eyes belied her smile. Her thoughts were not on this dinner. Her thoughts were with Jill Woodward. "Thank you for coming and putting on the tux."

"I feel like I've stepped back in time."

"I believe, at least in my father's mind, we've done just that tonight."

Vincent escorted Liz into the dining room. Seeing her, Emmett stood up, his eyes beaming pride. "My girl," he said, rising from his chair. Taking her hand, he kissed it, saying, "Oh, Elizabeth, how beautiful you are."

Tears filled Liz's eyes. "Thank you, Dad."

"No one has a daughter as lovely as you, Elizabeth."

Liz hugged her father. He held her, his chin resting in her auburn hair.

Elsie re-entered the room and said, "Dinner is ready."

"Then, Elsie, let's eat," Emmett said.

Liz stepped back from her father. Wiping a tear from her cheek, she said, "I'll help you serve, Elsie."

The dinner was incredible. Filet Mignon, garlic mashed potatoes, green beans, creamed corn, fresh baked bread and fabulous custard for dessert. Vincent ate and listened as Emmett, Lassiter, Mary and Elsie talked about the North Tonawanda of their youth. Emmett didn't slip once. True, he talked about the past. But he referred to it as the past; he knew it was the past. He even talked about his late wife without falling apart. Liz kept quiet, catching Vincent's eye a few times and gesturing in wonder at her father. Vincent could only shrug.

The meal ended shortly after eight o'clock. Elsie got up to clear the table and Mary Lassiter insisted on helping. Liz offered as well, but Mrs. Lassiter waved her away. "You visit with your friend there," she insisted, following Elsie out to the kitchen, both women carrying dishes.

Emmett turned to Lassiter. "Come, Douglas," he said, rising.

Lassiter stood up. "Excuse us, Vincent, Elizabeth," he said. "You're father and I must partake of a couple of old vices."

Liz smiled. "Then Vincent and I will stay clear of the parlor."

Once Emmett and Lassiter had departed, Vincent asked, "What old vices?"

"Pipes and brandy. Do you want to go partake?"

"Not a chance."

Liz sat back in her chair. "Douglas Lassiter has done amazing things for my father. He told me that you convinced him to come here."

"No, I didn't, Liz. I suggested. He had to make the move himself."

"Did you see Dad, Vincent? He was talking and laughing. He was…"

"What, Liz?"

"My father. For the first time in years, my father was in this room tonight. If it could only last."

Smiling, Vincent said, "I tend to think it will last, Liz. From what I see, your father is on his way back."

Faint hope in her eyes, Liz said, "I pray you're right."

❦   ❦   ❦

The phone was ringing when Vincent opened the door. He ran into the parlor and managed to snatch up the receiver before the answering machine kicked on. Collapsing on the couch, he said, "Hello."

"Hey, Vincent."

Her voice brought a smile to his face. "Hey, yourself."

"Where were you? I've tried three times."

Vincent unbuttoned his raincoat and untied his bow tie. "The Reilly's."

"How is Liz? I haven't connected with her in a few days. Phone tag."

"She's okay. Looking forward to seeing you this weekend. As am I. Are you still flying in Friday afternoon?"

She didn't reply, silence hanging heavy on her end. A red flag flew up in Vincent's brain. He sat forward on the couch. "You are still coming, right, Kate?"

"Actually, Vincent, I can't."

Don't yell. Stay calm here, Vincent. Into the phone, he said, "Can't come Friday or can't come at all?"

"I have to go to Indiana with Darren. I can't miss the event. He needs me."

"And I don't?" He fought to keep anger from his voice.

"I'll come in a few weeks, Vincent."

"A few weeks!" he yelled.

"Yes, how about the last week of this month? I'll make the reservations as soon as we hang up."

"You can't be serious."

"Yes, Vincent, I am."

"Damn it, Kate! This is ridiculous!"

"No, it isn't. This is my job."

"Which you don't need."

"Oh, because you say I don't. Don't you understand that what I do is a big part of me? Don't you get it?"

"No, Kate, I don't." He jumped up, pacing. "I don't get why you don't just quit and come here and write something worthwhile." *Shouldn't have said that, Vincent. You're giving in to your temper.*

"You don't think what I'm writing now is worthwhile?"

"Not really. You can do better than churning out political bullshit all day." She caught her breath on the other end of the line. "You could be writing your novel," he continued. "You could be writing something worth reading. Something that could make the world a better place. Something that matters." *You idiot, Vincent! She's going to hang up on you. Any ground you've gained, you're losing here.*

"Stop yelling at me, Vincent," she said, her voice filled with hurt.

Although he knew he should stop, he couldn't. He was out of control and he knew it. Still, he pressed on. "What happened to you, Kate? What happened to the woman I married who sat at the kitchen table writing for hours? Where in God's name did she go?"

"You're not being fair."

"Oh, is that so?"

"Yes. Not everyone is an artist like you, Vincent. Furthermore, not everyone wants to be."

He stopped in his tracks. "That's bullshit. You want to be. You've just sold out."

"I'm not arguing with you any longer. I'm not coming. That's it."

"Just like that. So you're blowing off Liz too."

"You just said that she's doing okay."

"I didn't say great, did I? Damn it, Kate, if you can't come to see me, at least come see Liz. You are supposed to be renewing your friendship with her. The friendship you walked out on twenty-one years ago as I remember."

"You are cruel." Her voice was cold. "You have no right to say anything about my past."

"The past you only seem to dole out when it suits you."

"What the hell does that mean?"

"Like you don't understand. God, I don't have a clue who you are anymore. Maybe I never did."

"Go to hell, Vincent," she said and hung up on him.

Vincent stared at the receiver until it started beeping at him. He slammed it into the cradle. "Damn you!" he cursed. But he wasn't cursing Kate. He was cursing himself for losing control. He ran a hand through his hair and said, "Idiot. I'm an asinine idiot."

He removed his coat and tossed it on the couch. He went upstairs to the bedroom and sat down on the bed. He had said some cruel things, things that should have been said in a kinder way, things he couldn't deny feeling. And yet, he couldn't stand there being anger between them. He picked up the phone and dialed the townhouse. She didn't answer. Clutching the phone, he listened to the recorded greeting on the answering machine. He hung up the phone without saying anything. What he had to say would not be said on a tape. He'd give her time to cool down before trying her again.

He changed into his jeans and Williamsburg shirt and went to his studio. Entering, he switched on the light. His hands itched to work in spite of his inner turmoil and anger. Hell, maybe he could paint anger. He would give it a face all it's own. He caught sight of the violin case on the table. He opened it and gazed down at Katherine's Stradivarius resting in the velvet. He plucked a string. The out of tune note rang loud in the studio.

He was done painting the violin. It didn't belong here any longer. He closed the case and lifted it from the table. He carried the violin down the hall and up the stairs to the third floor. He pushed open the door, stepped into the room and searched the air for the light pull. Finding it, he pulled. Light flooded Katherine's room. He placed the violin case on her bed.

He stood in her room for some time, wishing she were alive and there with him. His heart needed soothing. Her playing would do that. Sighing, he at last left the room closing the door behind him. He returned to his studio, but his hands no longer itched to paint. He switched off the light and went to his bedroom. He lay back on the bed still dressed. He realized that he thought of this room as his bedroom. It wasn't their bedroom. How strange was that? Kate had inherited this house and yet, he thought of it as his house now. His house, his bedroom, his studio, his—A broad smile crossed his face. One room in this house was Kate's. He'd made it so. Vincent rolled onto his stomach and hugged his pillow close. He had to get Kate here to see her room. Once she saw it, she'd have to see how much he wanted her with him. She would write. He would paint. Just the way they'd planned it when they got married. Once she was living here, filing the house with her presence, her own special light, it would be their house.

He snatched the phone up and dialed the Georgetown townhouse. Again, she didn't answer so he talked to the machine. "Kate, it's Vincent. I'm sorry. It's just that I want to see you. I miss you. And I planned a surprise for you. The last week of April is okay. Call me."

She picked up. "Hi." Her voice was heavy with tears.

"Hey."

She sniffed. "What surprise?"

"You'll just have to wait until the last week of April to find out."

"I'll call Liz. I promise."

"I know." He closed his eyes. Lord, he wanted to reach through the phone, drag her into his arms and talk some sense into her.

"I'm afraid, Vincent," she said.

"Of what?"

"Of the fact that you don't understand me anymore."

She was right. He didn't understand her. Hadn't for quite some time, in fact. Aloud, he said, "We'll work on that when you come. Truce for now?"

"Truce."

"Go to sleep. Call me before you go to Indiana."

"I will," she promised.

But she didn't.

CHAPTER 10

For the third day in a row, Vincent stared at the empty canvas. Nothing came. He threw his paintbrush and palette on the dresser and said, "Shit." *How could this be happening? I've knocked off three really good paintings in record time. I've reopened the well. How the hell could it have dried up already?*

He strode to the window and yanked it open. Cool air hit him and he leaned into it, sucking it in, letting it fill his lungs. It coursed through him, calming him and as it calmed him, he realized the reason for his dried up well. Closing his eyes, he bowed his head and for the first time in years, Vincent Vermay consciously prayed. "God," he said, clutching the windowsill, his knuckles white. "She didn't call. She said she would call and she didn't call." A sob escaped. "Help us."

The sweet sound of Katherine Malloy's violin immediately reached his ears. His eyes flew open. He didn't know what Katherine was playing, but it was both melodious and mournful. He stepped back from the window and turned towards the door. The music drew him and he let it carry him from his studio, down the hall, and up the stairs to the third floor. He reached for the doorknob, but stopped in mid-reach. The handle was different. It was made of multi-faceted crystal. Above it were three thick, wrought iron slide locks. He slid each lock open then turned the crystal doorknob. He pushed the door open and stepped inside.

Katherine Malloy played her violin in front of the bedroom's only window. She wore a powder blue dress, its collar round and lacy. From beneath its long, flowing skirt, he saw bare feet. Her hair—the same color and curly like Kate's—was pulled up on top of her head, ringlets falling down around her face. She played with her eyes closed and her body swayed as she played. Her gently angled face, free of makeup, was beautiful and so much like Kate's that it startled him.

He didn't disturb her, but listened as she played. She was in the music; she was the music as she slid the bow across the strings, body swaying. He watched her, amazed, knowing that were she on a stage, the entire audience would be as mesmerized as he. The piece ended abruptly with a final, short burst of notes. Eyes still closed, she lowered the violin, a small smile crossing her face. She bowed her head and softly said, "Amen." Raising her head, she turned towards the door and opened her eyes. She gasped and hugged the violin to her breast. "Why, Sir…" Her voice was lovely, holding a slight Irish accent, its tone sweet to the ears.

"Pardon me, Mrs. Malloy," Vincent said, bowing.

"How do you know my name?"

"I…" He didn't know what to tell her. In fact, he couldn't believe he was standing in the Victorian's third floor bedroom talking with Kate's grandmother.

"Are you an acquaintance of Jethro's?"

"Sort of." His heart pounded in his chest. He clasped his hands behind his back so that she would not see them shaking.

"He is most likely at church." She went to the bed and laid the violin in its case. "Although I don't know for sure. He did not come up to see me this morning."

Vincent remained silent.

She closed the violin case. Looking up at Vincent, she said, "Do you have a name, Sir?"

"Vincent. Vincent Vermay."

"I like the name Vincent," she said. "Like Vincent Van Gogh. I love his paintings. Are you one of Jethro's workers?"

"No."

"Then why are you here?" She hugged herself. "You shouldn't have come up here. Jethro would not like it."

"Why is that?"

She opened her mouth to speak but did not. Shaking her head, she said, "I have told you too much already. You, a complete stranger in my room."

Vincent glanced about the room. It was not the flowery room he'd seen the first night he'd gone to the third floor. Nor was it the room he'd seen in his earlier dream of her. This room was stark. The bed was wrought iron with a simple white bedspread. A pine armoire stood on the wall beside the door. A dresser to the window's left held a porcelain bowl and pitcher. A chamber pot sat beside the bed. A single yellow light bulb hung from the ceiling. There were no curtains on the window, only a yellowed window shade. The hardwood floor was scuffed and uncovered by carpets.

"You must leave," she said.

"I don't want to leave."

"You must. Why did you come up here?"

"I heard you playing. I wanted to meet the person who could make a simple violin sound so lovely."

She smiled in spite of her anxiety. "Thank you."

He gestured at the violin. "I have never heard anyone play as well or as beautifully as you, Mrs. Malloy. I hope you share your gift with the world."

She averted her eyes. "I used to."

"And now?"

"And now I am Mrs. Jethro Malloy. I play for my husband."

"Does he ever listen?"

Sadness filled her eyes. "You are too forward, Mr. Vermay."

"I apologize."

"Please, you must go. If Jethro comes home and finds you here..." She shuddered.

"I don't care what Jethro thinks. I want to get to know his talented and gifted wife."

She turned away. "There is no need to get to know her."

He stared at her back. She was thin. In fact, he thought her too thin. "Please don't dismiss me."

She didn't respond.

"I may be forward, but I think you're beautiful."

She turned back to him with tears on her cheeks.

He fought the impulse to go to her, take her in his arms and comfort her. Instead, holding his place, he smiled and said, "Come now, don't cry."

Sniffing, she wiped at her tears with her hand and managed a smile.

"Ah, that's better."

Her smile widening, she said, "You are not like any man I have ever known, Mr. Vermay."

"Why is that?"

"Why, you are forward and brash." She pointed at him. "And the way you are dressed on a Sunday, why, it's...at the very least unconventional."

He looked down at himself. He wore paint splattered jeans, loafers, and his Williamsburg shirt. He touched his whiskered chin. He hadn't shaved since Thursday. Lord knew what his hair looked like. He couldn't remember whether or not he had combed it after breakfast. He ran a hand through it.

Katherine chuckled. "You need a thorough scrubbing, as my mother used to say."

"I suppose I do."

"And yet you say you are not a workman. You say you sort of know Jethro, but you don't say how. You are quite the mystery."

"Do you like mysteries, Mrs. Malloy?" He stepped further into the room.

She took a step back, keeping the bed between them. "I have read a few. For you to be so bold, so unafraid of Jethro, I must ask you, did my husband send you?"

"I am a painter," Vincent said. "A portrait painter. I have come to paint your portrait." The words spilled out of him without prior thought. He had intended to tell her he was a painter and leave it at that. But the words had taken on their own life and after he had said them, Vincent discovered he was grinning. Yes, he thought, he would paint Katherine Malloy's portrait. His well had not run dry after all.

"But you have brought no paints or easel."

"One does not just jump into a portrait, Mrs. Malloy. One must first get to know his subject."

"Ironic," she said, wistfully. "My husband will not include me in his life and yet, he wants my portrait painted."

"Your husband has not hired me."

She frowned, tiny lines just like Kate's appearing between her eyebrows. "Then why do you want to paint my portrait, if you are to be paid no money?"

"Because I must, Mrs. Malloy. Yes, I must. I must paint the woman who plays such beautiful music on her violin."

"What will you do with this portrait when it is finished?"

"I will prominently display it for all the world to see."

"Jethro will never allow that, Mr. Vermay."

"Jethro can go to hell, Mrs. Malloy."

She stared at him, shock in her green eyes.

"Please let me paint you."

"I…certainly you can't mean—" She broke off and turned to the window. "He's home. You must go. Quickly."

Vincent ran to the window and stood beside her, their arms touching. He could feel the panic within her. He looked down at the driveway. Instead of concrete, he saw bricks. The 1924 Ford, the very one Vincent had seen in the carriage house, pulled into the driveway, a man in a derby bowler at the wheel.

Katherine grabbed Vincent's arm. "Hurry. You must go. Please, don't let him find you here? You don't know his temper. Please, I beg you?"

Vincent looked down at Katherine's hands tugging on his muscled upper arm. In spite of her frailty, her grip was strong, insistent. He laid his hand over-top of hers and with a reassuring smile, said, "I'll go. It's going to be all right."

She released his arm and he ran for the door. Turning back, he said, "May I come back? May I paint you?"

"Yes. I'll wait for you."

He dashed out the door and pulled it closed. He slid the slide locks over and ran down the stairs. He stopped at the bottom, wondering which way to go. Jethro was going up the driveway to the carriage house. Surely he would enter via the back door. Vincent sprinted down the stairs to the front foyer and hurried out the front door. He stopped on the front porch, blinking. His Rodeo sat in the driveway. "What?" he said, staring in disbelief at the Rodeo. He went back inside. His leather jacket and tweed cap hung on the coat rack. He ran up the stairs and down the hall. He took the third floor stairs two at a time. He stared in wonder at the door. The crystal knob was gone as were the slide locks. He grabbed the brass knob and opened the door. The flowery, cheerful room with the violin case on the bed greeted him. Vincent went to the window and stared down at the concrete driveway.

He turned from the window and leaned his rear on the sill. *What in God's name just happened to me? Did I really go back in time and talk with Katherine Malloy? Or did I imagine the whole thing?* He shook his head. He left Katherine's room and walked down the hall to his studio. He gazed at the empty canvas and grinned. He could already see Katherine's portrait. God had answered his prayer. It didn't matter whether He'd done it with a vision or Vincent's imaginative mind. What mattered was that He'd done it. And for the first time in three days, Vincent felt his heart rise in his chest.

Jessica Woodward opened the door and smiled in spite of her tiredness when she saw Vincent standing on her back porch. "Come in," she said.

He entered, stepped out of her way, and she closed the door. "I came to see, Jill, if it's all right."

Jessica nodded. "Yes, it sure is. Please, follow me. We've set her up in Mike's den. Actually, we moved his den up to her old room and her room down to his den." She stopped in the hall outside of the kitchen and he almost ran her down. "Sorry about that. Can I take your coat?"

He slid off his jacket and handed it to her. She pointed at his cap. He removed it and gave it to her. She stared at him a moment then said, "Look at those gorgeous locks of hair you have."

He felt his cheeks flush.

"Really," she continued. She reached out and curled a lock of his hair around her finger. "I bet the women drool over you at your art events."

"I never noticed," he said, his cheeks growing hotter.

She chuckled as she set his coat and cap on a Shaker-style bench and continued on to the foyer. Once again, Vincent found himself admiring the busts Tracy had done. Jessica stopped in front of the staircase and Vincent shot a quick glance at Jill's paintings, the glance confirming his belief that she had talent. When he turned his attention back to Jessica, her hands held the scroll shaped knobs on a pair of mahogany doors. "I should warn you though that this homecoming hasn't been easy on Jill. We've had some sleepless nights."

"Losing her leg has got to be a big adjustment for her."

Jessica sighed. "I can only imagine her inner turmoil, Vincent. I'll be in the kitchen cooking or in the family room straightening up and I'll hear her crying. I'll go into her room and she just clings to me. I look in her eyes and I see only pain and despair, no hope. She's lost and floundering. I don't know how to help her. I've talked to Liz, but she doesn't have the answer. In fact, she's so upset about Jill's illness that she's barely functioning."

"You noticed that?"

Jessica nodded. "She doesn't know I've noticed and don't tell her. But when you've been friends with somebody for so long…"

"You know."

"Exactly."

"Your secret is safe with me."

"Thanks." She tapped on the door then pushed it open. "Are you up for some company, honey?" She entered the room. Vincent held back, waiting for Jill's answer.

"Who?" Her voice was weak.

"Vincent Vermay. Liz's friend."

Jill said something that Vincent couldn't make out.

"I don't know," her mother answered. "Why don't you ask him and find out?"

Another unintelligible reply and Jessica stuck her head back out the door. She motioned him in.

Vincent entered. Jill's hospital bed ate up most of the room. It was positioned so she could see out the doublewide window that afforded a view of the quiet street beyond the house. The room's walls were papered in a blue and white stripe. His painting hung on the wall across from her bed. Next to the painting was a narrow shelving unit housing a television and VCR. The TV was on, an episode of *Touched By An Angel* playing.

Jessica pointed at a rocking chair beside Jill's bed. "Take a seat, Vincent. I have some more things to do in the kitchen."

She started to go, but Jill stopped her. "When will Tracy and Dad be home?"

"You father said not until late. We're not supposed to wait up. Visit with your company."

Vincent watched her exit, noting that she left the door open. He turned back to Jill. She looked awful. Her skin was pale, her eyes bloodshot and baggy. Less of her hair remained than the last time he'd seen her. She'd lost a tremendous amount of weight as well and he wondered why she wasn't still hospitalized.

She seemed to read his mind. "I couldn't stay there another minute. I needed to come home."

He nodded his understanding.

"Well, are you going to sit and stay now that you're here, Mr. Vermay?"

He sat down in the wooden rocking chair.

"That's a really comfortable chair. Which is a good thing since Mom has slept there the last two nights."

He rubbed the wooden arms. "Looks old."

"It was Mom's grandmother's."

"That's cool."

She gave him a half smile. Pointing at his painting, she said, "It looks good there. I get lost in it."

"I know, you told me."

She clutched the blankets with thin fingers. "Chemo sucks."

"I've heard that."

"That night, after the first treatment, I wanted to die." She looked sheepish. "In fact, I've wanted to do that a lot lately."

"I've heard that too."

"Mom says that you think I paint well."

"You paint wonderfully. You have potential, Jill."

"Is that why you're here? To get me painting again?"

"Only if you want to."

"I used to like painting."

"Good. You'll be an attentive student."

"Why would you do that? Why would you waste time on me? I could very well be dying."

Vincent sat forward. "You could be. But you could also live."

She looked away. "I doubt that. My prognosis isn't so hot."

He laid his hand over top of hers. The bones were sharp beneath her flesh. "Look at me, Jill."

She obeyed his command.

"I can't deny that this cancer just might kill you. I'm no medical man. I don't understand very much about what you have. I know it destroys healthy cells and it grows and spreads. But I also know that you've got a team of doctors who are working to prevent it from killing you."

"No one says they'll succeed."

"No one says they won't. No one says you won't beat this, if you really try. I also know that while you're fighting this disease, your life doesn't have to be just hospitals and pain and chemo. I know that it can have joy too."

"You think painting will bring me that joy."

"Yes, I do, Jill. And I want to be a part of that joy."

"Why? You're a famous painter. You don't even know me."

"Yes, I do. You are a passionate young woman. And whether it is cycling or studying, or loving your family, you give it your all. I believe you'll give this cancer battle your all too. And about my being a famous painter, strike that from your head. I'm just a man, Jill. Just a man who loves to paint and wants to help others who also love to paint."

She pulled her hand from beneath his and held it up. It shook, badly. "How can I paint with this, Mr. Vermay?"

He heard the anguish in her voice. He took hold of her shaking hand. "Does it shake every day?"

She shook her head. "Just mostly right after my one medication."

"Then we'll work around that. Are you in?"

She stared at him, doubt still in her eyes.

On the television Roma Downey was announcing, "I am an angel, sent by God…"

Jill turned to the television. "Do you believe in God, Mr. Vermay?"

"Yes."

"Do you believe in angels?"

"Yes."

"Do you think that God really does send them to help humans?"

"I'd lay money on it."

She gazed at him with sad yet hopeful eyes. "Okay, I wouldn't mind an art lesson or two."

Vincent grinned. "What time should I be over tomorrow?"

"The best time would be around ten."

"Ten it is."

❦   ❦   ❦

Light glowed in the windows of Liz's office. Vincent opened the door and stepped into the foyer. The waiting room door hung open so he entered. A loud bark followed by a deep growl greeted him.

"Hello? Who's there?" Liz called.

"Vincent."

Duke bounded down the hall, his tail wagging. Vincent knelt down, pet the yellow lab and was rewarded with several licks.

Liz appeared in the hall. She wore her lab coat, her hair pulled back, held in place by a gold clip. "Hey," she said. She looked exhausted, bags beneath her eyes, crow's feet pronounced.

Vincent stood up. "I thought you might be here."

"Am I that predictable?"

"You have been lately."

She motioned down the hall. "Come on in."

Duke walked between them, his nails clicking on the tile. When they reached her office, Liz collapsed in her desk chair. Vincent sat down in one of the leather guest chairs in front of her desk. He unzipped his jacket but left it on. Reaching down, he petted Duke who had lay down beside his chair. "I just came from visiting Jill?"

"How'd it go?"

"She's agreed to be my pupil."

Liz smiled, her eyes actually lighting up for a moment. "That's wonderful news. Hopefully, it will help her attitude."

"She is one depressed kid."

Liz nodded, the light leaving her eyes.

A mound of open books and journals covered the desktop. Pointing at them, Vincent asked, "What's that all about?"

"Bone cancer."

"Ahh."

"There's a ton of research out there." She tapped the top journal. "This study is particularly interesting."

Vincent scratched his chin. "Will any of it help Jill?"

Liz sighed. "I don't know. Two of the drugs are ready for clinical trials, but it depends how long…"

"She holds on," he finished for her.

"Exactly." She nearly choked on the word. Her hand went to her throat, massaging it.

"She's a strong kid, Liz," he offered, knowing the words sounded hallow.

"She's a very sick kid, Vincent," she stated, trembling as she spoke the words. She rose from her chair and went to the window. Duke followed her, sitting down next to her right leg, his tail thumping the floor. "Did you talk to Kate?"

"No. Have you?"

"Not in a couple of days."

Damn you, Kate! "Apparently she's too busy in Indiana."

Liz turned from the window. "You're pissed."

"Very. She promised to call and she didn't."

Liz leaned on the windowsill and folded her arms across her chest. "Do you still love her, Vincent?"

"Of course I love her. She's my wife. I just happen to be furious with her right now."

"Life is so fleeting, Vincent. Don't waste it on anger." Liz's sad, green eyes stared at him, penetrating into his heart as she continued, "We all have demons, my friend. Kate is no exception. Don't push her away because of them. Help her battle them."

Vincent sat forward in his chair. "What about your demons, Liz?"

She shook her head. "Don't worry about me. Just take care of you and Kate."

"I can't do that. You're my friend now."

She shuddered, as if hit by a sudden, overpowering pain.

He jumped up. "Are you okay?"

She didn't answer. She doubled over, her hand on her abdomen, a gasp escaping her.

He hurried to her side, his arm around her, supporting her. She fell against him, breathing hard. "Liz? What's wrong?"

"Cramps," she said, clutching his jacket. She shuddered again then straightened. Her skin was deathly pale.

Duke whined and paced anxiously, his eyes never leaving her.

"Maybe I should take you to DeGraff."

"No," she said, shaking her head. "Just…it happens when I don't eat and don't get enough sleep." She started for her desk chair and he helped her reach it. She sat down, leaning back, massaging her lower abdomen with her right hand. Vincent pushed a couple gray folders aside and sat on the corner of her desk. Duke sat beside her chair, his eyes still glued on her.

She gazed at her dog and smiled. "Mommy's okay, Duke," she assured him. "Don't you worry, boy."

Duke did not look reassured. And rightfully so, since Mommy's skin was still pale, and creases of pain lined her forehead. She closed her eyes and breathed through her mouth.

"Liz, I know you're a doctor, but maybe you should go over to DeGraff and get checked out. What would it hurt?"

Eyes still closed, she shook her head.

"Stubborn ox," he said.

She opened her eyes and looked at him. "In a lot of ways, you remind me of Alan." She grimaced. "Damn. God, I'm so tired. I just want to sleep."

"Well, if you won't go to the hospital, at least let me take you home?"

"Okay."

He helped her into her coat and put its hood over her head. She was wobbly and he slipped his arm around her. The wind had picked up outside and it overwhelmed Liz. She clung to the office door for support while she locked it, her hands shaking. Vincent didn't hesitate, but lifted her in his arms. Duke barked, jumping up and down, trying to reach Liz. "It's okay, boy," Vincent said. "Lets go home. Mommy is coming too."

The dog ran on ahead. As he walked, Vincent shielded Liz from the wind. "I can walk," she protested, but he ignored her. Giving in, she clasped her hands around his neck and rested her head on his shoulder.

Duke was waiting for them on the front porch when they reached the Reilly house. He barked at them as they came up the walkway. Vincent stepped on the first stair and the front door opened. Elsie Whiting stood in the foyer light. Opening the screen door, she said, "Is she all right?"

Duke ran inside and up the stairs. Vincent carried Liz inside. "She's—"

But Liz cut him off. "I'm just really tired, Elsie." Her voice was thin and barely audible.

Elsie motioned at the stairs. "Bring her up here, Vincent."

He followed Elsie to Elizabeth's room. Elsie switched on the lamp that sat on the nightstand next to Liz's sleigh bed and pulled down the blankets. "Lay her down."

He did as instructed then backed away from the bed. He watched as Elsie removed Liz's coat and tossed it aside. She removed the clip from Liz's hair, setting it on the nightstand. "We'll get you changed, baby," she said, gently stroking Liz's hair. "Then you can sleep."

Vincent knew he should leave. He shouldn't stay while Liz was undressed. Even so, he stood where he was, riveted, watching Elsie take care of Elizabeth as if she were her own child. And Liz let her do it, staring at Elsie like a small child stares at its mother, eyes trusting. Off came the lab coat, blouse and slacks. Seeing his friend exposed, her ribs too pronounced, told Vincent his thought about her being too thin was right on target. He also saw a scar where no scar had the right to be. It traveled around her side from her back snaking its way nearly to her navel.

"Vincent, grab her nightgown, please," Elsie said. "It's on the chair there."

A dark green, flannel nightgown lay on a wingback chair just to his right. He picked it up and carried it to the bed.

Taking it from him, Elsie said, "Sit up, honey."

Liz did, realizing that he was still there. Her right hand went to her side, trying to conceal the ugly scar.

"She volunteered at a free clinic during her first year of residency," Elsie said. "One of her patients knifed her."

Liz looked at him and said, "Ancient history." But he could see that like Alan's death, the incident was always in the back of her mind.

Elsie put the nightgown over Liz's head. "This boy came into the clinic high as a kite, Vincent. Liz tries to help him and he turns on her. How's that for gratitude to your doctor?"

"Elsie," Liz said, giving her a fond look. She put her arms through the garment's sleeves.

"Don't you Elsie me, young lady." She turned to Vincent. "She nearly died." Tears welled up in her eyes. "We nearly lost our girl."

"I'm still here," Liz said, lying back against the pillows.

Elsie turned to her. Their eyes met and Vincent saw the love pass between them. He didn't have to worry about Liz, at least not for tonight. She was in her house, in her bed, and Elsie Whiting was at her side. And while Elsie was not her mother, she was the next best thing. "I'll let you get some sleep," he said.

"Thank you, Vincent," she said. "You really didn't have to carry me home."

"No problem. Just get some sleep."

She looked from him to Elsie, a small smile crossing her face. Drawing a deep breath, she rolled onto her left side, her right arm circling round her abdomen, her eyes falling shut. Elsie pulled the covers up over Liz, tenderly stroked her cheek and then shut off the lamp. She closed the bedroom door as they exited and once out in the hall, said, "When she wakes up, I'll get some soup into her."

"I've no doubt you will."

"Well, I better go check on Emmett. He and Douglas were playing chess last time I looked in on them."

"They're still going well, Doug's visits?"

"Yes, they are." Elsie smiled. "More and more often, Emmett even seems like his old self. Mr. Lassiter has done wonders for him."

"That's great to hear."

As they walked down the stairs, Elsie said, "Elizabeth will always have residual effects from that knife wound. Especially when she doesn't take care of herself." She stopped with her hand on the newel post. "That was a horrible night. She lost so much blood. There was damage to her intestines and…" She shuddered. "It took her a long time to recover. Alan was still alive and he was wonderful with her. The way he took care of her, it was obvious how much he loved her." Elsie shook her head. "I can't tell you the number of times I've wished that boy hadn't died in that motorcycle accident." They reached the foyer and she opened the front door. "Thank you for bringing my girl home."

"You're welcome, Elsie. Call me if you need anything."

Vincent stepped out into the windy night. Hunching his shoulders, he started for the Victorian. He was halfway there when he saw the shadowy figure standing at the front gate. As he got closer, he recognized Doug Lassiter. The man stood with his head cocked.

"Doug," Vincent said.

Lassiter jerked, shook his head as if shaking cobwebs from his brain, and said, "Evening, Vincent."

"Heard you were playing chess with Emmett."

"I was. Damn doctor beat me."

Vincent chuckled. "Good for him."

Lassiter pointed at the Victorian. "You hear that?"

"What?"

"Listen, son."

Vincent listened but all he heard was the wind whipping between the houses and a train rolling down the tracks on River Road. "What are we listening for, Doug?"

"I could have sworn," Lassiter said, looking up at the Victorian's third floor. "Damn."

Vincent's heart kicked over in his chest. "You heard the violin, didn't you?"

"Most likely wishful thinking. I miss hearing her play. There will never be another like her. Too bad you never heard her."

Vincent smiled to himself. *But I have, Douglas. I most certainly have. In fact, I've met the woman who plays that violin.* He didn't tell the old man this. He didn't know why, but Vincent believed he shouldn't tell anyone about his time with Katherine. At least, he shouldn't tell just yet.

Vincent had just finished changing into his pajamas when the phone rang. He snatched it up, hoping it was Kate.

"Vermay," Doug Lassiter said in his ear.

"Yeah, what's up?"

"Elsie said you're a big history buff."

"I am."

"You might want to check out the historical society over in Tonawanda. It's a little brick building over by where the wife and I go to church—Salem United Church of Christ. The historical society is kitty corner from the church." Vincent heard pages flipping. "Here's the address…113 Main Street. You'll find lots of old photos of both North Tonawanda and Tonawanda there."

"Sounds interesting. I'll check it out."

Lassiter grunted. "And Vermay, will you do me a favor?"

"What's that?"

"Don't say anything to my wife about me hearing Katherine play the violin. She'll think I'm nuts."

"No problem."

"Thanks." Lassiter hung up without saying goodbye.

Vincent set the phone in the cradle and ran down the hall to Kate's office. Switching on the desk lamp, he pulled open the middle drawer and removed a piece of Malloy Lumberyard stationary and a pencil. He scribbled down the address Lassiter had given him. He knew what he'd look for first. He had to see what had been written in the newspaper when Jethro Malloy had brought his violin-virtuoso wife home. The articles in Norman Lassiter's scrapbook had all been from New York City papers. Vincent had to see what Jethro's fellow citizens had thought of his new wife.

The phone rang, breaking in on his thoughts and he picked it up. Kate's voice was in his ear before he said hello. "Vincent," she was saying. "Please don't be furious with me. I can explain. I'm sorry I've been out of touch but—"

"Stop, Kate. Just stop talking."

She did, breathing hard on the other end of the line.

He wanted to yell at her. No, he wanted to scream at her for neglecting both him and Liz. But he couldn't. Because in his mind he could hear Liz saying, "Life is fleeting. Don't waste it on anger." He thought of Alan Rourke being wheeled into the emergency room and Dr. Elizabeth Reilly watching her colleagues frantically trying to save his life and not succeeding. He saw her in his mind, holding her bloodied and broken fiancé in her arms. He silently counted to ten and he asked, "Are you okay?"

"Yes."

"Are you in Indianapolis?"

"Yes."

"With McMartin?"

"Yes."

Vincent sat down in the desk chair. "And you're really okay?"

"Yes, Vincent."

"Good. That's what's important." He was surprised to find that he no longer had the desire to scream at her. "Life is fleeting," Liz said again in his mind. Alan Rourke dying in a motorcycle accident while on his way home to his fiancée. Marlene Reilly losing her battle with cancer. *Life is fleeting.*

"You're wonderful," she said in his ear.

He bit his lower lip then said, "So what's new in Indianapolis?"

"I'm so sorry I haven't called, Vincent. It's just been crazy since the story broke about Darren's affair. I've been working day and night on things for him to say. We've written the same things over and over again. I feel like screaming."

"Affair?"

"You don't know?"

Vincent ran a hand through his wavy hair. "To tell you the truth, I haven't watched the news lately."

She laughed. "Oh, Vincent, you will never change."

"Fill me in."

"It seems that my boss, the good Darren McMartin was found cheating on his wife. It's been all over the news. The story broke Thursday."

"Proof?"

"In pictures, my love."

Vincent couldn't help grinning. "Serves him right. I assume he did do it."

"He did."

"What kind of excuses are you writing for him?" He winced as he spoke. Just thinking about her writing words that justified the man's infidelity stung.

"No excuses. He's owned up to it. The old 'I made a mistake, I regret it, please forgive me slant.'"

"Does he regret it?"

She didn't reply.

"Kate?"

"I don't think so. I think he loves his mistress."

"And you can still work for him?"

"Vincent, regardless of whether or not Darren regrets cheating, I have a job to do. Besides, even if he wasn't in the middle of a scandal, you still wouldn't want me working for him."

Vincent couldn't argue.

"In fact, I think you don't want me working at all. Since moving to that house, you've become a Neanderthal."

Vincent chewed his lower lip and fought the urge to shout at her. He saw the scar that ran from Liz's side across her abdomen. He saw Jill Woodward without her right leg. "Kate," he softly said.

She was silent on the other end of the phone.

"Let's not talk about this now. Not over the phone. We'll just argue."

"I know."

"When can you come? Liz needs you."

"I owe her a phone call."

"She really needs you."

"She's okay, isn't she?"

In his mind, Vincent saw Liz doubling over in pain. He remembered how light she had been in his arms. He saw how prominent her ribs were. He saw the scar. "Did you know she was stabbed in her first year of residency and nearly died?"

Kate gasped.

"She didn't tell you that, did she?"

"No."

"She still suffers effects from that wound."

"I'll call her first thing in the morning, Vincent. I have got to get her to open up to me more."

"You could do that better if you were here."

"True." He was surprised that she agreed with him. He was even more surprised when she said, "I'll be there the first week of May. I'll tell her that tomorrow. And I'll get her talking."

"Good."

"Okay. Well, I better get going."

"We need to talk too, babe."

She hesitated then said, "When I get there in May. Promise."

"I'll hold you to it. Goodnight, Kate."

"Bye."

The phone clicked in his ear. He sat there, listening to the dial tone and realizing that neither of them had said, "I love you."

❧   ❧   ❧

Jill sat in her wheelchair in front of the bedroom window, her tongue sticking out as she worked on her sketch. Vincent smiled at her intensity. The morning light filtered across her few strands of blonde hair, highlighting it with patches of bright yellow. She wore a forest green and gold, plaid flannel shirt. Her bottom half was hidden beneath a white, crocheted afghan. Still, he could tell her right leg was missing. His smile faded. He couldn't imagine how it would feel to lose a limb.

She looked up from her drawing. "What?"

"What?"

"You're staring at me. You're supposed to be working too."

Vincent sat in the rocker, his legs resting on the foot of her hospital bed. He held a pad in one hand and a pencil in the other. He glanced down at the pad. He'd sketched three different angles of Katherine Malloy's face. He didn't like any of them. None of them spoke to him. Something was missing. But what was it?

He tossed the pad and pencil on the bed and got to his feet. He walked over to Jill and peered over her shoulder. Actress Roma Downey stared back at him. Jill had sketched a head and shoulders view of her. "You must be a fan," he said.

"I am. Do you think she needs a hat?"

"Nope." He pointed at Roma's forehead. "You need to bring her hairline down a bit. And give her hair some body…some fullness." He ran his finger across Roma's chin. "A tad bit more of a curve here."

Jill stared at her work, her head nodding. "Yeah, the chin. The chin was bothering me." She looked back over her shoulder. "It's okay if I want to paint her, isn't it?"

"Sure. Although portraits can be tougher than landscapes."

She shrugged. "Everything's hard these days."

He patted her shoulder. He could think of nothing to say. *Gee, Jill, I guess it must be. Hell, it was just a leg, no big deal. Oh, it's just cancer. Piece of cake.*

"I didn't mean to make you uncomfortable," she said. "Sorry."

"No biggie." He gave her shoulder a light pat. He returned to the rocker, sat down and gently rocked. He wondered if Jill would live long enough to finish her painting. He pushed the thought away. "Are you going to stick with that view or sketch some more?"

"I like this one."

"Okay, then I'll bring the canvas and paints for our next session."

"Great," she said, grinning. Happiness filled her blue eyes.

"Hey, beautiful girl," her father said. Vincent turned in his seat. Mike Woodward stood in the doorway. "Lunch is ready."

"You came home," Jill said, joy in her voice. Vincent turned back to her. Her grin had widened and her eyes shone with love and warmth. Sitting there, in front of the window, the sun shining on her, Vincent noted that her father was right. She was beautiful, in spite of the ravages of her illness.

Mike Woodward came in, nodded at Vincent, and went directly to his daughter. He hugged her and kissed her forehead. She hugged him back, clinging to him, and Vincent could see that this father and daughter had a special relationship.

"Hey, Vincent," Tracy Woodward said, from the doorway.

He got up, gesturing towards the foyer. They both stepped out of the bedroom. "No school today, Trace?"

"Half day. How's Jill doing?"

"I believe she's enjoying herself." He glanced at his watch. "We've been at it for almost three hours."

"She's got to be getting tired. I bet she sleeps this afternoon." She took Vincent's arm. "Mom wants you to have lunch with us."

"Okay."

"Beep, beep," Mike Woodward said, pushing his daughter through the doorway. "Coming through."

"I'll push her, Dad," Tracy said, reaching for Jill's wheelchair.

Jill held up her hand. "I can do it, you guys."

Both Tracy and Mike backed away. They exchanged astonished looks. Jill put her hands on the chair wheels and got herself moving. Looking back over her shoulder, she said, "Well, don't just stand there. Come on. Mom is waiting."

"Coming," Tracy said, giving her father a final glance before following Jill down the hall.

"Wow," Mike Woodward said under his breath. "I don't know what you're doing, Vincent, but don't stop. Please don't stop."

Vincent gave Mike a puzzled look.

"That's the first time she's wanted to do anything by herself since her leg was amputated. What have you said to her? How are you motivating her? I've tried everything. Tracy and Jessica have tried. Liz too. Nothing could bring her out of her depression. I was beginning to think that if the cancer didn't kill her, the depression would."

Vincent scratched his chin as he said, "I don't really believe I've done anything, Mike. We just spent the morning sketching."

Mike gazed up the staircase at Jill's paintings hanging on the wall. "She loved painting when she was younger."

"That's what Jessica said. Look, Mike, all I'm trying to do is show her that there is always a reason to keep going. Just because she put painting on the back burner doesn't mean she's lost the passion for it."

"Sure you aren't secretly a shrink?"

Vincent laughed. "Nope. Just a painter."

"Come on you two," Jessica called from the kitchen.

"Coming," Mike said.

As they walked down the hall, Vincent thought of Kate and the fragile state of their marriage. Could he convince her to rekindle her old passion as easily as he'd convinced Jill?

❧   ❧   ❧

Vincent sat on the floor in his studio and watched as the afternoon light faded, the room darkening, hazy shadows appearing where defined objects had been. His sketchpad lay beside him, ignored. Duke's head rested in his lap and he absently stroked it. Katherine Malloy consumed his thoughts. He had to paint her. Her portrait would be his one magnificent painting. All the others would pale in comparison. He knew this as sure as he knew his name.

"Then why can't I find the right look?" he asked.

Duke moaned in response.

"Duke, I must see her again."

The dog raised his head and stared at Vincent.

"Yesterday was freaky, boy. It seemed so real. But it had to be a dream. What else could it have been? People don't just go back in time."

Duke licked his lips then laid his head on Vincent's lap again.

Vincent tapped the sketchpad. "This is the painting, Duke. I feel it in my soul. But maybe it's not time to paint it yet. Maybe I should concentrate more on fixing up the rest of the house and less on painting pictures."

Duke's tail thumped on the floor.

"You agree, boy?"

The tail thumped again.

Sighing, Vincent laid his head back against the wall and closed his eyes. He'd do the master bath next. He'd ask Kate if she had any preferences. He'd keep it Victorian. But color…he knew she'd want a say on the color scheme. The wall tile had to be replaced. Maybe Kate would like a ceramic floor. He'd ask her if she called later. He believed he could save the old tub. Its claw feet were priceless. He wondered if Kate would go for maroon or mauve. Or should it be green, linking it color wise with the fern-themed bedroom?

The violin crashed into his thoughts like a hurricane crashing into the shore. Vincent jerked, his eyes flying open. He was alone in the studio. Duke had deserted him. The music Katherine played wrenched his soul, the notes fast and furious, the violin screaming in agony. Chills coursed up Vincent's spine. He jumped to his feet and ran out into the hall, but stopped immediately. He must take his pad and pencil. Returning to the studio, he snatched them up then charged down the hall. He raced up the darkening staircase and slid to a stop before the third floor door. The crystal knob and locks greeted him. "Yes!" he exclaimed, sliding the locks over. He opened the door and rushed in.

Katherine stood beneath the single light bulb with her back to him. She played the violin with a recklessness and anger that shocked Vincent. He stood silent, watching her, wondering what had caused her such pain. She brought the piece to a loud, abrupt end. She lowered the violin and hung her head. Her shoulders shook.

"Mrs. Malloy," he said.

She whirled around. Tears streamed down her cheeks and a bruise was forming on her left cheek. A gash ran across her chin and the blood had dripped onto the lacy bodice of her green dress. In fact, the cut still bled.

"Who did this to you?" Vincent asked, stepping toward her.

She backed away, fear in her green eyes. "Stay away," she commanded.

He stopped. "Your chin."

Another drop of blood dripped onto the bodice.

Eying him warily, she backed up until her legs hit the bed and gave way beneath her. She fell onto the bed, the violin slipping from her hand. It hit the floor with a smack. Still staring at him, shock joining the fear in her eyes, she cupped her chin in her hand and said, "Oh, God."

"Let me help you," Vincent said.

She moved her hand away from her chin and looked down at the blood on her palm.

He didn't wait for her permission. He went to the dresser by the window, dropped his pad and pencil beside the washbowl and pulled open the top drawer. White cotton towels and undergarments greeted him. He snatched up a towel and hurried to the bed. Standing before Katherine, he pressed the towel against her injured chin. "Hold this," he said, reaching for her hand and pressing it against the towel.

She obeyed.

He picked up the violin and wiped the blood from it with his sleeve. He coaxed the bow from her right hand then set the instrument and bow on the pillow. Sitting beside her on the bed, he said, "Okay, let me see." He took hold of her hand and pulled it and the towel away from her chin. "We need to wash this cut," he said.

She stared at him with wonder in her eyes. "You came back."

"I told you I would. Let's get this cut cleaned up."

He stood up and she did too. She followed him to the pitcher and wash-bowl. He was relieved to find water in the pitcher and poured some into the bowl. "Go on, wash your chin."

She dipped the towel into the water and dabbed her chin.

"Do you have any bandages around here?"

"Downstairs, I suppose."

Vincent looked at the open bedroom door. He wondered what would happen if he walked through it. Would he step back into the year 2000?

She gingerly touched her left cheek. "Is there a bruise?"

"Yes. We should put some ice on it."

She looked alarmed. "Did I stain my violin?"

"No. It wiped right off."

She turned back to the bed. Seeing the violin and bow lying on the pillow, relief flooded her face. "Nothing can happen to it. My father gave it to me." She wandered back to the bed and sat down. She pressed the damp towel against her chin.

"You should go downstairs and get that bandaged," Vincent said.

"I don't go downstairs."

"Is there someone you can call up here?"

"Jethro left. I think he's gone to New York."

"City?"

"Yes. I begged him to take me this time. I miss it so."

Vincent stiffened. "Did he hit you?"

Her eyes told him he'd guessed correctly. But she didn't address the question. Instead, she said, "Do you still want to paint my portrait?"

"Yes."

"I don't know how you can. Jethro comes up here often."

"Well, he's not here tonight." He picked up his sketchpad and pencil. Sticking the pencil behind his ear, he carried the pad to the bed and sat down next to her. "Some poses."

She gazed at the sketches. "You're very good."

"I don't know about that. I can't seem to find one I like."

"Because you are drawing them from memory. You said yourself that one has to get to know a person before painting her. That's what is missing."

"What?"

"Understanding. Life. There is no life in my face in these drawings."

Vincent studied the sketches with a critical eye.

She touched one of the sketches. "No life in my eyes."

"You're right. You know what that means?"

"What, Mr. Vermay?"

"Call me Vincent. And if I may, I'll call you Katherine."

"That is very informal, sir."

"True. But what year is it?"

"1926."

1926. Shit. 1926. Smiling, he said, "Exactly. 1926. And formality is undergoing an overhaul."

"Maybe so, but you'll find that I'm old-fashioned. Still, if it will make you happy, I will call you Vincent."

"Excellent. And I may call you Katherine?"

"Yes, you may."

He said her name. "Katherine. It's a lovely name."

She looked away. "Thank you."

The blood was seeping through the towel. "You really have to get that cut bandaged," he said. He stood up. "I'll go and you—"

"No," she pleaded, grabbing his hand. "Don't. Please. I don't want to be alone tonight."

Vincent looked toward the open door. "He doesn't go to New York and leave you locked in up here, alone in this house, does he?"

"We have a maid."

She looked so distraught and fragile, her blood bright red where it seeped through the towel. "Why did you marry this man? This man who locks you up as if you were an animal. This man who beats you."

"You must not tell anyone, Vincent. Promise me."

Vincent took her by the shoulders. "Why? Give me one good reason why I shouldn't rescue you from this captivity?"

"You can't say anything," she insisted.

"I can and I will. You don't deserve this."

He got up and strode toward the door. He didn't know whether or not he would stay in 1926 when he stepped through it, but he was going to give it a try.

"Vincent!"

The panic in her voice stopped him and he turned back to her. She'd risen from the bed.

"If you do this, you'll ruin it for my baby."

Kate's relatives and dates flashed through his mind. *When did Katherine have her first baby? When?*

"Please? My child will be born into Jethro's wealth. If you expose him, God knows what he'll do. And what it will mean to my baby. I beg you."

Vincent stood shell-shocked.

"You've seen too much. Oh, God, I shouldn't even be with you. There's too much at stake."

Vincent had to think. He had to find out when Katherine's first baby was born. "Okay, I'll keep silent. For now."

She nearly collapsed before him.

He grasped her forearms and held her up.

She buried her face in his shirt. He stroked her hair and said, "I'll go now. You get your chin taken care of."

She looked up at him. "You'll come back, Vincent?"

"As soon as I can."

He turned from her and walked out the door. He closed it and slid the locks shut. As he walked down the stairs, he heard her calling a servant's name. He stepped outside and heard the unmistakable roar of a jet overhead.

❧   ❧   ❧

"1929," Kate said in his ear.

"Are you sure?"

"Of course I'm sure. Why this sudden interest in my grandmother's birthing activities?"

He heard the clicking of keyboard keys. He glanced at the VCR clock. 11 p.m. and she was still working. "Must be living in this house. It's peeked my curiosity."

"There should be a Bible in Jethro's library with the family history. At least there was when I was a kid."

"I'll have to rummage around in there." *Although it's no longer Jethro's library, Kate. No, now it's your office. If you would only get here and see it.*

"How's the painting going?" she asked, but the distance in her tone told him she would only half register his reply.

"Fine."

"Good."

"I'm going to start redecorating the master bath. Do you have any color preference?"

"Color for what, Vincent?" The keyboard keys clicked away.

He grit his teeth. "The bathroom."

"Which bathroom?"

Click. Click.

"The master bath."

"You should keep it compatible to the fern room, don't you think?"

"Green then?"

The clicking stopped. "Can you wait until I get there, Vincent? I need to stand in the room and feel it. You know?"

He wanted to say, you need to stop putting your energies into McMartin's screw-ups and come put your energies into our marriage, your abandoned novel and your depressed friend Dr. Elizabeth Reilly. "Okay."

"Great. I have to go. I have to finish this speech and I'd like to get to bed by midnight."

"I'll let you go then."

"I'll try to call tomorrow during the day. There's a function tomorrow night."

"Okay."

"Bye, Vincent."

She hung up before he could say goodbye back.

He set the receiver in the cradle and stood up. He went upstairs to Kate's office and flicked on the light. He didn't remember coming across a family Bible when he was rearranging the books, but that didn't mean there wasn't one. He could have missed it. He scanned the shelves and still found no Bible. He pulled open each desk drawer and again, didn't find the Malloy family Bible.

"Damn," he muttered, sitting down in the desk chair. Kate was probably right, but what if she was mistaken? Who might know? Doug Lassiter? Elsie Whiting? He snatched up the phone and dialed the Reilly house.

"Hello." It was Liz, her voice heavy with sleep.

"I woke you."

She coughed. "Yes, you did, Vincent. What's up?"

"I'm sorry, Liz."

"No biggie. I'm used to interrupted sleep. It goes with my occupation, I'm afraid."

"I know it's late but is Elsie still up?"

"No. What do you need her for?"

"I was wondering if she would know when Katherine Malloy had her first child."

"I can tell you that. 1929."

"You're sure, Liz?"

"Yes. But if you don't believe me, go down to the Historical Society over in Tonawanda. Katherine donated a lot of Jethro's belongings, including the family Bible. It lists the births and deaths in there. Kate is even listed in there. In fact, she's the last person Katherine added before donating the Bible."

"Really?"

"Yes."

Vincent drummed his fingers on the desktop. "1929. You're one hundred percent sure, Liz?"

"I am. Now I'm going to hang up the phone and go back to sleep. Goodnight, Vincent."

"Night."

He hung up the phone. If he was indeed stepping back into time, he was going back to 1926. Katherine had been married to Jethro since the fall of 1925. She believed herself pregnant. But history showed her first child being born in 1929. Which meant she was carrying a baby that wasn't going to live.

He bit his lip. *Listen to me, here I am believing I went back in time.* Time travel—physicists and sci-fi authors had long kicked the idea around, but no one had ever proved it possible. And yet, twice now, no, three times if he counted what he'd attributed to a dream earlier, he'd gone back to 1926.

Rising from the desk chair, Vincent went out into the hall. He walked up the third floor staircase. There was no crystal doorknob or sliding bar locks. He stood staring at the door for a long time.

❦   ❦   ❦

Vincent woke the next morning with a start. He sat up, breathing hard. He'd left his sketchpad in Katherine's room. Catapulting out of bed, he ran down the hall. It had to be there on the bed. It had to. He couldn't possibly be traveling back in time. He ran up the stairs, gripped the brass doorknob and pushed the door open. The faint morning light gave the room a hazy, surreal look. The roses on the quilt looked alive, as if they were breathing. The closed violin case sat in its usual spot. But there was no sketchpad on the bed. Could it be? Had he really gone back in time?

Vincent's legs turned to rubber and he crashed to the floor. He sat there on his rear, staring at the bed, his heart hammering in his chest, an ocean roaring in his ears. He had. Somehow, he had gone back in time. It was several minutes before his legs would hold him. Once on his feet, he stood there, clinging to the doorframe, and wondering if it would happen again. And if it did, could he possibly prevent the death of Katherine's unborn child? And if he could, should he?

CHAPTER 11

Vincent sat in the rocker next to Jill's bed, elbows resting on the chair's arms, hands folded as if he were praying. Jill lay curled up in a ball beneath the covers. Beads of sweat stood out on her forehead. She'd managed an hour of painting before giving in to nausea. He'd helped her into bed and covered her with the blankets. He wasn't going to leave her, not until Jessica got home. He might not be able to make her feel better, but at least he could sit with her.

"I'm sorry," she said.

"Didn't I tell you to stop apologizing?"

She grimaced. "You came over here for nothing today."

"No, I didn't. You got some painting done and your mom got to go out and run errands. I wouldn't call it a waste of time."

"I doubt what I did is worth anything. My hand was shaking."

"Then we'll start with a fresh canvas next time if you want."

"Don't you ever get depressed?"

"Yes."

"You could fool me." She grimaced again. "Oh, God…I feel awful."

Vincent sat forward and laid his hand on her shoulder. "It'll pass. Hang in there, Jill." She closed her eyes. He hated seeing her go through this. Hoping to comfort her, he gently massaged her shoulder.

"Talk to me," she said. "Anything. Just, please, talk to me."

"Okay. Let's see…if you could go back in time, who would you want to meet?"

"That's easy. Claude Monet."

"The young or old Monet?"

"When he lived at Giverny." She opened her eyes. "That would be so cool."

"What? Meeting Monet?"

"Going back in time. But if I could go back, I would go back to when my knee first started hurting and I would go to Aunt Liz right away. I…" She trailed off, tears spilling from eyes that pleaded with him to make it possible.

He bit his tongue, wanting to tell her that he'd gone back to 1926, but knowing he couldn't. *It's possible, Jill. I just haven't figured out how it happens yet.*

"I'm back," Jessica Woodward said, appearing in the bedroom doorway. Alarm crossed her face when she saw Jill and she hurried to the bed. "Honey. What's wrong?"

"She's nauseous," Vincent said, moving out of Jessica's way.

"Cramps too, baby?"

Jill nodded.

"Okay, hold on. I'll be right back." Jessica left the room and returned with a metal bowl filled with water. She set it on the nightstand. "Let's get you on your back, honey." Jill winced as her mother helped her roll over. Jessica soaked the washcloth in the water, squeezed it, rolled it and then put it behind Jill's neck.

"Oh," Jill said. "Oh, that's good."

"Where are the cramps, sweetheart?" Jessica asked.

"My thigh."

Jessica pulled the covers down and in spite of his effort not to, Vincent stared at Jill's stump. Compared to her complete left leg, it was a jarring sight. Jessica massaged the thigh above the bandage and Jill stared at her mother as if she were staring at a savior. "I love you, Mom," she said.

Jessica smiled down at her, her smile filled with a mother's special love for her child. "I love you too, baby girl."

Jill's eyes slipped shut. Still massaging her daughter's thigh, Jessica looked at Vincent and mouthed. "Ice cream. On the kitchen table. Put it in the freezer?"

He nodded and left the room. Out in the kitchen, he put away three bags of groceries, managing, he hoped, to put everything in the right place. He returned to Jill's room just as Jessica pulled the covers up to the girl's chin and lightly kissed her forehead. Turning away from the bed, she saw Vincent standing in the doorway and motioned towards the hall. "Thank you for staying until I got home," she softly said as she closed the double doors.

"No problem. Does this happen often?"

"Yes. The cramps cause the nausea."

"She tried her damnedest to keep painting, Jess."

"She's suddenly very determined. Thanks to you."

He waved her comment away. "Are the cramps real or just another form of ghost pain?"

"They'real. The muscles tighten up. They spasm. Dr. Fornier cut through them to remove her leg and…well…the trauma, you know?" She drew in a deep breath. "This is so hard, Vincent."

"No doubt."

Her bottom lip trembled, but she didn't cry. Instead, she said, "I'll be here for her. I'll be right by her side."

"I know you will, Jess."

❧   ❧   ❧

The Historical Society of the Tonawandas was housed in a small brick building with a sign informing him that it had once been a railroad station, serving in this capacity from 1870 until 1922. Vincent opened the door and entered. Glass showcases lined the room, holding models of various historical happenings such as the building of the Erie Canal. He saw models of canal barges, trolley cars, fire engines and police cars. There were maps of both North Tonawanda and Tonawanda showing how each city had grown over the years. Mannequins showed off uniforms worn by firemen, policemen and nurses in the late 1800's and early 1900's. Old street markers, fire hydrants and traffic signals sat at various spots throughout the room.

"May I help you?"

Vincent dragged his eyes off a female mannequin dressed in Victorian high fashion in a lovely purple suit and turned toward the voice. A tall, white-haired woman stood in a doorway that led to a back room. She wore burgundy slacks and a pale gray turtleneck. Glasses hung on a chain around her neck.

"I hope so. I was wondering if you have any newspaper articles or photographs from when Jethro Malloy married Katherine Mann and brought her home to North Tonawanda?"

The woman's right eyebrow shot up. "Ahh, Mr. Vermay," she said.

"My reputation precedes me?"

She chuckled. "I'm afraid it does. Elsie Whiting is my sister."

Vincent grinned. "Small world."

"Very. Especially in the Tonawandas." She held out her hand. "Mae Langford."

He shook her hand. "Vincent Vermay."

"Wait here. I think I have just what you'd like to see in the library room." Still talking, she went into the back. "Elsie says that you're planning on restoring the Malloy house. I'm thrilled by that news, let me tell you. That house was a beauty when Jethro built it. The showplace of Goundry Street, it was." Vincent could hear her rummaging through stacks of books. "Malloy kept the house in top condition while he was living. After he died, Katherine got a handyman. Abe, his name was. He kept the place in good shape too. But then he died and Katherine got old and one of her grandchildren dragged her off and…here it is." She returned to the main room carrying a thick, oversized book. She set the book on top of one of the showcases and said, "Listen to me babbling. You're married to Katherine's granddaughter, for Heaven sake. You know all this." She opened the book and tapped the page. "This is *The Evening News* from September of 1925. Take a look."

"Thank you," Vincent said, leaning over the book. Mae moved off, leaving him to his reading and thankfully, she quit talking.

Fascinated, Vincent read the articles and found that as he'd imagined, Jethro Malloy's marriage to the popular violinist Katherine Mann had caused quite a stir in North Tonawanda. The newspaper had celebrated with banner headlines and a front page spread. The paper's photographer had caught the couple stepping down off the train. Jethro wore a pinstripe suit, a derby bowler, and an elegant watch chain hanging across the front of his vest. His eyes were stern. Katherine wore a long, flowing white dress and a flowered straw hat. She was smiling, her eyes holding an innocence that struck Vincent. She had no idea what lay ahead—the physical abuse and captivity on the third floor of Jethro Malloy's house. She was a young bride anticipating a love-filled marriage.

"Beautiful, wasn't she?" Mae Langford said, peering over Vincent's shoulder.

"Very much so, Mrs. Langford."

"Call me Mae. Your wife takes after Katherine. I always thought that."

"She most certainly does," Vincent agreed. He looked at Katherine's young, innocent face again. "What you said before, about me knowing everything about Katherine and Jethro, I must admit, there's much I don't know."

Mae drew a long breath. "You and the rest of the town. She was an accomplished violinist, Vincent. And yet, she married Jethro Malloy, a man 35 years her senior, and virtually disappeared from public life. Why? I have always wondered why." She pointed at the photograph. "Look at her in that picture. She looks happy. She must have loved him."

Vincent closed the book. "Mae, did you know Jethro?"

Shaking her head, she said, "I don't think anybody really knew Jethro. Least of all, his wife. If she had, she wouldn't have married him."

"But you met him?"

"I'm seventy-five years old, Vincent. Jethro Malloy was an important businessman in this town when I was a young woman. Yes, I met him."

"And Katherine?"

"No. I never met her. Elsie's boss did though. Emmett and Marlene penetrated her world a bit, I think. Even after Jethro died, she was a loner. Except for Abe and her children, although the kids didn't visit her much. In fact, one of her sons moved into the house across from the Malloy house and never walked across that street to visit his mother."

"Nelson," Vincent said. "The son's name was Nelson. His daughter, Lydia, is the grandchild who dragged Katherine away from the house."

"Lydia. Lord, yes, I remember her. Spoiled brat. That girl had a mouth on her."

"Still does."

"Vincent," Mae said, folding her arms beneath her breasts and gazing at him with questioning eyes. "What has Kate told you about her time with Katherine?"

"Mae, my wife loved her grandmother. They had a bond. She accepted Katherine's shy ways."

"But how did she get to be a recluse, Vincent? There have long been rumors."

"And they would be?"

She gave him a knowing look. "Oh, I think you know."

I do know, Mae. I know those rumors are true. Jethro Malloy was an abusive bastard who kept his wife sequestered from the world. I know this because I saw it with my own two eyes just yesterday. "If you're asking me if Kate ever told me any of Katherine's secrets, I must say she hasn't. And considering that Jethro was dead before my wife was born, well, she couldn't tell me all that much about him either."

"You know what's funny, Vincent?" Mae said, picking up the archive book.

"What?"

"I never met Katherine Malloy and yet when I look through these old articles, I feel as if I'd missed out on knowing someone really special. I look at her face in these photos, and I think that she was one of those people who, just by their very presence, make the world a better place. Kate was very lucky to have had those summers with her."

Vincent thought of the lost child Kate must have been—her parents freshly divorced and prior to that, fighting all the time. He thought of Katherine, not young as she'd been in 1926, but older, graying, taking in her granddaughter and, in spite of her own years of loneliness and torture at her husband's hands, showing Kate what real love was. Katherine Mann Malloy had indeed been a special person.

"Let me put this away," Mae said, starting for the back room. "Anything else you'd like to see?"

"Yes. Dr. Elizabeth Reilly told me that Katherine had donated the Malloy family Bible. Could I see it?"

"Sure. I'll get it for you."

A few minutes later, she brought it out and set it on the showcase. Vincent ran his hand along the book's tooled leather cover.

"It's a beautiful, old book," Mae said. "Go ahead, look through it. Just, please, be gentle."

"I will." He opened the Bible. The pages were brittle and yellowed. The family tree went back to Ireland in the 17th century. Names repeated themselves down the line. There were Seans and Bryans. Several Elizabeths and Shannons. His finger trailed down the branches until it reached Jethro Malloy. Katherine Mann had been his only wife. Their first child had been born in 1929, a boy, named Sean Edwin Malloy.

Vincent exhaled a long breath. If he traveled back in time again dare he tell Katherine that the child she carried would not survive? What would telling her do? Would it save the child and change the Malloy family history? Or would history play out anyway? How did pre-destiny fit into this whole thing? The questions whirled around in his mind, questions that had no answers.

Vincent closed the physics book, set it on the coffee table with the other five physics books and picked up the postcard Sarah had sent him. On the front was a picture of downtown Philadelphia; on the back in her usual flowery handwriting was written, "I did better than call them, bro. Love, Sarah." Vincent smiled as he stared at the picture of the city where he and Sarah had grown up. He hoped the visit was going well. She'd reached out and he prayed that his parents accepted her olive branch with grace, that the differences could be resolved and he wouldn't be forced to spend another Thanksgiving and Christmas watching them play nice to one another but not really meaning it.

The doorbell rang and he glanced at his watch. Who was at his door at 10 p.m.? Tossing the postcard on top of the physics books, he got up and went to the front doors. He pulled them open and found Liz standing on the porch, Duke beside her, tail wagging.

"Hey," he said, motioning her inside.

She entered, Duke in step with her. Kneeling down, Vincent greeted the dog with pets and a kiss on the top of his head. Duke responded with licks.

"He really likes you, Vincent," Liz said.

"And I like him." Still petting the dog, he gave Liz a once over. She wore her running clothes, her hair pulled back in a ponytail that stuck out the back of a New York Yankees hat, but she didn't appear to have taken much of a run. In fact, with her pale skin and dark circles under her eyes, she didn't look like she should be running at all.

"I shouldn't have come over so late, but I saw your light on and…I…"

"It's okay, Liz," Vincent said, getting to his feet. He gestured toward the parlor. "Come in."

She kicked off her running shoes and followed him to the couch, falling on it. She patted the cushion and Duke jumped up, settling down with his head on her lap. She absently played with his floppy ears.

Vincent sat down beside the dog. "What can I do for you?"

She shrugged. Spotting the physics books on the coffee table, she asked, "Going into a new line of work?"

"Hardly. You know, I like to think that I'm a semi-intelligent American male. But all the different theories of time and the universe just befuddle me. And Einstein. He's so damn deep that…without a doubt the man was a genius."

"Why physics?"

Vincent eyed her, wondering whether or not to tell her about his travels to 1926. How would she react? Would she believe him? Or would she think that he'd lost his marbles?

"Why are you looking at me like that, Vincent? Do I look that bad?"

"No. But you do look tired."

"I'm not sleeping all that hot these days. But I think you knew that."

"How's your stomach?"

"You mean my intestines. They're still there." She picked up one of the physics books and thumbed through it. "Interesting? And, yes, very deep."

"You understand it?"

She laughed. "Poor, Vincent, I don't dare tell you what my IQ is."

"What is it?"

She shook her head. "You've got enough of a complex." She closed the book and hugged it to her breast. "Why physics? I would think you'd read art books."

Because I want to know how it is that I'm going back in time to 1926. "Mental stimulation, I guess."

She tossed the book on the coffee table. "Well, let me know if you have any questions. I might be able to help you out."

Vincent grinned. "You, Dr. Elizabeth Reilly, are an amazingly multi-talented individual."

"You think so?"

"I do. Now, what brings you out tonight?"

"Well, initially, I thought a run would pick up my spirits. But I cramped up so I quit and went to see Jill."

"How was she?"

"Still upset about cutting the art session short."

"Ah, she told you."

"She did."

"Well, she doesn't need to be upset. As the saying goes, tomorrow is another day."

"Thus said Scarlet O'Hara." Liz smiled. "You're a wonderful man, Vincent Vermay."

He waved her comment away. "Stop it."

"I hope my friend, Kate, realizes how wonderful you are."

"Has she called you lately?"

"Yes, she has. She really cares about me."

"You say that like it's a revelation."

Liz put her right hand on her lower abdomen and pressed, grimacing. "Damn." Duke sat up, whining. "Get down, boy," Liz said. "I have to stretch out."

Vincent got up and gently pushed Duke off the couch. The dog planted himself between the couch and the coffee table, eyes locked on his mistress. Liz lay on her back, stretching her legs out as far as she could.

"Can I do something to help you?" Vincent asked, noting she'd gotten paler.

"Ice pack would help. If you have one."

He retrieved one from the freezer in the kitchen. She slipped it beneath the waistband of her sweatpants and laid her hands on top of it. "Thank you."

He sat on the corner of the coffee table. "Are you sure you're going to be all right? I mean this thing keeps flaring up on you."

"I'll live. It's mostly muscular. I shouldn't have tried to run tonight."

"And they say doctor knows best."

She grimaced and laughed at the same time. "Obviously not this one."

Although he teased her, Vincent was worried about her. She looked awful. Scratching his chin, he said, "Maybe you should be examined by one of your colleagues."

"Maybe you should stick to painting."

"I'm worried about you."

"Don't be."

He sighed. "Damn, you are one stubborn lady."

"Inherited from my great Aunt Emma. At least that's what my mother always said." Duke laid his muzzle next to Liz's face and licked her cheek. The lick brought a smile to her face. "I love you too, Duke." The dog moaned.

Vincent reached across Liz and pulled the afghan from the back of the couch. He covered her with it and stood up. "Stay awhile." He picked up the physics book Liz had looked at and went over to the red velvet wingback chair. He sat down, opened the book and began reading. She was watching him. He could feel her eyes on him. "What?" he said, peering at her over the top of the book.

"I really shouldn't spend the night."

"So don't. Just rest a little while."

"Kate might get mad if I spend the night."

"No, she wouldn't. But do what you want."

"You know I will."

"Yep."

He returned to his reading. Three pages later, he glanced at her. Her eyes were closed, Duke still at her side. He finished the chapter, his head reeling from the mathematics and theories, and glanced at her again. Her chest rose and fell in the gentle, relaxed breathing of sleep. Quietly, he got up and turned off the lights. He went upstairs and called the Reilly house from the office phone. Elsie thanked him for letting her know where Liz was. She'd begun to worry. He read two more chapters before going downstairs to check on his guest. She'd rolled onto her side, the ice bag lying on the coffee table, Duke snoring beside her. She slept the night through and in the morning, looked the healthier for it. She even polished off an entire bowl of oatmeal.

❦   ❦   ❦

Duke stared up at him expectantly. Vincent chuckled. "I don't have anything, buddy." He pointed at the Victorian. "I'm just trying to figure out how I'm going to repaint this place. I want it to look like a work of art when I'm done."

Duke's tail thumped on the concrete walkway. Vincent sighed. "It needs more than two colors, Duke. It needs multi, complimentary colors. The carved trim needs to stand out. It shouldn't be just one shade."

Vincent backed up until his rear met the wrought iron gate. "We should work around the white. I like the white." He scratched his chin. "The mauve should stay, but…" A picture formed in his head and a smile crossed his face. "Yes, I see it."

The Victorian stood before him, resplendent, a blaze of colors. The intricate carvings on the trim and porch poles were painted gold, mauve and blue, and Vincent couldn't help but consider the amount of time such a job would take. The lattice beneath the wrap around porch was pale green as were the steps. The front of the house, beneath the porch roof, was white, the trim around each bay window painted maroon. The remainder of the first floor and the second floor was forest green and the third floor was pale blue. The widow's walk, towering above it all, commanded attention, it's shingles maroon, its wrought iron railings a rich, shining gold.

"Beautiful," he mumbled. "What do you think, Duke?"

He looked down, but Duke was gone. Frowning, Vincent looked over at the Reilly house but didn't see the dog. Where could he have gotten too? A car backfired behind him and Vincent whirled around. A 1925 Ford pickup truck drove past him, its engine struggling. Then he realized that violin music was floating down from the Victorian's third floor. As he listened, he realized that the air had grown significantly warmer and the sky was blue and cloudless.

It happened! The words screamed in his brain. After a week of waiting and hoping and wondering if he wasn't going crackers, it happened. He ran for the front porch but slid to a stop at the bottom of the steps. Dare he go inside? Was Jethro home? What about the maid? He stood, paralyzed, afraid to move, afraid of being discovered.

The double front doors opened and Vincent stared wide-eyed at a stocky, robust woman in a starched maid's uniform. She didn't seem at all surprised to see him. "Are ya with Norman?" she asked, her voice carrying a strong cockney accent.

"No," he said.

She put her hands on her hips and gave him a dubious look. "Then who be ya?"

"The painter," he said, not knowing what else to say.

"Aye," she nodded. "Mrs. Malloy mentioned ya. Mr. Jethro will like the gift. Have ya come fer yer pad?"

He nodded. Gift? Just what had Katherine told the maid?

"Well, ya best come in and go on up." She stepped aside. "Mr. Jethro will be home 'bout six. Both of ya best be gone by then."

"Both?"

"Mr. Norman is here. Now, get on up there."

She shooed him on as if he were a child. He hurried up the stairs to the second floor hall. As he strode to the third floor staircase, he heard applause and a man's voice, "Bravo. Bravo."

Katherine's bedroom door stood open and Vincent stopped in the doorway. Katherine stood in front of the window, holding her violin. Her hair was piled up on the top of her head and she wore an ankle length green skirt and a tan blouse. A man sat in a wooden rocking chair. He wore navy blue, pinstripe pants, a white shirt, and a red and white striped vest. His hair was wavy and brown, and he sported a thick but neatly trimmed mustache. He sat with his legs crossed, a tweed driving cap resting on his knee and Vincent knew him immediately. He was Norman Lassiter.

"Magnificent," Norman was saying. "I told you you could never lose your touch."

"Oh, Norman, I was horrible. You can't bring me new music and expect me to play it." She laid the violin and bow on the bed.

Norman grinned at her. "You, my dear lady, don't need a rehearsal."

She shook her head. "You are not objective."

"And you are too hard on yourself."

Katherine caught sight of Vincent. "Heavens," she said. "Vincent?"

Norman stood up, his cap falling to the floor and turned towards the door. "Who is this, Katherine?"

"His name is Vincent Vermay. He's going to paint my portrait."

Norman eyed Vincent up and down a moment then held out his hand. "Come in, good man."

Vincent shook Norman's hand, impressed with the actor's strong grip. He studied Norman's face, high cheekbones, jaw sharply angled and culminating in a square, dimpled chin. His blue eyes twinkled and spoke of one who took great pleasure in living.

"You've chosen a beautiful subject, Vincent," Norman said, glancing back at Katherine. "I've often told Katherine that she is the most beautiful woman in the world."

"Don't listen to him, Vincent," she said. But her eyes told Vincent that Norman's compliment pleased her.

She opened the top drawer of her dresser, pulled out Vincent's sketchpad and held it out to him. "I hoped you would come back sooner."

"I tried to. But..." He took the pad. He saw the faint scar on her chin, reminding him of Jethro Malloy's cruelty.

"I told Mrs. Collins that the painting is a gift for Jethro. She found the pad and..."

"You had to think of something fast."

"Yes."

"May I see?" Norman asked.

Vincent handed him the sketchpad. The actor carried the pad over to the window and studied Vincent's sketches. He grinned. "You are very good, sir."

"Thank you."

"How many portraits do you plan on painting?"

"Just one."

"No, you must paint one for me. I will pay you."

"No, Norman," Katherine protested. "You can't have one."

"And why not?"

"You know why not."

Norman brushed his mustache with his first finger and thumb. "You don't trust me with such a prize, Katherine?"

"How could I?" Her voice was indigent. "You would display it in your New York brownstone for all the world to see. Jethro would find out and—"

"Hurt you, Katherine?" Norman said, cutting her off. "You think I don't know how he treats you?"

Her hand went to the scar on her chin. She couldn't meet Norman's gaze.

He drew a deep breath. "I despise the day I introduced you to Jethro."

"Despite what you think, Norman, he does love me."

Norman shook his head in disgust. "He is a man who doesn't know how to love." He moved closer to Katherine and touched her cheek. "He can not love you like I do."

Katherine bowed her head.

Norman gazed at her a moment longer then said, "I have to catch the train back to New York." He handed Vincent the sketchpad and retrieved his cap from the floor. As he put it on his head, he said, "I'll be back next month." He cupped her chin in his hand and raised her head. "Promise me you'll be all right until then."

"I will be fine, Norman. Jethro would never seriously hurt me."

"He shouldn't hurt you at all."

"He's a complicated man. You just don't understand him."

"And you do? This is not the marriage you expected."

"He'll change."

Norman shook his head. Leaning close to her, he kissed her forehead, his lips lingering a moment on her skin. Then, turning to Vincent, he asked, "Will you watch out for her? Please?"

"I will. And I'll make sure you get a portrait. But you must promise me you won't show it off."

"I will hang it in a private place." With a quick nod, he was gone.

Katherine stood next to Vincent with dismay in her eyes.

"That man adores you," Vincent said. "He loves you."

Shaking her head, she said, "We won't discuss that. Have you come to work on your painting?"

"Yes."

"I should refuse you, Vincent Vermay. You have promised a portrait to Norman. That is against my wishes."

"You can't refuse me, Katherine Malloy. You are committed. Mrs. Collins is expecting you to surprise Jethro with a painting."

Katherine sighed. "True. Well, then, you still haven't brought your paints."

"Because I still need to find the correct pose." He scanned the room, his eyes falling on the rocker. "Let's see. Yes." He moved the rocker to the window, setting it next to the music stand. The piece of music Norman had brought laid open. "Okay, sit here, please."

Katherine sat down in the rocker.

"Your violin," he said. He retrieved it and handed it to her. "Okay, hold it like this." He showed her.

She did as he requested, resting the base of the violin in her lap.

"Yes. Yes. Good." He put the bow in her right hand. "Let it lie across your lap. Perfect." He sat down on the bed and flipped to a clean page in his sketchpad. He began drawing. The afternoon light lit Katherine with a glow that he could only describe as angelic. He drew swiftly and skillfully, catching the moment before it faded away.

He drew Katherine first, followed by the violin, the rocker and finally, the music stand with its sheet music. The sketch poured out of him like free flowing wine.

"You have found the pose, Vincent?"

"Definitely," he said, continuing to work.

He didn't know how much time had passed when she said, "Hurry. You must leave soon."

He did some final shading and said, "There. Come, see your sketch."

She came and stared at his drawing with awe in her eyes. "Oh, Vincent. Oh, it's wonderful. It's...it's alive. It's like I'm breathing."

He grinned. "You like it?"

"Yes, I love it. And so will Jethro." Vincent's grin faded. Not noticing, Katherine said, "Next time you must bring your paints."

"I will."

"You must go now. It's nearly six o'clock."

He rose and gazed down at her. "You will be all right?"

"You are as bad as Norman. I will be fine. Now, go."

He left her, closing the door and locking it. He walked down the stairs to the second floor hallway. The carpet was different than that of the present. This carpet was maroon and covered with white and pink flowers. Sketchpad under his arm, he walked down the hall to the stairs and on down to the foyer. Mrs. Collins stood in the parlor doorway. "Hurry," she said, motioning him towards the front doors.

He stepped outside and hurried down the porch steps. He walked part way down the walk and turned back to the house. It stood there in its multi-colored splendor. What, he wondered, should he do next? He turned to continue on to the gate and tripped over Duke. He protected the sketchpad as he fell, landing in the damp, brown grass. Duke barked at him. Ignoring the dog, Vincent looked back at the house. It sat there staring back at him with its peeling white shingles and mauve trim.

❦   ❦   ❦

"You okay, Vincent?"

Vincent looked toward the front gate and saw Doug Lassiter. "Yes," he said, motioning Doug inside.

Lassiter opened the gate and entered. He bypassed Duke, stopped in front of Vincent, and held out his hand. Vincent took it and Lassiter helped him stand.

They stood on the walkway, staring at one another. There was a knowing look in Lassiter's eyes. Grinning, the old man said, "Son, we have to talk."

❦   ❦   ❦

They sat at the kitchen table and talked over bottles of beer. Duke lay on the floor, head resting on Vincent's feet.

Lassiter spoke first. "I saw you disappear," he said, matter-of-factly, not an ounce of fear or wonder in his voice.

"You heard the violin, didn't you?"

"Yep." Lassiter took a swig of beer. "You were with her, weren't you?"

"How do you know?"

"It's the violin, Vincent. Every time it's happened to you, you've heard the violin first."

Vincent gaped at him.

"What's the matter? Cat got your tongue?"

"No…I mean…I…" He couldn't think of a coherent sentence.

Lassiter drank some more beer. "Okay, I'll level with you. When I hear the violin, like I've told you about, things change around me. The house turns into the looker it was back then. Mrs. Collins came out of the front door one time. Even saw Malloy sitting in a rocker on the front porch reading a newspaper once."

Vincent could only stare at him.

"But the thing is, Vincent," he continued, "I stand there frozen. I can't move. I can't talk. It's like I'm frozen there, just watching. But it's been different for you, hasn't it?"

"Different how?"

"You know. There's something special about you that has let you do more. Don't lie to me and tell me it isn't true."

Sudden, perfect, wonderful, pristine relief spilled over Vincent. He told Lassiter everything. Lassiter hung on Vincent's every word, his eyes misting over when Vincent talked of meeting his Uncle Norman.

When Vincent finished, Lassiter said, "Amazing." He shook his head in wonder. "I knew Malloy abused her. I just knew."

"Did your Uncle Norman tell you?"

"I never met my uncle. He died before I was born."

"I knew you said he died young, but I just assumed it was after you were born." Vincent raised his beer and drank.

"I was born in '30. Uncle Norman disappeared in 1926."

Vincent spit beer. It sprayed out of his mouth, landing on the table and his lap. "What?"

"Wipe your mouth, Vincent."

Vincent ran his sleeve across his lips. "What do you mean by disappeared?"

"Just what I said. He disappeared in December of 1926."

Vincent sat back in his chair, dumbfounded.

"My father always believed that Jethro Malloy had something to do with his disappearance. His body was never found. My father eventually had him declared legally dead. I got to know Uncle Norman through his scrapbooks and theatre reviews. I often wondered what Katherine's life would have been like if Norman had lived."

"What do you mean? I've only talked with the woman twice, but I can tell you she would never have divorced Jethro."

"Oh, I don't know about that. Uncle Norman loved her and, well, he wouldn't have given up the fight."

Vincent nodded, thinking of the young actor and how he had watched the man declare his undying love to Katherine.

Lassiter leaned over the table. "You realize that you're playing with fire, Vincent."

"Fire?"

"Yes, fire. Anything you do while back there could affect the future. Don't tell me you haven't thought of that."

"Oh, I've thought about it, Douglas. Katherine is pregnant. In 1926 Katherine is pregnant."

"But..."

"She doesn't give birth to her first child until 1929."

Lassiter's bushy eyebrows rose. "I see."

"Something happens that causes her to lose the baby. I don't know what, but something happens. And I've got the power to prevent it."

"By telling her what you know."

"Exactly."

"You think she'd believe you if you told her you came from the future?"

"I don't know. Probably not, but even if I got her wondering, maybe that would get her to be more careful and—"

"Whoa, son. Slow down." Lassiter leaned closer. "Don't mess with the past."

"And if I could prevent Norman's death? What would you say then, Douglas."

Lassiter swallowed hard. He hesitated for several moments before saying, "I would still say that you have no right to mess with the past."

"You'd still say that."

Lassiter nodded solemnly. "Yes, because any change could create havoc, Vincent. Think about it. What if Katherine does have this first child? Then maybe she wouldn't have the child that fathered your wife. Have you thought of that?"

Vincent bit his lower lip, his mind churning with all the different scenarios that could be *the present*. "Mind-boggling," he finally said, drawing in a deep breath.

"Promise me," Lassiter said. "Promise me that if you go back again, you won't change anything."

"Nothing says I will go back again. Hell, I didn't plan any of this. I don't have control. On top of that, each time I've gone back, the boundary has expanded. First it was the room, then outside the room, and now outside the house. I can't explain it."

"I'm no physicist either."

Vincent spread his arms wide. "I mean this last time could be it. It may not happen again."

"Oh, I think it will, Vincent. I think the next time you hear that violin, you'll go back."

"Why are you so sure, Douglas?"

The old man stared at him with envious eyes as he said, "I don't know. It's a feeling I have. I just think that you're supposed to."

❈   ❈   ❈

After Lassiter left, Vincent went upstairs to his studio, Duke following right behind him. He got his easel, canvas and paints ready. He put them outside the third floor bedroom door. He set the sketch of Katherine there as well. He was ready. If Lassiter was right and he was destined to go back again, he'd begin painting Katherine's portrait.

He lay in bed that night for a long time before falling asleep. "Don't mess with the past," Lassiter had admonished. "Promise me?" But Vincent hadn't promised him anything; because it would have been a promise he might not be able to keep.

CHAPTER 12

❀

Jill backed away from her painting and said, "What do you think, Vincent?"

Vincent got up from the rocker, came around the bed and studied the painting. "It's good."

"Do you think it really looks like her?"

"I think that Roma Downey would be pleased."

"It needs a lot more work."

"Well, God didn't create the world in one day, Jill."

She grinned sheepishly. "I guess. But he also got to work longer than me."

Vincent rubbed her shoulder. It was Good Friday and this was the first day Jill had been able to paint. God bless her, she'd tried. Every day, despite her shaking hand and weak body, she'd tried. And at the end of each session, she'd look at Vincent and say, "I have to start it again." So every day Vincent had brought a new canvas.

Jill gazed at her painting with triumph in her eyes. "Mom always says, 'If at first you don't succeed...'"

"So the saying goes. I'm proud of you."

"Thanks."

Vincent squeezed her shoulder. "I think you've done enough though. You look tired."

She nodded. "You don't have to stay though. Mom will be home soon. She just went for some last minute things for Easter dinner."

"I'm not going anywhere. I told your mother that I would stay until she got back and I will."

"Okay." She pointed out the window. "It's beautiful out there today."

"It is."

"Is it warm?"

"In the fifties."

"Take me out? Please? Take me for a walk?" Her blue eyes pleaded with him.

He squatted beside her chair. "You sure you're not too tired?"

"I'm fine."

"Okay, you're on."

He insisted she wear her ski jacket as well as a baseball cap. He also wrapped a scarf around her neck and covered her lower half with a blanket. He took her out the front door and down the four concrete steps to the walkway. Once on level ground, she took over moving the wheelchair. She stopped at the end of the driveway and drew in a long breath. "Yes," she said, her eyes animated. "Oh, God, smell it. Feel it."

She turned right and moved down the street. Vincent quickened his stride to keep up with her. They reached the end of Louisa Parkway and Jill stopped again. She looked up at Vincent, a smile on her pale face. "It's beautiful. So beautiful." She drew another deep breath. "I need to get out more."

"You think?"

"Most definitely." She turned the chair around and headed back to the house. "Mom is planning this really huge Easter dinner. She told me to ask you, but I said that your wife will probably be here."

"No, she's stuck in D.C."

"Bummer."

"Yeah, it is, Jill."

"Then come to our house."

"Well, thank you for the invitation, but I do have plans. I'll be at the Reilly's."

"Cool." Jill turned up the driveway, wheeled the chair back around to face the street and sat there looking around the neighborhood. "I feel good today, Vincent. For the first time since…" She looked down at her covered lap for a long minute, and then lifted the afghan and stared at the place where her leg used to be. "I didn't think I'd ever feel good again."

Vincent knelt beside her chair and laid his hand on her stump. She trembled, but didn't protest. "You're still a lovely, special young woman, Jill. This doesn't change that."

She placed her hand on top of his and said, her voice nearly a whisper, "Thank you."

"You can beat this thing, Jill. You can have a great life."

Nodding she said, "I promise you one thing, Vincent. I'm damn sure going to give it my best shot."

❖   ❖   ❖

Vincent sat on the steps leading up to Katherine's bedroom door. He waited for Katherine to play her violin as he'd been waiting for days now. Still, she did not play. He banged his head against the door. "Come on, Katherine," he said. "Play. Play."

Instead of the violin, Vincent heard Kate call his name. He stood up. Was he going crazy? Kate was stuck in D.C. with McMartin.

"Vincent!" she called again. "Are you here?"

He ran down the stairs, still not believing his ears. But when he reached the second floor hall, Kate was there, standing at the top of the staircase, smiling and holding out a large bag. "Hey," she said, looking both afraid and hopeful.

"Kate," he said. "I thought...what are...how..."

"I brought a Virginia baked ham from Colonial Williamsburg's Dubois Grocer," she said, setting the bag in his arms. "Your favorite." She leaned close and kissed him on the lips. "Happy Easter."

"You're here," was all he managed to say as he looked from her to the bag and back to her again.

She laughed at him. "For once my husband is speechless. Write this day on the calendar." She turned and started back down the stairs. "Come on, Vincent. That has to go in the fridge."

He trailed after her. As they walked through the foyer, he saw that she'd brought a suitcase. Still in shock, he said, "I thought you weren't coming until May first."

"I changed my mind. I'm a woman remember."

They entered the kitchen and she opened the refrigerator door. "Set it in there. I plan on cooking that for you tomorrow."

He set the ham on the top shelf then stepped back and she closed the door. "Now, greet me properly." She grabbed the front of his shirt and pulled him close. She wrapped her arms around him and kissed him.

He kissed her back, taking her in his arms.

"You taste so good," she mumbled. "Make love to me."

"Now?"

"This very second."

He scooped her up and carried her upstairs to the bedroom. Laying her on the bed, he straddled her, and tore his Williamsburg shirt up over his head. She unbuckled his belt and unsnapped his jeans. When she pulled his zipper down, he nearly exploded with his hunger for her. No matter their differences, he hungered for her touch.

They made love until, exhausted, he rolled off of her and lay on his back, panting. She moved beside him, snuggling, her hand resting in his chest hair. "I love you, Vincent," she said.

"I love you, Kate."

She said nothing else. He lay beside her, listening to her breathe. It wasn't long before she fell asleep, her hand still on his chest. He laid his hand over top of hers. Tomorrow he would show her the office. He would convince her to leave McMartin's employ. They would get back on track. Closing his eyes, Vincent fell into a sound sleep and did not hear Katherine playing her violin.

      ❧   ❧   ❧

"I surprised you, didn't I?" Kate said, grinning.

They sat together on the bedroom window seat. Kate wore his robe, her hair falling haphazardly about her shoulders. She hadn't put her glasses on yet and her green eyes still carried wisps of sleep.

He touched her cheek. Her skin was soft and warm. "You are beautiful," he said.

Tears welled up in her eyes.

"No, don't cry, babe."

She took his hand and clung to it. "I didn't know whether you'd be glad to see me or…"

He pressed a finger to her lips. "Shhh. I'm thrilled you're here."

"Happy Easter, Vincent."

"It is now."

She smiled. "I told Darren I wouldn't be back until the second week of May."

"What did he say?"

"He protested and whined, but I told him that was that. You'd have been proud of me. I was very inflexible with him."

"I suppose he's reserved the right to call you at his every whim."

"He has." She winked. "Doesn't mean I'll answer him."

"That a girl!"

She stood up and tugged on his arm. "I discovered something this morning and you have some explaining to do. Come on."

"What?"

She dragged him up from the window seat and led him down the hall to the re-decorated library. "This, Vincent. What is this all about?"

He shrugged. "I thought it would be a nice place for you to work when you're here." He used the term "work" on purpose. He didn't dare use the word write. Not yet. Now that he knew he had two weeks to persuade her, he could move at a slower pace. Let her try the office out first. Then subtly bring up her unfinished novel. Time was on his side now.

"This was the surprise you mentioned, wasn't it?"

"Yes. Do you like it?"

She stood in the center of the room and studied it. She sat down at the desk. She ran her fingers over the computer keyboard. "I can hook this into my office in D.C.?

He swallowed his protest and said, "If you want."

"You did this for me even though you've been upset with me?"

He leaned against the doorframe and folded his arms across his chest. "I did."

"Thank you. This is incredible." She held out her hand. "Come here."

He went to her, took her hand and they kissed. He sat on the corner of the desk and gazed at her, thinking that she had never looked lovelier.

She looked around the office again. "Just wonderful."

"The colors are okay, babe."

"Yes. It's so bright and…inspiring." She squeezed his hand. "But I can't dawdle in here today. I've a ham to cook." She started to rise, but he gently pushed her back down in the chair. "What, Vincent?"

"We'll be eating Easter dinner at the Reilly's house tonight."

She raised her eyebrows. "I see. What about our ham?"

"We'll cook that tomorrow."

"Okay. What should we do this morning."

"How about church?"

"Church? Lord, Vincent, have you found religion on me?"

He shook his head. "I just thought I'd go today and…well…say some extra prayers for Jill Woodward."

Kate smiled her approval. "You are such a softie at heart."

"Want to come?"

"Wouldn't miss it for the world."

❖   ❖   ❖

Vincent donned a navy blue suit with a white silk shirt and a pale blue tie. Kate looked resplendent in a white dress and pale purple blazer, her hair hanging free. He took her to Salem United Church of Christ near the historical society because Lassiter had mentioned attending there. The building was large, constructed of red brick, the chapel portion having three entrances. Each entrance had wooden double doors and concrete steps. As he escorted Kate down the tree-lined street towards the church, Vincent heard a familiar voice call his name. He turned and shielded his eyes from the sun. Mike Woodward walked beside Jill in her wheelchair.

"Hey, Jill, Mike."

He greeted Mike with a firm handshake and planted a kiss on Jill's cheek. She grabbed his hand and said, "I thought you said your wife couldn't come."

"She surprised me."

"Hi," Jill said, looking up at Kate. "I'm Jill Woodward and this is my dad, Mike."

Mike held out his hand and although Kate shook it, her eyes lingered on Jill and the pinned-up, pant leg where Jill's right leg should have been. Jill noticed, but Vincent had to give her credit, she didn't squirm under Kate's gaze. Instead, she said, "Mom and Tracy came to the sunrise service. I couldn't make that."

"Kate and I didn't make that one either."

The church bell rang, filling the air with melodious, reverberating sound.

"Better hurry," Jill said. She took hold of her chair wheels and pushed off.

Vincent and Kate stepped aside to give her more room. "See you in there," Mike said and followed her.

Vincent started following them, but Kate stopped him by grabbing his arm. "What?"

She trembled as she said, "She looks terrible, Vincent. Her skin tone, her eyes and, oh, Lord, her missing leg."

Vincent put an arm around Kate's shoulders. "I know."

"No wonder Liz is freaking."

Vincent drew her close. "That's why it's good you're here. You can spend time with Liz."

Kate shook herself and said, "We better go in."

The church was crowded and at first, Vincent thought they would have to stand. But then he saw Doug and Mary Lassiter. The old man waved him forward, pointing at two empty spaces in the pew beside him. Vincent and Kate slipped into Lassiter's pew and exchanged quick greetings just as the choir started walking down the aisle, singing an exuberant song about Christ's Resurrection.

The chapel held an old world, Middle Ages flavor. It's pews, choir loft, and pulpit were made of wood. Huge beams, from which hung lanterns reminiscent of Germany during the time of Martin Luther, ran across a cathedral ceiling. Tall, arched, stain glass windows depicting scenes from Jesus Christ's life were pure works of art. Red velvet carpeting ran down the aisle and up to the massive altar that was surrounded by rows of white Easter Lilies. But most impressive to Vincent was the painting of Jesus above the altar. Christ stood with arms outstretched, welcoming all those who entered this church.

"Magnificent," Kate whispered in his ear. She pointed at the painting.

"Truly," he whispered back.

The service sped by. It had been years since Vincent sang a hymn, but on this day, he joined in with all his might. Even Kate sang. The minister, a lovely woman with dark hair and glasses, stood in the pulpit and delivered a powerful message of love and hope. Vincent couldn't take his eyes off of her. According to the church bulletin he'd been handed upon entering the chapel, her name was Pastor McMichael.

They exited the church shortly after noon. As they came out the center door, Vincent saw Jill by the curb. She sat doubled over, one hand pressing on her stump.

He rushed to her, kneeling beside her chair. "Jill?"

She looked at him with pain filled eyes. "Dad's getting the car." She winced then said, "He wanted to park here in the handicap zone, but I wouldn't let him. Stupid, huh?"

Vincent could see the spasms in her thigh muscles.

"Is there anything we can do?" Kate asked, appearing beside Vincent.

Jill shook her head. Her breath came in short blasts. "I can't breath," she said.

Vincent rubbed her upper back. "Hang tight, kiddo." He could feel the eyes of other parishioners watching them. Douglas and Mary Lassiter stood just behind him.

Mike pulled his Jeep Cherokee to the curb and jumped out. He opened the passenger door then came to his daughter's side. "Let me lift you, Jill." He slid one arm beneath her thighs and the other around her back. He was just about to lift her when she said, "I have to throw up." She'd barely gotten the words out when the vomit came. It poured out of her mouth, a ghastly combination of breakfast and blood. "Daddy," she gasped. "Daddy, I think..." She went limp, falling against Mike's chest.

"Jill!" he said, panic in his voice. "Jill!"

She didn't move. She lay against him, her eyes open but not seeing. Her skin was ghost white.

"Oh, God, she's not breathing!" Mike yelled. "She's not breathing! Help me!"

"Call 911," a young man said. He pulled Vincent aside. "Get her out of the chair. Lay her down. I'm a doctor."

Kate pulled her cell phone out of her purse and dialed 911. Vincent stood watching as Mike and the doctor got Jill out of the chair and onto the ground. The doctor unbuttoned Jill's vomit covered jacket and blouse and bent close, listening to her chest. Somewhere in his terrified mind, Vincent thought, Christ, the doctor looks like a teenager. And he did, his hair long and golden blonde, a zit shining on his left cheek. But as if to belie Vincent's assessment of the physician's age, a girl of eight or nine ran up with a black leather bag. "Here, Daddy," she said.

Sirens wailed, growing closer. Pastor McMichael knelt down beside Mike Woodward and began to pray. He reached for the minister's hand and she gave it to him.

Lassiter's lips pressed against Vincent's ear. "She's gone, son," he said.

Vincent shot the old man a glance.

"I'm sorry, Vincent."

Vincent turned back to Jill. Lassiter was right. She was gone. He could feel it inside. The spot in his heart that had held Jill Woodward was empty.

The ambulance arrived. Jill was hooked up to IV's and monitors. They used paddles on her, her frail body jerking beneath the shocks. The young doctor and the two paramedics tried for what seemed like hours, but they couldn't revive her. Finally, the doctor said, "She's gone. I'm sorry." He laid a hand on Mike's shoulder. "I'm really sorry."

Vincent felt Kate slip her arms around his waist. He didn't bother trying to stop the tears that rolled down his cheeks.

People began walking away, shaking their heads, mumbling their condolences to Mike as they passed him. Mike moved close to Jill's lifeless body. He picked her up and held her. He tenderly stroked her few strands of blonde hair and told her over and over again that he loved her. He sat on the ground, holding his dead daughter and rocking her as if she were a sleeping baby.

"Damn shame," Doug Lassiter said.

"Poor child," Mary said. "So young."

The paramedics began packing up their equipment. The doctor looked at Salem's minister. She nodded. Sniffing, she laid a hand on top of Jill's head and said a silent prayer. Aloud, she said, "Michael. Michael, look at me."

Mike looked at her.

"The paramedics have to take her body now."

He clutched her tighter.

"Mike. Let her body go. Her soul is with God now. She's no longer suffering."

Mike kissed his daughter's cheek and gently laid her down on the concrete. The paramedics wheeled a stretcher over. Mike gave Jill a final look and said, "Daddy loves you, princess."

The minister stood up, took Mike's arm and helped him stand. "I'll take you home, Mike," she said.

He watched as the paramedics lifted Jill onto the stretcher, strapped her in and loaded her into the ambulance. As the ambulance drove off, he said, "How can I tell Jess? How?"

"I'll be with you, Mike," Pastor McMichael said and led him away.

Seeing Vincent, Kate, Doug and Mary still standing there, the young doctor said, "Was she a friend?"

"Yes," Vincent said, surprised that the word came out.

"I'm sorry for your loss."

"Thanks for your efforts," Doug Lassiter said.

The doctor nodded. He took his daughter's hand and said, "Come on, sweetie."

As they walked away, the little girl said, "You tried, Daddy. Don't be sad."

"I'll try not to be," he replied.

Kate squeezed him and Vincent gazed down at her. Tears stained her cheeks. He wiped them with his fingers.

"Someone has to tell Liz," Mary Lassiter said. "I will if you'd like."

Kate shook her head. "No, but thank you. Vincent and I will go over there now."

"Would you like Douglas and I to come along?"

"No. We can handle it."

Mary rubbed Kate's arm. "Well, you call if you need anything." She took her husband's hand. "Come on, Douglas. I must bake something for the Woodwards."

Vincent laid his cheek on top of Kate's head. He didn't want to go see Liz. He wanted to stay holding Kate in his arms forever. He wanted time to stop.

"We have to go, Vincent," Kate said.

Sighing, he said, "I know."

❧   ❧   ❧

Liz sat frozen on the couch. Kate sat next to her, holding her hand, talking softly to her. Vincent let Kate handle it. He couldn't talk to Liz right now because he would break down if he did. So he sat down on the steps in the foyer and buried his face in his hands. *Jill was dead. Sweet, young Jill. Gone. In a matter of seconds, gone.*

A moist tongue licked Vincent's hands. Duke stood in front of him. Emmett Reilly stood beside Duke. "What happened, Vincent?" he asked.

Vincent gave Duke a bear hug. The dog licked his face. Vincent released him, looked up at Emmett and said, "Jill Woodward died this morning."

"Oh, no," Emmett said, turning toward the living room door.

"It was awful, Emmett. God, it was awful."

"Liz needs me," he said, heading for the living room. Duke trotted after him.

Vincent sat on the steps and listened. "Elizabeth," Emmett said as he entered the room.

"Daddy!" Liz cried. Loud, choking sobs reached Vincent's ears. Vincent closed his eyes. He made out, "I should have been with her," amongst the sobs. "I let her down, Daddy. I let her down."

Vincent could listen no more. He got up and walked down the hall to the kitchen. Elsie Whiting stood at the kitchen sink staring out at the backyard. She heard Vincent enter and turned. "Mary Lassiter just called. She's going to make a potato casserole. I'll make a meatloaf."

"I didn't hear the phone ring."

"Yes, a large meatloaf will be good." She went to the refrigerator and opened the freezer portion. She removed a huge, frozen hunk of ground beef. "This will have to thaw first. I'll make the traditional meatloaf. I do have an Italian meatloaf recipe but I think traditional will be better for this situation. Don't you?" She set the frozen meat on the counter.

"She'll never finish her painting," Vincent said. "She had talent, Elsie."

Elsie peered at the spice rack. She removed three spice jars and set them next to the meat. "Lord, I hope I have bread crumbs. If not, I'll have to use crackers. It won't be as good with crackers though." She rummaged around in the pantry.

Vincent left her. He wandered back down the hall to the foyer. Kate came out of the living room. "Emmett will take care of her now."

Holding hands, they walked over to the Victorian. Vincent unlocked the door and they went inside. Kate hugged him. "What can I do, Vincent?"

He brushed her hair with his hand. "Nothing. I just have to deal with it. She was a great kid."

Kate nodded.

Vincent walked upstairs and down the hall to his studio. He leaned back against the wall and slid down until his rear hit the floor. He thought of his sessions with Jill. He stared at her rejected canvases, which rested against the wall below his studio window. He remembered how happy she'd been Friday after finally being able to paint without a shaking hand. She'd so enjoyed their short time outside. Her smile had lit up her face, erasing her illness, if only for a few moments.

It was so unfair. She was too young to die, too young and beautiful and talented to die. Why, God? he asked. Why did you have to take her?

No answer came. Vincent hung his head and cried.

❦   ❦   ❦

They buried Jill on Wednesday. Salem United Church of Christ was packed full of people. The service was short, but moving. Somehow, Tracy managed to get up and read a poem she'd written about her sister. Tears poured down her face while she read, but her voice came through strong and clear.

The drive to the cemetery was interminable. Vincent pulled through the cemetery gates and followed the line of cars along a curved roadway then parked on the shoulder of the road. Kate held his hand as they walked up the incline to Jill's freshly dug grave. He estimated the circle around the grave numbering well over a hundred.

Liz stood between Elsie and Emmett. Her eyes were hidden behind sunglasses, but Vincent didn't doubt that they were bloodshot. The Woodwards stood together, all dressed in black, Jessica looking haggard and sad. Tracy stared blankly at her sister's coffin. It was white with gold accents. As people arrived at the grave, they lay flowers on it.

Vincent couldn't believe that Jill lay lifeless within that wooden box. He looked up at the blue sky, wanting to see past the white clouds and into Heaven. He wanted to see Jill sitting with God. He imagined her finishing her painting of Roma Downey.

Salem's minister gave a brief message, culminating with the 23rd Psalm. People began moving off. Liz went over to Jessica and held out her arms. The two women embraced. Mike Woodward stood watching them, looking sadder than any man should ever have to look.

Tracy set a single red rose on Jill's casket and said, "Goodbye, Jillie. I love you." She turned away, saw Vincent and Kate, and came to them. "Thanks for coming."

"You're welcome," Kate said. "I'm sorry you lost your sister."

Tracy nodded. A tear slipped from her eye and she impatiently wiped it away. "Mom's going to hang the painting Jill started on the wall with her others."

"That'll be good," Vincent said.

"If it's okay with you, she also wants to hang the painting there that you gave to Jill."

"You gave it to her. I just painted it. And that's fine."

Tracy wiped another tear away. "She died happy because of you, Vincent. You gave her hope. The time she spent with you...She told me that it meant the world to her. Thank you."

Vincent could only nod his acknowledgement. The lump in his throat was choking him.

Tracy looked back at the casket. "I'm really going to miss her."

Kate laid her hands on Tracy's shoulders. "She'd want you to keep on living and pursuing your dreams, Tracy."

"I know."

"It's okay to be sad. You need to mourn. But go on too."

"I have to, Mrs. Vermay. I'm the only child Mom and Dad have left." She looked over at her parents. Jessica was still in Liz's arms. Mike Woodward hadn't moved. He stood staring at his daughter's coffin.

"Excuse me," Tracy said. She walked over to her father and slipped her arms around his waist. He pulled her close. He held her like a man afraid to let go of his remaining child.

"Let's go," Vincent said, turning away. He started down the incline.

"We have to go over to the house, Vincent," she said.

"No," he said, shaking his head. "I can't."

"Vincent, they'll expect us."

He opened the truck door. "I can't, Kate. I just can't."

He started to get into the driver's seat, but she grabbed his arm. "Let me drive."

He relinquished the keys. She was right. He was in no condition to drive.

He stared out the side window while Kate drove. They were halfway to the Woodward house when she said, "We have to show up, Vincent. You know that."

He turned to her. She had her eyes on the road but her jaw was firmly set. She wouldn't take no for an answer.

"You're right," he said.

❦   ❦   ❦

The dining room table overflowed with food and Vincent's stomach churned in protest. People surrounded him, people eating and talking and, my, God, even laughing. Jill was dead and her relatives and friends, all dressed solemnly in dark colors appropriate for the occasion, were still able to laugh. *How? How could they still laugh?*

He worked his way through the flood of people. He got through the living room. He stepped into the front foyer and saw Kate on the stairs with Tracy. Tracy was showing her Jill's earlier paintings. Vincent opened the door to Jill's bedroom and went inside. It was dark, the shades drawn. Liz sat in the rocker. "Close the door." she said.

He did and then stood waiting for his eyes to adjust to the dim light.

"You too?" she asked.

"Me too."

She ran her hand through her hair. "You okay?"

"No."

"Me neither."

Vincent sat down on the bed. "I really thought she could beat this thing, Liz. I really did."

Liz rocked a few minutes. "There is this hole inside of me, Vincent. And it hurts. They never stop hurting, you know. Those holes. Nothing fills them. Everyday, I wake up and I miss my mother and Alan. Now Jill."

Vincent said nothing. There was nothing comforting to say.

"Thank God Kate is here. If she weren't here I…"

"I'm glad she's here too. She's been great."

"Yes."

They sat together in Jill's room for a long time. They said nothing else. They didn't need to. Each knew what the other was feeling. And they took comfort in one another's presence.

※   ※   ※

After everyone had departed, Liz convinced Jessica to go upstairs with her. Kate sat with Tracy on the living room couch. The girl was curled up in a ball, her head in Kate's lap. Kate gently rubbed her shoulder. Tears ran freely down Tracy's cheeks. It was like someone had turned on the faucet that was her eyes and had forgotten to turn it off. But she didn't sob. Her body was too spent for sobbing.

"Vincent?"

Vincent turned. Mike Woodward stood in the doorway holding a can of nails and a hammer. "Yeah, Mike?"

"Help me hang the paintings?"

"Sure thing."

Per Jessica's wishes, they hung the unfinished painting of Roma Downey and Vincent's painting of the hansom cab on the wall above the stairs. They fit perfectly with Jill's other paintings. Vincent patted Mike on the back. "Jill would be pleased, Mike."

Mike nodded. "Thanks for everything, Vincent." He glanced up at the top of the stairs. "I need to check on Jess."

Vincent carried the can of nails and hammer down the stairs and set them on the Shaker bench. He went back into the living room. Kate pressed a finger against her lips. "She's sleeping," she whispered.

Tracy had fallen asleep with fresh tears on her face. Looking at her tore at Vincent's heart. He sank into a chair and sat staring at the floor.

Liz came into the room carrying her medical bag. She knelt beside the couch and laid her hand on Tracy's forehead.

"I gave Jess a sedative. Mike's with her." Liz straightened and gestured at Kate. "Come on."

Carefully, so she wouldn't wake Tracy, Kate slid out from under her. Liz put a pillow beneath Tracy's head and covered her with an afghan. She brushed a lock of Tracy's hair back from her forehead then lightly kissed her cheek. The girl stirred, rolled onto her back, but did not wake up.

Liz escorted Vincent and Kate to the front door. "I'm going to stay here tonight," she said. "I'll get the kitchen and dining room cleaned up then crash in the living room near Tracy."

"I'll help you," Kate volunteered.

"Go ahead," Vincent said. "I'll leave you the Rodeo. I can walk home."

"Are you sure?"

He smiled at her. "Yeah." He kissed her lips, slipped out the Woodward front door and headed for home.

Still wearing the black suit he'd worn to Jill's funeral, Vincent sat next to his art supplies, his back against Katherine's bedroom door. If there was ever a time he wanted to go back to 1926, it was now, to be free of the last four days, to put distance between them and where he was. God, he needed distance.

He closed his eyes and tried not to think, but to just listen. Minutes turned into hours and still he sat. He drifted in and out of sleep on rolling fog. The violin floated in on a gray cloud. Its tone was mournful, its music beckoning him. He jerked and his heart pounded in his ears. Had he been dreaming? No, there it was, the music soft and melancholy.

Vincent stood up, slid the bolts over and opened the door. The solitary light bulb dimly lit the room. Katherine sat on her bed playing her sad, penetrating song. Her hair hung down, falling past her shoulders in gentle curls. She wore a black silk robe. How like Kate she looked. How beautiful she was. Vincent cleared his throat.

She ceased playing. She lowered the violin to her lap. She did not seem surprised to see him.

"I know it's late," he said.

She smiled. "It's nearly midnight."

"Is that why you were playing so softly?"

"Yes."

"So Jethro won't hear?"

"No. Jethro has gone to Boston. He left this morning." She pointed at the rocking chair. "Please, sit."

He sat.

"I hope you didn't bring your paints. I certainly won't have you paint me in my robe." Red flashed in her cheeks.

"Actually, they're right outside. But I didn't come to paint you tonight."

"Then why did you come, Vincent?"

"To see you. I just wanted to see you."

"And I've missed you. That's why I was playing tonight. I hoped you would be walking by and hear."

It's the violin, Vincent.

"I don't know why," Katherine continued, "but it felt right to play a sad song tonight."

"Yes, it was right."

"You are dressed all in black. Has someone died?"

"Yes."

"Your wife?" she asked, alarm in her voice.

"My wife? How did you know I was married?"

She pointed at his left hand.

He looked down at his gold wedding band. "Ahh. I'm found out. But Kate didn't die. A friend did."

"I'm sorry. Death is a hard but necessary part of life."

"I guess it is."

"Would you like me to play some more for you?"

"I would. Please?"

He leaned his head back, closed his eyes and listened to her play. The violin's sweet sound soothed his soul and a smile crossed his face. Jill appeared in his mind. She was whole, standing on Monet's Japanese bridge at Giverny on both of her legs. She smiled at him, her eyes joyful and free of pain. "It's okay, Vincent," she said. "It really is okay." Jill was happy. The knowledge lifted his heart.

Katherine finished playing and Vincent opened his eyes. "Ending so soon."

"I've played for an hour, Vincent."

"Whoa. I guess I lost track of time."

She put the violin away then got up from the bed. "You should go now."

He stood up. "You are so much like my wife." The words came out on their own, surprising him.

She came around the bed and stood before him. "You said her name is Kate."

He nodded, still surprised by what he'd just said.

"My father called me Kate. Or sometimes Katie."

"Is he gone?"

"Yes. Shortly before I married Jethro."

"I'm sorry."

"Don't be. He is at peace now." She walked over to the open door. "You'll come again? This time to paint?"

"I will. Goodnight, Katherine."

"Good night, Vincent."

He stopped in the doorway and turned back. *It's the violin, Vincent.* "Katherine, when you want me, play the violin. If I'm nearby, I'll hear it."

"I don't know, Vincent. I've played it during the last several days and you haven't come."

"I'll come. I promise you." He tapped his ear. "I'll keep one ear open for you."

She smiled. "Then I will play to call you."

He answered her smile with one of his own then left her. He closed the door and slid the locks shut. He walked down the hall, feeling his way in the darkness. The house was eerily quiet. He stepped out the front door into a chilly drizzle. Street lamps cast ghostly shadows about him. He walked through the wrought iron gate and started up the street, heading for Payne Avenue. He passed driveways with vintage 1920s cars. The streets were void of life. He walked on, wondering if this time, he would not go back to his present. He crossed Payne and walked by a huge, brick mansion Liz had said was once the home of the DeGraff family—the same family that had founded DeGraff Memorial Hospital. As he drew closer to the intersection, he saw a Ford Explorer turn the corner, radio blaring. Relieved, he picked up his pace. Reaching the intersection, he stepped back into his present.

CHAPTER 13

The remainder of Kate's visit sped pleasantly by. They went shopping and chose the colors and curtains for the master bathroom, agreeing on a green and gold theme. They bought a toilet with a raised tank and pull chain and they replaced the corroded hardware with brass faucets and towel racks. While Vincent worked in the bathroom, Kate worked in her office. She wasn't writing fiction, but at least she was using her new space, so Vincent kept quiet. She also spent time with Liz, usually in the evenings. Selfishly, Vincent wanted her for himself, but he knew Liz needed her so he kept his mouth shut.

He visited Katherine twice during this time. On both nights, Kate was out with Liz and hearing the violin, he quickly changed into his painting clothes and hurried to the third floor. He began Katherine's portrait, having her pose exactly as she had for his sketch. Then he set the sketch beside her and he went to work. Her patience impressed him. Most models would not sit so long. Nor would they remain quiet and let him concentrate like she did.

When he left Katherine the second night, he had to walk further to exit 1926. The walk fascinated him and he drank in the things that were different from his present. Ford Model T's and Model A's, and Chevrolet Touring Cars and Roadsters sat in the driveways of the houses on Goundry Street that were in themselves, marvelous, because these same houses that were shabby and divided into apartments in his own time, served in 1926, as single family homes, looking fresh and meticulously cared for. He crossed Payne Avenue and continued on passed the DeGraff Mansion until he reached Vandervoort. He stopped and gazed for several minutes at trolley tracks in the brick street. Grinning, he crossed them, and still finding himself in 1926 and beginning to once again worry that he wouldn't make it back to his own time, he picked up his pace. But a four-story building brought him to a halt at the corner of Main Street and Goundry. Storefronts occupied the building's first floor and rows of windows wrapped around the second through fourth floors. A sign informed him he was looking at the Hotel Lincoln. He wondered when the building had come down and why.

Drawing in a long breath, Vincent debated which way he should go. He could continue up Goundry to Webster, turn left and go over the canal bridge. He glanced south, up Main Street, wondering if the Delaware Bridge existed in 1926. The darkness was thick, the light from the streetlights murky and faint, and he couldn't see if a bridge was there or not. Deciding to take Main at least as far as Tremont Street, he started walking, shivering both from the cold and from the thought that he would not make it back to Kate. He was nearly to Tremont when headlights approached, flickering in the darkness. Vincent watched as the lights sank lower, a smile crossing his face. Without a doubt, the one-ton pickup truck that passed him had come down over a bridge. He broke into a run, crossing over Sweeney and the Delaware Street Bridge. The air around him shimmered, seeming to press in on him as he came down off the bridge and to his relief, stepped into his own time.

Compared to the speed the pickup truck had been going, cars flew by him. He jumped back from the street and clung to a pole. A Corvette sped buy, music blaring. Vincent swung around and looked back over the bridge. The Corvette continued on its way, making a right onto Sweeney Street. He'd made it back this time, but what about the next time? How much farther would he have to walk? Which time when he traveled to 1926 would be the time in which he would not make it back to his own present? Dare he keep going back? Or should he stop? He was playing with something he didn't understand and he knew that he should stop playing with it. But as he walked home, he knew he wouldn't stop. Katherine's portrait must be painted.

Sunday came all too fast and because it was their last night together, Vincent took Kate to Schimschack's Restaurant for a farewell dinner. Located atop the escarpment in Sanborn on Upper Mountain Road, the restaurant was, Elsie had assured him, a local favorite. The building hugged the side of the escarpment, it's façade constructed of small, white, horizontal bricks. The inside was simple yet classic, a wooden bar on an upper level, wooden tables and chairs a few stairs below. Tablecloths of shimmering teal covered the tables and the chairs were antiqued and painted several different colors. An entire wall of windows overlooked the escarpment and Vincent was glad when they were shown to a table along this wall. Once seated, he looked out on the wooded hillside and farmer's fields below.

"Wow," Kate said, also admiring the view.

"For sure," he agreed. Turning from the window, he gazed at his wife. She was beautiful in a spaghetti strap, black dress, her hair curling around her face and shoulders. She'd worn a different pair of glasses, still metal, but black and they gave her an alluring look. Vincent had donned his navy blue suit for the occasion.

"Elsie was right about the view," Kate said, still looking out the window.

"The view at the table is lovelier," he said.

She flashed him a smile, gratitude in her eyes.

Once they had ordered their dinners and received a bottle of champagne, Vincent said, "I don't want you to go, Kate."

"I know. Part of me doesn't want to go, Vincent."

"Then stay."

She stared down into her champagne glass. "Is that why you did the office? So that I'd stay with you?"

"No, I did the office because I wanted you to have a place to write like I have a place to paint."

She sighed and shook her head. "Oh, Vincent, you are so transparent. Don't you think I know what you want? You want me to quit my job and come live solely for you."

"That's not it, Kate. I want you to pursue your real dream. Your real passion."

"What I do in D.C. is my passion, Vincent."

He shook his head. "I don't believe that."

She sat back in her chair and gazed at him with sad eyes. "Why can't you love me for me and not some woman you think I am? Some woman you want me to be?"

"Because I know who you are, Kate. And right now, I believe you've put that person in a vault and locked the door."

"People change, Vincent. I've changed. Please, you have to accept that and stop believing in a pipe dream."

"You like the office." It was a statement, not a question.

"I do. And when I come here, I will use it. But I will not give up my work, Vincent. Either accept that fact or…"

"Or what, Kate?"

"Or we have no future. At least we don't have a happy one."

He stared at his beautiful wife in disbelief. "Your way or no way?"

The waitress brought their plates. Vincent thanked her and looked glumly down at his filet mignon.

"I love you, Vincent. I do. But I won't give up my independence."

"Nobody is asking you to."

"It seems that way to me."

Vincent stuck his fork into the filet. "Let me just ask you one thing, Kate. Where is your novel?"

"You know where it is. It's in my desk drawer at the townhouse."

"Would you mail it to me? I'd like to read it again."

Suddenly, she smiled, her eyes laughing. "Yes, Vincent, I will. I want you to read it again. Because once you do, you'll see I'm right. Fiction is not really my shtick."

Vincent held out his hand. "Bet your wrong."

She raised her eyebrows. "You're on." She shook his hand. "If, after you read it, you still think it's good, I'll send it to my friend, Regina."

"Ah, your college friend. Where is she working now?"

"Random House. If she says it's publishable, I'll finish the book."

"You mean that, Kate? If she likes the book, you'll finish it?"

"Actually, she was my only college friend. Besides you, that is. And yes, I'll finish the book. But, here's your end of the bargain. If, after reading the book again, you realize my fiction stinks, or even if you insist I send it to Reggie and she says it's not publishable, you have to divide your time between the townhouse and North Tonawanda. Just like I do."

"You're tough, Katherine Malloy Vermay."

"Damn tough."

He grinned. "I'm going to win."

"Confident are we?"

"Most definitely."

As he ate his dinner, Vincent silently celebrated his victory. She was cracking. If she weren't, she never would have made the deal with him.

*   *   *

"What's she like?" Katherine asked.

"Who?"

"Your wife."

Vincent peered around the painting. "Kate?"

"Of course I mean Kate."

"She's beautiful. And talented."

"How long have you been married?"

"Fifteen years." He went back to painting.

Katherine absently plucked the strings on the violin neck. The notes were high and popping. "Do you love her, Vincent?"

The question startled him. He stood with the paintbrush poised in mid air. "Why would you ask me that, Katherine?"

"Because you don't talk about her."

Vincent set his brush and palette on the bed. He knelt before Katherine and said, "Yes, I love her. Very much. But she does have a stubborn, independent streak that is sometimes...well...very trying."

"Like how?"

"She doesn't always make what I think are the right choices."

Surprise flooded Katherine's eyes. "You allow her choices?"

"Yes. That surprises you?"

She shook her head in wonder.

Vincent chuckled. He straightened, went to the window and looked out. A produce delivery van ambled by. "I'm afraid I am what you would call a modern man, Katherine. I give Kate a great deal of liberty."

"A modern man," she repeated. "I can assure you that Jethro is not a modern man."

Vincent turned back from the window. "I would call a man who hits his wife and locks her in her bedroom a barbaric man."

Katherine hugged her violin. "He has not hit me for quite some time now."

"Does he know you're with child?"

She shook her head.

"Why not?"

"The time has not been right. I've tried to tell him but..."

"Has he even come up here to visit you, Katherine? Has he come since he hit you?"

Again, she shook her head.

Vincent's hands formed fists. He wanted to beat Jethro Malloy to a pulp. "How far along are you?"

"About three months."

"You'll begin showing soon."

Her eyes begged him to understand her situation. Trouble was, he did understand it. What he didn't understand was that she submitted to it. He tried to stare her down, tried to penetrate her fear and motivate her to tell Jethro. But as he looked deeper into her lovely green eyes, he saw the truth and he said, "It's not Jethro's baby, is it?"

She crumbled, tears pouring from her eyes. She hugged her violin tighter. He squatted, grabbed the rocking chair arms. "Whose baby is it, Katherine?"

"No," she stammered. "I...can't...tell you."

"Yes, you can." His tone was firm, commanding her to tell him.

"Norman," she whispered, helplessly.

The word punched Vincent in the stomach, stealing his air and he gasped, "Norman Lassiter?"

"Yes." She started sobbing.

Vincent stood up. He went back to the window, peered out, but he didn't register what his eyes were looking at. He ran a hand through his thick hair. "Norman Lassiter," he muttered.

Between sobs, she managed, "If I tell Jethro, he'll make me end my pregnancy. He'll...oh, God, what am I going to do?"

"You must not tell him, Katherine." Vincent sat down on the bed. "Let me think."

She buried her face in her right hand. The violin's bow slid from her lap and fell to the floor.

Norman's child. But this child was never born. Which meant she had told Jethro. Her sobs crashed into his brain and he covered his ears with his hands. *Think! Think, Vincent! Don't mess with the past. Shut up, Douglas!*

"Screw the past!" Vincent shouted. "Just screw it."

"What?" Katherine asked. She was settling down, regaining control of herself.

Vincent fell to his knees before her and took her hand. "Promise me you won't tell Jethro, Katherine. Promise me."

She nodded.

"Good. When will Norman be back?"

"I'm not sure. I never really know when he's coming. But he did say he would come this month."

"Okay, listen to me. When he comes, tell him you are pregnant with his child. Unless I miss my guess, he'll be thrilled. Pack your things and go with him."

"Go with Norman?"

"Yes. Give your child the loving father he or she deserves. This house, Jethro's money, it's not important. What is important is your safety and the baby's safety. And your happiness is important. Norman Lassiter can give you that. The man loves you more than life itself, Katherine."

"But I don't love him, Vincent. Not like a wife should love her husband."

"And you love Jethro that way?"

"Strange, but yes, for all his cruelty I do. I can't explain it, but I do."

"And yet you slept with Norman."

She turned away, ashamed.

"Why, Katherine?"

"You wouldn't understand."

"I think I would. You needed to feel loved that day. You needed warmth and human contact. You needed—"

"Stop it!" she pleaded. "Don't speak any more of that night." She grabbed the front of his shirt. "Stop!"

"You will do what I say? You'll leave with Norman?"

"I don't know."

"Katherine, you must protect this child. Jethro would never accept it. He will never let you carry it to term. You said that yourself. Could you go through with an abortion? Could you?"

She pressed her abdomen, alarm on her face. "No, no, Vincent, I couldn't. Not even for Jethro."

"Then do what I say."

"Katherine!" Jethro Malloy's voice boomed up the staircase. "Katherine, who is up there with you?"

"Oh, he's home," Katherine said, rising from the rocking chair. The violin fell from her lap, but Vincent caught it before it hit the floor. He straightened, stayed at her side, and faced the door.

Jethro Malloy appeared. He was a stocky man of medium weight. He wore a brown, pinstripe suit. His bushy eyebrows and mustache were as gray as his hair. His eyes were steel blue, lacking any hint of kindness. Vincent could only wonder what had made Katherine Mann fall in love with him. Jethro peered at Vincent with hard eyes. "What is going on here?"

"Jethro," Katherine said, forcing a smile. "You're home."

He ignored her. "And you are?" His eyes fell on the painting.

"Vincent Vermay, Sir." Vincent stepped forward and held out his hand. "Mrs. Malloy has hired me to paint her portrait."

Jethro accepted Vincent's hand. His grip was strong. To Katherine, he said, "Why are you having this done?"

She came to him, slipping her arms around his left arm. "For you, Jethro. For your birthday."

He gazed at his wife with unreadable eyes.

Vincent rubbed his hands together. "Well, Mr. Malloy, it looks like you have walked in on your surprise."

"Yes, it does look that way, doesn't it?" He disengaged himself from Katherine. "You are done for the day, Mr. Vermay. I wish to be alone with my wife."

Vincent didn't want to leave Katherine. He wanted to stay and protect her from this man she had married. It took every ounce of his being not to punch the man. "Then I shall go. Besides, my wife will be waiting for me."

The hard look in Jethro's eyes softened. "Then you understand my desires, Mr. Vermay."

"Very much so." He handed Katherine her violin. "Your violin, Mrs. Malloy. Don't forget to play it again soon."

"I always play it, Mr. Vermay," she assured him.

Vincent quickly capped his paints and stowed the palette and brush beneath the easel. He said his goodbyes and departed.

Mrs. Colllins met him at the front door. "He is very angry 'bout somethin'."

Vincent glanced back up the stairs. "Do you have any idea about what?"

"No, Sir. But I fear for her. I do."

"I'll be back soon. Can you watch out for her?"

"I'll try, Sir. I will."

"Good." He gave her an encouraging smile.

As he walked out of the Malloy gate, he saw a woman carrying a black leather bag walking up the Reilly front steps. Her hair was bright red and braided in one long braid.

"Dr. Reilly!" he called, running towards her. "Dr. Emma Reilly?"

She turned and watched him approach with questioning eyes.

"Hello, Doctor. My name is Vincent Vermay."

"Mr. Vermay. How did you know my name?"

"Katherine Malloy told me you live next door."

"Katherine did?" She gave Vincent a quizzical look. "I'm surprised the woman knows anything beyond the third floor of that house."

"Well, she does. I'm an artist. I'm painting her portrait as a gift for Jethro."

"A gift? As if the man deserves one."

Vincent let her remark go. "I was wondering if you would do me a favor."

"Which would be?"

"If you're here, at home when Jethro leaves, will you check on her for me?"

Emma Reilly gave him a knowing look. "Just how badly does he treat her? I've long suspected, Mr. Vermay."

"Very badly."

"And how do you expect me to get to her?"

"Mrs. Collins will let you in."

Emma nodded. "I will do what I can."

Vincent smiled. "Thank you. Thank you very much." Emma turned to go, but Vincent grabbed her arm. "Wait."

"There's more?"

"She's pregnant. Nearly three months along. You should know that."

"Yes, I should."

Vincent released her arm. "Okay, I have to go now." He gazed at her a moment. There were traces of both Emmett and Liz in her face. "Goodbye."

"Good day."

Vincent walked out of 1926 with fear in his heart. He knew by alerting Mrs. Collins and Emma Reilly, he'd done all he could to safeguard Katherine. But had he succeeded in convincing her to run away with Norman? He hoped so.

It wasn't until he reached the Victorian and opened the front door that he realized if Katherine had done as he'd advised her to then Kate could very well have not been born. Panic overtook him and he charged up the stairs. *Idiot! Can't you think? Damn you!* He snatched the phone out of the cradle and punched in Kate's cell phone number.

"Hello?"

He sank onto the bed, relieved. "Kate."

"Vincent, what's up?"

"Just wanted to hear your voice."

"How sweet. But I can't hang. I'm on my way to a meeting. Oh, watch your mail. I sent you a package."

"Great."

"Love you, Vincent."

"Back at you."

He hung up and lay back on the bed. He banged his fist on his head. "No more, Vincent," he said. "You will meddle no more."

✤   ✤   ✤

Kate's package arrived the next day. Vincent tore it open and read her note. *Vincent, here it is. Don't gag too much while reading it. Love, Kate.* He ran his hand over the cover page. He read the title, *Stranger in Town* by Katherine Malloy Vermay.

"I won't gag, Kate," he said.

He read the first three chapters at the kitchen table over a tuna sandwich and a cola. He was not a writer but he knew good writing when he read it and a broad smile crossed his face. She was good. Damn good. She would have to send it to Regina as promised.

He read for another hour, Kate's descriptive passages painting pictures that drew him in. Vincent found himself reading her grandmother's story, thinly disguised as fiction, but Katherine's story nonetheless. Kate's descriptions of the beatings Jethro gave his wife and the bruises and cuts they left behind jolted Vincent. He sat stock-still. How had she known about the beatings? Surely Katherine would not have told her about them. He remembered how she'd feared the third floor bedroom. How she had left the summer of her 18th year and not returned. While she had made peace with Katherine a year later over the telephone, she hadn't visited her again until Lydia had moved her to Maryland. Had Kate stepped back in time that summer and discovered her grandfather's cruelty? The questions rolled around in his head. And they likely would have kept rolling except that the doorbell rang, interrupting them. He left the manuscript on the kitchen table and went to answer the door.

Tracy Woodward stood on his front porch. "Hey," she said.

"Tracy, come in."

She entered, unzipped her jacket, but didn't remove it. She reached up to take off her Buffalo Bison's cap, thought better of it, and left it on. "I hope I'm not interrupting something."

"Not really. What's up?"

"I…" She trailed off. She looked tired and sad, and she had lost at least ten pounds. Dark circles were prevalent beneath her eyes.

"How about a sandwich? I've got tuna fish."

She shook her head, but then said, "Maybe I better. I haven't eaten yet today."

He led her into the kitchen and pointed at the table. As he collected Kate's manuscript and set it on the cupboard, he said, "Sit." He waited until she sat then asked, "How's your mom and dad?"

"Functioning. Mom never smiles anymore."

He quickly made her a sandwich; glad he hadn't eaten all the tuna. "It'll take time, Tracy. All three of you have to grieve."

"I guess. I miss Jill."

He set the sandwich in front of her. "That's normal. Soda, milk or water?"

"Milk."

He poured her a giant glass and set in on the table next to her plate. Sitting down across from her, he said, "Eat."

She took a bite, chewed then swallowed.

He pushed the glass of milk closer. "Drink." She obeyed, drinking a quarter of the glass. "What have you been up to?"

She shrugged. "I've seen Pastor McMichael a few times."

"The pastor from Salem?"

She nodded.

"That's good, Trace." He pointed at the sandwich. "Keep eating."

She took another bite, chewed, but was unable to swallow it. Alarm crossed her face and she jumped up, running to the sink. Vincent ran after her, reaching her just as vomit, filled with undigested tuna and a milky glaze, poured out of her mouth. He slipped his arms around her waist and held her while she threw up, gagging and coughing as she did. When at last she was finished, she leaned back against him, tears spilling from her eyes. Supporting her with his left arm, he turned on the faucet and said, "Rinse your mouth out, Trace."

She did as he instructed, cupping her hand and spooning the water into her mouth. Her hand shook and she got water on her neck and shirt collar. She spit, closed her eyes a second then said, "Okay."

Vincent turned off the water.

"You're sink," she said.

"Don't worry about it. I'll clean it later." Deliberately ignoring the mess she had vomited, he scooped her up in his arms and left the kitchen. She didn't protest, laying her head on his shoulder, her cold hands circling round his neck. He laid her on the couch in the parlor and covered her with an afghan. He sat on the coffee table and she gazed at him, her skin pale, her eyes filled with overwhelming pain and sadness. Resting his elbows on his thighs, he folded his hands and rested his chin on them. Neither of them spoke for several minutes. She continued gazing at him and he continued to wonder how he could help her.

"I'm sorry," she said, her voice strained. "I shouldn't have come here."

"You can come here anytime, Tracy," he said and meant it. He wanted to help this young girl who had so loved her sister and was obviously lost without her.

"Really?"

He nodded and held out his hand. "Friends?"

She took his hand. Her skin was still cold, her hand small and delicate inside his own. She was seventeen years old, but lying beneath the afghan on his couch, Bison's cap low on her forehead, she looked about ten.

"I miss her so much, Vincent."

He lightly squeezed her hand. "I know, kiddo."

"I can't sleep. I can't eat."

"You're grieving, Trace. Have you talked to your parents about this?"

She shook her head. "Dad's...he's...and Mom...they don't need to be worrying about me."

"Worrying about your children comes with parenthood. They love you. Believe me, they'll want to help you."

But still she shook her head.

Vincent sighed. She was a tough kid, but she couldn't go this alone. She'd been to see Salem's minister, but Vincent wasn't so sure Pastor McMichael was the person Tracy needed. He believed the minister could handle Tracy's grief, but it appeared as if Tracy wasn't letting her. Maybe because the pastor was a good friend with Mr. and Mrs. Woodward and while Vincent knew that Pastor McMichael would never break Tracy's confidence, Tracy might not believe that she wouldn't. So Vincent did something he'd never done for a teenager. He said, "Trace, when missing Jill gets so bad you can't stand it, call me. Okay? Promise me you'll call me? Anytime."

"Could I really?"

"Yes."

She managed a smile. Her eyes slipped shut then opened, searching for him. He gently squeezed her hand again. "Go ahead," he encourged. You're exhausted. I'll be right here in the house."

She closed her eyes and within minutes, he felt the tension leave the hand he was holding. She slept for four hours. When she awoke, he was sitting in the red wingback chair reading Kate's manuscript. She pushed off the afghan and sat up, flinging her legs over the side of the couch. "What time is it?"

"Almost five-thirty."

"I should get going."

"Want a lift home?"

She shook her head. "I can walk. It's not far."

He stood up, set Kate's book on the seat of the chair, and went to Tracy. "Then how 'bout I walk you home."

"Okay."

They walked in silence, but Vincent could tell she was glad he'd accompanied her. The air was unusually warm for May, although the sky was cloudy, promising rain. When they reached her driveway, she looked up at him and said, "Thanks."

"You have my regular phone and my cell phone?"

"I do."

"Don't forget your promise."

"To call you. I won't."

"Try to eat some dinner."

"I'll try."

He waited until she disappeared inside the house then headed back to the Victorian. She'd made him a promise and if he knew anything about Tracy, it was that she kept her promises. He felt confident about that. What he doubted was his ability to see the girl through the painfully sad days ahead of her.

❧   ❧   ❧

"Liz!" Vincent called, walking up the Reilly driveway. "Liz, are you here?"

"In the garage!"

She greeted him dressed in coveralls, a smudge of grease on her chin. The Mustang's hood was up.

"Problem?"

"No, just changing the oil. What brings you by?" She wiped her hands on a rag that hung from a hook in the garage wall.

He held up the box he was carrying. "This is Kate's novel. Would you read it and tell me what you think?"

"You mean she pulled it out of mothballs?"

"She did. I had to pull a few teeth though."

Liz laughed. "Of course I'll read it." She took the box. "The Mustang will be back on the road next week. I owe you a spin."

"Darn right you do."

She ran her hand along the car's fender. "I let Jill and her date use it for the senior prom last year. She was thrilled."

"I bet she was."

"God, I miss her, Vincent. I keep going over and over her treatment in my mind. I missed something. I failed her."

Vincent took Liz by the shoulders. "Stop that. You did everything you could."

"And it wasn't enough." Her lower lip trembled and tears filled her eyes. But she didn't cry, her body stiffening as she fought back the desire. She turned back to the car. "I have to get this finished here," she said, dismissing him.

Instead of leaving, he laid his hand on her shoulder. "How about we go grab a hot dog at Nestor's?"

She shook off his hand. "Not now. I'll take a rain check."

"Liz?"

Staring at the Mustang's engine, she said, "I said not now."

"Let me help you, Liz."

She slammed her hand down on the car's fender. "And just what do you think you can do, Vincent? Jill's dead. You sure as hell can't bring her back. You can't bring any of them back. Not Alan, not my mother, and not Jill." She stared at him with eyes so filled with deep caverns of hurt that he involuntarily stepped back from her. "Now leave me be." She turned on her heels and left him standing there, shocked, unable to fathom how anyone could live in that amount of pain and sadness.

❧   ❧   ❧

"She's in trouble, isn't she, Vincent?" There was fear in Kate's voice.

Vincent clutched the phone, wishing he didn't have to agree with Kate, but knowing he had to. "Yes. And she won't talk to me."

"Have you said anything to Elsie or Emmett?"

"No, not yet."

"I'll call them. I'll call Liz too."

"Good. I think if Liz could spend time with you, it would help too. When do you think you can get up here again?"

"I'm not sure yet. But I'll call Liz every day, without fail. I promise you that."

"Okay. But you're being here would be better."

"I know. I'll see what I can do about my schedule."

Your schedule? Screw it, Kate. Come home. Come home now and take care of Liz.

She interrupted his thoughts, asking, "Have you done any reading?"

"Yes."

"And?"

He wanted to ask her how she knew about Katherine's beatings, but he decided not to bring it up in a phone conversation. "Jury is still out. But I'm leaning toward Regina."

"Oh, you know, like this was even a fair bet. Of course you're going to say it's wonderful."

"I knew you were going to say that. So, I've given the manuscript to Liz to read."

"Really?"

"Yep. And if she thinks the same way I do you're cooked, love."

"You are sneaky."

Vincent laughed into the phone. "As you always tell me, don't pout."

"I'm not. But I'm glad you gave it to her. If only that it gives her something to do in her spare time. Maybe Liz has enough objectivity to see my fiction for what it is."

"Maybe," Vincent agreed. But he doubted it. The book was too good.

As he'd promised Katherine, Vincent kept his ear open, waiting to hear the violin. But the days passed by and each night he fell asleep wondering why she wasn't calling him. Had something happened to her that prevented her from playing her violin? Was he no longer supposed to go back in time? He refused to believe that he wasn't meant to finish her portrait. And he couldn't finish it without being with her, having her sitting in the rocker with the violin in her lap. To occupy his time, he scrubbed down each room in the house, cleaning every nook and cranny. He sketched ideas for the dining room and set them aside until Kate could see them. He wandered out to the carriage house, sat in the old Ford and decided he would get it running. Searching online, he found and bought new tires for it, having them shipped overnight service. He tinkered with it for two days before it started up. He whooped for joy then drove it out onto the driveway. Emmett Reilly stood on the sidewalk. Vincent let the engine run and jumped out. "What do you think, Emmett?" he yelled.

Emmett grinned. "Take me for a ride."

"It's not registered yet."

"Who the hell cares, son?"

"You're right. What the hell? Hop in."

They drove around the block, fellow motorists in their modern day cars honking and waving at them. They passed the Lassiter house where Doug was rolling his lawn. Seeing them, he yelled, "Now there's a real car!"

Vincent blew the horn. As they approached the Victorian, Emmett said, "One more time."

The second time around the block, Vincent saw Liz standing on her office porch. He nudged Emmett and pointed. They both waved at her. She waved back, actually smiling at them. They pulled into the Victorian's driveway and Vincent killed the engine. "Nice ride, huh, Emmett?"

"Beautiful."

Vincent climbed out. "Think I'll wash and wax her. It's warm enough today."

Emmett didn't hear him. "My Lizzie is sad, Vincent," he said. "I'm worried about her."

Vincent walked around to Emmett's side of the car and opened the door. "I know she is."

Emmett shook his head. "What can I do to help her?"

"Be there for her."

Emmett got out of the car. "I know how she feels. I dealt with Marlene's death by not dealing with it. I shut myself off."

Vincent closed the car door. "Everything takes time. You're dealing with it now."

The old man nodded. "Thanks to Douglas."

Vincent ran a hand through his hair. "What did he say that got to you, Emmett?"

"Wasn't so much what he said as how he is."

Vincent clapped a hand on Emmett's shoulder. "Then that tells you. Don't worry so much about what to say to Liz. Just be with her. Just be yourself."

Emmett sighed. "Trouble is, the state she's in, I don't know if that's enough."

CHAPTER 14

"I'm sorry about your friend, Vincent," Sarah said in his ear.

"Thanks, Sis."

"I know you hoped she'd make it."

"I sure did."

"At least she's not suffering anymore."

Clichés. Vincent ran a hand through his tangled hair. Conversations always resorted to them when someone died. He pushed the blankets down to his waist, scratched his bare abdomen and said, "How was Philadelphia?"

She giggled.

"What? Tell me."

"Are you sitting down?"

"I'm still lying in bed. It's five-thirty in the morning here, which means its three-thirty there. Don't you ever sleep, little sister?"

"Actually, I just got home."

"I didn't realize quiet little Silverton has a night life."

"You, dear brother, would be surprised. But, since you won't fall over when I say this, I'll say it. Mom and Dad agreed to come out here for Thanksgiving."

Vincent's eyes grew wide. "You're joking, right?"

"Dead serious. You and Kate better plan on coming as well."

"I'll tell her."

Sarah sighed. He heard the creak of bedsprings come over the line. "Guess I'll have to learn how to cook a turkey."

"I'll help you."

His sister yawned then said, "Good. Now, hang up. I need some sleep. Love you, bro."

"I love you."

Smiling, Vincent hung up the phone. Was it possible? Were his parents really giving in, accepting defeat where Sarah was concerned. Punching his pillow a few times, he rolled onto his side and went back to sleep, feeling for the first time in years, that Sarah and his parents just might work things out.

🍁   🍁   🍁

Vincent could stand the waiting no longer. He had to find out how Katherine was. If she wouldn't play the violin and call him, he would play the violin and call her. He didn't know if his playing the instrument would work, but he was not going to sit around any longer and do nothing.

He showered, slicked his hair back with gel and dressed in brown, pleated slacks, a white shirt and brown suspenders. The outfit was as close as he could get to 1920's fashion and since he wouldn't be painting this trip, he had to dress appropriately. He would just check on her, make plans for future painting sessions, and high tail it back to the present.

As he hurried up the stairs to the third floor, he repeated his new mantra, "You will not meddle. You will not meddle."

He switched on the bedroom light and went immediately to the violin case. He opened the case and removed the violin, admiring its craftsmanship once again. Then, standing in the center of the room, beneath the chandelier, he ran the bow across the strings. It screeched hideously, but he ignored the screeching and persisted, sliding the bow, pressing his fingers on the strings. "Katherine," he said. "Katherine. Let me go to Katherine."

And it happened. The air shimmered, pressed in on him and then he was standing under the single light bulb in Katherine's sparsely furnished room. She lay in bed with her eyes closed, perspiration covering her face, her hair damp from her sweat.

"Katherine?" He discarded the violin and bow on the rocking chair and went to her side. "Katherine?" He pulled the blanket down. Her white, ankle-length nightgown was soaked with blood at her groin.

"Oh, God!" he cried. He ran to the door and tried to open it. Of course it was locked. He hadn't come in through the door this time. He pounded on it. "Mrs. Collins! Mrs. Collins!" No one came. He pounded again. "Mrs. Collins!" He rammed his shoulder into the door. "Come on, open." He rammed the door again and again. At last, he felt it give. He rammed it twice more and the locks snapped. The door flew open and he nearly tumbled down the stairs. He grabbed the banister and saved himself.

"Katherine," he said, returning to the bed. "Katherine, can you hear me? It's Vincent. I'm going to help you."

He lifted her from the bed and she groaned. There was blood on the back of her nightgown as well. It was wet and sticky against his skin. He didn't hesitate. He took her to Emma Reilly. He had promised himself he wouldn't meddle. But there was one fact he knew. Katherine Malloy did not die in 1926. Getting her help should not damage his present.

He carried her out of the Victorian into a dark, cloudy night. Fog was rolling in off the Niagara River. He cut across Emma's yard and ran up the porch steps. He kicked on the door with his foot. "Dr. Reilly! Hurry! Dr. Reilly!"

The door opened and Emma stood in front of him wearing a maroon, flowered robe and holding a book. Her hair hung down. "Mr. Vermay?"

"Help her. Please."

"Follow me." She led him upstairs to what was now Liz's bedroom. In 1926, the room housed a bed, a roll top desk, file cabinets and a medicine cabinet. Emma pointed at the bed. "Lay her down."

When her body touched the bed, Katherine cried out, grabbing her abdomen.

Emma examined her.

"I think she lost the baby," Vincent said.

The doctor turned from her patient. "Wait outside, Mr. Vermay."

He almost protested. He could help. Remembering he was in 1926, he nodded and backed out of the room. He paced in the hall. Katherine's blood had smeared his hands and soaked into his shirt.

At last Emma emerged from the room. She was wiping her hands on a towel.

"Is she all right?"

"She's lost a great deal of blood. I want to hospitalize her but she refuses."

"She's conscious."

Emma nodded. "The bleeding was due to an abortion performed by someone who did not know the proper technique."

"Oh, God."

"I'll keep her here. I'll do all I can."

"Will she be able to have children?"

"It's too early to tell."

He wanted more details. Did she have an infection? Was she cut inside? But he again reminded himself that he was in 1926 and Dr. Emma Reilly would not answer his questions. He was a man, a man who was not Katherine's husband.

"She wants to see you. Not too long, Mr. Vermay. She needs to rest."

Katherine lay on her side, curled up in a fetal position. In addition to what she had done for Katherine medically, Emma had also changed her nightgown and washed her face. She looked peaceful in the pale office light. She heard him come in. "Vincent," she said, her voice weak and soft.

He knelt down beside the bed. "Hi."

"I prayed you would come."

"What happened?"

She shook her head.

"Okay. You can tell me later."

"He knew about the baby, Vincent. I don't know how but he knew. He sent Mrs. Collins away. He sent her to England to visit her sister. Then he brought this man who…" Tears filled her eyes.

"Shh." He laid his hand on her forehead. Her skin was hot. "Don't talk about it."

"It hurt. God, it hurt."

"I know." He stroked her hair.

"He murdered my baby." Tears fell from her eyes.

Emma Reilly came in. "You should go now. She must rest."

Vincent smiled down at Katherine. "You listen to your doctor. It's going to be all right."

"You'll come back?"

"You bet." He kissed her forehead. He didn't care how inappropriate the action was.

Emma walked him downstairs to the front door. Hand on the doorknob, he said, "Thank you."

"You're welcome."

"Do you need someone to sit with her while you work? I could do that."

"No. I'll send one of my nurses over to do that. Just come back and visit her. You may be just her portrait painter, but I see she's quite fond of you."

"I'm a married man, Doctor. I love my wife."

"I wouldn't suggest otherwise."

Vincent opened the door. "I'll be back tomorrow night to see her."

"Hopefully, you will find her much improved."

Vincent returned to Katherine's room within the dark and silent Victorian. The door hung open on one hinge, the wood busted around each slide lock. He fought the desire to hunt down Jethro Malloy and kill him. He picked up the violin. He had to take it back with him so he could come back to 1926. Or did he? He stopped halfway to the door. The violin case sat beside the porcelain bowl and pitcher on the dresser. It was open. Was it possible that this violin was in two places at the same time? He peered into the case. The violin lay nestled in the velvet. Vincent shook his head. *Two violins? Damn, I really am in the middle of something I'll never understand.*

Carrying the present day violin protectively under his arm, he left the Victorian and walked through thick fog until he crossed the Delaware Street Bridge into present day Tonawanda.

❦   ❦   ❦

Katherine was not alone when Vincent arrived the next day. Norman Lassiter sat on the bed beside her, gently wiping her face with a damp washcloth. He talked to her in soft, loving tones, tender eyes gazing down at her pale face. She slept unaware of his ministrations.

"Norman," Vincent said, entering the room.

"Vincent." He stood up, stretching out his hand.

They shook and Vincent said, "The nurse let me in."

Norman nodded. "The infection hasn't abated." He dunked the cloth in a bowl of water, squeezed it, and laid it on Katherine's forehead. She did not stir. "She had a bad night. She should be in a hospital, Vincent."

"She still refuses to go?"

"She doesn't want the town to find out about this."

"Who called you?"

"Emma did. I took the first train up from the City. Understand you found her."

Vincent waved his hand. "No big deal."

Norman's eyes held gratitude. "Thank you. I don't know what I'd do if..." He took hold of Katherine's hand. "She has to be all right."

Vincent laid a reassuring hand on Norman's shoulder. "She's strong, Norman."

He shook his head. "I want to kill him."

"No. Don't do that. She needs you free, not rotting in jail."

"She would be free of him."

"Norman, look at me." The young actor obeyed. "You can do more for her if you remain a free man."

Reluctantly, Norman agreed. "You're right."

Katherine moaned, her eyes fluttered, but did not open.

"I thought he loved her. That's why I didn't fight for her. She's fond of me, but she loved him so I let her marry him. You should have seen him court her, Vincent. He fooled me."

"Katherine too."

"Katherine too. Do you know where he is?"

Vincent shook his head.

"Did you know she was expecting?"

"Yes."

"She didn't tell me. Probably didn't want to hurt me until she had to. Just the thought of her having his child." Norman shuddered.

Vincent bit his tongue. As much as he wanted to, he couldn't tell him that the baby had been his.

"I'm staying with her, Vincent. I'm staying here until she's well. I have a brother over on Tremont. Place to hang my hat."

"And when she's well?"

"Maybe I'll just stay on forever. North Tonawanda is a nice town."

"What about your acting career?"

Norman laughed. "I'm no star, Vincent."

"There's always the future."

He adamantly shook his head. "No. I must stay here. I must convince Katherine to leave him. It's the best thing she could do. Surely, you agree, Vincent?"

Vincent stood silent. As much as he wanted to agree, he couldn't. Katherine had to stay with Jethro. If she didn't, he would lose Kate.

Vincent stepped out of the Reilly house into a warm Spring day. A blue, cloudless sky hovered above him, the sun beaming down, glittering off the cars and street lamps. Two small boys, dressed in knickers and tweed jackets, raced towards him. He jumped out of their way. "Sorry, Mister!" one called back over his shoulder.

"No problem!" Vincent replied.

He knew he shouldn't linger in this time period. He should walk back into his own time and leave Katherine in Norman and Emma's care. But could he? Or should he? What if Norman succeeded in convincing Katherine to leave Jethro? Was it possible? Or would his efforts be in vain because they were supposed to fail? Katherine had lost the baby she was supposed to lose. But Vincent had saved her. He'd brought her to Emma. Vincent scratched his chin. Who had saved her originally? By stepping into another's place and saving her, had Vincent altered the course of events enough to make Norman's efforts succeed? He shook his head. It was all too mind-boggling.

One thing he did know, he wasn't going to leave his unfinished portrait of Katherine in Jethro's house. He strode over to the Victorian. The front door was still unlocked. He entered, stopped in the foyer, listened, and heard only an eerie silence. As he climbed the stairs, he again wondered where Jethro Malloy had gone. He didn't wonder long. Jethro sat in the rocking chair in Katherine's room. He wore his usual brown, pinstripe suit, white shirt and brown and white striped tie. He smoked a foul cigar as he rocked back and forth, staring at her empty bed. Vincent fought boiling rage as he stood glaring at Jethro.

"I know you are there, Mr. Vermay," Jethro said without turning his head.

"I came for the painting and my supplies," Vincent said between clenched teeth.

"Where is my wife?"

"Do you really care about her welfare, Jethro?"

"Where is she?"

"Safe from you. She's being cared for." Vincent marched to the bed and tore the bloodstained sheet from the mattress. He held it up. "She nearly died." He shook the sheet in Jethro's face. "You did this to her."

Jethro took a long drag on his cigar. He blew a perfectly round smoke ring. His eyes moved from the bloody sheet to Vincent. "She brought it on herself. She is married to me. I will not raise another man's child."

"She's not a possession that you own, Malloy. She's a person, a human being who, God knows why, loves and believes in you. At least, she did until now."

"Where is she?"

Vincent dropped the sheet. "You're not going to find out from me."

"Tell me."

"No."

Jethro stood up. "She slept with Lassiter. And you expect me to believe that she loves me."

"She slept with Norman because she was lonely. Because she needed to be loved. She married a man she believed to be charming and kind, and you brought her back her and locked her up. And beat her." He pointed at Malloy. "What kind of monster are you?"

"I fear, Mr. Vermay, that you are the type of husband who gives his wife far too much liberty."

"My wife is my partner. She is my best friend and she is the love of my life."

Malloy gazed at him with amused eyes. "Ah, the young and foolish. Take your paints and your painting and get out of my house."

"Gladly."

Malloy watched Vincent pack up his things. "I'll find out where she is," he said, confidently. "This town keeps no secrets from me."

"If you hurt her again, Malloy, I'll kill you."

Jethro chuckled. "You could try."

Vincent gave Malloy a scathing, final look before departing. He carried his painting, easel and box of paints over to the Reilly house. The nurse opened the front door just as he reached the top of the porch steps. She smiled at him, but did not linger, walking down the stairs and heading home. Emma stood in the doorway. She reached out a hand. "Let me help you, Vincent." He gave her the box of paints. She grabbed the handle and said, "Is that the portrait you started?"

"It is."

He leaned the easel against the wall, slid the painting from beneath his arm and held it up.

"It's spectacular," Emma said. "You must finish it."

"I can't finish it over there. I can't take it home. I need to be with Katherine to finish it. I don't know why, I just do."

Emma nodded her understanding. "You can paint here. When she's ready to return home, you can decide whether or not to go back over there."

"Thank you."

She led him to a sunroom at the end of the second floor. She'd furnished it with white wicker and tall ferns. "This should do. You'll have a lot of natural light." She pointed at two pole lamps. "Those should suffice for evening."

Vincent grinned. "It's perfect."

"Then get to work, Mr. Vermay."

"I shall do so immediately, Dr. Reilly."

❦   ❦   ❦

"Amazing," Norman said. He sat in one of the wicker chairs with his legs crossed, hands resting on the arms.

"What is?"

"That you can do that. You've brought life to that canvas."

Vincent worked on Katherine's chin. "Katherine brought life to the canvas, Norman. I'm just the painter."

"What are you going to dress her in, Vincent?"

Vincent dabbed the canvas then stepped back from the painting. "I believe I will put her in her white dress. Do you know which one I mean?"

"Ah, I do. It falls to her ankles. It's lacy with white-on-white embroidery."

Vincent glanced at Norman. "You sound like a tailor."

He laughed. "My father was a tailor, Mr. Vermay. I picked up a few things."

"The afternoon light is fading," Vincent said, sighing. "I believe I'm finished for the day." He set his palette and brush aside.

"Will you come back tomorrow?"

"Most likely." He capped the paints.

"Norman? Vincent?" Emma appeared in the doorway. "I need your help. Please come?"

Vincent and Norman exchanged a questioning glance then followed Emma down the hall to Katherine's room. Katherine thrashed about the bed, delirious. "Help me," she mumbled. "Help me."

"We have to get her into the bathtub," Emma said. "Vincent, get ice from the icebox."

Norman lifted Katherine in his arms and followed Emma into the bathroom while Vincent ran downstairs to the kitchen. He grabbed the first bowl he saw. It sat on the cupboard by the sink. He opened the icebox and scooped every chunk of ice he could find into the bowl then ran back upstairs.

Water spilled from a copper spout into the large, claw-footed bathtub. Katherine, still in her nightgown, sat in the tub. Emma and Norman were splashing the water on her. Seeing Vincent, Emma said, "Dump the ice in."

He did, the chunks clanging against the metal sides of the tub. He dropped to his knees, snatched up a piece of the ice and rubbed it along her legs.

"Come on, Katherine," Emma said, washing her face and neck. "Stay with us."

Norman's hands shook as he massaged Katherine's arms with ice. "Don't leave me, Katherine," he pleaded. "I love you."

They worked on her for fifteen minutes. At last, she opened her eyes. She stared at Norman, exhausted but lucid. He kissed her forehead. "Oh, darling," he said. "Katherine." He held her hand, pressing it to his chest.

"I'm tired," she said, her voice barely above a whisper.

"Then you should sleep."

Her eyes traveled from Norman to Vincent and finally to Emma. "Why am I in the bathtub?"

Emma brushed Katherine's hair back from her face. "We had to cool you off."

"It feels good."

Emma smiled. "I'm glad." She gestured at the door. "You two get out of here. I need to get Katherine dried off and back to bed."

They waited in the sunroom. Norman sat with his face buried in his hands and Vincent wondered if he was crying. But when Emma came for them and Norman looked up, his eyes were dry.

Katherine lay on her back in bed, her skin ghost-white pale, creases of pain around her eyes. She looked so sick it was frightening. Still, she managed a smile when she saw them. Norman knelt beside her and took hold of her hand. Vincent remained in the doorway.

Norman didn't speak. He just stared at Katherine with complete love. She looked into his eyes and, her bottom lip trembling, tears falling, she said, "I love you too, Norman."

CHAPTER 15

"Hello, Vincent."

Katherine, wearing a blue silk robe with the initials E.R. on it, stood in the sunroom doorway. She leaned against the doorframe for support.

"Katherine." He set his palette and brush on a wicker stand and went to her, taking her by the arm. "Come in."

She leaned heavily on him. He helped her sit down in a wicker rocking chair. Just the small exertion of getting from the door to the chair drained color from her face. "I have never been so weak," she said in an apologetic tone.

He knelt beside the chair. "It's okay. You've been through a lot."

"You're very kind."

"You were sleeping so Norman went over to visit his brother. He's been sleeping on the floor—"

"Beside my bed. I know."

"You've made him very happy."

"I do love him."

"But?"

"But I'm married, Vincent."

Vincent's heart skipped a beat. "What are you saying?"

"I recited wedding vows. I can't ignore that." She winced and pressed her hand against her lower abdomen.

"Are you all right?"

"I'm still very sore." She closed her eyes. "Give me a moment."

"You should be in bed."

She shook her head and opened her eyes. "I love Norman. I never realized it until I opened my eyes and saw him next to the tub. The way he looked at me…"

Vincent remained silent, waiting for her to continue.

"He's been my friend. My only friend for so long." She winced again. "You should have seen Jethro the night we were introduced. He wore a gray suit, gold pocket watch and a derby bowler. He was so strong and charming. So handsome. He stole my heart."

"And Norman?"

"Would always be my friend."

"And now?"

She shook her head. "I love Norman. I want to be with Norman."

Vincent turned away. *Careful. Don't encourage her to go to Norman.* "But, as you said, you're married."

"Yes, I am married."

They were on dangerous ground. He couldn't, wouldn't talk anymore of her future. He had reminded her she was married. *Selfish bastard!* He stood up and pointed at the portrait. "What do you think?"

"It's wonderful."

"Well, that's because I have the perfect subject."

"You are too kind, Vincent." She closed her eyes again for a few moments then opened them. "Will you help me to bed? I don't think I can sit much longer."

He kept an arm around her waist as they walked slowly back to her room. He got her back in bed and pulled the blankets up to her chin. "You rest."

She grabbed his hand. "Will you go next door and get me my violin?"

He smiled. "Sure." He started to go but turned back. "Did Jethro tell you how he knew the baby wasn't his?"

He expected her to say the obvious. He expected her to say because they hadn't been sleeping together. Instead, she said, "Jethro is sterile, Vincent. He told me that after our honeymoon."

He could only stare at her in disbelief.

❧   ❧   ❧

Malloy was not home so Vincent had no trouble retrieving the violin. Katherine was sound asleep when he returned. He put the instrument on the bed next to her so she would find it immediately upon waking. He left

Katherine in the nurse's care. As he walked towards Tonawanda, all he could think was, *who had fathered Katherine's children?*

❦   ❦   ❦

"Vincent? Vincent, are you okay?"

Vincent slowly nodded.

"You looked so spacey," Tracy Woodward said. She kicked the kickstand down and let go of her bike. It was a sleek, red Diamondback road bike. She wore a black sweat suit. Her helmet was a loud, striped design of red, blue, gray and yellow. She sat down beside him on the wooden bench, unsnapped the helmet, and took it off. Fluffing her hair with her fingers, she said, "This is nice down here, isn't it?"

They sat in Gateway Harbor on the Tonawanda side.

"Yes."

"Jill used to come down here and read."

Vincent scratched his chin. "How you doing? You haven't called me."

She ignored his question. "People will get their boats out soon. This harbor will be filled with them all summer. And in July, for two weeks, there'll be the Canal Fest. Jill and I spent as much time as we could at the Canal Fest."

"I'll have to attend this year."

"Too bad you couldn't have a booth at the craft show and sell your paintings." Her cheeks flamed bright red. "What am I thinking? You are above selling your paintings at festivals." She shook her head. "Don't mind me, I'm crazy."

"No you're not. You're sweet and good-hearted."

"What were you thinking about?"

In his head, Vincent said, "Oh, I was just wondering who the hell fathered my wife's father. Why?" To Tracy, he said, "Just daydreaming. Enjoying the day."

She pointed at the Diamondback. "You ride?"

"Not for a lot of years."

"Jill and I rode all the time."

"Where'd you ride today?"

"Along the river. Wasn't much fun though."

Vincent clapped his hand down on her thigh. "Don't you have any school friends to ride with?"

"No. Jill was my friend." She drew a long breath. "I have a few friends that I go to movies with now and then, but I guess I'm pretty much a loner."

"I always was too. Until I met Kate."

"She's beautiful."

"Thank you. But you're beautiful too. You should get out more. Maybe you'll meet your special someone."

Tracy burst out laughing.

"What's so funny?"

"Man, if that wasn't a cliché." She smiled at him. "Think you might want to ride again. There's a great bike shop on Payne Avenue called Johnny's. You could pick one up there for a really good price. And he'd make sure it was a good fit."

"Who would?"

"Johnny."

"Ah, duh." Vincent screwed up his face and twirled his finger around by his ear.

Tracy laughed louder and he laughed with her. When their laughter was spent, they sat quiet, each pondering their own thoughts as they stared out over the canal. Finally, Vincent stood up. He held out his hand. "Think I will buy a bike. How about we go back to my place, get the Rodeo and head on down to Johnny's."

Tracy grinned. "You're on!"

❋   ❋   ❋

Johnny's was housed in an old building on the corner of Payne and Jackson. Bikes of all shapes and sizes filled the store window. Inside, rows of bikes lined the shop. Johnny, a handsome young man with blonde hair, stood behind the counter, water bottles, bike bags, and various other accessories lining the wall behind him. "Hey, Tracy," he said, when they entered.

"Johnny."

"Sorry about Jill, kiddo."

"Thanks. We got your flowers. That was sweet."

Johnny nodded, his face grim.

"This is Vincent. Think you can fix him up with a nice bike?"

Johnny shook Vincent's hand then looked him up and down. "I believe I have just the thing. Road bike?"

"Definitely."

"Color preference, Vincent?"

"Black. Very sleek."

Johnny nodded. "Just what I thought. Follow me."

Fifteen minutes later, Vincent walked out of the bike shop with his new bike. As he lifted it into the back of the Rodeo, Tracy said, "Meet me for a ride first thing tomorrow?"

"And just what time is first thing for you?"

"Six o'clock."

"As you would say, 'you're on.'"

❦   ❦   ❦

They rode along the Erie Canal, heading towards Lockport. It was a brisk, clear morning, mist rising off the water. They'd ridden nearly five miles, Vincent struggling to keep up with her, when he could pedal no more. "Tracy!" he called. "Hey, pull up!" He stopped and stood straddling the bike, breathing heavily. He pulled his water bottle out of its cradle and drank greedily.

Tracy circled back, deliberately squealing her breaks as she stopped beside him on the shoulder of the road. "What's wrong?" she asked.

Vincent squirted more water into his mouth before saying, "You're killing me. Are you forgetting that I'm 41 and you're…ahh…let's see, a mere 17?"

A silver Chevy pickup sped by. The driver came dangerously close to Tracy and Vincent grabbed her handlebars. "Move farther from the road, Trace." He stared after the pickup. "Asshole."

Tracy did as he asked. "You get used to that when you ride. Some drivers just don't like bicycles."

Vincent's head exploded with an image of Tracy lying bloody and broken on the road and he shuddered.

She touched his gloved hand. "What's wrong, Vincent?"

He managed a smile. "Just, when you ride without me, promise me you'll be careful. Your parents already lost one child."

She looked away, gazing out over the canal.

Vincent wanted to kick himself in the rear. *Idiot! This ride was supposed to take Tracy's mind off Jill and you bring up her death.* He dismounted and leaned his bike on its kickstand. He put an arm around Tracy's shoulders and gave her a light squeeze.

Still staring out over the canal, she asked, "Do you ever wish you could go back in time and change the past, Vincent?"

He caught his breath.

"Do you?"

"What brought that on?"

"I think about it a lot. I wish I could turn the clock back to last September when Jill first told me her knee bothered her." Tracy looked at him with eyes so filled with pain, that Vincent drew her closer. She laid her head on his shoulder. "I'd make her come home from Boston and go to Aunt Liz, even if it meant getting on a plane and going to get her myself. And I wouldn't promise not to tell Mom and Dad about her knee. They didn't know until she came home for Thanksgiving and she told them that she'd just hurt it, but I knew that she'd had a cortisone shot in October and…" She trailed off, tears slipping from her eyes.

"Tracy. You can't—"

"I want my sister back," she cried. "I never should have gone along with her and not told Mom and Dad. I…I shouldn't have…oh, Vincent, I let it happen. I let the cancer grow inside her and I—" She broke off, sobbing.

Vincent wrapped both arms around her. She clung to him, sobbing, grieving for her sister, her best friend. He held her and let her cry as they stood along the canal road, cars zooming by.

"Jill," she cried, her body shaking. "Jill, I'm sorry. I'm so sorry. I miss you."

When her sobs abated, Vincent said in a firm, authoritative voice, "It's not your fault, Tracy. It's not your fault." He lifted her chin, forcing her to look up at him. He wiped the tears from her cheeks with his gloved hand. "Jill made her choices. You didn't make those choices for her. You are not to blame. The past is the past. And even if you could go back, I doubt you could say anything that would make Jill change her choices."

"If I told her that she died because—"

"Shh." He placed a finger on her lips. "The past is the past. You can't change it, Tracy."

"I just feel that if I'd said something, Jill would still be alive."

"Maybe. But you made a promise and you kept it."

"Why, Vincent? Why didn't she go to Aunt Liz sooner? She could be alive. Damn you, Jill!"

"Mad at her, aren't you?"

"Yes." She slammed her right fist into the palm of her left hand. "I just want to grab her and shake her. And then I think of her not being in my life anymore and…She was supposed to be at my graduation ceremony this June. We were going to be each others maid of honor and throw baby showers for each other and…" She hugged herself. "She won't be there for any of those things. And…Vincent, I don't know if I can do this."

"Do what?"

"Live without her."

"You can. And you will. Tracy, everything you're feeling right now is normal. You're grieving. Let yourself grieve."

She nodded miserably. "That's what Pastor McMichael says too. She gave me a book on mourning."

"Did you read it?"

She nodded.

Vincent rested his hands on her shoulders. "Don't be so hard on yourself. Remember what you promised me. That you'll call me before doing anything crazy."

"Like killing myself?"

Vincent's heart froze at her words. "Have you thought about it, Trace?"

"Yes."

"Don't, kiddo. Promise me that you won't take your own life." He held out his hand. "Okay. I'll be here for you. Pastor McMichael will be here. You've got your folks. Come on, promise me."

She stared at his outstretched hand. "It's just that…" She closed her eyes. "I hurt so much."

"Trace. Look at me, Tracy."

She did.

"Listen, honey. Jill's death is not your fault. And it's okay to be angry with her. And it's okay to miss her so much; you don't think you can bare it. But you can. As time passes, you'll deal with it. Before you know it, memories of Jill will comfort you and keep you going." He shook his hand. "Come on, take my hand. You've taken the first step, Trace. You told someone what's going on inside you. Come on."

She took his hand and Vincent's heart kicked back on. He smiled encouragingly. She looked up at him with sad eyes. "Thanks, Vincent."

He kissed her forehead. "Come on. Let's ride back."

She nodded.

He mounted his bike and they set off. She stayed close to him on the ride back, holding her speed and he realized that she needed to be near him. They turned on to Louisa Parkway and Vincent saw Jessica Woodward turning over the soil in the front garden. They turned into the driveway. "How was your ride?" Jessica asked, leaning on her shovel.

"Good," Vincent replied. Jessica wore faded blue jeans and a black sweat-shirt. Her hair was pulled back in a ponytail and her face, though still carrying traces of sadness, had its normal color. She had lost her eldest daughter and she was grieving, but the look in her eyes told Vincent that she was pushing forward with life.

Tracy jumped off her bike, laid it on the driveway, and ran towards her mother. Jessica dropped the shovel and held out her arms. Tracy went into them, burying her face in her mother's sweatshirt. "Hold me, Mom," she pleaded. "I'm so scared."

"I've got you," Jessica said. She unsnapped Tracy's helmet and removed it, tossing it on the grass. She drew the girl closer. "I've got you, Trace." She looked over Tracy's head at Vincent, her eyes questioning him.

"We need to talk," he mouthed.

"Honey," Jessica said. "I'm right here with you." Tracy clung to her. "What happened, sweetheart?"

But Tracy couldn't explain. She could only cry and cling to her mother. Jessica stroked her daughter's hair and murmured reassuring words of love.

Vincent left them alone. He walked Tracy's bike to the garage and lifted it up onto the hooks on the back wall. Another bike hung beside Tracy's. Vincent ran his hands along the cold metal. No doubt this one belonged to Jill. He shook his head, turned to go, but his legs suddenly turned to rubber. He sat down on a box in the corner and drew in several long breaths. How close had they come to losing Tracy, he wondered? God, she'd been contemplating sui-cide. The picture of Tracy lying in a coffin whirled round and round in his head.

He didn't know how long he'd sat there before Jessica came for him. She was alone. "Where's Tracy?"

"Lying down in the family room."

"What did she tell you?"

Jessica pulled a small wooden barrel over and sat down beside him. "That she's nearly slit her wrists four times since Jill's death." She trembled as she spoke.

Vincent swallowed over the boulder in his throat. "Did she tell you she's been seeing Pastor McMichael?"

Jessica nodded. "She hasn't wanted to bother Mike and I. She didn't want to make us any sadder." A tear rolled down Jessica's cheek and she impatiently brushed it away. "I've been so absorbed in my own grief that I haven't been there for my only remaining daughter."

"You lost a child, Jess. You have a right to mourn."

"At Tracy's expense? I think not, Vincent." She leaned back against the garage wall. "Thank God she finally said something. Four times, Vincent. She nearly slit her wrists four times. Thank God you were there for her today."

Vincent shook his head. "Don't give me any kudos. I didn't see it. I thought she was doing okay."

"But you were there when the camel's back broke this morning."

"Pure luck, Jess."

"No. Providence." She brushed another tear away. "Tracy likes you. Jill was always the one she talked to. Now Jill is gone and…" She smiled. "You are there in her stead. Thank you."

Vincent shrugged, still doubting that he'd been all that effectual. "Did you call Mike at work?"

Jessica shook her head. "I can tell him tonight. Who I called was Pastor McMichael. She's going to come by this morning."

"Good," Vincent said, nodding.

"She said that Tracy may need professional help and she'll bring some names with her." She met his eyes and he saw pure gratitude.

He said again, "Don't overstate my role here."

"Tracy said that she couldn't sleep last night. She said that she sat on the edge of the bathtub with her razor in her hand for over three hours. And the only thing that kept her from slitting her wrists was the thought that she was going riding with you this morning. I don't think I'm overstating your role, Vincent." She stood up. "Now, I told Tracy I was inviting you to breakfast. Come on inside."

Vincent stood up. "Lead on."

Once inside, they found Tracy sleeping on the couch.

"Let her sleep, Jess," Vincent whispered. "I'll take a rain check."

She walked him to the front door. "I'll let you know what Pastor McMichael says." She opened the door.

"Okay. Bye" He stopped on the top step of the porch. Turning back, he said, "If she asks for me, call me. I don't care what time it is."

Relief flooded Jessica's face. "Thank you."

"We'll get her through this."

As he rode off on his bike, he gave Jessica a thumbs-up.

❧   ❧   ❧

He chained the bike to the railing outside Liz's office, ran up the steps and entered. All the waiting room chairs were occupied. Behind the window, Liz was showing her receptionist a file. Vincent knocked on the window and both women looked up. "I need to see you, Liz."

"Now?" She gave him an incredulous look. "I've got a waiting room full of patients. Or hadn't you noticed?"

"It can't wait."

She hesitated a moment more then said, "Okay, come on back."

She led him to her office. Pointing at the guest chairs, she took her seat behind the desk. Vincent sat down. "I thought you should know about Tracy."

"What about her?"

"She's depressed. She feels that Jill's death is her fault because she didn't push Jill to see you."

Liz shook her head. "That's ridiculous. Jill made her own decision."

"That's what I told Trace. Anyway, the bottom line is that she's thought of killing herself."

Liz sat back in her chair. "Suicide," she said, her face closed to him.

"Yes. Fortunately, she didn't do it. And she told me this morning."

Liz picked up a pen and began fiddling with it. "Does Jess know?"

"Now, she does. She called Pastor McMichael."

Liz tapped the pen on the desktop. "As much as I admire Pastor McMichael, I doubt she can handle Tracy's problems right now, Vincent."

"I think she knows that. She told Jess she'd bring over some names as a referral."

Liz opened her desk drawer and removed a pad. She wrote down a name and phone number, tore the sheet from the pad and handed it to Vincent.

He read what she'd written. *Dr. Nicholas Kostapoulis.*

"He's the best psychiatrist in the area."

"Call Jess and tell her."

"No. Give it to her." Liz rose from her chair. "I have to get back to my patients."

"Wait, Liz. You should recommend this guy to Jess. You're a doctor, plus you're Jessica's friend. It should come from you."

"No, Vincent." Liz started for the door.

Vincent jumped up and grabbed her arm. "What's going on, Liz? Have you talked to Jessica since Jill's death?"

She avoided his gaze and pulled her arm free. "I have patients, Vincent."

He grabbed her arm again. "You haven't, have you?"

"I have to go."

"Liz, look at me."

She refused, her head turned from him.

"What's going on?"

Liz stood mute.

"Liz?" he insisted.

Still, she stood silent.

"What are you doing, Liz? Jess needs her friend. You need each other."

"I don't need anybody," Liz hissed. "Now let me go tend to my patients."

He released her, stunned by her words. He watched her walk away and wondered where the compassionate and loving Liz had gone. Was she still inside, buried beneath a mountain of grief? Or had she disappeared forever.

CHAPTER 16

Vincent heard the violin the minute he walked through the Victorian's front door. Quickly, he changed into black slacks and a white cotton shirt. He wet down his hair and combed in some gel. Studying himself in the mirror, he contemplated a quick shave but changed his mind. Katherine was waiting and no telling how long she'd already been playing.

He hurried back outside, searching the air for what was now the familiar, faint shimmering between the past and the present. It was just beyond the front gate. Thunder rumbling off in the distance greeted him when he stepped into 1926. Black clouds hung in the sky, threatening rain. A cold wind hit him and he shivered as he ran to Emma Reilly's house. Just as he banged the brass doorknocker on the wooden door, lightening flashed, more thunder clapped and the rain came, pouring down from the sky in torrents, banging on the porch roof above. The wind blew the rain inside the porch, the droplets stinging his face. He reached for the knocker to bang it again and the door opened, Emma motioning him inside. As she closed the door behind him, she said, "Nasty storm out there."

"I just missed it."

"You also just missed Norman. He's gone to run some errands for me." She gestured at the stairway. "Listen. She's playing."

"I hear."

"She should be on a concert stage."

"She is marvelous."

Emma started up the stairs. "He nearly pounded the door down last night."

"Jethro?" Vincent asked, following her.

She stopped and turned. "He stood on the other side of the door bellowing how she is his wife and I have no right to keep him from her. He'd come to take her home, he said. Demanded I open the door."

"I take it you didn't."

"Of course I didn't." Her voice held indignation.

"I'm surprised he didn't drag the police down here."

"Oh, he tried."

"And?"

"Jethro Malloy is not the only man in this town with connections, Vincent." She winked. "The Reilly name carries some weight too." She started back up the stairs. "Especially when the Reilly in question successfully nursed the police chief's child through illness."

Vincent chuckled to himself as he followed Emma to Katherine's room.

"Vincent is here, Katherine," Emma said, tapping on the doorframe.

Katherine, wearing Emma's blue silk robe, stood by the room's wide window. Her hair hung free, curling around her shoulders. She turned, lowered her violin, and smiled at him. "Vincent," she said, her voice warm. "Come to me."

He took her outstretched hand, raised it to his lips and kissed her palm.

"You are so sweet," she said. "I've only known you a short time and yet you are dear to me."

"How do you feel?"

"Better."

"Her temperature has been normal all day," Emma said. "She's eaten and kept the food down. I pronounce her officially on the mend."

The two women's eyes met. Something passed between them, but Vincent could not see what it was. He turned back to Emma. *Talk to her*, Emma's eyes instructed. She left the room and Vincent turned back to Katherine. "What's going on?"

"Please, sit, Vincent."

He sat down in the chair beside Katherine's bed. She sat down on the bed, hugged her violin and said, "I'm going to stay with Jethro."

Vincent sat silent. His heart screamed at him. *Don't let her do this!* But his head told him that she had to do this. History showed she'd stayed with Jethro until his death. Still, the question of her children's paternity rolled around in Vincent's brain. Could it be that Jethro had lied to her and he really wasn't sterile? Had he hired someone to father children for him?

"I will not break the vow I took," she continued. "I've written Jethro a letter. I've apologized for my indiscretion and requested that he forgive me. Emma has promised to deliver it to him when she sees him come home."

Vincent could keep quiet no longer. "Forgive you? Lord, Katherine, he beats you. He endangered your life with a botched abortion. If anyone should apologize it is Jethro."

She smiled at him. "You are so radical in your thinking."

"You call treating your wife respectfully radical?"

"I cheated on him, Vincent. I had no right."

"If he had loved you as a man should love his wife, you wouldn't have cheated on him."

"It doesn't matter. I was wrong. I'm his wife."

"You are not his possession, Katherine."

"Vincent, I swore to love, honor and obey my husband. I have failed him. If he will let me, I will do right by him."

Shaking his head, Vincent let out a long breath. "Have you told Norman about this decision?"

"Not yet. If Jethro will have me, then Norman will be told."

"It will break his heart."

"I know."

She suddenly looked exhausted. Taking the violin from her, he said, "Lie down." She did as he stated. The violin case lay open on the desk. He put the violin inside and turned back to Katherine, pulling the blankets up to her chin. "You played so I would come, didn't you?"

"Yes." Her voice was soft. "Please understand why I must do this, Vincent. And please, above all else, be a friend to Norman."

"I'll be his friend, Katherine. Count on it."

"Thank you, Vincent."

He noted the gratitude in her eyes and responded with a smile. She reached for his hand and he gave it to her. Her grip was still alarmingly weak, but Emma had pronounced her on the mend, so he pushed his worry aside. He sat in the chair beside her bed until she drifted off to sleep. Lightly kissing her forehead, he left the room and wandered downstairs. Emma sat reading in the living room. The light from the lamp beside her chair was a soft yellow, a bright spot in a dark afternoon. Sighing, he sat down on the velvet couch. "Good author?"

"Henry James. She told you then."

"She did."

The rain pounded against the windows. Thunder roared overhead.

"I needn't tell you, Vincent, that I disagree with her decision. I don't want to take her letter to Jethro."

"But you will."

"I will because I have to. My patient has asked it of me."

"Well, I can tell you, Dr. Reilly, that I disagree with her decision as well. I believe she deserves better. A man does not own his wife. His wife is his partner, his lover and his friend. She is to be cherished, not ruled over."

Emma stared at him with admiration in her eyes. "May I just say, Sir, that if you weren't married, I'd consider marrying you myself."

Vincent laughed. "Why didn't you marry, Emma?"

"That, Mr. Vermay, is a story best saved for another day." Headlights flashed in the window. Emma closed her book and stood up. She went to the window and peered out. "Jethro is home."

"Would you like me to take the letter, Emma?"

"No. But will you stay with Katherine?"

"Of course."

"It shouldn't be too long."

Vincent watched her don her raincoat. As she buttoned it, he said, "Really, give me the brief version. Why aren't you married?"

Hand on the doorknob, she said, "Because I never found a man who would have a working wife."

"Then let me say that the men you have dated are nuts."

Smiling, she said, "Let me repeat, Vincent, you are a man out of time." She went out without waiting for his reply.

He stood in the foyer. She had no idea how right she was. He most definitely was a man out of his time.

❦   ❦   ❦

"Hey!"

Vincent looked down from the ladder. Liz stood on the grass. The brim of her Yankees baseball cap shielded her eyes from the sun. "What?"

"What are you doing?"

"Scraping paint in preparation for painting this fine old Victorian. Why?"

"Mustang is on the road. How about a ride?"

He grinned and started down the ladder. "Scraping can wait."

"Thought you'd say that."

They headed for Niagara Falls with the windows down, Vincent's hair blowing in the breeze. She drove along the Niagara River, the faint smell of fish in the air. "My mother loved this car," she said.

"I can see why." He ran his hand along the dash. "She took great care of it."

"Always."

They made a right on Williams Road then a quick left onto the LaSalle Expressway.

"You take good care of it too, Liz."

She didn't respond. She pressed the pedal down further and they sped along at seventy miles per hour. They shot off the expressway and onto the Robert Moses Parkway.

"Hoping for a ticket?" he asked, as they drove under the Grand Island bridges.

She kept her eyes on the road and didn't answer him. Two tall water intakes whipped by on their left. The intakes hugged the river's shoreline.

"Liz?" They were traveling so fast that Vincent couldn't read the names of the factories flashing by on their right. "Elizabeth!"

She let up on the accelerator and the car slowed. She took the first exit, turned left and pulled to a stop at the curb. She sat with both hands on the wheel, arms straight, breaths coming in short gasps.

He touched her right arm. "Liz. Talk to me."

She closed her eyes, her lower lip trembling. She fought for control.

"Liz."

She turned to him, her eyes filled with tears. "You better drive back."

"Talk to me," he said, again.

She opened the car door and tried to get out of the driver's seat but he held her arm, stopping her. She stared at his hand a moment, shook her head and pulled her arm free. She got out of the car.

"Liz, you need help."

"Don't tell me what I need. You have no idea."

He jumped out of the car. "Have you talked to Jess yet?"

"Did you tell her about Dr. Kostapoulis?"

"Don't ignore my question."

"Did you?"

"Yes. She wants to see you, Liz."

"No."

"Then maybe Tracy is not the only one who should talk to Kostapoulis."

She glared at him. "I promised you a ride. You've had it. Now will you drive me home?"

He nodded.

He went the speed limit on their way back. She stared out at the scenery and refused to talk. He pulled the Mustang into the driveway and shut off the engine. "Liz," he said. "Let's not argue."

She got out of the car. "You just get a little too personal sometimes, Vincent."

"You used to talk to me."

She looked at him with unreadable eyes.

He climbed out of the Mustang. "Anyway, I still owe you a ride in the old Ford."

"Don't worry about it."

"I want to worry about it. A deal is a deal."

"Another time. I finished Kate's manuscript. Wait here." She went up the back porch steps and into the house. Frustrated, he ran his hand through his hair. What the hell had happened between them? Why wouldn't she talk to him?

She returned with the manuscript in hand. Handing it to him, she said, "The book is wonderful and she should finish it."

"I was hoping you'd agree with me. But I wanted to make sure I wasn't being prejudicial because she's my wife."

"You aren't. Kate has written a story that needs to be told."

Slipping the manuscript under his arm, he said, "Have you talked to Kate lately? Last she told me, you two were playing phone tag."

"Still are."

She stood before him, looking sad and thin, her face haggard, her eyes void of life. He put his hand on her shoulder. "I've got an idea. Come with me to Georgetown, Liz. Get away from here. We can give Kate the news about her manuscript together."

A spark of desire flashed in Liz's green eyes then fizzled just as quickly as it had flashed. "I can't, Vincent. I have too many patients depending on me."

"I doubt they would begrudge you a vacation."

"Tell Kate hello for me."

She turned to go and Vincent grabbed her arm. "Liz. Promise me you'll get a hold of Kate and talk with her."

"There's nothing to talk about, Vincent. Life is what it is."

"Liz, don't do this. Don't withdraw into yourself."

She stared at him in stoic silence.

"Kate loves you," he continued. "I care about you. Your dad worships the ground you walk on. Don't throw it all away."

She drew in a long breath. She blinked back tears. But she didn't say anything.

He slipped his arm around her and pulled her to him. She resisted at first but then collapsed against him, crying. He let her cry, feeling her anguish and pain. "Call Dr. Kostapoulis, Liz. Don't battle this depression alone."

She got herself under control and pushed back from him. Her eyes held pain and misery. Still, she managed a smile and said, "I'll be all right."

"You'll call Nicholas Kostapoulis?"

"Maybe an antidepressant will help."

"Don't self medicate, Liz. Call Dr. Kostapoulis."

The pager she always wore on her belt rang. She peered at it, wiping tears from her face. "I have to go to DeGraff."

"Are you up to it?"

"Yes. I'll be okay." She climbed into the Mustang and started the engine. "I will take that ride in the old Ford another time, Vincent."

He smiled. "Great. Hang in there, Liz. Things will get better."

She didn't reply. She put the Mustang in gear and drove away.

❧   ❧   ❧

He called Kate immediately. He described the drive with Liz and asked when the last time was she had actually spoken with Liz.

"It's been over a week, Vincent. I get the feeling she's avoiding me."

Vincent sat on the couch with Kate's manuscript in his lap. "Babe, I know I promised to come to Georgetown once Liz had read your novel, but I don't think I should leave now. I'm very worried about her."

"That makes two of us." He heard flipping pages. "I can get out of here next Friday for a few days. I'll come up there."

"Excellent. I appreciate this. And once we get Liz back on track, I will come down to Georgetown."

"Deal."

"Speaking of our other deal…"

"Hush," she said. "I'll find out her opinion from her thank you. I don't trust you not to sugarcoat it, Vincent."

He laughed into the phone. "No sugarcoating needed. She loved it. You better get on the phone to Regina."

"My, my aren't we impatient. Now let me go. I have plane reservations to make."

"See you next Friday, love."

"Bye, Vincent."

The phone clicked off in his ear. He hung up the receiver then held up the manuscript. Grinning, he said, "We've got her now. Yes, indeed, we've got her now."

Katherine sat in a rocking chair on Emma's front porch. Her eyes closed, she softly played her violin. Her hair was pulled back and held in place with a gold comb. She wore a red silk blouse and a long black skirt. Five men in business suits and ten ladies in dresses stood on the sidewalk in front of the house listening as Katherine played, unaware that they were there. Vincent walked over to the group and stood beside a short, stocky man in a derby. The fellow glanced up at him and said, "Marvelous, isn't she?"

"She is."

"I saw her in New York in '24." He shook his head. "Damn shame she gave it up."

Katherine finished the piece and applause erupted. Startled, she hugged the violin, looking mortified at first and then, relaxing, she smiled. "Thank you," she said, inclining her head. Her eyes were alive with gratitude and joy.

The gentleman beside Vincent said, "Bravo! Bravo!"

The others on the sidewalk echoed his sentiment. As they all walked off, Vincent walked up the porch steps. Leaning against a column, he said, "It's good to see you outside."

"It's nice out here today."

"You should get out more often, Katherine."

"They clapped for me, Vincent." She said it with awe in her voice; like it was strange that anyone would still want to hear her play.

"They clapped because you play beautifully, Katherine. I told you that. Norman has told you that."

"So has Emma." Still hugging her violin, she looked out on the quiet street. She sat lost inside herself for some time before saying, "I hoped you would come."

"And I have."

"You're right, Vincent. I do need to get out more. The air smells so fresh and the sky is so blue." She sighed. "I'd forgotten how lovely it could be outside." She plucked the violin strings. Vincent recognized Beethoven's 5th Symphony. "It all seems so long ago."

"What?"

"New York…Vienna…playing before thousands of people in a theatre, traveling…a whole other life, Vincent. Somebody else's life. Certainly not mine."

"But it was yours, Katherine. You did play your violin for people all over the world."

"I started when I was nine. They said I was a musical genius."

"You still are."

She shook her head. "You asked me why I chose Jethro and an obscure life in North Tonawanda. I told you that he swept me off my feet."

"You did," Vincent agreed, nodding.

"It was more than that." She looked at him with eyes begging him to understand. "I couldn't live my life anymore. Every concert, every day before each concert, was torture. My father…my foundation…had died. I was filled with terror all the time. Backstage, before my introduction, I would shake, sweat; my heart would race, my ears practically explode with a rushing sound. I vomited so many times." She shook from the memories.

Vincent knelt before her chair. "Anxiety."

"What?"

"You were suffering from anxiety. You were having panic attacks."

"Whatever you want to call them, I couldn't live any longer like that. Jethro was my escape. He was strong, like my father had been. He was my salvation."

"Your father could not have been cruel like Jethro, Katherine."

"He wasn't. He was strict, but he loved me with all his heart. He traveled with me, all over the world, always by my side." Her eyes glowed as she spoke of him. "He made traveling fun. He kept my demons away."

"And then he died."

"Yes." She took a long breath. "Two years, Vincent. I tried carrying on without him for two years. And just when I thought I would lose my mind, Norman introduced me to Jethro."

"Did you ever tell Norman about your fears?"

"No. I couldn't. He had always thought so highly of me. I didn't want him to learn the truth."

"Oh, Katherine," Vincent said, taking her hand. "I understand now."

"Jethro is not the man I thought he was, Vincent."

Vincent could only nod his agreement.

"How could I have been so wrong about him?"

"You were living in a world of outright terror, Katherine. You saw what you wanted to see."

"I don't love him, Vincent. I doubt I really ever did. I just thought I did. I convinced myself I did."

Vincent squeezed her hand.

"He hasn't answered my letter yet. I want him to refuse to take me back, but I doubt he will."

Vincent forced himself not to comment. *Don't meddle, Vincent. What happens must happen.* Yet the thought of her moving back into the Victorian with Jethro tore him up inside.

❧   ❧   ❧

Norman appeared in the sunroom doorway holding a dozen, long-stemmed red roses. "For you, my lady," he said, kneeling before Katherine.

"They're beautiful, Norman," she said, leaning close to smell them. "They smell wonderful."

"Take them, my love," He set them in her lap.

She handed him the violin, gathered the roses in her arms and said, "I must put them in water."

Still on his knees, Norman watched her leave the room. Getting to his feet, he set the violin on the wicker rocker, and came over to where Vincent stood painting Katherine's portrait. He peered at the painting. "Magnificent."

"Thank you."

Norman sighed. "The painting you've promised me will be all I have of her, Vincent. She's going to go back to him."

Keeping his eyes on his work, Vincent asked, "Has she told you that?"

"She doesn't have to. I know her. She will not break her vows."

Vincent couldn't stop the words from coming out. "She loves you, Norman. She realizes that now."

"That may very well be true. But…" He trailed off.

Vincent wanted to yell, "Then fight for her! Damn it, man, fight for her!" But he didn't. He clenched his teeth and continued painting. *Jethro is sterile!* The words reverberated in his brain. He shook his head. *Even so, she must go back to him. Somehow, they have five children. She must have those children if Kate is to be born.*

"I will pay you for the painting you do for me," Norman said. "It will hang in my bedroom in New York." He backed away and sat down in a wicker chair. He watched Vincent paint, a glum look on his face.

What was it like, Vincent wondered, to love a woman and not be able to marry her? He thought of Kate. She had given his advances no rejection. They had clicked immediately. It was almost as if they'd run on the same cylinder. At least until the last year and a half, that is. Still, in spite of their disagreements, he loved her. She was his wife and friend. She was in his soul. As he painted Katherine's portrait under Norman's watchful eyes, he pitied the man.

"What shall I pay you for the portrait, Vincent?" Norman asked. "Make no mistake, you have earned the money. If you hadn't found Katherine the other night..." He shuddered, unable to finish his statement.

Before Vincent could reply, Katherine returned with the roses. She'd put them in a white porcelain vase. She sat them on the stand beside the rocker and assumed her pose again. Yes, Vincent thought, staring at the red roses. That's what the painting needs. They would give it a romantic, soft feel. Thank you, Norman.

Twenty minutes later, Emma appeared in the doorway. "Katherine," she said, obviously not wishing to do so. "You're husband is here."

Vincent felt Norman stiffen. Katherine closed her eyes a moment as if to prepare herself then said, "Show him up, please, Emma."

With a curt nod, Emma went to fetch Jethro.

Vincent turned to face the door, paintbrush and palette in hand. Norman shot out of his chair and knelt before Katherine. He grabbed her hand. "Don't, Katherine," he pleaded. "Don't do this. Come away with me. I love you. Katherine, God, please, I love you." He was near tears.

Katherine gently touched his cheek. "I love you as well," she softly said, her voice cracking.

He pulled her into his arms, crushing the violin between them. "I will give you all you desire. Come with me."

She ran her hands through Norman's hair. She held him tighter than he held her.

Vincent nearly bit his own tongue to keep from screaming, "Do as he says, Katherine. Go with him." *Kate. Remember Kate.*

Jethro Malloy entered the room. "Touching," he said.

Katherine pushed Norman away. The young actor fell on his rear. Seeing Jethro, his eyes glowed with hatred.

Katherine stood up. "Jethro," she said, her shoulders back, her head held high.

"I've spoken with your doctor," Jethro said. "She feels you will be ready to come home on Friday. Your room will be ready. I will expect you first thing."

Norman jumped to his feet. "You think you can just come here and order her around."

"You have nothing to say about this, Lassiter. She is my wife."

Norman's hands formed fists at his sides. Keeping his eyes on Norman, Vincent set his brush and palette on a nearby stand.

"You don't deserve her!" Norman shouted.

"She is mine," Jethro said, taunting him. "There is nothing you can do about it."

Norman lunged at him, overpowering him, getting his hands around Jethro's neck.

"Stop it!" Katherine cried.

Vincent tried to get between the two men. Norman's grip on Jethro was strong. "Let him go, Norman!" Vincent yelled, tugging on the actor's shirt collar. "Don't kill him, man."

Malloy gasped for air, his face turning red. He pulled at Norman's hands, trying to free himself.

"I won't let you hurt her anymore!" Norman shouted. "You won't hurt her anymore!"

Malloy's eyes bulged out.

"Norman, don't!" Katherine pleaded, joining the struggle.

The four of them stood entangled for what seemed an eternity. Finally, Vincent succeeded in pulling Norman off of Jethro. Norman fought against him, trying to get back to Jethro. In the process, he bumped Katherine, sending her sprawling backwards. She bounced off the rocker and crashed into the stand, knocking over the vase of roses. The sound of breaking porcelain stopped the three men. Jethro collapsed to his knees, holding his throat and breathing hard. Vincent held Norman in his arms.

Katherine fell on her left side, her left arm beneath her, on top of the shattered porcelain. She screamed in pain.

"Oh, my God," Norman said, shrugging Vincent off and hurrying to her. He took her right arm and pulled her away from the porcelain.

Vincent stared in horror at her left hand. A large, pointed piece of porcelain had run right through it, cutting her hand in half from wrist to fingers. Blood spurted out around the wound. She fell against Norman, fainting.

Vincent dashed from the room to the top of the stairs. "Emma!" he called. "Emma, we need you!"

He needn't have bothered. Emma was already on her way up the stairs, medical bag in hand. "What in God's name happened up here?" she asked, flying by him.

He followed her to the sunroom. "Jethro and Norman were fighting. Katherine got in the fray and—"

"Katherine," Emma said, dropping to her knees beside her injured friend. She quickly examined the wound. "Oh, God, her hand. She plays with this hand."

Vincent leaned back against the wall. His legs threatened to give way.

"Carry her to her room, Norman. Hurry."

Norman lifted Katherine in his arms and carried her from the sunroom. "I'm sorry, darling," he said as he carried her. "Katherine, I'm sorry."

Jethro got to his feet. "Can you save the hand?" he asked, still rubbing his throat.

Emma glared at him. "As if you give a damn, Malloy." She turned to Vincent. "Both of you stay out of my way." She ran from the room, hurrying to her patient.

CHAPTER 17

They sat together in the sunroom, neither speaking, the tension heavy in the air. Katherine cried out, her pain-filled voice floating down the hall as Emma stitched her wound. Vincent flinched, grinding his fist into the palm of his hand. He felt Malloy watching him, studying him, trying to get inside of him.

Unable to stand it any longer, Vincent said, "Why did you marry her?"

"Because she wanted me to. She asked me to take her away. So I did."

"I doubt she meant for you to put her in prison."

"She asked me to do that as well, Mr. Vermay."

"I seriously doubt that, Malloy."

Jethro chuckled. Red marks from Norman's strangulation attempt stuck out on his neck. "You think you know her. But you don't."

"And you do?"

"Yes, in fact I do. I married her and brought her home to a world where she no longer has to face people. She was going insane when I met her. Do you know that?"

"She was having panic attacks. She missed her father and was having panic attacks. They can be managed."

He shook his head. "It is not as simple as that, my radical friend. She couldn't eat or sleep. Her eyes were wild and helpless and she pleaded for escape. I've given her a world where she can play her violin and not worry about an audience or critics. She's amply fed. When Mrs. Collins returns from England, she will have company again."

Incredulous, Vincent shook his head. "You've locked her in a room away from life. That's not what she wanted or needed."

Jethro pulled out his pocket watch, opened it, read the time, closed the watch then put it back into his vest pocket. "And what, pray tell, do you think my wife needs, Vincent?"

"The freedom to come and go as she pleases; access to the entire house and this town. She needs friends. She needs to be able to play her violin for more than just herself. She needs a husband who loves and cherishes her, not one who locks her in a bedroom and doesn't visit her for days at a time."

"I suppose you believe that Norman Lassiter would be the husband she needs."

"I do."

Jethro laughed at him. "You, Vincent, are an imbecile. Lassiter is a penniless actor who could never support her. And as far as Katherine is concerned, she has nothing. Her money became mine when we married, thanks to an agreement she signed."

"I see, Malloy. She was so desperate to escape her life that you took advantage of her desperation."

Katherine cried out again and Vincent clutched the arms of the wicker rocker.

"I gave her the escape she wanted. In exchange, she gave me what I wanted—more money, a beautiful wife when I have need of her services. You must admit, after all, that Katherine is a beautiful woman."

"You bastard, Malloy. She's not a possession."

"Your ongoing theme, Vermay." He sat forward. "But she is a possession. My possession. And I will never give her up."

It took all his willpower not to finish the job Norman had started. The man deserved to die. Vincent got up and left the room. He hurried downstairs and out the front door. He stood with his fists at his sides and breathed in long breaths of the warm, afternoon air. He needed to cleanse himself of Jethro Malloy. He needed the man out of his system.

He sat down on the top porch step and buried his face in his hands. He sat this way for sometime, Katherine's pain-filled screams and Malloy's twisted words rolling around in his head. A hand touched his shoulder and he looked up. Emma sat beside him, her blue dress stained with Katherine's blood. He couldn't bring himself to ask her how Katherine was.

Emma smiled and pushed stray locks of hair back behind her ears. "She's lucky, Vincent. There was no damage to her nerves. She can still move her fingers."

"Thank God."

"Thirty-five stitches to close the wound."

Vincent shuddered.

"It's a very painful wound."

Vincent nodded his understanding.

Malloy came out the front door. He walked passed them and down the steps. "Will she still be able to come home Friday?" he asked Emma.

"I'll have to see how the wound is healing, Jethro."

"Very well." He turned to go.

"Bastard," Vincent said, standing up. "Did you even see her?"

Malloy stopped, his back to them. "What's the point? Lassiter is with her." He turned around. "That too will change when she returns home."

Emma laid a hand on Vincent's leg. "Don't," she said.

He took her advice and he went inside the house. As Malloy had said, Norman sat next to Katherine's bed. She lay beneath the blankets, her skin white, her left hand heavily bandaged. Although she slept, creases of pain lined her face.

Tears flowed freely from Norman's eyes. "I nearly took her violin from her," he said. "I nearly took away the only thing that makes her happy."

Vincent put his hands on Norman's shoulders and squeezed them. "But you didn't, Norman," he said.

※   ※   ※

Vincent rode his bicycle up the Woodward's driveway and parked it in front of the garage. He headed for the back door but stopped, glancing in through the arbor. Tracy sat on a wooden bench, her head bent over a book. "Hey," he said, removing his helmet.

"Hi, Vincent."

He went into the garden. The smell of freshly dug dirt hung heavy in the air. "What are you reading?"

She held up the book so he could see the cover—*A Year At Monticello* by Thomas Jefferson.

Vincent sat down beside her. "Have you ever been?"

"To Monticello?"

"Yes."

"No."

"You should go. It's a fascinating place."

"Jefferson was a fascinating man."

Nodding, Vincent gave her the once over. She wore an oversized flannel shirt, which made her thin body look small and frail. Dark circles under her eyes told him she still wasn't sleeping. He laid his hand on her thigh. "How are you doing?"

She avoided his eyes. "I have an appointment with Dr. Kostapoulis Friday morning."

"Good. Not sleeping though, huh?"

She closed her book. "Not really. Aunt Liz gave me something to help me sleep, but…" She shook her head.

"Taking medication isn't a sign of weakness, Tracy."

She shrugged.

"Too tired for a ride?"

"I really want to just sit here in the garden." She pointed at some tools and a box of marigold flats sitting on the stone walkway. "Mom's working out here. She just went inside. She should be out soon."

"I bet her gardens are beautiful once she's got them planted."

"They are. That's why I love reading out here."

Jessica came outside, two glasses of iced tea in her hands. "Vincent," she said, genuinely pleased to see him. "This is a nice surprise."

Vincent patted Tracy's thigh. "Just checking up on my girl here."

Jessica held the glass of iced tea out for Tracy, but she shook her head. "Vincent can have it."

Vincent accepted the glass. He caught the worried look in Jessica's eyes and gave her a brief nod of understanding. She took a long drink of her tea, set it on the ground by the bench leg and returned to her planting. Vincent gave Tracy's thigh another pat then got up, strolling over to Jessica. He watched her work with one eye and kept tabs on Tracy with another. When she had returned to her book, Vincent squatted beside Jessica and, keeping his voice low, said, "She's still pretty bad off, isn't she?"

Continuing to dig, Jessica said, "Yes. I've spent the last two nights in her room. She refused to take the sedative Liz prescribed."

"Why?"

"I don't know. She just won't take it. It's almost as if she's afraid of it." Jessica removed a marigold from the flat and placed it in the hole. "I asked Liz to talk to her but she wouldn't. She's pulled away from us."

"It's not just you, Jess. She's withdrawn from everybody. Maybe it's how she mourns."

"I told her she didn't fail Jill. She feels she did. I know her, Vincent."

Vincent watched Jessica adjust the dirt around the freshly planted marigold. "I think that it's more than just feeling like she failed Jill. I think that Liz just can't accept Jill's death"

"One death too many. I hear you. She's had some hellish years." Jessica dug another hole. "I'm worried about her. She's my friend."

"Kate's coming into town Friday. She's coming to talk to Liz, so don't worry. You take care of Tracy, and Kate and I'll take care of Liz. Deal?"

Relieved, Jess smiled. "Deal."

Vincent straightened and went back to Tracy. "You sure you don't want to go for that ride? I could use the company."

"Oh, Tracy, go with him," Jessica encouraged.

Indecision flashed across Tracy's face.

"Just a short one," Vincent said. "Just to get some blood coursing through those veins of yours."

Tracy looked at her mother. "Go on," Jessica said, nodding.

"Okay. A short one."

They rode side-by-side on the sleepy streets surrounding the Woodward home. Vincent let Tracy lead. The afternoon sun poured down on them and within fifteen minutes, Tracy pulled to a stop and peeled off her flannel shirt. She wore a dark green tank top beneath. As she tied the flannel shirt around her waist, she said, "You know you don't have to waste your time on me, Vincent."

"I don't consider this wasting my time. I'm getting exercise and spending time with someone I like. Now, catch me."

He took off, hoping she would chase him. And while she did follow him, she did not try to beat him. They rode another ten minutes, ending up at the edge of Pinewoods Park. She stopped and, straddling her bike, gazed at the ancient trees that lined the park. "Jill and I climbed those once. Dad just about killed us when he found out."

"They are pretty high up there. How old were you?"

"Eight and ten."

Vincent whistled. "Brave girls."

"Either that or stupid girls." She turned to him. "I'm scared, Vincent."

"Of what?"

"Dr. Kostapoulis."

"I'm sure he doesn't bite, kiddo."

"He's a stranger, Vincent."

"True. But he's also a professional who knows how to help someone who is depressed."

"Clinically depressed. I looked it up on the Internet."

"Then you know that Dr. Kostapoulis has the tools to help you."

"I guess." She looked up into the blue sky. "I never realized that the sun would keep on shining and the birds would keep on singing…and…life would go on even though Jill is de…dead. And that I wouldn't want to go on."

"What would Jill want you to do, Tracy?"

"Keep on living. Go after my dream."

"And what is your dream?"

Tracy's eye lit up. "You won't laugh?"

He held up his hand. "Scout's honor."

"I want to be a sculptor, like Michelangelo."

"Then pursue your dream."

Tears welled up in Tracy's eyes. "Jill was supposed to be with me."

"She will be." He pressed his finger against her chest. "She's right there. Forever."

Tracy looked down at the spot where his finger touched her chest.

"That's right, Trace," Vincent continued. "Jill is right there. And she'll never leave there."

Tracy looked up at him, revelation blooming like a flower in her tired eyes. A small, hopeful smile crossed her face. "Yes," she said, her voice barely a whisper. "She'll always be in my heart."

Vincent returned her smile as he nodded.

Her smiled broadened. "And in here." She tapped her bike helmet. "I'll always have her memory."

"Memories," he corrected. "Thousands of them."

Tracy's hands curled around the end of the handlebars. "And she'll be with me when I see Dr. Kostapoulis."

"You bet."

Tracy blinked and the tears spilled from her eyes, rolling down her cheeks. Still, she smiled and said, "Let's go home now, Vincent."

Nodding, he said, "Right with you, Trace."

❧   ❧   ❧

Wearing Emma's blue robe, Katherine sat in the wicker rocker in the sun-room, her bandaged left hand cradled in her right hand. Her hair hung free, falling down around her shoulders. She gazed out the window at the rainy May morning. Her skin was a pale gray, her eyes bloodshot, Vincent guessed, from crying. She didn't realize he stood in the doorway. She was lost in thoughts he couldn't imagine.

"Katherine?"

Startled, she turned towards him, catching her breath.

"I'm sorry, I didn't mean to scare you." He entered the room, pulled over a wicker stand and sat down on it.

"Vincent," she said, her voice hoarse.

"It's good to see you out of bed. The last two times I stopped in, you were pretty sick."

She looked down at her bandaged hand. "It's infected."

"I know. Emma told me."

"She called Jethro and told him that I'm not well enough to go home tomorrow."

"And she would be right."

Katherine reached out with her good hand and pressed it against his cheek. Her skin was hot. "You are such a kind man, Vincent." A small smile crossed her face. "Your wife is a very lucky woman."

He remained silent. He couldn't very well tell her that he was married to her granddaughter.

She drew in a long breath and coughed, turning away. The coughs were harsh and deep within her chest. She closed her eyes and leaned back in her chair.

"You should be in bed, Katherine."

Still coughing, she shook her head. "My back aches from laying," she said, between coughs. When at last the coughing subsided, she asked, "Have you come to paint?"

"The paint fumes wouldn't be good for you right now."

If possible, the coughing spell had turned her skin grayer. Her chest heaved with each breath. "I would like to meet her," she said.

"Meet who?"

"Your wife." She coughed again, doubling over from the effort. She reached for him. "Help me to bed."

He lifted her in his strong arms. She laid her head on his shoulder, her eyes closed. He carried her to her room. A young nurse with curly blonde hair was just changing the bed sheets and blankets when he carried Katherine into the room. She stepped aside so he could lay her down. Then she gently but firmly pushed him out of her way so she could tend to her patient. He watched as she gave Katherine a tablespoon of what he assumed was cough medicine. She helped her roll onto her right side and covered her with the blankets. "You rest," she instructed, placing a damp cloth on Katherine's forehead. Katherine stared up at her with feverish eyes. "Rest," the nurse insisted. Katherine's eyes fell shut. The nurse gestured at the door and Vincent followed her out into the hall.

"Pneumonia," she said before Vincent could ask the question. "I shouldn't have let her up, but she insisted. She thinks her backache is from being so long in bed." The nurse pointed at the space between her shoulder blades. "What it's from is the pneumonia."

Vincent looked back in through the door at Katherine, realizing that her death would mean Kate's as well. "Will she recover?" He wondered if the panic in his heart showed in his voice.

"Dr. Emma will see to it that she does. Don't you doubt that." She started for the stairs. "Now I have to make up some more broth for her. That's all she can keep down." Her hand on the banister, she asked, "You will sit with her until Norman gets back? He took the trolley down to Buffalo. Said he had some business to attend to."

"Yes, I'll stay."

"And don't go opening up those paints of yours. Those fumes could kill her right now." She headed downstairs.

Vincent returned to Katherine's bedside. He sat in Emma's desk chair, his elbows on the arms, his fingers forming a steeple. Katherine slept, her chest heaving, her breath rattling. Tears slipped from beneath her closed lids and trickled down her cheeks. He took the cloth from her forehead and gently wiped the tears away. "Norman," she mumbled, rolling onto her back. She coughed, her eyes opening and staring up at him, but not seeing him. She grimaced, crying out, "My hand."

"Easy," he said, brushing her hair back from her face.

She continued staring at him, her eyes laced with pain. "Where's Norman?" she asked, her voice barely more than a whisper.

"I'm right here," Norman Lassiter said, entering the room. Vincent vacated the chair and Norman took it, laying his hand on Katherine's forehead.

Feeling his touch, her eyes cleared, focusing on him and refusing to let him out of their sight.

"I'm right here," he said, again, taking her good hand.

"Don't leave me," she pleaded, coughing.

Norman leaned close. He kissed her lips and said, "I will never leave you, Katherine. Never."

Vincent left them, walking down the stairs with what he knew held within him. Come December, Norman Lassiter would disappear.

He met Emma on the porch steps. She wore a dark green overcoat and carried her medical bag. Her red hair was piled up on her head and held there with a silver clip. "Vincent," she said, pleased to see him.

"Emma. When did she develop pneumonia?"

"During the night. I'm afraid the infection caused by the abortion severely weakened her. Then the hand injury...well, her body is weak."

"Your nurse seems to think that you will see Katherine through to wellness."

Emma moved under the porch roof to get out of the rain. Vincent remained where he was, letting the cold rain beat down on him. He didn't know why, but the rain kept his emotions in check as he waited for Emma's next words.

"I will do all I can for her. She is a fighter. She has a good chance."

Vincent clutched the porch railing. "She still insists on returning to Jethro."

Emma's left cheek twitched. "I believe so, yes. I wish she wouldn't. I wish she would go with Norman."

So do I. But she can't, Emma. She can't. And I can't tell you why. "She loves Norman, that's for sure."

"And he her." Emma's eyes took on a distant look. "I've often wondered how that feels, Vincent. To love someone so completely."

"It is pure joy." Even as he said the words, he wanted to kick himself. They certainly would not comfort her, this woman who was destined to live alone the remainder of her days. "But if a man truly loves his wife, he will give her her head."

"Yes, you've noted that before. A most refreshing and thoroughly modern idea. Tell me, Vincent, how did you come upon it? For in so many other ways, you seem old-fashioned."

He shrugged his shoulders. "Reading, I guess."

"Books I'm sure your wife recommended."

No, not at all. In fact, I came upon it by growing up during the Women's Liber-ation Movement. I think, Emma, had you been born in my time, you would be happily married right now and still pursuing your medical career. "My wife is an accomplished reader."

"As I thought." She reached out and took hold of the doorknob. "I must check on my patient and get back to the office. One more thing, no painting until the pneumonia is gone."

"Agreed."

She went inside. Drawing a long breath of the wet air, Vincent sat down on the porch steps, the seat of his pants soaking up water. He placed his elbows on his thighs and rested his chin on his cupped hands. He hated himself. He knew this was irrational, but he couldn't stop the feeling. Katherine Malloy had to recover and return to Jethro. Norman Lassiter had to disappear. Facts were facts. History had to play out. Even so, Vincent couldn't stop hating himself.

Jethro Malloy's Ford rolled past the Reilly house. Vincent watched it, unaware that he was grinding his teeth. Malloy pulled into the Victorian's driveway. Vincent watched the car until it disappeared behind the house. It took all of his willpower not to march over there and kill the man.

❦   ❦   ❦

Vincent pulled the Rodeo to a stop in front of Liz's office shortly after five on Friday. Turning to Kate, he gave her an encouraging smile and said, "Good luck."

"I'll probably need it." She touched his cheek with her hand. "It's so good to see you. I miss you so much."

He took her hand and kissed it. "We can talk about that later. First things first."

Nodding, Kate looked out the passenger window at Liz's office building. "I hope she'll talk to me. I'll bring up the manuscript first and proceed from there."

"Good idea."

She leaned over and pecked his cheek. "I'll be home either when she kicks me out or I feel I can leave her. Whichever comes first."

"Okay."

She opened the truck door and slipped out. He waited until she went inside before driving off. Tracy Woodward sat on the Victorian's front steps when he pulled into the driveway. He shut off the engine, jumped out, and said, "Hey."

She stood up and waved.

He walked across the lawn. As he got closer, he saw that her eyes were red and swollen. She was dressed in pleated black slacks and a long-sleeved, white blouse. He put one foot on the first step, took hold of the railing and asked, "How'd it go?"

She rubbed her upper arms and shrugged.

"Bet Dr. Kostapoulis didn't bite."

She shook her head, her red eyes filling with fresh tears. She gave him an uncertain look.

He held out his arms and she flew into them, nearly knocking him over. He held her, waiting for a flood of tears. But the tears didn't fall. She squeezed him with all her strength then backed away, smiling.

"What?" he asked.

"I just wanted to thank you."

"For what?"

"If you hadn't gone riding with me the other day...well, I might have gone to see Dr. Kostapoulis, but I wouldn't have talked to him."

"I see."

"But I got there and I remembered what you said. That Jill will always be with me. I couldn't shut up. The guy probably thinks I'm nuts."

"I doubt that."

She glanced at her watch. "I have to go. Mom's making dinner. I'm going to work with this doctor, Vincent. I want you to know that."

"Okay."

"He gave me an antidepressant to take."

"It'll help, Trace."

She nodded. "But, can I ask you something?"

"Sure."

"If I ever need to talk to you...I mean can I still..." She trailed off, shaking her head. "No, you don't need to be bothered."

He dropped his hands on her shoulders. "It's no bother. We're friends. And yes, call me when you need to."

She hugged him briefly. "Thanks. See ya."

"See ya."

She ran off.

Vincent went inside, checked the answering machine and found a message. Sitting down on the couch, he pressed the play button. "It's Jessica, Vincent. Tracy's appointment went well. I think with the doctor's help, she can beat this depression. It'll take time, I know." A short pause. "Thank you, Vincent. And please, call me. Mike and I would like to have you and Kate over for dinner. Bye."

Smiling, he sat back. Tracy was going to be okay. He ran a hand through his hair. And then there was Liz. He prayed Kate could reach her. His thoughts turned to Katherine and Norman. They belonged together. They should be together. Frustrated, he grunted. He picked up the phone and dialed Douglas Lassiter's number. He got the answering machine. Not leaving a message, he slammed the phone down. *Who*, he asked himself. *Who fathered Katherine's children?*

He got up and went out to the front foyer. He grabbed his newsboy cap from the coat rack and smacked it down on his head as he ran down the porch steps. He continued running until he reached the Reilly's front door. He rang the bell and paced as he waited for someone to answer. The door opened and Elsie Whiting stood before him in her white apron, wiping her hands on a towel.

"Vincent?"

"I have to talk to you," he said, stepping inside without waiting for an invitation.

"All right." She closed the door. "But you'll have to do it in the kitchen. I'm making dinner."

"Fine. Whatever." He followed her into the kitchen. She offered him a seat at the table but he refused, pacing instead. She went back to snapping green beans in half. "I need to know something, Elsie. It's important."

"I'll help if I can, Vincent."

He pulled his cap from his head and worked it with his hands. "Where there ever any rumors about the paternity of Katherine's children?"

Elsie dropped the bean she was holding. It missed the bowl and fell on the countertop. Her body tensed and her back went rigid, as if there was a pole up her spine.

Vincent quit pacing and waited, aware of his own frantic breathing in his ears.

At last, Elsie turned from the sink. "No."

Disappointment coursed through Vincent. But then the look on Elsie's face told him that she knew more. She had his answers. And she stood before him, fighting an internal war. He saw it on her face and in her eyes. He didn't say a word even though he wanted to scream at her and beg her to tell him. He gave her the time she needed. When he thought he could remain silent no longer, she said, "Come with me."

She led him down into the basement. They made their way across the concrete floor, dust dancing in the fading afternoon light that shined in through the basement windows. The room was massive, the walls rough, gray stone. In the far corner, away from the furnace, she reached up and pulled a string. A single bulb flooded the area with yellow light and to his complete surprise, Vincent found himself staring at Emma Reilly's old desk—the desk that had sat in Katherine's room while she recovered in this house. Elsie opened the center drawer. She had to work the warped wood a bit, but managed to pull the drawer completely out. She set it on the concrete floor. Kneeling down and peering under the desk, she supported herself with her left hand and worked with her right. Vincent heard wood rubbing against wood. Seconds later, she pulled out a leather journal and handed it to Vincent.

Accepting it, he asked, "Is this the journal you told me she kept?"

Elsie got to her feet. "No. Emma kept two journals. Emmett doesn't know about this one. Neither does Liz."

"But you do?"

She nodded. "I told you my father worked in Malloy's furniture shop. He told me about the desks they made with secret compartments."

"How long have you known?"

"When Marlene was pregnant with Liz, she asked me to help her decorate the nursery. The room hadn't been redone since Emma's time and when I saw the desk…"

"You snuck a peak."

"I did. Don't think I haven't been sorry for doing so."

Vincent laid his hand on her shoulder. "You're only human, Elsie. And you were young."

"Maybe so, but I never should have read that book."

"But you did read it. And you've told no one."

"Until now."

"Why not?"

"What good would it have done? I had no right to take the Malloy children's inheritance from them. That's what would have happened."

"How? Katherine was their mother. She would never—"

"You don't know what Douglas Lassiter would have done. You like the man, I know. But if—"

"Lassiter," Vincent said, interrupting her. "Are you saying what I think you're saying?"

She gestured at the journal. "You'll read it all in there, Vincent. It will tell you how Norman Lassiter fathered all five of Katherine's children with Jethro Malloy's consent."

CHAPTER 18

Vincent sat in the red velvet, wingback chair in the Victorian's parlor and devoured Emma's journal. Astounded, he read how Norman Lassiter had found a gravely ill Katherine after her botched abortion. He had found her three hours later than Vincent had, but as Vincent had done, he'd taken her to Emma Reilly. Katherine's condition had been more serious since she'd lain unattended and bleeding for three hours longer, but, miraculously, she hadn't bled to death. She'd fought off the infection and had been visiting with Norman in the sunroom when Malloy had come to tell her he would take her back. A fight had ensued and Katherine had fallen on the vase of flowers, injuring her hand. The wound had infected and she had also developed pneumonia. It had taken her until the end of July to fully recover. Norman had stayed by her side and Katherine had filed for divorce. She and Norman had planned to marry. Then Norman had disappeared in December and Katherine had returned to Malloy.

Vincent shook his head in wonder. It had all happened the same way, even without him there. The only difference he had made was finding Katherine sooner than Norman had. Vincent flipped through the yellowed pages, scanning them, looking for more references of Katherine. Emma wrote about her often, but not recounting any time spent with her. Instead, there were paragraphs filled with concern for her friend's welfare and paragraphs of sadness over losing Katherine's friendship. Emma had missed Katherine and had hated Malloy all the more for taking her friend away. Then, on a night in 1955 Katherine had knocked on Emma's door and had asked her to come examine her already dead husband. Vincent bit his lower lip. What about Norman Lassiter fathering Katherine's children? Where had Emma recorded this information?

He rescanned the journal pages from Norman's disappearance to Jethro's death. Still nothing. He turned to the book's last page and Norman Lassiter's name jumped off the page. The entry had no date. He read eagerly.

Norman Lassiter is not dead, as long assumed. I saw him for the first time in 29 years the night of Jethro's death. He resembled not at all the man that I once knew. He had been living in Jethro Malloy's basement, chained to the wall most of that time. The vibrant, young, handsome actor was gone. In his place was a frail, emaciated, white-haired man who while alive, had no life in his eyes. They stared blankly, showing no emotion. That is, until Katherine walked into his cell. Then he could do nothing but stare at her with complete love and devotion. I could not believe my eyes that night. But there Norman was, sitting on a wooden chair with his left leg chained. Katherine went to him, unlocked his ankle cuff and said, "He is dead, Norman. You are free." He could only keep staring at her. She put her arms around him and drew him close. He cried then, like a small child. She held him and rocked him. I could not watch this and went back upstairs. I sat in the kitchen for some time and then they came upstairs. I wondered if Norman would know me or not, but he did.

Katherine asked me to examine him so I did. He sat quietly while I listened to his heart and took his blood pressure. Both were fine. I asked him how he felt and he just shook his head as one who is confused. Katherine kissed him and said, "You can go now, Norman. You're life is your own again." He laid his head on her shoulder and at last he spoke, his voice that of an old, defeated man. "I will not leave you." She held his hand as she said, "But you must. You must live your life now." He shook his head, his eyes not accepting her words and said, "There is no life without you."

Katherine knelt before him. "Then you shall stay, my love. Do you want to see your children, Norman? There are pictures." He nodded, a smile crossing his face. They sat together on the couch, thighs touching, looking through photo albums of children that North Tonawanda believes are Jethro's. But they aren't. No, Norman had fathered them all. Jethro had chained him to the basement wall and used him as a stud. How terrible it is to even write it!

How had this happened? I don't know. I may never know. Katherine will not explain. Norman barely talks. He will stay there with her. He will keep the place up for her. He has asked that I don't tell his brother or nephew that he is alive. Norman is dead to all but Katherine. To North Tonawanda, he is Katherine's caretaker. He said, "Emma, you must call me Abe. I will be Abe to all but Katherine."

I agreed. Why, I don't know. I told him the children should know their real father. I told him that Douglas and his father have a right to know. But he just shook his head and said, "What's done is done, Emma. Leave me in peace here with my Katherine." And so, I agreed. But every day, when I see him mowing the lawn or repairing the house or shoveling the snow and he calls his greeting and I reply, "Good day, Abe," something inside me screams at my culpability in their lie. But I made a promise and like Katherine, I will not break my promises.

I like to go out on the porch and sit in the early evening, especially now with the cancer so far advanced and my death eminent. I sit in my rocker, close my eyes and listen as Katherine plays her private concerts for Norman. She never lost her ability to play that violin of hers. It sings to me as I sit here and await my death. I know I should take their secret to my grave, but I can't. So I write it down here and put it in my desk and maybe someday, when the time is right, someone, possibly young Emmett, will find it. And when the Malloy children find out they are really Lassiters, I pray they forgive us—Norman, Katherine and myself. I pray God forgives me when I stand at His gate. That time is so very near. I have not told Katherine I'm dying. She holds me dear and I know my death will devastate her. I'm glad Norman is there to comfort her when I go.

This house will soon belong to Emmett. I hope he chooses to live here with his lovely bride. It is a good house. He can raise a family in this house. Lord, my chest hurts tonight. I think I shall go sit in my rocker. Katherine is playing. I do so love to listen to her. Cancer, not being able to work, it is not how I envisioned my final days. But Emmett will treat my patients well. Knowing that and my friendship with Katherine are my only comforts, especially on days like this, when the pain is so bad.

So, whoever reads these words, forgive me—no, forgive us for what we have done. Emma Reilly, M.D.

Vincent could do nothing but read Emma's words over and over again. How had Lassiter endured nearly thirty years as Jethro Malloy's prisoner? Had Malloy let him see sunlight? Human beings couldn't survive without sunlight. But if he had let Lassiter outside, how was it that no one had seen him? Questions whirled around in Vincent's head, questions that would never be answered. All the principle parties where dead. And while Emma's journal entry certainly confirmed that Norman had fathered Katherine's children, it did not explain Norman's willingness to let Malloy lay claim to five children that were not his own. Nor did it explain Jethro's willingness to do exactly that.

The front door opened and Kate called his name. Vincent jerked in his chair. Quickly, he closed the journal and stuffed it behind his back. Kate walked into the living room and collapsed on the couch. She laid her head back, closed her eyes and said, "What a night." She pressed the palm of her hand against her forehead. "God, I have a headache."

"Didn't go so great, huh?"

"No." She sighed.

Vincent slid Emma's journal under the seat cushion and went to Kate, sitting down beside her and taking her in his arms. He rested his chin in her hair, inhaling the gentle smell of lavender and realizing how much he had missed her closeness, her scent, and her love. He kissed the top of her head and was astonished when she started crying. Tears rolled down her face and she clutched his shirt.

"Hey," he said, drawing her closer. "What's going on here?"

She couldn't tell him. She could only cling to him and cry. He stroked her hair, soothing her with soft words of love. She pulled her glasses off and tossed them on the coffee table. She fought for and gained control of her tears. Furious with herself for breaking down, she wiped her face and eyes with the sleeve of her blazer. She laid her head against his chest and said, her voice thin and cracking, "I've lost her again."

"Liz?"

He felt her head nod.

"Tell me what happened."

"We went to dinner. I couldn't get her to talk. We walked along the Erie Canal. I couldn't get her to talk. She was there with me, but not there. The way she looked at me, like I no longer matter to her." Kate shuddered. "My Liz, the Liz I grew up with, the Liz I love, wasn't there. Her eyes..." Kate shuddered again. "Her eyes are so void of emotion and life. It terrifies me, Vincent."

I know what you mean. "Do you have plans to see her tomorrow?"

"Lunch and shopping. I had to jump through hoops to get her to agree." She played with a button on his shirt. "I know I deserted her once, Vincent. But since having her back in my life, even though it's been mostly by phone, I...well...her friendship means so much to me. I need her. She's filled a giant hole in my life. Can you understand that?"

"I can." His thoughts flew back over their married life. But for an occasional get-together with Regina, she had no friends. She had him and her work. "I'm sorry, babe," he said.

His apology brought her head up. "Sorry for what?"

"The lonely part of your life."

"Oh, Vincent." She tenderly touched his cheek. "It's not your fault. I'm the one who took off on Liz. I'm the one who doesn't make friends all that easily." She smiled. "You're so sweet."

"I love you," he said, amazed at how the words rolled off his tongue so naturally, amazed at how right they felt. In spite of their differences of late, he loved her. He would always love her.

"I love you." She lightly kissed his lips. "What I have to do is get a good night's sleep and wake up ready to fight for Liz tomorrow. And make no mistake about it, I'm going to fight and I'm going to win."

Vincent messed her hair. "That's my girl!"

She laid her head back down on his chest. "Hold me awhile, Vincent?"

"You bet."

She fell asleep in his arms. He carried her upstairs to their bedroom and laid her on the bed. Carefully, so he wouldn't wake her, he removed her clothing, leaving her in her bra and underpants. Her ribs were more pronounced than they should be and he estimated that she'd lost fifteen pounds since February. He knew why. He was no longer there to cook for her. Lord knew she never took the time to cook for herself.

Sighing, he pulled the covers from beneath her and she stirred, rolled onto her side, but didn't awaken. He covered her, bent, and kissed her tear-stained cheek. Returning to the living room, he retrieved Emma's journal and headed downstairs into the Victorian's massive basement. Where had the chain been? In what part of this damp, gray-stoned world had Norman Lassiter spent his time? He ran his hand along the cold stone. Must and mold assailed his nose and he sneezed. After several minutes of searching, he found a protruding piece of iron on the driveway wall below the window. The piece of iron ended in a round hoop, big enough to hold a substantial chain in place. Vincent turned back to the staircase. Malloy could stand halfway down the step and see Lassiter. What kind of evil maniac had Jethro been? And how had Malloy convinced Norman to father five children for him? Had Norman loved Katherine that much, that he'd actually give up his life and claim to his children for her?

Vincent climbed the basement stairs, switched off the light and wandered down the hall to the front foyer. He had to hide Emma's journal. He stood at the bottom of the stairs a moment, debating on a hiding spot. He decided on his studio. Kate hardly ever went in there. And when she did, it was to sneak a peek at whatever he was painting.

In the studio, he opened the armoire where he kept his paints and sketch-pads and slid the journal beneath a pile of pads. He closed the doors, turned away from the armoire then leaned back against it. Did he have the right to keep the truth from Kate? Could she deal with it? In essence, it meant that her entire life had been the result of lies. If she could accept it and the news was made public, how would it affect her inheritance? He remembered what Elsie Whiting had said about Douglas Lassiter. Katherine's children were actually related to him. Would Douglas fight for a piece of Katherine's estate? He shook his head. There was so much to consider. He certainly couldn't make a decision tonight.

He showered, slipped on a pair of pajama bottoms and crawled into bed beside Kate. She slept on, unaware that he'd joined her. He propped his head up on his arm and watched her sleep. Her chest rose and fell in a gentle rhythm. She looked small and younger than her age. Moonlight filtered in the window and fell across her face, highlighting her eyelashes. Her lids bounced with REM sleep.

If he were still living in Georgetown, he would lie beside her like this every night. He would have dinner ready for her when she came home from work. He would show her what he'd painted during the day. Their life had been so comfortable, so routine, so perfect, until his well of ideas had snapped shut. Now, here they were, he living in North Tonawanda, she in Georgetown; he wishing she'd quit her job and write fiction full time, she claiming he did not understand her anymore. If she could only see how wonderful it could be for them if she left McMartin? They could work at their respective crafts, together, in this beautiful house. And they would save this house. They would restore it to its former beauty.

He thought of Katherine and the choices she had made. She'd chosen a horrible life with Jethro instead of the concert stage. She'd allowed Jethro to hide her away from even the people of North Tonawanda. And she'd accepted having Norman's love according to Jethro's terms. He drew in a long breath. He understood neither of these two women.

If Kate was right about anything, it was the fact that he could not under-stand her need to toil away for Darren McMartin. How could she keep her tal-ent buried, locked away from the reading public? How could she think that being chained to Darren McMartin's every whim was better than pursuing her writing here in North Tonawanda? How?

Vincent lay awake for hours, unable to shut down his brain. Kate slept beside him, curled up in a fetal position on her right side. The first rays of daylight crept into the room and Vincent still lay awake. The phone rang, startling him, and he snatched up the receiver. Kate's eyes opened as he said, "Hello."

"It's Elsie, Vincent."

"What's up?"

"Is Kate with you?"

Vincent heard tears in Elsie's voice. He sat up, frowning. "Yes." He felt Kate staring at him.

"She'll need you."

"Elsie, what's wrong?" His heart thudded in his chest. *This isn't good. No, this isn't good at all.*

"It's Elizabeth, Vincent. She took...she swallowed—" A sob escaped her. "Oh, God, Vincent," she cried. "Elizabeth is dead."

❦   ❦   ❦

She looked like she was just sleeping, her auburn hair falling across the pillow. She wore a white, rose and green flowered nightshirt. She hadn't bothered with blankets. The empty bottle of pills and an empty glass sat on the nightstand.

Kate knelt beside the bed, tears streaming unchecked down her face. She held Liz's lifeless hand and cried, "Why? Oh, Liz, why?"

Vincent swallowed, forcing back his own tears. He couldn't cry now. Not in front of Kate. "How long ago?" he asked Elsie.

"I just found her."

"Does Emmett know?"

"He's not home. He went fishing with Douglas Lassiter. Some place in the Adirondacks. I have a phone number downstairs."

"He really went fishing?" Vincent must not have heard her right. He couldn't conceive of Emmett leaving his home for a day, let alone for a fishing trip.

"Left Friday morning. Took Duke with him. Emmett's been making such strides. What will this do to him? She is the light of his life. She is..." Elsie trailed off and covered her face with her hands.

Vincent placed a hand on her shoulder.

"She was like a daughter to me," Elsie cried.

Vincent bit down hard on his bottom lip, as if the pain this caused could mask the pain in his heart. Liz was dead. Kate's friend was dead. His friend was dead. Although he had only known Liz a short time, she'd forged a place in his heart.

Kate brushed Liz's hair with a gentle and loving hand. "My friend," she said. "Why didn't you call me? Oh, Lizzie, why this?"

Vincent couldn't look away from Liz's pale face. The emotional distress, the pain of losing Jill, Alan, and her mother, no longer showed. She was...*peaceful*. At last, she had found peace.

Kate climbed onto the bed. Sitting besides Liz's body, she took it in her arms. She held Liz close, sobs coming from deep within her soul. Vincent winced at the sound of these sobs. He wanted to run from this room. He wanted to run far away and convince himself that this had not happened. Liz had not committed suicide. But he couldn't run. This had to be dealt with.

"We have to call an ambulance," he said, his voice high and shaky. "Elsie, we have to."

Still crying, Elsie went to the bed and sat down on the other side of Liz. She massaged Liz's back. She seemed not to have heard him.

"An ambulance," he said again, in a feeble, unconvincing voice.

He watched helplessly as Kate and Elsie sat with Liz, their sobs and tears blending. He told himself he needed to comfort these two women and get them out of this room. He needed to call an ambulance so that Liz's body could be removed. He had to call Douglas Lassiter in the Adirondacks and have him bring Emmett and Duke home. Funeral arrangements had to be made. Overwhelmed, he turned from the bed and ran from the room. Out in the hall, he fought for air. *Liz was only 39. So young. So much more living to do. So many more patients to help.* But she was dead. Dr. Elizabeth Reilly was dead. He ran his hand through his hair. He had to keep control of himself. He had to go back into the bedroom.

But he couldn't get his legs moving. He collapsed on the floor. He sat there for what seemed hours. Conversations and times spent with Liz flashed through his mind. He reexamined their ride in the Mustang. Should he have pushed harder to make her open up? Should he have said things differently? He'd let her down. Somehow, they all had let her down. He closed his eyes. *Dead. Liz was really dead. Gone from us already, just her body lying in there, just an empty shell.* Tears slipped out from under his lids. Elbows resting on his knees, he buried his face in his hands and cried.

✤   ✤   ✤

When he had cried himself out, Vincent got up and did what had to be done. He called 911. He got Elsie and Kate out of the bedroom. He called the resort in the Adirondacks and left an urgent message for Douglas to call him on his cell phone. He dealt with the paramedics and the police. He watched as they loaded Liz onto a stretcher, covered her, and hauled her away. He held Elsie's hand while she explained to the police how she had gone to call Liz for breakfast and found her dead. He felt like he was in hell.

When the police, coroner and paramedics had finally gone, he somehow convinced Elsie to lie down. There was nothing more she could do until Emmett came home. He glanced down at his cell phone clipped to his belt. The green light flashed. It was on. He wouldn't miss Lassiter's call.

He walked Elsie up to her room. She lay down on the bed. He closed the door and stood outside her room a moment, listening. He wasn't surprised to hear her shedding fresh tears. He went looking for Kate. He'd lost track of her during the morning. He cursed himself. How could he have let that happen? She needed him. As he searched each room, panic grew within him. What if she had done the same thing as Liz? Shaking off the thought, he ran to the Victorian, bursting in the front door. She was in the parlor, curled up under a blanket on the couch, hugging a pillow to her chest. Relief flooded through him and his legs shook, threatening to give out. She gazed at him with damp, red eyes. He hurried to the couch and sat down beside her. Her right hand slid out from under the afghan and he took it. She didn't say anything. He saw her swallow with difficulty.

"I'm here," he said, trying to comfort her. He could think of nothing else to say.

She nodded then laid her head on his shoulder. They sat together like this, neither talking, each drawing comfort from the other's presence until the cell phone rang. Still holding his wife, Vincent answered it and told Douglas Lassiter what had happened. When he hung up the phone, Vincent realized how glad he was not to be the one who had to tell Emmett Reilly that his daughter had killed herself.

❀   ❀   ❀

Elsie stood in the funeral home foyer when they came in. Kate went to her, hugging her, asking her how she was. Elsie shook her head, her baggy, blood-shot eyes answering for her.

"And Emmett?" Kate asked.

Elsie gestured towards a closed door. "He's inside with her. He wanted to go in alone."

"How's he been?"

"Quiet. Undemonstrative. Frankly, he frightens me."

"Douglas said he took it hard when he told him," Vincent offered.

The funeral home front door opened and Jessica, Mike and Tracy entered. Jessica held her daughter's hand as they came up the four inside steps. Vincent nodded his greetings, his eyes studying Tracy. Profound sadness lay heavy in her eyes. She moved like a zombie. He met Jessica's eyes. They answered his unspoken question. Tracy was in bad shape. But then, Jessica wasn't doing much better. The sagging in her face and the red in her eyes told Vincent she wasn't sleeping. He watched as Jessica read the sign outside the parlor door—*Elizabeth Marlene Reilly, M.D.* She shuddered. Mike slipped his arm around his wife's shoulders and pulled her to him. He whispered into her ear. Vincent looked away, giving them their privacy.

"People are going to start coming," Elsie said. "The door has to be opened." Kate took Elsie's hand and Elsie stared down at it as if she hadn't been touched or comforted in years. "They'll want to see Liz. The door has to be opened."

Vincent laid a hand on her shoulder. "I'll talk to him," he said, hoping he sounded more confident than he felt. As he took hold of the brass doorknob, he wondered just what he could say to Emmett. How the hell did you comfort a man who had lost his only child, the light of his life?

Emmett knelt on a bench before Liz's coffin. He wore a black suit with a gray shirt and a black tie. His hands were folded in prayer, but he was not pray-ing. He was staring at his daughter. Liz lay in a mahogany casket with beige, satin interior. She wore a dark green blouse beneath a white lab coat, her stethoscope hanging around her neck. *Elizabeth Reilly, M.D.* was embroidered on the front of the lab coat. Her auburn hair was combed down around her shoulders. Her hands rested on her abdomen. Flowers surrounded the casket and lined the walls of the room. Their different smells assailed Vincent's sinuses and he sneezed. Emmett didn't move. He just kept staring at the child he loved and would bury tomorrow.

"Emmett," Vincent said, standing beside him.

"She's beautiful, isn't she, Vincent?" His voice was soft but steady.

"Yes, she is, Emmett." And in fact she was beautiful, even in death. One could almost believe that she was just sleeping.

"I should have been here," Emmett said. He touched Liz's hair. "She needed me and I wasn't here." He stroked her cheek. "I asked her Thursday night if she wanted me home. I offered to stay." He covered her hands with his own. "She hurt so deeply. She couldn't find her way out, Vincent. I knew what she was feeling. I begged her to talk to me."

"She probably didn't want to upset you."

"What did she think killing herself would do to me?"

Vincent could only shake his head. He gazed at Liz with a longing inside that slit his heart. He wanted his friend back. Kate needed her. Hell, he needed her. He wanted to take her by the shoulders, shake her and yell, "Wake up! Wake up and come back to us."

Fists clenched, he said, "People are arriving, Emmett. We have to let them in to see her."

"She wouldn't like this," he said. "She would have wanted no visitation. But her patients must be able to say goodbye to her. I pray she understands."

"She will." Tears pierced Vincent's eyes and he blinked them back. He couldn't cry here. Nor could he cry tomorrow, when they buried her. He must remain strong and in control for Kate's sake. She was barely holding it together. If he broke down…He shook off the thought.

Emmett got up. "I've lost my wife and my daughter. I've outlived them both."

Vincent wanted to reach out to Emmett, but he hadn't the strength. He just stood next to him mute.

Emmett finally took his eyes off Liz. He turned towards the door. "You're right, Vincent, we do have to let them in."

Still mute, Vincent nodded.

Emmett touched Vincent's arm. "I've nothing left, Vincent. I will put my baby girl in the ground and I will have nothing left. My wife and daughter, both gone."

"Elsie loves you," Vincent blurted out. "Don't you know that? Don't you see that, Emmett?"

"Yes, I have Elsie." He looked suddenly thoughtful, as if the statement was a totally new fact.

"You've had her for years, Emmett. For years."

A trace of a smile flashed across his face. Then he strode to the door and opened it. "Come in," he said. "Come give Elizabeth your respects."

More people had gathered in the hall. At Emmett's bidding, they began filing in, faces sober. They spoke to Emmett; they went to the casket, each saying goodbye in their own way. They were all ages, ranging from 18 to 85. Tears flowed freely. Elsie stood beside Emmett, accepting condolences. Jessica Woodward knelt in front of Liz's casket for a long time. She stroked her friend's hair and whispered into her ear. Mike kept his arm around Tracy when their turn came. The girl gazed down at Liz but didn't seem to see her, at least at first. And then, she pulled a framed picture from her blazer pocket. It was small, but Vincent could see that it was a photograph of Jill and Tracy together. Tracy laid the picture on Liz's chest, next to her stethoscope and said, "Goodbye, Aunt Liz. Hug Jill for me." She turned from the casket and buried her face in her father's shoulder. He led her away.

Somebody tapped him on the back and Vincent turned to find Jessica beside him. "You better go talk to your wife. She's sitting in a chair in the foyer."

"Thanks. I will. How are you?"

She glanced at Liz again. "Heartbroken."

Vincent nodded his understanding then headed for the door. Kate sat in a tan and blue-stripped, wingback chair. She stared at him with wounded eyes. He squatted before her and took her hand. "Kate."

"I can't, Vincent. I thought I could, but I can't see her like that. Not again."

"You have to. You'll regret it if you don't, babe."

She shook her head.

"Kate."

"No. I can't go in there. I can't say goodbye." She sniffed, tears rolling down her cheeks.

"You have to, Kate. She's gone."

"No."

"Yes." He stood up, tugging on her arm. "Yes, Kate. You have to say goodbye." He pulled her out of the chair. She swayed into him and he held her up, her body trembling. "I'll be right beside you. We'll do it together." He got her inside the parlor where Emmett immediately took her in his arms and patted her back. Elsie hugged her as well. She stared from one to the other, unable to speak. "Go say goodbye, Katie," Emmett said, somehow finding an encouraging smile.

They reached the casket and Kate fell on her knees. Vincent kept his hands on her shoulders, supporting her. She reached out, her hand shaking, and touched Liz's hand. "I don't want you to go," she said, fresh tears spilling from her eyes. "Why wouldn't you let me help you? I tried to help you." She sobbed. "You were the best friend I ever had, Liz. And I let you down so many times. I'm sorry. I'm so sorry."

Vincent blinked back tears and lightly squeezed Kate's shoulders.

"Remember how your mom used to take us for ice cream in the Mustang. And she'd walk us down to the Riviera so we could see a Saturday afternoon movie. We used to sit on your front porch and you'd say, 'I'm going to be a doctor just like my father.' I was going to be the greatest novelist ever. We…" She sobbed again. "You made it. You were a good doctor too. You…oh, Liz, I miss you. I don't want to say goodbye to you. Not again. Twenty-one years. All that time lost and now…now when I'm back and we had so much time left…" She trailed off, turning from the casket. She leaned against Vincent.

"Say goodbye, Kate," he whispered.

She turned back to Liz and in a voice barely above a whisper, she said, "Goodbye, my friend. I love you."

Vincent helped her to her feet. "I'll take you home now," he said.

* * *

Kate sat on their bed, her suitcase opened, but still empty. She held her manuscript in her hands. She wore blue jeans and a white sweatshirt, her hair pulled back in a copper clip. Her glasses rested on the end of her nose.

Vincent tapped on the doorframe. "Hey."

She looked at him with such profound sadness and confusion in her eyes that Vincent winced. He sat down on the bed beside her and put a comforting arm around her shoulders. She hadn't slept well since Liz's death and the lines in her face told him she was close to exhaustion. Dare he let her board the plane for D.C. today?

She seemed to read his mind because she said, "I'm not going. At least not today."

"Okay."

Her body was hot against him. He felt her forehead to make sure she wasn't running a fever. The action brought a smile to her face, something he hadn't seen there in days. He smiled back.

"You're sweet," she said, her voice soft and grateful.

"I love you."

She was silent a few moments and then said, "Liz told me during dinner on Friday that I should finish this book." She held up the manuscript. "She said that it's a 'phenomenal work.' She said I have to finish it. She was adamant."

"So am I."

"I promised her I would finish it and send it to Regina."

Vincent's heart rose. *Thank you, Liz. Thank you so much.*

Kate set the manuscript on the bed. "I don't know what to do, Vincent." Anguish hung heavy in her voice.

"Of course you do. Finish the book and send it to Regina."

She shook her head. "It's not that easy."

"But it is, Kate. You can work in the office I redecorated for you."

She stiffened. "That's you're ideal, isn't it, Vincent? Keep me in this house. Lock me in Jethro's old library."

"What? Kate, no, I thought you liked this house. I made the office the way I knew you'd like it."

She slipped from beneath his arm and got up. Hands on her hips, she said, "I'm not my grandmother, Vincent. I won't be possessed and locked up in this house."

Realization shot through Vincent like a flaming arrow. "Is that what you think? You think I want to do to you what Jethro did to Katherine?"

"And what else should I think? Since you moved to this house, that's all you push for. Getting me here. Taking me from my job and social world and—"

"Whoa," he said, jumping up. "No, Kate, I'm not Jethro Malloy. I'm Vincent Vermay, the guy who married you, the guy who loves you. The guy who has always believed you could be a fantastic novelist. You might have buried that dream deep inside, but I refuse to believe that you don't want what you said you wanted when we got married."

She deflated before him, stumbling backwards until her legs were knocked out from beneath her by the bay window seat. "I..." she began. "I want...I don't..." She hid her face in her hands and wept.

Vincent fought the urge to hug her. He had to let her think. He had to give her some space.

Finally, gulping, she said, "I don't know what I want anymore."

Vincent took her wrists and lowered her hands from her face, a face filled with misery and uncertainty, a face covered with tears. "You know one thing you want, Kate. You want not to be locked up in a room in this house. You don't want to end up like Katherine."

She nodded, swallowing hard.

"So take it from there. Think about what else you want."

"I want you," she blurted, fresh tears filling her eyes. "But I can't do want you want. I can't quit my job and move here. I can't, Vincent."

He closed his eyes a moment. Visions of the life he'd dreamed for them danced in his head. He drew in a long breath and opened his eyes. He chose his words carefully. He didn't want to upset her more than she already was. "Then don't. Finish the book in your spare time. Do it in Georgetown if you must. But do it, Kate. Finish the book."

"And you'll still love me?"

It baffled him that she didn't fully understand his love. After fifteen years of marriage, she still didn't understand that he loved her simply because she existed. She didn't have to do anything to earn his love. She didn't need to please him. All he asked of her was that she love him in return. He cradled her chin in his hand. "I will always love you."

She flew into his arms, knocking him over. They ended up in a clenched ball on the floor. She pushed him away and sat up, smiling. "I will finish the book, Vincent."

"Good."

"But I can't face working on anything just yet." She placed her hand on her chest. "It just aches in here. It aches for Liz."

He rubbed her upper back. "I know."

"I'm going to call McMartin and tell him that I'm staying here a few more days. I think I need to decompress."

"Okay."

"Do you really understand, Vincent? I need my outlet. I need my working life. I can't do what you do. I can't just be in this house everyday."

"I have to be honest, Kate. No, I don't understand." Her face fell. "But I can accept it. I can live with it."

"Thank you, Vincent."

"You're welcome." He kissed her lips then pulled her down on top of him. "We'll work it out, babe. We always work things out." But as he held her, he couldn't fight back the wave of disappointment inside him.

❧   ❧   ❧

She stayed three more days. They spent the days peacefully alone. They took walks. They read. She spent time in the office doing Vincent knew not what. He didn't ask her. He didn't want to intrude. He wanted her to view the office as her place where she could work undisturbed, where she would have privacy.

She slept through the second night, her head close to his shoulder, and left hand on his chest. He watched her, her eyelashes shimmering in the moonlight.

At the end of the third day, as they sat on the Victorian's front porch drinking iced tea, she said, "Have you painted anything since the violin paintings, Vincent?"

He slowly rocked, considering his answer. "I've sketched out some ideas. But actual painting, I'm afraid I've only done that on the exterior of the house."

"I did notice that. Where did you get the idea for the color scheme? I originally thought you were going to stick with the white and mauve."

The night was warm, the smell of lilacs in the air. The sun was setting, the sky a brilliant red and purple, promising a pleasant day tomorrow. "I did some research. Victorian houses should be colorful."

She stretched her legs out and rested them on the porch wall. "I like what you're doing."

"Good." He continued rocking.

"I'm going to leave tomorrow, Vincent."

Sadness flowed through him and its intensity surprised him. He liked having her here with him. He wanted her here with him always. But he had to let her go. He'd promised.

"What time is your flight?"

"8 p.m. I thought we could have one more day together."

He smiled. "That's good news. At least I don't have to say goodbye to you first thing in the morning."

She reached over and laid her hand on his forearm. He stopped rocking. "I appreciate you not fighting me on this, Vincent. Not many husbands would."

"Not many husbands love their wives like I do."

She smiled warmly. "I am going to finish the novel, Vincent."

"I don't doubt it, babe."

She toyed with his shirtsleeve. "God, I miss Liz."

"Me too."

She stood up, walked to the end of the porch and looked over at the Reilly house. "How do you suppose Emmett is?"

Vincent scratched his chin. "I don't know. I'm just glad Elsie is over there."

She sighed and pressed her forehead against the wooden post.

He kicked his foot off the porch wall and started rocking again. Minutes of silence ticked by. The colors in the sky deepened. A mother called her two children home. Kate turned around and stared at him. "What?" he asked, admiring her beauty.

She came to him, held out her hand and said, "Take me to bed, Vincent. It's been too long."

He accepted her hand and pulled her down into his lap. He kissed first her forehead, her nose, her chin and then her lips. She broke off the kiss, held his face in her hands and gazed down at him, her cheeks flushed. "Carry me upstairs," she commanded.

He did her biding. He set her on the bed and she grabbed the front of his shirt and pulled him to her. They kissed again. She tore at his clothes and he at hers. He felt her desire and knew she could see his own. He lost himself in her. He forgot about her impending departure. He forgot about Liz. He forgot about Katherine and Norman. Kate consumed his mind and his body. She consumed his soul.

❦   ❦   ❦

Douglas Lassiter was sitting in one of the rocking chairs on the front porch when Vincent pulled the Rodeo into the driveway. Illuminated by the porch light, Vincent saw he wore a windbreaker and a Buffalo Bison's baseball cap. Vincent threw the vehicle into park, shut off the engine, and climbed out. Lassiter remained seated, but waved a hand.

"Evening," Vincent said, as he walked through the lawn to the porch steps.

"Back from the airport?"

Vincent stopped on the top step and leaned against the post. Arms crossed over his chest, he said, "Yep."

"Saw you loading up her suitcase earlier. I was at the Reilly's."

"How is Emmett?"

"Grieving. Missing his daughter. But he hasn't slipped back, if that's what you really want to know."

"It is."

"He's sticking close to Elsie. That's good to see."

"Yeah. She loves him."

"True." Lassiter fell silent.

"It's always nice to see you, Douglas, but did you stop by for a reason?"

"I did." Lassiter gazed at him with probing eyes.

Vincent waited for Douglas to continue. He sat down in the other rocking chair and he drew a deep breath of the damp night air. He looked out on the neighborhood, windows shining in the dark, cars passing slowly by. A young couple walked by holding hands and talking softly.

"You still going back?" Lassiter finally asked.

"I am."

"Why? Because you can?"

"No. I have a portrait to finish."

In the pale porch light, Vincent saw Lassiter's cheek twitch. "Have you seen Norman again?"

"I have."

Lassiter's cheek continued twitching. "What is he like?"

"He is kind and witty and very much in love with Katherine. He is talented. You would like him Douglas."

The twitch spread to Douglas's eye. He clutched the rocker's arms, his knuckles white. "Will you be there, Vincent? Will you be there in December when Norman disappears?"

Vincent pushed the urge to tell Lassiter what he had read in Emma's diary right out of his head. He couldn't. Not yet. With Liz's death and Kate being home, he hadn't had time to think about what he should do with the information. So he chewed on his lower lip and he composed his words carefully. "I may be. But remember, Douglas, I don't know how the violin does it. I keep waiting for the time when it fails."

"It won't. I believe you are meant to finish your painting at least."

Vincent nodded. "I believe that too."

Someone drove by on a Harley, the roar of the motor smashing the peaceful night. Lassiter jumped in his chair. He waited until the motor had faded away before he said, "I want you to save him, Vincent."

"You know I can't."

"You can. You must. He deserves to live."

"What happened to not messing with the past?"

"The hell with it."

"You know you don't mean that, Douglas."

Lassiter sank back in his chair, deflating completely, looking suddenly much older than his seventy years. "Damn it all," he cursed.

"I can only paint. That's all I can do. I'm lucky that I haven't changed anything so far."

Lassiter sucked in a long breath of air then sat forward. "Forgive me," he said, standing. "I'll go now."

"I'm sorry, Douglas. But history can't be changed."

Lassiter started down the steps but stopped, turning back. "Do me one favor, Vermay?"

"If I can."

"If he's meant to die, don't let it be painfully."

Nodding, Vincent said, "I'll do what I can."

Lassiter gave him a curt nod then headed off. Vincent watched him walk away, his head bowed, his shoulders sagging. When he was no longer visible, Vincent got up, unlocked the front door and went inside. Tomorrow he would visit Katherine. It had been too many days since he'd seen her.

CHAPTER 19

"I've missed you, Vincent," Katherine said.

"And I you?" he said, entering the parlor.

She lay on the couch beneath a multi-colored quilt, a bouquet of red roses on the stand behind her head. Books were piled on the coffee table. The blinds were open, bright light flooding the room, dancing off the yellow pine woodwork. The parlor walls were painted soft beige, the color matching the beige in a blue, white and beige-striped, wingback chair. The couch of velvet fabric also had the same beige as the walls, but it also sported red and yellow roses with pale green leaves. Kitty corner from the room's double paned, front window was a fireplace surrounded by yellow pine panels and having a stone mantle. An ornate, oval mirror hung above the mantle, its glass concave and obviously old. Like the wainscoting and crown molding in this room, the stands at either end of the couch and the coffee table were yellow pine. Wrought iron table lamps sat on the stands and a wrought iron pole lamp sat next to the wingback chair. Emma's parlor was very different from what Marlene Reilly had transformed it into when she'd remodeled the Reilly house. Likewise, there was no mural of Monticello on the foyer walls.

Katherine smiled at him. She looked sick and her bandaged hand lay on her abdomen on top of the blanket. "Where have you been?" she asked, brushing a lock of hair back with her good hand.

He sat on the coffee table. "I was with my wife. She was going through a rough time."

"Is she all right now?"

"She's better."

"Good. You wore your painting clothes."

"I intend to work on your portrait. I've been quite remiss."

She smiled, obviously pleased. "I would like to pose for you, but I'm still very weak."

"You don't need to pose." He tapped his head. "It's right here."

"Will you help me upstairs so I can watch you work?"

"I think not," a firm voice said behind Vincent.

He turned and saw Emma standing in the doorway, black medical bag in hand. She wore her white lab coat and had her hair twirled into a coil at the back of her head. Vincent stood up and bowed. "Hello, Emma."

"Vincent." She entered the room. "You may paint, but Katherine may not be upstairs while you are doing it. She is still suffering from pneumonia. And make sure you open the windows while you work. That should minimize the odor."

Vincent saluted her. "Yes, Captain."

Katherine laughed, her laughter turning into a harsh cough. Emma took her by the shoulders, sat her up and patted her back. She snatched up the porcelain bowl that sat beside the vase of roses and said, "Bring it up, Katherine."

Katherine coughed repeatedly, expelling clumps of green and brown mucus. Vincent turned away, grimacing at the sound of her coughs.

"That's it," Emma said. "Good girl. Okay, easy." The coughing eased and finally stopped. "Okay, lie back now."

Vincent turned back around. Katherine lay propped up on a pillow, her skin white, lines of exhaustion in her face. She stared up at him with tired eyes while Emma listened to her heart and lungs with a stethoscope. Vincent walked around behind the couch. Offering Katherine an encouraging smile, he took her good hand. She squeezed his hand and he was disheartened by the weakness of her grip.

Emma pulled the quilt up to Katherine's chin. "I'll get you a glass of water. How's your throat?"

"Sore." Her voice was hoarse.

"That's from the coughing. You rest." She gestured towards the door.

Vincent released Katherine's hand. "I'll stop in to see you when I'm done painting today."

"Thank you," she whispered, closing her eyes.

He followed Emma down the hall to the kitchen. She rinsed out the porcelain bowl as she said, "She's not doing well, Vincent."

He picked up a dishtowel and held out his hand. Emma's eyes widened. She looked from Vincent to the wet bowl and then back at Vincent again.

"What?" Vincent asked.

Shaking her head in wonder, she handed him the bowl. "I've said it before, Vincent, if you weren't married, I'd snatch you up."

He dried the bowl. "I know; I'm a man out of time."

"Most definitely."

He handed her the dried bowl. "She's not getting better, is she?"

Emma shook her head. She can't seem to get over the pneumonia. She's extremely weak. She's keeping down very little of what she eats." She held up the bowl. "You saw what she expelled."

"I did."

"Her lungs are ravaged. I don't know if they'll ever regain their full capacity." Emma sighed. "To be honest, Vincent, I'm concerned that she's just going to waste away."

Vincent fought back a gasp. *No, Emma, Katherine can't die. She has to deliver five children. She has to live until a ripe old age and leave Kate the Victorian and eleven million dollars.*

Emma set the bowl on the counter, opened the cupboard and removed a glass. "She has good moments, Vincent. But they're coming fewer and shorter. What you just witnessed is a frequent occurrence." She filled the glass with ice and water.

"What does Norman say?"

"Norman hasn't been here for a few days now. I don't know where he is. If Katherine knows, she's not talking."

Norman couldn't be gone already? It was only June. It was too soon for him to be gone. *Unless,* Vincent thought, *my presence in Katherine's life is finally beginning to alter the timeline. Maybe Jethro has acted sooner. Maybe Norman is already chained up in the Victorian's basement. Or worse, maybe Katherine is going to die and never have her five children.* The thought that he would return to his own time and find that Kate had never been born caused an involuntary shudder.

Seeing it, Emma said, "I'm sorry, Vincent. I don't mean to scare you. But Katherine is not getting better. As her doctor, I'm concerned. As her friend, I'm frightened."

He bit his lower lip and fought the urge to run over to the Victorian and check the basement. Somebody knocked on the front door and Vincent jumped.

"Could you get that for me?" Emma asked. "I want to heat up some soup for Katherine."

"Sure."

Vincent snuck a peek into the living room as he walked to the front door. Katherine slept, looking frail and small beneath the quilt. Reaching the door, he opened it. Norman Lassiter stood on the porch, dressed in a black suit, gray and white, pinstripe vest, and gray derby, and carrying a dozen red roses.

🍁   🍁   🍁

"I have to say it again, Vincent, how do you do that?"

Vincent stopped in mid stroke. Norman stood in the sunroom doorway. He'd removed his suit jacket, unbuttoned his vest and rolled up his sleeves. "Do what?"

Norman sauntered in. Standing next to Vincent, he studied the portrait. "How do you take something from life, transfer it on to canvas and make it seem so alive? She almost breathes in this portrait."

Vincent shrugged. "I've just always been able to." He resumed painting. "How do you act? Now that's a mystery to me."

Norman grunted. "Not much of a mystery there. You just pretend you're something you're not."

"I doubt it's that easy."

Norman chuckled. He wandered away, going to the window to look down on the yard.

"How did your visit go?" Vincent asked.

"She's worse than when I left for New York."

"What was in New York?"

"Loose ends to tie up. I sublet the apartment."

"Then you're moving here?" Vincent's heart kicked into overdrive. *Has Jethro already cut some deal with Norman?*

"Yes, Vincent, I am. I intend to watch over her. I intend to make sure Malloy treats her properly."

"And you can do that? You can live here and watch the woman you love be with another man?"

Norman collapsed into a wicker chair and slung his leg over its arm. "I have to. I must protect her, Vincent."

"Have you told her?"

"I have."

Vincent continued painting Katherine's dress. "What did Katherine say about it?"

"I think she's pleased."

"You're not sure."

"She smiled and there were tears in her eyes. Although, I suppose the roses could have caused the tears. She loves red roses."

"So does my wife." Vincent saw Kate's face in his mind. He hated the fact that she'd returned to Georgetown. Too many miles separated them.

"I can't believe how much Katherine has deteriorated in three days, Vincent." Norman unbuttoned his collar. "I'm worried."

Vincent turned from the painting. "So is Emma. Damn, so am I."

Norman sat forward, elbows on his knees, chin on his hands. "I can't lose her, Vincent. She's…she's my only reason for living."

Vincent again saw Kate's face in his mind. Could he live without her? He prayed he never had to find out.

❦   ❦   ❦

"You are sad, Vincent Vermay," Katherine said, startling him. She stood in the sunroom doorway, bundled in a forest green silk robe, embroidered with the initials KM. He wondered if Malloy had sent over some of her things, or if the robe had been a present from Norman.

"You shouldn't be here," he said, setting his palette and brush aside. He went to her and slipped his arm around her. "Come on away from the paint."

He escorted her down the hall towards her room. She protested, saying, "Take me downstairs. Please. It looks like such a lovely day. Emma's parlor is so bright."

"Only if you promise me you'll rest."

"Heavens, Vincent, what else do I have to do?" She coughed and he thought she was going to start bringing stuff up like she did yesterday, but she didn't. Still, the spell weakened her, and she leaned heavily on him. Without asking, he scooped her up in his arms and carried her down to the parlor. He laid her on the couch and covered her with the quilt.

"Thank you, Vincent." Her voice was ragged and barely audible. She winced as she swallowed, her hand going to her throat.

He touched her forehead. Her skin burned beneath his hand. "You shouldn't tire yourself, Katherine," he scolded.

"I can't lie in that room by myself all day. Surely, you understand. I need—" Harsh coughs cut off her words. They came from deep within her chest, and they sounded painful.

He looked around for the porcelain bowl and found it on the floor beneath the coffee table. He snatched it up and held it out to her. She took it with shaking hands. He got his arm around her and lifted her to a sitting position. The coughs were relentless, her face contorted in pain. What she coughed up was yellow, green, and brown, and tinged with blood. He held her upright and helped her hold the bowl. He wondered if she were actually coughing up parts of her lungs.

At last, she collapsed against him, the spell over. He eased her back on the pillow. She stared up at him with glazed eyes. Her chest heaved up and down as she fought for air.

"I'll get you a glass of water," he said, and ran for the kitchen. As he turned on the faucet, he cursed himself for having sent the nurse home. How arrogant he had been to think he could care for her on his own.

She lay with her eyes closed. He knelt beside her. "Katherine?"

Her eyes opened, questioning him.

"Take a drink of this."

Hand behind her head, he lifted her head up off the pillow so that she could drink. She winced with each swallow. Pushing the glass away, she rasped. "No more." She held her throat as she said, "I'm dying, Vincent."

His heart stopped. He shook his head in protest. Two thuds in his chest and his heart kicked on again, but it only fluttered and he felt dizzy.

"I'm dying," she said again.

He leaned close. "No! You can't die, Katherine." He grabbed her shoulders. "You can't. You hear me? You can't die." He shook her, as if the shaking would force the life to stay within her.

Strong arms grabbed him and pulled him away from her. He was face-to-face with Norman. "What are you doing, man?" Norman shook him

"She can't die," Vincent said.

Norman threw him aside. Vincent stumbled and fell, landing in the wing-back chair. Norman knelt beside Katherine. "Darling," he said. "Darling, it's Norman."

She gazed at him but did not see him. She was drifting away from them. Her skin was ash gray. The quilt covering her bandaged hand was turning a bright red.

Norman pulled the quilt back. The bandage was solid red. Frantic, he turned to Vincent. "Call Emma. Hurry!"

What followed was a blur in Vincent's memory. He remembered picking up the clumsy black receiver on the antique phone and talking to an operator. But he didn't remember talking with Emma. He remembered standing in the parlor doorway watching as Norman talked to Katherine, telling her he loved her, and that he would die without her. And Katherine, he remembered how still she was. How she just laid there, eyes open but not seeing, her skin turning transparent so that he could see the bones beneath. And then Emma burst through the door. She pushed him aside as she rushed to Katherine's side.

He couldn't watch what Emma did to Katherine. He didn't think she could save her. Katherine was right. She was dying. She would die and Kate, his wife, his soul mate, his reason for living, would never be born. He didn't remember going out on the front porch but that's where he ended up, sitting in the rocker, head bowed, rocking aimlessly.

Norman appeared before him. "Is she gone?" Vincent stammered out the words, his voice squeaking.

"No."

Vincent didn't believe him. He stared at him, the disbelief shining in his eyes.

"Come with me," Norman said.

Vincent followed him, surprised at how rubbery his legs felt. But he made it up the stairs to Katherine's room. She lay on the bed, sleeping. Her left arm was cradled in a sling, the hand freshly bandaged. Her breathing, though raspy, came in normal rhythm. Emma leaned over her, stethoscope to her chest, listening to her lungs.

Seeing them, Emma motioned them into the room. "We nearly lost her," she said, tears in her eyes. Norman put a hand on her shoulder. Emma blinked back her tears and continued. "I've put a pressure bandage on her hand. It must be changed twice a day. The stitches didn't hold and I..." She trailed off, looking back at her patient again. "I'm not leaving her. I will stay by her side."

"I shouldn't have sent the nurse home," Vincent said. "I'm sorry."

Emma waved off his comment. "Katherine should not have gotten out of bed on her own. She shouldn't have exerted herself."

"We'll help you take care of her," Norman said. "You just tell us what to do."

Norman's shirt and vest were stained with Katherine's blood. His hair was disheveled, his face lined with worry.

Without taking her eyes off Katherine, Emma said, "The next several hours will tell us whether or not...You gentleman better go down to the kitchen and have something to eat. I'll eat after you. We'll take turns sitting with her."

Reluctantly, they did as Emma requested.

❦   ❦   ❦

Vincent lay on the canopy bed in Emma's guestroom. He lay in the dark, fully dressed, listening, counting the number of times Katherine coughed. He heard Norman pacing in the hall, the floor creaking under his feet.

Vincent stared into the darkness. He was torn. He wanted to go back to his present and see if Kate was still alive. Then again the thought of her not being there terrified him. He must stay here and make sure of Katherine's fate. Another part of him said he should take his portrait and flee this time period, never to return. But the artist in him would not forsake his portrait. He knew he would not be able to finish it if he took it to the future. He didn't know how he knew this, but he did.

His fingers played with the bedspread. *How long can I stay here? How long should I stay?* Questions rolled around in circles in his head. Did he really need to stay and learn Katherine's fate? He would know as soon as he got back to his own time and tried to contact Kate. If she didn't exist…He shook off the thought. Would his staying here make a difference in Katherine's recovery? God, he was so damn confused.

He didn't know when he'd fallen asleep, but he had. He awoke with a start, sweating, his shirt soaked. He sat up, listening. What had awakened him? There was no longer a creaking sound in the hall. He slid off the bed, went to the door and cracked it open. The hall light burned, but Norman no longer paced. Maybe he had relieved Emma.

Vincent stepped into the hall. Walking lightly, he went down to Katherine's room. Quietly, he opened the bedroom door. A single light glowed on Emma's desk. Katherine lay on her back, her eyes closed. Emma sat beside her bed. She looked at him with exhaustion in her eyes. She put a finger to her lips then stood up. She came to the door and Vincent stepped back, giving her room. She left the door cracked open and motioned for him to follow her. She led him to the sunroom, switched on the light and indicated he sit. He did, taking the wicker rocker. She took the other wicker chair. Sighing deeply, she said, "I finally convinced Norman to go to bed."

"You should go too. I'll sit with her."

Emma eyed him with suspicious eyes.

"What?"

"Isn't your wife wondering where you are, Vincent?"

"She's away visiting friends."

"I see." She ran a hand through her hair. "Maybe I will take you up on your offer then. I am tired. And Katherine has fallen back asleep."

"I heard her coughing."

Emma nodded. "I thought you might."

Lightning flashed and thunder rumbled in the distance.

"He hasn't come to see her since she injured her hand," Emma said. "The bastard sits over there in that house and doesn't come see her."

"Has he asked you when she can come home?"

"No. I've seen him twice when I've left for the office in the morning. He just glares at me and says nothing." She smoothed her eyebrows with her fingers. "I so want to shoot the man."

Vincent chuckled. "I never thought of you as violent, Emma."

"I never thought of myself as violent either. He brings out the dark side of people."

"Yes, he does."

The thunder rumbled closer. Vincent heard the sizzle in the lightning.

"I love her, Vincent," Emma said. "Since she's been here with me, I've come to love her. She's no longer just my patient. She's my friend."

Vincent didn't comment. He sat waiting for Emma to continue. She didn't disappoint. "When you choose the life I chose, you sacrifice a lot. Women doctors are still not well received. Girls I grew up with, well, let's just say they drifted away. It's a solitary life, Vincent."

"But a noble one, don't you think?"

She smiled. "That's what Katherine said. She said that I am 'noble and special.' She feels safe in my hands."

"Because she is. Malloy can't bully his way past you if you don't want him to."

Her smiled broadened. "True."

Thunder cracked above their heads. Lightning flashed dangerously close and the rain came, beating against the windows.

"I've said it before. I don't want her to go back to him."

"None of us do, Emma. Especially Norman."

Emma sighed. "But she insists. I don't understand it."

"She took vows. To her they are sacred."

"Do you really think God would judge her if she left that man?"

Vincent thought of the portrait of Jesus with his arms outstretched in the sanctuary at Salem Church. "No," he said, "I don't."

The thunder roared louder, the lightning coming fast and furious. Sheets of rain pounded the windows, threatening to break them. Emma stood up abruptly. "I will stay with her until dawn. Relieve me then."

"Okay." He knew there was no point in arguing.

He stayed in the wicker rocker, the flashes of lightning bringing Katherine's portrait to life. She held her violin. No, she cradled her violin like it was the only part of her life that mattered. As the flashes lit the painting first on then off, Vincent sat forward, forearms on his thighs, hands folded into a steeple, Norman's voice in his head, asking Vincent for a painting all his own. Various poses rolled around in Vincent's mind. He jumped up, turned on the light, and snatched up his pencil and sketchpad. He was still drawing when the storm moved off. He was still drawing with the first light of dawn.

She accepted the broth he offered, letting him raise her up to the cup. She drank it greedily. When she was finished, he eased her back down. She closed her eyes a moment then opened them, searching for him. He set the cup on Emma's desk and sat down in the chair beside her bed.

She stared at him, dark circles surrounding her eyes, contrasting sharply with her white skin. "Thank you, Vincent." Her voice was a low grumble in her throat.

"Would you like more?"

She shook her head. "You're still here."

"Yes. Norman is too."

"I know." She swallowed and while the action pained her some, at least she did not wince. "You never answered me, Vincent."

"About what?"

"You are sad. I can see it."

"I'm supposed to be happy that you are so sick, Katherine?"

"It's not me that makes you sad. Tell me, Vincent."

How could he tell her? What should he say? *Gee, Katherine, I'm sad because Emma's great niece killed herself last weekend. She killed herself and I couldn't stop her. Oh, and on top of that, your granddaughter, who just happens to be my wife, doesn't understand that I want her to live with me in your house. She thinks that I, her husband who would die for her, would to do to her what Jethro did to you. And I don't get it, Katherine. I don't understand why Kate would think that of me. What did I ever do that would make her think that?*

"Vincent?"

"You are uncanny. You see right through me."

"Is it your wife?"

He scratched his chin as he chose his words carefully. "I guess. She's away visiting and I miss her. I get melancholy when I'm away from her."

"You are such a dear man."

He took her right hand. "And you are a special woman. You deserve better than Jethro Malloy." He knew he shouldn't say this, but he couldn't help himself. He had to clench his teeth to keep from begging her not to return to Malloy.

"Don't you realize?" she asked. "I have used him as much as he's used me."

"No," he protested.

"But I have, Vincent? I used him to escape." She closed her eyes, turning her head away. "I needed to escape life. Jethro gave me that escape. But...oh, Vincent...I should have told Norman. I should have turned to Norman." Tears slipped from beneath her eyelids.

Vincent gently squeezed her hand. "Norman is here for you now."

She cried softly, her shoulders shaking. Vincent kept hold of her hand, hoping his touch comforted her.

Emma came in, saw Katherine's tears, and gave Vincent an inquiring look. "Past mistakes," he mouthed.

Emma nodded her understanding. She picked up the empty cup and smiled. Then, leaning close, she rubbed her hand along Katherine's tear-stained cheek. "Katherine?"

Katherine opened her eyes.

"Jethro wishes to see you. He's downstairs. I told him I would let him come up as long as I was in the room with you."

"Where's Norman?"

"Baring the staircase like a guard dog."

Vincent couldn't suppress a smile. *That a boy, Norman!*

Emma wiped Katherine's cheeks with her sleeve. "Do you want to see Jethro?"

"I want all of you here."

"Done," Vincent said, rising. "I'll get him."

"And Norman too," Katherine insisted.

Vincent winked. "And Norman too."

❁   ❁   ❁

Tension ruled the room. Jethro, immaculate in a brown, pinstripe suit, a bouquet of wildflowers in his hand, stood at the foot of Katherine's bed. Emma sat next to her, holding her hand. Norman leaned on the desk, arms folded across his chest, glaring at Malloy. Vincent sat on the windowsill, one eye on Norman, the other on Jethro. He could smell the flowers, their scent vibrant yet welcome. They overpowered the lingering smell of medicine that had lived in this room since Katherine had occupied it.

"Emma tells me you are quite ill," Jethro said.

"Yes." Her voice was guarded.

"I brought you some flowers."

"Thank you."

No one rose to accept the flowers so he kept holding them. "Mrs. Collins will be home this weekend. I was hoping that you could come home."

"I'm afraid that is not possible, Jethro. She is far from well, as I've already told you." Emma's tone was one of annoyance.

Malloy ignored her. "I miss you, Katherine."

A muscle in Norman's right cheek twitched. Vincent was ready to jump if necessary. There would be no fighting between these men today. Katherine's fragile state would not allow it.

"I will try to be a better husband."

"Is that possible, Malloy?" Norman blurted.

Emma sent him a scathing look.

Katherine opened her mouth to speak but coughed instead, what little color there was draining from her face. Emma leaned close, laying her hand on Katherine's chest. "Easy," she said. "If you're not up to this, you say so."

Katherine shook her head. "Jethro," she rasped. "I will no longer be your prisoner. I will no longer remain locked up in that room. I need to live. I need to be among people. I need—" Coughs cut off her words.

Malloy watched impassively while she coughed. When at last the spell ended, she laid back, her eyes closed. Emma gently massaged Katherine's chest. "You should go now, Jethro," she said.

"You will have the life you want," Jethro said.

He's lying, Vincent thought. *Plain, flat out lying. He has no intentions of being a proper husband to her. She is his possession. One he refuses to lose.* Vincent shot Norman a warning look, but it was not necessary. Norman's twitching face and angry eyes told Vincent that Norman was not fooled either.

"You expect her to believe that?" Norman asked. "Do you think she's stupid?"

"Norman, don't," Katherine pleaded, opening her eyes. She sought him out. "Please don't fight with him."

Norman dropped to his knees beside her bed. "Don't go back to him, Katherine. God won't hold you to this vow." He touched her cheek, brushed her hair with a loving hand. "Please don't go back to him."

"He is my husband," she whispered.

"He does not love you as I do. I love you."

She gazed at Norman with a look Vincent knew well. It was the same look Kate gave him. It was a look of complete love. "I know, Norman," she assured him.

"Then stay with me. I will give you all you ever dreamed of and more. I will hold you when you are sick and scared. I will give you your head when you need it. I will—" She laid a finger on his lips.

She turned to Jethro who stared back at her with steel eyes. He clutched the bouquet of flowers so tightly his knuckles glowed white. "I will not be coming home, Jethro," she said, her voice suddenly strong. "Take your flowers and go. Leave us in peace."

Malloy argued no further. He turned on his heels and stalked out. Vincent heard his footsteps on the stairs and then the slamming of the front door.

Norman's face was alive with pure joy. He gathered Katherine in his arms. "Thank God," he said, rocking her. "Katherine, my love, my life. Thank God."

She let him hold her, resting her head on his shoulder, her eyes closed.

"Not so rough, Norman," Emma admonished.

"It's okay, Emma," Katherine said. "Hold me, Norman. Never let me go."

"Never," he assured her.

Emma pointed at the door. Vincent followed her out into the hall. "I would say that our patient's prognosis just improved tenfold, Vincent."

"I agree." Still, Emma frowned. Vincent had no doubts why. "You don't think Malloy will give up so easily, do you?"

Emma sighed deeply. "No, Vincent, I don't."

CHAPTER 20

Vincent returned to the Victorian exhausted, but happy. He had been gone four days, having stayed in 1926 long enough to know for certain that Katherine would live. He entered the parlor and saw the message light flashing on the phone. Grinning, he pressed play, collapsed on the couch and listened. They were all from Kate, wondering where he'd gone and why he hadn't told her where he was going. Her tone went from annoyance in the early messages to downright terror by the last message. She'd even sent Elsie and Emmett over to check on him. Damn, he hadn't meant to scare her.

He sat up and dialed her cell phone. She answered on the first ring. "Hello. Vincent, is that you?"

"Hi, babe."

"Oh, thank God." He heard the relief in her voice. "I've been so worried. Where have you been? Why haven't you called? I...Oh, God." She was crying.

"Don't cry, babe," he said, suddenly sick to his stomach. He could only imagine how worried she'd been. He felt like kicking himself in the rear.

"I was about to leave for the airport. I called the police. Where have you been?"

"Okay," he said. "Calm down, Kate. You don't need to cry. I'm fine." She sucked in a long breath of air. "That's it, babe. Take a few deep breaths. I'm sorry. I was off doing some soul searching. Trying to get my creative juices flowing again." He hated lying to her, but he couldn't tell her where he'd really been.

"Where did you go?"

"No place really. I was actually close by. Anyway, I should have told you, but I figured you'd be so busy with McMartin you wouldn't miss me." He cringed after the words were out of his mouth. *Damn, why did I say that? Talk about stupid, Vincent. Really, stupid.* He waited for her to yell at him, accuse him of not understanding her, of not considering her work as important as his painting.

"I guess I deserve that."

He sat silent, not believing what she had just said.

"Vincent? Are you still there?"

"Yeah." He wondered if he looked as dumbstruck as he felt.

"Vincent," she said. "I started working on the novel again and…well…I hate to admit it, but I really enjoy doing it."

"You do?"

"Amazingly, yes, I do. A lot. In fact, the work for McMartin is getting in the way. I want to work on Chapter 44 and instead, I have to write one of his confounded speeches."

Was he hearing her correctly? Was she really telling him that she was disenchanted with putting words into Senator McMartin's mouth?

"So, I made a decision yesterday."

"Which was?"

"I gave McMartin my notice."

Vincent's eyes opened wide. "You what?"

"I gave him notice. I told him that I would stay on until the election, but after that, I'm stepping down." Vincent stood up. Kate continued talking. "I had dinner with Regina and gave her a copy of the manuscript, the first 20 chapters anyway. She called me this morning. She said her company wants to publish it. She'll be my editor. A contract is being drawn up."

"No shit!" he said, dizzy with excitement.

"No shit," she repeated then laughed. "I thought a lot about what you said, Vincent. How you believe in me."

"I do, Kate. Without a doubt."

"And if I come there, to North Tonawanda, to live with you there, it…I won't…"

"Be my prisoner?"

"I know thinking that way is irrational, Vincent. I know you aren't like Jethro. But that house, it does things to me."

"It's not the house, is it, Kate?"

She didn't respond.

"It's the third floor bedroom, Katherine's bedroom. And what you saw your grandfather do to her in that room."

She gasped.

"Did you see him beat her? Is that what you saw in that room?"

"How do you know?" she asked.

He almost said, "Because I've gone back in time myself." But he didn't, he couldn't, not yet. "I know that something scared you in that bedroom. There are ghosts there that tell stories. They get in your head and you see things that were."

"Yes," she cried.

He wished she were here, next to him, so he could hold and comfort her. He chose his words carefully. "I've no doubt that what you imagined really happened, babe. Jethro Malloy was an abusive, possessive man. I'm sure he hit her."

"He beat her so badly. She bled from her nose. She begged him to get Emma. He refused. And—" She broke off, sobbing.

"Kate," he said, his voice firm. "Kate, listen to me." She quieted down. "What you saw in your head, I know it was real to you. But the fact is Katherine lived until the age of 94. You spent summers here with her while growing up."

"I loved her."

"I know you did."

She sniffed, gulped then said, "I asked her, Vincent. I asked her if he'd really beaten her. She refused to tell me. I pressed her. I said if she didn't tell me the truth, I wouldn't come see her anymore. She still refused and in my young, stupid pride, I left and...oh, Vincent, I lost so much time with her. I didn't see her again until Lydia forced her to Maryland. I cut off Liz too. I couldn't go back to North Tonawanda. I couldn't tell Liz what had happened between Katherine and me. I...I...Vincent, until I met you..." She hiccupped. "You saved me, Vincent. You gave me life again."

Vincent ran a hand through his hair. He didn't speak, but listened.

"Oh, I still talked to Katherine on the phone. I...I sent her letters and gifts, but I just couldn't...I couldn't see her in that house. Just thinking of her in that house brought pictures of Jethro beating her into my head. He was so brutal. So hateful to her and...I should never have abandoned her. I should have helped her fight the move with Lydia, but I didn't. Oh, Vincent, I didn't." She sobbed into the phone.

"You made up before Katherine died, Kate," he said, his voice firm, penetrating her tears. "That's what's important."

"We never talked about Jethro or the night I asked her if he'd beaten her. Our relationship was strained. It was never like it had been."

"Maybe not outwardly, babe. But Katherine left you the house and eleven million dollars. What does that tell you about how she felt about you?"

She didn't answer at first. He gave her the time she needed to collect her thoughts. "Vincent," she finally said. "Will you come to Georgetown for a visit?"

He wanted to go to her. He wanted to get on a plane this very minute. But he couldn't. He had to stay in the Victorian. He had to keep painting Katherine's portrait. "I'll come when I'm done painting the house, okay. And the current portrait I'm doing too. Deal?"

"I suppose with the nice weather coming up there now, you should finish painting the house. I guess I can wait a bit to see you if you promise me you won't go off and not tell me again."

"Promise."

She sniffed. "I'll call the police and tell them you're no longer missing. Oh, and get that fireplace fixed so we can cozy up in front of it during the winter."

"Consider it done." He could feel the smile on her face. "Now, wash your face, Kate, and get back to work on that novel. I'm proud of you."

"McMartin is pissed."

"McMartin will live."

She laughed, her laughter lifting his heart. "I'm sorry I've been so impossible lately, Vincent. I was so scared and confused."

"Don't worry about it. Now go write."

"Okay."

"I'll see you soon. And, Kate?"

"Yes?"

"I love you."

❀   ❀   ❀

"She really quit her job?" Sarah asked, not believing him.

"Yep." Vincent sat in Kate's office, feet up on her desk, phone to his ear.

"Damn," Sarah said.

"Once the election is over anyway."

"Damn," Sarah said again.

"But that's not really what I called to tell you."

"What else?" she asked, her tone growing serious. "You are all right, aren't you, bro?"

He heard worry in her voice. "I'm fine. Just, I've lost another friend."

"Who and how?"

He told her about Liz, not at all surprised to find tears on his face when he'd finished his tale.

"Oh, Vincent, I'm so sorry. You should have called me. Why didn't you call me? We could have talked."

Vincent smiled. She was right. He could have talked to her and vented his sorrow. Like he'd always done in the past. So why hadn't he called her? "I don't know, Sis. Guess I just wasn't up to talking."

"How is Kate? She was renewing her friendship with this Liz, right?"

"She was. And she's hurting." Vincent led his feet drop to the floor and sat forward in his chair. "She could use a friendly voice. Other than mine, that is."

"What about you?"

"I'm okay. Painting and counting the days until November and the election."

"If you need me to, I could rearrange some things and fly out there."

"Sarah, your big tourist season is heating up. You can't leave Silverton. Besides, I'm okay. So hang up the phone and call my wife."

"You're sure?"

"Positive."

"Okay. But if you change your mind and want me to come out there—"

"I'll call. Now hang up and call Kate."

"You got it. Bye."

"Night."

The phone cut off in his ear. He moved the receiver away from his ear, resting it against his chest a moment. *Why*, he wondered? Why was it that he hadn't had to immediately call Sarah? All his life, she'd gotten him through his tough times. And yet now...Now there was Katherine, Norman and Emma. Now, for as long as it lasted, he had another whole life.

"I like it, Vincent."

Vincent looked down from the ladder. Tracy Woodward stood on the lawn, clad in denim cutoffs and a white polo shirt, her hair pulled back in a ponytail. Mirrored sunglasses hid her eyes.

"Hey!" he called down.

"I'm serious," she said. "It's going to be beautiful when you're done."

"Thanks." He stuck his paintbrush in the can of paint that hung on the ladder and climbed down. "I decided to go vintage Victorian."

"Does Kate like it?"

"Yes. So far, anyway." He pulled a rag from his back pocket and wiped sweat from his brow. "Time for a break though. Want an iced tea?"

"How about a beer?" She grinned.

"You're not legal."

She held out her hands. "Promise I won't drive."

He considered and then shook his head. "Sorry, iced tea it is. I don't want the wrath of Jessica on my head."

"Chicken."

They sat on the front porch in the wooden rockers and Vincent gulped his iced tea. The day was a steamy one for June. The sun burned relentlessly down and he could feel the heat coming off the paved street, the smell of burning tar filling his nostrils. Haze hung in the sky, turning its vibrant blue to a metal gray.

"Have you seen Emmett Reilly lately?" Tracy asked, worry in her eyes.

"No. I haven't seen Duke either. But Elsie Whiting is with them."

Tracy traced a *J* in the condensation on her glass. "I still can't believe that Aunt Liz actually did what I thought about doing."

"Well, she did, Trace." He shook his head. "I still can't believe she's gone. I keep expecting to see her car pull into the driveway over there."

"Did you know that she left me the Mustang, Vincent?"

"No, I didn't."

Tracy ran her tongue along her upper lip. "Pastor McMichael said she did it because she loved me."

"She did love you, Tracy."

"I know." She paused a moment and then said, "I went and put fresh flowers on her grave this morning. I drove the Mustang over there. I had thought about riding my bike, but it just seemed right to take the Mustang."

"What kind of flowers?"

"Lilies." She took a long drink of her iced tea. "I'm still seeing Dr. Kostapoulis."

"And your medication?"

"Still taking it."

"Good."

"I came over to see you because I want you to know that you don't have to worry about me anymore. I'm going to be okay."

"I'm sure you are." He laid his paint-stained hand on her forearm. "We'll still be friends, right?"

She grinned. "Of course."

"Great." He patted her arm, drained his glass and stood up. "I better get back to work."

"Can I help?"

"Sure. I've got lots of brushes."

He got another ladder out of the carriage house and set her to painting the back of the house. They worked in comfortable silence. She headed home just before 6 p.m. with a smile on her face.

❦   ❦   ❦

Vincent was washing his supper dishes when Duke came in the doggie door. The dog sat down on the kitchen floor and stared at Vincent with morose eyes. Vincent wiped his hands on a paper towel and sat down next to Duke. "Hey, boy," he said, petting him from head to tail. "How ya doing?"

Duke lay on his belly, his head in Vincent's lap. He let out a long, sorrowful moan. "You don't understand, do you, boy?" He rubbed the top of Duke's head. "None of us do. And we all miss her too."

"Duke! Duke! Where are you, buddy!" Duke's ears went up and he barked. Emmett Reilly came in the back door. "So this is where you've gotten to. Sorry, Vincent."

"Hi, Emmett. He's welcome anytime." He eased Duke from his lap and got to his feet, extending his hand. Emmett shook it, his grip firm. "I was thinking of coming over after I showered," Vincent added.

"I saw you and Tracy painting today," Emmett said, kneeling beside his dog. "Good to see this old house getting a fresh coat of paint. He rubbed Duke's back. "I'm afraid this guy is pretty sad these days."

"I see that."

"He doesn't understand why Elizabeth doesn't come home. He sits in front of the door waiting for her."

"What about you, Emmett? How are you?"

The old man's eyes filled with tears, but they didn't fall. "I'm doing. Elsie keeps me strong." He bent and kissed Duke's head. "I'm like Duke sometimes. Especially when I wake up from a late afternoon nap. I expect her to walk in the door." He shook his head, his white hair shimmering in the kitchen light. "I just can't believe that she's...I keep wondering if there was anything I could have done to prevent her from taking her life."

"Kate and I keep wondering that too."

Emmett gave Duke's head a final pat and straightened. "She'd just drawn up her will. She'd signed it the day before she took her life. She left me her practice. What the hell am I going to do with it?"

"Sell it."

"She was a good doctor, Vincent. I was so proud of her."

"I know you were. She knew you were."

"But it wasn't enough. My daughter suffered in silence. She lost her fiancé and her mother and she hurt deep inside, and I couldn't reach her." He shook his head. "What kind of father was I?"

"Liz loved you, Emmett."

He didn't hear him. He went on, still shaking his head. "And then the last straw. Jill's death and Elizabeth could take no more. And all I've been is a burden to her. Another worry. Another cause of pain."

Vincent grabbed Emmett's shoulders. "Stop it!" he shouted.

Emmett jerked.

"Listen to me. The past is the past. Liz loved you. And yes, she hurt. More deeply than you, or Elsie, or I, or Kate could reach. She chose to end her life. Her death is awful and painful. But we are alive, Emmett. Liz would want us to live."

"She would," he agreed, nodding.

"You have a wonderful woman over there, Emmett. You know Elsie Whiting loves you. She loved Liz as her own. Go home, let her comfort you and you her. Be together." He turned Emmett toward the back door. "Go on."

Emmett went without protest and seeing him go, Duke jumped up and ran after him.

❋   ❋   ❋

Vincent stepped back from Katherine's portrait and grinned. He had to show her. She must be the first person to see it finished.

She sat in an Adirondack chair in Emma's backyard. She wore a lavender dress, a white shawl around her shoulders, her bandaged left hand resting in her lap. Her hair hung free, tendrils blowing around her face. She sat with eyes closed, her face held up to the afternoon sun.

Vincent carried the painting across the lawn and she heard him coming, turning her head towards him and shielding her eyes with her good hand. "Is it finished?" she asked, excitement in her voice, a voice no longer hoarse.

"It is." He held it up. "What do you think?"

Wonder filled her eyes. "Magnificent." She looked it up and down. She shook her head and said, "She is so beautiful, Vincent. Surely, you embellished her. I am certainly not as beautiful as she."

"But you are, my love," Norman Lassiter said from the back porch. He came down the steps and strode across the lawn. Stopping behind her, hands on her shoulders, he kissed the top of her head.

"Norman. You are hardly objective."

He took her hand and squatted beside her chair. He looked handsome in a white suit and white straw hat. "Katherine is right, Vincent. It is magnificent. And now, you must begin work on my portrait of my beautiful, special Katherine."

Katherine inclined her head, embarrassed.

"No, my love," Norman said, taking her chin in his hand and raising it. "You are a treasure in this world." Tears pierced her eyes. He kissed her forehead with gentle lips.

The back door slammed, pulling Vincent's attention to the house. Emma came down the porch steps. Seeing the painting, she stopped, a wide smile spreading across her face. "Now, isn't that spectacular?" She hurried to them. "Oh, Vincent, you have truly outdone yourself."

"That he has," Norman said, straightening.

Emma pressed her hand against Katherine's forehead. "And how are you feeling today, young lady?"

"Much better. It is so lovely out here."

"Well, I'm afraid you must come inside now. It's time to change your bandage."

"My hand feels much better as well, Emma. It no longer aches."

"It is nearly healed. Still, with your propensity to infection, we must keep it cleansed and dressed. Now come on."

Norman helped Katherine up then watched as she walked with Emma across the lawn and up the porch steps. As the screen door swung closed, he said, "I still can't believe it, Vincent. I can't believe that she loves me. That she has chosen me."

"She has."

Norman gazed at the painting. "She is the loveliest woman in the world. Don't you agree?"

"Oh, I'm partial to my own wife for that title."

Norman's eyebrows shot up. "A wife we've yet to meet."

Vincent ignored the comment. "I better get this painting back inside. It needs to finish drying."

Norman fell in step beside him. "Take a walk with me?" he asked, hands in the pockets of his slacks.

"Where?"

"Over to Tremont. I've got something I'd like to show you."

❦   ❦   ❦

The house was small yet cozy, standing a story and a half tall, its roof slate gray, its shingles white, shutters blue. A hedged lawn and luscious, blooming gardens surrounded it, irises and azaleas dancing in the breeze. They walked up a narrow stone driveway to a carriage house with white doors adorned with blue trim. A black wrought iron fence surrounded the back yard.

Grinning, Norman asked, "What do you think?"

"You bought it?"

"I did. Come inside."

Norman led him back to the front of the house and they entered through the front door, stepping into a small foyer with a marble floor. The downstairs consisted of a kitchen, dining area and parlor. In the dining area and parlor, the crown molding, wainscoting, and baseboards were walnut, the floors honey oak. A marble fireplace commanded the living room. Walnut staircases led from both the kitchen and the front foyer upstairs to two bedrooms and a bathroom, all with slanted ceilings and French doors with stained glass windows. The bathroom had a pedestal sink and claw foot tub. The larger bedroom occupied the front of the house, sporting a wide, Palladian window that looked out on the street below.

"This will be her music room," Norman said leading him to a back bedroom.

Vincent scratched his chin as he asked, "And where will you put the children?"

Norman grinned. "We shall add an addition should we be blessed with children."

Vincent scanned the room. The walls were a soft white, one wall consisting of built in shelves and drawers. A black music stand decorated with gold g-clefs already stood before the window. A maroon, gold, black and white flowered carpet covered the wood floor.

"Do you think Katherine will like it?" Norman asked.

Vincent couldn't look at him. This man who loved Katherine so, who had bought her this house, who dreamed of a life at her side as her husband and had no idea that he would never live with her in this house. Vincent walked to the window. He looked down at the backyard, the afternoon sun flitting over the flowers. *Paradise.* It was the only word he could think of. Vincent ran his finger along the windowsill. But Malloy would never let them have their paradise

"Vincent?" Norman persisted.

Without turning from the window, Vincent said, "She will think it paradise."

Norman clapped his hands together. "Yes. Exactly. That's what I thought the moment I saw it. Of course, we will need furniture. But we will choose those items together. Although, I think I'm partial to a brass bed for our bedroom."

"Brass is nice." Vincent turned from the window. "But how? How did you afford this?"

Vincent chuckled. "Vincent, don't tell me you believe everything Malloy says. I am not the poor man he thinks I am. I may not have his wealth, but I have more than sufficient means to give Katherine what she needs."

"All she needs is you, Norman."

"She needs happiness. She needs joy. I will give her both."

No, Vincent thought, hoping his face did not reveal his thoughts. *No, you won't.*

They rode their bikes out to the cemetery, Tracy in front, the muscles in her legs pulsating as she pedaled. He could tell by the power in her legs and the fact that she was not winded by their speed that she'd been riding a lot without him. He struggled to keep up, but he did not ask her to slow down. The exertion helped melt away the tension he'd carried around inside since visiting the little white house with Norman. He thought of his recent talk with Douglas Lassiter. *I want you to save him, Vincent.* The fact that he couldn't and shouldn't had been clear to Vincent on that night. But since visiting Norman's house…Vincent shook the thoughts from his head.

The morning was overcast, fog slowly lifting off the fields. Cows ambled behind a fence off to Vincent's right. The air was cool, a gentle wind raising the hair on his forearms. His backpack bounced against his back. Smells of fresh cut grass, wet earth and young wheat filled the air.

Tracy shot through the towering cemetery archway, coasted down an incline, rolled through two curves and brought her bike to a stop. She pulled her water bottle from its cradle and squeezed it. A solid stream of water shot into her mouth. Vincent stopped next to her and drank from his own bottle. Her thirst quenched, Tracy sprayed her face, neck and chest with the water. She was fitter than she'd been prior to Jill's death, her body carrying solid muscle, her biceps and deltoids tight and pronounced, her bare abdomen showing the beginnings of a solid six-pack.

She realized he was studying her and said, "I started lifting weights." His eyebrows went up. "I met this guy at my grief support group. He's really nice and he works at Bally's. He's sort of turned into my trainer."

"You like doing it?"

"I do." She averted her eyes. "I go riding with him too."

Vincent slapped his hand against his heart. "Forsaken. Thrown aside for a younger man."

"I'm sorry, Vincent. It's just that he asked me and he thinks I'm pretty." She was genuinely upset, thinking Vincent was serious.

He smiled. "I'm joking, Trace. I understand." He laid a hand on her shoulder, feeling her muscled deltoid quiver. "And he's right. You are pretty."

"You're really okay about this? I mean I know I pushed you to buy your bike to go riding with me."

"I bought the bike because I wanted to. What's your friend's name?"

"Nathaniel. But he likes to be called Nathan."

Vincent put the bike's kickstand down. "Who did he lose?"

"His mother."

"Ouch."

"He's been in the group for a year. He says I make him smile."

"Then you must keep spending time with him." He slung his arm over her shoulders. "And don't worry about me. Now, come on."

They walked up the rolling hill to Jill's grave. Tracy dug two small pots of red geraniums and a digger out of his backpack. While she planted the flowers, he moved off, heading a few rows over to Liz's grave. She was buried beside her mother and Emma. It felt strange, looking at Emma's grave and knowing that he would see her alive in just a few hours. The stone that marked Liz's grave looked crisp and new next to the aging gray of Emma's stone. He knelt down and traced Liz's name with his index finger. *Elizabeth Marlene Reilly, M.D. Beloved daughter of…*He stopped, his hand dropping. Tears crept into his eyes.

He blinked them back and wiggled out of his backpack. He removed the last two geraniums and planted them. He continued fighting his tears as he worked. This was hard, coming here, doing this, but he had promised Kate he would do it for her. He set the flowers in freshly dug holes. Emotions rolled through him like speeding bullets. One minute he was sad, the next angry, and all the time wondering what he could have done differently to help Liz. He thought of Emma and the solitary life she had lead. She'd tended her patients by day and then she'd gone home to her empty house at night. Liz had had her father and Elsie, and even Duke to come home to. But she had shut herself off from them.

"Why?" he asked her as he packed dirt around the flowers. "Why didn't you reach out? We all loved you, Liz."

"Because she couldn't." Tracy knelt down beside him. "Because she was afraid of losing again."

Vincent met Tracy's eyes. The understanding and knowledge of what had happened in Liz's mind was so strong in them that Vincent fell back on his rear. Tracy ran her hand across the top of Liz's gravestone. "It hurt so bad when Jill died that I just wanted to die. I would look at my parents and think that I couldn't lose them too. That I couldn't go through their deaths and that most likely, since they're older than me, I would outlive them." She sat back, cross-legged, elbows on her thighs, and rested her chin in her hands. "And I had only lost my sister, Vincent. One person. Aunt Liz had lost her fiancé and her mom. Then Jill. As much as I hurt, I can't even imagine the pain she felt."

Vincent rested on his hands, his legs crossed in front of him. "I guess she was the doctor who tended to everyone else while letting no one tend to her."

"I miss her," Tracy said. "Yet, I feel her close to me. Especially when I drive the Mustang." She pulled a tuft of grass out of the ground and tossed it into the air, watching the individual strands fly away on the breeze. "I feel Jill too. All the time. Sometimes, when I wake up at night now, it's like she's holding me in her arms. Like she's lying next to me in bed, protecting me. Nathan says he feels his mother like that too." Fine frown lines appeared on her forehead. "Does that sound crazy, Vincent?"

"Nope."

She smiled shyly.

A flock of Canadian geese flew over them, their calls loud in the quiet morning. Vincent watched them, amazed at how their wings worked in simultaneous motion, almost as if they had one consciousness.

"We should get back," Tracy said. "I've got to go tour Buffalo State this afternoon."

"You've decided an art major then?"

She nodded.

As he rode behind her back to North Tonawanda, Vincent couldn't help but think how close she'd come to slitting her wrists. He thanked God that she had turned to him. He would always wish that Liz had done the same.

❧   ❧   ❧

When Vincent walked up Emma's front stairs that evening, he was surprised to find her sitting in the rocker, wiping tears from her cheeks. He stopped short, his left foot on the top step. Anger flared in her eyes and he knew that it was anger at herself for letting him see her like this. He leaned against a porch column, purposely looked out on the street, and gave her time to compose herself. A dog ran by chased by a young boy in knickers.

"Vincent," Emma finally said, her voice strained.

Still not looking at her, he said, "Evening, Emma."

"I'm sorry you saw such foolishness," she said.

"What foolishness would that be?"

She stood up, came to him, but leaned against the column opposite his own. "You are very kind, Sir. But I'm sure you saw."

"Crying is not a sin, Emma."

"I suppose not."

He gave her an encouraging smile. "What caused your tears tonight?"

She folded her arms across her chest. "She'll be leaving soon."

"Oh, I doubt she'll go anywhere until her divorce is final and she marries Norman."

"The nights will be so lonely without her. It sounds ridiculous, doesn't it? I have lived alone all my life and enjoyed it. But now, the thought of her going…How quiet and empty this house will be."

"She'll be over on the next street. No doubt she would love you to visit."

The front door opened and Katherine came out. She saw him, smiled then drew in a deep breath of the night air. Wrapping her shawl tighter around her shoulders, she said, "I wondered where you'd gotten to, Emma. I was hoping we could play cards. Will you join us, Vincent?"

"I'm afraid I can't. I just came to retrieve the portrait. What about Norman, will he play?"

Katherine frowned. "I haven't seen Norman all day. It is so unlike him not to even call."

Vincent froze, unable to comment. Once again he couldn't help but think that Malloy had struck early because of Vincent's meddling in this time period?

"I know he had business to attend to today. He took the High Speed Trolley Line down to Buffalo early this morning. But he should have called by now."

"It is unlike him," Emma said, touching Katherine's arm. "Let me call his brother and see if he's heard from him. She disappeared into the house.

Katherine rubbed her upper arms, her eyes locked on Vincent, asking him if he had any idea as to where Norman could be. He had an idea all right. One he certainly couldn't voice. "How's your hand feeling?"

She held it out for him to see. The scars on the hand's palm and its top were thick and red in the porch light. But all the fingers moved, although obviously with extreme effort and discomfort. "Emma has me doing exercises to regain my strength and mobility. I don't know if the scars will fade or not."

"They should."

"They are ugly." She gazed over at the Victorian. A single light burned in the library window. "Do you suppose he will really let me go, Vincent?"

"I doubt he'll go down without a fight."

She shivered, although the night was not cold. "Then I shall fight back."

And you will lose, Vincent thought. *In fact, you may already have lost.*

She cleared her throat and said, "I've been reading some of Emma's magazines. Many women are wearing short hair now. I wonder how it would look on me."

At present, her hair hung free, waving down around her shoulders. He tried to imagine it short and shook his head. "You would break Norman's heart."

She chuckled. "Yours too, no doubt."

"No doubt."

She grinned. "Women have begun wearing pants, you know."

"So they have."

"I know I am young and should be open to change, but I tell you, I don't know if that's a change I can embrace."

"Why not?"

She touched the folds of her skirt. "I guess because I am old-fashioned. My mother often said that had I been born in the 1800's, I would have been happier. I sometimes feel, Vincent, that I am a throwback to that time." She brushed a lock of hair back from her face. "Emma says that you are a man out of your time."

"She does," he admitted.

"She says that your ideas about marriage and women in general are not usual."

"True."

"I would like to meet your wife someday. Will you introduce us?"

Vincent scratched his chin and thought of Katherine's future, when she would hold her granddaughter Kate in her arms. "You shall meet her, Katherine," he said.

Emma came out the front door. "Norman is not with his brother. Timothy said that he hasn't heard from him since two o'clock when he stopped by after getting off the trolley from Buffalo."

Katherine's hand pressed against her chest, alarm flooding her eyes. "Where could he be?"

"Did Timothy say where Norman was going?" Vincent asked, managing to keep his voice level and panic free.

"To do some repairs at the new house."

"What new house?" Katherine asked.

Vincent ignored her question. Obviously, Norman had not told her of his purchase yet. "I'll go over there, Emma." He started down the stairs.

"Timothy has already checked there, Vincent. He's not there."

Vincent stopped on the walkway. He turned back, looking from Katherine to Emma. Emma's face was filled with fear. "Would somebody tell me what house?" Katherine insisted, stamping her foot.

"I'll check again. As well as a few other places. Take her inside and tell her about the house, Emma."

Nodding, Emma put her arm around Katherine and said, "Come inside. I will tell you about your new home."

Vincent waited until they were in the house and then he darted across the lawn, opened the wrought iron gate and charged up Malloy's front steps. The double doors were locked, Malloy's stained-glass face taunting him. He pounded on it with his fists. Finally, the doors swung slowly open to reveal Jethro standing behind them in his after dinner jacket, a pipe in his hand and a triumphant grin on his face.

CHAPTER 21

"Where is he?"

Still grinning, Jethro said, "Do come in, Mr. Vermay."

Entering, Vincent asked again, "Where is he?"

Malloy closed the front doors. "Where is who?"

Vincent took him by the collar and pushed him back against the doors. The pipe fell from Malloy's hand and Vincent kicked it. It skidded down the hall, spilling tobacco, smelling like vanilla flavored coffee. "You know who, Malloy. Where is Norman?"

Malloy's left eye twitched. "I would expect that he's hard at work on his nest."

"What have you done with him!" Vincent shouted in his face.

Malloy's eyes were two steel rods. "I've done nothing with him. Search the house. See for yourself."

Vincent checked the basement first. Nothing. He ran from room to room, ending in the third floor bedroom. No Norman. Malloy waited for him in the foyer, having reclaimed his pipe. He puffed on it and watched Vincent descend the stairs with cold eyes. "Are you satisfied?"

Breathing hard, sweat pouring out of his pores, Vincent said, "You've done something. The man just can't disappear."

"Can't he?"

Smug bastard, Vincent thought. It took all his willpower to keep from slugging Jethro.

"Now, could you please leave so I may finish my book?"

Vincent chewed his lower lip, his hands twitching with the desire to form fists and go to work. He clasped them behind his back. "She doesn't love you. Leave her be. Leave them be."

Malloy opened the front doors. "I trust you'll give Katherine my regards, Mr. Vermay."

Reluctantly, Vincent departed. As he walked over to the little white house on Tremont, his stomach curled in on itself and he pressed a hand against his abdomen. He knew that Norman would not be at the house. He knew it just as sure as he knew the sun would come up tomorrow. He also knew that Malloy had acted. Norman might not be chained in the basement yet, but he wasn't going to show up at Emma's with flowers for Katherine anymore.

Lights burned in the windows of the little house, beckoning Vincent inside. A can of paint, still open, sat on the front bedroom floor. The windows were open but still the smell of paint scorched his nostrils and Vincent sneezed as he took in the scene, the room half painted a soft rose, a ladder and brushes abandoned.

"Damn it!" Vincent cussed, running a hand through his hair.

Hands shaking, he capped the paint and closed the windows. There had been no struggle. Had Malloy held a gun on him? He searched the remainder of the house although he knew it was futile. He checked the small basement last and as he'd expected, no sign of Norman.

He locked the house on his way out. He walked back to Emma's, his heart aching in his chest. Aching for Katherine and the happiness that would never be. She was waiting on the porch, her shawl around her shoulders. Emma stood beside her. Their eyes questioned him. Vincent shook his head, "I couldn't find him."

Katherine shuddered, her legs buckling. Emma held her upright, an arm around her. "Where...where could he have gone?" Katherine asked, looking to Emma for an answer.

Emma didn't hold her suspicions back. "What did Malloy say?"

"Jethro?" Katherine asked. "What would he have to do with this?"

"He claims he knows nothing, Emma. He let me search the house then sent me on my way. I went over to the new house, but Norman wasn't there either. It looked like he'd been interrupted in the middle of painting the bedroom."

"Our bedroom?" Katherine asked.

"Yes," Vincent admitted.

Katherine held out her hand to him. "Vincent." He took her outstretched hand. It was cold and small. "He wouldn't just leave me. Something happened. You must find him. Please?"

"I'll do what I can," Vincent promised, even though he knew there was nothing he could do.

✿   ✿   ✿

Douglas stood beside Vincent, his eyes on Katherine's portrait. "How many days has he been missing?"

"Four."

"And you witnessed nothing?"

"Nothing. One day he was there, the next gone."

"How is she taking it?"

"She's seriously depressed. She won't eat. She's not sleeping. She just wants to sit on the porch watching for him."

Douglas reached out to run a finger along Katherine's hair but stopped an inch from the canvas. "She was so beautiful. No wonder Norman loved her."

"She's a lovely woman on the inside too. Very conservative and very shy, except when you put that violin in her hands. The transformation is amazing to see."

Douglas stared a while longer at the portrait then said, "He should not have disappeared this early, Vincent."

"I know. But he has. What else could have happened? Norman wouldn't voluntarily stay away from Katherine this long."

Douglas turned away from the painting and met Vincent's eyes. "Your meddling succeeded in depriving her of five months of happiness. Do you realize that, Vincent?"

"I do," Vincent said, swallowing over a lump in his throat. "Don't think I haven't cursed myself either."

Douglas nodded. "Will you be going back?"

"I shouldn't. I have my painting."

"But you want to paint more, don't you?"

"Yes."

"So you'll go back."

"Let's just say I'm trying to talk myself out of it."

Douglas snorted. "Good luck, Vincent." He started for the studio door but turned back. "I hate to be a pessimist, my boy, but I doubt you'll succeed."

❧   ❧   ❧

The violin dragged him out of a deep sleep. It wasn't her best playing, but even at her worst, with her handicapped hand, the violin sang to him. Vincent opened his eyes and found himself in the rocker on the Victorian's front porch. A glass with melting ice sat on the porch wall in front of him. He stood up. He couldn't go dressed as he was, in denim cutoffs and no shirt.

He ran upstairs and dressed quickly in black slacks, a white cotton shirt and black suspenders. He rushed down the stairs, sliding to a halt in the foyer. His hair was greasy and flecked with paint. He snatched his derby bowler from the coat rack and slapped it down on his head.

Outside on the porch again, he saw her through a shimmering fog. The violin blended with the clang of the trolley bell that floated over from the High Speed Line. He hurried down the steps and out through the front gate, walking into the fog without hesitation. By the time he reached the Reilly driveway, he'd crossed over. The afternoon was warm and humid, sweat instantly popping out on his skin. She saw him coming and ceased playing, lowering the violin, tears on her cheeks. And yet, in spite of the tears, she was smiling.

"You came," she said when he reached her.

"You called."

"Although not very well." She held up her left hand. She opened and closed it, grimacing. "I missed many notes."

"It was still beautiful, Katherine."

She came down the steps and hugged him, the violin banging against his back. "He's home," she said. "He's home and I couldn't wait to tell you."

Vincent eased her away. "Norman?"

She nodded, fresh tears spilling from her eyes.

"Inside?"

She nodded again.

Vincent thought he would explode with joy. He pulled Katherine close and kissed her forehead.

"Go see him," she said, pushing him. "But don't wake him. Please."

Vincent kissed her cheek then went inside. Emma met him at the top of the stairs. "He's in my room," she said. "Let him sleep."

"What happened?"

"After you see him."

Norman Lassiter had obviously been beaten. Bruises covered his face and upper body. A bandage encircled his head and another covered his nose. His bottom lip was split and sported dried blood. A bandage circled round his upper torso and his left arm rested in a sling.

Emma waited for Vincent in the hall. He closed the bedroom door and asked, "He'll be all right?"

"He will."

"Where did you find him?"

"I didn't. Two men brought him to my office today. They carried him in and dumped him on the waiting room floor."

"Who were they?"

"I have no idea, Vincent. I've never seen them before. I don't think they're from town. They came in, dropped him and left without saying a word."

Vincent bit his lower lip. "You think they work for Malloy?"

"I don't doubt that they do."

Katherine appeared at the top of the stairs, still carrying her violin. "I'm going to sit with him," she said. "Will you put this away for me?"

Emma touched Katherine's forearm. "You really don't need to, Katherine. He's sleeping fine."

"He sat with me when I needed him. Now I will sit with him." She held out the violin. Vincent took it and she slipped into the bedroom.

"She'll sit with him until he wakes up, you know."

Emma nodded. She pointed at the violin. "Why don't you put that away and join me on the porch?"

Ten minutes later they sat on the porch drinking lemonade. Emma sat in her rocker and Vincent on the top porch step, bracing himself against a column, his legs stretched out in front of him. Twilight was descending, the crickets singing all around them. A glorious sunset filled the western sky with shades of red, purple, orange and yellow. A gentle breeze blew a subtle smell of fish in off the Niagara River.

"He'd been drugged," Emma said. "His wrists bear rope burns as do his ankles."

Vincent drank a long drink of lemonade. It relieved his parched mouth, rolling refreshingly down his throat.

"But why did those men release him, Vincent? That is the mystery."

"I don't know. Have you told Katherine your suspicions?"

"I have."

"And?"

"She doesn't believe Jethro had anything to do with it. She may not love him, but she refuses to see the evil in him."

Vincent scratched his chin. "I don't think that Katherine could see the evil in anybody, Emma."

A faint smile flashed across Emma's face. "I believe you're correct about that." She took a drink of her lemonade. "Doesn't it surprise you, Vincent, that Katherine was so well traveled and had performed before thousands of people and yet, she is so naïve? So innocent and so ignorant regarding the ways of the world."

"She had her father, Emma. He protected her. He was the wall between her and the world."

Emma sighed. "If only he hadn't died so suddenly. The child was so unprepared to be alone."

"A fact that Jethro Malloy used to his advantage."

A crow flew by, cawing loudly. Vincent watched its dark shape streak through the sky above Malloy's house and in spite of the warm night, he shivered.

     ❦   ❦   ❦

Norman sat in an Adirondack chair in Emma's backyard, Katherine by his side in another. She was clad in her white, long, lacy dress, her head bent over a book. Her hair was pulled back in a gold clip, sunlight twinkling off the gold in blinding beams. Norman's eyes were closed; his head back against the chair. He wore a pair of tweed slacks and a pale gold robe. His feet were bare.

It was good to see them together. And yet, Vincent knew that it wouldn't last. Before the end of December, Malloy would have them each locked up in the same house, separated by floors. But five times they would be together, five precious times. Vincent sighed. God, this was so unfair. They deserved better than what Malloy would give them.

Kate. Her beautiful face jumped into his mind and warmth rolled through his chest. She deserved to be born. And although, if Vincent foiled Malloy's plan, Norman would still father Katherine's children, would they still have all five? Again he wondered if Kate's father was born, would being brought up in a loving home instead of boarding schools change him enough to prevent him from marrying Kate's mother? It was all so confusing. So befuddling. He shouldn't be thinking of changing Katherine and Norman's future and yet, he couldn't stop himself. What would Kate say? What would she want? Leave it as it is or try to change it? Would she take the risk? He had no right to make this decision alone. He realized that now. Kate had to know what he'd been doing these past months. She had a right to be included in this decision. She must be.

He turned on his heel and left Emma's yard without speaking to Katherine or Norman. He walked swiftly, urgently. He had plane reservations to make.

❦   ❦   ❦

A taxi passed Vincent as he walked down Goundry, the violin in his hand. It was not your normal yellow taxi. It was a dirty, off white, the name on the door unreadable, the paint obscured by accumulated grime. The car pulled to a stop in front of the Victorian, and Kate got out of the back seat. Vincent quickened his pace, watching as the driver, a heavy set man with gray hair pulled back in a ponytail, opened the trunk of the vehicle and removed Kate's suitcase and briefcase.

"Kate!" Vincent called, running now.

She handed the driver his fare then turned, smiling. Reaching her, he pulled her close and kissed her lips. They tasted sweet against his own, the smell of chocolate reaching his nose. The familiar feel of her, the scent of lavender sent him soaring. "I love you," he said, burying his face in her hair.

"Easy, boy," she said, pushing him away. "Why are you carrying my grand-mother's violin around?"

He heard more than saw the taxi drive off. He held up the violin. "Getting in the mood," he said. "I'm about to start another painting. Now, come here." He pulled her close again. He wanted to take her upstairs and make love to her. He wanted to hold her while she slept. He didn't want to ever lose her. And yet, he had to tell her everything. He had to see if she wanted to risk her very exist-ence to help her grandmother. The grandmother she had loved with all her heart.

Her eyes told him that she'd read at least one of his thoughts. She grinned, laughing. "You horny boy," she said.

He touched her cheek, her skin soft and warm. He felt tears pierce his eyes and he wondered if she saw them.

She did. "So serious," she said, kissing his cheek. "I love you too. And I want to do that as well. No need to cry about it."

"I've missed you," he managed, his voice a frog's croak.

She frowned. "What's wrong, Vincent?"

He swallowed over the ball in his throat. "Here, you carry the violin. I'll take these and we'll go inside."

He dumped the suitcase and briefcase on the fern room floor. She stood in the doorway, arms wrapped around the violin. "I thought I was supposed to be the next one to visit," he said, delaying the inevitable.

"You were. But I have good news."

"What?"

"You first. Yours seems to be of the bad persuasion. Bad news should precede good news."

He gazed at her. She was lovely in white, cotton shorts and a maroon, polo shirt that bore an embroidered Colonial Williamsburg insignia. Her hair hung free, well past her shoulders, curling haphazardly, outlining her softly angled face, so reminiscent of Katherine's face. New glasses rested on her nose. They were perfectly round, the frames black metal, showcasing her green eyes. They looked good on her and he told her so.

"Thank you, but tell me your news." She tapped her foot, the sole of her sandal causing a soft thud against the hardwood floor.

"Please, yours first, Kate."

Her foot stopped. His tone and the look on his face caught her off guard. She didn't say anything for a long, agonizing minute and then, when he thought he would scream, she said, "McMartin fired me."

"What?"

"Can you believe it? He fired me." She chuckled. "After he gave me this long sermon about how he needed me until after the election in November when I gave him my resignation and then yesterday, he comes into my office and says, 'I've replaced you, Kate. You can clean out your desk now.' I have to tell you, Vincent, I was thrilled. Yeah, can you believe it? Me, the work hound, was thrilled about getting fired. I don't know how you and Liz did it, but you turned me back into a real writer. I'm really enjoying working on the book again."

Vincent crossed the space between them in two strides. He couldn't talk. He couldn't do anything but hug her, the violin's neck whacking him in the chin. At last she'd come around. At last, the old fire was in her eyes. Eyes that shone like they had when first they were married and she had labored at the typewriter in the evening at the apartment's kitchen table. She believed in herself again. She'd escaped her demons and insecurities, and re-discovered her true self. And now, now he had to tell her what he'd been up to. How could he do it? How?

"We believed in you," he said, his voice cracking. "Liz and I. We both believed in you."

"Even when I no longer did."

He held her chin in his hand. He lifted her face so he could look into her beautiful green eyes. "I will always believe in you, Kate. Always. I'll support you too. Whatever decisions you make. You're my wife, my soul mate, and my best friend."

Worry filled her eyes. "Vincent, you're scaring me. What is wrong?"

"Nothing. And everything." He took her hand. "Come, I've something to show you."

She gasped when she saw Katherine's portrait. "Oh, Vincent," she said. She moved closer, discarding the violin on the dresser top where his palette sat. She looked the painting up and down, wonder in her eyes. "You've captured her," she finally said. "Oh, Vincent, you've brought her to life. This is her. This is my grandmother. She's in this painting. Her eyes. You've put her heart right there in her eyes. I'd swear that you knew her at this age."

"I do know her, Kate," he said, moving to stand beside his wife.

He saw her muscles tense and her shoulders pull back. She turned to look at him, and he was surprised to find a lack of surprise or disbelief in her eyes. Instead, he saw relief and understanding. "The violin," she said.

"Yes."

"Ghosts in the room. My imagination. Bullshit."

"I couldn't tell you then, Kate. It…it wasn't time."

She picked up the violin. "Liz and I had been at a movie and it was nearing midnight when she dropped me off. I planned to go upstairs and kiss Grandma goodnight without waking her. But when I opened the door, I heard the violin. I thought it odd that she'd be up so late playing. Then I thought that maybe she was waiting for me. After all, summer was almost over and I would be leaving soon. Starting college. I went upstairs and opened the bedroom door. Katherine was there all right. But not my old grandmother. It was Katherine as she is in your portrait. She was playing Beethoven, although I didn't know which composition. I just knew that it was Beethoven." Kate stopped talking, collecting her thoughts. She plucked a string on the violin and it's high, staccato slapped Vincent's ears and he jerked. Kate continued. "I stood there, shocked. I didn't know what to do or say. Or even if I should say anything. She quit playing and cocked her head as if she were listening for something beyond the music she'd been making. I remember thinking how beautiful she was. And then he came in. He stormed in. I flattened myself against the wall. Neither of them saw me. He pulled the violin from her hands and threw it on the bed. He shouted, 'You will not see him again! I will not allow it!' He was furious, Vincent. He grabbed her and squeezed her arms until she cried out. She tried to calm him down. She told him she didn't know what he was talking about. That she hadn't seen anyone behind his back, but he wouldn't listen. He just started hitting her. Oh, God, he beat her so badly. She begged him to get Emma. She was hurt. I tried to go to her. I tried to help. But something pulled me back. I saw her crumble to the floor as I was pulled away. And then I was sitting on the floor in her room and she was lying in bed sleeping, her gray hair flared out on the pillow." Kate's breaths came in short gasps.

Vincent took the violin from her and set it on the dresser. He laid his hands on her shoulders. "It's okay," he said.

She pressed her forehead against his. "How long have you been going back?" she asked, her arms slipping around him.

"Since April."

"I thought I was crazy, Vincent. I can't tell you how many times I've relived that scene in my mind, wondering if I'd gone back in time, or dreamed it or…or, damn, I didn't know."

"You're not crazy. And you did go back in time that night. What you saw was real."

"Grandma," she said, laying her head on his shoulder. "My grandma."

Vincent stroked Kate's hair and held her.

"She was the only adult who loved me, Vincent. When I was growing up, she was the only one. To know how horrible her life was with him…" She trembled and Vincent tightened his hold.

"I want to go with you," she said. "Please, Vincent, I must meet her. Please?"

"Kate, I don't think," he started to protest, but stopped in mid-sentence. "There are some things you need to know before we make that decision."

She raised her head to look at him. "What?"

"Sit with me."

They sat together on the floor, backs against the studio wall, facing Katherine's portrait. He told her all he could, his tale encompassing all that had happened since his first meeting with Katherine. She listened, wide-eyed, as he explained that Norman had fathered Katherine's children. When he had brought her up to date, she asked, "Norman and Katherine are both staying at Emma's right now?"

"Yes."

She pushed her glasses up her nose. He could see the wheels turning in her brain. "You and Emma really think that Jethro had something to do with Norman's beating?"

"We do."

"But you have no proof?"

"Not at present."

She pushed her hair back over her shoulder as she said, "Norman spent all those years in Jethro's basement and let himself be a stud. You realize that's what you've just told me."

"I do."

She shook her head in amazement. "He really must have loved her."

"He does. I mean, did."

She grinned. "What you're telling me is that I am not descended from Jethro Malloy. I have none of his genes."

"None whatsoever."

"Hallelujah." Joy shined in her eyes. "What a relief that is."

He took her hand, brought it to his lips, and kissed her palm. "Nice to make your acquaintance, Katherine Lassiter Vermay."

"That means that Douglas is my second cousin."

"Yep."

She giggled like a ten-year-old girl. "Do you realize that I inherited money that I've no right to?"

"That's wrong." He held up his finger. "Katherine inherited it from Jethro and passed it on to you. You have every right to it."

Doubt filled her eyes.

"You do, Kate."

She looked at Katherine's portrait again. "If Norman fathered Katherine's children anyway, couldn't…" She trailed off, stroking her chin with her thumb and first finger. She turned back to Vincent, her face solemn. "You've thought of this already, haven't you, Vincent?"

He nodded. "Except that other factors could come into play. If they live together as man and wife, Norman and Katherine may not have as many—"

She waved off his words. "She could be happy, Vincent. She could spend her life with a man who loves her more than life itself. How can we deny her that?"

"And if making that happen means that you're never born, then what, Kate?"

He saw fear flash in her eyes. She sat silent, clinging to his hand. Now that she was with him, her body close to him, her hand in his, he knew he could not lose her. He touched her cheek. Her skin was cold. She swallowed, the muscles in her throat taut. "Vincent," she softly said. "I have to think."

He pulled her to him. He closed his eyes and held her. Why had he told her? What had he been thinking? *Idiot!*

Her voice muffled by his shirt, Kate said, "Please take me to her, Vincent. Please, I want to meet her."

"No," he said, his voice hoarse. "If you meet her, you'll want…meeting her will make you want to save her."

Kate gently eased away from him. With resignation in her eyes, she said, "She won't have to make me want to save her, Vincent. I already do." She got to her feet and stretched out a hand to him. "Now, take me to her."

Reluctantly, he took her hand, got to his feet and said, "Okay."

CHAPTER 22

❀

Kate changed into a traditionally styled, short-sleeved dress with a white background and small, yellow flowers. She piled her hair up on her head, holding it there with crystal hairpins. They walked hand-in-hand to the carriage house. Vincent led her around the building to the back. "This is one of the good spots for crossing over because no one ever seems to come back here."

"Doesn't anyone hear the violin, Vincent?"

"No one seems to." He touched her cheek. Her skin was soft and warm beneath his fingers. "You look beautiful, babe."

She smiled. "Thank you. I hope Grandma approves."

"Don't call her that."

"I won't. Promise."

He could see the excitement in her eyes and could only imagine what it must feel like, knowing that you were about to meet your grandmother—the person you'd loved most in the world during your childhood—when she was still a young woman. He kissed Kate's lips, savoring their softness. "I love you," he said, searching her eyes, hoping she understood that he never wanted to lose her.

"I love you too," she said, and he knew she understood. She touched his chin then laid her hand against his cheek. It was warm and comforting. "Whatever decision we make, we will make together, Vincent. I promise."

He nodded. Stepping back from her, he lifted the violin. "It sounds awful. But it works." He ran the bow over the strings. She grimaced at the harsh sound. "Sorry, babe." He punched random notes as he moved the bow. Some notes sharp, some flat, and none of them forming a familiar song. Kate covered her ears with her hands. He played on. He wondered if, just maybe, it wouldn't work for both of them. He thought he might disappear on her. Or maybe because he was trying to bring her along, he wouldn't cross over either. But on both counts he was wrong. He saw the familiar flickering of light around them both. He gestured with his head as he raised his leg. She followed suit and they stepped into a sunny, North Tonawanda afternoon in July of 1926. The smell of fresh mowed grass was strong in the air. Children's voices traveled on the gentle breeze as they played in nearby yards.

Kate grabbed his arm. She glanced around, eyes wide, holding her breath. Vincent leaned close and spoke into her ear. "Welcome to 1926, Kate."

"Magnificent," she said. She ran her hand along the carriage house wall. "So this is where you got your color scheme for the house. And here I thought you just dreamed it up."

"Nope."

"Take me to her, Vincent. I can't wait any longer." Her face was alive with anticipation. She looked like a child on Christmas morning.

He stowed the violin behind a bush then took her hand. "Follow me." He led her along the side of the carriage house, stopping to steal a look inside the side window. The hansom cab was alone, the car missing. *Excellent.* They didn't need any complications from Malloy during Kate's first visit. He continued on until they reached the sidewalk. Stopping, he released Kate's hand. "Sling your arm through mine," he said. "It's more proper."

"Certainly, Sir," she replied, doing as he asked.

"They were in the backyard earlier," Vincent said as they reached the Reilly driveway. He was about to lead her to the backyard when the front door opened. Emma came out. As always on weekdays, she wore her white lab coat, her stethoscope around her neck and medical bag swinging at her side.

Kate gasped beside him. "Easy, babe," he whispered.

Waving, Emma came down the front steps. "Vincent. I was hoping you'd come today. You must talk to Norman." Reaching them, she smiled at Kate. "And who is this?"

"My wife. This is Kate."

"So this is the lady who claims your sensitive heart, Vincent." Emma touched Kate's forearm. "Welcome. We have all wanted to meet you."

"And I you," Kate managed to say, although her voice was an octave higher than normal. She could not take her eyes off of Emma. Vincent could see her thoughts. This was Liz's great aunt.

"I must return to the office," Emma said, regret in her voice. "Norman and Katherine are inside. In the parlor."

"How are they both doing?" Vincent asked.

Emma gave him a knowing look. "Talk with Norman. He is sore, but he'll live. As far as Katherine is concerned, I can safely say that both the pneumonia and the infection are gone. Her hand will require more exercising, but I believe she'll regain full mobility. She's itching to play her violin. I told her not to push it like she did yesterday."

"Good luck keeping her from the violin. That's like telling me to stop painting."

Emma grunted. To Kate she said, "Enjoy your visit. Hopefully, I'll see you again soon."

"Goodbye," Kate mumbled.

Emma walked off, and Kate stared after her in wonder.

"Kind of throws you at first," Vincent said, when Emma was out of earshot.

"That's an understatement. I just talked to Emma Reilly, who died before Liz was ever born. And now…now Liz is dead too."

Vincent squeezed her arm. "Come on, let's go inside."

He didn't bother knocking. He opened the front door and escorted Kate inside. She glanced around the foyer. "It's so different," she whispered.

"I know. Come on."

Norman lay on the couch, his eyes closed. Katherine sat in the wingback chair. She was looking down at her left hand, running the index finger of her right hand over the scar on her palm. She wiggled her fingers. Creases on her forehead told Vincent that she was worried. She was so intent, that she hadn't heard them come in.

"Wait here," he whispered, leaving Kate in the doorway. He didn't mean to startle Katherine, but he did. She jerked when he touched her shoulder. She covered her scarred hand with her right, holding it against her chest. Fear filled her eyes. "I'm sorry," he said, kneeling beside her chair. "Let me see."

She released her left hand and he took it in his. He touched the scar and she shuddered. "It's not as ugly as you believe, Katherine. It looks better than it did the other day."

"It's hideous." She pulled the hand back. "I'm scared, Vincent. Emma says I will play again like I could before but…"

"Emma would never lie to you. I hope you know that."

"I know." The words came out in a choke. She looked at the injured hand again and a tear slipped from her right eye. She wiped at it, aggravated with herself.

Vincent could feel Kate's eyes on them, her love for Katherine spilling over them. He knew that Kate could feel Katherine's anguish and uncertainty. He also knew that Kate wanted to take her grandmother in her arms and chase her fears and pain away.

Don't, Kate. He prayed she heard his thoughts. *Stay put. Please, stay where you are*

Norman stirred and opened his eyes. "Who are you?" he asked. He was staring at Kate.

Katherine followed the line of his gaze and her eyes grew wide. A large smile crossed her face, wiping away her worry. "You brought your wife, Vincent." She stood up and tugged on his arm. "Introduce us this instant."

Norman struggled up to a sitting position. "Yes, Vincent, introduce us."

Vincent went to Kate and took her arm. He led her to Katherine and said, "Katherine Malloy, this is my wife, Katherine Vermay. Everyone calls her Kate."

Katherine took Kate's hand. "It is an honor. Your husband has been so kind to me. Have you seen the portrait? Has he shown you?"

"Yes, I've seen it. It's wonderful." Kate's eyes were those of a star-struck fan who finally meets her favorite celebrity.

"Vincent made me look much better than I do."

"That's Katherine's opinion, not mine," Norman said. He held out his hand. "Vincent, my friend, help me up off this couch so I may greet your wife properly."

Vincent helped him up. Although unable to bow because of his injuries, Norman still kissed the back of Kate's hand. "Norman Lassiter," he said, grinning. "And I am very pleased to meet you."

Kate beamed at Norman. "Hello, Norman." The intensity of her scrutiny told Vincent that she was searching for traits that she might equate to herself. After all, she'd just learned this man was her grandfather.

"My father used to call me Katie," Katherine said.

Kate met her gaze as she said, "My grandmother called me Katie." She flashed Vincent a quick look. There was joy in her green eyes. "And, regarding your painting, Katherine, you are as beautiful as it depicts."

Katherine's cheeks went red. "You are too kind." Suddenly aware of her scarred hand again, she hid it behind her good one.

Kate saw the movement and said, "Don't be ashamed of your injury." She took hold of Katherine's left forearm. "Please. You've no need to hide it from me." Her eyes held love and tenderness.

Katherine held up the hand and Kate took it between her own. "It will heal as Emma says. I'm sure the scars will fade. Even if they don't, it doesn't change your beauty. That comes from within."

"Here, here," Norman said, moving closer to Katherine. He slipped his arm around her.

Katherine looked from Kate's face to the hands encasing hers and then back to Kate's face again. She sensed something. Vincent saw it in her eyes. He watched closely, his heart pounding, waiting for her to say something. Kate gave her an encouraging smile. Katherine smiled back, happiness flowing into her eyes. "I feel I have just met a special friend," she said.

"You have," Kate assured her. "Now, will you sit outside with me? It's a beautiful day, and we can let the men talk."

Katherine looked to Norman.

"You don't need my permission, my love. Go and be with your new friend. I do want to speak with Vincent."

She pulled her hand from Kate's grasp. "We can sit in the backyard and talk."

Kate followed Katherine from the room, giving Vincent a last glance on her way out. Her eyes spoke volumes. She was thrilled beyond belief.

Norman sat back down on the couch, grunting as he did so. He pressed his hand against his side. "Ribs," he said. "Sit, Vincent."

Vincent sat down in the wingback chair across from Norman. He crossed his legs, brushed a piece of fuzz from his pant leg, and said, "Tell me what happened."

"First, I must say, you're wife could be a double for Katherine. It's amazing. She's lovely, Vincent."

"Thank you." He didn't address how much the women looked alike, hoping the conversation wouldn't linger there.

But Norman said, "Do you suppose they notice how much they look alike?"

Vincent shrugged. "Now, what happened to you, Norman?"

"I was painting the room. I didn't hear anybody come in. One minute I'm painting and the next, nothing."

Vincent pointed at the bandage circling round Norman's head. "Whoever it was knocked you out then?"

"Yes. I don't remember much after that. I can tell you there were two of them. I remember different voices. They tied me to a bed and kept sticking a needle in my arm whenever I woke up. The last time I woke up, I endured a beating and then was dropped on Emma's waiting room floor."

"You never saw Jethro?"

"No. But when his cohorts were driving me to Emma's office—which I didn't know, I might add. I thought they were going to dump me in the Niagara River. Anyway, I was tied up in the backseat and I did hear the one driving say, 'Screw Malloy. I'm not into murder, for Pete's sake.' The other man said, 'He wants him out of the way.' To which the driver replied, 'Then he can hire someone else.'"

Nodding thoughtfully, Vincent asked, "And you told this to Katherine?"

"I did."

"And she said?"

Norman chuckled. "She wanted to go give him a piece of her mind." He raised his eyebrows. "Since spending so much time with Emma, I'm afraid our Katherine is becoming quite feisty."

"I hope you discouraged her from seeing him alone."

"Emma made her give her solemn promise that she wouldn't go over there on her own."

"Good for Emma."

Norman stroked his stubbly chin. "I know now that I must watch my back, Vincent. I'm not worried about myself. But Katherine...I worry that he will try to hurt her."

Vincent's left eye twitched. "He better not even think it."

His voice filled with venom, Norman said, "If he tries, Vincent, I won't be responsible for my actions. If he so much as hurts a hair on her head, I will kill him. I swear it."

Vincent could only nod his agreement. He felt the exact same way.

When Norman had laid down again to rest, Vincent wandered down the hall, through the kitchen, and out the back door. His wife and Katherine sat in the Adirondack chairs. From where he stood on the back porch, he could hear every word they said. He knew he shouldn't eavesdrop, but he couldn't help himself. So he slid his hands into his pants pockets, leaned against the porch railing, and listened.

Katherine was telling Kate about growing up in Manhattan. How she had fallen in love with the violin at the age of five. "When my father bought me the Stradivarius, I thought I would die of excitement. I was fourteen and my teacher had begun showcasing me at recitals. Before I knew it, I was traveling all over the world, playing for large audiences. My father went everywhere with me. He watched over me. He took care of the business end, the travel arrangements. He was a wonderful man."

"What did your mother say?"

"Until she died, she traveled with us too. At times she would tell me that I should concentrate more on learning how to be a good wife. I suppose I got most of my old-fashioned ideas from her."

"Did you enjoy performing, Katherine?"

"I suppose I did. It didn't matter how many people were in the audience because the only person I really played for was my father. He always sat in the front row. I only saw him. And then he died. We were in Vienna. He collapsed backstage one night. A heart attack. He died in my arms." Her voice broke and Vincent saw her wipe at her eyes.

"I'm sorry," Kate said, laying a hand on Katherine's arm.

"Has Vincent told you the rest? Did he tell you why I married Jethro?"

"Yes."

"I should have turned to Norman. But he had always idolized me so. I didn't want him to see how weak and afraid I really was once my father was gone."

"When did you meet Norman?"

Happiness born from pleasant memories filled Katherine's face. "Just after I turned sixteen. He worked at the music hall where I often played. He was so easy to like. We became fast friends. When my mother died, he was a great comfort to me. He found ways to lift my spirits and make me laugh even in my grief."

"And yet you did not turn to him when your father died."

"By then, Kate, I had risen to great heights in the music world. I felt Norman's feelings for me changing. He hadn't spoken of love, but...as I said, I thought he idolized me. That's how I interpreted what I felt coming from him. And I couldn't let the idol fall in his eyes. I did not think he loved me as a potential life partner."

"But he does."

"And, I now know, has for years." Her cheeks flushed slightly. "I have made so many wrong choices since my father's death, Kate."

"But now you are making the right ones," Kate assured her.

"If Jethro will let me." Her tone was wistful, her eyes bearing anguish. She took hold of Kate's hand. "It is so easy to talk to you. It's odd, but I feel I know you already."

Kate could not meet her grandmother's eyes. She looked away and when she did, something caught her eye. Vincent turned to see what it was. Jethro Malloy stood in his yard, hands clasped around the pointed tops of the wrought iron fence. Possessive eyes stared at Katherine.

Vincent hurried down the porch stairs towards Jethro. "What do you want, Malloy?" he said, reaching him.

Without taking his eyes off of his wife, he said, "As if that is any of your business."

Katherine charged him, Kate right behind her, calling her back. She ignored Kate's call and planted herself right in front of Jethro. Hands on her hips, she said, "How dare you, Jethro! How dare you attack Norman!"

Malloy didn't flinch. "You are my wife, Katherine. I will do whatever it takes to see that you remain so."

Vincent thought that Katherine was going to jump the fence and attack him like a panther. Kate grabbed her shoulders and held her back. "You've no right!" Katherine shouted. "I don't love you. I never loved you. And even if I did, you killed that love. You took my baby from me. Norman's baby. You will not take Norman from me. Do you hear me?"

"As if you could stop me." He looked at Katherine as one looks at an imbecile. "You are so naïve, Katherine," he said, shaking his head.

Katherine seized up, her face turning red, her body tense, fists clenched. "Leave us alone, Jethro. Leave us alone or…"

"What, Katherine?" he goaded her. "Or what?"

Vincent stepped between them. "Kate, take her inside." He met Jethro's gaze. "Killing Norman will not make Katherine love you, Jethro. Surely you realize that."

Katherine strained against Kate's hold, but Kate held firm. "Come on, Katherine," she said. "He's not worth your time. Come inside." She dragged her away.

"What do you know of it, Vermay?" Jethro said.

"Leave us alone!" Katherine yelled again.

Jethro gave her a final glance then looked at Vincent again. "Mark my words, Vincent," he said. "They will never live together as man and wife. I shall see to it." Then he turned and walked away.

    ❧   ❧   ❧

Vincent watched him go, seething inside. But he forced himself not to chase after him and kill him.

"Vincent!" Kate called from behind him.

He turned and found his wife kneeling beside Katherine, who was on her knees, a hand to her chest. She appeared to be choking, fighting for air. Vincent rushed to her side. He held her by the shoulders and said, "Easy, Katherine. Calm down. Breathe slowly. Come on, Katherine." Kate massaged her back. Still, she wasn't breathing. He remembered something he'd seen his mother do when babies got so mad they held their breath. He blew into her face. It worked. She took long, deep breaths and fell into him. Her body shook with her fury.

"Vincent," she said, tears falling. "Please, don't let him hurt Norman. Promise me you won't let him hurt Norman."

He held her as he said, "I'll do what I can, Katherine. I can promise you that." He looked at Kate. She still knelt beside Katherine, massaging her back. Her eyes showed him her inner turmoil. "I understand," he mouthed to her.

She took Katherine from his arms and hugged her while she cried. She stroked her hair and comforted her with quiet, soothing words. Watching his wife, Vincent wondered if he'd already lost her.

    ❧   ❧   ❧

Kate sat curled up on the bedroom window seat wearing one of his dress shirts. The bedroom lights were off and Vincent could see stars twinkling in the night sky. But she wasn't looking at them. She sat with her head against the windowpane, her eyes closed. Her arms were folded across her chest. Tears glistened on her cheeks. She wasn't wearing her glasses.

Vincent hung his bath towel around his neck and went to her. Sitting down beside her, he touched her damp cheek. The tears were warm on his skin. "Hey," he said.

She looked at him. "Done showering?"

"I am. Why the tears?"

She took his hand. "She's so young, Vincent. Nineteen years younger than I am now. And...so...so naive. All those summers I lived here, she never told me much about her childhood."

"Now you know."

"Yes, now I know." She drew in a long breath of air. "By the time I came along, she'd changed, Vincent. She was so quiet and so small. Her rich, brown hair had gone gray. There was a part of her that was always sad. But I could make her smile. My father would pull into the driveway. She'd be waiting on the porch and when I would get out of the car, oh, she would smile. Her eyes would light up." Kate shook herself, as if to dissolve the memories. "I knew Abe. Did I tell you that?" She didn't wait for him to respond but continued talking. "He loved her. I knew that. Even as a small child I knew it. It was in his eyes." She held up a fist. "And the whole time, this kind man who slipped Liz and I candy, who cared for this house, was my grandfather. And he knew it."

She punched the windowpane.

He grabbed her wrist. "Easy. Don't hurt yourself."

"Abe's death tore her heart out, Vincent. She was never the same after he died. She was resigned, hopeless. No longer able to fight. Thus, Lydia had her way with her. But for all her heartache and pain…a lifetime of it…she lived to be 94. And the majority of those years were so cruel to her. I wonder how she even survived them."

"I don't know, babe. But she did. And you were a source of joy for her."

"When does Norman disappear, Vincent?"

"In December."

"And we still don't know how it happens?"

"No."

Kate massaged her forehead. "God, I don't know what to do, Vincent. I love her. I want her to be happy. Part of me keeps thinking that since Norman is my grandfather anyway; let them be together as man and wife. But then I also know that more than just paternity made my father the man he was. I'm sure Jethro Malloy and a boarding school upbringing damaged him a lot."

"It keeps rolling around in your head, doesn't it? It's rolled around in my head for days."

Kate sighed, closing her eyes for a brief moment. Opening them again, she said, "I don't know what to do, Vincent."

"How could you?" He held out his arms.

She came into them, burying her face in his bare chest. He felt more tears fall from her eyes. "If it means anything, I don't want to lose you, Kate. I love you."

"I love you," she said, her body trembling. She fought for control and won. Looking up at him, she said, "I want to go back with you. I want to see her again."

He brushed her hair back from her face. "I don't think we should go, Kate. Maybe we should just walk away."

She shook her head. "No. Vincent, you have more paintings to do. She needs a friend. I can be that to her. At least for now."

"And when December comes?"

"When December comes…if we can still go back…if the violin still lets us, then we'll see. We'll talk and we'll decide together. Like we agreed. We'll make the decision together."

He didn't release her. He couldn't. He sat with her on the window seat, holding her close against him. He didn't want to ever let her go.

CHAPTER 23

It wasn't a spoken agreement, but it was an agreement nonetheless. They spent most of the following week at the Canal Fest and neither spoke of Katherine and Norman. They played the games on the Midway; Vincent winning Kate a giant stuffed Dalmatian on Saturday. They rode the rides, spending an obsessive amount of time on the Ferris Wheel. They sampled food at just about all the food vendors, Kate being especially fond of the funnel cakes covered with powdered cinnamon. The Fest, a joint venture sponsored by both North Tonawanda and Tonawanda, spilled over the canal bridges into both cities. Each night throughout its duration there were concerts in the band shell at Niawanda Park, along the Niagara River, featuring such acts as the nationally acclaimed Buffalo Philharmonic Orchestra to the local favorite Ramblin' Lou Family Band. Kate was especially moved by the voice of Linda Lou Shriver, one of Ramblin' Lou's daughters. Her version of *Blue* sent chills up Kate's spine she informed Vincent after the concert. The highlight of the Festival's final weekend was the craft show. Crafters from all over the region set up booths along North Tonawanda's Webster Street, flowing over the canal bridge to Tonawanda's Main Street, and hawked their wares. Throngs of people attended the craft show and the hum of their voices mingled with a jazz band that played on a small, wooden stage by the canal.

On Sunday, Vincent and Kate strolled hand-in-hand along Webster Street, examining each crafter's booth. There were booths showcasing stained glass, dried flower arrangements, paintings, photographs, furniture, wooden toys and much more. The sun beat down, the heat sizzling up off the tarmac. After they crossed the bridge over into Tonawanda, Vincent stopped at a food stand and bought them each a glass of lemonade. They drank as they walked, Kate stopping at a booth offering embroidered vests. She held up a black one embroidered with red, long stemmed roses. "What do you think, Vincent?" she asked.

He thought of Katherine and the fact that red roses were her favorite. "I like it. Try it on."

She did, slipping it on over her white t-shirt. As he watched her button it, he thought that the garment couldn't possibly look that good on anyone else. She modeled it for him. "Well?"

"Sold." He grinned.

She paid the young, red-haired woman for the vest and they started off again. It was nearly 4 p.m. when they finished perusing the crafts. Kate was sweating; tendrils of wet hair sticking to her face and forehead. Even though the lenses of her glasses had darkened in the sun, Vincent could still see the tiredness in her eyes. He slipped an arm around her shoulders and, as they both sidestepped a stroller with a sleeping baby, said, "How 'bout we call it a day?"

"Okay."

They headed home, walking side-by-side, holding hands. They walked down Goundry and had just crossed over Vandervoort Street when Vincent saw Tracy riding toward them on her bicycle. She wasn't alone. A tall, muscular, young man, his strawberry blonde hair waving out from beneath his helmet, rode beside her. They pulled to a stop, straddling their bikes. Grinning, Tracy said, "Hey, Vincent, Kate."

She wore white shorts and a pink halter-top, and in spite of the sweat pouring off of her, she looked lovely and at peace. Vincent had no doubts that Tracy's companion had much, if not everything, to do with Tracy's newfound peace. He stuck out his hand and said, "You must be Nathaniel. Vincent Vermay and this is my wife, Kate."

The young man's grip was strong. "Hello," he said, his voice deep, sounding older than his years. He shook Kate's hand as well, saying, "Trace has told me a lot about you both. Great to finally meet you." His eyes were soft hazel and carried a constant twinkle. His face was chiseled, cheekbones high, gentle laugh lines at the corner of his eyes, his chin squared and dimpled. Vincent thought him the subject of any teenage girl's dreams. And he was glad that Tracy Woodward, she of low self-esteem and loner tendencies, had found him. It was obvious by the way the young man looked at Tracy that he adored her. Vincent couldn't keep from smiling as he stared at young Nathan.

"On your way to the craft show?" Kate asked.

Tracy shook her head. "Nope. We did that yesterday. We're going to go ride the path by the river."

"Well have fun." Kate said.

"Good to meet you, Nathan," Vincent said. "You and Tracy stop by the house soon."

"Sure." The young man grinned.

As the couple rode away, Kate said, "They look good together."

"She needed him," Vincent said, not elaborating. He didn't have to. Kate understood.

The message light was blinking on the parlor phone when they reached the Victorian. The first message was from Sarah, just "checking in." The second was from Vincent's parents. They were off to London and would call him upon their return. The third was from Jessica Woodward, inviting them to a barbecue next weekend. Kate called her back to accept the invitation while Vincent poured them each a glass of iced tea.

"I told Jessica I'd bake a dessert," Kate said, coming into the kitchen.

Vincent handed her a glass of tea. "And what will I be baking?" he asked, teasingly.

Kate chuckled. "Whatever your little heart desires, Vincent."

They wandered out onto the porch and sat in the rockers. Sipping his tea, Vincent asked, "Any ideas for dinner?"

"I can't imagine what it must feel like," Kate said, seeming not to hear his question.

"What?"

"Losing a child."

"What brought that on?"

"I don't know. I guess talking to Jessica."

"How'd she sound?"

"Like she's working very hard at getting on with her life. But underneath, deep within her heart, she's bleeding."

Vincent sighed. "Jess is a strong woman. And she has Mike and Tracy."

Kate downed half her iced tea. She rocked slowly, her index finger tracing the rim of her glass. Condensation rolled down the sides of the glass, dripping onto her bare thigh.

"What are you thinking?" Vincent asked, watching her closely.

Without looking at him, she asked, "Why do you suppose we never had kids, Vincent?"

"I guess we just never got around to it. Do you want children?"

She looked at him. "We've been married fifteen years and…"

"And what?"

"It never entered our thoughts?"

Vincent shrugged.

"I'm thirty-nine."

"And I'm forty-one."

"If we had a kid now, I'm be fifty-nine when he or she is twenty."

"So?"

She started laughing and took his hand. "How strange, though, Vincent. We meet, fall in love and get married, and never discuss having kids. We must be two strange ducks."

He squeezed her hand. "No, we're just perfect for one another."

She leaned over the arm of the rocker and kissed his lips. As he returned her kiss, he thought about Norman Lassiter, December, and the decision he and Kate would all too soon have to make.

Life fell into a comfortable routine. Most days were spent with Katherine and Norman. Vincent painted, and Kate spent time with Katherine. Sometimes the women talked. Other times Katherine would read while Kate worked on her novel. She'd write her thoughts out in longhand and transfer them onto her computer at night, oftentimes working away in her office until well after midnight. Norman bounced back quickly and returned to the house on Tremont Street to finish readying it for the day he would bring home his bride. Vincent noted that Norman kept one eye on Jethro Malloy's movements. The actor would not be surprised again. Katherine's hand finally began responding to the exercises she so diligently performed. By the end of September she was playing her violin again like she'd never been injured. The joy in Norman's eyes when he listened to her spoke volumes.

When not in 1926, Vincent continued working on the Victorian. He finished painting the house, which was now the talk of the neighborhood. In fact, many of his neighbors had stopped while he was painting to tell him how much they liked what he was doing to "the tired, old place". He had to replace several rotten posts on the porch and was fortunate to find a local carpenter who helped him with the task. Then he began work on the kitchen. The red refrigerator and black stove went. The stove only had two burners that worked and Kate said that the red refrigerator was "hideous." The ceramic tile floor cleaned up nicely and Vincent was happy that it could be saved. The old cupboards were torn out and oak cupboards were installed. Vincent stripped the white paneling that ran halfway up the walls and discovered beautiful oak beneath. He painted the walls above the wainscoting an ocean blue and installed dark blue counter tops. Elsie happily jumped in and made them blue and white striped curtains for the kitchen windows.

Kate helped him with some of the work, but for the most part he left her to her writing and her developing friendship with Jessica Woodward. Since the Woodward barbecue, the two women spent a great deal of time together. Since they both needed a friend, Vincent was glad they'd found each other.

Norman claimed the fourth portrait Vincent completed of Katherine. He'd painted her from the shoulders up, her head slightly turned so that she appeared to be looking out of the painting. Her hair flowed down over her shoulders, curled strands falling over her throat. A trace of a smile on her lips made one believe she had just seen something pleasant. Her eyes glowed a bright green, commanding attention. Despite Vincent's protests, Norman insisted on paying for the portrait. Relenting, Vincent accepted the money and shoved it into his pocket.

Shortly after, on a day in late September, Vincent set out with Norman to hang the painting in its new home. The air was brisk and both men wore jackets, Vincent also wearing his tweed cap. Orange, gold, red and yellow leaves hung precariously to the trees. Dark, ominous clouds hung in the north sky, promising rain.

They reached the white house and Norman unlocked the front door. He led Vincent into the living room and pointed at the marble fireplace. "I wanted to put it above the mantle there, but I'm afraid Katherine has insisted that she not be on display in our parlor."

Vincent laughed. "Too bad. It would look good there."

Norman grinned. "It would look splendid there. But, I'm afraid it's been delegated to the bedroom."

They went upstairs to the room Norman hoped to share with his future wife. Unlike the last time Vincent was here, the room was completely painted and furnished with a walnut sleigh bed, dresser, nightstands, and armoire. A scroll-patterned, beige and rose wingback chair sat in front of the Palladian window, a stack of books sitting beside its left front leg. Norman pointed at the wall above the bed. "Right there, Vincent."

Working together, they had the portrait hung in less than ten minutes. Norman stepped back to admire it, a contented smile on his face. "Ah, she is beautiful, is she not, Vincent?"

"She is," he agreed, unable to meet Norman's eyes. In fact, if the truth be told, it was getting harder and harder to look either Norman or Katherine in the eye.

Norman rubbed his hands together and said, "Excellent. Now, follow me, Vincent."

"Where?"

"To my next venture. Come on, don't dawdle."

They headed up Tremont Street. Norman walked with his hands in his coat pocket, his head down. They had just crossed over Payne, when he said, "Katherine has filed for the divorce, Vincent."

"Then she's seen a lawyer."

"We went together. I will not let her go out alone. I'm sure you understand why."

"I do. Has Malloy been served yet?"

"He has."

"And?"

"He's stalling."

"That doesn't surprise me."

"Nor me. Timothy says that Malloy will hold on as long as he can."

"Does your brother know Jethro?"

"They run in the same circles, yes. Jethro is a man who is used to getting his way. He is a man who values his possessions above all else."

"And Katherine is his possession."

"In his mind, without a doubt, she is."

Vincent swatted a drowsy bee away and asked, "Why did you introduce them, Norman? If you knew what Jethro was like?"

"He was in New York. I knew him vaguely. I ran into him at one of Katherine's performances. He asked to meet her and I introduced them. I never thought anything would come of it. I don't have to tell you again that I could kick myself for doing so."

"Hindsight," Vincent muttered.

"Kate's been good for Katherine. You realize that don't you, Vincent?"

"I'm glad."

"Emma likes her too."

"Yes, she's told me."

Norman brushed his mustache with his thumb and forefinger. "Katherine is fascinated by Kate's writing ability. You know Katherine loves to read."

"Kate is fascinated by Katherine's violin playing so I guess you can call it mutual admiration."

"They look so much alike too. Katherine doesn't see it though. She shakes her head and says I'm crazy when I mention it."

Vincent didn't comment. There was nothing he could say. They did look alike. And he damn well knew why. They passed the police station on the Corner of Tremont and Main. The building sported wide windows surrounded by thick, wooden frames. Steps led up to a massive, wooden door with glass panels on each side. Etched in a glass panel above the door were black letters proclaiming, **POLICE STATION**. In Vincent's own time, North Tonawanda's police station was located on Payne Avenue, north of Goundry.

As they drew closer to downtown, Vincent felt a slight flush come over him. He hoped that Norman didn't mean to take him over the bridge into Tonawanda. He'd have to refuse to go. Once over the bridge, he'd return to his own time. And wouldn't that freak Norman out, seeing his companion disappear before his very eyes?

They drew closer to Webster Street and Vincent's eyes nearly popped out of his head. He pointed at the tall, brick building on the corner of Webster and Tremont. It stood six stories tall and towered over downtown, commanding attention.

"What?" Norman asked.

Vincent almost said, "What the hell is that building?" He stopped himself just as his mouth opened. *You're supposed to be living in this time period, stupid,* he scolded himself. "I've just always admired that building, Norman." God, he hoped he sounded convincing.

"Timothy works in there for Metropolitan Life."

"Really?"

They passed the building and Vincent saw signs for cigars, soda, and drugs on its striped, canvas awnings. Webster Street itself was a marvel of familiar buildings, different buildings, and buildings conspicuously missing. Quaint light posts lined the red, brick-paved street. Businesses long closed in North Tonawanda in Vincent's time were now open and thriving. He read their names in wonder: People's Clothing Store, Wilder Hardware Company, Federal Radio, Dollar Dry Cleaning Company, E.C. Smith, The Goundry Hat Shop, Paris Shoppe, Twin City Restaurant, Evening News, and the Niagara Domestic Appliance Company. People walked in and out of the stores, men in derbies and women in dresses with long overcoats, stylish hats on their heads, some of velvet and most bearing silk flowers. Fords and Chevrolets lined the street. There were Touring cars, Roadsters, Coupes, Model T's, Model A's and one ton pickup trucks. They were parked diagonally just like the cars did in the year 2000. Vincent saw a construction site ahead. Norman pointed at it. "There it is. My new venture."

A building was indeed under construction. All the steelwork and brick had been completed and the entire building roofed. The portion of the building facing Webster Street was narrow, the remainder of the building fanning out at an angle and ending on Main Street.

"A theater," Vincent said, realizing that this was the future Riviera Theatre.

Norman slapped his hand on the entrance framing. "She has just been named. She is the Rivera. Come on in. They're working on the basement, mezzanine and balcony floors now."

They entered a low-lit world of busy workmen who paid them little attention. The pounding of nails reverberated throughout the hollow building. Sawdust hung in the air, burning Vincent's nostrils and he sneezed three times. "And how are you involved in this, Norman?" he asked, sniffing.

"I told you I was involved in a new business here, didn't I?"

'You did."

Norman spread his arms wide. "Here it is. I'm a partner."

"Vincent scratched his chin. "Impressive."

"The Rivera will definitely be impressive when she's completed. She's scheduled to open in December."

"I see." Vincent saw the theatre's current marquee in his mind. The sign read Riviera. He wondered what year the name change had taken place.

Norman clamped a hand down on Vincent's shoulder. "She'll seat twelve hundred, Vincent. She's Italian Renaissance in style. She'll be gorgeous inside once her interior is completed." Norman's eyes burned brightly as he spoke. "She'll have an organ made by the Wurlitzer Company. She will have the most modern ventilating system of any theatre in Western New York. In addition to my financial stake in her, I am forming a company that will stage weekly vaudeville shows every Friday and Saturday night. There will be movies and there will be three plays a year. Opening night itself will be an event like this town has never seen." He leaned closer. "Plus, there is something you and Kate must help me do." His tone was conspiratorial, a wide smile on his face.

"And that would be?"

"Talk Katherine into performing on opening night."

Vincent's eyes moved from Norman to the half completed stage flooring and back to Norman again. He bit his lower lip.

"You're not saying anything," Norman said, his smile fading. "Don't you think it's a good idea?"

Still biting his lip, Vincent considered Norman's request. "I know she's told you why she married Jethro Malloy, Norman. And knowing that, how can you suggest that she step onto a concert stage?"

"Because she must, Vincent." Norman's face held resignation and the knowledge that what Katherine needed to do would be hard for her. "She must face her fear and overcome it. I am not a psychiatrist by any means, but since she told me of her fears and 'panic attacks' as you called them, I have done some reading. Of all the different theories, one stands out from all the others. Facing your fears. Beating them."

Vincent sighed. "What if she can't do that, Norman? Then what?"

"It will grieve me because it will mean that her demons will never be completely gone. But I will love her nonetheless. I promise you, I will make sure she knows that."

Vincent crossed his arms over his chest and gazed around the interior shell of the Rivera. The thought of Katherine playing her violin on its stage brought a warm pleasure in his heart. He could see her playing in this theatre. North Tonawanda would never forget it that was for sure. And Norman was right. It would help Katherine chase her demons away.

He held out his hand. "You've got at least one co-conspirator here, my friend. I can't speak for Kate although I will talk to her."

Grinning, Norman shook Vincent's hand. "We shall make Katherine whole again, Vincent. We will not only free her from Malloy, but we will free her from her fears.

Vincent grinned back. And as he grinned, he marveled at the fact that he could do so even though he knew that what Norman wished would never be.

❦   ❦   ❦

"I hate to see her go through that," Kate said, leaning back in the rocker and resting her jean-clad legs on the porch wall. She wrapped her quilted, flannel shirt tighter around herself. The night was cold and when she spoke, Vincent could see her breath. "But Norman's right. She does need to face her fears."

Vincent, settled in the rocker next to Kate, peered at *The Tonawanda News.* He could barely read the print in the fading evening light. He didn't answer his wife because her tone told him she didn't need him to say anything.

She paused, sipping her cup of coffee. "But wouldn't she shock the shit out of North Tonawanda if she did get on that stage and play for them? It would do both the town and her wonders."

Vincent raised an eyebrow. "Shock the shit?"

"Yes." Kate laughed. "What an image. Twelve hundred people crapping their pants."

He shook his head, squinted at the paper again, and an advertisement jumped out at him. "Hey, babe," he said, "Listen to this."

"What?"

"Friday night at the Riviera Theatre they're giving a tour of the theatre. After the tour, they'll show a silent movie accompanied by the Mighty Wurl-itzer. We should go."

"How much?"

"Five dollar donation per person appreciated."

"The Riviera," Kate said, her tone nostalgic. "Lord, Mrs. Reilly used to take Liz and I there when we were kids. Saturday afternoon matinees. Liz and I would sit up in the balcony. We had a ball. But the poor place was following apart back them."

"Well, it's not anymore. It's been restored. Liz said that it's beautiful now."

"Then she's been...she'd been there." Kate's voice wavered with the last three words.

"Yes, she had been," Vincent said, a wave of sadness welling up within him.

"I miss her," Kate said, quietly, just as Vincent was thinking how much he missed Liz.

He folded the paper and set it on his lap. He placed a hand on Kate's fore-arm, gently rubbing it.

She looked at him, tears in her eyes. "There's this part of me inside that is empty. It's Liz's spot. Even though I didn't see her for all those years, she was still alive. I knew that. I also knew that I could pick up the phone and call her. I never did but I knew I could."

Vincent kept rubbing her forearm. No words of comfort came. Losing Liz had torn him up as well.

Kate turned from him and stared down into her coffee cup. "You know what she told me that Friday night, the last night we spent together?"

He waited for her to go on.

"She said that I had to be 'off my rocker' to think that you would do to me what Jethro had done to Katherine. And I knew she was right. I knew that my thoughts were irrational, but they wouldn't go away. They took hold of me. They made me think you would do things that you would never do."

"Like lock you in the office upstairs and not let you out."

"God, when you say it, it sounds so ridiculous. But every time I came to visit you, and you mentioned my moving here and writing full time, I just freaked inside. I guess I was 'off my rocker.'"

"No, babe, you weren't." He leaned over the arm of his chair and cupped her chin in his hand. He gently turned her face towards him. "You were reacting to what you saw happen in this house that night when you stepped back in time. In some traumatized part of your mind, I wasn't Vincent anymore. At least not the Vincent you fell in love with and married."

"You didn't deserve being thought of like that, Vincent. I'm sorry."

"I know you are. It's over. You're here now."

"You should add, and not locked up in the office."

He smiled. "Don't be so hard on yourself."

She took hold of his hand and moved it from her chin to her lap. She held on tightly as if she didn't ever want to let go.

"What?" he asked, knowing she needed to say more.

"Liz also said that I was the luckiest woman in the world. I have a husband who loves me with all his heart, a husband who believes in me. I sat across the table from her and realized for the first time how lonely and depressed she was. That's why I pushed her to spend Saturday with me. But she…" Kate couldn't go on. She didn't have to. They both knew what had happened after that dinner. They had both lost a dear friend.

He squeezed her hand in a lame effort to comfort her. She forced a smile.

They sat together in comforting silence, holding hands, watching as the last remaining shreds of daylight gave way to darkness. Kate sat with her head back, eyes closed. Her breathing was even, almost rhythmic. Vincent thought she'd fallen asleep and was just contemplating carrying her up to bed, when she opened her eyes and said, "Tell Norman I will help convince Katherine to perform opening night. She must not spend the remainder of her life tortured by fear. I can tell her from personal experience it's not a fun way to live."

"Okay."

She moved closer, hunkered down, and laid her head on his shoulder. "I love you, Vincent," she said in a way he had never heard her say it before. He couldn't explain how or why it sounded different and more soulful and genuine than it ever had. He just knew that it did. And while his heart soared, his mind screamed with fear. December was only a few months away. What if she wanted to risk her life so that her grandmother's would be better? What would he say? Would he let her? Could he let her?

He looked down at their clenched hands. Her hand fit into his so perfectly, like it was meant to always be there. The thought of never holding her hand again sent chills up his spine. "I love you too, Kate," he said. *And I don't want to lose you*. He didn't say the words aloud, but he didn't have to. When she raised her head and looked at him, her eyes told him that she'd heard them nonetheless.

CHAPTER 24

Vincent stood on the sidewalk in front of The Riviera Theatre, Kate at his side. He'd donned his navy blue, pinstriped suit for this event. He'd matched the suit with a pale blue shirt and a red, white and navy blue-striped tie. Kate wore a silky white dress that hung to just above her knees. Her shoes were white with pale purple stripes. She wore a purple scarf around her neck, held in place by a gold and pearl clip. Her hair was pulled up, held in a coil at the back of her head by pearl and gold hairpins. She was, in Vincent's estimation, downright gorgeous.

While they waited in line, Vincent studied the theatre's façade. Constructed of tan brick, it loomed above them and was topped by two beautiful, terra cotta ladies. The marquee stretched out over the sidewalk, its running lights blazing. Noting the length of the line behind them, Vincent was glad they'd come early. The crowd represented a range of ages and most, like he and Kate, had dressed up for the occasion, harkening back to a time when dressing up was not so rare. Cars filled every parking spot along Webster Street, spilling down to Manhattan Street and the old Murphy's Department Store parking lot. The hum of voices filled the air.

Kate moved closer to him and he slipped an arm around her shoulders. "Cold?"

She nodded.

He rubbed her arm. "That's what you get for wearing a sleeveless dress on a fall night."

She jabbed him with her purse.

To make amends, he said in her ear, "You look ravishing, darling."

She stood on tiptoe and kissed his cheek.

"Want my suit coat?"

She shook her head. "And ruin my ravishing look?"

At last the theatre's exterior doors were opened and Vincent, keeping his arm around Kate's shoulders, led her inside. They filed through an entry area highlighted by an ornate glass, brass and marble ticket booth. Walking through another set of doors, Vincent stepped into a world so beautiful that he gasped. Intricately carved blue and gold moldings decorated the ceiling and the top of the walls. Burgundy material, beige plaster, and mirrors covered the lobby walls, and elegant crystal light fixtures hung from the ceiling. Two magnificent, marble staircases on each side of the lobby led up to the theatre balcony. Vincent was vaguely aware of Kate opening her purse, pulling out a $10.00 bill and putting it in a donation box just inside the doorway.

"Good evening, everyone," an amplified voice said.

A woman stood in front of the concession stand. She wore black slacks, a white, lacy blouse, and a nametag that read *Volunteer, Doris*. Her salt and pepper hair curled around a lovely face, and she had bright, pretty, hazel eyes. Vincent guessed her to be in her sixties.

"Welcome. I'm Doris and I'll be taking you on your tour this evening. We'll start in the balcony and work our way downstairs. Everyone ready?"

A murmur of consent from the crowd and then they were moving, climbing the marble staircases. The balcony was large, the seats burgundy complimented by brass railings. It afforded a fantastic view of the auditorium that was itself a work of art, decorated with elaborate moldings painted in the same color scheme as the lobby. The auditorium walls held tapestry panels and more carved moldings. The molding on the arch above the proscenium was painted gold, blue and ivory. The area above the arch showcased canvas paintings depicting vaudeville caricatures. Vincent tuned back into what Doris was saying. "The canvas paintings were designed by Willard P. Lusk and they were painted by Ferdinand Kebely. The caricatures consist of dancers, a clown, a Chinese magician, a saxophone player, bowery girls, minstrels, hula girls and a Cossack."

"Wow," Kate mumbled beside him. "This is incredible. Nothing like when we were kids."

A dome in the golden ceiling, high above the auditorium's burgundy seats, framed a brilliant chandelier that Doris pointed out, consisted of 15,000 French cut crystals. "The chandelier was not added until 1974," the tour guide explained. "It was salvaged from the Genesee Theatre in Buffalo before its demolition. Prior to that, the dome stood alone, but was impressive in itself."

"Amen," Vincent said under his breath. Kate slid her arm through his.

"Some interesting facts about the chandelier," Doris continued. "It measures ten feet in diameter and is 14 feet high. It has three circuits of 85 bulbs each."

"Impressive," a man near Vincent said.

Doris grinned and said, "Very."

As they continued on with the tour, Doris rattled off the history of the theatre from opening night on December 30, 1926 until present day. "It changed hands several times and fell into a sad state by 1980 when it was placed on the Register of Historic Landmarks by the United States Department of the Interior. On February 14, 1989 the theatre was purchased by the Niagara Frontier Theatre Organ Society and restoration of both the theatre and the organ began."

They were back down in the lobby, heading into the auditorium through wooden doors with stain glass windows. Each window bore an R. Finding himself close to the tour guide, Vincent asked, "When did the spelling of the theatre's name change from Rivera to Riviera?"

"In the 1930's. The theatre became a Shea's Theatre and the name was actually changed to Shea's Riviera."

She led them along the back of the auditorium. They passed tables of delectable refreshments. Vincent noted fruit and vegetable trays, pastries, and other desserts. They went down the left side of the auditorium, up a set of steps then down another to the basement. Dressing rooms shared space with the heating and air conditioning systems. "In 1926, however," Doris said, "There were more dressing rooms. Six of them in fact. State of the art for the time. However, I'm afraid the air conditioning eliminated some of them just as the office space eliminated part of the Ladies' Lounge on the second floor."

When they came back up from the basement, Vincent saw that the organ had been raised up on a platform. He moved closer to it, barely hearing their guide give the stage dimensions. The organ was astounding, a beautiful ivory with an array of whimsical scenes painted on it. Doris smiled at Vincent as she walked by him and took her place beside the organ. "It's a 3/11 Wurlitzer Special, opus 1524," she said. She tenderly stroked it's top. "It was shipped from the factory on Niagara Falls Boulevard on November 27, 1926. In its day, it was the latest technology. And tonight, during the movie, you'll hear it, and I'm sure you'll agree that it is marvelous."

Kate whispered in his ear. "I think Doris loves this theatre."

"I think you're right," he whispered back.

"Please help yourselves to the refreshments at the back of the theatre. I'll be around if you have any further questions." She glanced at her watch. "The movie will be starting in thirty minutes."

Kate tugged on his arm. "Let's eat."

Vincent munched on carrots, celery and broccoli. He scanned the crowd wondering if any of his neighbors were attending. He saw the young couple that had recently moved into the house across from the Victorian. They exchanged waves.

Kate, who had somehow disappeared, reappeared beside him, her plate piled high with fruit. "Let's sit in the balcony," she said. "Like Liz and I used to do."

"Lead on," he agreed, shoving a piece of broccoli into his mouth.

They went out to the lobby, working their way through the crowd. Vincent saw their tour guide at the bottom of the nearest staircase. Surprisingly, no one was talking to her. He gestured with his head. "Over there, Kate. I want to ask her something."

"Right behind you."

"Doris," he said when they'd finally reached her.

"Yes. What can I help you with?"

"Vincent Vermay," he said, holding out his hand. She shook it. "And my wife, Kate Vermay."

"Ahh," she said. "You are the painter."

"I am."

"You're living in the Malloy house."

"We are," Kate confirmed. "Katherine Malloy was my grandmother."

"Of course," Doris said, smiling. "You used to come here with Elizabeth Reilly. I worked the concession stand in those days. Marlene used to bring you."

"You knew Mrs. Reilly?"

"I did. Parent Teachers' Association brought us together." She shook her head. "So sad, what Elizabeth ended up doing. She was such a wonderful doctor. The best doctor I've had in my lifetime, I might add."

"I tried to help her," Kate said, her voice strained. Vincent didn't have to look to know there were tears in his wife's eyes. He put his arm around her shoulders.

Doris expertly changed the subject. "Well, you've both done wonders with that Victorian. It's alive with color and warmth again."

"Thank you," Vincent said. "But I do have a question for you."

"And that would be?"

"Do you have a list or a record of who performed here opening night?"

"You mean in 1926 when the theatre first opened?"

"Yes."

"I believe I can help you. Follow me." They headed up the marble staircase. "I have to say, Mr. Vermay, that you impressed me during the tour. I could see that you fell in love with this theatre the minute you walked in."

"I'm that transparent, Doris?"

"Oh, honey, for sure you are," Kate said. Both women laughed. "But never fear, I love you anyhow."

When they reached the top of the stairs, Doris made a left. She led them through a door that opened into a supply room. Next came a conference room, a small office and finally, a bigger office, decorated with old theatre posters, a desk, three wooden chairs and a wall of file cabinets. Doris pointed at the wall behind the desk. "The opening night poster."

"May I?" Vincent asked, not wanting to assume he could just walk behind the desk.

"Of course. You'll see it lists all the major features and events." She opened a file drawer. "And if you look below the big shots and the major features, Kate, I think you'll find something interesting. Unless of course your grandmother told you about it before she died."

Beside him, Kate pushed her glasses up her nose and leaned closer to the poster. "Oh, my Lord," she said, punching Vincent's arm. "Look."

Vincent was already looking. There, in black and white, was the announcement that *Katherine Mann, world-renowned concert violinist* was going to appear. Vincent looked at Kate who was grinning.

"Good for her. She didn't use her married name, Vincent."

Doris joined them behind the desk. "No, she was billed as Katherine Mann. *The Evening News* did an article on her prior to opening night. Here's a copy of it."

Kate took the article. She scanned it, her smile widening. "Listen to this, Vincent. It talks a little bit about her stage career then her marriage to Jethro Malloy. Let's see...okay, it talks about her being pretty much out of sight...Damn, Vincent, it says that she's now separated from Malloy and living with Dr. Emma Reilly, and that she's filed for divorce." Kate looked at him with incredulous eyes. "I can't believe she let them do this article. But here's her picture. She obviously posed for it."

"No mention of Norman?"

"Yes, there is. In the last paragraph. They quote her. 'No, I doubt I'll return to the stage fulltime. But I do hope to play here at The Rivera from time-to-time. And I also hope to be the wife of Norman Lassiter and the mother of his children.'"

Vincent let out a whistle. "That a girl, Katherine," he said.

"I guess once she decided to step back into life, she went full force."

Doris held out another piece of paper. "The review of her performance."

"You read it," Kate said. "Don't tell me if it's horrible."

Vincent read it quickly. "Far from horrible. Apparently, Katherine 'astounded' all those in attendance with her 'masterful playing.' It goes on, praise upon praise."

Katherine took the article. But before she could read it, Doris said, "Most people felt sorry for her after that night though."

"Why?" Kate asked.

"Well, they'd seen her shine. Heard her brilliance. And then, Norman Lassiter disappeared, and she returned to Malloy and became a recluse again. Story goes Norman was there in the wings watching her play. She performed four songs. When she came offstage, he was gone. He was never heard from again. And of course the article didn't come out until the next day, and Norman was already missing. She had mere moments of joy and triumph, and then her world came crashing down." Doris shook her head. "I didn't move to North Tonawanda until the 1950's, but people were still talking about it thirty years later."

"My grandmother was a beautiful person, Doris," Kate said. "My summers with her, well, they turned out to be wonderful. Although I doubted they would be when I first arrived."

Doris collected the clippings from them and went back to the file cabinet. "No doubt she was beautiful. I always say that for one to play music so beautifully, they have to have that beauty in their heart. Your grandmother had it. Although I wasn't born until 1929, I have to admit, every time I pull this review out of the cabinet, I wish I'd been there to hear her." She closed the file drawer, ushered them out of the office and said, "Now, we better get downstairs before the movie starts."

"Coming to bed?" Vincent asked, sticking his head out the front door.

Kate sat in the rocker, her legs curled up, arms encircling them. She wore one of his flannel shirts over top her white and rose-striped pajama bottoms. Her hair waved about her shoulders. She wasn't wearing her glasses. A white candle in a pewter candlestick sat on the porch wall, burning gold in the dark.

Kate sighed. "I should."

"It's 2 a.m."

"I didn't mean to wake you, Vincent."

He stepped out onto the porch, wrapping his robe tighter around himself, tying the belt into a knot. He hadn't put on his slippers and wet boards immediately dampened his bare feet. He shivered. He guessed it was below forty degrees. "You're going to catch your death out here," he said, moving behind her chair and sitting down in the rocker beside her. He crossed his right leg over his left and massaged his foot.

"Give me," she said, turning her rocker to face him.

He did the same with his chair and put his feet in her lap. She put the tail of the flannel shirt on top of them. "Now, that's better," he said.

"Good." She took in a deep breath of air then blew it out, the breath white. "Do you realize what I can't put out of my mind, Vincent?"

"What, babe?"

"If Doris is right, we now know almost to the minute when Norman disappears. He's with Katherine backstage. He probably kisses her, says he'll be right there in the wings if she panics and sends her off. And she doesn't panic. No, she plays four songs brilliantly. Malloy strikes during those four songs, Vincent. And if we are there we can stop Malloy."

Vincent's stomach lurched into his throat and he wondered if he just might throw up everything he'd eaten at the theatre. His voice came out in a croak. "But we haven't decided that yet, Kate."

"We have the upper hand now," she continued, not hearing him. "We have the time narrowed down. It's not just December. No, it's December 30th while Katherine is on stage."

Vincent couldn't speak. He knew if he opened his mouth, he'd vomit.

Kate ran her fingers through her hair. "Which means, we will succeed if we decide—" She broke off and leaned closer to him. "Vincent, are you all right?"

"If we decide what, Kate?" he barked at her. "Or is it, you've already decided?" After he'd said the words, he marveled at the fact that he hadn't puked in her face.

She tensed, one hand going to her cheek almost as if he'd slapped her there. "No, I haven't decided, Vincent. I won't decide anything on my own. I promised you that." She moved from her chair to his lap and put her arms around his neck. She kissed his lips, messed his hair with her fingers, and said, "I don't break my promises." He pulled her closer. She rested her head on his shoulder. "Now, that's more like it," she said, snuggling against him. "Hold me like this until morning, Vincent. Just like this."

And he did. He held her close, feeling her body relax as she fell asleep. He could have carried her up to bed, but he didn't. He stayed on the porch, in the chair, Kate in his lap. He didn't sleep. He watched the candle grow smaller and burn out. He listened to the cars over on the Twin Cities Memorial Highway. He heard a siren as an ambulance rushed into DeGraff's Emergency Room driveway. He heard trains roll through town over on the tracks alongside River Road. Kate slept peacefully in his arms. But he was still awake when the first streaks of dawn appeared in the night sky.

CHAPTER 25

"Look," Katherine said, pointing out over the canal. "There's Norman."

Vincent shielded his eyes from the blinding sun, and looked across the canal to the stage were Norman Lassiter stood beside a gray-haired woman with a lovely face. She was slender, her hair coiled at the back of her head, and she wore a navy blue overcoat with a fur collar. The coat traveled down to her ankles, protecting her stocking-clad legs from the crisp October air. Next to her stood a man in spectacles, a derby bowler on his head, his topcoat securely buttoned. He was clean-shaven, his face wide and made handsome by his smile. Vincent estimated him to be around 70, the woman younger than he.

"Who is Norman with?" Kate asked beside Vincent.

"That would be Mayor Mackenzie and his wife," Emma said, hugging herself. In spite of her heavy overcoat and flowered velvet hat, she was shivering.

The four friends stood amongst a throng of people on the Delaware Street Bridge. Vincent had to estimate that between those on the bridge and those on the docks, there were over 3,000 people. Although the sun was shining and the sky was blue, the air was cold, the wind holding the feel of impending winter. Leaves swirled about the crowd, blown up from the ground and down from the trees.

"Isn't he handsome?" Katherine said. She wore a green overcoat, white scarf and white hat, the ensemble another gift from Norman. Her eyes were alive with joy, and she did not appear to feel the cold air in the slightest.

Vincent couldn't help teasing her. "Who, the Mayor?"

"No, silly, Norman." She slipped her arms around Emma. "Here, let me warm you up a bit." Emma didn't protest.

Norman did indeed look handsome. He wore a black overcoat, black slacks, black boots, and a black top hat. In addition to Norman, the Mayor, and Mrs. Mackenzie, the stage held ten other men. They all were looking down the Erie Canal, waiting for a flotilla of boats to arrive. Vincent followed their gazes. The flotilla was not yet in sight. The anticipation within the crowd was infectious and Vincent waited just as impatiently as those around him. He was also excited just to be witnessing this historic moment. Here he and Kate were, sharing in the one hundred year celebration of the opening of the Erie Canal. The flotilla they waited for was retracing the inaugural journey, but doing it in reverse. In 1826, a boat had sailed from Buffalo carrying a flask of Lake Erie water, which had been dumped in the Atlantic Ocean upon reaching New York City. On this October 13th in 1926, the boats were traveling from New York City to Buffalo, a small cask of salt water resting on the bow of the packet freighter, the *Dewitt Clinton*. It would be dumped in the Buffalo Harbor the next day.

Vincent shot a quick glance at the tents of food vendors lining the canal on the North Tonawanda side between Webster and Main. The smoke from the fires filled the air and Vincent smelled sausage, burgers, hotdogs, pork, onions, popcorn, peanuts and soups of every variety.

"Do you suppose they have funnel cakes in 1926?" Kate whispered in his ear.

He smiled at her and shrugged. "If not, I'll get you the biggest hot dog they have."

Standing on tiptoe, she kissed his cheek, her lips smooth and warm against his skin. A loud horn blew and Vincent turned toward the sound.

"Well, folks," Mayor Mackenzie announced through a bullhorn. "Here they come."

Amidst cheers, whistles and applause, two boats appeared and slowly made their way up the canal. Sailors lined the deck of the *Dewitt Clinton*. Vincent saw the cask of salt water on the bow, the ship's captain in full dress uniform standing behind it. The boats pulled to a stop, several of the men waving and bowing. The Captain saluted the Mayor and those on the stage with him.

"This is wonderful," Emma said, smiling. "What a moment to experience. Don't you think so, Katherine?"

But Katherine had abandoned Emma. She leaned over the bridge railing, straining to hear and see better.

Vincent put his arm around the doctor and said, "I agree, Emma. I whole-heartedly agree."

Emma's eyes widened. She looked apologetically at Kate and slipped from beneath Vincent's arm. Her cheeks were bright red.

Vincent chuckled to himself, while at the same time silently scolding himself for forgetting he was in 1926, a time when married men didn't just put their arms around other women. Not even women who were dear friends. And especially not when their wives were with them. Kate nudged him playfully in the side.

The flotilla lingered just long enough for three important speakers. Congressman S. Wallace Dempsey of Lockport was introduced. He praised the engineering marvel that the Erie Canal was as well as former Governor Dewitt Clinton who had pushed to make the canal a reality. He reminded his listeners that the canal had helped make New York State into an Empire State. Dewitt Clinton's 80-year-old great-grandson, George, spoke as well. His speech called for all "Tonawandans" to be "boosters" of the Erie Canal. He received an enthusiastic promise from the crowd. Mayor Mackenzie spoke last, basically echoing the thoughts of the two men who had preceded him.

All too swiftly, the flotilla went on its way and the crowd slowly dispersed, heading for the food vendors. Vincent escorted Emma, Kate, and Katherine from the bridge. Patriotic music filled the air, played by a trio of men on a stage by the food tents. All three were thirty-something and they wore navy blue uniforms with shiny brass buttons and red berets. The shortest man played a banjo. Next to him was a tall, rail thin man playing a trumpet. The snare drum player was thick muscled, his biceps straining the fabric of his uniform.

"Norman said to wait for him here, remember?" Katherine said when they reached the first tent.

"Sure do," Vincent said. An overpowering smell of roasted peanuts assailed his senses and he could not resist. Stepping away from the women, he purchased a large bag of peanuts from the mustached vendor. The brown paper bag felt strangely solid and heavy in his hand, and he looked down at the paper. Dark brown in color, its fabric content was obviously higher than any bag made in his own time. This bag was made to last and be used more than once.

"Going to share?" Kate asked, appearing at his side.

He grinned at her. "Feel this bag, babe."

She did, humoring him. The band burst into *Toot, Toot, Tootsie, Goodbye*. Two young boys in knickers ran past them, weaving their way in and out of the adults. Kate smelled the peanuts and said, "Yummy."

"Did you feel the paper, Kate? It's so—"

She cut him off with a finger to his lips. Emma and Katherine came up behind her, Katherine protesting that they were straying too far from the appointed meeting spot. Vincent held out the bag of peanuts. "Have one, ladies."

Katherine shook her head but Emma helped herself. Katherine strained to see over the heads of those around her, looking back toward the bridge, searching for Norman. Vincent followed her gaze and saw him walking across the Delaware Street Bridge, the Mayor and his wife with him. Handing the bag of peanuts to Kate, Vincent slipped his arms around Katherine's waist and lifted her off the ground. "Wave to him, Katherine," he said.

"What…Vincent, for Heaven's sake, what are you doing?" she protested, slapping his hands. "Put me down this instant. Why, this is improper."

Vincent chuckled, as did those around him.

"Vincent!" she protested again.

The band broke into *Charleston* and Vincent twirled around, Katherine still his captive and still protesting. Her hand thumped down on his derby, knocking it askew. He ignored her protests and strode with her towards Norman. He met Lassiter and his companions at the end of the bridge and promptly set Katherine on her feet.

Flustered, cheeks fire red, Katherine said, "Help me, Norman. Vincent has lost his senses."

Grinning, laughter in his eyes, Norman took her hand and asked, "New form of transportation, darling?"

Vincent straightened his derby and said, "The lady was having difficulty seeing you in the crowd, so I thought I'd help her out."

"I, well, I…" Katherine cut in but faltered into silence.

A trace of a smile on his wide face, Mayor Mackenzie said, "Dr. Reilly, how are you?" He stepped around Katherine and Norman to greet Emma and Kate who were just reaching them. Mackenzie took Emma's gloved hand and kissed it.

"Mayor," Emma said, nodding. She turned fond eyes on Mrs. Mackenzie. "Mary." The women hugged. "You are due for a checkup, my dear."

"I suppose I am, Emma." She turned to Kate. "And who might your friends be?"

"Kate Vermay and her husband, Vincent."

"Ahh, the painter I've heard about," the Mayor said, looking Vincent up and down. "Norman here tells me that you are a master at capturing the true life of your subject." The Mayor's eyes moved to Katherine whose cheeks were still slightly flushed. "And you must be Katherine Malloy."

Katherine nodded but didn't speak, her throat muscles taut. She seemed suddenly socially inept. She looked toward Norman and he stepped to her side, taking her arm and saying, "Katherine Mann Malloy. Late of New York City and the concert stage."

Admiration blazed in Mackenzie's eyes. "A violinist like no other. Mary and I saw you in London."

"Really?" Katherine managed to croak.

Unable to bear her grandmother's discomfort, Kate said, "That was a wonderful ceremony, Mayor Mackenzie. A very fitting one hundredth year celebration."

The Mayor turned to Kate. "Why thank you, Mrs. Vermay. We had to do something to mark the occasion. The Canal was truly a boom to this area and…"

Vincent tuned him out, his attention solely on Katherine. She literally relaxed against Norman, pulling in breaths of air. "You're all right, darling," Norman said close to her ear. "You did fine."

Mute, she shook her head, close to tears. Vincent heard what she was thinking. *I failed him. I cannot be the social wife he needs to succeed in this town. He deserves better. I am hopeless.*

Norman bent closer to Katherine's ear and whispered. Vincent couldn't hear what he said, but he obviously said the right thing. The threatening tears did not fall and Katherine managed a grateful smile.

"Do you suppose she really cares about the history of this Canal?" Emma asked folding her arms across her chest.

"You mean Kate?"

"Look at her, Vincent."

Kate had led the Mayor back up on the bridge and was listening intently to every word the man said. Vincent caught her eye and mouthed, "Thank you."

Her right eyebrow shot up but she kept her attention on Mackenzie and his story.

The strains of *Bye, Bye Blackbird* drifted over from the bandstand. Mary Mackenzie glanced over at her husband and Kate, and said, "I'm afraid, Mr. Vermay, that your wife is in for an ear full."

"Is that so?"

"Mrs. Mackenzie is right," Norman put in. "The Mayor loves to talk."

"Especially to captive audiences," Mary added. Then, turning to Katherine, said, "I would love to hear you play again, Katherine. Do you think I could convince you to give me a private concert?"

"Oh, Mary," Emma said. "I'm afraid that Katherine is still recovering from a hand injury. I doubt she's ready for public performances yet. Are you, Katherine?"

Katherine stood clutching Norman's hand, shock in her eyes.

"Right, Katherine?" Emma pressed.

"Well, I...my hand..." She looked away from Mary Mackenzie, her eyes searching for then finding Vincent. *What should I do? What would you do? What?*

Don't let it beat you, Katherine, he thought, hoping like hell his face revealed his thoughts. *You can beat this.*

Stalling for time, Katherine said, eyes still glued on Vincent, "I'm not presently playing my best, Mrs. Mackenzie." Amazingly, her voice didn't waver.

"Well that may be true," Vincent said. "Your worst is better than some violinist's best, Katherine. Don't you agree, Emma?"

Mayor Mackenzie was escorting Kate down off the bridge. "No, I'm afraid I prefer Sandburg, Mrs. Vermay. Surely you've read *Abraham Lincoln, the Prairie Years*?"

"Well, I must admit I haven't. I'm still finishing up *The Great Gatsby*."

"A Fitzgerald fan, I see."

Kate gave him a slight curtsy. "Guilty as charged."

The Mayor laughed. "Mr. Vermay, you wife is a true delight." He slipped his arm from Kate's and turned her over to Vincent. "Are you aware you are married to an F. Scott Fitzgerald admirer?"

"I am, indeed, sir. However, while I have read *Gatsby*, I've also read *The Prairie Years*. I'm afraid I am a history lover."

Mackenzie took his wife's arm. "We must mingle, my dear," he said.

"Katherine must answer my question before you drag me away, James." She gazed at Katherine expectantly.

"And what question would that be?"

"If she would honor me with a private concert."

Mackenzie grinned. "Honor us, you mean. What do you say, young lady? Will you play for us?"

So many emotions flowed through Katherine's eyes that Vincent couldn't name them all—desire, frustration, terror and more. But she couldn't bring herself to say yes. Not yet, anyway. So she said, "May I get back to you on that? I need to practice some more."

"Then we shall wait to hear from you." The Mayor winked. "I shall pray your rehearsals go well."

Once North Tonawanda's first couple had taken their leave, Katherine buried her face in Norman's black overcoat and said, tears in her voice, "I'm sorry, Norman. I'm sorry."

"Shh," he said, lightly stroking her cheek with his thumb. "It will come, darling."

"And if it never does?"

Norman hugged her close, unmindful of those around him, and said, "Then I will love you anyway."

❈   ❈   ❈

"You would think, Kate, that you're husband could find better subjects to paint," Katherine said, pointing her parasol at Vincent.

He grinned at her but continued painting. He stood with palette and brush in hand, his easel set up some fifteen feet back from her. She wore a forest green, velvet dress, it's skirt spread out on the grass around her, hiding the legs he knew were crossed beneath it. The bodice was intricate, white lace, the collar round, and rising to just below her chin. Her hair was pulled back, held there by a gold and emerald clip—another gift from Norman—but Vincent had insisted it fall over her left shoulder, looking like a brown waterfall as it fell well past her left breast. The parasol matched the gown, repeating the green and white in its frilly material. Vincent had posed her in front of a row of stately old trees that miraculously, in spite of the late date, were still bursting with fall leaves of gold, orange, red, and yellow. As he'd hoped, she looked like she belonged in the late 1800's, not 1926.

Kate sat to his right, wearing a pair of gray, classically tailored slacks—reminiscent of those worn by actress Katharine Hepburn in her youth—and a pale pink, silk blouse. She wore her hair up in a coil at the back of her head. Needless to say, Katherine's eyes had just about popped out of her head when Kate arrived wearing slacks. "Well, Katherine, you know it's all the rage now," Kate had said, kissing Katherine's cheek.

Katherine had just shook her head and said, "My, I am so old-fashioned."

Vincent chuckled at the memory. "Put that parasol back over your right shoulder, Katherine," he said. "Don't break the artist's concentration."

Katherine started spinning the parasol, a rare playfulness in her eyes.

Vincent's brush stopped in mid-air. He stared at Katherine, soaking in the look in her lovely, green eyes. "That's it!" he exclaimed. "My, God, that's it!"

"What's it?" both women asked simultaneously.

Vincent didn't answer. He couldn't answer. He had to catch Katherine's playful eyes before they disappeared. As he knew they would. And all too quickly. He worked furiously, his brush taking on a life all its own. It painted what he'd seen as if his hand were guided by a higher power. *Thank you, God. Thank you.*

He heard Kate rise with a small grunt. He felt her standing beside him. "Amazing," she said, her voice just a whisper.

"Vincent," Katherine insisted, her eyebrows arching, the playfulness gone from her eyes. But it didn't matter. He'd gotten it. By the grace of God, he'd gotten it.

Going to her, he said, "Come here." He held out his hand. "You must tell me what you think."

She took his hand and he helped her stand. She walked ahead of him to the painting. She stood before it, studying it intently, parasol resting on her right shoulder.

Kate stood behind Katherine, hands on her grandmother's upper arms. She peered over Katherine's left shoulder at the painting. "Isn't it amazing, Katherine?" she asked.

"I look…" She trailed off, a smile crossing her face. "I'm teasing. I'm…happy." She leaned back against Kate and Kate slipped her arms around her.

"You are happy, Katherine," she said, pressing her cheek to Katherine's.

"Yes, I am. I truly am." She turned her eyes to Vincent. "I thought that I would never be happy again. But I am. Because of Norman. He loves me. He…" She stepped out of Kate's arms and turned to her. "He loves me no matter what."

"Yes, he does," Kate agreed, nodding.

Katherine tossed the parasol aside and hugged Kate. Kate looked over her grandmother's shoulder at Vincent, her eyes screaming her thoughts. *How?* they asked. *How can I let her happiness be destroyed when I can prevent it?*

Vincent held up his hands then turned away from them. He didn't want Kate to see the fear in his eyes.

❀   ❀   ❀

Vincent studied the hat dubiously. It was charcoal gray, round in shape, with a lavender band, and silk orchids decorating its right side. The brim was narrow yet sufficient enough to shield the face from the sun. The shop proprietor, a plump woman in her fifties, patiently held the hat up, giving him all the time he needed.

"Buy it, Vincent," Norman encouraged him. He stood leaning on the counter, his elbow resting beside a black, cast iron cash register. As usual, he was dressed to the nines in a brown suit, complete with matching vest, white silk shirt, and flowered tan, green, pink, pale blue and white tie. His brown derby bowler sat upon his head.

They were inside The Goundry Hat Shop at the corner of Oliver and Goundry Streets. Hats of every possible shape, size and style surrounded them, some on mannequins, and others on shelves and tables.

"She'll love it, my friend. Would I ever steer you wrong?"

"I suppose not."

"Suppose? You know not." Norman smoothed his mustache with his thumb and forefinger. "You told me you needed a birthday present for Kate. Now you will have one."

"May I?" Vincent asked the proprietor.

She handed him the hat.

The workmanship was exquisite, the material thick and fine to the touch. Each flower was unique both in shape and the way the different shades of purple blended on its petals. Without a doubt, Kate would love it. "I'll take it," he said.

"Amen," Norman said.

Vincent paid for the hat with 1920's money he'd purchased from a collector over the Internet. It had cost him a pretty penny to obtain, but it had been necessary. He and Kate were spending more time in 1926, growing closer to Norman, Katherine, and Emma and doing more things that required leaving the safety of Emma's yard and house, things like shopping, that required money.

Once outside the shop, Norman headed for The Rivera. Vincent tagged along, the hatbox under his arm. Unlike the day of the Canal celebration, the air was warm, a coat not needed. "Indian Summer," Emma had called it.

"I just want to check a couple of things," Norman said.

"Fine by me, I'm in no hurry."

"While I'm in the theatre, should you be so inclined, Vincent, you could see what else you might find Kate in the People's Clothing Store over on Webster. They have the latest fashions, you know."

Two gentlemen passed them going in the opposite direction. As the taller man stepped around them on the grass, Vincent heard him saying, "What I can't believe is that the Cardinals won the blasted Series. The Yankees had Gehrig and Ruth. What do you suppose happened?" Vincent couldn't hear his companion's response.

"I never was one for sports, Vincent," Norman said. "What about you?"

"Not really. I like a good baseball game now and then. Not as a steady diet though."

"Are you a theatre man?"

"I am."

They reached Main Street and Norman gestured to his left. "Let's go in via the back way."

They crossed Goundry, stopping at a newsstand. Norman bought a copy of *The Evening News* and scanned the front page as they continued on towards The Rivera. They walked past a somber *Evening News* building that in Vincent's time was painted bright pink and housed the Partners in Art Gallery. *The Evening News* had become *The Tonawanda News* and sat out on River Road.

"Good, Lord," Norman said, shaking his head. "Seems as if the government is still arguing whether or not to overturn the dry law."

"What do you think, Norman?"

"I think," he began, lowering his voice. "That if they overturn the law, Jethro Malloy will lose a great deal of his income."

Vincent stopped in his tracks. "You think he overseas a running operation?"

"I know he does."

"You're serious?"

"Where do you think he got the men who kidnapped and beat me? Rum-runners, they were. I heard them talking."

Vincent scratched his chin. "Damn." He'd always thought Malloy ran only legitimate businesses such as furniture making, real estate, and finished lumber.

"Surprised, Vincent? With what you know about the man. Come on now."

"Damn," Vincent said again. Because at that moment, it was all he could say.

❦   ❦   ❦

"Damn," Kate said, staring at him.

They sat together on the window seat in their bedroom. As usual, she wore one of his shirts. He wore only his pajama bottoms. Thunder rolled off in the distance.

"That's what I said too."

Kate pushed her hair back over her shoulder, drew up her legs and circled her arms around her knees. "You know, I hadn't thought about it, but 1926 is during Prohibition, isn't it?"

"It is," Vincent said, nodding.

Kate grinned. "Malloy a bootlegger. Damn."

"Well, as Norman said, with what we know about the man, we shouldn't be surprised."

"Oh, I'm not surprised, Vincent. I wonder if Katherine knew."

"Probably. Norman kept no secrets from her." Lightning flashed outside the window.

Kate sighed. "Too bad Jethro didn't get himself killed in the process."

Vincent reached out and laid his hand on her knee. Her skin was silky and warm beneath his palm. He remembered what her eyes had asked him that day in the park. *How can I let her happiness be destroyed when I can prevent it?* He shuddered and she saw it. She laid her left hand, the one with her gold wedding band, on top of his. He stared at the gold glowing in the bedroom light. Thunder rolled again, this time closer.

"I have made no decision yet, Vincent," she said.

But you have, Kate. You don't know it yourself yet, but you have. He nearly spoke these thoughts but managed not to. Instead, he said, "I know."

"Then, as you would say, be still." She smiled. "Now, on the eve of my 40th birthday, don't you think we could find something better to do then talk about Jethro Malloy?" Her eyebrows shot up. "I mean, really, Vincent."

He smiled back, leaning into her and kissing her warm, inviting lips as once again, lightning flashed outside the bay window. Her arms slipped around his bare back, her touch arousing him. She nuzzled his ear and she said, "Take me to bed, Vincent Vermay. Take me this instant."

He carried her across the room and laid her on the bed. He straddled her and watched as she slowly, teasingly unbuttoned her shirt one button at a time, gradually revealing her perfect breasts and slender abdomen. He cupped a breast in each of his palms, amazed as always at how firm and round they were. Her nipples rose, calling to him. He bent and kissed each one, moving up her chest to her neck. But as slow as she'd been to unbutton her shirt, she wasted no time tearing at his pajama bottoms. Responding to her urgency, he helped her remove them and then pushed her shirt off her shoulders. She shrugged it off, pulling him down on top of her and muttering in his ear, "I love you. I will love you forever."

"I love you," he assured her. "More than life itself."

They came together passionately as the thunderstorm rolled into North Tonawanda with a vengeance. Lightning sizzled on the street in front of the Victorian and thunder shook the house, but neither of them paid the storm any mind. They were too caught up in each other to hear anything but their own vows of love.

At dawn, they once again sat together on the window seat, Vincent in his pajama bottoms, Kate in his shirt. She lay back against him, his arms fitting naturally around her, his chin resting in her soft hair. Outside, the first rays of morning sun shone down on a leaf-covered street still filled with puddles of rainwater. Last night's storm had obviously been furious. Downed tree branches littered their neighbors' yards.

Kate was tired. He could feel the tiredness emanating from her. He could see it in the fine lines around her eyes; lines that only appeared when her body craved sleep. "You should go back to bed," he said.

She smiled. "I might."

"You will." He lightly nibbled her ear and she laughed, saying, "Stop that. Especially if you want me to try and sleep."

"Which I'm sure you didn't do last night."

"Guilty. But it was nice, lying beside you and listening to you breathe." She stretched her arms out and cracked her knuckles. They popped, the sound loud in the morning quiet. "I have to meet Jessica for lunch. So if I do go back to bed, you have to wake me at eleven."

"Okay."

But she didn't get up from the window seat. She stayed in his arms, one hand playing with the hair on his forearms. "Vincent," she said, her voice low and serious.

"What, babe?"

"Will you let me do something?"

"What?"

"Let me spend part of my birthday with Katherine."

"Actually that's already planned. We are having dinner at Emma's tonight. Katherine insisted, but you must act surprised or she'll be mad at me for telling you."

Kate turned to look at him. "She really planned a birthday dinner for me?"

"She did. She also wrapped the 1926 birthday gift I bought you for me."

"1926 gift? I'm getting more than one gift."

He disengaged himself from her and got up from the window seat. "You are," he said, going to the armoire. Opening it, he pulled a small box down from the shelf. He had pushed it to the very back of the shelf so that it had been up too high and back too far for her to see it. Returning to her, he held out the box. "Happy birthday, Kate."

She accepted the gift and as she tore the red ribbon off the little gold box, she joked, "Isn't this the birthday where I start to fall apart? The big Four O?"

He sat down beside her on the window seat and leaned back against the window. The glass was cool against his skin. "Yes, your mid-life crisis should officially begin, I believe."

"My breasts start to fall and I get fat."

He touched her right breast. "Never. Don't you ever fall."

She slapped his hand away. "Honestly, you are definitely a boob man."

Vincent crossed his arms over his chest. "I warned you of that when we were still dating, I recall."

She lifted the lid from the box and her eyes filled with both tears and joy. "It's beautiful, Vincent."

"You really like it, babe?"

She stared down at the gold, heart-shaped pendant resting on the velvet cushion in the box. "I…it's…" She could find no words.

He took the box from her and pulled the necklace out. He held it up and said, "The diamond in the center of the heart is my love for you, Kate."

A tear slipped down her cheek.

"We sailed some harsh waters lately, babe, but through it all, I never stopped loving you. I never will." He put the necklace around her neck. The heart rested on her chest just above the space between her breasts. "Now, whenever you wear this, you will have my love with you. No matter where you are."

She covered the heart with her right hand. "Thank you," she said and then her tears poured out. He held her while she cried. "I don't deserve you, Vincent." She laid her head on his shoulder and he stroked her hair.

"Okay, now," he said. "Stop saying that nonsense. You're exhausted and need to sleep." He felt her nodding hear head, her hair brushing his chest as she did so. "Come on then."

He walked her to bed. She lay down and he pulled the blankets up to her chin, the heart necklace disappearing beneath them. She grabbed his hand and refused to let go.

"What?"

"Stay with me until I fall asleep."

"Okay." He sat down beside her on the bed.

Still holding his hand, she closed her eyes. Before long, she was asleep, her chest rising and falling with gentle breathing. He had a ton of things to do—bills to pay, more work awaiting him in the kitchen, leaves to rake, and the gardens to ready for winter. But he did none of those things. He stayed with Kate. He lay down beside her and listened to each breath she took. She slept peacefully until he woke her at eleven.

They gathered in Emma's parlor, dinner concluded and the dishes done. Emma sat in the beige, blue and white-striped wingback chair. Katherine sat between Norman and Kate on the couch. Vincent, poker in hand, rearranged the logs in the fireplace.

"Your husband has wonderful taste, Kate," Katherine said.

Vincent felt Kate watching him and he turned to meet her eyes, seeing happiness within them. She wore the orchid hat on her head and she looked beautiful in it.

"I can't take all the credit, Katherine," Vincent said. "I must admit that Norman helped me pick it out."

Katherine looked at her fiancé. "I already know that you have wonderful taste, darling." She touched the lacy bodice of her new maroon dress, yet another gift from Norman. "Because you spoil me."

"And I love to do so."

Vincent's eyes traveled from Kate's face to the heart necklace resting on the bodice of her own dress. "Don't you ladies know it's a man's right to spoil the woman he loves?"

Emma grunted. "You are both a couple of romantic fools, if you ask me."

"Oh, now, Emma," Norman protested. "Surely you mustn't mean that."

"But I do, Norman," Emma answered, chuckling.

Orange flames sprang up in the fireplace. Stepping back, Vincent put the poker in its holder and went to sit on the arm of the couch, his hand on Kate's shoulder. He listened, amused, while Emma and Norman exchanged their different theories of romance. As always, Emma was practical, talking of the economics of marriage and how life takes a toll. Norman, even more the incurable romantic than Vincent, proclaimed that nothing could damage the marriage of two people who were truly in love with one another.

Kate laughed at them both and Katherine, grinning, kept shaking her head. Leaning closer to Kate, she softly said, "Didn't I tell you the two of them couldn't agree on anything? If he says it's raining, she says it isn't."

"I think they enjoy their little battles," Kate confided.

"I think you're right. And I love them both."

Clearing his throat, Vincent said, "Norman, how are things coming along down at The Rivera?"

Norman shot him a glance. "Very well. We are on schedule. However, there is still the matter of a manager. We haven't chosen one yet."

"Applicants?" Katherine asked. "Why, Norman, you should do it."

He held up his hand. "No, no, Katherine. I have too much on my plate already."

"How many people have applied?" Emma asked.

"Several. Of them all, I'm leaning towards James Kelly."

"Doesn't he manage the Avondale over on Oliver Street?"

"He does, Emma. But I think the potential of The Rivera could lure him away."

"Do your partners like him as well?"

"I think so. But we will interview everyone before making the final decision."

"Well, if you plan to open the place by the end of December, you better hurry up. It's late October already."

"Emma, Emma," Norman said. "Do have faith in me."

"I do, Norman. But the clock is ticking."

And Norman and Emma were at each other again, this time debating whether or not the new theatre would open on time.

"They are impossible," Katherine said.

Vincent leaned back, rested his arm on the back of the couch, and listened to them argue, thoroughly enjoying the show.

* * *

Vincent had gone to the foyer to retrieve he and Kate's coats from the stairway closet when Norman came up behind him. "Want to have some fun tomorrow night?" he asked, mischief in his eyes.

Vincent laid the coats over his left arm and closed the closet door. "Doing what?"

"Malloy has a shipment of booze coming in from Canada. I've arranged a surprise for him."

"What kind of surprise?"

Norman grinned. "Come and see for yourself."

"You better not be putting yourself in danger, Norman. Katherine needs you."

"Don't worry, we'll be watching from a safe distance. Now, will you come?"

Vincent scratched his chin. He gazed at Norman, considering.

"Well?"

Grinning, Vincent said, "I wouldn't miss it for the world."

CHAPTER 26

The smell of fish was strong in Vincent's nose and water lapped steadily on the rocks below his hiding place. He sat beside Norman, engulfed by darkness on an outcropping behind a massive boulder, their position affording them a view of both the Niagara River and the Malloy Lumber Yard. The yard, filled with piles of lumber that looked like black hulks in the dark, sat kitty-corner from their position, and beyond the lumber sat the small office. The future marina was, in 1926, a furniture shop, painted white like the office. In the fog seeping in off the river, the building was a colossus, its windows accusing eyes, its body threatening.

Vincent shook himself, wrapped his arms around his shivering body, and turned his eyes back to the river. Norman chuckled beside him and whispered, "What's the matter, spying got you all worked up?"

"It's damn cold out here," Vincent said, eyeing his friend. Although Norman was nothing more than a vague blob beside him, Vincent knew that like himself, Norman was dressed completely in black, his newsboy cap down low on his forehead. "We've been sitting here freezing for three hours and so far, nothing."

"Be patient, my friend."

"But it's 2:30 a.m."

"It's early yet. Trust me."

Vincent hunkered down against the boulder, closed his eyes and listened to the water below them. It hit the rocks in a gentle, rhythmic pattern. In spite of the cold and dampness, he could easily fall asleep to this rhythm, thoughts of Kate in his head.

Norman slapped his arm. "Vincent," he whispered, urgently. "Wake up."

"I am awake."

"You've been sleeping for an hour. Look, by the furniture shop. And listen."

Vincent turned and peered back at the colossus. A light above the back door now burned bright in the darkness. In the distance he heard the unmistakable sputter of a motorboat.

"It's coming up from Buffalo," Norman said, peering down the river.

As the engine drew closer, Vincent could discern a pale light in the fog. He heard the shop door open. Malloy stepped out, followed by two men.

He tapped Norman's arm. "Recognize them?"

"No. Hard to see their faces in the light."

"Well, whether you can see his face or not, that's definitely Malloy. You can tell just by the way he carries himself."

Norman didn't reply, but turned his attention back to the approaching motorboat.

A lone man sat in the boat just in front of the engine, crates piled in front of him. It was a wonder he could see where he was going. He killed the boat's engine, letting the vessel drift up to the massive dock behind the furniture shop. Malloy and his men met him there, Malloy himself tying up the boat. Vincent couldn't hear what was said but he had no doubt Malloy had given instructions. The boatman began unloading the crates. Malloy's boys carried them down to the dock, across the lumberyard and into the furniture shop. Vincent watched fascinated by the swiftness with which the men performed the task.

The boatman had just heaved up the last crate when North Tonawanda's finest accompanied by federal agents showed up. Or a better description would be, popped out from numerous hiding places behind piles of lumber. Beside him, Norman chuckled with glee.

Malloy whirled around and shouted, "What the hell!"

A tall, trench-coated man standing on the dock and holding a machine gun, said, "I wouldn't move a muscle if I were you, Mr. Malloy. A signal from me and all these boys start shooting."

The man who had taken the last crate of liquor from the boatmen dropped it, shooting his hands in the air. The crate hit the dock hard, the sound of breaking glass echoing down the river.

"Idiot!" Malloy barked. He kept his eyes on the man with the machine gun.

"Game is over for tonight," the agent said. "Get to it, boys."

Four uniformed policemen, service revolvers ready, walked down the dock to Jethro and his rumrunners. The taller policeman cuffed Jethro's hands behind his back. Vincent watched in wonder, feeling like an extra in an episode of *The Untouchables*. "Now this is fine entertainment," Norman whispered in his ear. "Better than theatre."

The boatman, unlike the others, had no intentions of submitting to arrest. He dove from the boat, hitting the water with a loud splash.

"Shit," the agent closest to Norman and Vincent's hiding place said then took off running. He dove in off the shore, just clearing the rocks below, his dive a graceful arc. He cut the water neatly, emerging from beneath the dark surface right behind the unfortunate boatman. He grabbed the man's collar, turned him around and promptly punched him in the face. The boatman went limp in his arms. As the agent dragged his victim back to the dock, one of the policemen standing beside Jethro said, "It would seem, Mr. Malloy, that all you hire are idiots."

"Just shut up and get on with the damned arrest already," Jethro hissed back.

Forty-five minutes later, the lumberyard was once again dark and quiet. Jethro, his rumrunners, and the liquor had been hauled away. "Show's over," Norman said, whacking Vincent on the back. "Now you can go home and climb into bed beside your wife."

"And you?"

"I will go home and dream of climbing into bed beside Katherine." Norman jumped down from his perch. "Thus, I envy you, my friend."

Vincent jumped down as well, his shoes landing in dirt that was on the verge of becoming mud. Brushing wrinkles from his slacks, he said, "Dreams do a man good, Norman. Didn't your mother tell you that?"

"I believe she did. Come on."

Hunching his shoulders against the cold, Vincent walked beside Norman down River Road to Goundry. He could feel Norman's joy at what they had just witnessed. "How did you know about tonight's drop off, Norman?"

Norman grinned. "I have friends. They have eyes and ears."

"And who might those friends be?"

Norman shook his head. "No, Vincent. It's better you don't know."

They crossed railroad tracks and Vincent felt the cold steel through the soles of his shoes. He shivered involuntarily. "Do you suppose he'll figure out it was you?"

"I doubt it."

"How can you be sure?"

Norman stopped. "Did you know, Vincent, that sometimes, you are worse than a woman? All you do is worry."

"Is that so?"

Norman slung an arm around Vincent's shoulders. "Yes, it is. Now, come on, lighten up, stop worrying and do what I'm going to do."

They started walking again. "And what is that?"

Grinning once more, Norman said, "Enjoy reading the front page of *The Evening News* tomorrow."

Kate slapped the copy of *The Evening News* down on Vincent's bare stomach and said, "You're lucky I don't knock you over the head with this. I can't believe you didn't take me with you."

Vincent picked up the paper he'd brought back from 1926 and read the headline: **JETHRO MALLOY ARRESTED IN RAID.** Laughing, he said, "And how would I have explained dragging my wife along to Norman Lassiter."

Kate lay back on her pillow, folded her arms across her chest, stared at the ceiling, and said, "Shit."

"You know I'm right. I couldn't take you. It was just us men."

"Us men," she snarled.

"Hey, at least I was thoughtful enough to bring *The Evening News* back for you."

She rolled onto her side and rested her head on her hand. "Aren't you just the sweetest guy, Vincent Vermay?"

"I believe I am, my love." He shook the paper in her face. "I believe I am."

She grinned. "So tell me about this little adventure you went on while I was sleeping the night away."

He did and she listened intently, eyes wide with wonder. She teased him when he mentioned how cold it had been. "Honestly, Vincent, stop whining." She laughed when he told her the federal agent's comment about Jethro hiring idiots. "Damn," she said when he ended the tale. "I wish I could have been there."

"I wish you could have been too, babe. It was a gas."

She tapped the newspaper. "So, does he go to prison for this little indiscretion?"

"How should I know?"

"Oh, come on, Vincent. I know you. Surely while I was writing this afternoon, you hightailed it down to the Historical Society?"

Vincent grinned. "Yep."

"So, does he?"

He rolled onto his side and faced her. "Funny you should ask. No, he doesn't."

Her eyebrows shot up. "Really?"

He nodded. "There were some articles about a possible trial and then, nothing. Apparently, Jethro Malloy had friends in higher places than we first thought."

"That figures." Kate sighed. "That had to be a thorn in Norman's side."

"I'm sure it was."

Kate picked up the newspaper and scanned the article again. "You know, even if he'd gone to prison, he could still order Norman's kidnapping."

"True."

Her eyes sad, Kate said, "Katherine."

Vincent touched his wife's cheek. He needed to feel her soft skin against his own, to know that for the moment, she was still with him. "Shh," he said. "Not now. Let's not talk about it now."

She smiled but the sadness didn't leave her eyes.

He tossed the paper to the floor and drew her closer, her warm cheek resting on his bare chest. For the moment, she was safe in his arms. He kissed her hair, closed his eyes and wished that they could remain here in their bed, just as they were, forever, and that he would never have to leave her.

Two weeks later, Kate emerged from her office shortly before dinner. She walked into the kitchen, held up a CD case and said, "Finished." She looked triumphant and disheveled. Her tangled hair revealed that she'd been playing with it while she wrote. Her glasses sat on the end of her nose. The collar of her blue button down was unbuttoned, one side up, the other down. The blouse itself was open to her breasts, her cleavage shining in the incandescent kitchen light. Her belt was not buckled, probably forgotten after her last trip to the bathroom. She wore a fuzzy slipper on one foot and just an argyle sock on the other. Her eyes shone with accomplishment and joy, and she was totally and completely beautiful as she stood there smiling at him.

"It's ready to send to Regina?" he asked, wiping sauce from his hands on a paper towel.

She nodded, still grinning.

He tossed the used towel on the counter next to the pan of lasagna he was making and went to her. He took the CD case from her hand and looked at the silver disc inside the plastic. "You better label it before you send it, dear," he said, teasingly.

She snatched it back. "Can you believe it?" she asked, shaking it at him. "I really did it. I really finished the damn book."

"I always knew you could."

"So did Liz." Her grin faded. "God, I wish she was here."

Vincent ran his hands through her tangled hair. "I know, babe."

She batted his hands away. "Don't do that. You know where it always leads."

"And what's wrong with that?"

He reached for her but she dodged him, going to see what he was making. "Yummy," she said. "My favorite."

"I know." He came up behind her, resting his hands on her slender shoulders.

She looked up at him, tugged on his apron strap, and said, "You look good in kitchen finery."

"Thank you. Now move aside so I can finish dinner."

"I'll make the salad," she said. She set the CD on the table and opened the refrigerator. She rummaged around inside of it, filling her arms with lettuce, tomato, celery, mushrooms, pepper, carrots, and hardboiled eggs. She kicked the door closed with her leg and dumped everything on the counter next to the cutting board. Perusing the bottom cupboards, she asked, "The salad set? Did you bring that up here with you?"

"Nope." He gestured at the cupboard to her immediate left. "Use the big glass bowl in there."

She retrieved the bowl then went to work. She remained quiet, concentrating on cutting the vegetables.

Vincent finished the lasagna and put it in the oven. He washed his hands, took another paring knife from the drawer, grabbed a tomato and began cutting.

"You don't have to, Vincent," she said. "You made the lasagna."

"I want to," he said, smiling at her. *Damn, she was beautiful.*

She smiled back. They worked in silence and were comfortable with that silence, Vincent realizing that they were more in tune and more together than ever before.

She must have read his thoughts, because she said, "Kind of neat, isn't it, Vincent?"

"What?"

"Us. Now. This moment."

He nodded.

She dumped a bunch of chopped carrots into the bowl. "For the first time in my life, Vincent, it's all coming together. I'm happy. You and I are back on track. I finished the book. And yet…" She sighed, heavily. "Come December 30th, I could be giving it all up."

"You could if you decide to." Vincent swallowed over the lump in his throat.

She shook her head. "God, what the hell should I do?"

"Have you thought what Katherine would want for you?"

She began cutting an onion. "I have. And, Vincent, I think she would change my childhood if she could."

"But would she want you to give up your life for her? Do you honestly think for one minute that she would risk your very existence?"

"You mean if she knew that by preventing Jethro's men from kidnapping Norman, I could very well prevent my own birth, would she allow me to do it?"

"Yes, even if she knew your childhood would be awful, do you still think she'd want you to never exist?"

Kate grew pensive, her knife falling idle. Vincent kept working, giving her the time to think. At last, she reluctantly said, "No. She would want me to live."

"Then you better consider that, Kate."

She stared at him, her eyes filled with the realization that up until this moment, she hadn't considered Katherine's wants for her granddaughter. And that's who she was, Katherine's granddaughter. The only one of her grandchildren to give her comfort and joy in her old age. Kate set her knife to the onion again and said, "There's a lot to think about regarding this decision, Vincent. And every time I think I've made it for sure, another twist comes along and puts doubt in my mind."

He bent and kissed her cheek. "Nobody said it would be easy, babe." She nodded, discouraged. "May I offer a suggestion?"

"Which is?"

"Live your life. Enjoy your now."

She touched his chin, the smell of onion strong on her fingers. "I think that's just what I'll do. Because I have to say, Vincent, that my 'now' is far superior at this moment than any other 'now' I've ever had." That said she kissed him full on the lips.

He dropped his knife and took her in his arms, returning her kiss. He took her knife from her hand, threw it on the cutting board, and lifted her in his arms. He carried her up to their bedroom, laid her on the bed, and straddled her. Tearing at his shirt, she asked, "What about the lasagna?"

"The oven will take care of it," he assured her, unbuttoning her blouse.

She giggled and said, "I hope the timer is loud enough for us to hear it up here."

He didn't care about the timer. He didn't care about the lasagna. All he cared about was Kate.

They were still making love when the timer went off down in the kitchen.

❀   ❀   ❀

Kate sat across from him at the kitchen table, her plate piled high with burnt lasagna. She wore his bathrobe, her hair tied back with a red ribbon. She squinted at him, having left her glasses upstairs on the nightstand.

"What?" he asked around his mouthful of rubbery noodles.

"Are you really going to eat it?"

"I suppose so. Unless you want to order a p—" He broke off, listening. "Kate, do you hear it?"

She smiled. "Katherine." She cocked her head."

"Want to?"

She glanced down at her lasagna and playfully asked, "What about dinner?"

"I'm sure we can sacrifice," he assured her.

She laughed as she rose to her feet. "And here I was thinking I actually had to eat the horrid stuff."

"Oh, you're going to pay for that."

He chased her up the stairs, down the hall, and into their bedroom. Lunging, he knocked her down on the bed. Still laughing, she rolled from beneath him. "Not now, Vincent. We have to change."

He grinned up at her. "Wear the slacks again. I love the way she gets in a tizzy over you wearing slacks."

She slapped his knee and went to the armoire. Opening it, she tossed him his black suit and said, "Now, get dressed. It's evening so you must look your best."

He caught the suit, but he didn't start dressing. Instead, he sat watching her. She pulled out a white dinner dress with spaghetti straps. Arching his eyebrows, he said, "Now that, my love, is a fine choice." She pulled out a green silk shawl. He let out a long whistle.

She turned to him, glared, and said, "Get dressed, Vincent."

Chuckling, he said, "Yes, dear."

❦   ❦   ❦

Emma greeted them at the door. She wore a black gown and had her hair piled up on top of her head, diamond studded hairpins holding it in place. She looked lovely and more feminine than Vincent had ever seen her look. When she smiled, her face shone with beauty he had missed before, and he found himself wondering how the men of Emma's era could have been so stupid as to let this dynamic woman remain single.

"You're here!" she exclaimed, taking Kate's hand and pulling her inside. "I didn't know how to get in touch with you to invite you. Do you two realize that you've never even told us where you live here in town?"

Vincent entered and closed the door behind him. He shot Kate a guarded glance. Her eyes shooting him understanding, she kissed Emma's cheek and said, "Invite us to what?"

"Listen." Emma gestured at the stairs.

"Katherine is playing," Kate said.

"Yes," Emma said, excitedly. She turned to Vincent. "But not just for herself. Nor just for me. Come, let me show you."

They followed her up the stairs and down the hall to the sunroom. Emma stopped just outside the door, leaned close to Vincent, and whispered. "See?"

Katherine, in the white, lacy dress she loved so much, stood before the window, playing her violin. Norman sat to her right. Three other people sat next to him. Vincent recognized Mayor Mackenzie and his wife. He'd never seen the other gentleman before. He was younger than Mackenzie, most likely pushing 40, his hair fair, carrying a hint of red.

Emma took Kate's arm and moved further down the hall, where their talking wouldn't disturb the concert. "I still can't believe that Katherine agreed to play for them. But she did. I wanted to invite you, but you hadn't been by the last several days and as I pointed out, I don't know where you live." She stepped back from Kate and looked her up and down. "But it seems that you dressed for the occasion even though you didn't know about it."

"Oh, actually, we were just out for dinner and thought we'd stop by," Kate said, thinking quickly.

Vincent quietly moved back to the sunroom doorway. Katherine was playing the climax of a piece he could not identify. She was playing magnificently, but Vincent could see she was not comfortable. Her body was tense, her jaw clenched, and she avoided looking towards her audience. Instead, her eyes were focused on the wall and they held fear of nearly an insurmountable proportion. Vincent did not know how many songs she had already played, but he could tell that she would not make it through another.

She brought the piece to a resounding end, her audience jumping to their feet, applauding. "Bravo!" the Mayor exclaimed.

The younger gentleman agreed, "Magnificent, Mrs. Malloy."

Katherine lowered her violin. Her head bowed, eyes averted, she said, "Thank you." Her voice wavered.

Vincent stepped into the room, clapping, echoing the Mayor's "Bravo." They all turned to look at him, but he ignored them and went straight to Katherine. "Katherine," he said, smiling encouragingly. "You were wonderful." He took her elbow and felt the panic within her. He pushed her with his hip, getting her moving, taking her to Norman.

Norman slipped his arm around her shoulders. "Lovely, darling," he said. He turned her towards the guests and Vincent wanted to slug him. How could he, this man who loved her with all his heart, not see the state she was in? Somehow, she withstood their compliments and handshakes, but she was not enjoying herself.

Kate appeared at Vincent's side. She hugged Katherine, whispered something in her ear that Vincent could not hear, then turned to Norman. "Introduce us to this fine gentleman, Norman," she said, gesturing at the stranger. She kept her arm around Katherine.

"This is James Kelly, manager of the Avondale Theatre over on Oliver Street. I'm seriously trying to entice him to come manage The Rivera."

Vincent shook the man's hand. His grip was firm, his face handsome and his eyes friendly. Releasing Vincent's hand, James said, "Surely, the concert isn't over. Please, Mrs. Malloy, play another piece."

Vincent saw the shudder go through Katherine and he opened his mouth to protest, but Norman spoke first. "I'm afraid that's it." He raised his hand against their protests. "No, Katherine mustn't overdo it. Her hand is still tender." He bent and kissed Katherine's cheek. "We'll see you downstairs." He ushered the North Tonawanda dignitaries from the room, Emma following the group out, but only after a knowing glance at Vincent. Once they were gone, Katherine fell back against Kate, her body shaking uncontrollably. Vincent took the violin from her and Kate helped her to the wicker loveseat. Sitting down beside Katherine, she held her grandmother while she shed tears of frustration. Kate spoke words of congratulations and encouragement. "You did it, Katherine," she said. "You made it through and you played beautifully."

The violin case sat on a small stand beneath the window. Vincent laid the violin on the soft velvet then closed the case. He pulled a wicker stand over in front of Katherine and sat down. Elbows on his knees, he rested his chin on his folded hands and waited for her to cry it out.

Eventually, sniffing, she looked at him and said, "I can't believe I just did that."

"Well, you did. And you made it through." Kate squeezed her. "I'm so proud of you."

"I could never play an entire concert," Katherine said.

"Sure you could," Kate said.

She leaned her head on Kate's shoulder. "I'm so glad you are here," she said. "I...I need you both."

Kate kept her arm around her. "I'm glad we decided to stop."

A tear slipped down Katherine's cheek.

Kate wiped it away with gentle fingers. "Don't cry, Katherine. It's okay. You did it."

"The entire time I was playing, I thought...it was just like before. It was like the concerts I played after Daddy died. I felt like I was going to breakdown." She trembled and Kate pulled her closer. "It doesn't matter if there are thousands of people or three. It feels just as awful."

"No doubt it does," Vincent said.

Kate kissed Katherine's forehead.

"Will it ever go away, Vincent? Norman thinks it will. He says that each time I play for people, it will get easier. But I don't know. I just don't know."

Kate kissed Katherine's temple.

"I don't want to disappoint him," Katherine continued. "I don't want him to think I am a failure."

"He would never think that," Kate assured her. "He loves you and just wants to help you get over this. And I think that he may be right. The only way to beat a fear is to face it down."

"But what if it beats me, Kate? What then?"

Kate shot Vincent a questioning look. *What do I tell her? What do I say to make her believe in herself?*

"Katherine," Vincent said in a firm voice.

She looked at him.

"What do you want?"

She blinked back tears and said, "To be Norman's wife. To make him proud."

"Beyond being Norman's wife. What do you want?"

She gazed down at her hands. "I don't want a concert career. Not like I had. It doesn't mean anything to me now. Not without my father at my side."

"But?"

"I want to be able to…I…" She sighed. "I hate being afraid, Vincent. I want to be able to pick up my violin and play for whomever I choose without panicking. Whether that person is Mayor Mackenzie, or an audience in the park, or my neighbors. I don't need to pack concert halls with thousands of people. But I do need…" She hit her thigh with her fist. "I need to be free of this fear. I hate what it does to me. What it turns me into."

"What does it turn you into, Katherine?"

She met his eyes as she answered, "It turns me into a blubbering fool. I wish you could have known me before…before my father died." Saying the word "died" nearly choked her. Tears filled her eyes and a small sob escaped her.

"It's all right, Katherine," Kate said. She smoothed Katherine's hair with a loving hand. "It's all right to miss him." Katherine's lower lip trembled. "It's all right to mourn. Oh, my dear gr—friend, let yourself mourn."

Kate's words pulled the plug and for the first time since her father's sudden death, Katherine expressed her grief. Words spilled out. Words mixed with sobs that made most of what she said incomprehensible. But what Vincent did comprehend was just how much she had loved her father. He could only imagine how tortured she'd been inside—desperately missing her father, married to a man who had held her captive, too afraid to face the world and ask for help, wanting only peace. It was a miracle she had survived with her sanity.

"Katherine," Norman said behind Vincent. He sat down beside her on the loveseat's arm and tenderly touched her face. "My love. Why are you crying?"

She lunged for him and he took her in his arms. "I want him back, Norman," she cried, her words still tangled up in her sobs. "I want my father back."

Kate slipped from beside her, allowing Norman to take her seat.

He rocked her, stroking her hair, telling her he loved her and would always be with her.

Vincent stood up. Norman looked at him, anguish in his eyes. Vincent gave him a nod, hoping he understood just what his presence and love had done for Katherine since her father's death. Only Norman had kept her sane. He had been the one true friend, the one true light in her destroyed world. And now, he was her soul mate. Her life.

Norman looked from Vincent to his sobbing fiancée and back at Vincent again, realization dawning in his eyes. Assured that he understood, Vincent turned away, took Kate by the arm, and led her out into the hall.

Kate looked back in at Norman and Katherine. "She's bottled up that grief for much too long, Vincent."

He leaned back against the wall. "Yes, she has."

Kate shook her head, a trace of a smile crossing her face.

"What?"

"It's amazing. I'm so like her." She put her arms around his neck and kissed him.

"What was that for?"

"For being my Norman."

❧   ❧   ❧

Emma closed the door behind her departing guests then leaned back against the door and said, "Thank you."

"For what?" Kate asked.

"Rescuing me. I'm not much at entertaining and once Norman disappeared, I was pretty much floundering."

"Oh, I doubt that," Vincent said, loosening his tie. "You are quite the charming lady."

Emma laughed. "Sure. Just give me my patients and medical records, and I'm just fine, thank you." She pulled the hairpins from her hair, letting it fall down around her shoulders, looking suddenly very young and very beautiful. Once again, Vincent found himself thinking that Dr. Emma Reilly would have made someone a challenging but wonderful wife. His thoughts traveled to Liz and how she too had lived her life without a husband. He wondered how dif-

ferent things would have been for her if Alan hadn't died in a motorcycle accident. He also wondered what Emma would have thought of her great-niece.

"Vincent is right," Kate said. "You are charming."

"And you both are blind," Emma said. She looked up the stairs. "How was
she when you came down?"

"Upset," Vincent said. "But with Norman."

"Norman is who she needs." She headed for the kitchen. "If you want to talk
more, I'm afraid you'll have to follow me. I've got some dishes to wash."

"I'll help you," Kate said.

"Don't be silly. You didn't even eat with us."

"That doesn't mean I can't help you."

She started after Emma. Vincent let her go and went into the dining room.
He collected up dessert dishes, piled them on the wooden serving tray resting
on the sideboard, and carried them out to the kitchen. It took him four trips to
get all the dirty dishes and glasses. When he set the last tray full of dishes down
on the counter, Emma said, "Kate, do you know how lucky you are? Good
Lord, any man I've ever known wouldn't help clear dishes."

Hands in the soapy dishwater, Kate glanced back at Vincent and winked. "I
have him well trained, don't I, Emma?"

Vincent winked back and leaned against the counter, arms crossed over his
chest. "What else do you need me to do, Emma?"

Plate in one hand, dishtowel in the other, Emma shook her head. "Like I
keep saying. You are a man out of time."

The glass Kate was washing fell from her wet hands, splashing soap up onto
the cupboard. Vincent saw her shoulders go rigid. Fortunately, Emma didn't
notice.

"I must say," Emma continued, "Katherine did rather well this evening.
She's been worried about this dinner for days. But, she did just fine." Emma
smiled. "I'm so glad for her. I could tell she was scared, but still, she did it."

"Did Norman tell you he wants her to play at the opening of The Rivera?"
Kate asked.

"He did."

"What do you think?"

"I believe she can do it. She's been restless lately, like she's growing bored
with spending her days here in this house. Norman takes her out when he's not
working, but, well, she seems to be a bundle of energy wanting to get out."

"And to grieve," Vincent said. "That's what she was upset about upstairs.
Her father's death."

Emma nodded. "It doesn't surprise me, Vincent. It is hard for her to talk about him or her life prior to his death. It was obvious that she hadn't allowed herself to fully grieve. I'm not a psychiatrist, but...well, I did study a little bit. She's been simmering for quite a number of days now. Which reminds me, where have you two been? It's been two weeks since you last visited."

"I know," Kate said. "But I've been working on a project. It absorbed me."

"That writing of yours?"

"Yes, that was it."

Vincent heard Norman's voice in the hall. A moment later he and Katherine entered the kitchen. Katherine had washed her face and pulled back her hair, but her eyes were puffy, her nose red from blowing it. She went directly to Emma and said, "I will be leaving for a few days, Emma. I'll be going to New York with Norman." Her voice was hoarse, revealing the large amount of crying she had just done.

Emma glanced at Norman then back at Katherine. "Whatever for?"

Her voice raw with pain, she said, "To visit my father's grave."

CHAPTER 27

It was strange being back in Georgetown. Vincent stood beside the Rodeo and stared down at the bricks beneath his shoes. Slowly, his gaze traveled from the familiar bricks of the street to the familiar brick façade of the townhouse he and Kate had shared for fifteen years. So familiar, and yet, no longer home. He thought it odd how quickly the thought came to his mind. *No longer home.* Shaking his head, he went up the townhouse steps and unlocked the front door. He stepped into the foyer he'd stepped into so many times before and thought how strange it felt and how stale it smelled, dust seeming to fill every crevice. He shuddered off the strangeness and went into the living room. As he'd hoped, the message light flashed on the answering machine. He hit play. "I miss you, Vincent," Kate said. "I got to New York without a hitch. Settled into the Waldorf just fine. I'm having dinner with Regina tonight. I'll call you when I get back to the hotel. I love you." He smiled. Her voice was music in his ears. He hit the repeat button and listened again, smile widening.

He had to force himself not to listen a third time. Instead, he returned to the Rodeo and unloaded his paintings. He carried them up to his old third floor studio and arranged them in the order he'd painted them. He'd brought them all except for the one he'd given to Jill and the one he'd sold to Norman. As he studied them, arms folded across his chest, he wondered if David would think him nuts or obsessed for having spent so much time painting one woman and her violin. In fact, he might laugh in Vincent's face. And yet, while Vincent knew this was a possibility, he didn't really believe it would happen. The paintings were brilliant. They were, in fact, his best work to date. Surely, David would see that too.

Vincent glanced at his watch. It was 4 p.m., and David wasn't due for another three hours. To occupy himself while he waited Vincent grabbed a quick shower, changed into a pair of black Dockers, a white shirt and a solid black tie, and then ran out to the grocery store to stock his fridge with a few essentials to get him through the next couple of days. He finished putting the food away at 6:45 and found himself so anxious about what David would think of his paintings that he could do nothing but pace around the living room.

The doorbell rang promptly at seven and, his heart pounding in his chest, Vincent opened the door. David stood on the front porch, wearing his usual red beret, tweed jacket, and turtleneck sweater. He grinned at Vincent, genuine pleasure in his green eyes.

"David," Vincent said, motioning him inside.

David held out his hand. "Long time, my friend."

"Months," Vincent agreed as they shook hands.

David looked older. Gray hair tinged his temples, a stark contrast to his usual dark black mane. His mustache, once a thick black, looked thinner and splattered with gray. Crows feet spread out from the corners of his eyes.

"Nearly two years, Vincent."

Vincent closed the front door. "How are things at the gallery?"

"They could be better. Especially since my best selling painter…"

He didn't need to finish the statement. Vincent hung his head. "I'm sorry, David."

"I know." He smoothed his mustache with his thumb and forefinger. "With Carol on the team, we've stayed afloat."

"Your wife is a genius at marketing, David."

He nodded. "Oh, she can get the people in the door, that's for sure. But what they buy just doesn't fetch as much as your work, Vincent."

Fetch. Even after all his years in Washington, D.C., David's rural roots popped out every now and then. "Well, I hope what I'm about to show you will benefit us both."

"I trust it will."

His heart still pounding in his chest, Vincent led David up to his studio. "Here they are," he said, his voice squeaking. His hand went to his throat. His Adam's apple felt as big as a grapefruit. He hung back, letting David view the paintings in silence. He watched with trepidation as David viewed each painting for what seemed like hours.

Finally, when Vincent was close to screaming, David turned to him with a huge grin. "What?" Vincent barked, standing on tiptoe.

David rubbed his hands together as if preparing to pick up a knife and fork and devour a filet mignon. "They're magnificent. The ones of the violin are inspiring. And the woman, oh, Vincent, she's beyond beautiful. Who is she? Where did you meet her?"

"You really like them?"

"Oh, yes, my friend." He turned back to the paintings. "You are going to be an even bigger star in the art world, Vincent. Now, who is this lovely woman?"

Vincent came up beside David. He had to tread lightly here. Only so much truth could be told. "She is Kate's grandmother. Her name was Katherine Mann Malloy."

"The woman who died last spring and left you guys all her money?"

"She didn't leave us all of it, David."

"Damn near." He bent close to one of the portraits. "She's so alive in these paintings, Vincent. So young. How did you capture this from a ninety-four-year-old woman?"

Vincent ran a hand through his hair. He wanted to tell David the truth. He wanted him to know how beautiful Katherine really was. Instead, he said, "From photos at the North Tonawanda house. And from stories heard from people who knew her."

David drew a long breath. "Marvelous." He turned to Vincent. "That speaks volumes for your talent, Vincent. That you could bring this woman to life from just that."

Vincent avoided David's eyes and shrugged.

David slapped him on the back. "Don't deny your talent, Vincent. Revel in it. I'll have the contracts drawn up Monday. Why don't you stop round the gallery on Tuesday at 2 p.m. to sign them?"

"Our usual terms?"

"Sure."

Vincent shook David's hand. "Then I guess I'll see you Tuesday."

"We'll open the exhibit up with a grand party, my friend. Kate must come. We are on our way. Yes, indeed." David turned back to the paintings. "We are about to turn the art world on fire. And at long last, Vincent, Faragomi's Gallery of Art is going to be a gallery to be reckoned with. And Vincent Vermay will be the undisputed king of the art world."

🍁   🍁   🍁

"Did I wake you?" Kate asked in Vincent's ear.

He glanced at the bedside clock. It was midnight. "No, I'm lying in bed, but I'm awake. How did it go with Regina?"

"Great."

"What did she say about the book?"

"She gave me back a paper copy of the manuscript with some suggestions. I scanned them. They seem quite elementary, really. In fact, she said I don't need much editing."

Vincent heard joy in Kate's voice. "That doesn't surprise me, Kate."

"How'd it go with David?"

"I'll be signing the contract Tuesday."

"Damn!" Kate said.

He could imagine the look on her face. He could see the twinkle in her eyes and her wide, warm smile. He wished she were in bed with him and not in New York City at the Waldorf Astoria.

"He's going to arrange an opening party. I'm not sure when, but he wants you to come."

"I wouldn't miss it." He heard the creaking of bedsprings on the other end of the phone and then she said, "I went to her father's grave this afternoon."

"And?"

"I felt her there, Vincent. Or maybe it was my imagination. But as I knelt there in front of his stone, I swear she was there too, at that exact moment, only in 1926."

"Maybe she was."

"I hope so. I hope she was there and could somehow feel me, her friend Kate Vermay."

"Norman is with her, Kate. Remember that."

"I know. Her mother is buried there as well."

"Beside her father?"

"Side-by-side. Their stones are works of art. Katherine spared no expense on them."

Vincent remained quiet. He could tell there was something more she wanted to say. The silence hung there, but it was not an uncomfortable silence. She needed to collect her thoughts. He listened to her breathe, again wishing she weren't so far away from him.

At last, she said, "I want to be buried at your side, Vincent."

He closed his eyes. "You will be."

"Not if we decide to save Norman and I end up never existing."

"Kate. Don't think about that now."

The bedsprings creaked again. She sighed.

"Kate?"

"You know what bothers me more than the fact that I may not exist?"

"What?" He could hear the strain in his voice.

"The fact that you may have no memories of me."

Vincent swallowed hard. He could not say what he thought. That he hoped he would not suffer her loss. That he would step back into his present and if there had never been a Kate, he would never feel any pain. She would be gone from his soul and his brain. He would just be Vincent Vermay living his life. No, he could not tell her this for it would cut her too deeply. "I will never forget you, Kate," he said. "You will always be in my heart. Always. No matter what happens."

Tears in her voice, she said, "I love you, Vincent."

"I love you, Kate."

❦　　　❦　　　❦

He pulled into the Victorian's driveway and shut off the Rodeo's engine. He was tired, the drive up from Maryland interminable, but he was happy. At last he was home and he knew Kate was waiting for him. He expected her to be sound asleep since it was nearing 2 a.m., but she wasn't. She was in her office, scrapbooks and photo albums scattered over the desktop. The lamp on the corner of her desk cast a yellow, circular light over the pages. She didn't hear him come up the stairs. He stood in the doorway, watching her, smiling to himself, thinking how beautiful she looked. She wore no makeup and her glasses sat on the end of her nose. Her hair hung freely about her shoulders, shining in the pale light. Her legs were bare and curled up beneath her, red wool socks covering her feet. She wore his red and green plaid, flannel shirt.

She turned a page in one of the scrapbooks and a wistful smile crossed her face. She traced something on the page with her index finger. "My great-grandfather, Vincent," she said, looking up at him. "Come see him."

"So you did hear me?"

She didn't answer but motioned him to her. He came and stood behind her, hands on her shoulders, loving how they felt beneath his palms.

"Wasn't he handsome?"

Vincent peered down at the man in the photograph. He had thick, dark hair, and a pencil thin mustache, his chin square, his face narrow, features classically chiseled and, without a doubt, handsome.

"This was taken at Katherine's sixteenth birthday party. He was only thirty-four. She was born during his eighteenth year."

Vincent kissed the top of Kate's hair. "Seems awful young to be a father."

"From what Katherine told me today, he was a damn good one."

Vincent raised his eyebrows. "You went to see her?"

She craned her neck back and looked up at him. "I did. And let me tell you, I play that confounded violin worse than you do."

Vincent laughed and slipped his hands around her neck. She laid her hands on his forearms. He kissed her forehead then said, "How was her trip to New York?"

"Hard. Norman said she collapsed at her parents' graves and cried for over an hour. He stayed nearby, but let her cry it out."

"Good."

"Yes. She needed to do that." Kate pulled another scrapbook from the pile on the desk and opened it, flipping pages until she found what she was looking for. She pointed at a photograph. "This was the last picture of Katherine and her father together. He died the next day."

Vincent studied Frederick Mann's face. While still handsome, losing his wife had taken its toll. His hair had thinned and was peppered with gray, deep lines surrounding his eyes, eyes that were weary and lonely. He stood with his arm through Katherine's, a smile on his face that belied his inner pain. "He wasn't happy anymore, Kate. Frederick missed his wife."

Kate nodded. "Yes, he did. If you ask me, Vincent, I'd say he died of a broken heart."

"Katherine and her career were not enough for him. He wanted the love of his life back."

Kate nodded. She closed the book, slipped from inside Vincent's arms and stood up. Facing him, she said, "I wish I'd known him."

"He was dead long before your father was conceived, babe."

"I know. But…" She sighed. "I would have liked him."

Vincent brushed a lock of hair off her forehead. "I imagine he would have loved you." He kissed her lips. They were sweet, tasting of chocolate. "I missed you, Kate."

She put her arms around his waist and laid her head on his chest. He stroked her hair. Outside, the wind picked up.

Several minutes passed by, Vincent not caring about them. He could stand here holding her forever. But Kate had other ideas. She lifted her head, took off her glasses, and tossed them on the desk. "Make love to me, Vincent," she said, one hand massaging his chest.

She didn't have to ask him twice.

He awoke in the morning to the smell of coffee and an empty space in the bed beside him. He sat up, finding her sitting curled up on the window seat, a huge mug in her right hand. Another one of equal size sat on the window seat beside her.

He kicked the covers aside and jumped out of the bed. She turned and watched as he slipped into his flannel pajama bottoms.

"What?" he asked, tying the waist string.

She grinned. "Come here."

He obeyed, picking up the coffee mug and joining her on the window seat. She leaned close and kissed his cheek. She smoothed his hair with her free hand. "You look like a tousled-haired, ten-year-old boy right now."

"Then I must be irresistible."

"Totally." She gestured out the window. "Check it out."

A blizzard was raging outside the window. The snow was so thick he couldn't see the yard below. "Damn, I'm glad I drove in last night."

"I'm glad you did too. I put the radio on while I was making the coffee. Schools are closed and even some businesses."

Vincent scratched his whiskered chin. "And here I was teasing Sarah about how early it snows in Silverton. It's only mid November here."

"According to the D.J, this is the earliest it's stormed here in years."

"How nice of it to do this for us then, don't you think, Kate?"

She chuckled, sipped her coffee, and said, "What do you suppose it's doing in 1926 right now?"

"Don't know. Why?" He took a large drink of his coffee. It was strong, the way she liked it, but it warmed him as it traveled down to his stomach.

Ignoring his question, Kate said, "We have to see Katherine and do what we promised Norman we would do, Vincent."

Vincent bit his lip.

"He's already broached the subject with her."

"And?"

"From what he tells me she's in conflict. A part of her wants to do it and the other part doesn't."

"Do you think going to her father's grave will help her with her fear, Kate?"

"I do. But it's not like she turned off some kind of fear switch. She still has to take the first steps. What I think going to Frederick's grave and crying did is give her more strength to face her fears."

"And you think that by knowing that we believe—"

She cut him off with a wave of her hand. "Not us, Vincent. We don't come into the equation here. We know she takes the plunge. History told us so. No, Norman and Emma are the ones who convince her."

"Then why should we go try to talk her into it?"

"Oh, Vincent," Kate said, shaking her head. "We did promise Norman we'd talk to her, didn't we?"

The wind gusted outside, snow banging against the window. Vincent felt cold air seep in through the window edges. He shivered.

Kate laid her hand on his leg. "Let's go see her today, Vincent."

"Okay."

They fell silent, each finishing their coffee. He could feel the wheels turning in his wife's mind. She grew pensive, drawing within herself. Then, without warning, she handed him her empty mug and stood up. She started for the armoire, but stopped, turning back to him. "God, Vincent, do you realize it's mid November? Time is speeding by so damn fast." Panic filled her eyes and she started trembling, her legs starting to give way beneath her. He dropped the mugs on the window seat and rushed to her, catching her in his arms. She buried her face in his chest and sobbed, "I can't do it, Vincent. I can't risk my life. I can't. I love her, but...oh, God, Vincent, I want to see my book published. I want to grow old with you. I want...I want to live, Vincent. I want to live my life."

"Then live it, Kate," he said, holding her close, his lips to her ear. "Katherine's life is over. But yours isn't. We'll go see her today, Kate. We will. We'll encourage her to play opening night at the Rivera and then we'll come back here, to our time, to our life together, and we won't go back to 1926 again." He grabbed her chin, pushed up on it, forcing her to look at him. "Agreed?" he asked.

Still sobbing, the tears spilling from her eyes, she said, "Yes."

CHAPTER 28

Vincent opened the heavy wooden door and stepped into the theatre vestibule. He stood just inside the door for a moment, eyes scanning the buzz of activity. Workmen were busy installing a ceramic tile floor, it's pattern consisting of one inch by two inch rectangular tiles set at right angles, it's colors varying from light yellow to deep purple brown, giving the effect of fallen leaves. Squatting, he touched the tile, noting that even though this same floor still held its beauty in his own time, it was magnificent in 1926—so smooth, shiny, and new.

"Can I help you, Sir?" a dust-covered workman asked, his black, curly hair sticking out from beneath a tweed cap. He was chewing tobacco.

Vincent straightened. "I'm looking for Norman Lassiter."

"Inside," the man said, gesturing with his head.

"Thank you." Vincent pointed at the floor. "It's lovely."

The man pushed his wad of tobacco from his left cheek to his right and nodded. "Yes, it is. One of the newer floor patterns, called Golden Pheasant. I'm kinda partial to it, myself."

A younger man with red hair, tiles in his hands, called from the corner where he was kneeling, "Don't you listen to him, Mister. He's partial to every pattern. Just depends on which one he's working on at the time."

The tobacco chewing workman waved off his co-worker's comment with his hand and said, "You go on in now. Mr. Lassiter should be in the auditorium."

Vincent gave the red-haired workman a wink and headed on into the theatre lobby. He stopped in the lobby's center, taking time to admire the marble staircases, their brass railings shining in the afternoon light. The unmistakable hum of voices flittered out through the auditorium doors. The smells of paint and plaster were heavy in the air.

"Vincent?"

Vincent turned to his left and found Norman coming down the staircase. He removed his derby, bowed, put the hat back on his head, and said, "Do come upstairs, my friend."

Vincent trailed Norman up to the balcony. They looked down on a beehive of activity. Artists on scaffolding, crowded practically elbow-to-elbow, were working on the heavily ornamented proscenium arch. Snatches of several different conversations reached Vincent's ears.

"He's a solid baby, that one. Ten pounds when he was born."

"Might snow tomorrow, I hear."

"The Thompson boy is trying to get into West Point. His mom ran into Evy at the Dollar Dry Cleaning yesterday."

Norman sat down on the balcony's top step. "She's almost done, Vincent," he said, pride in his voice. "The organ should be here in a week or so. Seats a week or so after that."

Vincent sat down next to Norman. "She's beautiful."

"Ahh, so she is." He grinned. "My partners, Yellen and Henschel, and myself, hell, we're all pleased." He rubbed his hands together. "Now, all that is left is convincing Katherine to play opening night."

"You have broached the subject with her?"

"I have."

"And?"

Norman's right eye twitched. "She's petrified. But that's to be expected. I believe she can do it."

Vincent flicked a piece of fuzz off his thigh. "Well, you will be happy to know that as we speak, Kate is talking to her about it."

"Excellent."

They fell silent, watching the workmen below, Vincent putting off telling Norman what he had come to tell him. Finally, no longer able to postpone the inevitable, Vincent said, "I've got some news, Norman."

Norman turned, eyebrows raised, eyes questioning.

Vincent sighed. Damn, he hated doing this. But it had to be done. He and Kate had agreed. It was time to move on with their lives. He'd accomplished what he'd set out to do by continuing to come back here. He'd jump-started his creativity. He was painting again. Ideas flowed through his mind like blood through his veins and arteries. He no longer needed to be in 1926 to paint.

Kate's life was turned around as well. She was on track, achieving her dream. As selfish as it was they would let history run it's course.

"What is it, my man?" Norman asked.

Vincent scratched his chin. Sighing again, he said, "Kate and I are leaving North Tonawanda, Norman."

Norman's eyes grew wide.

Vincent couldn't look at him. Instead, he gazed out at the workmen and said, "It's my painting. It's time to move on with it. This country is vast and there is so much subject matter. I must go paint it. I'm sure, being creative yourself, that you understand." The words came out in a rush, like words do when one is futilely trying to explain the unexplainable.

But to Vincent's surprise, Norman said, "I do, Vincent." Vincent dared glance at Norman. His friend's face held both sadness and understanding. "Kate is willing to go?"

Vincent nodded. "She can write anywhere."

"I suppose she can." He removed his derby and brushed at it with his hand. "When will you leave?"

"Tonight."

Norman whistled. "What about your house here?"

"It's all handled."

"Then you've known for a while."

Not really. Just since this morning. "We have."

Norman rolled his derby around on his index finger. "This will tear Katherine's heart out, you realize. She loves both of you very much."

"She'll have you and Emma."

"This could set her back."

Vincent shook his head. "No, it won't. Katherine is on the forward road now. With you and Emma at her side, she won't fail."

"Will you write her?"

"Of course," Vincent lied. *After all, how would they? They were going to be years and lifetimes apart.*

Norman laid his hand on Vincent's knee. "We'll both look forward to your letters."

Guilt shooting through him, Vincent said, "Then we better make them entertaining." He stared down at Norman's hand. *This man does not deserve what his future holds. He deserves a happy life with Katherine. And, by God, I love this man. This man is my friend.*

Norman lifted his hand from Vincent's knee and held it out. Clearing his throat, he said, his voice sincere, "I will miss you, Vincent Vermay."

Vincent accepted Norman's hand. He shook it, gripping it hard, and he said, "I'll miss you too."

❧   ❧   ❧

"Vermay!"

Vincent looked up from the sidewalk. Jethro Malloy stood just outside his front gate, bowler on his head, brown overcoat hanging nearly to his ankles. His arms hung at his sides, gloved hands forming fists. Vincent debated whether or not to acknowledge Malloy. He reached Emma's front walkway, stopped, glanced from the front porch to Jethro and nearly turned towards the porch. And most likely would have if Malloy hadn't taunted him.

"Can't face me like a man, boy!"

Vincent met Malloy's cold, steel eyes. The pure hate within those eyes was staggering. But Vincent didn't fear that hate, and he strode over to his nemesis. "Malloy."

Jethro looked him up and down, his left cheek twitching.

"Say what you want to say," Vincent demanded. "I have more important things to do then stand here with you."

"I know it was Norman who tipped them off."

Refusing to cave under the man's stare, Vincent said, "I have no idea what you are talking about."

"Oh, but I'm sure you do. I'm sure you and Lassiter enjoyed the show that night."

Vincent said nothing.

Malloy's fists opened and closed. "Deny what you will, Vermay, I have my sources. And you can assure your friend that he has caused only a temporary nuisance for me."

"Are you through, Malloy?"

Jethro grinned. "You're dying to hit me, aren't you, Vincent?"

As a matter a fact, I am. "Don't consider yourself so important that I would risk arrest for assault over you."

The old man laughed. "But I am important. I hold their destiny in my hands. You know it. Norman knows it. And Katherine knows it. She'll never have this divorce. They will never be man and wife."

"You can only delay it so long, Jethro."

"You'll see how long I can delay it, Vermay."

So that they would obey him and not swing at Malloy, Vincent thrust his hands into the pockets of his wool coat. "You're wasting my time," he said and turned to go.

Malloy grabbed his elbow and his grip sent shivers up Vincent's spine. "You've become quite the pest as well, Vermay. Quite the pest indeed. I suggest you keep a close eye on your wife. Wouldn't want anything to happen to her now, would we?"

Vincent's heart froze and he had no doubt that Malloy could see the panic in his eyes. *Calm down. His threats are meaningless. You and Kate will not be coming back here after today.*

Malloy released his arm. "Tell my wife I wish her a Happy Thanksgiving. I assume you'll be dining with her on that day." He pushed open the front gate, stepped inside then closed the gate, the latch clanging loud in Vincent's ears. "I hope that Norman and Katherine enjoy their brief time together. And be assured, Vincent, it will be brief."

"Bastard," Vincent spat.

Jethro shrugged his shoulders then continued up the walkway. He climbed the porch steps and went into the house, the door with his stained glass face swinging shut behind him.

Vincent stared at Malloy's image and fought the urge to go up to the door and bust the window. He took several long, deep breaths then turned from the Victorian. Black clouds were forming out over the Niagara River. The temperature had dropped considerably during the afternoon, the air heavy, promising snow. Vincent shivered in spite of his wool coat.

Emma answered the door with tears in her eyes. She motioned Vincent inside and closed the door against the cold.

"Kate told you?"

"She did. Do you really have to go, Vincent? Aren't there more subjects around here that you could paint?"

"I'm afraid it's time to move on."

Emma put her arms around him. He hugged her back, a sudden, strong memory of holding Elizabeth coursing through him. Elizabeth, who had been so like the great aunt she'd never known; Elizabeth, the friend that both he and Kate still ached to have back in their lives. If only she had had Emma's emotional fortitude. If only she had reached out to him, to Kate, to Emmett, Lord, even to Elsie. If only.

As if suddenly realizing what she had done, Emma wiggled out of his grasp and straightened her skirt. Clearing her throat, she said, "You had better go tell Katherine goodbye. She and Kate are in the sunroom."

Vincent took hold of her hand. "You will stay at her side."

Emma smiled through her sadness. "Of course. She is my friend."

"You'll be all right?" he asked while thinking, *At least until cancer gets you many years from now.*

"I'll be fine. Go on up, now."

Leaning close, Vincent kissed her cheek. "You're a magnificent woman, Emma Reilly."

She blushed but did not comment. She pointed at his outerwear and said, "Now, give me those garments."

Vincent removed his coat and hat and handed them to her. He took the stairs two at a time and hurried down the hall to the sunroom. Kate and Katherine sat side-by-side on the wicker loveseat, Kate's arm around her grandmother's shoulders. Although she was crying, Katherine wiped impatiently at her tears. Seeing Vincent in the doorway, she said, despair and disappointment heavy in her voice, "You are taking my friend away from me, Vincent Vermay."

He held up his hands, admitting his guilt.

"I should be angry with you." She wiped at her tears again and sniffed. "What is calling you now that you must paint?"

"Scenery," he said, surprising himself with the answer.

A lock of hair had escaped from the coil at the back of her head and she absently pushed it back from her cheek. "I suppose it must be the Rocky Mountains. You do realize they are two thousand miles away from here?"

"I do."

She took a possessive hold of Kate's hand. "Must you take my friend away with you?"

Vincent knelt before her. "Am I not your friend as well?"

She squeezed Kate's hand harder and Kate winced. Katherine didn't notice. "Yes, you are, and I don't want either of you to go."

Vincent looked at Kate. His wife's eyes spoke of incredible inner turmoil and yet, they also told him she had not changed her mind. As painful as it was, she was going to walk away from Katherine and let what would be, be.

Vincent laid his hand on Katherine's thigh. "You will be fine no matter where Kate and I go. You have Emma and Norman. You have your violin."

Katherine's eyes dropped to her scarred left hand.

Vincent covered her scar with his hand. "Don't torture yourself over your scars, Katherine. You can still play your violin."

She smiled wistfully. "Yes, thank God, I can." Doubt filled her eyes. "Do you know that Norman wants me to play opening night at The Rivera."

"And you should."

Katherine's eyes filled with fresh tears. "How can I? How?"

"The same way you played here in this very room not so long ago."

"I was terrified."

"But you got through it."

Katherine turned to Kate. "But you won't be there. I couldn't do it...not unless you both are there."

"Yes, Katherine," Vincent insisted. "Yes, you can. You don't need us. Emma and Norman will be there."

Katherine adamantly shook her head, tears spilling from her eyes. "No, you have to be there. I need you there. Please, please, you must come."

Kate's eyes found Vincent's. *Could we? Just for that night, Vincent?*

Jethro Malloy's voice screamed in his brain. *I suggest you keep a close eye on your wife. Wouldn't want anything to happen to her now, would we?* Going against his better judgment, Vincent nodded his consent.

Relief flooding her eyes, Kate touched Katherine's tear-stained cheek. "Then we will come back. We will be at the theatre that night."

Katherine shot Vincent an incredulous look.

"We will be there," he assured her. "Promise." *And if Jethro Malloy or any of his men come within five feet of Kate, I'll kill them.*

Someone started clapping and they all turned their attention to the doorway. Norman stood there, Emma at his side, smiling. "Now that," she said, "Is the best news I've heard today."

Vincent wiped a large tear from Kate's cheek. She snuggled closer to him in the bed, sniffed, then said, "I thought you were sleeping."

"Nope."

"I didn't mean to wake you."

"You didn't."

It was pitch black in the bedroom, thick clouds obscuring the stars and moon. Harsh winds banged the Victorian, blowing snow from its resting place on the ground up and around, wiping out any light the street lamps may have cast into the room.

She laid her hand on his bare chest, her fingers kneading his flesh. "That was so hard today."

"It was."

Her fingers worked harder against his skin. "I'm going to miss her."

He drew a long breath. "Me too."

He felt a tear hit his bicep. Kate sniffed again. He wrapped both of his arms around her. "You'll see her again, Kate. We made a promise and we'll keep it. We'll go watch her play opening night."

"Her finest hour."

"Yes."

"That will be so amazing."

"It will."

He closed his eyes, his cheek resting on her soft, thick hair. He lay listening to the wind howl around the old Victorian. The bay window rattled in its frame.

After what seemed like hours had passed, Kate softly said, "Vincent?"

"What, babe?"

"After December 30th, it will be over. Finally and completely over." He didn't say anything, feeling, knowing she had more to say. "I'm forty, Vincent. I'm not getting any younger and I know that we never really thought about this or talked about it, but...well...do you think we could have a child?"

"A child?" He wondered if she could feel his heart thudding beneath her hand.

"Yes. A little Vincent or Kate."

He grinned. "What brought this on?"

"I don't know. Maybe having been so close to Katherine and seeing her talent and her beauty. I'd like to keep passing that on."

"You think we might have a little violin player?"

"Or a painter. Maybe even a writer."

He stroked her hair. "Sounds like a good idea to me." And oddly, the idea was suddenly appealing and desirable.

"Really?"

"Yep." He searched for, found, and kissed her lips in the darkness. They were warm and welcoming.

She cut off the kiss seconds later and said, worry in her voice, "Given my history, do you think I'll be a good mother?"

"Do you want to be a good mother?"

"Yes. I want to be like your mother, Vincent."

He saw his mother's kind, lovely face in his mind, and warmth and love rolled through him. He patted Kate's arm. "Then talk to her, Kate. She'll tell you her theories on motherhood."

"Do you think she would help me with the baby?"

"I'm sure she would, babe. She's always wanted a grandchild. And with Sarah's lifestyle, you know she won't get one from her. And don't forget about me. I intend to be a hands-on father like my dad was."

"Do you want a boy or a girl?"

He touched her cheek. "Either."

"Me too." She reached up and took his hand. "After the 30th then. We start trying."

"After the 30th," he agreed.

She fell asleep soon after, her breath warm against his chest. He continued holding her; his mind filled with thoughts of a child—their child, growing up here in North Tonawanda, in the Victorian, surrounded by love. Of course they would take him to D.C. too. Or her, he reminded himself. Unless they sold the townhouse. He'd have to talk to Kate about it. Maybe she'd want to keep the townhouse as a place they could visit a few times each year so their child could experience the nation's Capitol.

Their child. He couldn't stop grinning at the thought of it.

The wind gusted outside and Kate woke with a start. She pushed off of him and sat up. "What was that?"

"The wind." Snow ticked against the window glass. Vincent laid his hand on her shoulder. "Come on, it's okay, lay back down."

He felt her shiver. "Feel that draft." She threw her legs over the side of the bed. "I'm going to close the curtains." He heard rather than saw her walk to the window. Brass curtain rings squeaked on the brass rod. "That should keep it a little warmer in here, Vincent."

The wind gusted again, screaming shrilly, the bay window shaking then giving way, glass shattering, wood cracking. Kate screamed in pain and he heard her fall, calling out his name. Gritty snow, ice, and freezing air poured into the room. Vincent sprang from the bed, stepping on shards of glass. They pierced the bottom of his feet, but he didn't notice. He switched on the pole lamp and searched the floor for Kate. She lay in front of the window amidst a mess of fabric, glass, and wood. She was screaming, clutching at her head. Blood poured out between her fingers. A chunk of glass, glittering in the lamp light, stuck out of her right cheek, blood oozing out around it.

Vincent snatched the phone from the nightstand and dialed 911. He'd barely gotten the words out of his mouth when he heard sirens and silently thanked God the Victorian was only three minutes from DeGraff hospital.

Kate screamed his name, her voice riddled with pain and confusion. He had never heard such pain in her voice in all their years together. He wanted to take her into his arms and comfort her. He wanted to stop the blood that was pouring out of her. Instead, he ran from the room, down the hall, and down the stairs to the front door. He got it open just as the paramedics pulled into the driveway. "Hurry!" he shouted, watching the attendants unload their equipment. *God, they were taking forever.* Upstairs, Kate kept screaming his name.

At last they came towards the door. There were two of them—a man with dark hair of medium weight and a woman, young, probably in her twenties, with hair that reminded him of Liz. As he led them upstairs to the bedroom, Vincent wished to God that Liz were still alive and here to take care of Kate.

The woman went immediately to Kate. "What's her name?" she asked.

"Kate," Vincent said, hanging in the doorway, staying out of their way and wondering how he could be so terrified and still function.

The man spread out the equipment and opened up the cases.

"Kate," the young woman said, firmly but gently. She took hold of Kate's wrist and eased her hand away from her head. "Kate. My name is Stephanie. I'm going to help you. Can you hear me, Kate?"

Kate's entire body shook. Her eyes stared at Stephanie, but she didn't seem to hear her.

"She's in shock," Stephanie said.

Vincent clutched the doorframe. It took all he had within him to stay where he stood. He wanted to hold his wife. He wanted to take care of her, but he knew he would only hurt her if he got in the way. Then he saw what he could do. He ran to the window and closed the part of the curtains that still hung. While they didn't keep the cold from coming in, they at least held the wind back, deflecting it from Kate and the paramedics.

Stephanie and her partner moved quickly, working in unison, each knowing what the other would do. They took Kate's vitals, hooked her up to an IV, and applied a pressure bandage to the cut on the side of her head. They left the chunk of glass in her cheek.

"It's better not to remove it at this point," the man said. His nametag read Stan.

Kate had ceased shaking and her eyes were closed.

"You better get some clothes on if you want to ride along to the hospital," Stan said.

Vincent opened the armoire, snatched up a pair of khakis and a flannel shirt, and slid into them. He didn't bother with socks. Two more men appeared in the hall. They carried a stretcher. Vincent wondered when they'd arrived.

He watched helplessly as Stephanie, Stan, and one of the other men lifted Kate onto the stretcher. She moaned, her eyes fluttering, but falling shut again. She was deathly white.

Vincent ran down the stairs ahead of them. He put on his hiking boots, his hands shaking as he tied the laces. The bottom of his feet felt sticky, but he ignored the feeling. He shrugged into his jacket, not bothering to zip it up. He followed the stretcher outside. Elsie and Emmett stood on the walkway, Elsie's flannel pajama bottoms sticking out from under her parka. "What happened?" she asked, her eyes watching the paramedics carry Kate to the ambulance.

"The bay window busted. The glass got her. I have to go." He ran towards the ambulance, reaching it just as they finished loading Kate inside.

"I'll fix the window!" Emmett called after him.

Vincent didn't answer him. He climbed into the ambulance and sat beside the stretcher. In the harsh glare of the interior ambulance lights, Vincent saw bruises forming on Kate's cheek around the chunk of glass. Blood was seeping through the pressure bandage. His hand shaking, he took Kate's hand. He felt no response. "I'm here, baby," he said. "I'm with you, Kate. I love you."

The ambulance started moving, its siren wailing, sounding hideously feeble in comparison to the wind.

CHAPTER 29

"Vincent."

He awoke with a start.

"Vincent, it's Sarah."

She knelt beside his chair. His sister, wearing her ever present blue jeans and cowboy hat, knelt beside his chair.

"How did you get here?" he asked, touching her arm. "The storm?"

She smiled. "I chartered a plane."

He stared at her in wonder. She was beautiful, her dark hair falling about her shoulders, blending in with the brown and gold plaid of her flannel shirt. She wore a tan turtleneck beneath the flannel shirt and she looked as if she belonged to the earth and it to her. She spent most of her time outdoors and even after traveling so far to reach him, she smelled of Colorado pine.

She straightened, leaned in and kissed his cheek. Then she turned to the bed where Kate lay, still unconscious, tubes in her arms and nose, the right side of her head bandaged, her right cheek severely bruised, her skin as white as the sheets on which she lay. "How is she?"

Vincent took a long breath.

"Vincent?"

He blinked back tears. "Her skull is fractured. She could have brain damage."

"Oh, God."

"They don't know what abilities she's lost until she wakes up. If she wakes up."

"Lost?"

"Then again, she may be lucky and not lose anything. But the doctor thinks…"

Sarah laid a hand on his shoulder. "What does he think she lost?"

"Possibly memories, motor abilities or speech."

"Will she be able to walk?"

He shrugged.

Sarah cupped his chin in the palm of her hand, her touch warm and comforting.

"Mom and Dad couldn't get here yet," he said. "The storm. But they keep checking in. As soon as the planes are flying out of Philadelphia again…"

"Vincent, I'm sorry," Sarah said.

He nodded, unable to stem the tide of tears. His sister held him while he cried.

❧   ❧   ❧

Four interminably long days crept by before Kate died. She never woke up during that time and Vincent never left her side. He held her hand, talked to her, watched for some sign of life. He prayed and he hoped. His parents arrived and sat with him. Kate's mother and stepfather came. Sarah made sure he ate and drank. And then on the morning of the fifth day during one of the rare moments he was alone in her room, she left him. He was standing at the window, looking out at the winter wonderland that was Tremont Street when the monitor straight lined. He felt her leave, felt the hole open in his heart, the pain nearly more than he could bear. Doctors and nurses rushed in. They worked feverishly. They used paddles on her. He watched, detached somehow, as they fought to revive her. But he knew they wouldn't succeed. He knew because she had taken her final leave of him. He'd felt her go, taking with her the biggest part of his heart.

When they had given up and pronounced her dead, her doctor came over and said, "I'm sorry, Vincent."

Vincent looked at him. He was young, younger than Liz had been, but he'd done his best for Kate. Vincent doubted that Liz would have faulted anything the man had done. Vincent felt that he should tell him that and so he said, "Thanks for everything you did. I know you did all you could."

"I'm sorry I couldn't do more," the doctor said, running a hand through his blonde hair.

"Don't be. You did your best." He almost added, "Dr. Elizabeth Reilly would be proud of you, Doctor." But he didn't. He wondered if this man had known Liz.

"Would you like some time with her?"

"Please."

The doctor shooed the medical personnel from the room. Once they were gone, Vincent went to the bed, lay down beside Kate and took her into his arms. He didn't cry as he held her lifeless shell. He searched the room for her. He stretched his heart out, every fiber of his being searching for her, calling out to her. But she was gone.

He released her body and got out of the bed. He smoothed her hair with his hand and gazed down at her face. He leaned down and kissed her lips. They were already cold. He gave her a final look, memorizing her features, promising her he would never forget what she looked like, and then he pulled the covers up over her face.

❦   ❦   ❦

They buried her the day before Thanksgiving. It was sunny and warm, although snow still covered the ground. The sky was a royal blue; white clouds here and there, the sun shining down. Vincent's father stood on one side of him, his mother on the other, Sarah next to her. Elsie was there with Emmett. Douglas and Mary Lassiter stood beside them. Jessica Woodward was crying, her head on Mike's shoulder. Tracy, Nathaniel at her side, held her mother's hand. Nathaniel looked somber in his dark coat and slacks, and Vincent thought how honorable it was that Nathan had come to the funeral of a woman he'd met only briefly so that he could support his girlfriend.

Kate's mother cried silently, her tears streaming down her face. She clutched her husband's hand. He was a stocky man with graying hair and a round face. He kept whispering into his wife's ear, as if his words would hold her together. But they didn't. The tears kept rolling down a face that looked nothing like Kate's. No, with her blonde hair, blue eyes, and sharp facial features, it seemed impossible to Vincent that this woman had born his wife.

Kate would rest beside Elizabeth. Emmett had insisted. The grave had originally been meant for him and thus, the Reillys would have lain Emma, Marlene, Elizabeth and Emmett. Now Emmett would move to Emma's other side, leaving the spot next to Kate for Vincent.

Vincent didn't hear anything Pastor McMichael said. He was fixated on Kate's coffin, a lovely, stunning box of mahogany and gold. His wife's body was inside of this box. Her body was but she wasn't. Her beautiful soul, the soul he had loved above anything else on earth, was gone and he was painfully alone. For the rest of his days he would be painfully alone.

It angered him that Senator McMartin had not bothered to show up for her funeral. But Freeholder, the Congressman she'd left to go work for McMartin, was there with his wife. David and Carol had come. They stood holding hands. Regina was there as well and she was crying. She'd lost an old friend and friends were hard to come by. Vincent knew that from personal experience.

Pastor McMichael finished speaking and asked if anyone would like to say something. Between sobs, Regina said, "I assure you her book will be published. Her writing is brilliant." Regina's devotion to Kate's novel brought momentary warmth to Vincent's heart. Then, to his own surprise, Vincent said, "I am going to miss her. She was not only my wife, but she was my best friend and soul mate. I knew her I think, better than she knew herself. I can tell you that she would not have been happy living in a diminished capacity which, had she lived, would have been the case. She would no longer have been the woman she wanted to be." His father took his hand. He liked the way it felt, holding his father's hand even though he was 41 years old. He stared down at the coffin. "I love you, Kate. Wait for me."

"She will," Sarah said behind him.

But she hadn't spoken alone. Kate had spoken with her, lovingly whispering, "I will," in his ear.

❦   ❦   ❦

"Come to Silverton with me," Sarah said.

She stood in the office doorway, arms folded beneath her breasts. Vincent figured that by stating rather than asking, she believed she could solicit his agreement. "You should have gone to the Woodward's with Mom and Dad."

"I have nothing to celebrate this Thanksgiving Day."

"Neither do Mom and Dad."

She nodded. "I know. Actually, I think Mom went to see how Jessica is doing. You know Mom, she may have just met the woman but when someone is in that much distress—"

"Margaret Vermay to the rescue."

"Exactly. She drove Kate's mother and stepfather to the airport this morning. Did you know that?"

Vincent nodded, remembering what Kate's mother had said before leaving. "Kate and I haven't always had the best of relationships, but she was my daughter, Vincent. I loved her. And lately, we'd been growing closer. But did she truly forgive me the ugly past. I don't know."

Vincent had smiled encouragingly and said, "She did. I'm pretty sure she did."

"Did she tell you that?"

Vincent had touched his mother-in-law's arm and had said, "She didn't have to. The fact that she offered you a share of the inheritance told me."

His words had eased his mother-in-law's grief, if only just a little. Pushing the memory away, Vincent picked up Kate's picture, leaned back in the chair, and put his feet on the desktop. He stared at his late wife for several minutes. In the picture, she sat on the townhouse front porch steps, her hair hanging out from beneath a Baltimore Orioles baseball cap. She was smiling, her green eyes dancing behind the lenses of her wire-rimmed glasses. She wore blue jeans and a white, tan and green plaid, flannel shirt. She looked playful and incredibly beautiful. He held up the picture. "I love this picture of her." He ran his finger along the glass. It was cold beneath his skin.

"I miss her too, Vincent," Sarah said, and the honesty and pain in her voice grabbed his attention. Her lower lip was trembling.

"Even though you didn't see her much."

"With modern technology, distance was no obstacle." She came into the office and sat on the corner of the desk. She held out her hand and he gave her the photograph. She stared down at it, a tear rolling down her cheek and falling on Kate's face. Sarah wiped the glass with her shirtsleeve. "She understood me, Vincent."

He nodded then asked, "Did she tell you about our marital problems?"

Sarah's left eye twitched. "She did. She blamed them all on herself though. Because of her screwed up childhood. Did she tell you that?"

He nodded again, a lump as big as Montana in his throat. How Kate had tortured herself.

"She also told me how much she loved you and how, once she got her head on straight, your love was even deeper."

He almost asked her if Kate had told her about the time travel, but he held his tongue.

"I envied you that, Vincent."

"What?"

"Your love. In case you hadn't noticed, I'm still single."

"You're a terrific woman, Sis. You'll find somebody."

She shrugged off his words. "I hate to think of you here in this house, alone. Kate wouldn't want that. Come to Silverton with me. Or go home with Mom and Dad."

"No. I belong here. This is my home."

"Can you really do it, Vincent? Can you really live here without her?"

"I don't know. But I have to find out."

She touched his arm. "Why don't we go over to the Woodward's house?"

He shook his head. "I'm not up to that." He took Kate's picture from her and gazed down at it. "She's gone, Sarah. A freak accident and she's gone." Sarah squeezed his forearm. "We were going to make a baby after the first of the year. Hell, we decided it just an hour or so before the window broke."

"Jesus, Vincent."

He set Kate's picture on the desktop. "Let's get out of this room. It still smells like her."

"Okay."

They went downstairs to the living room. Vincent sat on the couch, Sarah in one of the wingback chairs. Vincent picked up the remote and hit the power button. The television came to life. He scanned the channels, but nothing caught his attention. He was painfully aware of the empty space beside him on the couch. He shut off the TV and glanced at Sarah. She met his gaze, her eyes questioning him. He nodded and she came to him, sitting down and slipping an arm around his shoulders.

"I love you, Vincent," she said.

He looked at her through his tears and managed to croak, "I love you too, Sis." Then he lay down, curling up into a fetal position, his head in her lap. She stroked his hair. He thought how comforting and loving her touch was. He thought how empty the Victorian would be once she and his parents had departed. He thought how horrible Kate's death was for Jessica Woodward. She'd lost a daughter and two friends, all so close together. But most of all, he thought how unfair Kate's death was to him, and he wondered how the hell he was going to survive it.

❦   ❦   ❦

He could stand the silence no longer. It was deafening. So he put on his boots, cap, and jacket and he left the Victorian, an empty casserole dish in each hand. He went to the Reilly house first. Elsie answered, sympathy and understanding in her eyes. She invited him in, took back her casserole dish and accepted his thank you. "Come, Vincent," she said. "How about some hot chocolate?"

"Sure," he said, even though he didn't really feel like eating or drinking anything. His stomach hurt. Constantly.

He sat at the Reilly kitchen table and watched her prepare the hot chocolate. She didn't use a mix, but made it the old-fashioned way with cocoa and milk. "Where's Emmett?" he asked.

"Out walking with Duke."

"Oh." He toyed with the edge of his white and blue, plaid placemat. Kate would have liked the mat's design. He almost told Elsie this but didn't.

"Your parents and sister got off okay?" she asked, stirring the hot chocolate.

"Yeah. Sara flew Mom and Dad to Philly then headed back to Colorado. She's supposed to call me when she gets there. She figures it'll be around ten our time tonight."

Elsie turned off the burner, the gas flame extinguishing abruptly, just like Kate's life had ended—abruptly, without warning, without rhyme or reason; just ending and shattering his heart.

Elsie poured two mugs of hot chocolate and brought them to the table. She set one down before him on the placemat and then took a seat across from him. She set her mug on her placemat, gazed at him a moment, and said, "If it's too lonely next door, Vincent, you could stay over here with us for a few days."

He ran his finger along the rim of the cup, the steam from the liquid burning him. It hurt like hell, but it felt good.

Elsie said no more, but sat quietly across from him. She didn't touch her drink. Steam blew up from its surface.

"Do you suppose I've been ignoring it this past week?"

"Ignoring what?"

"Dad and I replaced the bay window. Mom somehow managed to get the blood out of the rug. You see, while they were there with me, I could...it was like...I stood and watched my mother scrub the rug. Dad and I hauled the pieces of wood out onto the back porch. Sarah got rid of all the glass. I don't know how, maybe using a vacuum and a broom. I worked right along side them. And I knew why it had to be done. I knew the window had busted, glass and wood had hit Kate and she..." His hands formed fists. "But they left today. My family left and Kate..." He stared at his fists. "And Kate isn't coming back." He looked at Elsie. "She's not coming back." Tears spilled from his eyes, rolling down his cheeks. And then he was in Elsie's arms and he was crying harder than he'd ever cried in his life, his chest heaving, gasping for air. And he hurt. In fact, every fiber of his being hurt, and the pain was suffocating him. He heard someone screaming in pain. Unbelievable pain and it was he, he was the one screaming.

Elsie Whiting stood beside him, holding him, rocking him and telling him it was okay to cry. It was good to cry.

So he cried and wondered as he did so, if he would ever be able to stop.

🍁   🍁   🍁

Vincent raised his head from Elsie Whiting's soft breasts and saw that the kitchen was growing dark. He wiped his face with his shirtsleeve. Elsie brushed his hair back from his face, kissed his forehead, and returned to her seat across the table. She took a few sips of her hot chocolate and made a face. "Cold."

"Thank you," Vincent said.

"You're welcome."

He swallowed over the phlegm in his throat. "I can't stay here."

"Why not?"

"The Victorian is my home."

She nodded.

"I don't know what I'm going to do without her." He picked up his cold cup of hot chocolate and downed half of it, not even realizing he was doing so. "David and Carol have moved my exhibit opening to January 2. But I could care less if I ever paint again."

"That will change."

"I doubt it."

"I don't."

He raised his cup to drink again, but didn't, putting it back down on the placemat.

Elsie reached across the table and touched his hand. Her touch was comforting. He gazed into her eyes and waited for her to add comforting words to her touch. But she said nothing. And he knew why she said nothing. There was nothing comforting to say.

🍁   🍁   🍁

Darkness had fallen when he left the Reilly house. Emmett and Duke hadn't returned yet, but Elsie wasn't worried. Most likely they'd stopped to visit Douglas and Mary Lassiter.

Vincent stopped in front of the Victorian's wrought iron gate. The windows were all black. He hadn't thought to leave a light on. He shivered in the cold night air and turned away from the house. He had one more casserole dish to return.

Light burned bright in the Woodward's home on Louisa Parkway. He trudged up the driveway to the back door. He raised his hand to knock, but Jessica's quiet voice stopped him. He turned. She sat on the wooden bench in her snowy English garden. She wore a parka and earmuffs. Her hair hung free, touching her shoulders. A kerosene lamp sat on the stone walkway in front of her, casting a yellow glow on the white snow.

He walked to her, holding out the casserole dish. "Just wanted to return this. And thank you."

"Tracy made it," she said. She took the dish and set it on the bench beside her.

"It's cold out here," Vincent said, rubbing his hands together. They were gloveless. It had been warmer when he'd headed over to the Reilly's house.

"Yes, it is. We're having a snowy December."

He shoved his hands in his coat pockets. "Mike home?"

"No. Teaching a night glass this semester."

"Tracy?"

"Out with Nathan. Studying I think. At the library."

Vincent picked up the casserole dish, sat down on the bench, and set the dish on the walkway beside the lamp. He pressed his shoulder against Jessica's. "You okay?"

She looked at him. Her eyes were sad. "Are you?"

He shook his head. "No."

"Jill would have been twenty today."

"Damn."

She sat back, folding her arms across her chest. "What a year, huh? My daughter and two of my friends...three strikes and you're out."

Vincent felt tears in his eyes again. He wondered where they'd come from. Hadn't he cried them all out in Elsie's arms?

"I was hoping," Jessica said, "That if I sat out here in the cold, I would go numb. I'd stop feeling. At least for a little while. I really need to go numb."

"Sounds good to me too?" She tugged on his arm. "What?"

She held out her hand. It was covered with a deerskin glove. He gave her his hand, the deerskin soft against his skin. "What do you say we sit here awhile, Vincent?"

"Okay."

And they did. And somehow, doing so, just sitting there grieving together, made them both feel better.

🍁   🍁   🍁

He couldn't sleep in their bed. In fact, he hadn't slept in it since the night of the accident. He lay down on the couch and waited for Sarah's call. He drifted off and didn't hear the phone until the start of the fourth ring. He didn't reach it before the answering machine picked up and when it did, he sat frozen, listening. Because it was Kate's voice on the tape, saying, "Hi, you've reached Vincent and Kate. Leave a message. We'll call you back."

He didn't pick up. He didn't hear what Sarah said. He just sat there, staring at the phone. And then he did something he found himself doing over and over again as the days passed by. He listened to Kate's voice again.

🍁   🍁   🍁

Vincent sat in the desk chair in Kate's office; her picture propped up on the desktop. Christmas was three days away. He would be leaving for Philadelphia tomorrow. That is, if he went. He didn't want to go. He didn't want it to be Christmas. Not without Kate.

He traced his finger along her chin, the glass cold like his heart, like his life. He stared at Kate's smiling face. He wanted her back. He didn't want to spend any more nights alone in this house. He didn't want to stand in his studio and realize that without her, he had nothing left to paint. Which was odd, he knew, because Kate had not been the one who had brought him out of his artist's block. Katherine had done that. And yet, something inside of him, the part that told him to paint, which told him he could paint, had died with Kate.

He sat back in the chair and hugged Kate's picture to his chest. The frame's sharp edges dug into him. He closed his eyes and ached for her softness, her skin, and the feel of her body against his own. The phone rang. He deliberately didn't answer it, knowing that the answering machine would pick up and he would hear Kate's voice one more time. The machine kicked on and her voice filled the old Victorian—her sweet, melodious, comforting voice. He listened closely, savoring every syllable.

"Vincent," Regina said when Kate's message ended. "Vincent, come on pick up. And, Lord, change the message already. Do you have any idea how freaky it is to hear Kate on the line?"

He didn't pick up, even though the portable sat on the desktop.

"Vincent. Come on. I know you're there. All right, then just listen. I need a picture of Kate for the book jacket. Call me. Bye."

Vincent looked down at the picture of Kate on the townhouse front steps. He supposed he could give Regina a copy of it for the book. He sighed, set the photo on the desktop, and stood up. He went to the window and peeked out through the Venetian blind. The sun shone down on the snowy street below. A father was pulling two laughing children in a sled. The kids were bundled from head to toe in snowsuits, boots, hats and scarves. The sled was like the one he and Sarah had grown up with—wooden with steel red blades; a good, solid sled built to last.

He turned from the window. He and Kate had been married for so long and only when it was too late, they'd decided to have a child. What had taken them so damn long in making that decision?

Vincent left Kate's office, her picture in hand. He started downstairs but stopped halfway. He couldn't go into the parlor today. He couldn't look at the spot in front of the bay window where she would have put their Christmas tree. He would have dragged it into the house and set it up for her, following her instructions, both of them laughing. He went back upstairs and wandered into his studio. He stood in front of his easel, staring at the blank canvas. He held up his right hand. He stared at it and he felt nothing but its uselessness. He used to look at this hand and feel its desire, its need and ability to paint. He found it hard to believe that he had so recently filled canvases with brilliant, beautiful portraits of Katherine.

Katherine. Are you and Norman celebrating Christmas? And Emma, are you celebrating? His glance fell on his sketchbook. He went to the table and opened it, gazing down at his preliminary sketches of Katherine. He drew in a long breath of air. He and Kate had told her goodbye. They were supposed to be traveling out West, not to return until December 30, 1926. So far, Vincent had honored the promise he and Kate had made to one another about not going back until that date. But standing here now, alone in the giant Victorian, Katherine's sketches on the table before him, Vincent knew he could no longer honor that promise. He had to see Katherine. He must see her. She was so much like Kate. At least, he could have that.

So Vincent did something he hadn't done in days. He showered, shaved, and combed his hair. He put on a pair of black dress slacks, a white, puffy-sleeved shirt, red, black and white-striped suspenders, and argyle socks. He went upstairs to Katherine's third floor bedroom and picked up the violin case. Downstairs in the foyer, he put on his leather jacket, boots, and newsboy cap. He slipped out the front door and trudged through the snow to the carriage house. Behind it, where he had last gone back to 1926 with Kate, he removed the violin from its case, laying the case in the space between his feet. He raised the violin and bow and began to play, his eyes closed, praying that it worked.

He knew it had before he opened his eyes. He felt the change in the air. He felt the change within him. He looked around. There was still snow, but less of it. The temperature was at least ten degrees warmer. He put the violin back in its case and stowed it in his usual hiding place. He darted up the side of the carriage house to the driveway. The street was quiet, except for laughter and voices that he recognized immediately. Hearing them again brought a trace of joy to his broken heart.

Emma Reilly stood on her porch, hands on her hips, her face sporting a look of disbelief. Katherine and Norman were lugging a huge evergreen tree up Emma's front walk. "Now, just where do you two think I'm going to put that?" Emma scolded.

Norman and Katherine ignored her protests, Katherine's laughter music to Vincent's ears. It was so much like Kate's. He ran toward them, calling, "Let me help with that!"

Katherine turned, dropping her end of the tree. It fell to the ground, releasing tiny green needles in the snow. "Vincent!" She ran towards him, her arms outstretched and for a moment, a very brief moment, she was Kate running towards him. But when he held her, he knew she wasn't Kate. Still, it felt good to hold Katherine's slender, feminine body close. He kissed the top of her head, knocking her earmuffs askew.

"Vincent," Norman said, reaching them. He held out his hand.

Releasing Katherine, Vincent shook Norman's gloved hand.

"Where's Kate?" Katherine said, peering behind him. "Are you hiding her?"

Emma arrived, her look of disbelief replaced with one of happiness. "Yes," she said, first taking his hand, then hugging him. "Where is Kate?"

He looked at the three of them and he realized that he hadn't thought about this. He'd have to tell them. He wondered how each one of them would take it. He dropped a quick kiss on Emma's cheek, cleared his throat and said, "Why don't we get that tree in the house and then I'll explain."

Katherine would have none of that. Her beautiful, so like Kate's green eyes told him she knew something was wrong. She grabbed his hand and tugged it. "Vincent, what's wrong? Why are you alone?"

He suddenly found himself crying, standing there surrounded by them, crying and blurting everything out. He told them about the storm, how the window in their room had broken, how the glass and wood had hit Kate and killed her. "She didn't wake up. She laid there in the hospital and she didn't wake up." He collapsed on his knees, not even feeling the wet snow seep through his pant legs. Arms held him. Emma's arms, a distant, still functioning part of his brain told him. "She's gone," he sobbed. "My Kate is dead."

Someone knelt beside him. Another set of arms encircled him. A voice, a loving, soft, sad, yet comforting voice said, "Oh, Vincent, my dear, Vincent. I am so sorry. Please, come inside with us. Come inside and I will hold you."

He looked toward the voice. It was Katherine, tears on her cheeks, pain in her eyes, but strength there too. She pulled him to his feet. She held his arm and led him down the sidewalk, up the walk past the fir tree, and into the house. She removed his coat and cap and handed them to Emma. She led him into the parlor and sat with him on the sofa, her arms around him. He laid his head on her breast and he cried. He clung to her, because in her were parts of Kate, and those few parts were all he had left of his wife.

When he could cry no more, he raised his head and looked at Katherine. She managed a small smile, but the red in her eyes and the sorrow in her face told him she was hurting too.

"Norman!" she called. "Emma!"

They came from the kitchen. Their eyes revealed that they had been crying.

"I'm sorry, Vincent," Norman said. "She was a wonderful woman."

"Yes, she was," Emma added.

Still clinging to Katherine's hand, he said, "It happened before Thanksgiving." He felt sudden, intense shame. "I'm sorry. I should have told you sooner."

"If we had known, we could have come to the funeral," Norman said. He came to the sofa, sat on the arm nearest Katherine, and rested a hand on her shoulder.

"Is she buried in town here?" Katherine asked. "May I go see her grave?"

He couldn't meet her eyes. He couldn't tell her that Kate's grave lay years into the future. "No. It's quite a distance away."

She accepted his explanation with a resigned nod of her head. "You've been wandering aimlessly, haven't you, Vincent?"

"Yes, I guess I have." He thought of his heart and the aimlessness within it.

"You must stay with us, Vincent. For now." She looked at Emma. "You have room for him, don't you?"

"Of course."

"He could stay with me at the new house," Norman offered.

"No," Katherine said. "He must stay with Emma and I." She touched Vincent's tear-stained cheek. "He needs a woman's touch now. He needs to grieve. It is easier to do that with women."

Vincent stared at her face, so much like Kate's, and for an instant, he wanted to kiss her and when he kissed her, he wanted her to be Kate. He wanted to stay here, in Emma Reilly's house with Katherine. At least he would feel closer to Kate. But he couldn't. He had to go to Philadelphia for Christmas. His parents and Sarah would be worried beyond belief if he didn't show. Releasing Katherine's hand, he said, "No, I can't stay with you. I have business I must attend to in Philadelphia. But I'll come back for opening night, like Kate and I promised. I'll be there."

Katherine smiled. "I will compose a song for her, Vincent. I will play it that night. I will play a song for my dear friend Kate."

Vincent smiled in spite of his pain. "She would be honored. She loved you dearly, Katherine."

"And I her." Katherine's eyes spoke volumes as he gazed into them. They told Vincent just how special Kate had been to Katherine. And they told him just how much she would miss her.

"At least you can stay for dinner," Emma interjected.

"Of course he will." Norman said, leaving no room for argument.

"I will," Vincent said. "But after dinner, before I go, will you do something for me, Katherine?"

"What, dear Vincent?"

"Will you play your violin?"

She nodded. "For you I would play all night."

❦   ❦   ❦

Dinner over with and the dishes cleared away, they gathered in the sunroom and listened to Katherine play. Norman and Emma shared the wicker loveseat while Vincent settled into the rocker. She began with a simple, soothing piece that Vincent could not identify, but knew that Kate would have loved it. He closed his eyes, saw her face in his mind's eye and he held it there, cherishing it. Arms folded across his chest, he stayed inside the music, keeping Kate's beautiful face in focus. He longed to remain here, in this chair, Katherine's violin working its magic, easing his pain, letting him forget his loneliness, and letting him believe that Kate was still with him.

He fell asleep, his head falling sideways, nearly touching his left shoulder. He slept for hours, unaware that upon conclusion of the song, they all left him, turning out the light and closing the door. He awoke at dawn, heart pounding in his chest. He looked frantically about the room, wondering where he was and then remembering. He bolted from the chair, threw open the door and ran out into the hall. What time was it? He had a plane to catch. He ran to the top of the stairs, started down then stopped, hearing voices. He squatted on the stairs, looking down into the foyer.

Norman and Katherine stood in each other's arms before the front door. He wore his bowler and overcoat. She wore a flowered, flannel robe. He kissed her, promised her he would be home by five then opened the door. Cold air poured into the house, traveling up the staircase. Vincent shivered.

Katherine closed the door behind Norman and turned, catching sight of Vincent. She smiled. "Good morning."

"Hello."

She motioned him down. "Please, you don't have to stay on the stairs, Vincent." He straightened and walked down to the foyer. He took her outstretched hand. "That's better." She squeezed his hand. "I'll get you breakfast. Emma and Norman have both left for the day."

"No," he said. "Ah, wait." She raised her eyebrows just like Kate always had. "What time is it?"

"Nearly nine." She looked down at herself. "And I should be dressed."

"You're fine." He considered her offer of breakfast even though he knew he didn't have time. "I wish I could stay, but I have a pl—train to catch."

"I see."

He pulled her hand to his chest and placed it over his heart. "Thank you for playing for me last night. It helped."

"I wish I could do more."

He averted his eyes. How could he tell her that just being with her, touching her, made him feel close to Kate? He couldn't tell her. No, he couldn't tell her who Kate really was.

"I will miss her friendship," Katherine said, touching his whiskered chin with her free hand. "I meant what I said, Vincent. Some day, I would like to see her grave."

He nodded.

A tear slipped from her eye, rolling down her cheek. She ignored it and pressed on, saying, "I will see you on the 30th."

"Of course. I'll be there."

"I will have a song for her that night. I promise."

He nodded, his throat closing, preventing him from speaking his reply.

"And you will come to our wedding. You must."

He nodded again.

Her hand slipped from his grasp and she went to the closet beneath the stairs. He watched as she retrieved his coat and cap. She handed them to him. "Norman and I want you to be forever in our lives, Vincent. You are a dear friend."

"Thank you," he said. He put on his coat and hat.

"Until the 30th then." She stood on tiptoe and kissed him lightly on the cheek. "Have a safe trip."

He gave her a final look then slipped out the door, the cold air biting into his very bones. He ran down the sidewalk past Malloy's house. He ran until, if Katherine was watching him, she could no longer see him. He waited a good fifteen minutes then returned to the Victorian, running up the driveway and alongside the carriage house. He came around the corner; eye on the bush where he'd stowed the violin the night before and nearly ran over Jethro Malloy. Katherine's husband stood on the snow-covered lawn, beside the bush, the violin case in his gloved hands.

CHAPTER 30

"Hello, Vincent," Jethro said, his face impassive but his eyes triumphant.

"Malloy."

Jethro held up the violin. "Does Katherine know you have this?"

"That's not hers."

"Oh, but it is. I looked inside this case. I would know this instrument anywhere."

"It really isn't. Go ask her if you don't believe me." Vincent's heart thumped in his ears. He wondered if Jethro could hear it. "There's more than one Stradivarius in the world," Vincent added.

Malloy's left eye twitched beneath the brim of his derby. He grinned. "I suppose there is." He tossed the violin and Vincent lunged at it, thinking he wouldn't catch it and somehow, doing so. "Is she teaching you to play?"

"No."

"That's good. Because a good student wouldn't leave his instrument in a bush now would he?"

Vincent stood silent, clutching the violin case as if it were a precious jewel. And in a way, it was. Because it brought him back here, to Katherine, who was so much like Kate.

Malloy's eye twitched again as he stared at Vincent. He licked his lips and said, "They will never be together. I will make sure of that one way or another."

"You son of a bitch," Vincent said, pushing back the urge to kill Jethro.

"You really have no idea of the power I have in this town do you, Vincent. You see a few buildings over on the river and you think that is all I own. Well, it isn't. Look at the bars on Oliver Street. Look at three-quarters of the police department. Look at the politicians. I am this town."

"What you are is an evil, pompous ass."

Malloy laughed, the wickedness in the laughter sending chills up Vincent's spine. Still laughing, he walked past Vincent, starting for the back steps. He stopped; right hand on the railing and turned back. "No matter what you think of me, I will win, Vincent. I have never lost." He pointed at the violin. "And whatever you are doing with that, make sure I don't find it stuck in my bush again. I'd hate to see it used for firewood, wouldn't you?"

Vincent stared at him, hatred in his eyes. Malloy turned and walked up the steps. On the top step, he said, his back to Vincent, "I do love her, Vincent. You may not understand my love. Nor does she. But I do love her." He opened the back door and went inside, the storm door banging shut behind him.

Vincent sat in his father's easy chair beside the Christmas tree. The house was quiet except for the ticking of the clock on the fireplace mantel. The smell of pine filled the darkened room. Only the tree lights burned, their many colors falling across the pile of Christmas gifts beneath the tree. Opened boxes of shirts and sweaters, DVDs and compact discs, a new curling iron for his mother, a new laptop for Sarah, two collector edition books for his father and more. He was alone in the house. His parents had gone to a neighbor's house. Sarah had gone to visit an old friend.

He'd made it through the Christmas Eve service and the party his parents always held. Relative after relative had expressed their sympathy for his loss. Then came Christmas morning, exclamations of surprise as gifts were opened. Christmas dinner, which he dutifully ate but didn't taste, while painfully aware that Kate was not sitting next to him at the table. He'd tried to follow the conversation, but couldn't. He must have looked like a moron, constantly asking, "What?" whenever anyone asked him anything.

And now it was the next evening and at last, he was alone. Alone with his pain, alone with his grief, and alone with the image he couldn't get out of his head. It was constantly there. It was even in his sleep. Norman and Katherine, arm-in-arm in front of the door, saying goodbye. The loving way she had looked at Norman and the tender way he had held her, kissed her, and promised her he'd be home by five. If any two people belonged together, it was Norman and Katherine. Their love was special. Their love was complete. Vincent knew how love like that felt. He'd had it. For fifteen years, he'd had that special, complete love with Kate. And he knew the crushing pain that came when that love was taken away. Neither Katherine nor Norman deserved that pain.

He heard the front door close. Someone was home. Sarah, it had to be Sarah. There was no talking. His parents would be talking.

Moments later, she called his name, "Vincent!"

"In the living room."

She came to him. "Hey." She sat down on the floor at his feet, her legs crossed. She stared at the tree. "That's nice. Mom always does a great job."

"She does."

She touched the laptop. "I can't believe they did this. These things aren't cheap."

"They love you."

"Yes, they do. Lately, I realize that I miss them, Vincent. Even though I love what I do in Silverton, and I love Colorado and don't want to ever live anywhere else, I miss them being there for the everyday things."

"They never should have let you go on that church trip out there when you were sixteen."

"Well, they did. And the mountains bit me."

"And hooked you."

"Without a doubt." She leaned back, resting on her hands and peered at him, the tree lights dancing in her eyes. "Are you okay, Bro?"

"No."

"I guess it will take you awhile."

"I guess."

"Mom and Dad are coming out to Silverton for New Year's. Why don't you come with them? You haven't been out since I built the log cabin house."

"Afraid I can't, kiddo. Got commitments."

"Your opening at the gallery? Hell, I can fly you to D.C. myself in time for that."

"Not just that."

"Then what?"

He gazed at her. *Gee, Sarah, I have to go to the opening of The Rivera on the 30th in 1926. And I need a date. Want to come?* He sighed and smiled in spite of his sadness. *What,* he wondered, *would you say if I told you the truth?*

"Vincent?" she pressed.

"Some other events I committed to. After all, don't you think it's about time I get back to living my life?"

"Can you do that?"

"I have to do that. Kate would want me to."

Sarah got up off the floor, sat in his lap, and wrapped her arms around his neck. She kissed his forehead and said, "I love you, Vincent."

"I know." He touched her cheek. It was still cold from her walk home. "I love you too."

She laid her cheek on his head. "Vincent, promise me something."

"What?"

"That you won't do anything crazy."

"Like what?"

She didn't speak for a moment, but her grip on him intensified. Her voice soft, she said, "Just promise me no matter how depressed you get, you won't shut me out. You'll call me."

Something in her tone, in the seriousness of it, told him what she was thinking. He closed his eyes, bit his lower lip then said, "I haven't thought about killing myself, Sarah." He felt the instant relief in her body. He put his arms around her and drew her closer than she already was. "I promise you that I wouldn't do that, Sis. I...I would call you first."

"Thank God," she whispered.

They sat together like this for several minutes and then she said, "Vincent, promise me something else?"

"What?"

"That you will come out to Silverton next year. We'll go hiking. Just you and me."

"I'll come," he said, although he wondered if he really could go back to Silverton without Kate.

Vincent arrived back in North Tonawanda on December 29th and he went immediately to the cemetery. He had to talk to Kate and tell her his decision. He pulled the Rodeo in through the cemetery gates and drove the winding road to the hill where his wife lay. He parked the truck, jumped out and closed the door, feeling suddenly inadequate and foolish as he stood looking up the incline towards Kate's grave. He had forgotten flowers. He should have stopped on his way from the airport. He should have gotten red roses.

Sighing, scolding himself, he started up the hill, boots crunching the snow. Thick, ominous clouds filled the sky around him, and he could feel the impending snowfall in the air. It penetrated his bones and he shivered. He was halfway up the hill when he saw Jessica Woodward kneeling in front of Kate's grave. He stopped and watched her. She set a pot of geraniums in the powdery snow, just below the writing on the marble stone. Snow obscured part of Kate's name and Jessica brushed it away with a gloved hand.

"Hey, Jess," he said, starting forward again.

She stood up and turned. He saw dark, wet knee stains on her blue jeans. She wore a blue pea coat and blue furry earmuffs, her blonde hair blowing in the breeze. She smiled; genuinely pleased to see him, and she held out her arms. He went into them, hugging her, enjoying the feel of her feminine body against his own. He loved that feeling and with Kate gone, he missed it. Especially at night, holding her while she slept, listening to her gentle, rhythmic breathing and knowing that at least for the time she was in his arms, no harm would come to her. But it had come to her, he reminded himself, the memory harsh and merciless. It had come to her in their bedroom with him at her side.

Jessica eased him away and she asked, "How was Philadelphia?"

"Okay. How have you been?"

She glanced back at both graves, Kate's and Elizabeth's, identical stones side-by-side, and then turned her gaze to the east, towards the hill where her daughter lay before looking at him again and saying, "Hanging in there. Mike and Tracy have been wonderful. But it was the first Christmas without Jill, my firstborn. That was hard."

He nodded his understanding.

"Your Christmas, Vincent?"

"Void."

She rubbed his arm. "Did you just get back?"

"Just now. I wanted…" He pointed at Kate's grave.

"I better get home," she said, giving his arm a farewell pat. "Why don't you stop over on New Year's Eve? Nathaniel and his father are coming over. Just a small gathering."

"To celebrate the New Year, Jess?"

She shook her head. "No. Just to be together."

Vincent bit his lip. He wondered what the world was going to be like for them all come December 31st. But he couldn't tell Jessica he suspected it was going to change. That was something he had to talk to Kate about. Not that standing there talking to her gravestone was going to change his mind. The decision was made. He'd finalized it on the plane back but deep inside, he supposed he'd actually made the decision the day they'd put Kate's coffin into the ground. "I'll think about it, Jess."

"Please. And don't be a stranger. Stop over whenever you want."

"Thanks."

She kissed his cheek, her lips warm against his cold skin. He watched her walk down the hill and along the road towards the hill where Jill was buried. Most likely, that was where she'd parked her car.

He turned back to Kate's gravestone. He squatted before it and touched it with his gloved hand. He ran his finger along her name—*Katherine Victoria Malloy Vermay*. How beautiful she had been. He smiled. And how infuriating she had been at times as well. He closed his eyes a moment, steadying himself and then, opening them, he said, "I'm going to do it, Kate. I'm going to keep Jethro from taking Norman away tomorrow night. And I pray it will be as theorized. I will return and there will have been no you." His throat tightened but he forced the words out over the tense muscles. "Because I can't take it anymore, babe. I can't live without you. It hurts too damn much. I would rather have never known you than live like this. Please understand." He leaned close to the stone and kissed her name, his lips sticking to the cold marble. He pulled them free, oblivious to the pain of tearing flesh. He straightened and stared down at Kate's grave for a long time. He read her name over and over again. Doing so somehow helped ready him for what he was about to do. Because the truth was, he had no idea just how many lives would change after tomorrow night. And he didn't care. He had to free himself from his loneliness and sorrow.

Vincent touched Kate's gravestone one last time then walked down the incline to the Rodeo. He drove back to the Victorian, parked the truck in the driveway and went in the front door. He knew Elsie had picked up his mail and newspapers for him, but he had no desire to retrieve them. He had to shower, change, and go to 1926. He would spend the night at Emma's. He would follow Norman around the entire day, just in case he and Kate had guessed wrong about the time Jethro's henchmen had struck.

He was ready by 4 p.m. He had his tuxedo and Katherine's violin in his suitcase. He slipped into his black, wool overcoat and new bowler he'd picked up in a Philadelphia historic hat store. Clutching his suitcase, he went into the parlor. He gazed down at the answering machine. His finger lingered over the message button. He took a deep breath, pressed the button, and stood savoring Kate's voice. "Hi. You've reached Vincent and Kate. Leave a message. We'll call you back." He knew it might very well be the last time he ever heard it. When he came back, if he was lucky, his memory of her as well as this message would be gone. In fact, if all went as planned, he would not return to the Victorian. If there had been no Kate, she would not have been here to inherit it. It was mind-boggling; the extent of what could change after tomorrow night.

He shook himself into activity. Although he didn't know why he did so, he left a single lamp burning in the parlor. Outside, in the fading afternoon light, he stood on the walk and studied the Victorian. It truly was a beautiful house. He hoped it remained so even if he was never to know it. He turned away. He would walk down the street a ways past the Reilly house then play the violin. He no longer gave a damn if anyone saw him disappear.

He was latching the front gate when he heard Katherine begin playing. She was playing a song with such reverence and beauty that tears came to his eyes. He blinked them back. He heard children's voices across the street. He turned and saw four young boys building a snowman, complete with a top hat and scarf. A milk truck passed by on the street, the driver blowing the horn at the boys and waving.

Vincent grinned. How quickly it happened now. Just a few notes when Katherine played, not more than five minutes when he played. Emma's house was decked out in red bows and evergreens. The greenery encircled the columns and hung around the door and the windows. The Christmas tree that Norman and Katherine had hauled inside sparkled brilliantly in the front parlor window. The music came from the backyard. He ran up the driveway and past the garage, stopping just behind it.

Katherine stood on the back porch. She wore a long, forest green coat with a green and red plaid scarf. Her hair hung free from beneath a brown fedora. In spite of the cold, she played without gloves. He watched, awed and moved by what she played. He'd never heard the piece before.

Suddenly aware of him, she ceased playing in mid note. "Vincent?"

"No, don't stop," he said, approaching her. "It's magnificent." He reached the steps, stopping with his boot on the first step. He gazed up at her, searching her face for all its similarities to Kate's.

"It's called, *For Kate*. I'm glad you like it."

He couldn't speak.

"I wanted it to reflect her goodness and beauty."

He tried to assure her that it did but could only gulp.

Katherine cradled the violin and bow under her left arm and held out her right hand. "Come inside. I'm so glad you came today."

He came up the steps, set down his suitcase, and took her hand. He brought it to his lips and kissed its palm.

"Oh, Vincent," she said, touched by his gesture.

"How are you?" he asked, meeting her lovely green eyes. "Tomorrow is your big night."

"Surprisingly, I'm not nervous. It's strange, Vincent. But I know that Norman, Emma, and you will be there. And…"

"What?"

"And Kate will be there as well. She will be in the music. The music she inspired."

Vincent bowed his head, tears spilling from his eyes. Katherine touched his cheek. "My poor, Vincent. When will your sorrow ease?"

He didn't answer. He couldn't. She must not know what her future could have been. No, she must live her life with Norman, happy, never knowing what Vincent had prevented. He wiped at his eyes with his sleeve and after a hearty sniff, said, "In time, I suppose. Because it's said, Katherine, that time heals all wounds."

She smiled. "Yes, yes, Vincent, it does. Now, come inside and have dinner with us. And spend time with those who love you."

He nodded and followed her inside.

❦   ❦   ❦

It was still Christmas on Webster Street. Multi-colored lights decorated the building façades and street lamp poles. Bright wreaths and evergreen trees lit up shop windows, lights dancing on the snow that lined the road. People went in and out of stores, bells ringing when each door opened. Children ran up and down the sidewalks, dodging piles of snow. Everyone living and loving life; joyous on this festive evening, many still in the Christmas spirit. But then, this was 1926 and life was slower and simpler. There was time for savoring the holiday, for making it last as long as possible.

Standing outside the crowded Mary Lincoln Candy Store, Vincent found himself wishing for the umpteenth time since arriving at Emma's earlier that Kate were experiencing this evening with him. She would have so enjoyed the scene playing out on the street before him. A shop bell jingled behind him and Vincent turned. Norman came out of the candy store with a giant brown bag in his hand. He held it up. "Three pounds should do it, I think, Vincent."

"Three?"

"Definitely three. Don't let Emma tell you otherwise, but she has quite the sweet tooth." He opened the bag and Vincent looked inside. The smell of chocolate sent him reeling and reliving all the times he had smelled the candy on

Kate's breath and how much he had liked smelling it there. "Famous Mary Lincoln chocolates," Norman was saying. "Emma's favorite."

Vincent managed to say, "I'm sure Emma will be pleased."

Norman closed the bag and pointed at The Rivera. Tonight, its marquee was dark and it stood silent, teasing, anticipation of its opening night in the conversations of those bustling about Webster Street, unable to keep from glancing over at North Tonawanda's new showplace. "Tomorrow night, Vincent," Norman said. He drew in a long, satisfying breath. "This theatre will shine, my friend. And Katherine, my beautiful Katherine will shine as well. North Tonawanda will see what a truly lovely and gifted woman my lady is."

"She will take them by storm."

Norman slapped Vincent on the back. "Most definitely. And now, to the jewelry store."

"For what?"

Norman propelled Vincent forward. "To pick up a very special broach. One I had made for Katherine to wear tomorrow night. I pray she likes it."

"I'm sure she will."

"Ahh, Vincent, there is nothing like the love of a good woman, is there?" He had no sooner said the words then he stopped walking, a hand on Vincent's shoulder. "How insensitive of me. I'm sorry. I shouldn't have—"

Vincent waved the apology away. "No need to apologize for speaking the truth."

"Still…" He cleared his throat. "Vincent, you do know how sorry I am that you lost Kate."

"I do."

Norman started walking again and moments later, they entered a small jewelry store. Cases displaying rings, necklaces and bracelets of every shape and size lined each side of the store and led up to a counter manned by a gray-haired man with silver-rimmed glasses. He wore a white, cotton shirt and a black vest. The vest was open, the sleeves of his shirt rolled up to his elbows, revealing forearms covered with thick, black hair. Seeing Norman, the proprietor grinned and said, his Russian accent heavy, "Cutting it close, Mr. Lassiter. I was just about to lock up for the night.

Norman removed his pocket watch, opened it, peered at it, and said, "Now, Alexie Gudunov, I have a good five minutes yet."

Alexie laughed and held up his hand. "I think I know what you've come for. Let me get it for you." He disappeared through a door that led to the back of the store.

Norman stowed his watch back into his vest pocket. "Alexie is the best diamond cutter in Western New York, Norman. Once Katherine's divorce is final, I will have him make her an engagement ring." He sighed and leaned on the counter. "For now, I must settle for just a broach."

Vincent squatted so he could see the jewelry in the case beneath the counter. "You would buy Katherine the world if you could, wouldn't you, Norman?"

"I'm afraid that's true."

Vincent spotted a dainty diamond ring. The stone was oval in shape, the diamond surrounded by rubies. Kate would have loved it. He saw the ring on her finger and the smile on her face as she looked at it. Shaking the image from his mind, he straightened. *You only have to get through tomorrow night, Vincent. You can survive these flashes of Kate until then.*

Alexie returned and held out a box covered in black velvet. Taking it, Norman opened the box and said, "What do you think, Vincent?"

The broach lay on red velvet. Its diamond was multi-faceted and cut in the shape of a heart. Emeralds the exact color of Katherine's eyes surrounded the diamond. Vincent shook his head. He had seen this broach before. Katherine had been wearing it the first time Kate had taken him to meet her. He remembered how surprised he had been to see such a broach on Kate's frail, wheelchair bound grandmother; a woman who at that point was completely ruled by Kate's cousin Lydia. Lydia had taken her grandmother's independence away. Why hadn't she taken such an obviously expensive broach away as well?

Katherine had barely spoken that afternoon, but Vincent had realized she was sizing him up. She'd shaken his hand, her grip weak; the fine bones in her fingers fragile and he'd been afraid they would break in his hand.

"Vincent?" Norman pressed.

"It's marvelous," he said, finding himself smiling and, amazingly, feeling happy in the knowledge that Katherine's life was going to be different after tomorrow night. It would be a happy life and he, Vincent Vermay, would be the reason why. Damn, it had been so long since he'd felt happiness.

"Would you like me to wrap it for you?" Alexie asked, scratching his square chin.

Norman closed the box. "A white bow is all it needs."

Vincent watched, impressed, as the jeweler turned a plain white ribbon into a three-tiered bow. He worked quickly, his hands agile, fingers moving in fluid motion. Vincent could see why he was the best diamond cutter in Western New York.

Norman paid cash and Alexie walked them to the door. "I will be at your opening tomorrow night, Mr. Lassiter." He opened the shop door, cold air blasting them. "I would not miss a chance to see your lady play again."

"Again?" Vincent asked.

Norman stepped outside. "He saw her in Vienna."

"I did indeed."

"Alexie lived there for a bit after leaving Russia."

"A few short years, yes. But always, I save to come to America."

Norman held up the jewelry box. "And I, for one, am very glad you did."

"You tell Miss Katherine that she will have a fan there tomorrow night, Mr. Lassiter?"

"I will."

Alexie locked the door behind them. They walked past the dark Rivera, heading for Goundry Street. "He lost his wife in the Revolution, Vincent," Norman said.

"In 1917?"

"Yes. She was pregnant with their first child. She died in his arms."

Vincent looked back at the jewelry store. The shop windows went dark.

"He is only 34 years old, Vincent."

Vincent looked back at Norman and nearly fell over a patch of ice. Norman grabbed his arm and kept him upright. "That's younger than me, for God's sake. He looks much older."

"Inside he is. What he has seen in his lifetime…well…they are sights I can't even imagine. But he is a good friend. He could help…" He trailed off, sighing. They turned right onto Goundry. "Vincent, I'll be blunt. Are you going to stay after tomorrow night?" He didn't give Vincent a chance to answer but kept on talking. "You should stay. You have people who love you here. And now you have met Alexie. He has experienced your grief. He could help you. There, I've said it. I want you to stay. Katherine and Emma want you to stay. So, damn it, stay."

Vincent was touched, but he couldn't stay. He had to go back to his own time, the time when he had been born, the time in which he must live. And after tomorrow night, when he got to his own present, if he were right, all memories of Kate would be gone. And his pain would be gone.

"Well, Vincent?" Norman asked.

"I'm not sure what I'm going to do yet," he lied.

"Then you will think about staying?"

"I will."

Vincent sat in Emma's parlor, the day's edition of *The Evening News* spread out in his lap. The paper had done a special Rivera Theatre edition. All the articles were filled with praise for the new theatre. The paper proclaimed that tomorrow night's opening promised to be a grand event.

"Can't sleep?"

Vincent closed the paper and looked up. Emma stood in the doorway. She wore a red, flannel robe and her hair hung well past her shoulders. In the Christmas tree lights she looked much younger than her forty some years. She was beautiful and feminine and he again felt sadness that she would never marry.

She hugged herself. "Why are you staring at me like that?"

"You are beautiful," he said. It was time someone said it to her. She deserved to hear it. She may think him forward, or insensitive to Kate's memory, but his time here was short, and he wanted to show her that a man could find her attractive.

Her cheeks turned red and she averted her eyes.

"You don't believe me, do you?"

She remained silent. He stood up, dropped the newspaper on the chair and went to her. Taking her by the upper arms, he firmly said, "Look at me." Reluctantly, she did and the depth of insecurity in her eyes astounded him. *What have the men of your past done to you?*

She must have read his mind because she said, "That is history, Vincent. Let it rest."

He touched her chin, her skin warm and smooth. "Fools."

She slipped away from him and went to stand before the tree. He joined her, making sure there was space between them. She didn't want to talk about her past. He would respect that. But he was glad he had told her she was beautiful. She wouldn't forget what he said. Somehow, he knew that.

Most of the ornaments on the tree were Victorian in style, handmade with lace, velvet, buttons, and bows. There were some painted glass ornaments here and there, as well as some ceramic ones. She pointed at one of the ornaments near the top of the tree. It was a ball of green and red velvet with white lace. "My mother made it." She pointed at a blue ball further down the tree. "This was my first attempt. It didn't come up to her standards."

Vincent examined them. "I don't know. I think they both show skill."

She shook her head, tendrils of red hair dancing in the tree lights. "She wanted me to marry Charles Melon. I was to stay in Albany and be a good wife. I was to produce scores of grandchildren and generally spend the remainder of my life emulating her."

"I take it you rebelled."

She pointed at a ceramic Santa Claus. "Charles gave me that. It was in the first wrapped box that year. A diamond engagement ring occupied the second box."

Vincent raised his eyebrows.

"I refused it. It really was quite a scene, Vincent. Mother shouting. Me shouting. Right there in the parlor around the Christmas tree."

"What did you father say?"

A warm smile crossed Emma's face. "Nothing, at first. He sat there in his big, wingback chair and said nothing. Embarrassed, Charles stormed out. Mother followed him, pleading my case. Something about how she'd talk me into my senses. My youngest brother sat by the fire, drinking eggnog, and enjoying the entertainment."

"I take it she didn't convince Charles to stay."

"She didn't."

"And you stood your ground."

"I did." She laughed and her laughter was robust and music to Vincent's ears. "I calmly explained to her that I was going to medical school. I was going to be a doctor just like my father."

"Did she have a stroke?"

"Nearly. I left her fuming in the parlor. I grabbed my brother by the hand and insisted he take me ice skating in the park."

"Which he did?"

"I think he knew by the look on my face that he didn't dare refuse." She laughed again. "Dear Edward. He has always been my knight in shining armor. He still lives in Albany. He's an attorney. And he recently did something at the age of forty that shocked his colleagues. The self-proclaimed bachelor got married." Emma's eyes twinkled with joy. "Poor mother is just beside herself. He married beneath him."

Vincent burst out laughing.

"I dare say, Vincent, you wouldn't like my mother very much."

"Well, I would find her a challenge to say the least."

Emma grinned. "You would have liked my father. He was wonderful."

"He passed on?"

She nodded. "In 1920. Heart attack." She drew in a long breath and touched a red and silver, pear-shaped glass ornament. "He gave me this when I was ten. He bought it on one of his trips to New York City." She was silent a moment and Vincent joined her silence. Emma turned from the ornament and said, "The night I turned Charles down he came to my room with a briefcase. He sat beside me on the bed and opened it. It was filled with money. I couldn't speak. I just sat there staring at all those bills. He pulled a train ticket from his breast pocket. 'This will take you to Buffalo. An old friend of mine will meet you. Her name is Ida Jacobs. She has agreed to help you get into medical school. You can have a room in her house if you want it. Or find a place of your own if you'd rather.' There were tears in his eyes as he spoke. 'There's enough money here for eight years if you are careful. Take it. Take the tickets and leave here. Because if you stay here, with your mother so close...' He didn't finish the statement but he didn't have to. I knew he was right, Vincent. One can only withstand Mother for so long before one breaks down."

"So you left Albany."

"I boarded the train the next day. Father and Edward saw me off. Mother refused to come to the train station."

"Not surprising."

"No." She pointed at the portrait that hung on the wall. It was a head and shoulders painting of a dark-haired woman in her fifties. She was not beautiful, her nose slightly too large, her chin seeming to roll into her neck, but there was dignity and grace about her. Kindness ruled her eyes and Vincent could see that once one got to know this woman, one would find her appealing. "Ida Jacobs," Emma said. "She was a nurse. And she was my father's true love."

"I see," Vincent said, nodding.

"Even though he broke her heart by marrying my mother, she remained his friend. She was a phenomenal woman, Vincent."

"Why didn't he marry her?"

"Thus you found the chink in Daddy's armor. She was poor. My father came from a wealthy family. Sons of wealthy families did not marry someone of Ida's social standing."

"So he gave her up?"

"He did. And spent the rest of his life regretting it. But he wouldn't let me do that, would he? No, he wouldn't let me give up my dream as he'd given up his." She pulled the collar of her robe tighter around her neck and shivered. "It's cold in here."

"Have you ever regretted getting on that train, Emma?"

She shook her head. "No. I admit I'm sometimes lonely. But I wouldn't have been happy not being a doctor." She looked up at the ceiling. "Just like Katherine wouldn't be happy if she returned to Jethro. Choices, Vincent. We all must make choices in this life. Rest assured, I don't regret mine." She went to the window and pushed the drapery aside. "What do you suppose he's planning over there?"

"What do you mean?"

"Come now, my friend, you really don't think he's going to let Katherine choose Norman, do you?" She turned from the window. "I know you aren't that naive."

He wondered if she would read his mind again as she had seemingly done earlier. Despite this fear, despite the dryness of his tongue, he said, "What do you think he's planning?"

"I don't know. Which is why I can't sleep. Tomorrow night Katherine performs in front of the whole damn town. Jethro will be there. I just can't help feeling an overwhelming sense of…of foreboding."

"Have you said anything to her?"

"Good, Lord, no. Miraculously, she's not nervous about this performance. I certainly don't want to make her nervous."

"Norman?"

"Yes."

"And he said?"

"Not to worry about anything. He would be there to take care of her."

Vincent took her hands. "Then listen to him. Stop worrying. He will be there to take care of Katherine, and I will be there to take care of him."

She shuddered. "And I will have my medical bag."

CHAPTER 31

December 30, 1926, opening night, and The Rivera had finally opened its outer doors to the throng of people waiting impatiently to get in. They filled the lobby and spilled out onto the sidewalk outside, their conversations humming like a beehive in Vincent's ears. He stood on the left staircase, dressed immaculately in his tuxedo; hair slicked back, white gloves on his hands. He shook his head and he grinned, awed by the scene below him. It was so much like the night he and Kate had come to the theatre for the silent movies and tour, and yet it was so different. For on this night The Rivera was opening for the first time. There was joy and anticipation in the air. North Tonawanda now had a grand theatre, a showplace finer than any public venue the city had known before. Vincent ran his hand along the brass railing, still not believing that he was here, witnessing this night, reliving history. *If only Kate were here.* He pushed the thought away. He must not dwell on his own loss tonight. He had a job to do. He walked down the steps, pausing on the first stair to unhook the red, velvet rope serving to keep the crowd at bay. Once through it, he hooked it shut again and heard an elderly gentleman to his left mutter disapproval. He shook his head. Even in 1926, people hated waiting for the show to start.

He scanned the crowd one more time but saw no sign of Jethro Malloy or of anyone else acting suspiciously. Mayor Mackenzie and his wife were talking with James Kelly near the ticket booth. Mrs. Mackenzie was gorgeous in a long, black and silver silky gown and matching hat adorned with feathers. Vincent made his way slowly through the crowd, pushed open one of the auditorium doors, squeezed through and closed it tight. Turning, he met a tall, sandy-haired man with questioning eyes. Vincent flashed the pass Norman had given him, side stepped the usher, and continued on his way. He hurried across the back of the auditorium and down the side. Reaching the steps that led up to the wings, he stopped to listen a moment to the organist. He was playing *Toot, Toot, Tootsie, Goodbye*, rehearsing one last time before the auditorium doors opened. The mighty Wurlitzer organ was raised up on its platform. For 1926, the ornate, hand-painted instrument was a technological marvel.

Vincent went up the steps and through the wings to the stairs that led down to the dressing rooms. The organ music trailed him down but once he reached the basement, the music was drowned out by the chatter of the various acts scheduled to perform in the vaudeville portion of the show. A man pushed by him, carrying a cello, his collar still unbuttoned, his bow tie not yet tied. A woman stood outside the nearest dressing room door, her hand on her throat, practicing the scale. She hit each note perfectly. Her golden hair was piled up on top of her head and her face was covered with what looked to be an entire makeup case worth of makeup. But her gown was stunning, white lace on turquoise silk, the fabric shimmering with multi-colored sequins, somehow making her a pleasure on the eyes.

Vincent nodded at her as he passed by. He walked to the last dressing room and knocked on the wooden door. The door opened immediately, revealing Norman Lassiter looking handsome in a black tuxedo with a forest green cumber bun. "Vincent," he said, pleasure in his voice. "Come in."

Vincent stepped inside and found Katherine standing in front of the dressing table. She wore a forest green, velvet gown with a long flowing skirt that fell to the tops of matching green and silver shoes. The diamond and emerald broach Norman had bought her was pinned to a forest green, velvet ribbon encircling her neck. Diamond, heart-shaped earrings adorned her ears. She wore very little makeup but then she didn't need much. Like her granddaughter, Katherine possessed a natural beauty that needed no embellishment. She had her hair pulled up to the back of her head, held in place by diamond hairpins. Stray tendrils hung about her face, softening her look, making her seem very young and very innocent.

She held out her hands to him, stepping forward. She smiled but in her eyes he saw fear. He had hoped that she'd not experience fear on this night. He took her hands and lightly squeezed them. He met her eyes, and he wished that he could tell her he was there to make everything all right. She need not fear anything.

Norman came to her side and kissed her cheek. "I have to get upstairs. You should come to the wings and watch the show for a bit. There's no need for you to sit down here worrying."

"He's right, Katherine," Vincent said. "I'll go up with you if you like."

She looked at Norman and said, "Go, darling. Do what you must. I'll be fine." The trembling in her voice told Vincent just how close she was to breaking down and giving into her fear and anxiety.

Norman slipped his arm around her. He bent close as he said, "You are so lovely this evening." He touched her cheek. "I love you. You are going to be magnificent."

He kissed her lips, gave Vincent a knowing look then departed, closing the door behind him.

Still holding her hands, Vincent said, "He's right. You will do fine, Katherine."

"I'm terrified," she said, tears welling in her eyes. "It hit me this morning. God, I'd hoped..."

"I know."

She stepped closer to him, and he released her hands and wrapped her in his arms. She laid her head on his chest. "I had so hoped," she said, again.

"You know what this is, Katherine. It is just anxiety. You can beat it. You know that now. You know it won't hurt you."

She hugged him tighter. "I'm going to do it. I'm going to play. I don't care how frightened I am. I'm playing Kate's song. And if that is the only song I get through, so be it, but I'm playing it."

He felt her determination in the tautness of her muscles. The tenderness and love in her voice when she referred to Kate touched him. He stepped back from her and said, his voice cracking, "Kate will be with you tonight, Katherine. I know she will." Their eyes met and he swore he saw Kate looking back at him, encouraging him, agreeing with his decision and being right there beside him to carry it through.

"I'm counting on that, Vincent," Katherine said. She slipped her arm through his. "I wish Emma were here."

"As do I."

Katherine sighed. "Why do her patients always need her at the most inconvenient times? I so wanted her to see me perform."

"She might make it back in time. Now, come upstairs with me."

She inclined her head. "I think I will go up and watch the show for a while. I won't be on until after intermission. I don't need to warm up yet."

He escorted her from the dressing room and as they passed her fellow performers, greetings and good lucks were exchanged. The golden-haired woman in the turquoise dress kissed Katherine's cheek and said, "I saw you in Milan, Miss Mann. I am so thrilled to share the same stage with you."

"Thank you. I'm not sure how I'll do. It's been some time since I've played in front of a large audience."

With a warm smile, the woman said, "Your talent is natural. You will be triumphant. I've no doubt."

"Thank you," Katherine said, again.

Vincent gave the woman a look of gratitude and gently pushed Katherine on her way.

They stood in the wings, listening to Mayor Mackenzie's speech. He praised everyone involved with the theatre. He read congratulations telegrams from New York State Governor Alfred Smith and Hollywood movie producer Cecil B. DeMille. He pointed out the organ, talking it up and congratulating the Wurlitzer factory on making such a marvelous instrument. Vincent moved to the door and peered out at the crowd. It consisted of North Tonawanda and Tonawanda's finest and wealthiest families. Every man wore a tuxedo, every woman a long, gorgeous gown. There wasn't an empty seat in the theatre.

When the Mayor finished, theatre manager James Kelly introduced the first movie; *Upstage* starring Norma Shearer. Vincent led Katherine down the steps and stood with her along the side of the auditorium. Norman joined them halfway through *Upstage*. He bent close and whispered something in Katherine's ear. She nodded, smiling in spite of her nervousness. Vincent kept one eye on Norman and the other on the movie. The time had come when he must keep his full attention on Norman.

They escorted Katherine down to her dressing room just as intermission began. Once inside the room, Norman said, "I can't stay, my love. You know I must be upstairs mingling with our supporters." She managed a smile as she nodded. He hugged her, kissed her cheek and hand on the doorknob, said, "You will be magnificent. I'll be right in the wings with you before you go on." She nodded again.

"Norman, wait," Vincent said. He flashed Katherine a final glance. She was shaky but he couldn't worry about that now. Giving her an apologetic look, he said, "I'll go with you."

Norman frowned. "Vincent," he said, "I thought that maybe you—"

"Miss Mann?"

All three of them looked to the doorway. The woman in the turquoise dress stood there, her arms folded in front of her abdomen.

"I understand that I go on right before you. I was wondering if you'd like to keep me company while we wait our turns. We could go up together when it's time."

"I..." Katherine began then trailed off.

Vincent jumped in. "Thank you, Miss..."

"Constance. Constance Landingham." She came into the room, went directly to Katherine, and slipped an arm around her waist. "You two gentlemen go about your business. We'll be fine here."

Vincent couldn't help but grin at the singer. She winked at him, her eyes two vats of knowledge and understanding."

"Katherine?" Norman asked.

Katherine looked from Norman to Constance and then to Norman again. Her body relaxed and when she spoke, there was no waver in her voice. "I would love to have Constance keep me company. She's a fan, you know. She saw me in Milan."

"It's settled then," Constance said. She pointed at the violin case sitting on a sideboard on the far wall. "Now, let's get that instrument warmed up."

Slipping free of Constance's grasp, Katherine stepped closer to Norman, stood on tiptoe, and pecked his cheek. "Go," she said. "I'll be fine."

He smiled at her, touched her cheek then said, "Come on, Vincent, and let's go. I have some socializing and deal making to do."

Vincent followed Norman out of the dressing room, closing the door behind him. They made their way through the other performers, up the stairs to the wings then down the stairs to the auditorium. People stood in the aisles, talking, eating and sipping coffee or tea. Vincent remained at Norman's side, nodding and saying brief "hellos" whenever Norman introduced him. They made their way to the lobby and up the left staircase. Norman had to meet Max Yellen and some other men in the theatre offices, he explained, indicating that Vincent should wait outside.

Reluctantly, Vincent waited just outside the office door. He leaned back against the tapestry wall, arms folded across his chest, eyes watching, scrutinizing the crowd. The murmur of the crowd was loud up in the balcony. Cigar and cigarette smoke burned his nostrils as it floated up from below. Intermission ended and still Norman did not come out of the office. Vincent's mouth went dry, his heart rate picking up. What was going on in there, he wondered? Who were these men? Could Yellen be in on Malloy's plan? Could it be that Norman would never come out of the office?

He shook the thoughts away. Norman had to come out. History said that he had been in the wings with Katherine right before her performance. The man with the cello had taken the stage and, at last, Norman came out of the office, Yellen at his side. They shook hands, Yellen nodded briskly at Vincent and continued on his way. Norman clapped Vincent on the shoulder. "Done deal, my friend," he said, beaming.

"What deal?"

"If all goes well with her performance tonight and she wants to when I suggest it, Katherine will have a monthly show here at The Rivera."

"Excellent."

"Indeed." He gestured toward the marble staircase. "Come on. We should get to the wings. Katherine and Constance should be there already. I don't want Katherine to be alone when Constance goes out to perform."

They were halfway down the stairs when Vincent saw Jethro Malloy.

❧   ❧   ❧

But for the concessionaires, Jethro stood alone in the lobby. He wore his perpetual brown, pinstriped suit and derby bowler. No tuxedo for him. A cigar hung from his mouth.

Norman stopped, his hand on Vincent's arm. "I wondered when he would show up."

Vincent met Jethro's dark eyes and saw dastardly intent within them. *Could you be here to carry out your evil deed by yourself, Malloy? No henchmen this time?*

Jethro approached the staircase and Norman started down again, Vincent on his heels. They met at the bottom, Jethro looking Norman up and down as if he were already his prisoner. "Nice theatre," Jethro said, no emotion on his face.

Norman glared at him.

Malloy took a drag on his cigar, blew the smoke in Norman's face. Somehow, Norman managed not to cough. "You really think she's going to pull this off tonight, Lassiter?"

"She will."

Jethro shook his head. "She's a frightened, little, daddy's girl who is paralyzed without him. Why do you think she married me?"

"Before long, she won't be married to you any longer."

In the auditorium, James Kelly introduced Constance Landingham. Vincent gave Norman a slight push. "Forget about him, Norman. Constance just went on."

Norman pushed past Jethro and strode to the auditorium doors. Vincent followed him, giving Jethro a threatening look as he walked by him.

Malloy watched them go without a word. And that made Vincent's skin crawl. *What the hell did the man have planned? And who the hell was going to carry it out? And am I strong enough to prevent it?*

Katherine stood just offstage, violin and bow in hand, watching Constance sing. Vincent had to admit that the singer was good even though he wasn't a big opera fan. Norman slid his arm around Katherine's waist. Standing there together, they fit perfectly. Just as he and Kate had fit perfectly, Vincent thought, sadness welling up within him. He pushed it away. Not now. He could not waste time grieving now.

Movement at the top of the stage steps caught his eye. *Emma.* She'd made it back. She wore a long black gown, her auburn hair held up on top of her head with gold hairpins. She came to him and even in the dim backstage light; he saw the blood stain on her front. She hadn't had time to go home and change after her medical emergency. His eyes questioned her about the welfare of her patient. She mouthed, "He'll be all right." Then she went to Katherine. She took her friend's free hand and kissed her cheek. The smile that crossed Katherine's face when she saw Emma nearly moved Vincent to tears. He did not doubt that if he was successful tonight, these two women would remain friends, their lives entwined daily.

"You made it," Katherine said, reaching out to hug Emma.

Emma stepped back, pointing at the bloodstain on her dress. "Don't get this on you," she said.

Katherine's eyes widened.

"It's not mine. And my patient will be fine." She took Katherine's hand again. "I can't wait to see you out there."

Constance brought her song to a crescendo, her voice echoing throughout the auditorium.

"I hope I don't disappoint you, Emma."

"You won't."

Constance held the song's last note until Vincent thought he would run out of air in sympathy. When she finished, the audience jumped to its feet, clapping and cheering. She curtsied twice and came offstage. Grinning, she said, "They're all yours, Katherine. Knock them dead."

Norman took Katherine by the shoulders, turned her towards him, and said, "I'll be right here. If you get scared, look over here. Look at me. I'll never let you down, my love. Never. I love you, Katherine."

"I love you, Norman."

On stage, James Kelly said, "And now please welcome one of the finest violinists of our time. And, I'm pleased to say, a resident of our fair city. Ladies and gentlemen, I give you Katherine Mann."

The applause shook the theatre. The audience was already on its feet and Katherine hadn't played a note. Vincent held his breath as she walked out on the stage. *Don't look at the audience, Katherine. Just lift your violin and begin playing. Don't look at them.*

At first she seemed to hear him. She lifted the violin, nuzzled her chin against it, and raised her bow. She played a few notes then stopped. She raised her head and looked out at the mass of people.

No! Vincent silently cried. *No!*

But she held her ground. She looked out at her admirers and she said, her voice soft yet reaching them due to the overhead microphone. "This first song is dedicated to a dear friend who died a short time ago. I wrote it for her. It's called *For Kate.*"

The audience was deathly quiet, all eyes on Katherine. She began to play and but for her violin, there wasn't a sound in the auditorium. Vincent felt Emma's hands on his arm, squeezing, holding on for dear life. He looked at Norman. Lassiter's eyes were glued on Katherine. She was the love of his life. She was his future. She was his reason for being.

And her violin sang out, flooding the auditorium, touching everyone, making its way into everyone's soul. She had never sounded better, at least not to Vincent. But he did not watch her for more than seconds at a time. He kept his eyes on Norman and the dark, shadowy corners of the backstage area. This was the dangerous time. This is when Norman disappeared and if Vincent died trying, he would do all he could to prevent that from happening.

Katherine made it through *For Kate*, bowing slightly at the resounding applause. She glanced towards the wings and seeing Norman, smiled, raised her violin again, and began to play Mozart.

"She's doing it," Emma said in his ear. "Dear, Lord, she's doing it."

Stagehands had gathered with them to watch Katherine. Norman pulled his pocket watch from his pants pocket, peered at it, and then slid it back into his pocket. He leaned close to Vincent. "I'll be right back. Five minutes at the most."

"Where are you going?"

Norman didn't answer but started off. Vincent extricated his arm from Emma's grasp, ignoring her protests that he was leaving. He caught up with Norman halfway up the aisle to the back door and grabbed his arm. "What are you doing, man? You can't leave her. She needs you now."

Norman pulled his arm free. "Go back. I'll only be five minutes."

"Why?" Vincent insisted.

"Look, Malloy said if I meet him in back of the theatre during Katherine's performance, he'd discuss not dragging out the divorce any further."

"And you believe him?"

Norman pulled a folded piece of paper from his inside suit coat pocket. He held it out to Vincent. "He signed his name to it. He came to my house a few days ago and—"

"He's lying, Norman. I know this man. You know this man. That piece of paper means nothing."

"I have to meet him, Vincent. He's tortured Katherine long enough. I have to try. For her."

"Then I'm going with you."

"Come on then. I'm already late."

They passed by an usher at the top of the aisle. The woman didn't even see them she was so entranced by Katherine. Norman pushed open the back door and they stepped out into a cold winter night. It was pitch black, thick clouds hiding the stars.

"It's about time," Jethro Malloy said in the darkness.

Norman whirled around. "Where are you?"

Jethro emerged from the shadows. He held a revolver, aiming it at Norman's chest.

Norman stepped back, bumping into Vincent. Vincent held him upright.

"I told you to come alone," Malloy said, his tone annoyed but not angry.

"What the hell is that?" Norman asked, pointing at the gun.

Vincent stepped out around Norman and placed himself in front of Katherine's fiancé.

"Brave man, Mr. Vermay," Malloy said, sarcasm heavy in his voice. "But then you don't have anything to live for anymore, do you? Tell me, how did the little lady die, anyway?"

Vincent felt Norman grip his shoulder. Vincent held his ground. "Why the gun Malloy?" he asked. "You know you're not going to kill him. You can't. Not if you want this plan of yours to work."

"You know, Vermay, I don't like you. You are more of a thorn in my side than he is."

"Why? Isn't my sperm good enough?" Vincent's words hung in the air between them. Strong, crude words for 1926.

"What the hell are you talking about?" Norman asked, breaking the icy silence.

"He plans on taking you prisoner, Norman," Vincent said. "He's going to chain you to the wall in his basement and have you father five children with Katherine which he will claim as his own. He's sterile."

"Christ," Norman said.

"What I don't get," Vincent went on, "Is why you aborted Katherine's child, Jethro. You would have had your heir then. It was Norman's baby. Why did you care then only to now want the man to father her children?"

"Let's say I had a change of heart."

"Well, it's not going to happen," Vincent said. "I won't let it. You will not hold this man prisoner. You will not force him to father five children for you. I'll see to it."

"Vincent," Norman said, panic in his voice. "How do you know this? How?"

Vincent was surprised at how calm he felt now that the moment was upon him. Jethro didn't scare him. Jethro's gun didn't scare him. In fact, the thought of dying actually appealed to him. After all, Malloy was right, he really didn't have anything to live for. Kate was gone.

"Vincent?" Norman persisted.

Jethro cocked the trigger. "I guess you'll just have to come along as well, Mr. Vermay. I do have a rather large basement. But then you know that, having already been in it looking for your friend here not so long ago."

"We're not going anywhere with you?" Vincent said, still shielding Norman.

"Don't make me shoot you, Vermay."

"Do what you want, Malloy. You always do anyway."

Malloy stood considering his next move. Vincent felt Norman's heavy breathing on the back of his neck. *Trust me, Norman. Let me do what I have to do here.*

"You're crazy, Malloy," Norman said. "I'm not going with you. Katherine and I are going to have a life together."

"Really? I could shoot you and Vermay right now."

"But you won't," Vincent said. "That would be too messy, wouldn't it, Malloy? How would you explain it to the police? Two against one and we're not even armed."

Malloy's gun hand shook with anger.

"So go home. Leave now and stay out of their lives."

Malloy shook his head. "I'll never leave them alone. And she'll never be free. Never. She's mine."

Vincent felt Norman move and he reached for him. "No, Norman, don't!" He got his hands on Norman's back and pushed him hard. Norman crashed to the pavement with a grunt just as the gun went off, the bullet whizzing by Vincent's ear, embedding itself in the concrete theatre wall. Vincent sprang at Jethro, expecting to take a bullet. But there was no bullet. The gun misfired. Vincent grabbed it, the metal cold against his skin. Malloy fought him. They fell to the ground, entwined, struggling over the weapon. They rolled, the gun barrel pointing at Vincent's head. Vincent fought hard, the barrel slowly turning away from him towards Malloy. For his size and age, Malloy was strong. He fought like an angered lion, snarling and cursing. Vincent heard Norman calling his name. He ignored him, concentrating on Jethro. Again, they rolled and Vincent ended up beneath Malloy. Snow and cold penetrated his tuxedo. The gun pointed at Malloy's chest now. Vincent put his finger over Jethro's on the trigger. He didn't hesitate. It had to be done—for Katherine, for Norman, for Emma, and, for Kate.

The gun went off, jumping in his hands. Malloy deflated on top of Vincent like a rag doll. He died instantly, the breath pouring out of him, hot and stale on Vincent's face.

Vincent lay still, breathing hard, feeling Malloy's blood soak into his white shirt. It was over. He had changed history. Dear, God, he'd done it.

Norman pulled Malloy off of Vincent, rolled the dead man onto his back, and knelt beside him. "Christ," he said, staring down at his nemesis. "Holy Christ."

Vincent sat up. Shivering, he said, "Go inside. Tell the usher to call the police. Send Emma out here."

Norman just stared at him.

"Go inside," Vincent said, again. "Tell the usher to call the police. Send Emma out here. Go, now."

"He's already dead," Norman said.

"I know that, Norman. Go!"

Norman went. Vincent got to his feet and stood looking down at Malloy. He could think of nothing but his own time and what it was like there now. Had Kate been born? Had they met, fallen in love, and married? And if so, had she still died in their bedroom in the Victorian or…He shook his head violently, pushing all thoughts away. It was done. Whatever was awaiting him in his own time awaited him.

He looked up from Malloy out at the street lined with cars, the Methodist church rising above them. It had begun to snow.

CHAPTER 32

Katherine stared down at her dead husband in silence, her emotions hidden. She seemed small and fragile, dwarfed by Norman's jacket wrapped around her shoulders. Norman stood next to her, looking solemn and, Vincent noted, appalled at himself. Vincent understood why Norman was appalled. After all, a man lay dead on the snowy, cold concrete and yet those close to this man, those who knew him well, secretly celebrated. Vincent was celebrating inside. Hands handcuffed behind his back, policeman holding his arm, Vincent celebrated. He had succeeded and Malloy would no longer ruin Katherine's life.

People surrounded them, most having poured out of the theatre to watch this new, more intriguing show. A reporter from the *Evening News*, a tall, rail thin man in a derby shouted questions at both the police and at Vincent. Cameras clicked, bright flashes blinding Vincent. He blinked the spots from his eyes. Snow continued falling, big, thick flakes coming down fast. They landed on Katherine's shoulders, twinkling in the light from the kerosene lamps held by the policemen surrounding Jethro's body.

She looked at Vincent, her eyes questioning him, wondering how he, a sensitive painter, could kill a man. He wanted to tell her that he'd done it for her. That it had to be done. Was she angry with him? Was she not glad that Malloy would be forever out of her life?

Emma knelt beside Malloy, a policeman at her side. She'd unbuttoned Jethro's coat, vest, and shirt. "He die quick?" the policeman asked, watching her work.

"Instantly," she replied. She pointed at the bloody hole in Jethro's white, cotton shirt. "Bullet went through his heart."

"Damn," the policeman muttered, getting to his feet. He gestured at Vincent.

The policeman holding Vincent's arm—a powerfully built man with curly red hair and matching beard—tugged on Vincent's arm. "Let's go," he said, his voice gruff.

"No!" Norman exclaimed. He stepped away from Katherine. "That man saved my life. Jethro Malloy was going to shoot me."

The policeman beside Emma held up his hand. "We can sort this all out at the police station, Mr. Lassiter."

The crowd around them burst into protest. One man yelled out, "Come on, you can't be serious." Another agreed, adding, "The man's done this town a favor. Don't be locking him up for it."

"My brother doesn't tell lies," a third man said, pushing his way past the ring of policemen. He wore a black wool coat and bowler, and he looked disconcertingly like Norman.

"Now, Timothy," the policeman said, "No sense everyone standing out here in a snowstorm. We'll go down to the station and sort it all out."

"Norman told you want happened. Don't you believe him?"

"I've no doubt what your brother says is true, but we must follow police procedure."

"Norman," Katherine said. He turned to her. "Let the police do their jobs. I'm sure the truth will prevail." She looked past the brothers to Vincent. Her eyes begged he cooperate. There had been enough violence, enough tragedy for one night. He gave her a curt nod.

Emma got to her feet. She touched Norman's shoulder. "You go with Vincent. I'll take Katherine home."

As he was led away, Vincent heard Katherine say, "No, Emma. I must go to the police station."

🍁   🍁   🍁

It was a short walk across the snow-slicked street to the police station. The red-haired policeman led Vincent up the concrete steps and through the massive wooden door. Oak desks, each with a black phone and piles of papers, lined the room. The floor was wooden and stained from years of use. Vincent was led down a narrow aisle between the desks and on into the cell area. As the metal door of bars clanged shut behind him, Vincent was grateful that no one else was in the cell. He sat down on the bunk on the cell's right wall and watched the policeman lock the door. The man left without a word. Out in the squad room, Norman and his brother were yelling. Vincent smiled. He had no doubt that he would not be jailed for long, not if the Lassiter boys had their way.

The cell was sparse, gray cement block walls, no window, and the metal bar door. There was another bunk across from him and a chamber pot sat on the back wall. Definitely not a five star hotel, Vincent mused. The only light came from a lone bulb hanging from the ceiling just outside the cell. But it was enough light to see Jethro Malloy's blood on his shirt. Vincent gazed at the blood and felt no remorse. He had killed a man. Shouldn't he feel remorse, even though the man had been a bastard to the nth degree? Was this how murderers generally felt? Not the least bit remorseful; no regret for what they had done?

He wasn't sure how long he'd sat in the cell when a man appeared at the door. "Seems you're a hero, Mr. Vermay," he said. He was muscular and dressed in a tuxedo, obviously having been one of The Rivera's patrons this evening. He rested his big hand on the cell door's bars. "I'm Chief Kinsky by the way." Vincent didn't say anything. He wracked his brain trying to remember just when the Miranda Warning came into being. "Apparently Malloy was going to kill Norman Lassiter. Seems you fought the man and the gun went off during the fight." The chief's eyes were unreadable. "Like I said, you're a hero. There's a whole squad room full of Malloy haters saying so."

Vincent met the Chief's eyes, but still said nothing.

Kinsky's eyes didn't waver. He didn't blink. He scratched at his beard with one big hand. "Lady wants to talk to you. Normally, I don't allow women back here but...Hell." He walked away.

Five minutes later Katherine came to the cell door, her hair a tangled mess, Norman's tuxedo jacket still around her shoulders. Vincent jumped to his feet, his heart pounding. *Don't be angry with me. Don't hate me, Katherine. Please? I couldn't bear it.*

She stared at the bloodstain on his shirt, horrified. He thought she would cry, but she didn't. She slowly raised her head until her eyes met his and to his relief, he saw gratitude in them. "Thank you," she said, her voice barely more than a whisper. She stuck her right hand through the bars. "My dear, dear friend."

He took her hand. Her skin was cold, her hand small in his larger one.

"I've no doubt he would have killed Norman," she said.

Vincent nodded.

"You have given me my happiness this night. I know that. Norman and I may marry now. Have children and watch them grow. You have given me so much and I...I am unable to give to you the one thing that would make you as happy as you've made me."

Tears pierced Vincent's eyes. "Just live your lives, Katherine. Kate would want that."

"She would be proud of you, Vincent. I'm proud of you." She squeezed his hand. "I love you, dear friend. You come to me when the police release you."

Vincent nodded, although he knew he would not go to her. He would return to his own time and see what awaited him there. He forced a smile and she smiled back. He memorized her face in that moment, willing himself to never forget how her smile lit up her face and how her beautiful green eyes shimmered in the pale hall light. Nor would he forget how good it felt to hold her hand and know that he had saved her from a life of Hell on earth.

❈   ❈   ❈

The clang of metal on metal jerked Vincent awake. Heart in his throat he rolled off the bunk, landing on his hands and knees on the cell's concrete floor. The red-haired policeman stood with the cell door open. "Get up, Mr. Vermay," he said. "You're free to go."

Vincent got to his feet. "I am?"

"You are. Come on, now."

Vincent followed him out into the squad room. A couple of detectives worked on paperwork at their desks. The Chief stood at the front of the room, his suit coat discarded, thumbs hooked in his suspenders. Other than that, the room was eerily quiet and empty. When they'd reached the Chief, he said, "It's true. You can go."

Vincent swallowed. "Can't say I enjoyed the accommodations."

Chief Kinsky laughed. It was infectious and Vincent laughed as well.

Then, just as suddenly as he'd started laughing, the Chief stopped. His face serious, his eyes daring Vincent to argue, he said, "If I were you, I'd make myself scarce. One never knows what Malloy's associates might do."

"You mean leave North Tonawanda?"

Kinsky didn't respond. Instead, he moved aside so Vincent could leave.

Vincent walked by him. With his hand on the doorknob, he said, "Thank you, Chief. Officer Flannery."

Flannery grinned. The Chief just nodded.

Vincent pushed open the door and stepped outside into the frigid, snowy night. Tremont Street was deserted, snow having accumulated a good six inches. Hatless and coatless, Vincent hugged himself and walked down the police station stairs. Wind whipped at his hair, snow stung his face, but he walked on. The going was slow; his dress shoes not the best for plowing through snow. He walked with trepidation, wondering if Malloy's so-called associates were watching him. Were they hidden behind the next bush, ready to spring on him? Would they beat him to death? Or would they shoot him? As he played the different scenarios of his own death in his mind, he discovered that, much to his surprise, he didn't want to die. *Could it be,* he wondered, *that I could live without Kate?* He saw her face in his mind and with it came suffocating depression. He shook himself. Maybe he no longer wanted to die. But, Christ, how could he live in a state of perpetual depression?

He reached Payne Avenue and turned left. He supposed he looked like a walking snowman. The tips of his ears burned from the cold and he wondered why the snowplows weren't out. He covered his ears with his hands and continued walking. What he had done was right. He knew that now. In fact, he'd known it the minute Katherine had said, "Thank you," back in the jail. And Kate, well, Kate would be proud. He could imagine her nodding her approval in Heaven. He had no doubt that Kate was in Heaven. He prayed she was happy there. He reached Goundry Street and turned right. He stopped in front of Emma's house. He should go inside and get his suitcase. The violin was inside it. He should take it back to the year 2000. He shook his head. But then, he didn't need it any longer. He wasn't coming back here again.

Emma's house was dark. They were asleep; Emma, alone in her bed. Emma, who would never marry but have the love of a nephew named Emmett. Emma, who would die painfully of cancer after having spent a lifetime healing others. And Katherine, now sleeping alone for the short term and who would soon sleep beside the man who loved her more than life itself.

Norman! His name reverberated in Vincent's brain, filling his ears and sounding as loud as a million decibels. Norman could very well be the difference. Norman, sleeping over in the little white house on Tremont Street, happy, because he knew that soon Katherine would sleep beside him. Joy welled up in Vincent's heart. *Yes, I have to talk to Norman before I cross over.* Vincent took off at a run, slipping and sliding on his dress shoes, as he headed back to Tremont Street.

✳   ✳   ✳

Vincent pounded on Norman's front door a good ten minutes before it finally opened. Norman stood there wrapped in a flannel robe that bore his initials. His feet were bare, his hair a tangled mess. He stared at Vincent a moment and then said, "Good, Lord, man, you must be frozen. Get in here."

Vincent stepped into the tiny foyer. In fact, he was frozen, his teeth chattering.

Norman shut the door. "I'll make you some hot tea."

Vincent followed him down the hall. "I'm sorry I woke you," he said through his chattering teeth. "They just released me."

Although tiny, the kitchen was charming, having white, glass front cupboards, and blue countertops. The floor was white and blue checked ceramic tile, the blue in the tiles matching the blue of the plaid kitchen curtains. An oak table with two chairs occupied a wall beside the back door. The stove and icebox were blue, both appliances trimmed in gold.

Norman put the kettle on the burner and turned on the stove. "You should have called me. I would have come down to get you." He pointed at the stove. "Watch the kettle while I get you some dry clothes to put on."

Vincent sat down at the oak table and waited for Norman to return. He wiped the snow from his hair with his hand and tried to figure out just how he was going to put his question.

Norman came back carrying a pair of brown corduroy slacks, black socks, and a white, cotton shirt. He handed them to Vincent. "Go on, change. Use the basement stairwell."

By the time Vincent had slipped off his wet clothes and slipped on the dry ones, Norman had made two cups of tea. They sat together at the table. Vincent cupped his hands around his cup, letting the warmth seep into his hands.

Norman brushed his mustache and said, "They shouldn't even have held you as long as they did."

Vincent shrugged. He didn't care about the police anymore. He had other things on his mind.

"I owe you my life," Norman said, gratitude in his eyes. "But I still have to wonder why you think that Jethro was going to take me captive and use me as his stud. Did he tell you that?"

"No."

Norman shook his head. "It looked to me like the man wanted to kill me, not take me captive." Norman pushed his cup aside and leaned on the table. "You, my friend, have some explaining to do."

Vincent looked away. Dare he tell Norman the truth?

"Vincent?"

Vincent bit his lip as he looked back at Norman. He gazed at him for several minutes, the debate raging in his mind. *Tell him. Don't tell him.* Finally, unable to take it any longer, knowing that this might very well be his only chance for happiness, Vincent said, "Because in my time, that was history."

"What?"

Vincent pushed his own cup of tea aside. "You're going to think I'm crazy, but I'm not. What I'm about to tell you is true. I only hope that you can believe it."

"Then spit it out, man."

Vincent did. He told Norman everything that had happened from the moment Kate had inherited Katherine's money and house until he, miserably alone without Kate, had decided to change history. As he spoke, he watched Norman's face go through a range of emotions—disbelief, incredibility, denial, and at the end, miraculously, belief.

His story finished, Vincent picked up his tea and drank greedily, not caring that the liquid had grown cold while he spoke. Norman got to his feet and paced. Vincent remained quiet, letting him work through his thoughts. Ten minutes later, when Norman had retaken his seat, Vincent said, "You believe me."

Norman nodded.

Vincent reached across the table, took Norman's hand, and asked, "Then will you promise me something?"

"That you should even have to ask. Good God, Vincent, you've given Katherine and me our life together. Whatever you wish."

"Promise me you will have five children."

Norman let out a long, low whistle then asked, "Kate's father was our fifth child?"

"He was."

Norman ran his free hand through his messy hair. "Vincent, surely you realize that even if we have five children...well, things will be different and—"

"I know," Vincent interrupted him. "But at least if you have the five kids, then, maybe Kate will still be born."

"And when you return to your own time, maybe you two still would have fallen in love and married, and maybe she might still be alive?"

"I know it's one long shot after another, but it's all I've got, Norman."

Nodding, Norman said, "Then I promise, if Katherine can have them, we will have five children."

"Thank you."

"No, thank you. Will you stay the rest of the night and say goodbye to Katherine in the morning?"

"No. It's time I go." Vincent stood up. "Give her and Emma my best."

Norman got to his feet. "You can have one of my coats, a pair of boots, and a hat too. If you insist on going back out in this storm, you must dress properly."

In the foyer, Vincent put on Norman's boots, derby and coat. "I'm afraid I won't be able to get these back to you," Vincent said.

Norman's eyes were sad. "They can be your souvenirs." He held out his arms and the two men hugged. Then, pushing Vincent away, Norman said, "I hope she's there, my friend."

"Not as bad as I do, Norman."

With a final handshake, Vincent went out into the snowy night. He didn't go immediately to the bridge. He went back to Emma's to take a final look. *Goodbye, Emma. Goodbye, Katherine.* Finally taking his leave, he headed for the Erie Canal. He opted to use the Webster Street Bridge for his return to the year 2000 and arriving there, he stopped, looking across the bridge into his own time. Streetlights burned and no snow fell. The sky was clear, the first streaks of daylight pushing out the night. What awaited him over there? *Kate. Please, dear God, let it be Kate.* Stealing himself with a deep breath, Vincent walked over the bridge.

CHAPTER 33

Kate's alive!

The thought pierced his brain like a bullet the minute he stepped into the present. *She's alive!* And he knew he wasn't kidding himself. He knew because he felt her in the spot she'd occupied within him while alive, the spot that had been empty since her death. Vincent started running, dodging patches of ice, his heart pounding, the distance between the Webster Street Bridge and Goundry Street seemingly forever.

He was in front of The Riviera when he heard someone call his name. He skidded to a stop and turned toward the street. Liz sat in the driver's seat of her Saturn, the passenger window open. "Vincent," she said, motioning him to her. "Come on, we're holding up traffic."

Indeed, cars were piling up behind her. Vincent jumped a snow bank, cut between two parked cars, and reached the Saturn. He opened the door and climbed in. Liz started the car moving again. Reaching for the button to raise the passenger window, she said, "Damn, Vincent, Kate has been worried sick about you. And Katherine's recital is this afternoon." The window next to Vincent went up with a soft whine. "The poor kid has been crying all night, afraid you weren't going to make it. Kate has had her hands full."

Katherine. My daughter. Our daughter. Vincent grinned. Yes, he and Kate had a daughter. He knew that. He didn't know how he knew that but he did.

Liz turned onto Goundry Street. "I have to stop by the office a minute. Then we are going straight to your house."

Liz was not dead. That didn't surprise him. He stared at her. She was healthy; physically fit, and just the right weight; not at all like the too-thin Liz who had committed suicide. *But she hadn't killed herself. Not in this life.* Vincent's grin widened.

Liz turned right onto Main and then left onto Tremont. "Anyway," she continued, "Kate has fielded calls for you from David too. So, where the hell have you been?"

"I haven't been gone that long," he said, hoping her answer would give him some clue about the length of his absence. Had it been from the 29th until the 31st for them as it had been for him? He thought so.

"Right, Vincent. You told Kate two days ago that you were going for a short walk. You left with your sketchpad and pencil in hand."

"Short walk?" he asked, although he remembered doing just that.

She shot him a quick glance. "Yes, short walk. Do you realize that it's now New Year's Eve?"

"Yes."

She pulled the car to a stop across the street from her office and opened the driver's side door. "Wait here. I'll just be a minute."

He watched her sprint across the road, run up the stairs, and go inside the house where her office was located. Except that it wasn't just her office anymore. Before he looked at the sign, he knew what it would read. *Reilly Family Practice: Emmett Reilly, M.D. and Elizabeth Reilly, M.D.*

Liz returned a few minutes later with a small, red and white box. Getting into the driver's seat, she tossed the box into his lap. "Hold that, will you? I have to drop it by the Woodward's for Jill."

He held up the box. "Is this a brace or something? For her knee?"

Liz pulled away from the curb. Nodding, she said, "It's a wrap. It'll give her knee support and keep it warm so it doesn't stiffen up on her when she's cycling. She's going to try while she's off on Winter break and see if she can ride again."

"What do you think?"

Liz turned left on Niagara Street. "Nothing ventured, nothing gained. Hell, the kid has been through chemo, radiation, and surgery. Removing the tumor was no easy task and the knee was severely traumatized. She went through a lot of pain, both emotional and physical." They turned onto Goundry. "At first, I wasn't sure she would walk again. I know I mentioned that to you."

"I remember," he said and he did. In fact, he knew that Jill had seen Liz immediately about her knee pain. A fact made easier because instead of Boston, she attended school at Buffalo State. Earlier detection had made all the difference.

"But one thing about Jill, she's determined. I think that when she went back to Buff State last August, she just wanted to pour herself into the books. Now, she's ready to move forward. And with her determination, no doubt she'll ride again."

"I told her that myself, Liz. I've no doubt she'll ride again." Vincent thought of Jill, how she'd come to the Victorian a few weeks ago to talk with him about trying to cycle again. They'd sat at the kitchen table, drinking hot chocolate and talking. Jill, who once again had a full head of lovely blonde hair, who no longer looked sick, and who, thank God, had beaten cancer. Vincent shook his head in wonder. She wasn't the only one who'd beaten the disease. Marlene Reilly had as well. Vincent knew that and he also knew that Alan Rourke had died his gory death in Utah.

Liz pulled the Saturn to the curb in front of the Victorian. "Okay, out. Vincent. Go face your wife and daughter."

He leaned towards Liz and kissed her cheek. He smiled at her. He thought of Alan Rourke again and he wanted to do more. He wanted to take Liz in his arms and hold her. And yet, she didn't need him too. Not in this life. She missed Alan and sometimes thought of what could have been had she married him, but still having her mother, and Jill winning her battle with bone cancer had strengthened her. *And Kate, Vincent*, he reminded himself. *Don't forget Kate and the fact that, in this new life, there was never a twenty-one year separation for the two friends.*

Reaching over him, Liz opened the passenger side door and said, "Now, get out. I'll see you at The Riviera this afternoon for Katherine's recital."

He got out of the car then leaned back in. "Will your mom and dad be there?"

"Yes."

He closed the car door and watched Liz drive off. He drew in a long breath, turned from the street, and nearly fell over Douglas Lassiter. The old man was bundled in a blue parka, a gray tweed cap on his head, sunglasses hiding his eyes. But Vincent didn't need to see the old man's eyes to know he knew. The knowledge was in his grin. "Your Uncle Norman told you, didn't he?"

Douglas's grin widened. "He did." He scratched his cheek. "Malloy left the house here…" He pointed at the Victorian. "To Katherine. Damn fool hadn't changed his will since he never intended to lose her. Norman and Katherine moved in after marrying. Raised five kids in it. Norman kept the white house on Tremont and rented it out. Stayed in the family over the years. My youngest daughter lives in it now with her husband and kids."

Vincent looked from Douglas to the Victorian and back to Douglas again. "I know, Douglas," he said. "I know it all." He pointed a finger at his brain. "It's all here. All the changes."

Lassiter chuckled. "Why do you suppose that is, Vincent?"

Vincent scratched his chin. "I'm not sure. But, it could be because I lived it."

Douglas shook his head. "But if you lived it, how could you still have painted Katherine's portrait? Which you did, by the way."

"I know."

"But why did you go back? There was no need for you to go back."

"The violin, Douglas. Kate still inherited this house and I still had my artist's block."

Lassiter shook his head again. "I don't understand it and I'm not going to try. All I will say is welcome home." He paused a moment then said, "Vincent, Uncle Norman told me everything you told him that night. I know what my life should have been. It's different because Uncle Norman was alive instead of dead." He held out his hand. "Thank you."

Vincent accepted his hand and while they shook, said, "The whole thing is a miracle. What were the odds that Kate's father would marry the same woman? That he would still divorce her, gamble his life away, and kill himself in a Las Vegas hotel room?"

"Destiny? Fate? Hell, Vincent, what else could it be?" Douglas bit his lower lip. "You must also know, then, that Elsie Whiting still works at the Reilly medical office."

"Except now she's Elsie Kopinski, happily married, and the mother of three boys."

"Grown men now."

Before Vincent could say anything else, the Victorian's front door flew open and his seven-year-old daughter ran towards him. "Daddy!" she called. "Daddy, you're home." She flew through the gate and jumped into his arms. She wore a pair of flannel pajamas with Winnie the Pooh on them. Pooh-head slippers covered her feet.

Vincent caught her and twirled her around and around. She screamed in delight. Through her screams he heard Kate's voice. "Katherine, for Heaven's sake, you get back in this house! It's the middle of winter out there!" And then, "Vincent. Oh, thank God, Vincent." Still holding his daughter, feeling her nuzzling against his neck, he looked at Kate. She stood on the front porch, clad in blue jeans, a red turtleneck sweater, and red socks. Her hair curled about her shoulders. Behind the lenses of her wire-rimmed glasses, her green eyes burned with relief and joy. His heart soared and he ran to her.

"Daddy," Katherine was saying. "Oh, Daddy, I was so afraid you were going to miss my recital."

"Never," he said, running up the porch steps. He pulled Kate to him with his free arm and kissed her lips, savoring them, his heart swelling with his love for her.

She clung to him. "God, Vincent, you have to stop doing this."

"What?"

"You know perfectly well what." She pushed him away. "Disappearing on me. I suppose you were off sketching things for your next series of paintings."

He didn't answer her. Instead, he kissed her warm lips again. Katherine tugged on his collar. "Daddy, Mommy finished her new book."

"Let's get in out of the cold," Kate said, leading them inside. "David keeps calling about final details for your opening, and I have to keep making excuses for you." Holding his hand, she pulled him into the parlor. She pointed at a pad beside the phone. "Eight calls from him, Vincent. You have to call him back right away."

Vincent stared at the painting above the fireplace, feeling like he was seeing it for the first time and yet not seeing it for the first time. Katherine sat in a chair surrounded by her five children, Norman standing behind her with his hands on her shoulders. They looked to be in their forties. Kate's father was in his mother's arms, still a toddler. A wide, satisfied smile crossed Vincent's face.

Kate pulled Katherine from his arms and set her on her feet. With a gentle pat on her rear, Kate said, "You go finish your oatmeal. Daddy and I will be right in." The child ran for the kitchen. Kate slipped her arm inside Vincent's. "I love that painting. I miss her. I miss them both. And yet, even though she's only seven, when our daughter plays that violin, sometimes, Vincent, I swear it's my grandmother playing." Vincent looked at Kate. A tear slipped from her left eye and rolled down her cheek. He wiped it away with his thumb. She took his hand. "So, did you sketch other things to paint now that you finished your series on my grandmother? I do so wish she could have seen the paintings you did."

Oh, but she did, Kate. She did see them. In fact, she sat for them. Except this time, Kate had not traveled back with him.

"David said that the *Katherine Series*, as he calls it, is going to seal your stardom in the art world."

"What do you think?"

"That he's right." She kissed his cheek. "Now, all I need to do is win the Pulitzer Prize and we'll be all set."

"Maybe novel number ten will do the trick, babe."

She laughed and laid her head on his shoulder. "I doubt it's that good, Vincent."

"Yes it is." He closed his eyes. *Oh, Kate, in this life you've published nine novels and just finished number ten. You never set your dream aside or buried it deep within your soul. You never lived those tortured years.*

She tugged on his arm. "Come on. Let's go have breakfast with our daughter. Then we have to get ready for the recital."

"You go on. Let me call David quick."

She pecked his cheek and left the room. He sat down on the couch, surprised to find himself trembling. One action had changed so much. He'd stepped out of 1926 into a very different life, a life so much better than he could have imagined, a life he himself had been living. He shook his head. Mind-boggling. People were alive who had been dead. He and Kate had a child. She'd written ten novels already. And through all the changes, he had still painted Katherine. And crazily, he felt like he'd actually lived two lives.

He picked up the phone and dialed David's number, wondering if he would always remember his old life. Or would his memories meld, mixing those things that were the same in both lives and wiping out what was different in the old life? He knew one part he would definitely like to forget. Yes, if he could, he would choose to forget trying to live without Kate. David answered on the fourth ring and did most of the talking, telling Vincent that the opening was sold out. He gave Vincent flight information for the trip to D.C. He would stock up the townhouse for them. "Carol can't wait to see Katherine again," David said. "She's bought a ton of presents for her. You know how much my wife loves your little girl. Don't be mad at her for spoiling her."

Vincent assured him that he wasn't mad.

"Great. See you soon, my friend."

"You bet."

Vincent hung up the phone, sat back, and thought of Jethro Malloy. Jethro, whose stained-glass face no longer graced the Victorian's front door. No, Katherine had had the window replaced with a floral design. Vincent chuckled then scolded himself. *Get up and go into the kitchen, Vincent. Now.* He stood up, took a step towards the front foyer, and stopped in his tracks. Someone was playing the violin. Mozart floated down from the third floor. He tore up both flights of stairs and threw open the bedroom door. The violin case lay on the bed, an envelope beside it. He opened the envelope with trembling hands, tearing it nearly to shreds. Katherine's gentle, flowing script read, *Dearest, Vincent, please, you must have no regrets. What you did was for the best. Forget your old life. And please, dear friend, cherish your new one. Just as I shall cherish the one you've given me. All my love, forever, Katherine.*

He sank down on the bed, holding the note to his chest. *Believe me, Katherine, I have no regrets. And yes, I will cherish this new life. Don't ever doubt that.*

Vaguely he heard a phone ring. He stood up, wondering how long he'd been sitting on the bed. Tiny footsteps reached his ears then his daughter ran into the room. She snatched up the violin. "I have to practice one last time. Mommy says your oatmeal is ice cold. And Aunt Sarah's on the phone."

Sarah. Yes, I still have Sarah.

"Vincent," Kate called up the stairs. "Sarah's on the phone. She wants to talk to you. She's chartered a plane. She'll fly to Philly, pick up your parents and come on to Washington. Now, get down here, talk to your sister, and then eat your breakfast. You can warm it in the microwave. I have to grab a shower."

He tousled Katherine's hair with his hand. Smiling, heart about to burst with happiness; Vincent dropped a kiss on Katherine's head and called back, "Coming!"

0-595-27340-8

Printed in the United States
214563BV00001B/14/A

9 780595 273409